"Place is empty." Keld grunted. **"Been that way a while, by the looks of it."**

Byrne nodded, her eyes returning to the table.

"But I did find this." Keld held out the object he had bundled in his cloak.

Byrne reached out and unwrapped the object; a series of emotions flittered across her face as she recognized it. Sorrow, anger. There was a slight tremor in Byrne's hands as she revealed it.

A sword.

Drem knew it immediately, even if it was still in its scabbard with a long belt wrapped around it. Its size and length made it obvious that this was no ordinary sword, that it had belonged to a giant or giantess.

Sig's sword.

Drem felt a fist clench in his gut at the sight of it. He had known Sig for such a short time, but she had left an irremovable mark upon his heart. An example of true friendship, of loyalty. Of love.

Of truth and courage.

A TIME OF
COURAGE

Of Blood and Bone: Book 3

JOHN
GWYNNE

www.orbitbooks.net

Copyright © 2020 by John Gwynne
Excerpt from *Cold Iron* copyright © 2018 by Miles Cameron
Excerpt from *The Obsidian Tower* copyright © 2020 by Melissa Caruso

Cover illustration by Paul Young
Map artwork by Fred van Deelen
Author photograph by Pan Macmillan

Orbit
Hachette Book Group
1290 Avenue of the Americas
New York, NY 10104
orbitbooks.net

First Edition: April 2020
Simultaneously published in Great Britain by Macmillan,
an imprint of Pan Macmillan

Orbit is an imprint of Hachette Book Group.
The Orbit name and logo are trademarks of Little, Brown Book Group Limited.

The publisher is not responsible for websites (or their content)
that are not owned by the publisher.

The Hachette Speakers Bureau provides a wide range of authors for
speaking events. To find out more, go to www.hachettespeakersbureau.com
or call (866) 376-6591.

Library of Congress Control Number: 2019942512

ISBNs: 978-0-316-50231-3 (trade paperback), 978-0-316-50229-0 (ebook)

Printed in the United States of America

LSC-C

Printing 3, 2022

For my beautiful son, William, who has inspired a hero in this tale.
Of course you have, because you are a hero to me.
Love you x

Cast of Characters

Ert—veteran sword master of Drassil. Trainer of the
    White-Wings.
Ethlinn—Queen of the Giants. Daughter of Balur One-Eye.
Fia—a White-Wing of Drassil.
Jost—a White-Wing of Drassil.
Riv—half-breed daughter of Aphra and Kol. Trained as a
    White-Wing, though she has become disillusioned with
    the Ben-Elim and White-Wings.
Sorch—a White-Wing of Drassil.
Vald—a White-Wing of Drassil.

ORDER OF THE BRIGHT STAR

Dun Seren and Other Garrisons

Byrne—the High Captain of Dun Seren. A descendant of
    Cywen and Veradis, Drem's aunt.
Craf—a talking crow of Dun Seren.
Cullen—a young warrior of Dun Seren. A descendant of
    Corban and Coralen.
Drem—a trapper of the Desolation. Son of Olin, nephew of
    Byrne. He has joined the Order of the Bright Star.
Durl—a talking crow of Dun Seren.
Fen—one of Keld's wolven-hounds.
Friend—a great white bear who has followed the Order of the
    Bright Star's warband and saved Drem during the Battle
    of the Desolation, against Fritha and her warband.
Halden—a warrior of the Bright Star. Leader of the garrison
    at Brikan.
Hammer—a giant bear.
Kill—title for the captain of Dun Seren's warrior school.
Keld—a warrior and huntsman of Dun Seren.
Rab—a white talking crow of Dun Seren.
Ralla—one of Keld's wolven-hounds.
Shar—Jehar warrior.
Tain—the crow master of Dun Seren. Son of Alcyon.

Cast of Characters

Utul—Jehar warrior.
Reng—a warrior and huntsman of the Order of the Bright Star.

Kurgan Giant Clan

Raina—wife of Alcyon.
Ukran—Lord of the Kurgan.

Ben-Elim

Dumah—captain of the Ben-Elim and White-Wing garrison at Ripa.
Hadran—loyal to Kol. Riv's guardian.
Kol—High Captain of the Ben-Elim of Drassil. Father of Riv.
Meical—once High Captain of the Ben-Elim. Recently released from his captivity within starstone metal, where he was sealed for over a hundred years with Asroth in Drassil.

Kadoshim and their Servants

Aenor—Lord of the acolytes.
Arn—acolyte of Gulla, from Fritha's crew. Father of Elise.
Asroth—Lord of the Kadoshim. Recently released from his captivity within starstone metal in the Great Hall of Drassil.
Bune—a captain of the Kadoshim, close to Asroth.
Choron—one of Asroth's elite guards.
Elise—acolyte of Gulla, daughter of Arn. Healed by Fritha into a creature half-woman, half-wyrm.
Fritha—priestess and captain of the Kadoshim's covens.
Gulla—High Captain of the Kadoshim.
Morn—a half-breed Kadoshim. Daughter of Gulla.
Rok—Lord of the Shekam giant Clan, allied to the Kadoshim.
Sulak—Kadoshim captain, leader of the southern covens.
Wrath—Fritha's draig.

THE
BANISHED
LANDS

Kavala mountains

Grinding Sea

gard

Void

Drassil

Oriens

FORN FOREST

Isle of Kletva

ARCONA

Haldis

THE FAITHFUL

Brihan

Bairg mountains

Halstat

Jerolin

Agullas Mountains

Balara

Tethys Sea

Ripa

TARBESH

PELSET

NERIN

Telassar

"Better to fight and fall,
Than to live without hope"

The Völsunga Saga

CHAPTER ONE

DREM

The Year 138 of the Age of Lore, Hound's Moon

Drem threw his grapple-hook high. He felt it reach the apex of its climb and then drop. There was a *thunk* as it connected with wood. He pulled, felt it catch in timber, gave a tug to check it had caught properly and would hold his weight.

Drem was huddled tight to the wooden wall of a stockade. The only sound he could hear was his heart pounding, echoing in his skull and the rasp of his breath. Just being back here, where it had all started—it set him on edge.

The mine at the edge of the Starstone Lake.

Upon Byrne's orders, he and a few score huntsmen of the Order of the Bright Star had crept out of the northern woods in the full dark and made their way to the walls. Drem had noted that the hole Hammer had made in the stockade wall had been repaired. Emotion had swept through him as he'd looked at the spot where he had last seen Sig alive, where the giantess had made her last stand.

The mixture of grief and anger set his blood thrumming in his veins, even as he'd crept through the heather and rocks; it had not left him yet. And now he was here, pressed tight against the wall, waiting to go over, just as he had, twice before.

This time, though, I am going over with sixty of the toughest, hardest men and women I've ever encountered. Hunters of the Order of the Bright Star. There was a reassurance in that. His hand went to the hilt of his seax and brushed it lightly. There was a reassurance in that, too. He rolled his shoulders, shifting the weight of his mail coat, wincing as it rubbed on raw skin, even with two layers of linen and wool between the mail and his flesh. He'd lived and breathed in it for more than a ten-night, slept in it as well, as they'd made a forced march from the battle-ground in the heart of the Desolation to here. He'd learned the value of his mail at that battle and, no matter how uncomfortable it got, he was not taking it off any time soon.

The grey dawn was seeping into the land around him. With the dim light he could just make out the deeper shadows of another man and woman either side of him, twenty or thirty paces away. They had cast their grapple-hooks, too, and they were all waiting for the signal.

An owl hooted.

Keld.

Drem sucked in a deep breath and climbed, hauling himself up the rope, feet scraping on timber. He was a big man, heavy, but he was strong, stronger than most, and the climb was little effort to him. In a few heartbeats he was at the top; he rolled over, lowering himself to the walkway, crouching low.

A nod either side to his companions and then he twisted off the walkway, hung suspended, then dropped to the ground. A moment's pause, holding his breath to listen, and he was slipping his seax and short axe into his hands and moving into the complex.

The mine was a place of shadows and grey light, of muffled sounds: a door creaking on old hinges, the skittering of rats, in the distance the lapping of the lake. Drem made his way slowly from building to building, pushing doors open, checking for any inhabitants, searching the shadows. He saw tracks and crouched to inspect them. They were not a man's, being too long and distended, the ground scarred by claws, but they were not an animal's, either. Drem had seen too many tracks like this for his liking, lately.

A Feral's.

But they were old, the soil hard and dry.

A moon at least, maybe longer.

And the fact that they had not been scuffed away by new tracks was a confirmation of what he'd suspected. The mine had long been abandoned.

Drem moved on, continuing his methodical search, opening every door, scrutinizing every track. His path led him ever inwards until, abruptly, a space opened up: a square bordered on three sides by an assortment of buildings. To the north a slab of rock rose to the sky, like a cliff face. Deeper patches of shadow scattered across its darkness hinted at caves. Drem knew what they were, had seen them before.

Cages for Fritha's experiments.

In the centre of the clearing was a table.

Drem shivered as memories crawled out of the dark corners of his mind.

Memories of blood and fire. Of Fritha, Gulla the Kadoshim and of words of power. He had seen Fritha cut Gulla's throat and cast him upon that table, along with the body of one of the Desolation's giant bats and the hand cut from Asroth's body. He remembered the sensation of bile rising in his throat as he had watched that dark magic at work, the bloodied, frothing steam, the writhing and melding of the forms on the table, and finally of Gulla rising, born anew, born as something different.

The first Revenant, he called himself.

Drem shook his head and took a step into the open courtyard. Other forms separated from the shadows: more hunters of the Order who had made their search of the mine, all of them moving like a tightening noose towards this place, the heart of the complex. They stood in silence. Dawn was claiming the land, banishing the murk, and Drem saw more evidence that the place had long been deserted. The buildings were cold and empty, fire-pits stripped of ash by rain and wind, the only signs of life the occasional scuttle of rats or scratching of birds in eaves. The hard-packed earth was rutted with tracks. Drem imagined a gathering of many here, a mixture of animal and human, but the tracks were all hard and dry.

A final gathering before Fritha's warband left, marching out to meet the Order?

The sun was rising higher now; the morning light washed over the huge table in the centre of the courtyard, where it squatted like some sleeping, malignant beast. Chains and manacles of iron were set deep into the timber, darker stains scattered in pools on the grain.

Blood always leaves a stain.

In the pale-streaked skies above, Drem made out the circling of crows. Others were scattered elsewhere above the mine, landing on rooftops, winging through unshuttered windows. One of the crows above Drem spiralled down to the courtyard, a pale bird, white-feathered where the others were all dark. It cawed and beat its wings, alighting on Drem's shoulder. He felt Rab's claws flex and dig into him, and was glad again for his coat of mail.

"*Gulla gone,*" Rab squawked.

"Aye, looks that way," Drem said.

"*And no Twisted Men?*" Rab croaked.

"None that I can find," Drem told him, knowing that Rab was referring to Fritha's Ferals.

"*Good,*" Rab muttered, shaking and puffing his feathers out.

A figure strode from a street to the west. An older man, dark hair turning to grey, an elegance and intensity to his movement. An assortment of knives and short axes bristled from his belts. Keld, huntsman of the Order and Drem's friend. Two huge wolven-hounds were loping at his flanks, one slate grey, the other red. In one hand Keld had something long wrapped in a cloak.

A spear?

Keld strode to the centre of the clearing and paused beside the table, looking at it with a glower. Then he lifted his gaze and stared around the circle, meeting the eyes of each and every hunter. Drem shook his head when Keld's eyes locked with his.

No sign of the living.

With a nod, Keld put a horn to his lips and blew upon it.

An answering horn echoed in the distance. Soon Drem felt a tremor in the ground.

It is hard for the warband of the Order to move stealthily, especially when there are over a hundred giant bears amongst their ranks.

Shapes filled a wide street to the west, which cut through the mine from its main gate and led here. Mounted figures spilt into the clearing. At their head was Byrne, the High Captain of the Order of the Bright Star, and Drem's aunt. She was a stern-faced woman, dark hair drawn back tightly to her nape, her mail coat and leather surcoat thick with dust from their ride here. A curved sword arched across her back. Drem considered how unassuming she looked, no ostentatious embellishments, no gold or silver, just plain, though expertly made equipment. To see her, no one would guess just how deadly Byrne truly was. Drem thought back to the recent battle: Byrne trading blows with Fritha, using both blade and the earth magic. Fritha had clearly been outclassed. Drem felt a rush of pride and affection for Byrne. She had saved his life in that battle. She was his kin and, with both mother and father dead, the only kin he had— that meant a lot to Drem. More than that, she had shown him love and kindness, and that counted for far more in these bleak and desolate times.

At Byrne's shoulder a huge bear lumbered, upon it a dark-haired and pale-skinned giantess, Queen Ethlinn, a spear in her fist with its butt resting in a saddle-cup. Ethlinn's eyes scanned the clearing, focusing on the table.

To the other side of Byrne, another giant strode, his white hair braided, a creased lattice of scar tissue where one eye had once been. His coat of mail and leather jerkin did little to hide the slabs of muscle that padded his frame. He gripped a war-hammer in his huge hands. Balur One-Eye, father of Eth-linn, most famed warrior of the Banished Lands.

Behind these three rode the warband of the Order: an assortment of giants upon bears with mounted warriors, more riders coming out into the clearing from smaller streets. Drem saw red-haired Cullen riding close behind Byrne. The young warrior's eyes sought out Drem and he gave him a wry grin. Keld had spoken for Drem and his skills as a huntsman and tracker, and had easily accepted him into the hunter's order. Cullen had wanted to accompany Drem into the mine with the other scouts, but Byrne had forbidden it. Cullen was not a hunter, with neither the patience nor aptitude for stealth. He *was* skilled with a blade, more than most—far more than Drem—but he was hot-headed and acted before thinking, so Byrne had ordered the young warrior to stay with her. Cullen had been none too pleased about that.

Byrne rode up to the table and reined in, the others rip-pling to a halt behind her. With practised ease, Byrne slipped from her saddle. She approached the table, stopped before it and stared at it with a scowl. Ethlinn followed, holding a hand out over the table, her lips moving, and then she winced, as if seeing the terrible acts that had occurred upon it. Balur lifted one of the chains and curled a lip, let it drop.

"Keld?" Byrne looked to her huntsman.

"Place is empty." Keld grunted. "Been that way a while, by the looks of it."

Byrne nodded, her eyes returning to the table.

"But I did find this." Keld held out the object he had bun-dled in his cloak.

Byrne reached out and unwrapped the object; a series of emotions flittered across her face as she recognized it. Sor-row, anger. There was a slight tremor in Byrne's hands as she revealed it.

A sword.

Drem knew it immediately, even if it was still in its scabbard with a long belt wrapped around it. Its size and length made it obvious that this was no ordinary sword, that it had belonged to a giant or giantess.

Sig's sword.

Drem felt a fist clench in his gut at the sight of it. He had known Sig for such a short time, but she had left an irremovable mark upon his heart. An example of true friendship, of loyalty. Of love.

Of truth and courage.

A tear ran down his cheek.

Byrne nodded, holding the sword up high for all to see.

"You should take this," Byrne said, turning and offering it to Balur One-Eye.

The old giant blinked. He slung his war-hammer over his shoulder, reached out a tentative hand, then drew it back.

"No," the giant said. "It should go to someone in your Order. Sig was a warrior of the Bright Star, through and through."

Byrne lowered the blade, resting its scabbarded tip upon the ground. "So are you, in here," Byrne said, touching a hand to her heart with one hand.

"Huh," grunted Balur, not a denial, Drem noted. "But I have not taken your oath."

"You *knew* Corban, *knew* what he fought for. You were his *friend*," Byrne said.

"I was," Balur breathed, "but I never took his oath. Only one oath guides me. To guard my daughter's life with my own." He reached out a calloused hand and touched Ethlinn's cheek.

Ethlinn wrapped his hand in her own and smiled. "That oath would never conflict with the oath of the Order," she said. "Sig was dear to you. You should take the sword."

Balur stared at it and nodded.

"Aye, all right then." He reached out a hand and took the blade from Byrne, drew it from its scabbard and held it high. It glinted in the summer sun, though dark patches stained it.

"I'll avenge you with this sword, brave Sig," Balur shouted, his voice echoing from the buildings and down empty streets. A cheer rang out from the warriors around him. Drem's voice was one of the loudest.

You have already fulfilled part of that promise, Drem thought, remembering Balur fighting the giant, Gunil, Sig's killer and a traitor to the giants. Balur had crushed his skull with a blow from his war-hammer.

Drem had felt a huge sense of satisfaction at seeing Gunil slain, not only as revenge for Sig's death, but Gunil had also been one of those responsible for the murder of Drem's father, Olin.

Just Fritha left to face justice for that, now, Drem thought, his hands involuntarily clenching into fists at the thought of the woman who had slain his father.

"And it is rune-marked," Byrne said quietly to Balur, with a small smile as the cheering died down, and Balur slipped the sword back into its scabbard. "That may come in very handy in the coming days."

"Aye." Balur nodded.

During the battle against Fritha they had been attacked by a swarming host of Revenants, twisted offspring created by the bite of Gulla and his chosen. They were human in shape, but fought with an utter disregard for their own safety and were near-impossible to kill. Drem had seen decapitation put one down, but other than that they just kept coming at you. Unless they were stabbed with a rune-marked blade. When struck with a blade that had been inscribed with runes of earth power the Revenant would fall, every time. Drem had stabbed the host's captain, Ulf, with his own seax, rune-marked by Drem's father, Olin. Ulf had died and, with his death, the whole of his Revenant host had collapsed and died as well.

Every single one of us should have a rune-marked blade.

But they were rare, only belonging to those whom Byrne had deemed trustworthy enough to teach the earth power to. She said it was a great responsibility, learning the earth power, and so only a small portion of the Order of the Bright Star wielded such weapons. Sig had been one of them.

Now, though, after the battle with Fritha, there was a need for all to carry a rune-marked weapon, whether they knew the earth power or not. Otherwise there would be no standing against these Revenants.

Balur shrugged his war-hammer off his back and slid the sword over his shoulder, fumbling at the belt straps. Byrne helped him cinch them tight. The giant rolled his shoulders.

"I'll have to learn how to use this thing," he muttered.

"I'll teach you, One-Eye," Cullen called out. A few chuckles echoed around the clearing.

"I'll hold you to that, you young pup," Balur growled. He bent and picked up his war-hammer. "But for now, I'll stick to this." He hefted his war-hammer and smiled at its familiar weight.

Byrne looked back to Keld. "Will Balur get to wield his new blade here?"

"Not likely," Keld said. "We've scouted the place—not a living soul 'cept rats and the like. Only place we haven't looked is in there." The huntsman nodded towards the cliff face. "I wasn't going to send a handful of my crew in there until there were more swords at my back." The rock was pocked with scores of small caves, all of them set with iron-barred gates. Now open. Drem remembered all too well the inhabitants of those cells: Ferals, mutations of men, women and children, somehow warped into a malformed half-life, created by Fritha's twisted mind and her dark blood magic.

Set amongst the cells was a deeper blackness: a massive cave entrance which looked as if it ran deep into the rock face. Drem had a recollection of howls echoing out from that dark hole during the battle here on that nightmare-filled night.

Byrne lifted her eyes and stared at the black hole in the granite wall.

"Spread out, search every last handspan of this place," she called out. "I need to know where Gulla is."

The warband spread out into the surrounding buildings. Ethlinn and Balur remained, alongside a score of warriors, Byrne's honour guard with Cullen and Utul, Byrne's captain from the south. He was dark-skinned with a hooked nose, streaks of grey in his otherwise jet hair, and deep lines about his eyes—evidence of his near-constant smile. A curved sword hilt arched over his shoulder, similar to Byrne's, but with a longer grip. He was one of the deadliest swordsmen Drem had ever seen, and he'd had the privilege of seeing a few, lately.

"Drem, you're with us," Byrne said to him. Rab gave a croak, spread his wings and flapped into the air.

"You know this place better than any of us," Byrne said. "I want to take a look in there." She nodded towards the cave entrance and started walking, Ethlinn, Balur and the others following. Keld was already at the opening, striking sparks from flint and stone into a torch he'd taken from a sconce set just inside the cave entrance. Flames sparked and flared, sending shadows dancing. In the new light Drem saw the cave ran deep into the rock, sloping downwards.

Keld strode into the cave, holding the torch high. His two wolven-hounds, Fen and Ralla, followed him, though Drem could see their hackles were up, their noses twitching. Byrne ordered half her honour guard to remain at the cave entrance, the other ten following her as she marched after Keld. Ethlinn, Balur, Cullen and Utul accompanied her.

Drem drew in a deep breath and hurried after them.

CHAPTER TWO

JIN

Jin nocked an arrow, drew and loosed, repeating the action twice more before her first arrow thumped into the linden wood of a White-Wing's shield. Her second arrow *tinged* off an iron helm, the third punching into the warrior's eye. He fell back, causing a ripple in the shield wall as another stepped over his corpse to fill the gap.

A sharp scream somewhere above, a looming shadow, and a Kadoshim crashed to the ground, wings and arms splayed, blood pumping from a tear in its ringmail. Jin's horse danced sideways, treading on bodies, searching for even ground. Smoke billowed across the courtyard in great clouds, the reek of blood and death, the screams of battle and the dying everywhere.

Jin was holding the gates of Drassil, her oathsworn guards about her, others of her Clan dismounted now and in the gate tower. Arrows whistling down from above told her they had taken the towers and were on the wall. She gave a snarled grin at her success and snatched a moment to look and assess the battle.

She and her Cheren Clan had wreaked havoc with their initial assault, the gate guards thinking she was their ally and opening the gates for her and her warriors. She had swept them away in a tide of blood. But Drassil's White-Wings were regrouping now: a shield wall formed in the centre of the courtyard, pushing towards her. Fritha's acolytes were pouring through the open gates, a wave of shaven-haired warriors, grim-faced and resolute. They were men and women who had rebelled against the rule of the Ben-Elim and allied themselves to the Kadoshim, some of them having lived from hand to mouth in the wild for many years, outlawed for their audacity in spurning the Ben-Elim's iron Lore. Now was time for their revenge.

It had been a long time coming.

I want so much revenge. Against the Ben-Elim and their White-Wing puppets who have kept me a captive in this disgusting, barbaric hole when I could have been riding free upon the Sea of Grass with my kin about me.

With my father.

She still felt his death as if it was a physical blow. His murder was imprinted upon her mind, like when she looked at the fire too long, nothing else to see except the flames. Bleda's blade stabbing into her father's throat, sawing through it, a gush of blood.

I will kill you for that, Bleda, if it is the last thing I do.

Even killing Bleda's mother a few moments later had not softened her need for vengeance. It burned inside her.

He made a fool of me. My betrothed, meeting in secret with that half-breed winged bitch! To think I pleaded with my father to let him live, to allow us to wed. Her shame twisted her mouth into a snarl, too much for her to control.

The acolytes slammed into the shield wall, horses rearing, neighing. Screams rang as short-swords stabbed out from the shields, the White-Wings killing efficiently. But there were so many acolytes, more of them riding into the courtyard with every heartbeat, and behind them Jin glimpsed a rolling tide of mist. She knew what was hidden within that.

Time to move.

Gulla had assured her that his creatures in the mist would not harm her or her Cheren warriors, but she had seen what they had done to the Sirak. It was a risk she'd rather not take.

"With me!" she cried, a squeeze of her knees, and her mount responded, carrying her away from the gateway. A clatter of hooves and hundreds of her warriors followed her, in deels of blue and coats of mail, recurved bows in their fists, hawk banners snapping in the wind. First amongst them was faithful Gerel, close by her shoulder as always, her oathsworn man and guardian.

Jin reined in, seeing her new location opened up angles and gaps for her arrows to penetrate the wall of enemy shields. She reached for her quiver and nocked an arrow, cursing as the muscle twinged in her shoulder, not yet fully healed from an arrow wound taken during Bleda's escape.

That winged bitch put an arrow in me. If her aim was any better…

The White-Wings were still standing, holding the tide of acolytes, no matter that they were overwhelmingly outnumbered. They looked like a boulder in a river of shaven-haired warriors. Many acolytes were sweeping around the shield wall's flanks, ignoring them entirely and rushing towards the goal. Asroth, their frozen king. Jin ignored the protest from the frayed tendons of her shoulder and loosed, once, twice, three times, her Clansmen doing the same, a hail of arrows raining into the shield wall. The *clatter-thump* of arrows in shields, screams as some found the gaps and sank into flesh.

Mist moved in Jin's peripheral vision, a cloud of it boiling through the gateway's tunnel, into the courtyard, and Jin glimpsed figures in the mist, long-limbed arms and taloned hands, heard the slavering snarls and sibilant hissing as her new allies swept into Drassil and over the shield wall, sweeping around it.

A few moments silence and then the screaming began.

The crack of shields breaking, torn from arms, swords stabbing. Jin knew the sound of steel punching into meat, and of blows, the tearing and rending of flesh. Screams rose in pitch, fear-laced, and the shield wall was rippling, fracturing into a hundred pieces.

There is no holding back those…things.

The mist swept on, fragmenting, roiling into the street that led to Drassil's Great Hall.

"This is done: the courtyard is ours," Jin muttered to Gerel. He nodded, eyes fixed on the mist-shrouded carnage, streaks of blood punctuating the air.

Jin clicked and her horse moved on.

"Where are you going?" Gerel called after her.

"Looking for more White-Wings to kill," Jin said.

"Gulla said to take the gate and hold it," Gerel reminded her.

"I am not his whipped hound," she snapped back. "He is my ally, not my master. Besides, the gate is taken, there will be no coming back from this. And I have not killed nearly enough of my enemies."

Gerel nodded at that and urged his horse after her. Cheren warriors followed, their hooves mixing with the sound of battle.

Jin reined in, staring.

Wide streets led away from the courtyard to all parts of Drassil's fortress. The heaviest fighting was filling the street that led to Drassil's Great Hall, where Asroth was held in his iron prison. But Jin had seen something in one of the other streets, one that headed eastwards. A group of White-Wings, running across, away from the Great Hall, away from the battle. Some were limping.

One of them had stopped, was staring aghast into the courtyard. She had dark hair, cropped short like all of the White-Wings, but Jin recognized her, had watched her training in the weapons-field for so many years. There was a confidence and fluid economy in her movements that only the finest warriors possessed.

"Aphra," Jin whispered.

The figure turned and ran on with her companions, disappearing from view.

"If I cannot kill the half-breed bitch right now, then I will make do with killing her sister," Jin said, with a savage grin.

She touched her heels to her mount.

CHAPTER THREE

RIV

Riv swayed in the sky as her wings powered her, one hand carrying a dazed warrior through the air. All about her Ben-Elim and Kadoshim were locked in battle, a savage aerial conflict that filled the sky with blood and feathers.

She swung her short-sword at a Kadoshim who flew too close as he stabbed and slashed at a Ben-Elim. Her blade sliced through the meat of his wing and sent the demon tumbling towards the ground.

The Ben-Elim she had saved gave her a curt nod, then his eyes widened at what she was grasping in her left hand.

Not what, but *who*.

Another Ben-Elim, long black hair tied at the nape, a series of scars running across his forehead and down one cheek.

Meical, once High Captain of the Ben-Elim, though for more than a hundred years he had been locked within a cage of starstone metal, none knowing if he were alive or dead.

Riv had rescued him from Drassil's Great Hall, where Gulla and his Kadoshim had been moving to slay the newly awakened Ben-Elim, and now they were in the air above the courtyard beyond the hall. Bodies littered the ground, combat swirling in knots below them.

Meical had been dazed when she grabbed him and carried him from the hall.

Well, a sleep one hundred and thirty-eight years long would do that, Riv thought.

Now he was gazing around, eyes more focused, taking in the carnage. He looked at Riv, his lips moving, but Riv could not hear what he was saying over the din of battle echoing around them.

"Where's Corban?" Meical shouted louder to her.

Riv blinked. It wasn't a question she'd expected.

Corban? The founder of the Order of the Bright Star?

"He's dead," Riv called down to him.

Confusion, shifting to grief. The sense of pain and loss emanating from the Ben-Elim's eyes was so acute that Riv's breath caught in her chest. "For nearly eighty years," she told him.

"No." She saw his lips make the word.

Behind them a cloud of Kadoshim burst out of the doors of the Great Hall, Gulla leading the charge, larger than the other Kadoshim. His face was twisted in a rictus of hatred, head twitching like a predatory bird's as he scanned the courtyard.

He hunts Meical.

Riv closed her wings and dived, settling upon a rooftop and dragging Meical under an overhang and into deep shadows.

"What do you mean, eighty years?" Meical said.

Riv peered out into the sky, saw Gulla leading his Kadoshim south-east, towards Drassil's main gates.

She looked back at Meical and sucked in a deep breath.

"You've been asleep for one hundred and thirty-eight years," Riv explained. Of course, the day he had been frozen had been a day of battle, much like this.

She waved a hand at the conflict all around them. "This isn't your Day of Wrath, when the Kadoshim were defeated and you and Asroth were encased in starstone metal. That happened a *long* time ago."

Meical rubbed a hand over his eyes and pinched his nose, processing Riv's words. He sighed and let out a long breath.

A lot for him to take in, but I don't have time for this. Riv needed to find Aphra, and below that emotion was a deeper, darker pool tugging at her, that ever-present current of rage whispering to forget all else and just kill every enemy she encountered. There were Kadoshim and their followers everywhere, and they needed to die.

A hand gripped her shoulder.

"Tell me," Meical said, his eyes focusing on Riv, his confusion and grief of moments before gone, the pain in his eyes shut away.

"The Kadoshim have attacked Drassil," she said quickly, "released you and Asroth from your gaol." She thought about that. "They set Asroth free, and you were just a by-product of that."

Meical nodded. "They were about to kill me," he whispered, eyes distant, remembering.

"Aye," Riv agreed. "They still might, if we don't get out of here."

"Who leads the Ben-Elim?"

Riv shrugged. "Kol, if he's still alive."

"Kol? What of Israfil?"

"Israfil's dead." She held a hand up to Meical's questioning look. "There's no time," she snapped, the screams of battle still loud. "Drassil is fallen, our only hope is to escape. Now!"

"Flee?" Meical said, his lip curling.

"Yes, flee," Riv growled. She didn't like the thought of running away, either—it left a bad taste in her mouth—but living was better than dying. With a beat of her wings, Riv shrugged off Meical's grip and rose into the air, hovering above him. Meical's eyes took in her dapple-grey feathers.

"You are not Ben-Elim," Meical said, eyebrows knotting. "What are you?"

"I told you, there's no more time for talking," Riv said, her patience fraying, thinking of Aphra out there, fighting, needing her. "If we get out of here, I'll answer all your questions, but right now we need to get moving." She twirled the short-sword

in her fist. "I'm leaving. You can stay and die, or fly and live."
She beat her wings, climbing higher into the air, and looked
down at him.

Meical stared at her, then looked beyond her, at the battle-
stained skies.

"Give me a sword," he snarled.

She grinned back fiercely, threw her short-sword to him and
drew her other blade from its scabbard.

Meical caught the sword, hefted it for balance, then crouched
and leaped into the air. His wings were wide and bright white—
a pure-bred Ben-Elim, unlike her "tainted" half-breed blood, as
the others considered her.

The courtyard below was a swirling maelstrom of combat, clusters of White-Wings in their shield walls still holding
against the Kadoshim's acolytes swarming around them. Here
and there Riv glimpsed darker groups of the pale-faced, sharp-
toothed *things* that she had fought in Forn Forest. They were
shaped like men and women, but they fought like nothing Riv
had ever seen before, an unfettered ferocity that was more animal than human. And they were hard to kill, decapitation seeming to be the only way to put one of them down permanently.

Riv had seen three war-hosts of these creatures swarming
towards Drassil's walls. She knew there was no standing against
them—they were too many.

In the air about them Ben-Elim fought with Kadoshim and
their half-breed offspring. Riv twisted and turned through the
combat, part of her desperate to wade in and spill the blood of
her enemy, but she had helped Aphra and a few score White-
Wings fight free of Drassil's hall, and now she feared what had
become of them since she had turned back to rescue Meical.

A blast of turbulent air was her only warning. She twisted,
seeing the leathery wings and flat features of a Kadoshim half-
breed, the glint of steel as a sword stabbed at her. With a few
strong wing strokes, she halted her trajectory and defended.
Sparks flew as she deflected the blade, but the half-breed's

momentum carried him on. He crashed into her and they spun through the air together, locked in battle, snarling and spitting in each other's eyes as they fought to be the victor.

Riv wrapped one arm around her attacker's waist, dragged herself closer and slammed her forehead into his face. Cartilage shattered, blood spurted, but the half-breed just spat curses at her and tried to smash his sword hilt into Riv's skull.

She turned, felt air rush past her face as the hilt skimmed her. A twist of her arm as she drew back her own weapon for a killing thrust.

The half-breed suddenly stiffened, eyes and mouth wide with surprise, a tide of blood bubbling from his lips, his lungs pierced and flooding. Then he slumped, plummeting to the ground.

Meical hovered in the air, his sword red, his face cold and hard with hatred. He threw Riv's short-sword back to her, another, longer sword in his fist now, plucked from the half-breed's dying fingers.

"I had him," Riv snarled, resenting Meical for taking her kill.

"You said we need speed," Meical reminded her.

Aphra.

Riv bit back an angry retort, sheathed her swords, tucked a wing and turned northwards.

The main gate into Drassil was on the western wall, and that was where the fighting had been fiercest. Cheren horse-archers, led by their traitorous queen, Jin, had taken the gate and held it for the Kadoshim's acolytes, allowing them to pour into Drassil, and close behind them had come the cloud-shrouded monsters from Forn Forest.

There would be no escape for any on foot through *those* gates.

But, for those with knowledge, there were more ways out of Drassil.

Riv beat her wings faster and soon the air was clearing of fighting Ben-Elim and Kadoshim. A glance over her shoulder showed that Meical was close behind. She veered right, twisting and diving low, speeding along mostly empty streets, buildings rearing either side of her. Here and there people were running, not warriors—the White-Wing barracks were all situated to the south of the fortress—but traders and their families. Riv's heart went out to them.

How can they defend themselves against the Kadoshim and their host?

"MAKE FOR THE EAST GATE!" Riv yelled to them as she sped over their heads.

A turn southwards, the sound of screams drifted on the air, growing louder, the clatter of hooves. Riv's gut instinct was drawing her to the sounds of battle, but with an act of will she veered left, down another empty street, heading eastwards.

Again, the sounds of battle faded and Riv gave herself to her wings. They beat a storm, speeding her through Drassil's cobbled streets, whipping up a trail of leaves and dirt in her wake. The speed ripped tears from her eyes, sending her fair hair streaking in the air like a wind-whipped banner. Fear for Aphra, her sister—no, her *mother*—gave her wings even more strength, buildings passing by at a dizzying pace.

The thought of Aphra lying in a pool of her own blood with a Kadoshim standing over her would not leave Riv's mind.

A riderless horse jolted her back to the present. A warrior's foot was tangled in the stirrup, his body dragging along the ground.

One of the Cheren. Riv recognized the rider with his shaved head and warrior braid. Battle-cries echoed from the direction the horse had appeared. Riv swept on, turned a corner, and the street and buildings disappeared as Drassil's weapons-field opened up before her. Riv had grown up in Drassil, and most of those seventeen years had been spent on this field. It was the place she loved most, the place she had learned to become a warrior, and even though much violence had been practised here, it had always felt like a place of safety, of camaraderie.

And now it was filled with blood and screams.

CHAPTER FOUR

DREM

"Drem," Byrne called, and he hurried past the bulk of Balur to walk alongside his aunt. To either side, carved out of the cave walls, were more open cells, iron bars rusted. Here and there a smaller tunnel branched off. At each of these one of Byrne's guards stopped, a guardian against any hidden foes creeping up on them out of the darkness.

This is not a good place to be caught in an ambush, Drem thought.

Balur stuck his head inside one of the open cells, holding a torch he'd taken from the wall and lit with Keld's. He wrinkled his nose and spat.

"When you came here before, did you enter this place?" Byrne asked Drem.

"No," Drem replied. He had been to the mine twice: once on his own, searching for his father's murderers, and once with Sig, Keld and Cullen. "I did hear...things, in here, though."

"What things?" Byrne asked.

"Ferals, I think," Drem said, straining his memories. "It was the night Sig fell. We were fighting, out there." He nodded back towards the circle of daylight disappearing behind them. "Cullen was standing on the table, I was with Sig." He paused, frowning. "Keld opened the cages in the cliff face, letting the Ferals who weren't loyal to Fritha out. It was chaos, you understand, but I can remember hearing howling, like a storm, deafening, echoing out of the tunnel mouth."

"Hmm," Byrne said. "Ferals." She nodded, looking either side of them. "A lot of empty cages."

"They're not here now, though, more's the pity," a voice said behind Drem. Cullen, he realized.

Byrne looked at Cullen and frowned. "So, where are the Ferals now?"

"Food for crows," Cullen said, grinning. "We carved them all up back in the Desolation."

Drem shook his head. "There are a *lot* of cages down here," he said.

Byrne nodded. "We fought many Ferals, but *this* many?"

Ahead of them the torch stopped moving. Keld was standing and staring at something ahead. Drem saw Fen take a few steps ahead of Keld, muscles tense and coiled, as if he was hunting something. Ralla, the red-furred hound that had belonged to another hunter lost in the battle at the Desolation, paced forwards with a deep-throated growl, to stand beside Fen.

The group moved to join Keld, staring ahead to where the tunnel entered a large chamber. The scuff of their boots on stone echoed into the dark. The path curved left and right into the darkness.

A cavern?

A terrible smell pervaded the air. Decay, faeces and urine.

And before them was a drop, their torchlight flickering down into what looked like a pit, the sides too uniform to have been made naturally. It was deep, but in the dim light Drem saw shadowed shapes on the ground, utterly still. Without thinking, his seax was in his fist.

Balur stepped to the side and raised his torch to a sconce in the wall, lighting another torch, its flames crackling into life and illuminating more of the room.

Cullen slipped past them and walked along the left pathway, taking the torch and lighting others set into the walls.

Light slowly seeped into the chamber. Drem saw that the motionless shapes in the pit were cadavers, piles of skin and bone. Misshapen skeletons with long claws and too many teeth, elongated spines, sometimes a clump of fur.

"Ferals," Utul said.

"Dead Ferals," Cullen said, looking down into the pit with interest. "Anything that did walk or draw breath is long gone." He wrinkled his nose. "Or long dead."

A sound drifted out of the darkness.

A scraping and wheezing.

The sound was coming from the pit.

Something crawled out of the shadows, human-like in shape, in that it had a head, two arms and two legs, but there were patches of fur on an elongated skull, its lower jaw was distended, teeth like tusks curling out over its snout, and its hind legs were bunched and misshapen with muscle. With one long-clawed hand it reached forwards to dig into the hard-packed earth and drag itself along. The other arm was twisted tight to its body, like an old, arthritic man's. It made a snuffling, rasping sound from deep in its throat.

Fen and Ralla's growling grew deeper, more malevolent.

A Feral, Drem thought, though it didn't resemble the creatures he had fought in the Desolation. They were all mutated, twisted beings, animals and humans merged with dark magic. But the animal part of most of the creatures Drem had fought resembled wolven. This thing before him looked more as if it had started life as a boar.

"I'll put it out of its misery," Cullen said, with a grimace.

Before Byrne could say anything, Cullen had jumped into the pit. He threw his torch behind the crawling *thing*, revealing an empty space behind the creature.

Cullen's sword hissed from its scabbard.

The thing on the ground had seen or smelled Cullen and dragged itself towards the red-haired warrior. It left gouged tracks in the ground behind it, and in its wake some kind of dark fluid moistened the hard earth.

It crawled to a stop before Cullen, taking deep snorting breaths, apparently exhausted.

"Poor beast," Cullen said.

It sniffed, a wet snorting, its one good arm hovering in the air, its hind legs scrabbling, bunching under its torso.

"Get out of there, you idiot," Byrne called down to Cullen furiously, "until we have this room lit."

"It's as weak as a newborn," Cullen assured her, eyes fixed on the creature at his feet. The thing looked up at Cullen, then, in a shocking burst of speed, it erupted towards him, hind legs propelling it forwards. Its one good arm wrapped around Cullen's leg and it sank its tusks into his calf.

Cullen screamed, shock and pain mingled, and he hacked down at the thing. His blade bit, but not as deep as Drem had expected; the thick folds of skin on the creature snared Cullen's sword. Blood welled.

Byrne was shouting orders as Drem leaped down after his friend. It had not been a conscious decision. His seax and small axe were in his fists, gleaming red and gold in the flickering torchlight as he broke into a run.

Sounds came from the darkness: snorting, scrabbling noises.

Drem heard Byrne's voice, followed by Balur One-Eye's battle roar and the ground trembled as the giant jumped into the pit after him. Drem was close to Cullen now and raised his axe as he ran.

Something slammed into Drem's side, sending him flying through the air. He hit the ground hard, air punched from his lungs, and tumbled with something heavy on him, another Feral—solid, all muscle, coiled strength and a frenzied, ravenous hunger. The sharp stench of urine and blood filled his senses. He struck at it, felt his axe bite, then lost his grip on it as they rolled. He had a glimpse of tusks and rowed teeth, of snapping jaws and fetid breath. Still rolling, he stabbed with his seax, which did better than his axe. He felt the blade pierce the thick hide and sink deep, felt blood well over the hilt, over his glove and soak into his linen undershirt. With a high-pitched squeal, the creature pulled away. Drem yanked on his seax but it grated on bone, was snagged somehow, and the blade was ripped out of his hand.

Drem crashed into one of the cadavers. It exploded, covering him with stinking strips of skin and gnawed bone. He scrambled to his feet, breath heaving, a hot pain radiating from his ribs where the thing had connected with him. There were rents in his mail, rings hanging. In his peripheral vision he glimpsed Cullen still hacking at the creature trying to eat his leg, many more of the beasts attacking a handful of Byrne's honour guard who had joined them in the pit, and Balur One-Eye swinging his hammer.

Drem realized he was standing a dozen paces from the boar-thing that had attacked him, with no weapons in his hands.

Then it was coming at him again.

Stumbling away, he reached for his father's sword, sheathed at his hip, had a moment to wish he had a boar spear with a cross-bar, probably the best way to kill one of these things and keep it from goring him with its tusks. His draw turned into an upward cut, the blade's tip shearing through the beast's lower jaw, cutting through one tusk and up, through its cheek and on, carving through its brain and exploding from its skull in a spray of teeth and blood, brain matter and fragments of skull. The Feral's charge powered it on a dozen paces before its body realized it was dead and it crashed to the ground, skidding to a halt.

Drem had half a heartbeat to stare at the dead Feral before another one crashed into his legs, hurling him into the air. This one was bigger. Its momentum carried it on beneath him as Drem slammed into the ground behind it, feeling a sharp pain in his shoulder as he started to rise. The beast skidded, already turning, its feet scrambling for purchase on the bones and carcasses scattering the cavern floor.

It came at him again, snorting and squealing, tusks gleaming. Drem desperately tried to lever himself upright with his sword, knowing he was too slow.

Two snarling wolven-hounds collided with the onrushing

creature, knocking it off course, and it stumbled past Drem. Fen and Ralla, their jaws wide and biting, ripping chunks out of the Feral.

It came to a halt, twisting and spinning shockingly fast, its head catching Fen, hurling the wolven-hound into the air. Ralla snarled and threw herself onto the creature. Drem was on his feet now, rushing forwards, sword raised, and then Keld was there, sword and axe a blur, blood in the air.

The creature screamed, gurgled, legs spasming as it collapsed.

Keld wrenched his axe from the dead beast's skull.

"*LASAIR!*" Byrne's voice yelled behind Drem, and he turned to see her in the pit with them. Her sword was covered in blood, Ferals lying dead about her, and Utul was close by, chopping, slicing and stabbing at a trio of attackers. Byrne raised her hands and pointed towards an unlit torch upon the pit wall. It sparked into life, almost immediately followed by the one next to it, and then all of the torches in the chamber were bursting into flame, a wildfire chain reaction rippling around the huge cavern, light flaring bright.

The pit was revealed in its entirety: a broad stinking hole scattered with half-decomposed remains and hunger-mad creatures. One of the Ferals that appeared dead still moved, just raising its head where it lay, too emaciated and debilitated to move. Others had clearly been feeding on the weakest and were still strong.

Ethlinn was in the pit, standing close to Balur, stabbing with her spear. A handful of Byrne's honour guard were hacking at the frenzied creatures. Balur One-Eye's hammer swung in a deadly rhythm, his new longsword strapped across his back.

This is hammer-work, little grace to it, or needed.

Bones were smashed to kindling.

And then it was all over.

A Feral's squeal quietened to a weak rattle and then a final sigh. Cullen kicked and shook himself free of the creature that had clung to him, dead now, Cullen's sword red to the hilt. He surveyed the room, his eyes coming to rest on Byrne, who was scowling at him, and he gave a shame-faced shrug.

"See, I said I'd put it out of its misery," he said.

Only the sound of warriors breathing hard, and then Balur's rumbling laughter.

"What is this place, anyway?" Cullen muttered, looking around.

"It looks like Fritha's breeding chamber," Drem said, his toe nudging a pile of gnawed bones. They were small—a cub, or a bairn.

Or both, combined.

"Aye," Byrne agreed, a look of sorrow on her face.

"Why were they not with Fritha, at the battle in the Desolation?" Cullen murmured.

"Perhaps these weak, deformed ones remained behind," Ethlinn said, "and they bred."

Drem nodded; he thought that made sense, though he placed a hand on his throbbing ribs.

Not that weak.

"This Fritha has unleashed a new evil upon the world," Ethlinn said to herself, as she crouched and rested a hand upon one of the dead Ferals. "I can feel the earth power in it, twisted and tainted." She sighed. "These poor creatures. What has this Fritha done?"

Drem hadn't thought of that, Fritha's creations unleashed upon the world, breeding and mutating, adapting. The Banished Lands were dangerous enough, without Fritha's new terrors stalking it.

Fritha has much to answer for.

There was the slap of feet, echoing louder down the chamber. They all turned, weapons ready, as a figure emerged from the tunnel entrance and looked down into the pit.

It was Shar, a Jehar warrior and Utul's captain. Her long

dark hair was plastered to her head with sweat and she was breathing hard.

"We've found something," she said.

Drem stood on the shore of Starstone Lake, its slate-grey water glistening in the summer sun. To the south beyond the lake there was a smudge of green-topped hills, and to the east Drem heard the faint sound of gulls, a reminder of how close they were to the Grinding Sea. Decades ago, a canal had been dug by the first inhabitants of Kergard, leagues long, joining what had once been this huge crater to the sea. And then the waters had flooded in, filling the crater and turning it into a lake. That had been the beginning of the Desolation becoming habitable once more.

Since then more and more people had crept into the north, fleeing the strict rule of the Ben-Elim, or just wanting a more solitary life. Drem and his da had been part of that movement. Kergard had been a thriving town when they had come north, and had grown with every passing year.

Kergard is thriving no more. It is an empty, desolate place now.

Drem had passed through the town the day before. Part of it had burned down, gaping holes in the stockade wall, buildings— including Hildith's mead-hall—little more than ash-filled foundations. But much of the town stood as Drem remembered it. Just empty. Like a dead, soulless corpse.

A number of piers and jetties jutted out over the lake's water and the ground showed signs of a lot of movement. The shore was rutted with wide wheel tracks, the evidence of many boots lay all along this stretch of land. Abandoned cranes on the piers creaked in the breeze.

But this was not what Drem was staring at, alongside Byrne, Ethlinn and the others. They were standing before a boatshed, one of many along the lakeshore. Within it was a large timber scaffolding frame, discarded tools and offcuts of timber, empty barrels lined along one wall. Keld approached one and looked in.

"Pitch pine," he muttered, then looked at Byrne. "Caulking for a ship's hull."

"Now we know why Gulla was not with Fritha, or to be found anywhere in the Desolation," Balur One-Eye rumbled. "He's sailed away, with a warband far larger than the one we fought."

"Where is the sneaky bastard, then?" Cullen said. His calf was bandaged and he'd walked from the mine with a limp.

Drem turned, looking out across the lake, towards the wide canal that led to the Grinding Sea. He remembered a dark night, watching as ships rowed towards one of the piers, Kadoshim flying in the sky above them. He remembered what those ships carried.

Asroth's hand, cut from him in the Great Hall of Drassil.

He looked to Byrne.

"There is a reason that Kol and his Ben-Elim have not joined us," Byrne said, arriving at the same conclusion as Drem. "Fritha was a lure, to keep us in the north, and out of Gulla's way."

She looked at them all with a sombre gaze.

"Gulla has attacked Drassil."

CHAPTER FIVE

RIV

Riv slowed to a standstill and hovered for a moment, taking in the scene before her. The weapons-field of Drassil was a battle-ground. Fear snatched her breath away; she had told Aphra to come here, had arranged to meet her here because the eastern gate was only a few hundred paces from the weapons-field. She'd assumed the bulk of the fighting would have been between the main gate to the west and Drassil's hall, further north. Her eyes frantically scanned the field.

Where is she?

Meical drew up alongside her.

Bodies littered the ground, dead or dying, a mixture of White-Wings, Cheren and acolytes.

The drum of hooves drew Riv's eyes to the centre of the field, where Cheren riders, hundreds of them, were encircling a block of White-Wings. Riv glimpsed a familiar face behind a rectangular shield and her heart lurched in her chest.

Aphra.

Riv had hoped the Cheren would have held their position at Drassil's main gate, but somehow a large body of them had made their way here, deep into the fortress.

The Cheren were constant motion, circling in a steady canter around the warriors on foot, losing a hail of arrows at them. Most of those thudded into the rectangular shields of the White-Wings' shield wall, but Riv heard screams, saw gaps appear in the wall as arrows found cracks in their defence.

Elsewhere, Riv saw other knots of White-Wings, out-numbered and surrounded by shaven-haired acolytes of the Kadoshim.

A glance around her showed the skies were relatively clear; the Ben-Elim and Kadoshim's aerial battle was happening else-where, over the southern and western regions of the fortress. With a pulse of her wings Riv flew higher. She flicked open the leather strap that held her Sirak bow in its case, gifted to her by Bleda. She snatched a handful of arrows from her quiver and began shooting at the Cheren riders.

She took no time to aim, just loosed arrow after arrow at the Cheren. They were riding in tight order, almost a solid wall around the White-Wings, so that it would have been hard for even Riv's poor marksmanship to miss. She saw a horse jolt and rear, throwing its rider, another Cheren swaying with an arrow sprouting from their shoulder, another fall as blood spurted from their throat.

A beating of wings beside Riv.

"I thought escape was the plan, that we had no *time* to fight," Meical said.

"I cannot leave them," Riv grunted.

"Explain," Meical snapped, as he gazed around the field.

"My mother leads those White-Wings," Riv grated, nod-ding down towards the encircled shield wall.

Meical stared at the fighting warriors. "Tell me who to kill," he said.

"The riders are our enemy, allied to the Kadoshim, and those with the shaven heads, they are Kadoshim acolytes, fanat-ics sworn to the Kadoshim's service."

Meical dipped his head, and then his wings were beating and he was speeding towards the Cheren riders, his sword held out straight before him.

Warriors amongst the Cheren realized they were under attack, some heads turning in her direction, seeing Meical speeding towards them.

Riv recognized one of the Cheren: a woman, shaven-haired apart from a dark warrior braid, sharp, proud eyes and intelligent features, features that Riv hated. Hot rage swept through her.

Jin.

Once-betrothed to Bleda, and now the new Queen of the Cheren since Bleda had cut her father's throat. Jin had been due to wed Bleda. She had clearly loved him in her way, but now that love had transformed into a white-hot hatred, for both Bleda and Riv, because Jin had seen them together in a moonlit glade.

Riv saw the Queen of the Cheren shift her weight in her saddle, bow arm turning towards Meical. Riv knew how deadly Jin was with a bow.

Without thinking, Riv loosed her whole handful of arrows at Jin, reached into her quiver to snatch more. The first arrow flew over Jin's head, the second slammed into her mount's neck, the third into Jin's thigh.

As her mount staggered, the arrow Jin had aimed at Meical flew wide. She snarled at the pain, gripping the arrow in her thigh and snapping its shaft. Her eyes searched the sky and met Riv's.

Jin's face shifted into a cold smile, a mutual hatred pulsing between them. Riv could see Jin shouting orders to her warriors, and half a dozen Cheren around her shifted in their saddles, their bows snapping towards Riv.

Uh-oh.

Cheren archers could take the eye from a hawk in flight.

I'm dead.

Then Meical slammed into the line of riders.

Cheren flew from their saddles with the impact, horses neighing and stumbling, breaking the Cheren line and flow. Meical's wings beat, pulling him back, his longsword swinging in wide circles. Blood sprayed. Riv saw a head sail through the air, droplets of blood tracing a bloody arc.

Riv drew her wings in tight and dropped like a stone to the ground, restrapping her bow into its case. The air whistled past her cheek as another arrow flew above her head, then her wings were out and she was rushing to the ground, a pulse and shift of balance sending her skimming above the bodies of the fallen.

Jin was still upon her horse, shouting orders. Some of her warriors were replacing their bows in their cases and drawing swords to fight Meical, others further out moving to take aim at Riv.

She reached out a hand, snatched up a shield from a dead White-Wing and held it in front of her as she hurtled towards the Cheren, felt the drum of arrows thumping into the wood, one arrowhead bursting through, cutting the leather and linen of her glove to pierce flesh.

The pain just made Riv angrier.

More arrows punched into her shield, splinters of wood spraying in her face as she drew closer, the force of the arrows' impact greater, and then she was amongst them, smashing the shield boss into a face, drawing one of her short-swords and slashing, blood spurting. Horses neighed and reared, the Cheren struggling to control their mounts. There was a glimpse of white feathers as Meical swirled amongst them, leaving death in his wake. Riv hacked her way to him, and together they fought amongst the Cheren, guarding each other's back.

A battle roar made her look up. The sound of bodies crashing together, and the White-Wings were there, charging in perfect formation, a wall of shields carving into the Cheren.

"RIV!" a voice screamed, Aphra, and Riv veered towards her mother, with Meical following. The weight of the shield on Riv's arm was like lead, but her rage carried her on, stabbing, spitting and snarling, and Cheren died before her.

And then Aphra was in front of her, dark hair close-cropped in the White-Wing style. Blood sheeted from a cut across her forehead, but her eyes were sharp and focused. They shared a fierce smile, Riv glimpsing her friends Vald and Jost in the shield wall that was reforming around Aphra.

Aphra bellowed a command and the shield wall took a step deeper amongst the Cheren riders, forcing a wedge, pressing their advantage as they stabbed with short-swords, carving bloody ruin. Horses screamed; one close to Riv reared and toppled, pinning its rider beneath it. The shield wall strode over them, swords stabbing down into the trapped warrior under their feet.

The Cheren circle broke apart. Shouted commands filtered through the roar and din of battle, and Riv saw the Cheren attempting to withdraw.

They need space for their bows to tell.

Aphra bellowed orders, trying to keep the Cheren engaged, to keep the shield wall amongst them.

Riv yelled wordlessly, leaping into the gap that was forming, dropping her splintered shield and dragging a Cheren warrior from her saddle, trying to maintain a link with their enemy, to foul their withdrawal and reformation. She punched her sword through a shirt of mail into the woman's belly, twisted her blade as she ripped it free, throwing the warrior to the ground. But the Cheren were too good to be snared like this and, in heartbeats, a space was opening, widening. The Cheren were cantering away, their line reforming, swords slipping back into scabbards, bows emerging from their saddle-cases.

With a burst of strength, Riv flew after them and grabbed a trailing rider, dragging him from his mount, the warrior twisting, elbowing Riv in the mouth, the two of them falling to the ground as the horse galloped away. Riv spat and cursed, stabbed and punched, but the Cheren warrior avoided her blade and drew a knife. Then the man was being hauled away from her; Vald's bulk was standing over them. His sword cut the Cheren's throat and he cast the dying man away.

"You can't kill them all single-handedly," Vald said with a grin as he grabbed Riv's wrist and pulled her to her feet.

A whistle of arrows and Vald turned, raising his shield over them. A drum of impact as arrows punched into wood.

"Fly," Vald said to Riv.

"I'll not leave you like a fish in a barrel," she grunted.

Then more shields were slamming down around them: Aphra and her shield wall forming. Riv grinned at her mother.

"What now?" Jost's voice called out.

Riv bunched her wings and launched herself skywards, rising above the shield wall, hovering to take in the field.

Below her, seventy or eighty shields were tight around Aphra, elsewhere combat still raged in smaller knots: handfuls of White-Wings trying to stand against a swarm of acolytes.

The shield wall can hold for a while against the Cheren, but it won't be able to march and reach the East Gate. The Cheren are too accurate, will exploit the gaps in the wall that movement brings. And every moment we are held here we risk the Kadoshim and their dark creatures finding us.

Shadows flitted across the ground and Riv looked up.

Oh no.

Kadoshim and Ben-Elim, a rolling battle in the air that swept their way like wind-blown storm clouds. Some of the Ben-Elim surged down from the sky, spears and swords stabbing at the Cheren, who were turning, aiming their bows skywards.

Another roar rose from the west and Riv saw figures swarming into the field: men and women, even children, rushing into the weapons-field, snatching up the practice weapons that lay in racks and barrels. Riv recognized some of the traders she'd seen in Drassil's streets, the ones she'd urged to head for the East Gate. There were many more of them now. They charged at the Cheren and Kadoshim acolytes. Riv felt a swell of pride at their bravery, these ordinary people. The Cheren line fractured again as swords were drawn to deal with this new foe.

"Now!" Riv shouted as she turned to Aphra. "To the East Gate, NOW!"

Aphra hesitated a moment, staring at the Cheren line.

Riv felt it, too, the compulsion to stay and fight. To help those brave people that had attacked the Cheren. But if they stayed, the end was inevitable. She had seen the Kadoshim war-host.

"NOW!" she bellowed again at Aphra.

Her mother stood a moment longer, then she was turning, yelling orders, and the White-Wings took off eastwards. Riv saw them smash into the rear of a few score acolytes and scatter them, freeing a beleaguered knot of White-Wings, who joined them in their dash for the East Gate.

Riv hovered a moment, looking back towards the Cheren and those brave souls who had rushed them.

I cannot leave them, she realized, and made towards them.

The Cheren had recovered from the surprise of that first onslaught and were setting about carving the people of Drassil into bloody strips.

Riv reached them, chopped into a Cheren's neck, wrenched her sword free as she flew past. Meical scattered a handful of Cheren with his sword and wings.

"FLEE FOR THE EAST GATE!" Riv yelled to the people of Drassil around her. Some of them looked, breaking off from their combat, running for the gate.

A Ben-Elim and Kadoshim suddenly crashed to the ground in an explosion of feathers and dust.

In a heartbeat Riv and Meical were there, hovering. Together they stabbed down, piercing the Kadoshim's torso. He screamed, wings spasming, and then flopped still. Meical dragged the corpse off the Ben-Elim and Riv reached down, gave the survivor her arm.

It was Hadran, the warrior Kol had set as Riv's guardian during those early days in Drassil when she had been revealed as a half-breed. He staggered to his feet, sweat-stained and bloody.

"I am glad you are still alive," he said to Riv.

"You almost weren't," she said, a flash of her fierce grin.

"My thanks," he acknowledged, a dip of his head. Then his eyes shifted to Meical. He blinked, took a step back, eyes widening.

"Meical," he breathed.

Meical stood before him, silent. Then nodded. "Hadran," he said.

"But, if you're . . ."

"Aye. Asroth walks amongst us," Meical said grimly.

Hadran took another stumbling step backwards.

"Hadran." Riv shook him. "Look at me. The battle is lost. Where's Kol?"

The Ben-Elim's eyes focused on her. "Up there." Hadran gestured to the skies above them.

"Tell him of Asroth, tell him that we must flee now, live to fight another day."

Riv saw shame ripple across Hadran's face. "Flee the Kadoshim?" He rubbed a hand across his eyes. "How has this happened?"

"No time to question," Meical said, glancing at Riv. "Do as she says. This is one battle, not the war." He stepped close to Hadran, gripped his wrist. "Do not sell your life on the Kadoshim here. Live, and gather as many of our kin as you can. This need not be the end."

Hadran blinked, then nodded. "What of you?" he asked.

"I'm following her," Meical said, then looked at Riv.

"The cabin in Forn," Riv shouted to Hadran, and then she was leaping into the air.

Something drew Riv's eye further westwards, to the wide entrance to the weapons-field.

A dark cloud appeared, spilling from the street beyond, rolling onto the field like a mist. She glimpsed figures moving within it.

Riv had seen the damage just one of those *things* could do. Shouting a warning, she watched in horror as it washed over the rear ranks of those who had attacked the Cheren.

The screaming followed quickly.

With a savage growl, Riv rose higher in the air. She knew there was no defeating those *things* right now. People were screaming, the sound of death and slaughter spreading fear through their ranks. They began to break apart and run, but with the Cheren before them and the mist behind, there was no escape.

Riv dived, seeing a familiar face, blond hair and terror-filled eyes. Tam, the child of a wool-trader. He had never looked at her, a half-breed, with fear or disgust, only awe and excitement—she had let him ride on her shoulders once. She grasped his hand and heaved him into the air.

In Riv's arms the boy screamed as he watched the people he knew and loved slaughtered beneath them, but Riv knew there was nothing she could do against those creatures.

She turned and flew with all her strength, Tam's cries filling her world. Tears flowed from her eyes as she beat her wings and sped after Aphra. Meical caught up with her and together they overtook the White-Wings, coming to the smaller East Gate. Riv set Tam upon the ground and moved to the gate. It was barred, but Riv and Meical made short work of it, heaving the iron bar out of its brackets and throwing it to the ground. They put their shoulders to the gates and thrust them open.

A tunnel led beneath Drassil's thick walls. Light at the end of it revealed the empty plain beyond.

Riv turned and swept Tam back up into her arms. He was still crying.

Aphra reached them and Riv ushered her through, Jost and Fia, behind her, baby Avi strapped across Fia's chest, then scores more White-Wings, sixty, eighty, a hundred, more. Each one of them nodded to Riv as they passed into the tunnel. She was pleased to see the old weapons-master Ert amongst them, old, white-bearded and limping, but his face set in resolute lines and his sword red to the hilt in his fist. Behind him came Sorch, the White-Wing she had fought with more than once, even carried into the air and threatened to drop him. His eyes fixed on the sobbing Tam and he drew to a halt before her.

"I'll take him," Sorch said gently. He reached out a hand to Tam.

"I've got him," Riv said.

"You're injured," Sorch said, staring at her wings.

Riv frowned, glancing at herself. She was covered in blood, most of it not her own, although there were countless cuts and scratches on her limbs. She became aware of a dull ache in her back, from her wing. Glancing over her shoulder, she saw that her wound from a Cheren arrow on the muscle of a wing-arch had reopened. It pulsed blood in time with her heartbeat.

"Won't be able to fly far with that and extra baggage," Sorch said with a small smile.

He bent down to Tam. "Trust me, little man, I'll take care of you."

"Go on," Riv said, giving Tam a pat on the shoulder. "Sorch'll look after you for now. I'll catch up with you soon."

Tam nodded and allowed Sorch to sweep him up, then without another word the big warrior was running into the gate tunnel.

Riv waited until the last of the survivors had passed through and then searched the ground and sky behind them.

Where is Vald?

Riv had not seen her friend pass through the gates.

Without thinking, she beat her wings, began to move back towards the weapons-field.

Combat was still raging in a few knotted clumps, but most of the field was dominated with the enemy.

"Where are you going?" Meical called to her.

"My friend," she replied, hesitating. "I think he is out there."

Meical joined her, staring at the field.

Even as they both looked, the last knot of defence collapsed.

"If he is, he is dead," Meical said. He gripped Riv's hand. "Live," he said, "and avenge him."

I do not fear death, she snarled inside her head. *But to die here, now, would be pointless.*

"Ach, Vald, you big bull," Riv murmured.

"Revenge," she said brusquely at the field. With Meical she

retreated, closed the gates, reset the iron bar and took to the air, climbing higher and higher until they reached the top of Drass-il's walls. They hovered there a moment, looking back.

Drassil was in chaos, flames blooming, pillars of smoke curling into the sky.

It was hard, turning her back on her home, the place where she had grown up.

And now the Kadoshim have taken it from us. My home. I will come back here, Riv swore to herself, *and when I do, I shall make a mountain from the corpses of my enemies.*

CHAPTER SIX

FRITHA

Fritha stared up at Asroth, into the black pools of his eyes.

"We are betrothed," she repeated to him.

"Betrothed?" Asroth breathed, his voice a dry crackle.

Fritha was kneeling before the King of the Kadoshim, holding his hand. Power exuded from him like a living thing. It was as if she were sinking into a deep well, the world around her fading, Drassil's Great Hall, Kadoshim and Ben-Elim, blood and feathers, all the world blurring except for Asroth, who stood before her like a god made flesh. He wore a coat of mail, black and oily; dark veins mapped his alabaster skin, pale as milk. His long, silver hair was tied in a thick braid, his face sharp lines and chiselled angles, a white scar across his forehead. But it was Asroth's eyes that drew her, black and deep as forest pools at midnight.

Fritha blinked and shook her head, trying to pull herself back from the dark depths that were enveloping her. Part of her loved this feeling, part of her hated it.

"Yes. We are betrothed," she said quietly.

He is beautiful, she thought.

Asroth gave her a look of disdain and shook off her hand. He gripped her throat, hauling Fritha to her feet, then into the air, his face thrust in close.

"You are *human*." His eyes burned. "One of Corban's *maggots*." Revulsion twisted his lips and he began to squeeze.

Fritha tried to answer, but only a rattle came out and abruptly she couldn't breathe, could only feel the power in his fist as he crushed her neck. He seemed to be in no rush, watching her squirm. She clawed at his hand as he slowly tightened his grip.

He's going to kill me...

She reached desperately for her sword. Dots appeared before her eyes, blood pounded in her head, lungs screaming for air as blackness began to envelop her. Panic swept her, but her body wasn't responding, her limbs becoming heavy, uncoordinated.

Then something smashed into Asroth, sending them both flying through the air, crashing to the ground. Asroth's grip was gone and Fritha landed on the corpse of a White-Wing warrior. She lay there, sucking in great, ragged breaths, each one burning her throat. A bulky shadow loomed over her protectively, a taloned claw thumping down beside her head.

Wrath.

Her draig stood over her, bigger than a bull, a mass of muscle and fang and claw. "*No,*" Wrath growled. His tail lashed, sweeping corpses behind him.

A ragged strip of flesh hung from the draig's jaw.

Asroth climbed to his feet, eyes fixed like a predator on them. His right arm moved, as if reaching for a weapon, but his hand had been severed at the wrist. He held his arm up, seeing his disfigurement for the first time. He stared at the stump in shock, then looked about the room, at the corpses strewn all around him, at the Kadoshim and White-Wings fighting.

Fritha pushed herself to her knees.

There was a turbulence of air and Kadoshim were landing about Asroth, a score at least. They dropped to their knees. One of the Kadoshim remained standing, clad in blood-spattered mail, his hair shimmering darkness, a spear in his fist.

"Bune?" Asroth said, as if dragging a name from some distant memory.

"My King," Bune said, dropping to one knee with the other Kadoshim.

Asroth hesitated and pinched his nose, frowned. "Where is Meical?"

"He fled," Fritha answered before Bune could speak. She clambered out from beneath Wrath's bulk. The draig nuzzled her with his head. "Gulla has gone after him."

"Gulla," Asroth said, "my captain." He nodded. His eyes focused on Fritha, took in Wrath. The draig spread his wings, a ripple running through them, and growled. Fritha put a hand upon Wrath's jaw.

Bune looked up to see Asroth glaring at the two. "Lord, they are our allies..."

"What is happening here? Where is that maggot, Corban?" Asroth said. "And explain *this* to me." He waved his stump at Fritha and Wrath.

"You are newly awakened, Lord King," Bune said. "You and Meical were frozen within starstone metal. Fritha—" Bune pointed to Fritha with his spear—"she set you free."

A pause as Asroth took that in.

"How long?" he asked.

"One hundred and thirty-eight years," Fritha said. She saw the Starstone Sword upon the dais and took a slow step towards it.

"Corban? The battle?" Asroth touched the white scar on his head.

"We...lost," Bune said, bowing his head. "You and Meical were frozen," he repeated, "a sorcery of the enemy."

"That witch, Corban's sister," Asroth spat.

"Aye, Cywen," Bune said. "After you were trapped, we were routed and scattered. Gulla saved us from destruction and from that day to this we have fought. A hundred and thirty-eight years we have struggled, survived and planned for this moment."

A shriek above them. Two figures fell from the sky, two

pairs of wings, white feathers and dark skin. The two rolled on the ground, frantically stabbing at each other.

Asroth pulsed his wings to stand over the fighting warriors. He stamped down upon a white-feathered wing, grabbed the Ben-Elim's arm and twisted. There was an audible crack and the Ben-Elim cried out. Asroth grabbed a fistful of the Ben-Elim's hair and put a foot in the small of the warrior's back, then heaved. The Ben-Elim screamed again, arms flailing, his face purpling, eyes bulging, and then there was a series of concussive cracks, vertebrae snapping, the Ben-Elim's limbs flopping. Asroth dropped the corpse back onto the leathery-winged warrior, a rattling sigh escaping the dead Ben-Elim's throat.

The dark-winged figure shrugged off the Ben-Elim's corpse and stood. It was Morn, Gulla's half-breed daughter. She was blood-soaked and broad, slabbed with muscle, her close-cropped head slick with sweat and blood.

She looked about her, giving Fritha a curt nod. Then she dropped to one knee before Asroth, her eyes filled with awe.

"What are you?" Asroth said, frowning at Morn, studying her. As a half-breed she had the leathery wings of a Kadoshim, but her features were coarser, her frame squat and broader than the long-limbed, fine-boned Kadoshim.

"Gulla's daughter," Bune said. "We have not been idle. We have sired an army of half-breeds in this world of flesh, to replenish our numbers. Our losses were heavy on that day, but we have bided our time and made new allies."

"Allies, humans and half-breeds," Asroth growled, his lip curling as if the words had a foul taste. His eyes fixed on Bune a long moment, then snapped from Morn to Fritha.

"Aye. *Allies*," Fritha said, feeling her anger stir. She had sacrificed much, all, to bring this moment about, and Asroth sounded *ungrateful*. She took a few steps and stood over Morn, placed a hand on the half-breed's shoulder. "We are the difference between defeat and victory. Look about you, Lord King."

She gestured a hand around the huge chamber that was Drassil's Great Hall.

In the air above them combat still raged, Ben-Elim and Kadoshim fighting with all of their aeon-fuelled hatred. Kadoshim and their half-breeds had formed a kind of protective dome around Asroth, the remaining Ben-Elim hurling themselves against it, desperately trying to break through, but their numbers were dwindling; the end was looking close. On the ground the combat was even more one-sided. Pockets of White-Wings fought against shaven-haired acolytes, while further away a tide of Gulla's Revenants were decimating all in their way, a boiling mass that overwhelmed any who dared to stand against them.

As Asroth looked about the hall, Fritha bent and picked up the Starstone Sword.

"Victory," Asroth breathed slowly, tasting the word. He looked back to Fritha, holding her gaze, and again she had that sensation of sinking, drowning, but this time she resisted, her anger giving her strength.

Asroth smiled.

"This one has some strength to her," he said, and Fritha felt for a moment as if the sun shone upon her face. Asroth's attention shifted from her to Bune and the Kadoshim before him. "I was entombed in starstone metal?" Asroth said.

"Yes, my King," Bune said.

"Where is it?"

Bune shrugged, looked around. The dais and floor of the Great Hall were littered with congealed fragments of the black metal, hardened again after Fritha's spell had melted and shattered Asroth's skin-hugging gaol.

Asroth stooped and picked up a black shard, turning it in his hand.

"Gather it all," he said. "Now, before the battle is ended."

"Yes, my King," Bune said, and he and the other Kadoshim set about their task.

There is a lot of metal there. She looked at the Starstone Sword she held. *I could do so much with such a resource.*

"Except you, Bune. You follow me. And you," Asroth said to Fritha. He strode from the dais. "And you." He brushed a hand across Morn's shoulder.

Fritha shared a look with Morn as they marched across the dais onto the chamber floor, passing beneath the protective circle of Kadoshim above them. Fritha felt a tremor in the ground—Wrath was following her.

"Don't tell him we lost the battle against the Order of the Bright Star," Fritha whispered to Morn. "Don't tell him. Or Gulla."

The half-breed frowned at her. "I should tell my father," she muttered.

"Please, not yet," Fritha whispered. "Give me some time, a few days." She knew her fate and future stood upon a knife-edge. *I must make my mark now, consolidate my place before Gulla hears of our defeat.* She looked pleadingly at Morn. "We are bound, you and I," Fritha said, "the unwanted and despised, sisters of combat." She twisted her arm round to show the scar on her palm where she had cut herself and mingled her blood with Morn's. A pact, an oath between them. "Please."

Morn's scowl deepened but she gave a short, curt nod.

Asroth made towards the closest knot of combat, two score White-Wings fighting in a shield circle, beset by Kadoshim acolytes. Fritha glimpsed helms and faces behind the locked shields, saw the familiar short-swords stabbing out into the mass of warriors assaulting them. Blood was flowing, the shield wall holding. A tide of the dead lay at their feet. At the sight of Fritha's old comrades, respect and hatred tugged at her.

A ripple passed through Asroth's wings and he hefted his short-sword in his left hand, though it looked more like a knife in his fist.

"No, Lord," Bune said, hastening in front of Asroth and grabbing his arm, "you are newly awakened, not recovered. It is too dangerous."

Asroth froze, looked down at the grip on his arm, then raised his gaze to Bune's eyes.

"Two thousand years I laboured and plotted to bring us into this world of flesh," he said, his words calm, quiet. "And once I am here, within a handful of moments I am caged in starstone, for..." he looked to Fritha.

"One hundred and thirty-eight years, my King," Fritha said.

"Two thousand, one hundred and thirty-eight years I have waited for my revenge on Elyon. To be flesh, to *feel*." He paused, drew in a deep breath, as if savouring the reek of battle, of blood and sweat and excrement. "I will wait no longer," he snarled.

Bune's hand slipped from Asroth's arm and he dipped his head.

Asroth's leathery wings snapped out, and he was airborne, rising above the horde of acolytes, passing over the White-Wing shield circle and alighting within it. Fritha saw him smile as he skewered a warrior through the back, the short-sword punching out through mail and leather, an explosion of blood.

Bune and Morn took to the air, following their lord, landing beside him even as some of the White-Wings turned to face him. Fritha's face twisted in anger at being left behind.

"Wrath," she yelled, vaulting onto his back, and the draig was lumbering into motion, powerful bowed legs working, claws gouging the stone. His wings beat to launch himself at the enemy. Fritha screamed a battle-cry, Wrath opened his jaws and roared. It felt to Fritha that the whole world shook with their coming.

Acolytes leaped out of their way and Wrath slammed into the wall of shields. Bodies erupted into the air, Wrath's jaws snapping, claws slashing, Fritha with the Starstone Sword in her fist, chopping either side of her. Mail, leather, flesh and bone, all parted like butter for the black sword. In heartbeats the shield circle was breached, acolytes flooding into the rent Wrath had made, and it turned into a slaughter.

Fritha looked up from her death-dealing to see two White-Wings attacking Asroth. The Kadoshim kicked out, stamping a foot at the raised shields, the two warriors stumbling apart. Asroth's wings beat, rocking them more and propelling himself between them. He backhanded one with the stump of his wrist, sending the warrior spinning through the air, and chopped his sword into the other White-Wing, hacking deep from shoulder to ribs, leaving the blade stuck in bone. Asroth kicked the falling corpse away, released his grip on his sword and swept up a spear. He looked around for the warrior he had backhanded just in time to see Wrath rip the woman's head from her shoulders. Asroth looked up and met Fritha's eyes. He grinned, and then he was airborne, rising higher, stabbing at a Ben-Elim who was locked in combat with a half-breed.

The Ben-Elim's back arched as Asroth's blade pierced it; a scream, the Ben-Elim's wings were failing, and he dropped to the ground.

Fritha looked around for the next enemy to kill and realized Asroth's opponent was the last of the Ben-Elim still fighting. She saw a few flashes of white as Ben-Elim survivors fled the battle, speeding out of the Great Hall's high windows. Then the air was clear above them, only Kadoshim and half-breeds swirling in the high-domed reaches.

Further away a horde of Revenants were swarming over the last resistance, another shield wall falling.

The last screams echoed and faded. A silence fell upon the hall as Asroth glided down to the dais, his chest rising and falling, a look of joy sweeping his face. Spatters of gore were dark upon his alabaster skin. He licked blood from his lip.

"This world of flesh tastes good." He sighed.

He raised his spear, bellowing his wordless exultation, and then the hall was echoing with the roar of victory from Kadoshim, half-breed and acolyte lips.

"ASROTH, ASROTH, ASROTH."

Fritha added her voice to theirs.

The horde of Revenants had drawn closer, a mass of them standing on the steps of the hall. They were motionless now, as unnaturally still as they had been all frenzied motion only moments ago. Strands of mist seemed to leak from their bodies, to swirl about them.

Asroth regarded them a long moment, taking in their elongated limbs, their gaunt features and sunken dark eyes, their mouths slick with blood, clawed hands dripping gore.

"And what are these foul, beautiful creatures?" Asroth asked.

"They are mine," a voice called from above. Gulla swept into the chamber, circling and descending with a few score Kadoshim behind him. He landed before Asroth and dropped to one knee, bowing his head.

"Meical?" Asroth asked.

"He has evaded us, for now," Gulla said bitterly.

A dark rage swept across Asroth's features. "A shame," he said.

"I will bring him before you in chains, I swear it," Gulla said.

"Good." Asroth nodded. "In a way I am glad you do not have him. Now I have something to look forward to. Rise," he said, resting a hand upon Gulla's head. "You are...changed."

He is, Fritha thought, *part Kadoshim, part Revenant, by my hand.*

"Yes, my King," Gulla said. He was taller and thicker-muscled than most of the Kadoshim about him, though Asroth still stood half a head taller than Gulla. Where he had been coldly handsome, like many of the Kadoshim, Gulla's sharp-angled face had become more severe, the skin taut. One of his eyes was gone, only a talon-scarred hole where the white crow had raked him, and the other eye was a red glowing pit. Sharp teeth protruded from his drawn lips. A shadow seemed to outline Gulla, shimmering about him like a black halo.

"I have become something *new*," Gulla said, his voice low, but feeling to Fritha as if it spread through the great chamber, scratching on the inside of her skull. He held up a long-fingered hand, nails grown to talons. "It was the only way to free you, the only way we could stand against the Ben-Elim and their pawns."

"How?" Asroth breathed.

Gulla nodded at Fritha. "Our new allies. She is talented, a powerful sorceress."

Asroth looked at Fritha with appraising eyes as she sat upon Wrath's back. The draig's wings were folded now as he crunched contentedly on the leg of a dead White-Wing.

"And these are my children, now," Gulla said, gesturing his hand at the Revenants gathered on the tiered steps behind them.

The clatter of hooves echoed into the chamber and Fritha saw riders canter through the flung-open gates of the Great Hall. A rider reined in and stood there, silhouetted a moment: a woman with jet black hair. More riders filled the space behind her, then they were riding into the chamber and down the steps towards them. Wrath looked up from his feasting and growled; Fritha hefted her sword. Gulla called out a greeting and Fritha realized these were the allies Gulla had spoken about, the ones she had seen fighting at Drassil's gates.

The Cheren. One of the Horse Clans from the grass plains of Arcona.

Gulla gestured and the Revenants parted for them, making a pathway for the Cheren to ride through. They reached the floor of the great chamber, thirty or forty riders. Most of them reined in there; the woman rode on alone, approaching Asroth and Gulla. With effortless grace she dismounted and walked the last few paces to them, though now she was on foot she limped. Fritha saw a bandaged, bloodstained patch on one thigh. She was small-framed, though Fritha recognized a strength in this woman, both in the honed leanness of her musculature and the way her eyes met Asroth's as she walked towards him. She was clearly moved by his presence, but Fritha could see a determination not to be awed. A curved bow was sitting in a case at her belt, a quiver of arrows on the other hip. A sword hung from her saddle. She wore a coat of mail, beneath it a sky-blue deel of felt and over it a vest of leather lamellar. Blood was congealed on a scabbing cut across her forehead.

She reached Asroth and Gulla and stood before them,

meeting their eyes. Then, slowly and awkwardly, she dropped to one knee, though she did not bow her head.

This one does not like to kneel.

"Another ally, Lord King," Gulla said. "Jin, Queen of the Cheren. She took the gates of Drassil and held them open for us. Without her, the assault upon the fortress would have been far from certain."

"Yet another ally—how things have changed," Asroth said, a smile twitching the edges of his mouth. "Well met, Jin of the Cheren."

Gulla touched her shoulder and Jin stood.

"Welcome to the Banished Lands," Jin said, her accent harsh and guttural.

Asroth's smile grew broader. "I have been here longer than you, Jin of the Cheren, long before you were born, but I was sleeping, so in a way you are right, I am newly come to this world of flesh. There is much to learn, much to savour."

"I brought you a gift," Jin said, and raised a hand. "Gerel," she called.

A rider clicked his horse forward; he was a man, head shaved apart from one long warrior braid. The warrior held a rope in his hand, was leading a line of men and women on foot. A score of prisoners: White-Wings, mostly, all of them battered and bloody. Fritha's eyes were drawn to one man in particular, a young warrior, though he was built like a bull, his hair close-cropped, the muscles of his upper back so big he appeared neck-less. One eye was purpled shut and he held a blood-drenched arm cradled to his chest.

Gerel led them to Asroth, where they shuffled to a halt. One warrior collapsed.

Asroth took a step closer, came to stand in front of the White-Wing built like a bull.

"You should kneel before your King," Gulla said in his scratching voice.

The warrior looked from Gulla to Asroth. He was broad and tall, only a little shorter than Asroth. "He is no king of mine," he said, and spat in Asroth's face.

Five hundred Kadoshim blades left their scabbards.

Asroth held a hand up, then slowly wiped spittle from his cheek. He smiled.

"So much to savour," he said. "So many things to experience, so many feelings. Joy. Exhilaration. Anger. Fear." He paused, leaned close to the warrior. "Pain." He looked to Jin. "My thanks for your gift. I will enjoy them."

"More like him escaped," Jin said with a frown. "By your leave, I would go and find them. Bring them back on their knees."

Asroth's smile cracked into a laugh. "Are you humans always in so much of a rush?"

Jin scowled.

"We will find any who have escaped us, will hunt them down. Will crush them," Asroth said. "All of them, along with any who oppose us. But this is a hunt that should be savoured. I am newly come to this flesh, and I would enjoy it."

"But, they are..."

"No," Asroth said, like a door slamming shut. His smile was gone now. "This will not be rushed. Long I have waited for this moment, and I would savour it. The hunt will begin soon, but before that there is much to plan, and much that I want explained. The last hundred years. The strength and whereabouts of my enemy." He looked around at the assembled host. "Have you left anyone for me to kill?" he called out. Laughter rippled through the Kadoshim in the hall.

There is an army in the north for you, Asroth. The Order of the Bright Star are definitely up for a fight. But I don't think that's information I want Gulla to know about, just yet.

"So many questions," Asroth said. "What happened to my hand. And what exactly is that beast." He pointed to Wrath, and then he looked to Fritha. "So tonight, we shall feast, and enjoy our victory, and I shall have my questions answered."

CHAPTER SEVEN

BLEDA

Bleda unbuckled his weapons-belt and laid it upon the ground, making sure his bow-case and quiver were in reach, and then he sat on a stump of wood at the foot of an old cabin and set about fletching a bundle of arrows. His oathsworn guard Ruga stood behind him, her head shaved apart from one long warrior braid lying across her bandaged shoulder. She held a strung bow in one hand, a fistful of arrows in the other, and her eyes were never still, constantly prowling the forest gloom about them.

There are enough guards on duty out there to warn us of any danger, but she will not stop.

Bleda reached into a bucket where deer-sinew was soaking in warm water, then separated it into strands, selecting one to bind a goose tail-feather to a shaft of birch. Carefully he wrapped the sticky sinew about the feather, binding it tight, then repeated the process with two more feather vanes, careful to space them evenly. When he was finished, he tied it off and laid the finished arrow with the bundle beside him, then started another.

He'd hoped the task would distract him.

It wasn't working.

Images of his mother swam in his mind's eye. Her face beaten and bloody, one eye purple and swollen shut. Of Jin standing over his mother, a sword in her hand. The blade stabbing down...

The sinew in his hand snapped.

His eyes blurred with tears, grief and anger mingled, as he remembered his mother's words to him.

Stay strong.

He sucked in a deep breath.

I will, for you. For vengeance's sake.

Jin's face filled his world: once his friend, then his betrothed, and now the most hated person in his entire world.

Jin, I will watch the life drain from your eyes, if it is the last thing I do.

The arrow in his hands broke and he looked down to see his knuckles white.

"Waste of a good arrow," a voice said behind him, and Ellac appeared, the old warrior squatting down in the forest litter beside him. "Think of the enemy that arrow might have pierced."

"I am," Bleda muttered, cuffing away his tears. He saw Ellac studying him, but for once the old warrior held his tongue and did not lecture him on the Sirak Iron Code, on the cold-face and the mastery of emotions. Bleda knew it all, knew the benefits of discipline and control, but his anger was like a stallion that would not be broken.

Is this how Riv feels, all the time?

He suppressed a chuckle at that idea. The thought of Riv was the only light in his dark world. Without thinking, he looked up, though it was not as if he would be able to see her winging down to him out of the clouds, because all he could see was trees, thick boughs laced above him like a latticed tapestry, only a few scattered beams of spring sunshine piercing the treetop canopy.

"It is too soon," Ellac said.

"Aye," Bleda answered. Riv had been gone less than a ten-night. Too soon for her to fly to Drassil and then make her way here, to their cabin in the woods. Perhaps another ten-night, if she had kin on foot with her.

Every day would be an agony of waiting.

He remembered watching Riv fly away, towards Drassil, and every day since then he had felt an ache in his chest at being parted from her. She had saved him, flown into the heart of the Cheren camp and plucked him from certain death. Her, and Ellac and a score of Sirak warriors who had ridden out of the darkness in a desperate attempt to save him and his mother, Queen Erdene.

"She will come," Bleda said, "soon." He was not sure if his words were for Ellac or himself.

Ellac said nothing, just scrutinized Bleda. They both knew that there was no guarantee of Riv's return. She had flown to Drassil to warn the Ben-Elim, and to save her kin. But Bleda had seen their enemy, had been given a taste of what Drassil and the Ben-Elim were facing: Kadoshim, winged half-breeds; Ferals, savage, unstoppable beast-men, and worse, the creatures in the mist.

"She will come," he said again.

"Huh," grunted Ellac. "How long will you wait?"

Bleda shrugged. He had not dared to think of that question, did not want to acknowledge the possibility that Riv would not return to him, and what that would mean.

"If she does not come soon, we should go," Ellac said.

"No," Bleda muttered.

"If she does not come soon, then she is dead," Ellac ploughed on. "Staying here will not bring her back from the dead."

Bleda looked at Ellac, felt his knuckles whitening again.

"Don't say that."

"You are our leader now, our king. You must lead us."

Leader? King? I have only led you into defeat. Love, revenge, duty—these things claw at me, drag me in different directions.

"Lead you where?" Bleda muttered.

"To Arcona. To our people. They need you."

Bleda knew it was logical, that Ellac's words were wisdom, but the thought of leaving, of riding away and turning his back on Riv—it took his breath away.

"She will come," Bleda whispered.

Twigs crunched and Bleda looked up to see a score of Sirak warriors approaching, Yul at their head, more joining them.

Yul was no more than thirty summers old and looked like

any other Sirak warrior, shaven-haired in a long coat of mail split in the middle for riding, the sleeves cut short above the elbows to allow for bow work. He moved with a grace and effi- ciency of movement that marked him as dangerous. He had been Erdene's first-sword. Champion and guardian to the Sirak Queen. Bleda could see that her death still sat heavily upon him.

Bleda and his Clan had arrived here only three nights ago, injured and exhausted from eight days of struggling through Forn Forest. It was only a timber cabin and a small grove of cairns, but they had already turned the area into a defensible position. They had cleared trees, dug the foundations for a stockade and used the trees they'd felled for timber posts to make a wall. A paddock had already been made; their first priority was to look after their mounts, because without a horse a Sirak was only half a warrior. Rows of felt gers lined one side of the encampment, pots hang- ing over fire-pits. Bleda was keenly aware of their vulnerability to attack, but they had to rest somewhere, there were too many wounds to heal, and he had agreed to meet Riv here. Even if they managed to complete their encampment, Bleda knew it would not stand against a concerted attack from their enemies, but it would help, would buy them some time at the very least, and it had given them something to do other than *wait*.

Yul skirted the cairns that lay beyond the cabin, each one the size of a bairn, testament to the terrible secret Kol and his Ben-Elim had been keeping for over a hundred years. Half- breed children, the progeny of relationships between Ben-Elim and humans—killed or died—and buried in this lonely clearing.

Until Riv. She could have ended up in one of those cairns, if not for Aphra.

They have changed the world.

As Yul drew close, yet more warriors fell in behind him, until it looked as if the whole company was gathered.

What is happening here?

Yul stood before Bleda, who remained sitting upon his stump, looking up at the warrior.

"There are things that must be said," Yul croaked. A gash across his throat had been stitched, blood crusted on it, and a dark bruise covered one side of his face, orange and green now as it began to fade. Bleda had found Yul on the road where the battle had taken place. After Riv had left him, Bleda had led his small band of followers, just over a score of his own honour guard that had survived the attack in the forest, back to the site of their defeat, to the road where they had been ambushed by Kadoshim and Ferals.

And betrayed by the Cheren.

There they had gathered arrows, weapons, food from saddle-bags, tools and provisions, and said words of respect over their dead. Bleda and his band had wanted to wrap them in shrouds and light their balefires, but that would have alerted every living thing within ten leagues, so they had left the dead where they lay.

During their search of the battle site, Bleda had been thrilled to find survivors. Injured, wounded, but alive. They found more scattered and lost in the forest, and now their group numbered almost a hundred. Half of them were too injured to ride or draw a bow, but they would heal.

If we are given the time.

Bleda had dragged Yul out from beneath his dead horse and the huge carcass of a Feral. Yul was unconscious, half-crushed by his horse as it fell, and he had a claw slash across the throat that would have ended him if it had cut only a little deeper. But he was alive.

"What things?" Bleda asked.

"Some here have served you, trained with you, at Drassil," Yul said. His voice ground like breaking ice.

"Aye, my honour guard," Bleda said. "What is left of them." *Little more than twenty left from a hundred. I let them down, led them into a trap.* He sighed and looked at his hands, remembering the blood of Tuld, his oathsworn man. He had died in Bleda's arms. He looked back up at Yul. *They don't want me to lead them. And who can blame them? Not me.*

"But we were oathsworn to your mother, to Erdene, the Falcon of the Sirak. We have not ridden with you."

Old Ellac stood.

"He is your *Prince*," the old warrior said, not quite keeping the snarl from his voice. "And now your King."

Bleda felt Ruga tense behind him.

"Peace, Ellac," Bleda said. "Let him speak."

Bleda stood, too, his coat of lamellar plate chinking. It was a weight upon his shoulders, but he was always dressed for battle, now.

"We had not seen what kind of a man you are. What kind of a leader you are," Yul continued quietly. "We have, now."

Quicker than Bleda thought possible, Yul reached over his shoulder and drew his curved sword, before he, Ellac or Ruga could react, and stabbed it into the soil. All the while Yul held Bleda's gaze. He reached for his bow, took it from its case at his hip, and then he knelt, placing his bow reverently on the ground between them. The four score men and women gathered behind him did the same.

"You slew Uldin, King of the Cheren, lord of our sworn enemy. You slew Uldin our betrayer, in the heart of his camp, before his sworn honour guard and before his heir. You slew Uldin, our blood-sworn foe, in the sight of Erdene, our Queen. My Queen." Yul paused, a tremor running through his cracked voice. "For that, if we knew nothing else about you, we would follow you to the ends of the earth. Our bows, our blades, our lives are yours."

"*HAI!*" shouted the kneeling warriors, making crows squawk in the canopy above. Each of them took an arrow from their quivers and sliced their palms. Fists were made, blood dripping onto their sword blades.

"With our blood we swear this," Yul said.

Bleda stared.

"*HAI!*" cried the Sirak.

CHAPTER EIGHT

FRITHA

Fritha sat at a table, drinking wine from a pewter goblet. Asroth sat one side of her, Morn on the other.

Well, this is surreal, she thought, draining her cup and looking about for some more wine.

They were still in Drassil's Great Hall, but it looked markedly different now. The corpses had been removed, though the ground was still slick with pooled blood. Fritha's feet had stuck to the floor as she'd walked to her seat. The hall was filled with the stench of it, cloying and thick.

Tables had been found and dragged from all parts of the fortress, because Asroth wanted to feast. Hundreds of them were there: Kadoshim, acolytes, half-breeds, Cheren warriors, all eating and drinking. Upon the dais that had held Asroth and Meical entombed in starstone, a ring had been fashioned, spears rammed into the ground and ropes of human entrails hung between them, glistening in the flickering torchlight. Within this space a handful of prisoners had been made to fight. At first, they'd refused, but Fritha had let Wrath eat one of them, and not too quickly. That had persuaded the onlookers to cooperate. Fritha had earned a respectful nod from Asroth for that, which had given her a thrill of happiness.

She sat back in her chair and looked up, taking in the huge domed ceiling on the hall. Dark pockets gave away where the Ben-Elim had built fly-holes into the walls and roof.

I spent so many days in here, on my knees, praying, reciting the Ben-Elim's Lore. Being brainwashed, having my life ruined. They took my reputation, my child . . . my life away from me.

And now I am here, eating and celebrating their defeat.

Outside, Gulla's Revenants prowled, the countless many in their rolling mist; a hundred half-breed Kadoshim kept vigil in the sky. There would be no stealthy counter-attack that could get past them while Asroth feasted this night.

And feast is what we're doing. Fritha leaned forwards and speared a joint of lamb, dragging it closer so that she could cut a small slice. It tasted wonderful, spiced and crusted with some-thing sweet and delicious.

I'll say one thing for the Ben-Elim—they had good cooks in Drassil.

Laughter drew her attention and she looked along the table to where Asroth was leaning to whisper in Jin's ear, who sat the other side of him. Asroth was commenting on the duel before them, two White-Wings half-heartedly circling one another. Asroth laughed again, and even Jin smiled, an expression that looked out of place on her face.

Fritha felt a tinge of jealousy.

The atmosphere was euphoric, but she did not feel safe. Gulla was sitting opposite Asroth. He sipped something red from a goblet, like Fritha, though she knew he was not drinking wine, and every now and then his red eye fell upon her. Of all of his Revenants, only his captains remained within the hall. Some stalked the shadows, while others stood as still as stone. There were five of the Seven that Gulla had turned that night in Star-stone Lake. The Seven, who had become his generals, spreading Gulla's blood throughout the Desolation and beyond, gather-ing to themselves their own disciples, as they were Gulla's. She saw scar-faced Burg, who had once been a brigand. Fritha had fought with him when he was newly come to Kergard, because he had leered at her. Now his face was as pale as ash, and his deep-sunken eyes no longer sought her out as they once had, because he lusted for other pleasures. Blood was all that he cared about. Close to Burg stood Rald, prowling softly in the shadows, like some restless wolf. He had been an acolyte, one of Fritha's Red Right Hand. His lips and chin were crusted with blood. Elsewhere, still as a statue, stood Tyna. She had been another resident of Kergard, once the wife of Ulf the tanner, now a blood-hungry killing machine. Thel and Ormun stood close together, perhaps some shred of their kinship remaining, for they had been brothers. They watched those in the duelling ring with famished eyes, each drop of blood drawing their gaze like the predators they were.

Only two of the Seven had not come to the battle. Arvid, who had been sent into the west to sow destruction and gather a host. She had gone to Ardain and should be somewhere on the way to Drassil. And then there was Ulf, the Revenant who had stayed with Fritha, had supposedly been her secret weapon, her surety in defeating the Order of the Bright Star. But somehow he had found himself in a fight with Drem, and Drem had taken Ulf's life with a rune-marked blade. Ulf had died, and his war-band of Revenants had died with him. That had been the end of Fritha's chance, the end of all hope of victory.

Ulf, the idiot. If he had only stayed hidden in the shadows, as I'd told him. Stayed out of the battle. His hunger ruled him.

Fritha's eyes flickered to Gulla.

What will he do when he finds out that Ulf is slain, that his Revenant is dead? That I lost the battle against the Order of the Bright Star?

She drank a large gulp of wine.

Wrath won't be able to protect me from Gulla's anger. There are only so many Revenants he could eat. I must consolidate my position before Gulla finds out.

She reached out a hand to Asroth, hesitated a moment, then touched him.

Asroth's head snapped around, regarding Fritha with a flat stare. She jerked her hand away.

"It was I who took your hand," she said.

"My hand," Asroth echoed, a twitch of his lips that could have been a snarl. He looked at the stump of his wrist.

"We tried to free you, but the attack was too weak," Fritha carried on. "And Ethlinn was here. She is no weakling, I can tell you." She gave Asroth a wry smile. "I warned Gulla of the risks, but he was determined. Even so, I thought that if we failed to free you, perhaps we could take something that would help us to release you later. I told Gulla of an alternative plan. A way to fashion victory from a defeat."

Asroth shifted his weight, turning his back on Jin.

"Go on," he said.

"I told him of a way we could build a new warband, of creatures utterly loyal, and very hard to kill. Gulla's Revenants." She nodded at Gulla. "But to do it I would need something of great power, not inanimate, like the Starstone, but something living, or that had recently lived. Something that had pulsed with blood. My work, I use blood…"

Asroth continued to stare at her.

"There is something in our blood," Fritha said, "when Elyon created flesh, blood was the key. It is…magical," she breathed.

"Aye," Asroth said, a dip of his head.

"So, when the battle to free you was clearly lost, Gulla ordered me to take your hand." Fritha held her breath and looked into Asroth's eyes, could read no emotion there. It was unsettling. She knew this was a risk, that it could go badly wrong.

"You took my hand," he said, quiet as a whisper, and the sound of it turned Fritha's blood to ice.

"On Gulla's order," she answered.

Asroth's one hand drifted to a knife hanging at his belt.

Telling him was a mistake.

Shouts from the duelling arena grew loud, Fritha and Asroth both looking. It was the big White-Wing, the one who had spat at Asroth.

He was refusing to fight. Well, not exactly that. The sword

song was ringing out as blades clashed, but it was immediately clear to Fritha that he was fighting defensively, making no effort at all to attack. He was retreating, circling, parrying, but there was not one strike, and even with one arm crusted with blood and curled tight to his torso he clearly outclassed his opponent.

The spectators were booing and hissing, Cheren warriors shouting insults. Gulla stood from his chair, legs scraping.

The big White-Wing saw, and quick as a blink he darted forwards, smashed the hilt of his sword into his opponent's temple, dropping her.

"Bring him to me," Asroth ordered. "If he won't fight, I'll find a different entertainment in him."

Gulla slipped from his chair, a snap of his wings as they extended and took him into the air, over the ropes of entrails and he glided down into the ring.

The White-Wing looked at Gulla, froze a moment, then launched himself at the Kadoshim.

Gulla flicked his wings, sidestepping with unnatural speed, a knife suddenly in his hand, and he clubbed the White-Wing across the back of the head, sending him crashing into the intestine ropes, falling, tangled.

Gulla snapped his fingers and two acolytes leaped forwards to grab the White-Wing, who was groggily trying to rise. They dragged the man towards Asroth, though he struggled against them.

A sensation inside Fritha's skull, like a whisper, or the flutter of moth's wings.

Frrrithaaaa...

She knew that voice.

Elise. You live! A moment of pure joy. It had torn Fritha's heart to fly away from Elise, her friend, her creation, part woman part white wyrm. It had hurt her to leave all of her followers, her Ferals, Arn, her Red Right Hand.

Now that Fritha was concentrating, she could feel Elise. It was like a thrumming in her blood. At the same time she became aware of her Ferals, so few now compared to what there had been. They filled her with a quick joy. She felt so vulnerable here, so alone. She needed her creations around her, her children. Wrath was all she had, but now there were more.

Oh, my Elise, she whispered back, and felt a thrill of pleasure, knowing that Elise had heard her. *My babies. Come to me, Elise, come to me, all of you. I need you.*

"What are you smiling at?" a voice asked, Morn, beside her.

"Elise lives, she is coming," Fritha said. "Help them. Fly out and find them, guide them home."

"Father has tasks for me. Scouting," Morn said with a frown.

"I am not asking you to disobey Gulla," Fritha said quietly, "but you could scout to the north and west, could you not? Maybe travel a little further in that direction?"

A hesitation.

Fritha looked down at her cuirass, the white wings embossed upon it now stained a deep, dark red. A reminder of Fritha's and Morn's blood mingled. A reminder of their oath, to help each other in their vengeance.

"I will do what I can," Morn said, her attempt at a whisper more like gravel rattling in a pot.

And then the White-Wing was thrown onto the table before Asroth, scattering trenchers and spilling Fritha's wine.

Asroth stood, towering over the young warrior, who struggled to free one hand, punching an acolyte and sending them reeling.

Asroth raised his knife, the White-Wing lifting his hand in a futile defence.

"Don't kill him," Fritha blurted.

Asroth froze, knife hovering.

"Why not?"

"Because I need his hand," Fritha said, looking at the White-Wing's fist. It was big, almost as big as Asroth's.

Asroth frowned.

"I can give you a new hand." She smiled. "A better one."

A moment's hesitation, then Asroth slammed the knife down, deep into the table beside the White-Wing. Asroth gripped the White-Wing's face.

"What is your name?" he asked.

The White-Wing didn't answer.

Asroth squeezed, Fritha seeing the warrior's skin starting to tear, his eyes bulging, the crackle of cartilage and bone. The warrior screamed.

"Your name," Asroth said, calmly, his expression fascinated, studying the man as if he were some kind of insect.

"I know his name," a voice said. It was Jin. She was leaning forwards and staring at the White-Wing. "His name is Vald."

"You are sure?" Gulla asked her.

"Yes. He is a friend of the half-breed bitch."

"Who?" Asroth said.

"The Ben-Elim half-breed. The one who rescued Meical."

"Ah," Asroth said. "You are fortunate, Vald, because you will get to live a little longer. My *betrothed* tells me she needs you alive. But not whole." Asroth looked at Fritha and she shook her head.

Asroth adjusted his grip and pressed his thumb into Vald's eye, pushing, gouging, a steady increase of pressure. His face was not calm, now, a snarl of pure hatred twisting his features.

Vald screamed again, higher, piercing, and then his eye popped, a spray of blood and jelly. Vald's shrieks rose to a new level; Asroth cuffed him away. Vald collapsed to the ground, hands to his face. Gulla signalled and acolytes dragged Vald away.

Asroth looked at Fritha and licked jelly from his thumb.

"So, this is what pain tastes like."

CHAPTER NINE

BLEDA

Bleda's feet drummed on the timber stairwell and then he was at the top of the wall, looking out into the gloom of Forn. It was a cold spring morning, mist carpeting the forest floor, moving like a slow, languid sea.

He and his warriors had cleared a space beyond the wall, twenty or thirty paces deep. Not much, but enough to make their arrows tell should their enemy find them.

And perhaps they have.

Scouts had returned, telling of movement in the forest. Bleda had ordered the call to arms and now seventy Sirak warriors were spread along the wall, bows strung and fists full of arrows. The rest of his small warband were mounted and close to a rear gate, ready to sally and strike, or cut a path to freedom.

"I can't see anything," Ellac grunted, as he climbed the last few steps and settled in beside Bleda. The old warrior had a round shield strapped to his right arm, a spear gripped in his left hand.

"That is because you are old," Bleda said, eyes searching the gloom, though in truth all Bleda could see was mist and trees.

"Eyes above," Ellac warned.

Ruga and a few others about him looked skywards.

Let it be her, Bleda thought, and raised a hand to his chest, feeling the bulge of flower and feather wrapped and tucked beneath his coat of plate and tunic. Then he took a fistful of arrows from his quiver.

Hope for the best, be ready for the worst.

Mist coiled out from the trees, churning sluggishly. It reminded Bleda of creatures hidden in the mist.

He nocked an arrow.

A rustle and creak from above and his eyes snapped to the canopy. A shadow, descending. *Was that wings? One figure, or two?*

"Hold," he cried, unsure if it was friend or foe. Kadoshim wings were dark as leather, Ben-Elim white as snow, but Riv—her wings were dapple grey, beautiful, and well suited to be hidden amongst the shift of branches and leaves.

And then the figure swept through a shaft of sunlight. Blonde braided hair, a White-Wing cuirass. Bleda grinned, his arrow falling away from his bow, because Riv was there, appearing out of the shadows.

Her eyes found him and she smiled, then her wings were beating and she was free of the canopy and speeding down to him. They fell into each other's arms, Bleda staggering and feeling the breath crushed from his chest as Riv's wings wrapped around him and she squeezed him tight. He had forgotten how strong she was. His lips found hers and for long moments the world faded around him.

Riv was alive.

"I feared—" he said, Riv cutting off his words with her lips. The world faded again. They parted and she grinned at him.

"It is good to see you, Bleda ben Erdene," she breathed.

Bleda just looked at her, took in her blue eyes and pale, freckled skin. She was cut in a hundred places, blood-crusted, bruises, a bandage around her back and wing-arch, but she seemed as full of life and strength as ever. He smiled and nodded. They separated and Bleda became aware of those around him: Ellac, Ruga, Yul, many more.

The world is changing, our lives in the balance. A kiss is not so big a thing.

Riv looked around, at the wall, the rowed gers and paddock. "You've been busy," she said.

Another figure flew down out of the canopy, a Ben-Elim. Bleda did not know him, though he seemed strangely familiar. Long dark hair, bound tight at the nape, white scars raking one side of his face. He gripped a spear in his fist and wore a long-sword at his hip. Bleda frowned, trying to place him. Then it came to him. A statue he had studied in Drassil's Great Hall, many times.

"Meical," he gasped, hardly believing it.

Riv grinned as Meical alighted beside them. He was tall, stern-faced, his eyes a deep purple.

"Then that means..." Bleda said. "Asroth..."

"...is awakened, and free," Riv said.

A Sirak called out, pointing to movement in the trees.

Bleda's bow arm rose, but Riv touched his arm.

"My mother, with the survivors of Drassil," she said.

"Open the gates," Bleda cried.

Figures appeared out of the mist, Aphra at their head. She was sweat-stained and gaunt, her cuirass and coat of mail torn, blood staining her undertunic. Others materialized behind her, looking in a similar condition. White-Wing warriors, some others, even a child. Bleda watched in silence as they trailed through the gates into the stockade.

"How many?" Bleda said.

"A hundred and twelve," Riv said. "All that is left of Drassil."

Bleda shook his head, feeling the weight of that settle in his belly. Drassil and the Ben-Elim. All his life they had been a tower of strength, sometimes considered his enemy, his oppressor, but never had he thought the power of the Ben-Elim and the walls of Drassil questionable. The possibility of their defeat was unimaginable.

"Eat, rest," he called down, and Sirak warriors were already running to help the injured through the gates, others moving to the cook-pots and water barrels.

"A good idea," Riv said. "I'm starving."

"And then we shall talk of war," Meical growled. "I have not woken from a hundred years of sleep to spend my life running."

Bleda nodded, liking this Ben-Elim already.

Bleda sat in the wide space outside the cabin. Everyone was there, other than the guards on walls and scouts lurking in the forest.

Ellac sat one side of Bleda, Riv on the other. Aphra and Meical were close by. Fai was there with her baby boy Avi strapped across her chest.

He was born here, Bleda thought as he watched the bairn stirring in his sleep. *A half-breed child—one day he will have wings, like Riv.*

Yul and Ruga stood behind Bleda. Yul appeared to have assumed the role of Bleda's first-sword. Bleda was not sure that Ruga was happy with that. On the far side of the circle, a White-Wing stood behind those seated. He was broad and muscular; a fair-haired child sat upon his shoulders. Bleda recognized the warrior. Sorch, a trainee White-Wing who had attacked him in the weapons-field, and later had spat at Riv, calling her a half-breed, as if that were a curse.

Bleda felt anger coil in his belly at the sight of him, but he mastered it.

Of all those to survive, I would not have chosen him. But if he fights the Kadoshim and Cheren, that is enough for me. For now.

Sitting in front of Sorch was Jost, tall and thin as a stick, his short hair spiked with sweat and grime. He looked as if he could be blown over with a breath, but Bleda had seen him fight, had stood beside him and knew his worth. Jost looked more than exhausted, he looked devastated, broken, his eyes flat.

Then Bleda realized there was someone missing.

"Where is Vald?" Bleda asked Riv.

Her face darkened.

"He fell," she said, a twist of her lips. "He saved me, in the weapons-field, and then he was gone."

Bleda felt a stab of grief at that news. Vald had been a friend to Bleda, and he had experienced few enough of those. He shook his head and squeezed Riv's wrist.

"He will be avenged," Bleda said.

"He will," Riv answered, her eyes boring into the ground.

Aphra stood up, a bowl of stew in her hands.

"It is good to be here, amongst friends," she said. She spooned some into her mouth, swallowed and smiled. "You Sirak make good stew."

A ripple of laughter at that, other voices amongst the White-Wings calling out their agreement.

She looked about them, then, her smile fading. "I am guessing that word has spread amongst you, but let me make it plain for all. Asroth is risen from his gaol, Drassil fallen, the Ben-Elim routed."

Meical grunted and shifted, a ripple through his wings, but he said nothing.

"And the question stands: what are we to do, now?"

A silence, all eyes on Aphra.

"But before that, I would ask: what are *you* going to do?"

Bleda blinked at that, felt Ellac shift beside him.

"You are Sirak," Aphra said, "in a strange land, your home a hundred leagues from here. We were allies of a sort." She glanced at Bleda. "But I am no fool. I know that there were tensions between your people and the Ben-Elim. And yet, you are here." She turned a circle, looking at them all, coming to a rest with her eyes upon Bleda.

Slowly, Bleda stood. He felt the weight of this moment, knew the fate of his Clan hung on his words.

"You speak the truth," Bleda said. "There has long been a tension between the Ben-Elim and us Sirak. I was taken from my Clan at the point of a blade, saw my brother and sister's heads cast before me." A surge of emotion swept through Bleda, as if saying the words out loud opened a floodgate. The heart-break, anger and fear that he had felt as he had been carried away from his home was abruptly as vivid as the day it had happened. "Allies?" He shrugged. "That is not the word I would have used. The Ben-Elim ruled us with a rod of iron, kept me as a leash to tether my mother, and now, in a blink, the Ben-Elim have no power over us, no leverage over me or my people. So, yes, we could go. Given the way we have been treated by the Ben-Elim, we *should* go." He took a moment to steady himself, his emotions a constant swell that threatened his composure and clarity. "And yet, as you say, we are here." He blew out a long breath, feeling good to be speaking truths that had so long been bottled within him.

"The reason why *I* am here is not so hard to understand." He looked at Riv, stroked her face and her smile lit up the world.

"But for my Clan, we would be fools to walk away. We have seen our enemy. Kadoshim and their half-breeds. Feral beast-men, and worse—" he suppressed a shudder—"the mist-walkers." He rubbed his head, feeling stubble scratch his palm. "Where would we go that is far enough away from those creatures? Arcona? I do not think that is far enough. They are not just your enemies, they are enemies of all who tread these Banished Lands, and I suspect that nowhere is safe."

"Asroth dreams of tearing this world to bloody strips," Meical said.

Bleda nodded. "We have fought the Kadoshim, they are an evil that cannot be bargained with, or escaped. We must continue to fight them. And then there are the Cheren."

Behind him Yul growled and spat on the floor.

Bleda saw a few surprised expressions amongst White-Wings at that: it was an emotional display for a Sirak warrior.

"You may think of us as cold, aloof," Bleda said, "because we wear a face of stone, but that is our shield, for our enemies. Inside we are fierce and proud, passionate." He punched his chest. "Our love is a fire, our loyalty a rock, our enmity a curse."

A shifting amongst the Sirak, standing taller, rumbled agreements. A fire in their eyes. Bleda saw Ellac sit straighter and realized the old man was looking at him with pride in his face.

"The Cheren are our ancient enemy, and they slew our *Queen*. My mother." Bleda paused, controlling the emotion that constricted his throat. "They are allied to the Kadoshim. So, I say we *are* allies, now, because we face the same enemy. We will stand with you, bleed with you, win or die alongside you."

He sat down again.

A silence settled, then Aphra smiled at him.

"That is good to know," she said, and Bleda could see the weight of worry drain a little from her eyes.

"So, the next question is: how do we kill our enemies?"

"That is a question I like," Meical said.

Eyes turned towards the Ben-Elim.

"This is Meical, High Captain of the Ben-Elim," Aphra said. "He is Asroth's ancient foe. No one knows Asroth and the Kadoshim better, so we should listen to him. It is wisdom to know your enemy."

"That is a truth," Yul breathed.

"I am not High Captain of the Ben-Elim," Meical corrected Aphra. "But I *am* Asroth's foe, and friend to any who would fight him. And yes, I know him as well as any, though that does not mean I know him well." He shrugged, his wings undulated. "My guess is Asroth will want to consolidate his forces. He is newly awoken, like me, and it has taken me some time to come to terms with all that has changed. Asroth will need that, too, a time of adjustment. He will want to fight, to be *involved*, to rend and tear and destroy. For two thousand years this is what he planned and schemed for, and he would not rush it, nor would he miss it."

"What if you are wrong?" Yul asked.

"Then Asroth and his forces will hunt us sooner." Meical shrugged. "Either way, he *will* hunt us."

Footsteps ran on the stockade's palisade.

"WARE THE SKY!" a voice cried out, and then all were on

their feet, weapons in fists, Bleda sweeping his bow from its case at his hip. He snatched at arrows, nocked and drew, searching.

Deep shadows moved in the canopy above, silhouettes of winged figures. An arrow whistled from a Sirak bow.

"PEACE!" a voice bellowed from above, and then Bleda saw the flash of white wings, Ben-Elim materializing from the murk. Bleda recognized one, blond-haired, a scar through his cheek and lip.

Kol. Riv's father.

His coat of mail was torn, a glimpse of bloodstained bandages below his chest.

Bleda aimed at the Ben-Elim's heart. It was Kol who had slain his brother and sister, cast their heads at his feet.

I hate him.

Something stopped him from releasing the arrow. Moments passed, his arm starting to quiver with the strain. Then he dropped the arrow.

He is Riv's father. I cannot kill him like this.

He blew out a long breath.

And then the Ben-Elim were landing amongst them, three, four, five score, many of them injured, all of them bearing the signs of hard-fought battle.

Kol landed in their circle, Hadran beside him, reaching out a steadying hand that Kol shrugged off.

"We thought you had fallen," Aphra said, striding over to Kol.

"Not yet," Kol said, a grimace twisting his bitter smile. "Though they tried their hardest." He raised a hand to the wound on his torso. Close up, Bleda could see that Kol was pale, his face worn with fatigue and pain.

"What happened?" Riv asked matter-of-factly as she joined Aphra and Kol, who gave her a curt nod. It was hardly the loving reunion of a father and daughter, but then Riv disliked him almost as much as Bleda did.

"We lost," Kol said.

"We fled Drassil after your warning," Hadran said. "Tried to make it here, but there were too many wounded." His eyes flickered to Kol. "We had to stop, to stitch wounds, set bones. We flew on as soon as we could."

"What is happening here?" Kol said, eyeing the circle suspiciously.

"A council of war," Aphra said.

Kol looked from Bleda and the Sirak to the bedraggled White-Wings. He curled a lip.

"Then it is a good thing I have arrived just in time."

"What do you mean by that?" Bleda said. He could feel his hatred fluttering in his veins.

"I mean that I am High Captain of the Ben-Elim, Lord Protector of the Land of the Faithful. The White-Wings serve me. You are my ward, and the Sirak my ally." He stared at Bleda, a cold arrogance in his eyes, even with his coat of mail torn and blood seeping from a wound in his torso. "I *mean* that I command here."

"Things have changed," Bleda told him. "I am your ward no longer. You do not *command* me, or my people. I saw you fly away and leave my mother to die." A ripple of anger then that he could not contain. He felt a presence at his shoulder: Ellac, Ruga, Yul, all close behind him.

The Ben-Elim around him tensed, as did the Sirak warriors about the encampment. Hands went to hilts and bows creaked as they were drawn.

"Peace," a voice said. Meical stepped between them. "This is not the time for blows. As you said so eloquently, Bleda, we are all enemies of Asroth. All other grievances should be put aside, for now." He stared at Bleda.

"I will not fight him," Bleda said slowly. "But I will not *serve* him, either."

Meical nodded. "Agreed," he said, that slight twist of his lips that passed for a smile.

"And who made you lord and king?" Kol spat, staring at

Meical. "You lead no one, have no authority here. The last I saw you, you were in chains, and that's where you should still be."

Meical turned to face Kol.

"I would like to see you try," Meical said with a small smile, his hand dropping to the hilt of his sword.

"We have our own grievances, Kol, and I have not forgotten them," Meical continued. "But Asroth is loose, Drassil fallen, the Ben-Elim routed. This is not the time for the enemies of Asroth to fight amongst themselves."

"Meical is right," Aphra said. "This is a council of war amongst equals. Allies united against a common enemy."

Kol looked at them all, then at his battered followers. Slowly he nodded, then waved his hand. "So, what has been decided?"

"Decided? Nothing," Aphra said.

"Meical was speaking to us," Bleda said. "Telling us of Asroth."

"Oh, really?" Kol said. "Then please, continue," he said to Meical with mock formality.

"I have been absent a hundred and forty years, so much has changed," Meical said. He looked at Riv. "Our fierce friend here has filled me in on much, on the events of our Long War over the last century. From what I understand, you have allies. The Order of the Bright Star." He paused there, a ripple of grief sweeping his face, a twitch of his head to master it. "And there is Ethlinn and Balur One-Eye, and their giants. I would like to see old One-Eye again." He looked to Bleda. "And you are a king, I am told, of the Sirak Horse Clan."

Bleda frowned. The title felt unfamiliar on his shoulders, and unearned. But he nodded.

"How many could you muster and bring to the fight?" Meical continued.

Bleda looked at Yul.

"Three thousand, if the Clan is gathered," Yul said.

Meical nodded. "And White-Wings?" he asked Aphra.

"We numbered ten thousand, but over two thousand swords

were at Drassil. If the other garrisons have not been hit, then seven to eight thousand. The largest garrison after Drassil is Ripa in the south."

"Eight thousand for the shield wall, two thousand horse," Meical said. "The Order of the Bright Star, and Ethlinn's giants. This is a warband that could stand a fighting chance against Asroth, Gulla and their hordes."

"If we can gather them," Aphra said.

"Aye. But what else can we do but try?" Nods and murmurs of agreement. Bleda saw Hadran beside Kol murmuring his assent. It earned the Ben-Elim a dark look from Kol.

"Good, then we have the beginnings of a plan," Meical said. "Now, let us make it happen."

CHAPTER TEN

JIN

Jin sat at a table in Drassil's Great Hall, forcing herself to remain seated. She glanced behind her and saw Gerel, her oathsworn man. He stood at her shoulder, his hand resting on the bow in its case on his belt. His expression was flat, but she knew he felt the same.

Why are we still sitting here, when my father's murderer is out there?

Asroth was seated opposite her. No matter that she loved her own Clan above all things, her eyes kept drifting towards the Lord of the Kadoshim. His coat of mail clung to his form, ridges of muscle clear beneath it, his face pale and angular, dark eyes drawing her gaze.

He is . . . exceptional.

Asroth was reclining in a huge oak-carved chair, one leg draped across the arm, and he was eating cheese. He seemed to be enjoying it a great deal. Around him sat his captains, Bune the Kadoshim, who was a constant at Asroth's shoulder, alert, always checking for danger. Gulla was there, his gaunt face and the unsettling shadow that glimmered about him setting him apart from the other Kadoshim. Standing a dozen paces behind him were a handful of his Revenants. They stood unnaturally still, wisps of mist curling about them.

Also at the table was Morn, Gulla's half-breed daughter, who looked permanently angry, a deep scowl ridging her brow, and Fritha, whom Jin had heard called *priestess*. Jin had spoken to Fritha twice, once during the feast on their victory night, and then the next day. Jin found it hard to fathom her. At times Fritha seemed coldly focused, then, the next, it seemed she had forgotten that Jin was there.

Aenor was also at the table. A broad, squat man with a face that looked as if it had been flattened in the pugil-ring, his nose broken and set wrong. He was the appointed lord of the acolytes, those humans who followed the Kadoshim with fanatical loyalty.

Asroth put another slice of cheese into his mouth, chewing and swallowing with obvious satisfaction.

Jin coughed and shifted in her chair. Bune's eyes snapped onto her. Asroth smiled.

"You would be away from here, hunting your enemies," Asroth said. He sat up straighter, shifting his leg from the arm of the chair. "I understand the need that drives you. I feel it within me, too, in here." He tapped a long, fine-boned finger to his chest. "The Ben-Elim are my ancient enemies. Thousands of years our blood-feud has raged, and now their annihilation is so close."

"So why are we sitting here?" Jin asked. "Seven nights I have been here. Waiting. Let us ride out together, slay our enemies."

"I like you, Jin, you have a fire within you." Asroth smiled. "That is why I will allow you to question me, this *once*." His voice was amiable, charming, but there was an edge to it, enhanced by the way Kadoshim around the hall paused, all of their eyes abruptly upon Jin.

Asroth cut another slice of cheese and slowly, deliberately ate it. He licked his lips.

"We will wait because this is a moment that should be savoured, like good food, and wine, and...other things." His eyes flickered to Fritha with amusement, and then back to Jin. "I understand your need. Let me assure you, it will be satisfied.

You have served me well, accomplished great deeds. You are worthy to be allied with us Kadoshim."

Jin felt a warmth fill her at Asroth's words, sounding so much like praise, but deep within her a small voice bridled.

... *served us well*... It reminded her of how Bleda had spoken to her father, calling him Gulla's slave. She had felt a sharp anger and deep shame at Bleda's words.

"*Served you*," she said to Asroth. "I am your ally, not your servant." Jin made sure that she spoke slowly, so as to keep the emotion from her voice.

Asroth waved a hand languidly. "Of course," he said. "Now, to business." He looked at Gulla. "How many of our Kadoshim kin are with us?"

"Eight hundred here," Gulla said, his voice scratching, like nails on slate. "A thousand in the south with Sulak."

"And your half-breed offspring?" Asroth said, his lips twitching. Jin was not sure if it was the hint of a smile or a grimace of revulsion.

"Close to a thousand here, the same again with Sulak in the south."

Asroth grunted. "And acolytes?"

"One thousand, eight hundred and forty-six," Aenor said. "There are more trying to approach the fortress, close to two thousand in various covens, but they are...hesitant, to approach Drassil's walls."

"Hesitant?" Asroth asked. "Why?"

"They are afraid," Aenor said. "Afraid that they will get eaten. By Gulla's mist-walkers."

"Ha." Asroth barked a laugh. "This world of flesh is so full of hunger." As if to prove his point, he took another bite of cheese.

"Even Revenants must eat," Gulla said, with a rasping sound issuing from his throat that Jin realized was laughter.

"This is a serious matter," Asroth said. "I cannot have my allies eating one another. Especially not before the war is won."

He smiled, softening the words, though Jin would not forget them.

"Gulla, you must control your children."

"They are hungry." Gulla shrugged. "They know they cannot touch any within this fortress, so they have taken to hunting in the forest. They are having to travel ever wider to slake their thirst." Gulla paused a moment. "It would be better if we marched now. There will be no shortage of blood once we find our enemies."

Asroth's brow furrowed. "We will march when I *say* we march," he said, his voice abruptly empty of charm and humour. A cold power radiated from him.

Gulla held Asroth's gaze with his one eye a long moment.

Jin felt something change around her, a chill in the air. One of Gulla's Revenant captains appeared from the shadows, tendrils of mist curling around him, his eyes fixed upon Asroth. Jin saw Bune's hand drift to his sword hilt.

Gulla dipped his head. "Of course, my King," he said.

The tension melted away. Jin looked over her shoulder to see the Revenant gone.

"How many of your Revenants are there?" Asroth said, his voice reverting to its earlier charm.

"In the region of ten thousand," Gulla said.

"Hmm," Asroth mused. "That is a lot of mouths to feed. We must move them away from the fortress, allow our *allies* to join us here, and find a way to keep your Revenants satisfied until we march. I will think on it."

Marching to war would be the obvious answer, Jin thought. *As Gulla says, find our enemies and let your Revenants glut themselves.* She held her tongue, though. Partly because she had trained all her life to give nothing away to her enemies, and deep in her heart she considered anyone who was not of her Clan to be an enemy. There had only been one outside of the Cheren of whom she had thought differently. Had loved.

Bleda.

The other reason she did not challenge Asroth's judgement was because she feared him. Even so, she could not stay silent. She was a queen now, and felt the weight of that: a responsibility to her people that she had to live up to.

"If not now, then when?" Jin asked.

"Soon," Asroth said. "The time is approaching for us to march. Our enemy are scattered. Where are we likely to encounter their strongest force?"

"In the south," Bune said. "Drassil was always the Ben-Elim's greatest stronghold, but as they moved to conquer and rule more territory their forces were focused on the edges of their land."

"Just so," Gulla nodded. "Ripa in the south holds a large White-Wing garrison, and there would be more Ben-Elim there. There could be up to six or seven thousand White-Wings, maybe a thousand Ben-Elim." He looked at Asroth. "There are other garrisons. Haldis, Dun Bagul, but Ripa is the strongest."

"And what of Ethlinn's giants and this Order of the Bright Star?" Asroth said. "Founded by that maggot, Corban." His hand strayed to the scar on his forehead.

"They have been dealt with," Gulla said. "By Fritha."

"I led them away from Drassil," Fritha said, "far from here. I kept them from giving aid to Kol and his Ben-Elim. I fought them in the north."

"A great victory," Gulla said, looking at Fritha keenly. "They have been a formidable enemy over the last hundred years. Worse than the Ben-Elim in their tenacity."

"Good," Asroth said. "Then we shall march on Ripa, as that is where we shall find the largest number of our enemy to kill." He grinned.

"What of those that fled Drassil?" Jin said, feeling her frustration bubbling in her veins.

What of Riv? She will lead me to Bleda.

"We will find them. I would think that they will seek to join their comrades." He shrugged. "I wish to see Meical's head on a spike and his wings hacked from his back, but chasing after them through Forn Forest will only waste our time. I think perhaps we will meet those that fled Drassil upon the battlefield at Ripa. Meical and the Ben-Elim will think to fight us, but first they must gather their strength. Where else would they go?"

You might be right. Bleda will follow his half-breed bitch like a dog in heat, and Riv will go where the Ben-Elim go. Jin felt her fingers twitch for an arrow. *Twice she has put an arrow in me,* Jin thought. *Her, the worst archer in the world.* The need to put Riv in the ground was almost as strong as her desire to slay Bleda. Almost.

"But before you ride with me to Ripa, you have a warband to raise," Asroth said, snapping Jin from her anger.

"What?"

"You have five hundred riders here, yes?"

"Aye," Jin said. "Five hundred horse-warriors. The best in the Banished Lands."

"Five hundred is not enough. I want you to return to your land, this Sea of Grass, and raise your Clan. Every man and woman who can ride a horse and wield a bow. How many can you raise?"

Jin looked to Gerel.

"Three thousand at least," Gerel said. He shrugged. "More."

"Ha," Asroth said, slapping the arm of his chair. "Now *that* is a number I like. You shall bring them to Ripa. But first, destroy your ancient enemy, the Sirak."

Jin blinked.

"What did you say?"

"Every last man, woman and child. Destroy them, trample them into the dirt. Ride for Arcona, gather your Clan and slay the Sirak. They are an enemy that I do not need at my back. Make it as if their Clan never existed."

Jin could not control herself, she felt a grin spread across her face.

CHAPTER ELEVEN

DREM

Drem crested a hill and saw the traders' town of Dalgarth on the plain below. The sun was sinking into the west and Dalgarth looked eerily still, no columns of smoke or hum of noise emanating from it, like the first time he had seen the town. Now it was a desiccated husk, sucked dry of all life. When Dalgarth had first fallen silent they thought it had been hit by a plague, but now they knew better.

It was a plague, in a way. Ulf and his Revenants, infecting all those that they feasted upon, turning them into the same blood-hungry creatures.

He rode on, part of a line of scouts preceding their main warband. Keld was closest to him, twenty or so paces to his left. Crows wheeled in the sky above and wolven-hounds loped ahead of them.

As they made their way down the slope Drem's horse whickered, head raised, and took a snorting breath.

"Almost there," Drem said, patting the neck of his roan mare, Rosie. She had carried him all the way north, into battle and then to the starstone mine, and now they were making their way home. She knew they were close to home.

Dun Seren. *Home. Strange that I have so quickly come to think of it as that.*

He saw it in the distance, beyond a wide sweeping river. A dark tower upon a hill, surrounded by clustered buildings and tiered walls. Columns of black smoke rose from the fortress. Heralds of the coming war from the forges of blacksmiths. Almost immediately after the battle with Fritha, Byrne had sent a contingent of warriors back to Dun Seren: all of their skilled smiths. Kill, Byrne's captain, had led them.

The ground levelled into a rocky plain that led to Dalgarth and Dun Seren beyond. Drem heard the thump and scrape of bear-claws as Queen Ethlinn and her giants crested the peak of the ridge behind him, and then the warband of the Order was spilling down the slope.

They rode in silence past Dalgarth, choosing to skirt the town rather than ride through it. They passed a copse of trees, twisted and wind-blasted, though green with summer's leaves. Something moved in Drem's peripheral vision and his eyes snapped around, searching. One hand went to the sword at his hip.

It was the white bear.

You are remarkably silent and stealthy for a creature almost the size of a barn, Drem thought with a smile.

The white bear had joined them at the battle, perhaps responding to Hammer's bellowing call when she was injured. Whatever the reason, the white bear had saved Drem's life and helped to turn the battle against Fritha's creatures, her winged draig, the Ferals and her snake-woman. Drem shuddered at the memory of her. He still had fading bruises across his ribs from where her coils had squeezed him and he remembered her breath on his face, her voice in his ear, sibilant and reptilian.

After the battle Drem had found her tracks, leading south-east, away from the conflict. There had been blood in them.

Did she find some place to die, or is she still out there?

He didn't like the thought of that.

Drem watched the white bear as it made its way through the group of trees, following them.

What will you do now? Will you cross the bridge and join us? Or will you part ways with us again, the bridge and Dun Seren too much for your wild heart to cope with? I know how you feel...but I'm getting better with people and walls. Maybe you would too if you gave us a chance...

Drem's hand drifted to his neck, the thought of the fortress raising his anxiety. With two fingers he searched for his pulse, the rhythmic beat calming him.

Soon Rosie was cantering over the stone bridge that arched the river before Dun Seren. He looked back over his shoulder, saw the column of their warband crossing the bridge and stretching back beyond. He could just make out the shadow of the white bear, sitting off to the west amongst a stand of trees, watching. And then he was turning a bend and riding up to the walls and open gates of Dun Seren. He passed through the gates and into a huge courtyard. A small crowd was waiting to greet them in the shadow of the Order's founder, the statue of Corban and his wolven, Storm.

I wonder what he was like.

The statue looked serious, but there were laughter lines carved at Corban's eyes, and something about the set of his mouth that spoke of kindness.

It is a strange thing, to think my bloodline goes back to that man, and his sister.

Kill, Byrne's captain, was standing beneath the statue. She was tall and dark-skinned, her black hair tied back into one thick warrior braid. She nodded a greeting to Keld, who was first to ride through the gates at the head of fifty of Dun Seren's huntsmen.

Drem followed close behind Keld. They rode around to the right, making room for Ethlinn and her giants.

Stablehands rushed to take Drem's reins as he dismounted. Young lads and lasses, too young to fight. The fortress had been almost stripped bare of warriors, only a skeleton garrison left to protect those too old or too young to go. Drem thanked the young lad trying to take his reins, but told him firmly that he would see to his own mount.

"She has looked after me, so it's only fair that I should look after her now," he said. That was what his da had taught him, all their years living a solitary life in the wild. The stable-lad nodded and moved on to the next rider.

Ethlinn, Balur and a few hundred giants and bears were filling the courtyard now, Byrne riding in behind with her honour guard, as well as Utul, Shar and Cullen. Drem nodded to his friend.

Byrne rode towards the statue of Corban, slipping from her mount and striding forwards to greet Kill. They took each other's arms in the warrior grip, then Byrne turned.

"We've travelled far, and fought hard," she called out. "Rest and eat, you've earned it." And then she was striding towards the keep, deep in conversation with Kill. Ethlinn and Balur followed her.

"Come on, then," Drem said, as he patted Rosie's neck. "Let's see if we can find you some oats and a good brush."

Drem walked towards the bridge, a spear in one hand, a sack slung across his back. He stepped into the torchlight and raised a hand to the guards, two men and a woman. He strode across the bridge, his long legs taking him quickly to the far side, where he stopped a moment to let his eyes adjust to the darkness. Behind him the fortress stood like a deeper shadow, torches glinting through shuttered windows and upon walls. He turned his back on it and strode west, along the riverbank, pulling his cloak tighter about him.

Trees loomed and he paused, looking up. Stars punctuated the night sky. Drem had a sense of something, the skin on his neck prickling. A flicker up above, stars winked out and then back, quick as a blink.

He hefted his spear, searching the sky for some clue.

Kadoshim or their half-breeds? Would they come so close to Dun Seren? Scouting?

Drem stood there for a long time, hunting the sky, but there was no sign of anything.

Perhaps it was a bird. An owl or a heron?

He drew in a deep breath, feeling his lungs expand with cold air, as if shrugging off a heavy cloak. Drem felt comfortable in the silent landscape. Far more comfortable than he felt within the walls of Dun Seren, with people and stone crowding all around. He had sat many a night in the wild, only his da for company.

He walked a few dozen more paces under the trees until he entered a clearing, and then he stopped, setting his bag on the ground. Leaves scratched and rustled in the breeze, the creak of branches, beyond that the gurgle of the river.

"Where are you?" Drem muttered as he searched the gloom, but he saw nothing but trees and crow-black shadows. He rummaged in his bag and took out a big clay pot, grunted as he unstoppered it, then wafted it around, the scent warm and sweet.

"Come on," Drem called, and set the pot on the ground.

He sat and waited.

It was not long before there was a vibration in the ground, and then the cracking of foliage as something large made its way closer. A deeper darkness formed, growing larger, and then the white bear was lumbering into the glade. It towered over him, its muzzle twitching as it snuffled. Drem held up the pot, took a ladle from a cloak pocket and scooped out a spoonful of honey.

The bear snorted its pleasure and took a big lick of the spoon, its rough tongue rasping across the back of Drem's hand.

"I thought you'd be hanging around," Drem said. "You've got too used to your honey."

And us.

Drem had fed the white bear every night after camp had been set. He'd elicited curses from the healers when he had stolen pots of honey from their tent, but Byrne had waved their complaints away.

"*He saved enough of us,*" she had said. "*The least we can do is share something of what we have with him.*"

Drem ladled out more honey, the bear sat down, slurping, the lips and fur of his muzzle sticky and dripping. When the honey was all gone, it scratched at the pot with long claws, one of them missing from his front paw. Drem put a hand to the claw hanging about his neck.

"It's a strange world," Drem said, "that you and I should start off with you trying to eat me, and now I am the one feeding you."

He bent down, stoppered the pot and wiped it on the ground before stuffing it back in his bag. Slinging it over his shoulder, he gave the bear a pat on a huge shoulder. He was not sure when he had started doing that, or when the bear had made it clear he would tolerate being touched, but now it felt quite natural.

"I'll bring some more tomorrow," Drem said, and walked away.

The bear lowed mournfully behind him.

"It's all gone," Drem said, and carried on walking. A dozen heartbeats later and the ground was rumbling. Drem didn't look back and carried on walking. The bear followed. It paused when Drem began crossing the bridge, but only for a few moments. Drem heard its claws scratching on stone.

The outer guards stared as they walked past. They had not seen the white bear, but tales had spread of his part in the battle. His huge head swayed from side to side as he assessed them with his small dark eyes.

Together they followed a wide road that skirted wharves and barns and then passed beneath the sweeping walls of Dun Seren.

Guards saw Drem and the bear approaching and the gates swung open. Drem slowed down, falling back to walk almost alongside of the bear.

When they reached the gates, the white bear stopped and regarded the walls suspiciously. Drem stopped, too, looking up at the looming fortress.

"I know how you feel," Drem said, resting his hand on the

bear's neck. "When I first came here it felt as if someone's hands were about my throat, everything was so closed in, and there were so many people. You and I are creatures of wood and sky, we love the open spaces. But it's not that bad, it just takes a bit of getting used to. It's worth it, for a warm bed, hot food and good friends."

The white bear looked from Drem to the open gates. Drem set off again, and after a moment's hesitation the bear followed. Their steps echoed through the gate tunnel and then they were in the courtyard. Drem didn't hesitate and led the way through the city until they came to a large building, more like a stone complex, a paved courtyard edged with what looked to be large stables. Drem approached one of them and a bear's head appeared over a stable's half-gate.

It was Hammer.

She rumbled a greeting to the white bear, who approached her, growled and then rubbed his muzzle against hers, their teeth *clacking* together.

Drem unbolted the door and opened it. The stable was huge, large enough for three bears. The white bear took a deep snorting breath and then lumbered in, Hammer rumbling and growling in welcome.

Drem stood in the doorway and watched as the white bear scratched at the straw-covered floor, sniffed at a barrel of apples and turned in a circle. Then it looked up at Drem.

Drem returned the bear's gaze, the two of them frozen for long moments, then the white bear snorted and stuck his head into the apple barrel. There was a lot of crunching.

"You're welcome," Drem said. He bolted the stable door and walked away. He was smiling.

Drem's door rattled; someone was pounding on it with a fist.

"What?" he groaned, rolling out of bed and stumbling to the door.

Cullen was there in his training leathers.

"Your white bear's smashed a stable door to kindling and I'm not quite sure where the beast is."

Drem tugged on clothes, grabbed a tunic and ran out of the door.

Dawn was seeping into the sky in pinks and orange, Drem's breath misting as he ran into the bears' stable enclosure. The door he had bolted last night was splintered and spread over a wide area; Hammer and the white bear were nowhere to be seen.

"Oh dear," Drem muttered.

"Aye," Cullen breathed, skidding to a halt as he caught up with Drem. "Oh dear, it is."

The courtyard was empty, though bears were sticking their heads over stable doors and peering into the courtyard.

"Over here," a voice called. Keld appeared at the far end of the courtyard, Fen and Ralla at his heels. Drem hurried over.

Keld was leaning on a post-and-rail fence, looking into a huge paddock. Drem blew out a sigh of relief. In the shadowed grey of first light he could see the white bear was in there, with Hammer. Both of them were standing in a stream, scooping at fish.

"I guess he doesn't like feeling shut in," Drem said.

"Aye," Keld said, eyeing the shattered stable door. "You can say that again. Some of us just don't like bars."

"I suppose that's fair enough," Drem said.

"Say that once you've cleared up his mess," Cullen said, grinning and patting Drem's back.

"Come on, we'll help you clean up before Ethlinn's giants start arriving," Keld said, and looked up at the brightening sky. "Any moment now."

"Stooping falcon," Byrne called out, and fifteen hundred swords were drawn and raised into the air.

Drem was in the weapons-field, standing with most of the warband of the Order, going through the sword dance. Byrne stood at their head, Kill one side of her, Utul the other. Unless the Order of the Bright Star were actually fighting, it seemed that missing the sword dance as their morning ritual was unthinkable.

"Lightning strike," Byrne cried, and every sword slashed diagonally downwards.

Drem had come straight to the weapons-field from the bears' enclosure. Keld and Cullen had helped him clear the debris, though he wasn't quite sure what he was going to do about repairing the smashed door before sunset.

Maybe the white bear will be happier in the paddock.

Giants had arrived while Drem and his friends were cleaning up, Alcyon first amongst them with his twin axes crossed upon his back, dragging a wain full of fruit and berries. His son, Tain the crow master, was with him. They were deep in conversation.

"It is time, long overdue," Alcyon was saying. "Please, Tain, send one of your crows to find her."

"They are not *my* crows," Tain said, "and they are needed. They do an important job."

"I *know* that. Have a conversation with Craf, then. He will not begrudge this."

Tain was silent.

"Tain, your mother should be here. Should have been here a long time ago."

"I do not think she will come," Tain said.

Alcyon stopped, gripping Tain by the shoulder.

"There is only one way to know that. Please, send her the message."

Tain nodded. "I will talk to Craf about it, and Byrne."

Alcyon grunted and they carried on into the courtyard. He raised an eyebrow when he saw the smashed door and looked at Drem.

"Takes a while for a bear to settle in, sometimes," was all he said.

"Boar's tusk," Byrne cried. Drem lunged forwards and up,

like a gouging boar, and held the position. He was starting to sweat, now, steaming in the fresh morning air. He liked this time, when the world faded for a short while and all that existed was the burning in his muscles, the tip of his blade and the trembling in his fibres, the pleasure when he executed a manoeuvre and stance well. And deep in the back of his mind the knowledge that his parents had once been here, going through exactly the same routine. It was comforting, somehow.

And then before Drem knew it Byrne was sheathing her sword across her back and facing the gathered warriors.

"We are at war," Byrne addressed them. "You have fought well, and we are all grieving for those we have lost."

A ripple through the warriors around Drem, bowed heads as comrades were remembered.

"We shall never forget. But we shall avenge them," Byrne shouted.

"Captains, with me," she called out, and strode away. Utul and Kill followed her. Drem and Cullen made for the weapons racks.

"Drem, this way, lad," Keld said to him.

Drem raised a quizzical brow.

"You're coming with me, to Byrne's council of war." Keld gestured for him to follow.

"I don't understand," Drem said. Byrne had requested her captains, and Keld was captain of the Order's huntsmen, but Drem was newly arrived, hadn't even taken his weapons trial or sworn the oath yet.

"Didn't I tell you? You're my apprentice now." Keld stopped. "Byrne approved my request last night. And that means you go everywhere I go, and I'm going to the council of war, so..." He shrugged.

"Ach, that's not fair," Cullen moaned. "I should be there, too."

"Ha," Keld said. "We all know what *your* input would be."

"Oh, do we? And what would that be, then?" Cullen said.

"Attack. Attack now."

Drem held back a smile.

Cullen shrugged. "Seems like the obvious thing to do," he said sullenly.

"As it happens, Byrne asked me to bring you along, too."

Cullen grinned, bright as the morning. "She's realized I'm invaluable," Cullen said to Drem.

"Ah, Cullen, good," Byrne said, as they walked into a high-vaulted chamber where Byrne sat at the head of a table. "I've asked for you to be here because I want to keep my eye on you."

Cullen opened his mouth to speak.

"Sit down, be silent, and perhaps you'll learn something," Byrne said with a frown.

She is still mad with him for jumping into the Feral pit at the starstone mine, Drem thought.

Queen Ethlinn and Balur One-Eye were there, along with Tain Crow Master and the old crow, Craf, perched on his shoulder. Utul and Kill sat either side of Byrne.

"So," Byrne said, "we need to decide what to do? We know Gulla has sailed with many ships, his target likely Drassil, and we have had no word from the Ben-Elim. Has Drassil fallen? The silence makes that seem likely. So should we march on Drassil? Gather our full strength here before we move out? Or send out word to the other garrisons of the Order, and meet somewhere on route?"

"Gulla has to be stopped, we should move quickly," Cullen said.

"But not blindly," Drem said to his friend, frowning. "We've been led by the nose enough."

"Aye," Balur rumbled. "We need information."

Byrne looked to Tain and Craf.

"*Gulla bad man,*" Craf squawked. "*Craf like to peck his eyes out. Must be stopped. But Craf's children in danger. Skies not safe.*"

"I know," Byrne said. "But we need to know. These are dark times, and your crows could save lives."

"*Yes, yes,*" Craf muttered, wagging his head. "*Craf heard it all before; Craf fly here, Craf fly there, tell us this, watch that. Craf do it for friends. For Corban, for Brina, for Camlin, even when Craf scared.*" The crow's claws dug into Tain's shoulder, but the giant only stroked Craf's ruffled feathers.

"You are brave, Craf, and so are your children," Tain said.

Craf bobbed on Tain's shoulder. "*Craf's children brave,*" he murmured. "*Flick was brave.*"

Drem felt a twinge at that, because Flick had been the crow who had found Drem, Keld and Cullen in the Desolation, when they had been fleeing Fritha. Flick had disappeared, it was assumed he was dead.

"Flick was brave," Tain said. "He fought for our cause. For friendship, and against the darkness of the Kadoshim."

"*Bad men,*" Craf agreed. He rubbed his beak against Tain's head. "*And Tain my friend. Byrne my friend.*" The crow looked at them all, hovering over Ethlinn and Balur. "*Even old One-Eye a good friend.*"

"Careful who you're calling *old*, you old crow," Balur grunted.

Craf squawked, the noise sounding like laughter. "*My children will fly, be your eyes in the sky,*" he said.

"Thank you, Craf," Byrne said, dipping her head to the crow.

"*Welcome,*" Craf croaked.

Horn calls drifted in through an open window and they all stopped, Byrne rising to look out. Drem could see the pale blue beyond her.

There were winged figures in the sky.

CHAPTER TWELVE

FRITHA

Fritha woke and stretched. High above, she saw the silhouette of Kadoshim wings, flying in lazy circles beneath the Great Hall's domed rooftop. Dawn's light seeped through the fly-holes built into the chamber, casting the world in shadow and beams of grey light. She was lying on a bed that had been carved and built upon the dais in Drassil's Great Hall. The dais where Asroth and Meical had recently been entombed in starstone metal. The bed was huge, big enough for half a dozen giants, but one thing she was learning about Asroth.

He liked excess.

Looking about her, she realized that Asroth was gone. Rolling to the bed's edge she grabbed her breeches and tugged them on, then dragged her linen shirt over her shoulders, hiding the bruises. Her body ached, purpling fingermarks a testimony to Asroth's tastes. After the feast he had come to her, asking her to explain why she had called him her betrothed. He had listened stone-faced as she'd explained to him about the Kadoshim covens and Acolyte Assembly, about how Gulla had negotiated a deal with humankind, the beginning of an alliance that promised a new future for both races. If the Ben-Elim were defeated.

"*So, you are the bridge between our worlds, between Kadoshim and mortal-kind,*" he had said.

"*I am to be your bride,*" she had answered with a shrug, "*a symbol of our races' futures together.*"

95

"So much is new," he had breathed, eyes locked on hers. *"Not how it was supposed to be. But, I think I am liking this new world and its compromises."*

He had smiled at her then, and after that he had taken her to his bed. They had not had the handbinding ceremony yet, but in all other ways they were now wed.

She put a hand to her belly.

A sound behind her; she turned and saw Asroth.

He was standing with one arm outstretched, his hand against the trunk of Drassil's great tree, about which this whole chamber and the fortress beyond were built. The bark was knotted and ridged, stippled with patches of moss and age-old vine. The trunk was wider than any of Drassil's towers.

Fritha rose, buckled on her weapons-belt and padded over to Asroth. As she walked past, she glanced at the huge chest Asroth had ordered built to hold the shattered pieces of star-stone metal. It was closed and bolted, but Fritha fancied that she could sense the power of the metal within, a tingling deep in her blood. Asroth never moved far from it.

Fritha reached Asroth and rested an arm upon his bare back, ran her fingertips down the alabaster flesh, following a tapestry of blue-black veins.

"What are you doing, my love?" she whispered.

He ignored her, his hand tracing the knots and whorls of the great tree. He was whispering, at first the words alien and meaningless to Fritha.

"Geata rúin, taispeáin duit féin," he muttered, over and over again. Slowly the words coalesced in Fritha's mind.

"Gateway of secrets," she murmured, "show yourself."

Asroth froze, his black eyes turning to regard her.

"You are a *remarkable* woman," he said quietly. "I must never forget that. And if you breathe a word of what I am saying to another living thing, I will kill you."

Fritha recoiled, took a step back.

"I would never," she said. "We are wed, bound."

Asroth stared at her long moments, his face expressionless, but Fritha's skin goosebumped, as if caressed with frozen hands. He held her gaze a moment longer and then turned back to his task, resumed his muttering. Abruptly he stopped, his hand finding something in the bark, not quite a hole, more like an old wound, as if the bark had been stabbed. Amber resin had leaked like blood from a sword-cut, scabbed and hard now. Asroth's fingers probed and he continued to mutter. "*Geata rúin, taispeáin duit féin, geata rúin, taispeáin duit féin, geata rúin, taispeáin duit féin.*"

There was a cracking sound, like an axe splitting wood, and a line appeared, spreading, an arched gateway was outlined against the bark, wide as two giants. Asroth gripped inside the hole he had found and pulled, and with a creaking and hissing of air long-captured the door swung open.

A stairwell stood before them, carved out of the heart of the tree, leading downwards. The air was musty, thick with mould, but there was something else there, too. Fritha inhaled, scenting the tang of metal, like a blacksmith's forge, but as faint as morning mist.

Bune flew down from above them, landing with a soft scrape of leather on stone.

"A torch," Asroth commanded, and Bune swept one from a sconce on the wall, handing it to his master.

Asroth stepped into the stairwell, touched his torch to a bowl mounted upon the wall. Blue flame crackled and Fritha recognized it for the oil she had once found in giant ruins. More of them lined the stairwell; Asroth lit them as he descended.

Fritha followed, stepping quickly in front of Bune.

Her fingers traced the wall as she spiralled downwards. They came away sticky with sap, the scent of resin thick in the air. And then the stairs were levelling out and they were entering a circular chamber. Asroth touched his torch to a trough built into the wall and it flared with blue fire, spreading around the room with a hiss and crackle, and the stench of oil. Fritha took a moment to take in the room. It was edged with racks filled with giant weapons: war-hammers, battle-axes, spears and swords. Further on, tools replaced the weapons: tongs, pincers, hammers of all sizes, chisels and awls. In the room's centre stood a huge anvil, and behind it a bellows and forge loomed, still banked with ancient charcoal and cinder.

Asroth approached the anvil and, almost reverently, laid his hand upon it.

Fritha saw runes inscribed upon the wall, and other things, symbols. The whole circle of the wall was filled with them. One looked like a spear, another like a double-bladed axe, elsewhere a cup.

"It is a map," Asroth said, watching her. "Of the Banished Lands, and of where the Seven Treasures were kept."

"The Seven Treasures," Fritha whispered. So many tales of them: cauldron, spear and axe, dagger, torc, necklace and cup. All of them were said to have been created from the Starstone, and all had power. She touched a hand to the hilt of her sword.

"Yes, like your blade," Asroth said, "though that is a crude thing compared to these treasures. The giants used them in their war, when their Clans were sundered."

"It is all true, then," Fritha breathed, the tales of antiquity in this place feeling like a real weight, heavy and bearing down upon her.

"Oh, aye," Asroth said. "And this is where they were forged." He patted the anvil, a meaty slap. "But those treasures are no longer where the map says they are. They are all up there, in my wooden chest."

Fritha looked at him.

"All of the treasures were cast into the cauldron, by Corban and his witch-sister, Cywen. They were undone by her sorcery, melted and made new again as my prison. A skin of starstone metal. Ach, how it burned." His face twisted in a snarl.

"But they will be made new again, and I shall wield them."

Fritha looked at him with a fierce smile. *And I shall be by your side when you do.*

CHAPTER THIRTEEN

RIV

Riv began the descent to Dun Seren, far below her.

The fortress was a dark smudge upon a green hill, the river Vold curling around its northern walls like the black carcass of a great serpent. Riv could hear horns blowing, see pinpricks moving upon walls. She glanced at Meical, who flew silently beside her, his face set in hard lines.

"They've seen us," Riv shouted over the roar of air as they swept downwards. Meical stared ahead, eyes fixed on the fortress.

"That is Dun Seren?" he called to her, his face shifting, emotions rippling.

"Aye, you know it?"

"By another name. It was Gramm's Hold then, a hall of timber and thatch, and it was in flames when I left it. Dun Seren," he said, a smile ghosting his lips. "Fortress of the Star."

"The Order of the Bright Star," Riv corrected him.

Meical said nothing.

Riv did not know what to make of Meical. All her life she had seen him as a symbol of the fight against the Kadoshim. A literal image of that battle, locked in combat with Asroth for all to see. Though now, looking back, Riv realized that during all of her history and Lore lessons her Ben-Elim teachers had barely mentioned Meical or Corban. That was strange. And, judging by the words Meical had exchanged with Kol back at the cabin, something had happened to sour Meical's relationship with his kin.

A flicker of white wings and Hadran overtook them, another dozen Ben-Elim with him. Kol had sent them with Riv and Meical, as protection against Kadoshim and half-breeds, Kol had said, but Riv knew that was no truth. Kol wanted to keep a leash on Meical. He was a threat.

If Kol doesn't like Meical, or trust him, then that alone is a good reason for me to like Meical.

Riv felt no bond of daughterly love for her Ben-Elim father, who she knew would have slaughtered her as a child, had her mother Aphra not concealed her existence.

She knew Kol would have been here to watch Meical himself, but he had another task to accomplish. The debate at the cottage in the woods had swept back and forth for half a night about the best course of action. The next day they had separated, all going about their own tasks, each one vital. Each one dangerous.

I miss Bleda. Riv felt his absence like a punch in the gut. She had felt such a rush of joy at seeing him upon the wall at the cabin, after so much fear and death, and now they had been separated again. She pictured his face, his beautiful almond eyes, could for a heartbeat feel his fingers upon her bare skin, the sensation of his lips against hers.

I will see him again, she vowed.

Dun Seren was much closer now, the tower and courtyard clear, a crowd forming. Hadran led them down in a slow spiral, making sure that all below could see that they were Ben-Elim, that their wings were white feathers, not leather and gristle, like the Kadoshim.

They circled above the courtyard and touched down between the statue in the centre of the yard and the wide stone steps that led up to the keep. Riv saw Ethlinn and Balur One-Eye emerge from the keep's shadows and could not keep the smile from her face at seeing the old giant. Byrne, High Captain of the Order, emerged between them. Riv felt nothing but respect for the woman who had bested Kol in this very courtyard, not so long ago, to Riv's surprise and great satisfaction.

Others were with Byrne. A slender giant Riv remembered as Tain. Craf the old crow was on his shoulder. There were five human warriors as well, a dark-skinned woman and four men. One she recognized: Drem. He had been the reason Kol and Byrne had fought—some old grievance between the Ben-Elim and the Order of the Bright Star.

Byrne saw Riv and dipped her head in a greeting.

Hadran stepped ahead of Riv and the other Ben-Elim, and took a few paces up the steps towards Byrne.

"Drassil has fallen. Asroth is free," he said, loud enough for all to hear.

Gasps and oaths muttered around the courtyard. Byrne jolted to a stop, her face turning ashen.

"No," Ethlinn said.

Balur One-Eye made a growling sound.

Riv looked around for Meical and realized he was not standing with her or the other Ben-Elim. He was standing behind her, gazing sadly up at the statue in the courtyard, of a warrior and a wolven.

Corban, the founder of the Order, and his wolven, Storm.

Riv stepped close to Meical, saw that his lips were moving, though she could not hear what he was saying.

A loud squawking filled the courtyard.

"*MEICAL, MEICAL, MEICAL,*" and Riv saw the old crow on Tain's shoulder hopping up and down and flapping his scraggly wings.

Meical turned and stepped out from behind the Ben-Elim. He smiled at the exuberant crow.

"I did not expect to see you here, Craf," Meical said, striding up the steps. He stopped before Byrne and dipped his head.

"You must be Byrne," he said, "the High Captain of this Order."

"I am," Byrne said, no emotion on her face. "And you are Meical. I have seen you before, frozen in starstone metal." She took a long moment to study his face, holding his gaze.

"I am free, now," he said. He rolled his shoulders and looked from Byrne to Ethlinn. "It is good to see you, Lady."

"And not so good to see you," Ethlinn replied, "for to see you means that a hundred years has been undone. Asroth is free."

"Aye, he is," Meical said. "But that means he is also free to die. To be sent back to the Otherworld, once and for all."

Riv liked the sound of that.

"And you, old One-Eye," Meical said. "It is good to see you, too."

Balur stared at Meical with his one eye, a scowl on his face.

"You caused us a *lot* of trouble," Balur grunted.

"I did," Meical said, a pinching of his eyes.

"Corban said Meical redeemed himself, at the end," Ethlinn reminded him gently, reaching a hand out and resting it on Balur's arm.

Balur nodded. "And that is why I have not taken this winged man's head," he growled. "But still…"

Craf flapped his wings and took off from Tain's shoulder. The bird rose unsteadily, winged through the air, a few feathers drifting down to the ground, and landed on Meical's shoulder.

"*Meical good friend,*" the crow croaked. "*Craf saw Meical save Corban, fight Asroth.*"

Meical scratched Craf's head.

"No, Craf, it was Corban who saved *me*," Meical said.

"*Corban saved us all,*" Craf squawked. "*And Cywen.*"

"The victory was won by many," Ethlinn said.

Riv looked at Meical. *That's not how most Ben-Elim would have us know it. They told us they were the saviours of humankind. There was little mention of Corban and his followers…*

"How is it that there's still breath in your beak, old friend?" Meical said to Craf.

"*Secret*," Craf cawed, with a touch of smugness to his tone.

"There is much to speak on," Byrne interrupted. "War is upon us. Hadran, Meical, join us in council, there is much we need to discuss." She paused, eyes shifting to Riv. "And you, too," she added.

Horns blew loud behind Riv, from the gate tower.

"Riders approaching," a voice boomed down to them.

CHAPTER FOURTEEN

DREM

At the alarm, Drem followed Byrne as she hurried towards Dun Seren's gates. He watched Riv open her wings and take to the sky, flying upwards in a tight spiral. Craf squawked from Tain's shoulder and spread his wings, flapping awkwardly into the air.

"Be careful," Tain called up to the old bird. Other crows cawed and croaked above them, flying south to where the riders were approaching. Drem saw the white smudge of Rab amongst them.

When they reached the battlements' top Byrne walked until she stood over the gate, Ethlinn and Balur either side of her.

Drem put a hand over his eyes and stared to the south.

Dun Seren spread in tiers below them, shifting into rich green pastures. A road cut through the green, and upon it a plume of dust marked riders approaching.

"What do you see, lad?" Keld muttered beside Drem. He knew Drem's eyes were excellent.

"Three riders," Drem said. "Warriors." He strained his eyes, but they were too far for him to tell anything else.

A flapping from above and Craf descended, alighting clumsily on Tain's outstretched arm.

"*Craf tired, too far,*" the crow muttered.

"Your children will do your flying," Tain soothed.

They waited.

The riders drew closer. It seemed to take a long while but

Drem could tell they were riding hard. He saw a winged figure swoop down, circling the riders: Riv, he thought, from the
colour of her wings, though he could not be sure at this distance. Crows circled above them. Then the winged figure was
speeding back to them, straight as an arrow's flight, crows following in her wake.

Drem was right, it was Riv. She approached at a dizzying
rate, wings spreading and checking her when she was almost
upon them. Her feet touched gently onto the stone wall before
Byrne.

"Riders from Ardain," Riv said. "They say they are scouts
of Queen Nara, who follows behind them. They have been
attacked."

"Who by?" Byrne asked.

Riv pulled a face. "Monsters in the mist, they said."

Byrne looked at Ethlinn, then turned to the honour guard
beside her.

"Sound the call to arms," she said. "Every warrior with a
rune-marked weapon rides with me."

The riders clattered through Dun Seren's gates as Drem rode
back into the courtyard, Keld and Cullen either side of him.

Byrne was already waiting there in her war gear, her coat of
mail and iron helm gleaming, and mounted ahead of a score of
her guards, waiting for the riders of Ardain. They were mud-
spattered, eyes dark with exhaustion. Byrne cantered to them as
stablehands ran to help them. One warrior slid from his mount
and lay still on the stone-flagged ground. Men ran to help him.

A trembling of the ground and Drem looked over his shoulder. He saw Ethlinn approaching, mounted upon a bear, a spear
in her fist, two score giants upon bears behind her. All of the
bears bore coats of mail, strapped with leather and iron. They
were a formidable sight, muscle rippling beneath their riveted
mail. Alcyon was there, the sides of his head freshly shaved and
his two axes slung across his back.

"What news?" Byrne asked. Drem rode as close as he could to hear. "Is it true that Queen Nara is behind you?"

"Ardain is fallen," one of the warriors panted, a younger man, tufts of beard on his chin.

"What?" Byrne blinked, leaning forward in her saddle as if she had misheard.

"The monsters in the mist, they have swept Ardain like a plague. Queen Nara tried to fight them, but it was impossible. In the end she gathered the survivors and fled the realm."

"She is coming here?" Byrne asked.

"Aye. We had nowhere else to go. But they have followed us, and they are gaining. They were almost upon us when Queen Nara bid us ride to you."

"Lead us to her," Byrne said, calling for fresh mounts for the riders.

"I'll find them," Riv said, spreading her wings, "lead you to them."

"No," Byrne said.

"Why not? You don't trust me?" Riv scowled.

She doesn't like being told what to do, Drem observed.

"Not that," Byrne snapped. "It's too dangerous."

"I'm not *scared.*" Riv bridled.

"I didn't say that, either," Byrne said, frowning at Riv. "You must learn to listen," she added. "Did you not hear my orders, on the wall."

"Something about runed blades," Riv said. She put a hand to the two short-swords at her hip. "I don't need runed blades. These are all I need."

If you want to die a quick death at the hands of Gulla's Revenants, Drem thought. Drem's sword and seax were both rune-marked, both of them forged by his father, Olin. Drem had raised an eyebrow at Cullen when he had appeared at the stables and saddled his horse. He knew Cullen didn't have a rune-marked blade, and so should not be preparing to ride out with Byrne, but he'd learned not to tell Cullen he couldn't do something. That was the surest way of getting Cullen to do it.

"Not against these creatures," Byrne said, "if they are the same that we fought in the Desolation. Only a rune-marked blade can slay them. I forbid anyone to trade blows with these creatures unless they are wielding a rune-marked blade. I'll not have my people dying in a fight they can't win." Her face softened. "Or you."

"These mist-walkers, I've killed them before," Riv grunted.

They are called Revenants, Drem silently corrected.

Byrne raised an eyebrow. "Have you? How many?"

A long pause.

"One," Riv muttered. "And that wasn't...easy." A longer pause. "And I had some help."

Cullen barked a laugh.

"Rune-marked blades kill them. Hurt them like any blade would hurt us," Drem said.

Riv stared at Drem a long moment, then looked back to Byrne. "Well, have you got one of these blades I can have, then?" she said.

Byrne smiled, looking to her left, where Kill and a dozen warriors were leading a horse and wain into the courtyard. They creaked to a halt before Byrne, and Kill pulled back a waxed sheet to reveal a mound of weapons. Spears, swords, axes, some bundled arrows.

"Not enough," Kill grunted, "but this is all we have been able to craft in the last moon."

"How many?" Byrne asked.

"Forty swords. Seventy spears. Sixty-five axes. Fifty arrows."

"It will have to do, for now," Byrne said.

Riv edged closer, peering into the wain.

Meical stepped forwards.

"We are not of your Order, but it would be wise to give us Ben-Elim a weapon. We can fly out, could be a great help in bringing Nara and her people back within these walls."

Byrne looked at him, and at Hadran and the dozen Ben-Elim behind him.

"Trust us," Meical said. "Trust *me*. I will not let you down."

Byrne gave a curt nod.

"Take spears," she said.

"My thanks," Meical said, and stepped closer. Kill handed him a bundle of spears to distribute amongst the Ben-Elim.

"Can I have a sword?" Riv said, looking in the wain. "And some arrows." She patted the curved bow in a case at her hip and looked up at Byrne in her saddle. "Please," Riv added.

Byrne nodded to Kill and then Riv was walking away with a sword and a sheaf of arrows, which she began threading into her belt quiver.

"Spread the weapons amongst the mounted," Byrne said, as she reached down and gripped a spear. "Make sure Cullen has a rune-marked sword," she added.

The crack of hooves as more riders cantered into the court-yard from the direction of the stables: Utul and Shar, other warriors of the Order who possessed rune-marked blades, all of them in mail and leather. Behind them there was the creak and roll of empty wains drawn by horses rather than auroch, as was usual for the big wagons. It was a convoy of them, more than Drem could count.

"And remember," Byrne cried, standing tall in her sad-dle, "protect yourselves at all costs. A coat of mail, iron helm, gloves, or you don't ride out with me. If these things bite you, you're finished." She looked at her warriors. "More time and we could have rune-marked helms and shields, our armour." She shrugged.

Drem's hand shifted to the iron helm strapped to his sad-dle. It was more of a cap, and he hated wearing it, but knew that Byrne was right. He was already wearing his gloves, thick, boiled leather with strips of iron stitched in to protect the knuckles.

Meical, Riv, Hadran and the other Ben-Elim leaped into the sky, wings beating. Byrne turned her mount and cantered for the gate. "WITH ME!" she cried, and with a roar Drem was swept through the courtyard and out of the gates of Dun Seren.

Three leagues south of the fortress, Drem saw the host of Ardain. The sun was high in the sky, a pale light behind dark-ening clouds. A sharp wind brought the taste and scent of rain to Drem. At first the host before Drem was little more than a dark smudge across the land, a sheen of dust hovering in the air above them. Riv, Meical and the other Ben-Elim had already flown out to the vanguard and given word of Byrne's coming. Now the Ben-Elim flew above Byrne's riders, crows smaller dots flapping amongst them. Drem glanced up, saw Rab flying close to Riv. They looked to be talking.

The survivors of Ardain were spread across the land, a swirl of people thousands strong, disappearing over a ridge on the horizon.

I have never seen so many people in my whole life, Drem thought. He felt a shifting in his belly, still a sign of his inherent dis-comfort at such crowds. Muscles in his arm twitched, fingers wanting to search for the steady reassurance of his pulse. With an effort he kept both hands upon his reins and drew in a long, steady breath, as his father had taught him.

"You all right, lad?" Keld called to him.

"Aye," Drem grunted. He looked at Keld, felt something was missing. Then he realized.

"Where are Fen and Ralla?" he asked.

"Told them they couldn't come. They've not got rune-marked teeth or claws, they wouldn't stand a chance against those Revenants."

He's right. As vicious as Fen and Ralla are, tooth and claw won't stop Gulla's Revenants.

A hand drifted to his seax, feeling the smooth-worn bone of the hilt.

A loose line of riders stretched ahead of Ardain's host, the glint of steel from weapons and mail.

Ahead of him Byrne touched her heels to her mount, picking up the pace. Drem and the other mounted warriors matched her, eighty or ninety riders, a gap opening between them and the column of empty wains that were being driven across the land. Ethlinn and her bear-riders broke into a loping stride, matching the speed of Byrne's riders. Drem glimpsed Balur One-Eye with Sig's sword across his back, and Alcyon upon Hammer. Behind Alcyon and Hammer there was a flash of white fur. The white bear had followed them and was loping along close to Hammer and Alcyon. Drem felt a twinge of worry for the bear.

I didn't know you'd followed us. Hope you don't get into any trouble if this comes to a fight.

The drum of hooves filled Drem's ears and soon they were close to the sprawling host. Some were on horseback, here and there was a wain crowded with too many people, but most were on foot. Gaunt, hollow eyes gazed up at Drem and the others. A ripple of cheers rose from them as Byrne and her riders approached. A warrior rode out from the vanguard, a woman, dark hair tucked beneath a helm, her warrior braid sweat-stained and stuck to her skin. Byrne slowed.

"Where is Nara?" Byrne called out to the warrior.

"With the stragglers and the rearguard," the warrior shouted, gesturing over her shoulder with a spear.

"Wains are coming, fill them with the neediest first," Byrne called, and then she was urging her mount on and breaking into a canter, riding along the outskirts of the host. Drem and the others followed.

"Where are they?" Cullen said, riding close to Drem. The red-haired warrior was staring ahead, searching the distance.

"Who?" Drem called to him.

"Our enemy," Cullen shouted, a grin on his face. "My arse is getting sore and I need to stretch my legs." He had a flush in his face and a gleam in his eye that Drem was starting to recognize.

Drem glanced up, saw the outline of Ben-Elim above them, and ahead the dark spots of Dun Seren's crows, circling.

I think they've found our enemy.

They crested a ridge, cantering down a gentle slope. The crowd was thinning, only a few score stragglers hobbling up the slope. A little further down the ridge was a line of horsemen, five, six hundred of them, spread in a long row. All were warriors, spears and swords in their fists, the grey-checked cloaks of Ardain fluttering from their backs in a sharp breeze. They were facing away from Byrne and her companions, towards the bottom of the ridge where the ground levelled out. A black mist seethed and boiled there, filling the land to the horizon, like storm clouds rolling in a sullen sky. It was moving steadily towards them, against the breeze. Drem felt a shiver's chill course through his veins.

Gulla's Revenants.

He guessed it was no more than three leagues away.

A banner snapped and rippled in the middle of the horsemen, a snarling wolven, teeth bared. Byrne rode towards it.

Faces turned to them: a woman, straight-backed and dark-haired, skin pale, a coat of mail beneath a thick cloak.

That must be Queen Nara. She had a drawn sword in her hand, resting across her saddle. To one side of her was an older warrior, broad-shouldered and mail-clad, a short beard upon a stern face. On the other side of the Queen sat a man in leather and mail, slimmer, dark-haired, his warrior braid coiling out from his helm. His eyes flitted across Byrne, Drem and the others, hovering on Ethlinn and Balur to the rear of Byrne's companions. Something about the way he sat on his horse, his posture and his sharp glance told Drem this was a dangerous man.

"Well met, Queen Nara," Byrne called out as she reined in before the dark-haired woman. Byrne dipped her head in greeting.

"You have come, but I wish now that you had not," Nara said with a calm gaze. "It is too late. They are almost upon us, and I would not have you or your people risk your lives for the impossible."

"You should not be waiting here for them," Byrne said.

"That's what I said," the older warrior muttered, his voice as stern as his face.

"Elgin," Byrne said with a nod.

"My Lady," Elgin replied with a dip of his head.

"I will not *run* while my people stand and die," Nara snarled at the older warrior. He did not wither before her anger, just nodded soberly.

"Aye, that is what makes you the queen you are," he said slowly, "but with you Ardain lives or dies. I would rather it live on. We could stay, fight, buy you the time you need to escape. You should go while there is still hope."

Drem got the impression this was not the first time they'd had this conversation.

"No," Nara said. "There is no hope, now. They are too close, and there are too many. You would buy us some time with your courage, Elgin, but not long enough for my people to reach Dun Seren's walls. Better that we shall die fighting together, on our feet, steel in our fists and facing our enemy, not showing them our backs."

"There *is* hope," Byrne said grimly, "but you need to leave." She drew her sword, a rasp of steel and leather and held it in the air. "This blade is rune-marked and can kill those things in the mist," she cried, her voice loud, carrying along the line. "Each warrior here with me carries such a weapon. We can kill them. So, let us stand, guard your rear while you tend to your people. We have wains, beyond the ridge, to carry your injured, your children and old folk to Dun Seren's walls, and fresh horses. Go, save your people. They need you."

Nara looked at Byrne, then to the roiling mist in the valley.

She has made her peace with death. It is hard to come back from that place.

"My Queen, go to your people, and we shall meet you at Dun Seren," Byrne urged.

Nara blew out a slow breath, looked away from the mist and into Byrne's eyes. She nodded.

"Ardain is forever in your debt," Nara said.

"No debt. We are allies, and friends," Byrne replied. "Besides, one day soon you may be returning this favour."

A ghost of a smile on Nara's lips. "Gladly," she said, then reached out and gripped Byrne's wrist.

"Kill those bastards," she hissed. "They have torn my land and its people to pieces."

"We will make them pay dearly for it," Byrne said.

"Good," Nara snarled. "Madoc, sound our withdrawal." The dangerous-looking warrior put a horn to his lips and blew, three short blasts, and Nara turned her mount and cantered up the ridge after the last of her disappearing people. Her warriors turned and rode after her, Madoc first to reach her.

Byrne watched them go.

"Right," she said, turning back to Drem and the others. "Let's get ready for a fight."

CHAPTER FIFTEEN

FRITHA

Fritha blinked sweat from her eyes as her hammer rose and fell, the clangour filling her head, echoing through the room. She was in the forge room of Drassil, this wondrous place secreted right at the very heart of the fortress, a chamber carved out within the great tree's heartwood. She liked it here; she felt as if she was party to some ancient secret.

And I am. The Seven Treasures were forged here. And out of their molten destruction, something new shall be reforged.

Fritha paused in her work, muscles burning in her arm, shoulder and back. She wiped sweat from her face and looked to one corner of the chamber. Blue giants-fire flickered in the trough set around the circumference of the room, warring with the white-orange blaze of the forge. Combined, the two light sources cast an eerie glow on the huge chest in which Asroth had stored the shards of starstone metal that had once been his gaol.

The lid was open.

Fritha looked down at the shape on the anvil before her. An iron glove of black metal, riveted and articulated for ease of movement. It was big, made to fit a large hand, larger than most men's, though smaller than a giant's hand.

"He will be here soon," a voice said, Choron, standing close to the chamber's entrance. He was one of half a dozen Kadoshim in the chamber, all of them watching her every move. It was an honour that Asroth trusted Fritha to be in this room, to be carving and making something from his horde of starstone metal, but he did not trust her completely.

Not enough to leave me to work in peace. I have to have their black eyes watching me.

If Wrath were down here you would speak to me with a different tone, she thought, staring at Choron. Her draig was too wide now to fit down the stairwell that led to this chamber, even though it had been built by giants, for giants. Fritha knew that he would be waiting for her in Drassil's Great Hall, though.

She bit back a retort and reached for her tongs, gripped the glove and thrust it into the forge fire, held it there until it glowed white-hot, then laid it back upon the anvil. She took up a small, sharp knife and neatly sliced her palm, another red line that would soon join the myriad scars that were testament to her dark work.

Everything has a price, especially power.

Blood dripped from her palm onto the white-glowing metal, sizzling and spitting, then she picked up a small hammer and an engraver's chisel and hunched over the glove, tapping in careful, measured beats.

"*Réalta dubh, foirm nua, saol nua. Bí láidir, ná sos, crush do naimhde*," she breathed as she tapped. "*Réalta dubh, foirm nua, saol nua. Bí láidir, ná sos, crush do naimhde*," she repeated, again and again as she carved runes into the backplate of the iron gauntlet.

A blast of air made the forge fire roar, flames leaping hungrily, and Fritha looked up from her work. Footsteps echoed on the stairwell and Bune appeared, and behind him, Asroth himself.

"Is it done?" Asroth asked, approaching Fritha.

"Yes," she said, taking the gauntlet in tongs and dipping it hissing into a vat of oil. She pulled it out, held it up for him.

Asroth took it in his one hand and studied it, turning it this way and that. He saw the runes carved into it.

"Unbreakable, foe-crusher," he whispered. Slowly a smile spread over his face. "I like it. Now I just need a hand to wear it upon."

"Yes, you do," Fritha said with a sharp smile. "And that is what we are here to do." She waved her hand over a table full of tools. Razor-edged saws, spikes, tongs, knives, a wide-bladed cleaver. Strips of leather cord, bone needles and twine. Fritha looked over to the Kadoshim Choron and nodded. He shifted his weight, pulling on a chain, receiving only a groan in response, drifting up from a shadow at his feet. Choron spat a curse and kicked the figure on the floor, dragging on the chains again. The figure slowly stood, a tall, muscled man, swaying unsteadily. Vald, the White-Wing warrior who had spat in Asroth's face the night of their victory feast.

He did not look like the same man now. His hair had grown out from the close White-Wing crop and now hung lank and greasy, one eye was barely open in a swollen mass of purple bruising, the other eye a black, scar-puckered hole where Asroth had gouged it out. His lips were macerated against chipped and broken teeth. In his half-open eye, though, Fritha saw the same defiance and strength of spirit that had led him to spit in Asroth's face. It was a stubbornness that no beating would put out. Fritha knew, because she had administered much of the torture; she had tried to snuff it out, and failed. She was still a little annoyed about that, though also felt a grudging respect for the warrior.

"Bring him here," Fritha said.

Choron jerked the chain and led Vald shambling across the chamber to stand before Fritha and Asroth. It was not just Vald's face that had been beaten. He dragged one leg, blood crusted on cuts and burns all over his torso, the burns weeping yellow pus.

"Your new hand," Fritha said, gesturing at Vald.

"It is still attached," Asroth pointed out.

"Aye. You must take it and give it to me."

Asroth smiled, brushing his fingertips over the cleaver upon Fritha's table of tools, then nodded at Choron.

The Kadoshim dragged Vald forwards, but somehow, despite his condition, he gathered untapped reserves of strength and threw his body towards Choron, taking the Kadoshim by surprise. Choron fell onto Fritha's table and Vald rose with an iron spike in his fist, stabbed two-handed at Choron, burying the spike deep into Choron's shoulder.

The Kadoshim shrieked, stumbled backwards.

Bune and other Kadoshim surged forwards, but Asroth was ahead of them. He slammed a fist into Vald's face, pulping the man's nose, then wrapped his fist in Vald's hair and smashed his face into the flat of the anvil. Vald went limp, a pool of blood spreading around his face.

"Hold him," Asroth snarled, and Bune and others pinned Vald to the anvil.

"His hand," Asroth said, reaching for the cleaver with his left hand and raising it.

Choron gripped Vald's right hand and pulled it forwards, then Asroth's arm was rising and falling. A thunk and crack as the cleaver carved through meat and bone, blood sprayed. Vald screamed.

Fritha licked blood spatters from her lip.

The cleaver rose and fell again, crunching into Vald's skull, his scream cut abruptly short.

Asroth lifted the severed hand and gave it to Fritha. Vald's corpse was released to slide off the anvil and fall in a heap to the ground.

"Thank you, my King," Fritha said. She took the hand, measuring it against the iron gauntlet, and smiled to see her calculations and measurements matched perfectly.

"What now?" Asroth said.

"Now I will bind this hand to your flesh," Fritha said. She offered him a strip of leather. "You may want to bite on this," she said. "I suspect this is going to hurt."

Asroth took the leather, looked at it and tossed it on the ground. "Pain will not master me," he said, curling a lip.

"Put your arm on the anvil," Fritha instructed.

Asroth did, eyes fixed on hers.

"Do not fail me," Asroth said.

Fritha wrapped leather cords about Asroth's forearm, binding it to the anvil. Then she turned to her table and selected a saw. She touched the sawblade to the puckered flesh of Asroth's stumped wrist, hardly hearing Asroth's words, her focus on the task ahead, her blood pounding with the thrill of it.

Bune wrapped a hand around her wrist.

"If any harm comes to our King, you will know pain you could never imagine."

She ignored him.

"My King?" Fritha said, looking into the black pools of Asroth's eyes.

"Make me whole. Make me *more*," he said. "Your rewards will be . . . great."

"*An chéad ghearradh, breith na maitheasa,*" Fritha chanted into the chamber, her voice echoing, then a silence fell.

Fritha began to saw.

Asroth opened his mouth and screamed. Then, slowly, the screaming shifted to laughter.

CHAPTER SIXTEEN

DREM

The wall of mist was a mere half a league away now, if that. The Revenant host had covered over two leagues at shockingly quick speed.

A blast of air from above and Drem looked up to see Meical and some of the Ben-Elim descending. Riv was with them. They hovered close above, the air from their wings stirring the grass.

"Ethlinn," Byrne said. "I think our enemy needs to come out from behind its cloak. We need to see what we are facing."

"Aye," Ethlinn said, "just what I was thinking."

"ELEMENTALS!" Byrne called out.

Riders drew up either side of Byrne, forming a line that faced the black mist. Ethlinn, Balur, Alcyon and Tain were amongst them. Keld rode over to Byrne's side and Drem made to guide his horse after the old huntsman. Cullen grabbed Drem's reins.

"This isn't for the likes of us," Cullen said.

"What do you mean?" Drem frowned.

"We are not Elementals."

Elementals—those who have learned to use the earth magic. Byrne had used that word when she had taken him into the secret passages beneath Dun Seren and shown him the Order of the Bright Star's sacred book. It was a great responsibility, she had said, and only those judged capable of handling that responsibility were chosen. They were the elite of the Order, and most of them were gathered here. One of the marks of an Elemental in the Order was that they rune-marked their own blades. Byrne had spoken of teaching Drem the earth power, had showed him the chamber where the Elementals learned their craft. She had hinted at teaching him, and Drem had felt both scared and excited at that thought.

Byrne and Ethlinn were at the centre of the forming line. Balur, Alcyon and Tain were the only other giants there, the rest hanging back on their great bears. Utul and Shar joined the line, along with two score Jehar that had ridden with Utul from the south. Utul drew his curved sword from his back and ran it across his hand.

"*Lasair*," he said, and flames ignited along its blade. He held it up in the air.

"Always the show-off," Shar said beside him.

Kill, Keld, all of Byrne's honour guard and a few score other warriors from the Order rode up to the growing column. Drem and Cullen remained close to the giants, all of them separate from Byrne's gathering. Drem figured there were about ninety riders spread either side of Byrne, all facing down the ridge.

"What are they doing?" Drem whispered to Cullen.

"Patience." Cullen winked.

Drem frowned. *Of which you normally have none.*

Ethlinn and Byrne pulled knives from their belts, drew them along their palms and cast their hands into the air, spraying speckles of blood.

"*Cumhacht an aeir, scrios an dorchadas seo ón talamh*," Byrne called out, and repeated the words, Ethlinn adding her deep voice to Byrne's. The words rose and fell, washing over Drem. They set a tingling in his blood, like the thrum and vibration of a bowstring.

Others in the line drew blades from scabbards and more blood was welling. They raised their hands and joined their voices to Byrne and Ethlinn's.

"*Cumhacht an aeir, scrios an dorchadas seo ón talamh*," they cried. "*Cumhacht an aeir, scrios an dorchadas seo ón talamh*." Over and over again, voices ringing like a wake dirge, and even though Drem did not understand the words, he felt them seep into him and twist and twine through his veins.

"*Cumhacht an aeir, scrios an dorchadas seo ón talamh.*"

"*CUMHACHT AN AEIR, SCRIOS AN DORCHADAS SEO ON TALAMH,*" the voices rang like a thunderclap.

A gust of wind rose up, tugging at Drem's hair, building to a roar in his ears. It swirled around him, growing stronger, and within two dozen heartbeats became a howling wind that swept down the slope, stirring up a dust cloud in its wake. Drem could almost see the forms of warriors in the wind, a sharp-edged gale that slammed into the tenebrous mist, cutting into it. There was a moment where the mist swelled, holding and bending like a dam under pressure, and then it began to tear and fracture, ripping like an old desiccated parchment. The outlines of figures appeared, a seething mass. They were too far away for Drem to make out their features, but he had seen their like before: long-taloned, pale-faced, hollow-eyed creatures. Once these beasts had been men and women of Ardain—Drem even saw the silhouettes of children amongst them—people who had had lives, friends, families, dreams and hopes. Now they were Gulla's Revenant horde, driven by a baser hunger.

They were moving at a steady, uniform pace, but Drem saw many of them falter as the tattered mist dissipated around them, faces looking up to the sky, black eyes blinking, confused. Others came on, seeing Byrne and the warband ahead of them. Some of them broke into a run.

"They're *running*," Cullen said, beside him. "Half a league away and they're running. Ha, they will be running *away* when they see me and my sword."

Somehow, I doubt that.

There were thousands of them. Drem looked at Byrne's line of warriors and the other two score giants close to him.

A hundred and thirty of us, maybe a hundred and forty. He looked up, saw Riv and the dozen Ben-Elim. *A hundred and fifty.*

Back to the horde of Revenants surging up the slope.

We are outnumbered, twenty, thirty to one, maybe more. Even with our rune-marked blades, how can we hope to defeat so many?

A tingle of fear twisted in his belly.

Byrne lowered her hands and looked either side of her.

"Too many for us," Kill said. "We should retreat."

"Then they would catch Nara and her people," Byrne said. "We must slow them, somehow." She looked at the approaching mass, then at the warriors about her. "TWO LINES!" she bellowed. "The Order and giants mixed. First line hits them, retreats, second line hits them, giving the first some room to get out. Second line retreats..." She looked up at Meical and the Ben-Elim. "You strike then, help the second line to get out."

Meical gave a stern nod.

"Then we retreat, see what having a taste of our blades does to them. Once they know they will die easily, it may give them pause."

Or it may not, Drem thought, remembering the Revenant horde they had fought in the Desolation. *They are capable of thought, Ulf spoke to me, remembered me, but it was through a veil. Their bloodlust made them more like the Ferals than humans.*

"Once we are all out, we shall see. Maybe harry their edges, but keep our distance." Byrne rose up in her saddle, raising her voice for all of them gathered about her. "We slow them, but this is no last stand. I need you for the war ahead. Do not throw your lives away." Her eyes flickered across everyone, lingered on Cullen a few moments. "And remember," she cried, "DO NOT let them bite you. You know what will become of you if that happens. One day at most and you will become one of them."

Drem shivered at that. The thought of becoming one of those blood-mad creatures turned his stomach to ice. He unbuckled his iron cap from his saddle, slipped it onto his head. He shifted it around to get the leather and sheepskin liner that padded it more comfortable and tried to buckle up the chin-strap. He spent a while fumbling at it, getting nowhere.

"Straps first, gloves last," Cullen whispered to him with a smile.

Drem took off his gloves with his teeth, buckled his helm's chinstrap with ease, and pulled his gloves back on.

"There's a lot more to the art of war than stabbing what's in front of you," Drem muttered.

"Now we can see them, it's easier to kill them," Balur bellowed. He drew Sig's longsword from behind his back, swept it through the air in a figure of eight. Warriors shouted their approval. Somehow the act checked the fear that sat like a coiled wyrm in Drem's gut.

"And that's what we are going to do," Byrne called out. "WARRIORS, ON ME!" she cried, and nudged her horse into a walk down the slope.

"*Now* it's time for us," Cullen said, slapping Drem on the shoulder and kicking his horse on. Drem followed, feeling something shivering through his veins, the echoes of magic, Byrne's words, a combination of both. He drew his father's sword as he joined the line.

Byrne turned and saw him, beckoned him over.

"When you slew their leader in the Desolation, they all died," she said.

"Yes," Drem agreed.

"And you told me his name was Ulf. That he was one of the Seven that Gulla turned."

"Aye," Drem nodded. He knew where Byrne was going with this; his thoughts were taking him a few paces down the same road.

"Do you know who all seven were? And would you recognize them now?"

Ulf. Tyna, his wife. Burg, the man who tried to hang me. The brothers Thel and Ormun, trappers who wintered at Kergard, like me and Da. He closed his eyes, picturing that dark night, black pools of blood glistening on the table. Gulla, teeth bared and arms open, wrapping people in a deathly embrace. *A man, tall, lean, but not someone from Kergard. And Arvid—she was one of Hildith's strongarms.*

"I...think so. Six of the Seven, yes. Five were from Kergard, my home. Two weren't. I'm guessing they were acolytes from the mine—one of them tried to hang me, so I won't forget his face in a hurry. The other one, maybe."

Byrne nodded. "If you see one of them, tell me. Or kill them. Then, with luck, the whole horde will die and save us the job of killing them one by one."

Drem nodded.

"Here, beside me," she said, making a space for Drem to stand to her left. She looked to Cullen. "And you, in the front row. Keep an eye on Drem."

Cullen grinned at Drem's frown.

Horses jostled, bears growled, gouging at the turf with long claws. Drem rolled his shoulders, shifting the weight of his mail coat. He smelled the sweat and grease that coated the riveted mail.

The Revenants were surging up the slope, now, all of them seemingly accustomed to the daylight.

And not as hindered by it as I'd hoped.

The slither of fear in his belly uncoiled, worming through his body.

How have I come to be here, standing before a horde of snarling creatures who want to kill me? I don't even like crowds.

He fought the urge to be sick.

I hate battles.

And then he remembered his father's shattered body, holding his da's hand, trying to stroke the blood away from his lips. His father's last breath. He remembered the oath he had sworn, of vengeance, the oath that had set him upon this course.

These Revenants were born of Fritha's magic. Born of the Starstone Sword my father made, that was stolen from him. That he was killed for.

His fear was still there, but he felt a sliver of anger, a resolve that tempered the terror, that kept the dread from ruling him.

A horn blast and the first row moved into a canter, swords drawn, spears levelled. Despite his fear, Drem did not hesitate. To his right Byrne held her reins loosely, sword in her fist, to his left Cullen was grinning as if it was his name-day.

The Revenants were rushing to meet them, running with unnatural speed, mouths gaping, sharp teeth glinting, saliva hanging in thick threads from their mouths.

Thousands of them.

Drem sucked in a deep breath, snarled a curse at his fear.

The first Revenants were five hundred paces away. His eyes flickered across them, searching for something familiar, for one of the Seven.

"TRUTH AND COURAGE!" Byrne cried, a hundred voices echoing her, and the first line charged. Drem squeezed Rosie's flanks, a whispered word as he bent close to her ears, and she obeyed instantly, leaping forwards from canter to gallop in a burst of muscle and power and speed.

The world became a thunder of hooves, blood pounding in his head, voices screaming the Order's battle-cry. Dimly he realized he was yelling it, too. And then they crashed into the Revenants, a wave of horse and bear smashing into meat, a concussive crack as bones broke and bodies were flung through the air. Drem glimpsed Ethlinn and her bear, Revenants hurled like so much kindling, her spear stabbing about her. He slashed with his sword, a spark of blue light as his blade crunched into a skull, his arm wrenched as his mount's momentum carried him on, but managing to keep a grip of his sword as it ripped free of the skull, trampling Revenants, cutting to either side of him with his blade, eruptions of blue light all about him as blades bit into their blood-hungry enemy, wounding, maiming, killing.

They carved deep into the Revenants, their enemy falling away. Those that weren't crushed and broken by hoof and claw were stabbed and skewered by magical blades, but then the charge slowed. The weight of bodies in mounds underfoot were a growing pressure before them, until Drem felt as if they were wading through water. His sword rose and fell, hacking, chopping, his arm and shoulder burning. Sweat blurred his eyes. To his left Cullen was laughing and singing, dealing out death like a reaper on harvest-day.

A hand grabbed at Drem's hip, talons raking his mail coat, a Revenant hauling itself up, its mouth gaping wide, teeth bristling. Drem stabbed into its mouth, a burst of blue light and he ripped his blade free, teeth flying as the creature slumped back into the throng.

Three more leaped at him. He thrust, pierced a chest, feeling ribs crack, then his wrist was grabbed in an iron grip and he was dragged forwards.

A sword swipe, a blue explosion and Drem was leaning back in his saddle, a severed hand still gripping his wrist, Cullen laughing even as he stabbed another Revenant in the face.

Drem brushed sweat from his eyes and snatched a glance at Byrne, saw her slicing and stabbing at a dizzying speed, though each stroke was economical and tight. The line had not broken, but Revenants were pushing between Drem and Cullen now.

Much longer and we will be swamped.

Byrne shouted something to one of her honour guards and a horn blew, sounding the retreat. Drem swung with his sword, a flurry of blue bursts of flame as his father's blade carved through flesh and bone, and he tugged on his reins, Rosie neighing, rearing, lashing out with her hooves and half-turning.

A face in the horde, eighty, a hundred paces away. A tall woman, the remnants of a muscled physique visible through a thick-grimed tunic. Once it had been fine wool, embroidery on the neck and sleeves. Her eyes were fixed on Byrne. She looked less *feral* than the other Revenants, more in control, something calculating in her expression. And she held a hand-axe in her fist, the first Revenant he had seen with a weapon beyond its teeth and talons. Revenants were grouped around her, a protective mass.

He knew that face, though it took him a moment to place her, changed as she was.

Arvid.

Rosie's hooves slammed down, Revenant bones splintering. Cullen was yelling; Byrne had already turned, kicking her mount away, back up the slope. Drem hesitated, stared into the Revenant horde.

Arvid. Kill her—the battle is won.

But there were five hundred Revenants between them.

Not possible. Get out, tell Byrne, maybe another charge.

He tugged on his reins. Rosie shifted her weight, then there was a thud as a Revenant leaped up behind him, arms wrapping around his waist and chest. Teeth bit down into his shoulder, and Drem screamed.

CHAPTER SEVENTEEN

RIV

Riv swooped low over the Revenants, slashing with her sword. Arms reached out to grab her, some Revenants leaping startling heights to grasp at her, but she twisted and rolled, avoiding them, chopping and hacking limbs and heads, always just out of reach, as if she were skimming the surface of a turbulent lake.

A lake full of flesh-hungry monsters.

Well, I want to kill you as much as you want to eat me, she thought, losing herself in the joy of battle. It was the simplicity of it she loved the most. Gone were the politics of Ben-Elim and half-breed, all the precepts and rules of the Lore that she had lived her life by, the confusion and anger-inducing betrayals of the last year. With the Revenants it was simple: kill or be killed.

A shape lunged at her from the mass below and her sword slashed, a ripple of blue light as the blade sliced the lower jaw from a Revenant's head.

I love this sword.

The Revenants were still unnaturally fast, their strength incredible and their single-minded drive to tear the life out of anyone in front of them was daunting, but with these blades they felt pain and could die just as any normal human.

Riv smiled as she killed them.

A voice, faint, filtered through the din of battle and Riv's own bloodlust. Calling her name. She angled her wings, sweeping higher, twisting away from the horde below.

"RIV," the voice called.

Meical.

He was hovering above her, Hadran and the other Ben-Elim around him. She flew up to join them. Riv could taste the moisture in the air, the tingling of imminent rain.

"We will be needed soon," Meical said when she reached him.

Riv turned and looked down at the battle beneath them. She had watched with a mixture of envy and respect as Byrne had led a charge into the oncoming Revenants.

Sixty or seventy riders in that first line, against thousands, and Byrne at the front.

She had looked at Meical. "We should go and help."

"I cannot," Meical answered with a frown. "Byrne asked for our aid; we are needed for the extraction of the second charge. The timing will be vital, I cannot risk becoming embroiled in my own separate battle."

She had looked down at the conflict below, watched as Byrne and her warriors had carved a wedge deep into the onrushing Revenants. It was hard to watch other people fight her enemies.

"I can't just stay here and watch," Riv said with a growl.

"I am not your captain, but *I* gave Byrne my word," Meical said, his face unreadable, but Riv saw something in his eyes.

Approval.

"I'll be back soon." Riv grinned, tucked her wings tight and drew her rune-marked sword as she plummeted towards the ground.

"Return when I call you!" Meical had shouted after her.

And she had. She hovered now with the rest of them, heard the horn blast sounding the retreat of the first line, saw Byrne, Ethlinn, Alcyon and a few score others turn and ride out of the destruction they'd caused. One of the riders had not pulled away with the others. She stared harder, saw that it was Drem. *He's in trouble.*

Before she realized it, her bow was in her fist, her other hand unclipping the quiver, and her wings were propelling her down towards the battlefield. She saw another warrior in the retreat turn, heading back to Drem, other heads turning. A streak of white feathers shot past her and sped towards Drem. It was the white crow, Rab, whom she had spoken with on the flight here.

Speaking with a crow! The world is stranger every day.

Rab flew at the Revenant attacking Drem, talons raking at its head, beak pecking. The Revenant swept a hand up, but Rab's wings beat, taking him out of reach, and then he swept back in again. At the same time the second charge was beginning, two groups sweeping in from the flanks. She was vaguely aware that Balur One-Eye was leading one side, a huge sword in his hands. She was closing in on Drem now, an arrow nocked, but the Revenant that had leaped onto Drem's horse was wrapped around him and Rab was still hovering at its head, raking shreds of skin and flesh from the Revenant's skull. Riv knew she wasn't the best of shots with a bow and didn't want to risk putting an arrow into Drem, or Rab. Another Revenant leaped out of the crowd at Drem and her arrow punched into his chest, a blue flash of light and the creature fell back, mouth wide in a scream. Riv's wings shifted, sending her in a spiral, swerving behind Drem, and now she had a clear shot of the Revenant grasping him. Another arrow nocked, drawn, loosed, and this one slammed into the creature's back. It arched, threw its head back, but did not let go.

Revenants were everywhere, all around Drem, grabbing and tearing at his horse. Riv heard it scream, saw it rear, saw Drem draw his short-sword and stab it behind him, into the belly of the Revenant that was clutching him. It fell away, another of Riv's arrows punching into its face as the gap between it and Drem appeared. The horse's hooves thumped into the enemies, but there were more, sweeping over Drem and the horse like a tide of rats. The horse swayed, then fell with a crash. Rab flew skywards, escaping a flurry of grasping hands, and hovered over the fallen Drem, squawking in panic. Another two arrows drawn and released in as many breaths, and then Riv was slipping her bow back into its case, snapping the leather clip into place, drawing her sword and was speeding towards the ground. A voice filtered down to her from above, *Meical?* But the red haze was filling her mind, a rage swelling with every breath.

She crashed into the Revenants swarming Drem and his mount, her wings buffeting a handful of them to the ground. With a choked snarl she slashed and stabbed, a cascade of blue light erupting as she hacked her way to the fallen warrior. He was on the ground, one leg pinned beneath his horse, which was clearly dead, blood sluicing from a hundred wounds. Drem was desperately fending off Revenants with two blades. Riv powered towards him, took the head from a Revenant as it turned towards her, sliced another in the gut, ripped her blade free, spun and crunched her sword into another's skull, but more were flooding in between her and Drem. A rider appeared: red-haired Cullen, chopping either side of him, forging a way towards them, but he too was held back by the Revenants. Riv screamed her frustration, leaped into the air, wings beating, slashing down as she tried to reach Drem. A taloned fist grabbed her ankle, tugging her down, and Riv twisted but missed the Revenant, cutting at air. She felt herself sinking, saw teeth and talons rising towards her.

There was a turbulence of air above her, spears stabbing down, and Meical was there, with Hadran and the other Ben-Elim, and the Revenants fell away like wheat before the scythe. Meical skewered the Revenant clutching Riv, whipped his spear free and thrust it into the mouth of another foe. In heartbeats a space opened up, littered with the dead.

Riv alighted beside Meical, gave him a quick nod of thanks and moved to Drem. His face was bloodied and twisted with pain. She put her arms under him and pulled, trying to drag him out from under his dead horse, but he did not move.

"Rosie?" Drem breathed.

"What?" Riv grunted, tugging to no avail.

"My horse," Drem said.

"She's dead," Riv grunted again, saw Drem's face twist, a wash of grief.

The thud of hooves and Cullen was there, leaping from his horse to help her, another rider appearing, the old huntsman, Keld. Meical and Hadran faced into the enemy horde, the other Ben-Elim forming up either side, making a protective fist about Riv and the others as a fresh tide of Revenants came at them. All about them battle raged. Riv heard Balur yelling a battle-cry, the screams and snarls of Revenants, other voices, horses neighing, bears roaring.

Riv, Keld and Cullen tugged and pulled at Drem, leaned into the horse, trying to raise it even half a handspan.

"We can't hold them much longer," Meical yelled, as wave after wave of Revenants swarmed around them, the line of Ben-Elim bending and curling ever tighter around Riv and Drem. She shared a look with Cullen and Keld. The two men threw themselves against the dead weight of the horse; Riv dragged at Drem. He moved a handspan, then was stuck again.

"Leave me," Drem grunted.

A Ben-Elim fell across him, blood jetting from his throat, a Revenant wrapped around him, teeth ripping at the warrior's face. Riv, Keld and Cullen all stabbed the creature in the same moment. It screeched, spasmed and flopped off the Ben-Elim, but it was too late for him. Another Ben-Elim staggered back into them, fending off teeth and talons. Meical and Hadran fought back to back, Riv standing over Drem and snarling. Cullen and Keld stepped in either side of her, the three of them covering Drem the best they could.

"FLY!" Meical shouted at the remaining Ben-Elim. They took to the air, eight or nine of them, Meical and Hadran the last to leap skywards, hovering low, still stabbing at the Revenants who now ran at Riv, Keld and Cullen.

"Leave!" Drem shouted up at them.

"Shut up!" Riv and Cullen shouted back in the same breath.

Then Revenants were hurling themselves at Riv and the

others. Keld and Cullen shrugged shields from their backs, locked them together over Drem, stumbled as bodies slammed into them. Riv snarled a curse and cut at a belly in front of her, opening up a blue-lined gash. She knew she should fly, take to the air, live to fight another day, as she had done time and time again, but something held her feet to the ground; perhaps it was the courage of the two men standing and fighting over Drem, a loyalty that resonated in her very core.

She stabbed and slashed, beat her wings, pushing a Revenant back, others all around her now. They were an island fighting the incoming tide. She could only see enemies, the roar of battle building around her, growing louder, like the sea in a storm.

Talons raked her wings, feathers exploding. She stabbed the Revenant in the face, a blue-crackled explosion of teeth and bone. Her sword arm was grabbed and she was yanked forwards, stumbling onto one knee. A Revenant's jaws opened around her arm and bit down, her sleeve of mail blunting it, the teeth grinding, grating, but the links of mail held, though pain exploded in Riv's arm. A spear thrust from above stabbed down into the Revenant's back and it collapsed. Meical's face appeared, his hand reaching out for her, but more creatures threw themselves at Riv, and she was rolling on the ground. Bodies blotted out the sky, Riv rolling, trying to swing her sword.

I'm going to die, the realization hit her. Bleda's face filled her mind, the thought of never seeing him again. She screamed in rage and frustration.

The roaring grew louder.

CHAPTER EIGHTEEN

DREM

Drem swung his sword, chopping into a Revenant's ankle, at the same time he swept his seax up, cutting into the open mouth of another Revenant bearing down upon him, seemingly intent on biting his face off. He sawed with the long knife, cut deep into the soft tissue of the creature's mouth, grated on teeth, and it recoiled. Drem glimpsed booted feet: Cullen and Keld. A flash of Riv's grey-speckled wings, the warrior on her knees, enemies swarming her.

I'm getting them all killed. A terror and rage built within him and he writhed, heaving with every ounce of his strength to free himself from Rosie's corpse. Rosie, who had carried him, obeyed him, fought for him and who would now be the death of him and his friends.

The roaring grew, bears' and warriors' voices mingled.

Not bears. Bear.

One of the Revenants grappling with him disappeared. A white-furred paw swept across Drem's vision, leaving behind a cloud of eviscerated flesh and bone hanging in the air. A deafening roar right above Drem, and a gaping maw and fangs appeared, clamped around the remaining Revenant's head and shook, tearing the head from its shoulders. The headless corpse swayed and fell away from Drem.

Two huge white paws slammed down either side of him, the white bear standing over him, roaring its defiance, spittle flying. It swiped left, raking flesh and smashing bone, freeing Cullen and Keld, then swiped right, ripping a Revenant from Riv's back.

Drem tugged on his leg, felt a little give, leaned up and pushed futilely at Rosie's dead weight.

The bear looked at what Drem was doing with his small black eyes, then swiped at the dead horse, lifting it off Drem's leg as easily as a cat swatting a mouse. Drem rolled away, gasping as jolts of pain shot up his leg, but he was free. He sheathed his sword and grabbed a fistful of the white bear's leg, dragging himself upright. Hands gripped him, Keld heaving him up onto the bear's back. Cullen was hacking at Revenants that were grappling with Riv. In a burst of wings she was airborne, a hand reaching down for Cullen, grabbing his wrist and hoisting him into the air. Revenants leaped at him, Cullen slashing at them, more Ben-Elim appearing, stabbing down with spears.

The white bear shifted, looked around to regard Drem on its back.

He's going to throw me off, Drem thought, but instead the bear turned, a swipe of a paw decapitating a Revenant, and then it was moving, smashing a way through the sea of creatures about them. Drem reached down and grabbed Keld's hand, hauled him onto the bear's back. They both clung on desperately, wrapping their fists in fur as the bear's muscles heaved and bunched, ploughing its way through wave after wave of Revenants.

They were not as alone as Drem had thought. Byrne and Ethlinn were close by, Alcyon upon Hammer, his twin axes swinging. More giants and warriors were riding in a wedge behind them, trying to cut back into the Revenants.

Byrne saw Drem atop the white bear and she yelled a wordless cry.

A dozen paces of being tossed like a branch on a storm-racked sea and the white bear made its way to Byrne, all of them fighting now to break away from the horde. Bodies were everywhere, the ground thick with Revenant corpses, bones and meat crunching and bursting with every step of the bear's rout. A snatched glance behind showed the ridge was still dense with living Revenants, too many of them to count. They were spreading wide, starting to encircle Byrne and her company.

A shadow passed over Drem and he looked up, saw Riv carrying Cullen above them. He was white-faced, his maniacal smile gone.

Utul was close, a savage grin on his face, Shar at his side, her mouth a stern line, as always.

Utul fought with his flaming sword. He chopped downwards; a Revenant fell away, flames licking its blue-edged wound. Another slash of Utul's blade and more were reeling away, flames catching in their tattered garments. A gap opened up around Utul.

"BYRNE!" he cried. "They don't like my fire." He slashed again.

Byrne reached inside a cloak, came out with something in her fist, a vial. She threw it to the ground amongst a swarm of Revenants, sliced her palm and threw droplets of blood after the vial, shouting, "*LASAIR!*" Fire erupted, a wave of heat, and Revenants screamed, a dozen of them going up in flames, staggering and stumbling, falling to their knees. Others paused in their frenzied rush, some even stepping hesitantly backwards.

"Give them fire!" Byrne cried, pointing to the effects of her flames, and in a few moments all around her warriors of the Order were throwing vials, shouting "*LASAIR*," and flames were bursting around them. The white bear sniffed and snorted, breaking into a shambling run up the ridge, away from the Revenant horde and the spreading flames. Close to the top of the ridge it slowed and stopped, turning around to look back down the slope at the conflict.

Rab flapped down out of the sky and alighted on the bear's back, his feathers ruffled.

"*Drem safe, safe,*" Rab squawked. "*Rab happy.*"

"My thanks for your help, brave Rab," Drem said, stroking the crow's head.

"*Brave Rab, brave Rab,*" the white crow croaked, head bobbing up and down.

Islands of fire burst into life in a rough line, quickly feeding on Revenants and the dry plains grass, spreading to form a wall of flame, the Revenants reeling away, standing and hissing at the blaze. Byrne shouted orders and riders were moving left and right, throwing more vials, shouting words in their Elemental tongue, and in a score of heartbeats the wall of fire had spread huge distances across the ridge. In another thirty heartbeats it was out of control, the wind swirling and spreading the flames in all directions.

Byrne came galloping up the ridge, her face covered in black soot, the survivors following behind. Ethlinn was bleeding from claw marks across her cheek; many others were wounded, but it looked to Drem as if most of their number were still standing. Byrne reined in next to Drem and the white bear.

"You were too slow," Byrne said breathlessly, her mouth a stern line.

"I saw Arvid," Drem explained, shifting on the bear's back. "One of Gulla's Seven."

Byrne's mouth softened a touch. "Where?" she said.

Drem tried to see through the flames, but black clouds of smoke were billowing across the ridge, flames crackling as high as a stockade wall. He shrugged. "She was close when the horn sounded, but not close enough."

Byrne put a hand on his shoulder.

"I am glad you're not dead," she breathed, a flicker of relief and emotion sweeping her face. She looked back at the sheet of fire and the faint outline of Revenants beyond. Heat was rolling up in great, pulsing waves. Drem could feel the hairs on his face prickling. "That will slow them, at least. And it will allow Nara and her people to reach Dun Seren safely."

Something landed on Drem's cheek. He looked up at the sky, dark clouds bunching above them. Another raindrop splashed on his nose.

He looked back to the fires blazing on the slope.

Byrne held her hand out, raindrops landing on her palm.

She stood tall in her saddle. "Well fought," she cried. "Now for the walls of Dun Seren while the fires still burn. I don't think our enemy will be far behind us."

A flapping of wings and Riv was descending from above, Cullen held tightly in her grip. His face was pale as milk.

"You could be more *grateful*," Drem heard Riv say, as Cullen's feet touched the ground. He dropped to his knees.

"Don't let her near me, ever, ever, again," Cullen said with shaking hands.

"What's wrong with you?" Drem asked.

"I don't like heights," Cullen managed to say before he vomited onto the grass.

Rab made a squawking, croaking noise that sounded to Drem suspiciously like laughter.

CHAPTER NINETEEN

FRITHA

Fritha cut the leather cords binding Asroth's arm to the anvil, then stepped back, her own arms from her hands up to her elbows thick with blood.

Asroth's blood.

She smiled, looking slowly around the chamber. A dozen Kadoshim were all staring, but not at her.

Asroth stood with his right arm raised in front of him. He looked at his new hand, a thick line of stitches around his wrist, clotted blood crusting around seared flesh. Asroth made a fist.

"It feels...strange," he said. Knuckles cracked and popped as his fist clenched tighter. He spread his fingers, wiggled them, looked at Fritha. "Will this ever feel right?"

Fritha shrugged. "Ask Wrath," she said. "His wings work well enough."

Asroth smiled at that. "Ask a draig," he muttered, shaking his head.

"It will feel stiff and alien at first," Fritha continued. "The more you use it, the more natural it will feel. And it will feel better with the gauntlet on," she added.

Asroth reached for the gauntlet, lifted it and slipped his new hand into it.

"It is cold," Asroth observed.

"I am not finished, yet. It needs a leather liner. Let me help you." Fritha stepped closer, reaching for leather cords that threaded under the wrist.

When it was secure Asroth flexed it, twisting his hand. After long moments of studying it, flexing the fingers, twisting to test the articulation, Asroth looked at Vald's corpse.

"Lift him up," he said. Bune and Choron grabbed the dead White-Wing and held him before Asroth.

"On the anvil," Asroth grunted, and they lay him upon the huge slab of iron. Asroth stood over him, then raised his hand, curled it into a fist and slammed it into Vald's face.

The head exploded, blood, bone and brain spraying. Asroth pulled his fist away and there was nothing recognizable of Vald left, just a pulped mess of meat and fluid.

"Huh," Asroth grunted, "it works, then." He looked up at Fritha and wiped a chip of bone from his cheek. Then he took a step towards her and wrapped an arm around her waist, pulling her close to him, crushing her lips to his.

For long moments Fritha was lost in a dark storm, a whirlpool of black water pulling her ever deeper.

"Ha!" Asroth exclaimed, as he released her from his embrace. "And to think, once I hated all you humans. I have to concede, Elyon may have been onto something in your creation. You can be quite useful when you set your minds to it."

Kadoshim laughter rippled around the chamber, more like hissing and spluttering. Fritha found it unsettling, though she was only dimly aware of them. Asroth's closeness and his attention were dizzying. She could still taste him.

Something filtered through the haze of pleasure that was filling Fritha's head. A tickling at the back of her skull, a whisper in her mind.

"*Frithaaaaaa,*" the voice said.

Fritha jerked away from Asroth.

"Elise?" she said.

"*Frrrithaaaaa,*" the voice in her head said again.

Asroth frowned, raised an eyebrow at Fritha.

Fritha heard Wrath growl, somewhere up in Drassil's great chamber.

"Elise, where are you?" Fritha said.

"*I am heeere*," the voice said.

Without thinking, Fritha was leaping up the stairs. She burst into Drassil's hall, past the bulk of Wrath, who had been sleeping close to the doorway. Fritha took a few steps and then froze, staring up at the entrance to the chamber.

Elise was slithering down the wide steps of the hall, part woman, part white wyrm, her great coils sinuously looping and bunching. She still wore her coat of mail, though it was ragged and torn, streaked red with blood and rust. Beside Elise strode a tall, lean warrior—Arn, Elise's father, and Fritha's friend. He was grey and travel-stained, his hair long and lank. Behind them both were a few score warriors, men and women of Fritha's warband. And around them were other creatures. Part man, part beast, creatures of tooth and claw, hunched and muscled, limbs elongated.

My Ferals.

Fritha sighed, a sense of joy blooming in her belly.

They were surrounded by acolytes, looking more like war-riors now that Drassil's armouries had been thrown open to them. They were clothed in coats of mail and boiled leather, iron caps on their heads, swords at their hips and spears in their fists. Aenor, Lord of the Acolytes, led them; despite his new-found and very fine war gear, he still looked more like a brigand than a warrior, short and squat, barrel-chested.

Above them Kadoshim flew in lazy circles. Fritha saw Morn and smiled at her. Morn did not return the smile, her face flat. She nodded her head, directing Fritha's gaze ahead of her.

Fritha met the cold, flat gaze of Gulla, who was staring at her, his face twisted with rage.

He knows about Ulf. Elise or Arn must have told him.

Of those on the ground, the Ferals saw Fritha first, a ripple of whimpering passed amongst them. They bounded towards her, claws scraping on stone.

Fritha held her hands out, the Ferals swarming around her, nuzzling her, grunting and snuffling. There were more than Fritha had dared hope after the terrible slaughter in the Desolation, forty or fifty of them.

Gulla swooped down from above, the blast of his wings opening a space before Fritha. He landed, striding towards her, his one red eye blazing.

"You lied," he snarled, a long-taloned hand reaching for her throat.

Fritha stepped back, Ferals filling the gap between her and Gulla. They crouched low, snapping and snarling at the Kadoshim. They felt his power, like terriers before a wolven.

But even so they would protect me. Fritha smiled at them, stroking fur.

"Call them off, else they will die," Gulla snapped, his hand moving to the hilt of his sword. In the edges of Fritha's vision she saw mist-wrapped shadows detach from dark recesses in the hall.

Gulla's Seven. Or Five, now that Ulf is dead and Arvid is hunting in Ardain.

"You owe everything to me," she said. "I found the Star-stone Sword, took Asroth's hand. I *made* you."

"Ulf is dead, you lost the battle; you *lied* to me," Gulla answered, knuckles tightening around his sword hilt. His Revenants were closer now, mist-wrapped pillars of death, standing motionless beyond her Ferals, all of them staring at her.

"You will die for your deception," Gulla snarled.

Wrath growled, a deep tremor that Fritha felt through her feet.

"*Touch Fritha, you die,*" the draig rumbled.

"You dare threaten me," Gulla said. He half-drew his sword.

"*No threat,*" Wrath growled. "*Promise. I will* eat *you.*"

"What is all this?" Asroth's voice called out, as he emerged from the blue-flickered stairwell carved into Drassil's great tree. He strode into the chamber, Bune and a dozen Kadoshim spreading wide behind him. More Kadoshim and half-breeds appeared, the sound of leathery wings above as Drassil's hall filled.

"Gulla, what are you doing?" Asroth asked as he drew close. His voice was calm, but Fritha detected something within it, an undercurrent of deep malice that gave her pause. Asroth stopped at the Ferals, stared at Fritha. She whispered a command and the Ferals parted for him, until he was only one step away from Fritha and Gulla.

This is the moment. Life or death, on a knife-edge. I must be cunning.

"Ulf, one of my Seven," Gulla said, sucking in a deep breath and trembling with the effort of controlling his rage. "I left him and his warband with Fritha, to help her fight the Order of the Bright Star. She told me they were defeated, that she had won. But survivors of the battle have arrived." He gestured to Elise and the others; Asroth's eyebrow rose as he saw the wyrm-woman.

"Another of your creations?" he said to Fritha.

"Yes," Fritha said, the sight of Elise filling her chest with pride.

"Fritha lied to me, to us all," Gulla said. "She *lost* the battle, Ulf is dead, his warband destroyed."

"They were impossible odds," Fritha said. "I held the Order in the north, took their attention away from Drassil. If they had been here, Asroth would still be in his prison. I had five hundred swords against two thousand, what did you expect?"

"I gave you Ulf!" Gulla said, fury cracking his voice. "He had *thousands* of Revenants in his warband."

"It was *Ulf* who lost us the battle," Fritha snapped. "I *told* him to stay back, to stay hidden, but he could not control his bloodlust. It was his own fault he died."

"You failed and you LIED!" Gulla yelled, spittle flying from his razored teeth. "And now you stand before me, in Drassil's Great Hall, and you threaten *me*. Me, Gulla, High Captain of the Kadoshim. I have fought the Ben-Elim in this world of flesh for over a hundred years, saved my kin from extinction, orchestrated Asroth's freedom, and you dare to threaten *me*."

"I did not threaten you," Fritha said.

"Your draig did, and you control him," Gulla hissed.

"He is loyal," Fritha said with a shrug. "That is no crime."

Gulla took a step towards her.

"No," Asroth said. "You—" he pointed at Elise and Arn— "come here."

Aenor led them over, Elise's coils scraping on the flag-stoned floor. Fritha could not help but smile at her, though Elise regarded Fritha with pain in her eyes. Arn's stare was flat and cold.

"You left usssss," Elise said to Fritha.

"My friend, I am sorry but I *had* to be here," Fritha said. "I vow I was coming back for you. I sent Morn to find you."

Gulla twitched at that, a twist of his lips.

Fritha held a hand out to Elise, who remained where she was, though her tail-tip rattled, and Fritha saw her fingers move involuntarily.

"You are survivors of the battle in the Desolation?" Asroth asked them.

Elise and Arn were staring at Asroth with expressions of awe.

"Yessss, my King," Elise said first.

Asroth regarded her, his black eyes taking her in from tail-tip to head. "You are a work of art," he breathed. "Fritha, you are nothing if not...talented."

Fritha smiled.

I know. And Elise is just a fraction of what I can do.

"What happened in the Desolation?" Asroth asked Arn and Elise.

"We fought the Order of the Bright Star," Arn said, his voice flat, as if he were reporting after an uneventful patrol. "Pits were dug, the Order was tricked. Ulf's Revenants flanked them. The battle was going well." Arn stopped.

"What happened then?" Asroth prompted.

Arn looked to Gulla. He had been Arn's commander for countless years, the figure of highest authority in his life. Arn opened his mouth, but no words came out.

"Tell him what you told me," Elise hissed at her father.

"Tell me," Asroth commanded.

"Ulf came out from hiding and was seen by Drem," Arn continued. "Drem slew Ulf. The Revenant host died."

"See, I *told* you," Fritha said to Gulla. "Ulf disobeyed my order and died because of it. The battle was almost won, the idiot just had to stay alive."

"He was my firstborn," Gulla said, teeth grinding.

"He was a witless fool," Fritha retorted.

"I will see you on a spike for this," Gulla hissed.

"You would have to fight through my children first," Fritha snarled at him.

"You think I cannot? I have legions ten thousand strong beyond these walls."

"Your word is no longer the last say, *you* are not lord here," Fritha said loudly. "You may think yourself Lord of Drassil, but you are just another captain, no different from me."

Gulla's face twisted in a paroxysm of rage; he lunged forwards and grabbed Fritha by the throat, heaving her into the air.

All around the chamber motion blurred. Gulla's Revenants burst forwards, the Ferals crouched, snarling, muscles bunching. The hiss of blades drawn in the air above. Wrath let out a deafening roar, claws scratching on stone. Elise jerked towards Gulla, lips pulling back to reveal long fangs. Gulla's grip tightened about Fritha's neck; there was a pounding of blood in her head. Her hand reached for her sword hilt, her palm still slick with Asroth's blood.

"HOLD!" Asroth's voice boomed. He stepped in, his new gauntleted fist clamping around Gulla's forearm.

All movement around the chamber stopped, a frozen, sharp intake of breath.

"Release her," Asroth said, quiet as death.

Gulla's one red eye snapped from Fritha to Asroth.

"She lied to me, betrayed me, lost the battle," he hissed. "And she is a human *worm*."

Asroth looked from Gulla to Fritha, whose face was purpling, eyes bulging. His eyes shifted to his new hand.

"She is *valuable*," Asroth said thoughtfully.

Gulla's eye widened, but he did not release Fritha's throat.

Asroth squeezed, the gauntlet constricting. Fritha heard bones grind and suddenly she was free, dropping to a heap on the ground, her legs weak. Wrath's bulk was beside her, his fetid breath washing over her.

Asroth released Gulla. The Kadoshim stepped back, holding his arm tight to his chest. He was staring at Asroth, and at his gauntlet.

"You would choose her, over me?" Gulla hissed.

"It would do you well to remember this," Asroth said, wings snapping wide behind him and beating slowly, lifting him from the ground. "I am king here, not you." He held Gulla with his baleful eyes, then looked at his new hand, flexing it into a fist. He smiled at the sight of it. "And Fritha is my bride and shall be your *queen*."

CHAPTER TWENTY

DREM

Drem sat on a bed in Dun Seren's hospice while a healer prodded at his shoulder.

"You're lucky," Aelred the healer said. "It's bruised but doesn't look like its teeth broke your skin."

Drem blew out a sigh of relief. He'd seen what Gulla's fangs had done to those he bit.

After the journey back to Dun Seren, all the wounded had been ordered to pay a visit to the fortress' healers. Keld had accompanied him while they waited to be seen.

They had stood in silence and watched as healers strapped down Giluf, a warrior of the Order with seven Kadoshim kills notched on his sword. He was bandaged around the throat, fresh blood seeping through the fabric. A Revenant had tried to tear his throat open, just missing the artery. It was a deep and ragged wound, though, and Giluf had deteriorated on the journey home. He was acting disoriented, now, his face pale, and he was struggling with the healers.

Drem had spoken to the healers helping Giluf, had advised that they use more straps, and kept a very close watch over the young warrior, and any others bearing signs of puncture wounds from Revenants' fangs.

"It must be someone else's blood," Aelred said, still examining Drem's shoulder.

"Good," Drem grunted, a wave of relief flooding him as he

proceeded to struggle back into his ringmail and strap his belts back on.

He was feeling exhausted, and downcast. He was glad to be back inside Dun Seren's walls, but every time he closed his eyes he saw Rosie's corpse. He knew she was a warhorse, bred and trained for battle with the Kadoshim, and that this life of violence often ended quickly. But he felt he'd let her down. That she'd carried him faithfully, trusting his guidance, and she had died because of it.

What kind of creature did Fritha create that wants to suck the world dry and watch it crumble? Does she have any idea what she's unleashed?

Drem was slow to anger, but he felt it building within him, now, deep in his core. A rage fuelled by the injustice of it all, the acts of murder and slaughter. He had seen too much death recently: his father, Sig, the battle in the Desolation, and now this.

All of it flowing from that one night at the starstone mine, when Fritha transformed Gulla into a monster. He jerked his weapons-belt tight, buckled it with white knuckles.

"You all right, lad?" Keld asked him.

"No," Drem said, blowing out a long breath. "I'm angry. At Gulla, Fritha, the Kadoshim and their acolytes. Those blood-drinking Revenants. At all this death and bloodshed."

"I meant your wound," Keld said, pointing at Drem's shoulder.

"Oh." Drem frowned. "Aye, that's fine. Just bruises, nothing more. Thanks to this." He slapped his mail, the blow dispersed in a gentle ripple. "How about you?" Drem nodded at a bandage on Keld's arm.

"Just a scratch," the huntsman said. "Claws, not teeth, apparently, so it wasn't deep. And I'll not become a Revenant by morning."

"Well, that's always good to know," Drem said.

A horn blast rang out, echoing through the hospice building, repeated again, and then again.

"Call to the walls," Keld said. He looked at Drem.

"They're here."

Drem stood with a groan, muscles aching and stiff. He picked up his helm, tucked his gloves into his belt and then they made their way out into the darkness. He looked briefly towards the bear stables and paddocks, where he'd left the white bear. He had ridden home on the bear's back, but the animal had growled and curled his lip at Keld, showing his teeth, until the huntsman had dismounted. Drem, though, the bear seemed to tolerate happily for the entire journey back to Dun Seren.

Drem had felt strangely...honoured.

Horns sounded again.

"Come on, lad," Keld called back to him. "We are needed."

Drem hurried after Keld. It had taken half a day to get back to Dun Seren from the skirmish with the Revenants. They had caught up with Queen Nara and her people, many loaded on the wains from Dun Seren, and the sun had been sinking into the horizon when the last rider passed through the gates of the fortress. Now it was deep into the night, a blustery wind whipping rain into Drem's face.

The courtyard was crowded. Drem and Keld threaded their way through people who were making their way into the great keep, most of them inhabitants of the outer ring of Dun Seren, tradespeople and their families.

Byrne had ordered the outer fortress evacuated. It was protected by a stone wall, but Byrne wanted the keep manned only by warriors who carried rune-marked blades, and they would be spread too thin on the outer wall. In truth, they would be spread thin on the inner wall, too, but it was better than the alternative. No warrior was permitted to carry more than one rune-marked blade, allowing for closer to three hundred warriors to line the walls, rather than the hundred and fifty who had ridden out earlier that day. Drem had loaned his sword to a warrior of the Order. He felt more confident with his seax, had spent a decade with it in his fist, whereas he was still adjusting to fighting with a sword. He'd rather fight with the seax than a sword.

Drem climbed the stairwell beside Dun Seren's gates and found Byrne on the wall.

She was surrounded by Ethlinn and Balur, Kill, Tain and Utul, Alcyon with his twin axes, and a dozen of her honour guard. Meical was also there, and Drem saw Cullen lurking close by. He grinned to see Drem and Keld. All those with rune-marked blades were gathered close on the wall, waiting.

A fluttering of wings and Rab swept down out of the darkness.

"*They are here,*" the white crow squawked. "*Bad people every-where, filling the shadows.*"

More wings from above and Riv appeared. Drem had not had a chance to thank her for helping him.

For saving me. I was trapped and buried, thought it was the end of me, and then she was there. And she did not leave.

"Mist-walkers are swarming through the gates of the first wall," she said to Byrne, who nodded. Byrne jumped up onto the wall's rampart and turned to face everyone.

"Our enemy are within the walls of Dun Seren," she cried. "We are outnumbered, but we have this wall, we have our blades, but greater than that, we have TRUTH AND COUR-AGE!" She brandished her sword, Drem and three hundred others answering her with a battle-cry that echoed from Dun Seren's stone walls.

"Drem," Byrne called, and he made his way to stand before her. She offered him a hand and gripped his wrist, pulling him onto the battlement beside her, though he felt uncomfortable standing before so many.

"The leader of these Revenants," Byrne called out. "Kill her and the rest of her brood die, just like the horde in the Desola-tion. Drem knows her." She looked at Drem. "Describe her."

Drem closed his eyes, picturing Arvid as he had once known her, as he had seen her that night at the mine on the shores of

Starstone Lake. She had been one of Hildith's enforcers. Tall and broad, long-limbed and muscled. Then Gulla had sunk his teeth into her neck.

"A woman named Arvid," Drem cried out. "Tall, a muscled physique. Long dark hair. Her clothing was once rich, her tunic of fine wool, embroidery on the neck and sleeves, though it is in tatters now. There was something about her when I saw her: she had more control than these other Revenants, seemed more *human*, more calculating. And she held a hand-axe in her fist, the first Revenant I have seen with a weapon beyond their teeth and talons. There were other Revenants grouped around her, like an honour guard." He shrugged. "That is all I can say of her."

"That is enough," Byrne said. "If you see her, kill her!" she shouted. "And remember, DO NOT let them bite you." A moment's silence as they thought on the consequences of that. "Now, to your stations," Byrne called.

With that, Drem was jumping back onto the stone walkway and making his way a few hundred paces along the wall. Every twenty paces or so was a burning brazier, a stack of oil-soaked torches piled either side.

Drem buckled his helm on, shook his head to check the strap was tight enough, then pulled his thick leather gloves on.

"Ah, you're learning, laddie," Cullen said with a grin, and thrust a shield at Drem. He didn't really like working with a shield, preferred to have a blade in each fist, which he told Cullen.

"It's not about liking something," Cullen said, his face serious for once, "it's about choosing the right tools for the job. You have one rune-marked blade, not two. And your blade is not so long—you will have to get close to these vermin to use it. You need a shield to hold them off; you know, to stop them from biting your face off while you stab them."

"Cullen's right, much as it pains me to say it," Keld said, hefting his own shield and a sword.

Drem thought about it, knew that the logic was sound and so took the shield. He slipped his hand into the grip behind the shield boss, tested the feel of the iron handle, a bar wrapped in leather riveted to the back of the linden boards. He hefted the shield, measuring its weight. It was large and round, banded in iron, painted black with a four-pointed white star upon it.

The Bright Star.

"My thanks."

He looked out over the wall.

The night was as black as pitch, rain clouds hiding any sign of moon or stars. Bonfires blazed in the street surrounding the wall, crackling and hissing in the wind-whipped rain, buffeted beacons of light in the darkness.

That is what we are, Drem thought, *standing against the darkness of Asroth and his Kadoshim. They spread evil like a plague.*

"Where are they?" Cullen muttered beside him.

And then elongated shadows were detaching from the night, a swarm of long-taloned shapes surging towards the wall, mouths gaping.

"Truth and Courage," Drem whispered, as he drew his seax.

CHAPTER TWENTY-ONE

RIV

Riv stepped off the wall and spread her wings. She glided across the open space between the inner wall and the buildings of the lower fortress. Below her, Revenants were breaking away from the darkness, outlined and silhouetted by the beacons Byrne had ordered built.

Not a night for archery, Riv thought, cursing the wind and rain, because this was just when she could use a bow: a swarming mass of her enemy, no allies she did not want to risk harming amongst them.

The first Revenants reached the wall, leaping and snarling, claws scraping on stone as they tried to climb. It stood as high as six men; even the Revenants' unnatural speed and strength would not be enough for them to scale those walls.

She swooped low over the invaders, lifted higher, over the first buildings. The darkness was so dense that even her sharp eyes were struggling to discern the Revenants' movements.

Byrne asked me to track them, but they're all heading for the gate, so I might as well go and stab a few of them.

She sped back to the walls.

Revenants were swarming the huge gates, tearing at the wood, splinters flying, great gouges, but the gates were holding.

They're trying to eat their way in.

But the gates of Dun Seren were thick, and banded with iron.

It will take them a moon to get through.

As Riv flew closer, she saw flaming torches hurled from the wall's battlements, arcing down to land amongst the heaving mass before the gates, trailing sparks in the dark. A Revenant caught fire, gave a hissing scream, staggering away from the wall. More torches were thrown from above, setting many of the creatures alight, but they either stumbled away or were trampled beneath the press of hundreds.

Riv drew her sword, swooping low over the mass of heaving bodies, slashed down, felt her blade bite, saw the crackle of blue flame that had come to give her so much pleasure. Then she was at the gates, hovering over the mass, which was rising as Revenants climbed on one another in their frenzy to reach their prey.

Slowly the tide climbed higher, becoming a kind of living ladder or tower made of limbs and torsos.

Riv slashed and roared, kicked one Revenant in the face as it bunched its legs and launched itself at her. Others saw her now, more propelling themselves at her.

A beating of wings and Ben-Elim were dropping from the night sky: Meical, Hadran and the others, all of them stabbing with long spears, skewering Revenants as they leaped, killing others as they clambered up the seething mound that was slowly reaching towards the battlements.

A snapping and snarling behind Riv, and she snatched a glance left and right. Black shapes were bursting from the darkness as far as she could see all along the wall, gathering in clusters, massing together to form more living ladders, knots of bodies merging, rising like a swarm of ants that Riv had once seen as they massed together to cross a stream. The Revenants surged higher at startling speed.

The noise behind her again and she spun around in the air, saw a dark knot of shapes in the shadow of a building. She strained her eyes, her wings taking her a little closer, and saw two or three score Revenants. There was something different about them. They were still, staring, watching, their attention focused towards the centre of their circle, not the walls.

Then Riv saw her, a Revenant standing half a head taller than those around her. She was broad, had long dark hair and an axe in her fist.

Arvid.

Arvid was gesturing with her axe, giving orders. Revenants were running where she directed, at the darkest points on the wall, between the reach of the bonfires. Here they were linking together, forming their organic, living ladders, rising with shocking rapidity towards the battlements; all the while, new Revenants were rushing to join them.

Riv heard shouts and screams, the sound of battle drifting down from above, marking where the Revenants had reached the top.

Glancing around, she saw Hadran and flew to him, shouting in his ear over the din of battle. Together they turned and flew straight at Arvid, Hadran's arm pulling back, hurling his spear.

A dozen Revenants leaped into the air in front of Arvid. Hadran's spear skewered one of them, threw it back into the wall of a building, pinning it there, a crackle of blue fire rippling through its chest.

Riv stabbed a Revenant in the mouth, cut another's hand off, slashed another across the throat, caved another's skull in, but where one fell, two more threw themselves at her. Hands grasped at her, talons raking her, mouths open unnaturally wide, until Riv veered upwards, flying out of reach.

Hadran hovered there, his sword in his hand, but it was not a rune-marked blade.

"Where is she?" Riv yelled.

"That way," Hadran said, "I think. She fled with a score or more around her."

"Come on, then," Riv said.

Hadran looked back to the battle at the wall, where screams and the din of battle were echoing from the battlements, snatched and swirled by the wind and rain. Riv could see at least four ladders of bodies where the Revenants had coiled together and breached the wall.

He turned towards the darkness where he had seen Arvid running.

"You go back to the wall, Riv—they need your sword arm, and your rune-marked blade. I've lost my spear, so I'll follow Arvid, see where she's going. They won't see me."

A moment's hesitation. With every fibre of her being, Riv wanted to kill Arvid and end this. But she could have disappeared, and the screaming from the battlements sounded desperate.

Riv nodded. "Don't get yourself killed," she said.

Hadran smiled at her, something she'd never seen him do before. "I'd give you the same advice," he said, and then he was winging into the darkness.

Riv flew towards the wall. Meical and the other Ben-Elim were fighting above the gates, spread around Byrne and Ethlinn. She glimpsed Balur swinging a two-handed longsword. Revenants' body parts were flying in myriad directions. Further along the wall, a breach to the right, the fighting looked more desperate. Two Revenant ladders were dividing and crushing a section of the wall's defenders. Alcyon was there, with his two axes. Then she saw Drem, stern-faced, smashing his shield into a Revenant as it scaled the top of the wall.

So many to kill—where do I start?

She gave a bloodthirsty grin and headed to where she thought she'd be needed most.

CHAPTER TWENTY-TWO

DREM

Drem grunted, slamming his shield into a Revenant as it scaled the wall, its claws raking his shield, clinging on as he propelled it back into open air. He teetered for a moment, stabbing it frantically. It fell away, a flare of blue light exploding in its torso, but it was too late. Drem stood a moment, arms flailing, feet scrabbling for purchase, but the stone was slick with rain and blood. He fell. Keld lunged for him, but the huntsman was too far away. A scream built in Drem's throat, and then a hand grabbed hold of him. He glimpsed wings and feathers, and then his feet were on solid stone.

Riv laughed breathlessly.

"Can you avoid getting into trouble just for a little while?" she asked, turning to ram her sword into the face of a Revenant.

Drem stepped to the left, took a taloned blow on his shield that would have ripped one of Riv's wings off, plunged his seax into the Revenant's belly. He shoved its body away as he tore his blade free. "I don't think that's a realistic request," he grunted.

Riv gave him a grin, crouched and leaped into the air, flew straight up, then looped and came back. She kicked an invader in the face, sending it hurtling off the wall, stabbed her sword through another's back, the blade bursting out of its chest.

Drem swiped rain from his eyes and snatched a glance along the wall. He couldn't see far, but the situation didn't look good. Revenants were everywhere, two of their multi-limbed ladders latched onto the wall within fifty paces each side of him. Along from him, Alcyon swung his two axes, sending heads flying, but there were too many dead warriors of the Order lying in pools of blood, Revenants upon them, tearing at their flesh. Keld and Cullen were close, fighting back to back, holding off a tide of black shapes. Revenants were dying, but for every one that died, four more were scaling their living ladders.

Even as Drem watched, Keld was reaching inside his cloak and throwing a vial, shouting, "*LASAIR!*" A Revenant erupted into flames, stumbling off the wall and falling, a blazing torch.

Those ladders, unless they are stopped…why doesn't Keld just set them all on fire? But even as he thought the question, the answer was obvious.

Not enough fire. How many vials does he have? Five, ten? He would need ten times that. There are just too many Revenants.

He looked around wildly, flames from the brazier whipped in the wind, highlighting the scene in shifting flame and shadow. And then he was moving, ducking low under the swing of a clawed hand, stabbing up into the Revenant's sternum as he rose, deeper into the chest cavity, blue light pulsing through a map of veins. He shoved the dying creature away, slammed his shield into another face, stabbed around the shield rim into a shoulder, ripped the blade free and slashed across the creature's throat, hacked another across the face from scalp to chin. He stepped over it to reach the brazier.

It was only a pace or two away from a Revenant ladder. He grabbed one of the torches leaning against the wall, shoved it into the flames to ignite, then he was swinging the torch with his shield hand, stabbing and hacking with his seax. Two Revenants caught fire, falling away into more of their kind, careening off the wall.

"KELD, CULLEN!" Drem yelled as he threw the torch at another, its face igniting, melting, then he dropped his shield and crouched, wrapping his arms around the brazier's base, hoping that his friends had heard him and that they could reach him in time.

The base was huge, as wide as a man. He grunted with the strain, barely able to lift it a handspan from the ground. Heat washed him as the wind tugged at flames. He ignored it, heaved again, veins bulging, feeling as if his head would explode, every sinew in his body straining. There was movement close in his peripheral vision, the gaping maw of a Revenant looming close. Drem screamed defiantly, determined to finish his task even as the teeth lunged for his face.

And then the face was gone, a stump upon shoulders left where the head had been. The creature's body toppled to the side, Alcyon's bulk appearing beside him. The giant swung his two axes, blue light erupting as he cleared a space about Drem. Keld and Cullen reached him a breath later. Seeing what he was about, they both grabbed the brazier, helping him lift it. Slowly it rose, the bowl scraping against stone. A blast of air and Riv landed, crouched and put her back under the brazier's base, then began to stand. She yelled as she stood, face red, eyes bulging.

The brazier lurched higher, then it was teetering above the ramparts and Drem was shoving it, guiding its fall. Flames washed out of the bowl, white-hot coals and fire cascading over the wall, a waterfall of flame pouring down onto the seething ladder. The first Revenants burst into flames, an explosion of heat, not even time to scream. The flames spread greedily down the dried, desiccated creatures, the Revenants' limbs and bodies so intertwined that it was impossible for them to disentangle themselves in time to avoid the fire. In moments the ladder was an inferno collapsing in upon itself.

Drem and the others stood and peered over the wall. Bodies writhed and twitched, flames pooling and spreading along the base of the wall. The tide of Revenants that had been feeding the ladder was now scattered and retreating to the shadows in dismay.

Alcyon grinned at Drem and the others. Almost immediately the fighting along their section of the wall lessened, with Revenants dying and not being replaced. Alcyon set about hastening that process, hacking at a knot of invaders who were tearing at a handful of warriors.

"Well, I'm glad your da forgot to teach you not to play with fire," Cullen grinned at Drem. Riv barked a laugh.

"Don't encourage him," Keld said to her with a sigh.

The screams of battle echoed along the wall and they all looked towards the gate. Battle was still raging there. Cullen slapped Drem's shoulder and pointed at another brazier.

"ALCYON!" Riv shouted as she flew into the air, wings beating. Drem and the others linked their shields and started fighting towards the next brazier. The wall-top was just wide enough for them to form a shield wall four men wide. Alcyon joined them, standing behind and towering over them. His axes sang their song of steel above their heads as he chopped at Revenants beyond their small wall of shields. It was Revenants now who were caught between enemies from two sides, and in a few dozen heartbeats Drem and the others were at the next brazier. With Alcyon's help this one rose more easily and they heaved it over the wall onto another ladder of Revenants. An explosion of flames and sparks, hissing and screaming, and the ladder was collapsing.

"Next one," Riv said to them, and she soared off the wall, Drem and the others linking shields again. They pushed towards the gate, stabbing and cutting down any enemy before them, but before they reached the next brazier Drem saw Balur and Ethlinn heaving it into the air and hurling it down upon the next ladder.

Three ladders had been incinerated now. The Revenants on the ground beyond the wall were more hesitant for the moment, retreating to the shadows beyond the bonfires. Riv alighted on the battlements next to Drem and the others.

"There are more braziers further along, beyond the gate," she said, "but I've told Byrne; they're going to throw them over."

Even as the words left Riv's mouth, Drem saw a burst of fire and flame flaring bright in the darkness, an implosion of sparks as another ladder caught fire and was decimated.

There were still invaders upon the wall, and Drem and the others set to slaughtering them. The Revenants were fast and unnaturally strong, but the combination of rune-marked blades and their small wall of shields worked well against them in a tight space. Alcyon drove them back, and Riv swept in and out of the darkness, her sword leaving trails of blue sparks.

Drem chopped at taloned fingers that clutched his shield rim, slashed his seax into the Revenant's throat as it fell back. He looked for the next one to kill, saw one crouched on all fours, snarling over a dead warrior of the Order. It saw Drem and the others, bunched and leaped at them, but as it flew into the air Drem saw Queen Ethlinn appear behind it.

She stabbed the Revenant with her long spear, skewering it, the blade bursting out through its chest. Blue light stuttered through its veins as Ethlinn lifted it high and hurled it out over the wall. Drem watched it crunch to the ground and roll, coming to a stop before one of the bonfires.

He nodded a weary thanks to Ethlinn.

The wall was clear for the moment, at least as far as Drem could see either way. Byrne was there, yelling orders, blood sluicing down her forehead, slick in the rain. She ordered the Revenant corpses to be thrown over the wall, then oversaw as the healers arrived to treat the injured and screaming. Some were put on stretchers and carried off.

"Here," Keld said, tapping Drem with a water bottle. Drem took a sip and abruptly realized he was thirsty beyond all understanding. He lifted the bottle and drank deeply.

"Is that it, then?" Cullen said, glaring out over the wall at the brooding shadows. He sounded disappointed.

"They'll be back," Meical said, a whisper of wings as the Ben-Elim emerged from the night above them and alighted on the wall. "There are many more of them out there."

The slap of feet, and Drem saw Revenants surge out of the darkness, running in their peculiar gait past the bonfires on the street below. Hundreds, thousands of them. It was as if the mountains of their dead piled along the wall had not dented their numbers, or their fury. They knew what they were doing now—no frenzied hurling themselves at a thousand points on the wall. This time they filtered into columns and swarmed together in clusters along the wall, their limb-knotted columns rising.

Drem looked at Keld and Cullen; the two warriors were hefting their shields, setting their feet.

There are no more braziers.

Byrne looked at the approaching enemies and nodded to Kill, who was standing beside her. The warrior lifted a horn to her lips and blew. One long, lingering note, wavering on the snatching wind.

"FALL BACK!" Byrne yelled.

Keld turned, grabbing Cullen's wrist when the young warrior did not move.

"I'm not running," Cullen growled.

"It's an order from Byrne, so you are," Keld said.

"No," Cullen snapped, eyes fixed on the Revenants swarming at the walls.

"Ach," Keld spat. "This is not the time for brainless heroism, lad."

"Cullen," Drem said, resting a hand on his shoulder. "You've sworn an oath to Byrne and your sword-kin. To protect and obey. Byrne is chief, here; to disobey her is to disrespect the Order, and to break your own word." He paused, Cullen's head twisting round to stare at him. "I hope one day that I am worthy of taking that oath, of saying those words and pledging myself to you all, and to our cause. Do not dishonour it or yourself."

Cullen frowned, glaring at the climbing Revenants. He spat a curse, then turned with Keld, and the three of them were making for the stairwell. Drem saw a hand-axe lying on the wall, close to a fallen warrior of the Order. He slung his shield across his back and snatched the axe up as he strode past, hefted it for weight.

That's better.

They swept down the stairwell and pounded across the courtyard, other warriors and giants all around them.

Byrne had spoken of the possibility of falling back, knew that the wall was long and their numbers were few. They made for the keep, where most of the population of Dun Seren was taking refuge, the huge doors open, bristling with warriors. Nara, Elgin and many more who had wished to be on the walls but had been forbidden by Byrne were determined to keep them safe.

Looks as if they'll get their chance to fight soon enough. There are not enough of us with rune-marked blades to man every door and window of the keep.

A sound filtered through the wind and rain, from the east. Drem's footsteps faltered and he stumbled to a halt, straining to hear. And then he heard it again, swirling on the wind.

Roaring.

He looked at Keld.

"The bear enclosure," they said together.

Without thinking, they both broke into a run, away from the keep. Cullen joined them, following without question. Drem ignored everything, just ran, only one thing in his mind.

The white bear.

CHAPTER TWENTY-THREE

RIV

Riv was hovering above the gate's battlements, stabbing at the first Revenant to scale the wall. It fell back with a shriek, blue flame crackling from a hole in its throat.

"Riv, come on," Meical called to her, the Ben-Elim winging back towards the keep. Riv saw the first warriors reaching the keep's open doorway, others sprinting across the courtyard. The wall was clear of them, now, and that had been why Riv had lingered: to protect any stragglers. She saw a rune-marked spear on the wall, its owner dead; she sheathed her sword and swept down to it, plucked it up, beat her wings and gained some height as Revenants started to swarm over the battlements.

A noise on the wind, swirling louder and then quieter, snatched away, blurred by the hiss of rain. A roaring.

Then she saw a handful of figures change direction in the courtyard, her sharp eyes picking out Drem, Keld and Cullen. Alcyon was close behind them, a few more warriors followed, one of them the man with the flaming sword. Riv couldn't remember his name, though she liked his fighting style—all-out attack, no thought of defence. They were heading away from the keep.

Riv flew into the courtyard, swirled around the statue of Corban and started to fly after Drem and the others.

"Riv," Meical called again. He was hovering above the steps of the keep. He saw her hesitate, her eyes staring after Drem and the others, and he flew to her.

"We'd be no use inside the keep," Riv said. "We should go with them." She nodded into the darkness, where Drem and the dozen others had disappeared. Something about Drem, Cullen and Keld reminded her of her friends Vald and Jost. A camaraderie they shared, a friendship forged in blood.

The thought of Vald caused a knot in her gut, like a fist wrapping around her intestines.

He's dead. Fallen on the field protecting me.

"They'll need our help," she shouted.

Meical stared. The sound of bears roaring swirled around them. There was an edge to it that Riv didn't like.

It sounds like...pain.

"The mist-walkers must have scaled the wall," she said. "Come on."

"Byrne needs to know," Meical said.

"No time to wait, I'm going after them." Riv shifted and beat her wings, speed building as Meical wheeled away, back to the keep.

In heartbeats she was alone, twisting through a wide street, wind and rain whipping into her face. The sound of feet, figures appeared out of the darkness: Alcyon, Drem, half a dozen others charging towards the building ahead of them. As the group drew near, the door exploded open, splinters of wood, two figures careening out into the street. Two men, both dressed in the Order's dark mail. They rolled on the ground, came to a halt. The one on top looked...strange, then his head thrust down and his jaws clamped around the other's throat. A savage wrench, a spray of blood.

A Revenant! How?

Riv swept lower, almost level with Drem and the others.

Keld was closest to the creature in the street. His sword arm came back, began to swing, but the creature saw him, ducked with unnatural speed and rolled to the side. Keld's sword hissed over its head and Keld's momentum was carrying him on, his feet skidding to check his speed and he was turning, his backswing catching the Revenant as it leaped at him. A flash of blue fire, but the creature kept coming, crashing into Keld, and the two of them flew through the air, crunching to the ground, rolling. They slowed, limbs thrashing, the Revenant on top, one hand over Keld's face, pinning him, its mouth opening wide, bearing down.

Riv saw movement at the edge of her vision, heard a savage growling, and two wolven-hounds burst from the shadows, crashing into the figure on top of Keld, hurling it off him.

The wolven-hounds set about ripping the still-rolling Revenant to pieces, tearing chunks of flesh from its arms and legs. It came to a halt, got one knee beneath it and rose, the hounds snapping, snarling, ripping. The Revenant lashed out with a taloned hand, sending one wolven-hound stumbling away, grabbed the other one by the fur of its neck and opened its mouth wide, fangs dripping. The wolven-hound squirmed and bucked, growling and whining in the Revenant's grip, but its hold did not loosen.

Riv's spear took the Revenant through its open mouth, a spatter of blue fire and the creature flopped into a puddle, its grip on the wolven-hound abruptly loose. Now Riv was closer, she could see the hound was red-furred, the other one a dark slate grey, like storm clouds.

"My . . . thanks," Keld panted as he rolled to his knees. The wolven-hounds pushed themselves close, licking his face.

"Ach, you two, you're a pair, so you are," Keld said, ruffling their fur, hugging them. "I told you both to stay out of it. I can't rune-mark your teeth and claws, and I'd not have you ripped open or infected by one of *them*." His lip curled, a glance at the Revenant.

"Love and loyalty thinks not of itself," Alcyon murmured.

Riv looked at the giant—something in those words struck a chord in her.

Drem gave Keld his arm, helping the huntsman up.

"I'm fine, lad," Keld said to Drem's worried look. Keld sounded angry with himself. "The sight of him, it shocked me. Slowed me down." He pointed to the Revenant.

"It's Giluf," Drem said. "We left him in the hospice with a bite wound in his neck."

Screams echoed out behind the shattered door.

The warrior with the flaming sword was first through it: no hesitation, he charged in, curved sword raised high. A woman followed, stern-faced, wielding a curved sword.

A crash, grunting, a scream. Riv was desperate to get inside, but Alcyon's bulk filled the doorway, then he was through, Cullen after him and Riv close behind.

She paused a moment, blinked. The stench of death was thick in the room, blood and excrement.

A healer's room, by the number of beds and the way they were laid out, and by the cupboards lining the walls, bottles and jars full of herbs and plants. Now everyone was dead.

The room was a slaughterhouse, blood everywhere, sprayed across the walls, glistening pools on the floor. The flaming sword chopped into a Revenant's neck; its head spun through the air.

Alcyon's axes swung, an explosion of blue light as another Revenant fell, body opened up from shoulder to gut.

Then it was silent, punctuated by the groans and wet rattle of the dying.

"Four, five Revenants did this," Drem whispered, nudging corpses with his boot. "I told them to strap Giluf and the others tight, to watch them close."

"Not tight enough, not close enough," Cullen snarled, stabbing a dead Revenant; its body twitched.

"It's dead," the warrior with the flaming sword said.

Cullen shrugged. "Makes me feel better, Utul," he grunted.

Utul stuck his sword into a dead Revenant. He looked up at Cullen and grinned. "So it does," he said.

"Tsk," chided the woman at Utul's side.

"They have turned so quickly," Keld muttered.

"Come," Alcyon grunted, "they are all beyond our help here, but the living still need us."

Another roar swept through the open doorway on a gust of wind, this one louder.

Alcyon ran into the night, the others following, Riv running out through the door and into the air, beating her wings.

CHAPTER TWENTY-FOUR

DREM

Drem ran through Dun Seren's streets, the image of slaughter in the hospice imprinted on his mind.

These creatures are a plague. Setting brother upon brother, friend upon friend. Gulla needs to die for this crime against nature, and Fritha, for creating this pestilence.

The roaring from the bear enclosure was ringing in the air now.

It made his legs pound harder, overtaking all except Alcyon, though he drew level with the giant.

Please be alive, please be alive, he repeated to himself again and again, *not like Rosie.*

The rain was fading, the glow of moonlight leaked into the air from behind ragged clouds.

And then they were skidding around a bend, into the courtyard of the bear enclosure.

Torches flickered, swirling in the wind, sending shadows dancing. All was movement; confusion and chaos as Drem's eyes adjusted, trying to make sense of the scene before him.

Bears filled the courtyard, too many to count. Some were moving, some were not. Smaller shadows flitted around them: Revenants everywhere, leaping, biting, tearing. Blood glistened like black pools on the ground, stable doors had been smashed to kindling.

"HAMMER!" Alcyon yelled. Drem looked straight to

Hammer's stable, the door that he had only repaired yesterday smashed and splintered again, then his eyes were searching the courtyard for a glimpse of Hammer and the white bear.

If Hammer answered Alcyon's call it was impossible to tell—the roar and clamour was almost deafening. Without thinking, Drem was moving, running into the courtyard. He hefted his seax and hand-axe, chopped into a Revenant as it leaped at a bear, a blue flare of flame as the axe hacked through ribs, the Revenant dropping to the ground, rising, and Drem's seax punched through its mouth. He kicked it away and strode on.

Behind him Alcyon roared, axes swirling. Cullen stormed into the enclosure, a berserker scream on his lips and spittle flying as he killed. Utul's blade flamed and flared as it carved through Revenants, Shar beside him, silent and deadly. Keld and his wolven-hounds worked together, jaws pinning arms as Keld's blade took lives. A shadow flitted over the moon and Riv was amongst them, spear flicking down, a trail of blue in her wake.

A Revenant crashed into Drem, sending him flying. He crunched into a dead bear, the stench of fur and blood engulfing him. He stabbed and chopped with his two weapons, the Revenant hissing and screaming as it lost half a hand to the axe blade, a blue hole in its waist from the seax. Nevertheless, it came relentlessly on, jaws wide as teeth sought his flesh. Drem tried to throw himself away—Giluf's corpse was a stark reminder of what a Revenant's bite could do to him—but the bulk of the dead bear held him there.

An explosion of flame and blue light, the Revenant's skull gone, Utul's grinning face filling the same space.

"Give me your hand, brother," Utul said, hoisting Drem to his feet.

Brother.

Drem liked that.

This is my family.

And then Utul was moving, his sword tracing incandescent sparks in the air; a Revenant fell. Another jumped at his back, talons reaching, but Shar cut it down, the head and body rolling in different directions.

"You going to lie there all day and watch?" she asked Drem, as she took the head from one more.

He staggered to his feet, moving through the courtyard, chopping and killing.

They went from bear to bear, saving the living, avenging the dead, and there were already so many of them. The bears were fighting with all of their prodigious strength, the ground littered with dead Revenants, but these creatures just did not stop, biting and clawing, latching onto bear flesh like terriers around a bull. Too many bears were still and silent.

And then Drem saw the white bear.

He was close to the gateway to the paddocks, standing before the bulk of a slumped shadow.

Hammer.

Drem's heart felt as if a fist had closed around it. He broke into a run. Revenants came at him, he ducked swiping claws, stabbed into a belly, slammed into the dying creature, spun around, ripping his blade free, his hand-axe swinging, taking the lower jaw from another attacker, teeth and bone spraying, stumbled on.

Shouts behind him, Alcyon bellowing a battle-cry, to the side a Revenant went down under Fen and Ralla's savage attack, Keld stabbing down.

Drem was almost there, the white bear looking at him, black stains all over his white fur, which glowed silver in the fractured moonlight. Half a dozen Revenants were hurling themselves at him. Drem saw claws swipe at one, eviscerating it, intestines and shattered bone slopping onto the ground. The bear's jaws clamped onto another's head and shoulder, a savage shake and the Revenant was in pieces, its torso collapsing. But there were too many. Others leaped onto the bear, talons sinking deep, climbing up onto the white bear's back. One cast its head back, mouth opening wide, teeth bared.

Drem threw his axe, heard it crunch into the side of the Revenant's skull, saw it topple bonelessly from the bear's back. Then Drem was beside them, a moment as he rested his palm on the huge beast's muzzle, looking into its eyes.

He's exhausted, lost so much blood.

A snatched glance at Hammer lying upon the ground. She was still alive, her sides moving with breath. Black blood caked her jaws, pooled around her body, a mass of dead Revenants littered the ground.

Tears blurred Drem's eyes. The anger that had been bubbling away inside him suddenly boiled over. With a scream, he wrenched his hand-axe from the skull of the dead Revenant, swung and slashed at the shadows that were latched upon the white bear, clawing and biting. Drem slaughtered them, moving with a strength and speed that only rage provides. His world became a red haze punctuated by lunging talons and snapping teeth, their hissing screams as he tore their lives from them, the burn of muscles and crackle of blue flame as his axe and seax carved through flesh and bone.

Dimly he was aware of Cullen close by, of Keld and his wolven-hounds guarding one flank of Hammer and the white bear. The flash of Utul's sword, Shar guarding his back. Alcyon's booming battle-cry. Revenants piled up about them like a tide-line.

A Revenant came flying out of the darkness, straight at Drem, no time for him to even lift a blade. He braced himself for the impact. A spear hurled from above skewered his attacker, pinning it to the ground, its legs drumming, twitching, then still. Riv swept low, hacked with her sword, more taloned hands grasping for her, one catching her wing and dragging her down. She slammed into the ground, fell, dazed. Drem leaped forwards, chopped his axe between the neck and shoulder of the creature that had torn Riv from the sky, stabbed it in the gut with his seax, ripped both his blades free and stood over her.

She rolled to one knee, pushed herself upright, drew her sword, looked at him.

"Guess that makes us about even," she said breathlessly.

They set their feet, standing to one side of the white bear.

A new wave of attackers were rushing out of the darkness.

Drem gritted his teeth.

The air above came alive: white-feathered wings, and Meical and Hadran were there, the Ben-Elim about them, swooping and stabbing with their long spears.

"TRUTH AND COURAGE!" a voice bellowed, and Balur One-Eye appeared, his longsword sweeping around his head, chopping limbs from three Revenants at the same time. Ethlinn was beside him, her long spear stabbing, and then Byrne was beside Drem, sword and shield in her hand, her honour guard sweeping through the courtyard, and in short moments the last Revenant was hissing its dying breath into the stone-cobbled ground.

Byrne squeezed Drem's arm.

"You live," she panted.

He nodded, numb, turned to the white bear. It stood beside Hammer, lowered his head to nudge the female bear.

Hammer rumbled a mournful growl.

All about the courtyard a silence fell, only the wind, the rumbling growls of bears.

Drem moved to inspect the white bear's wounds. Ice shifted in his belly as he saw countless puncture wounds made by Revenant fangs. He knew what that meant, had seen what had become of Giluf, and so quickly.

"I am sorry," he whispered. "I should never have brought you here. I should have left you north of the river."

One of Byrne's honour guard stepped close to them. "They are all the same," the warrior said. "Every bear that still breathes bears the same wounds."

Drem knew where this conversation was going to go. The only logical answer was to kill the bears now. To put them out of their misery before the Revenants' infection took hold.

Gulla's infection.

But he could not do it. To take a blade to the white bear, after all they had been through, after the loyalty and friendship this creature had shown him.

Alcyon was on his knees beside Hammer, cradling her head.

Byrne put a hand to her sword hilt.

"There is another way," Drem said desperately.

"What way?" Byrne said. "I pray there is, for this is a task I cannot abide."

"Arvid. We must find her and we must kill her. *Now.*"

CHAPTER TWENTY-FIVE

RIV

Riv wiped blood and sweat from her brow, stepping closer to listen to Drem and Byrne. Byrne was talking about killing the surviving bears.

They have been bitten by these mist-walkers, are infected with their disease. It is the logical thing to do, but...

She looked at the white bear, then around the courtyard. Many of the bears were already dead, but more were standing.

How can we kill them? They are so...noble, and we need them.

"How can we kill Arvid?" Byrne muttered, frowning. "She could be anywhere."

"I saw her," Riv said. "In the street beyond the gate. Hadran and I tried to kill her, but she fled. Hadran followed her."

"But that does not help us," Byrne said. "Where is she now? Where is Hadran?"

Riv looked around. She had glimpsed Hadran close to Meical.

"Hadran," she called.

"I am here," Hadran said.

"Arvid. Where is she?" Riv asked.

"I followed her," Hadran said. "While the gate and wall were assaulted she led a force of Revenants north-west, around the fortress, circling it. They reached the river and found a tunnel."

"What?" Byrne said. "Where? Describe the tunnel?"

"To the north of the fortress," Hadran said, "west of the

bridge. It is on the riverbank, concealed by an overhang of trees and roots."

"How did they find out about *that*...?" Byrne broke off, her face pale. "We must go, now. Hadran, would you do me the service of flying to the keep and telling Kill what you have just told me. She will know what to do."

"The keep is swarming with Revenants; how will I get in?"

"A window high on the north side of the tower, it is my chamber. There are not enough Revenants here to build their tower of bodies that high."

Hadran nodded.

"Warriors, with me," Byrne cried. She slung her shield across her back and set off at a run, shouting orders, calling out the names of those she wanted to stay and tend to the injured bears.

Drem shared a look with Riv, turned and buried his face in the white bear's fur.

"I'll be back soon," he said. "Don't you *dare* die on me." Then he was setting off after Byrne, weapons still gripped in his fists.

"Here, I found you a new spear," Riv said, handing her weapon to Hadran.

"My thanks," he said, dipping his head. "I'll try and keep hold of this one."

Meical alighted beside them, along with the other Ben-Elim. Eight were there, where there had been twelve.

"Where is Byrne going?" Meical asked.

"Arvid, the chief of these Revenants, has entered a tunnel to the north of the fortress. Kill her and they all die."

Meical nodded.

"Good. A chance to finish this, then. Let's do it," he said, and spread his wings, launching into the air. Hadran's wings took him into the sky, though he veered away from the other Ben-Elim, flying towards the keep.

Riv felt a wave of weariness, the muscles in her back that powered her wings were burning, but she ignored it and followed after Meical. She was eager to finish this, too. The way the Order had fought against these creatures had filled her with respect for them: their bravery, and their military strategy. She had seen how the Revenant hosts in Forn had rolled over the defenders of Drassil. Byrne and the Order had proved that these creatures could be defeated, or at the very least, that they could be fought and held.

She caught up with Meical and the other Ben-Elim, then with a shift of her wings she spiralled upwards. Moon and stars shone silver beyond ragged clouds, the air fresh up here, as if the rain had washed the grime of the world away. Below her Dun Seren was a place of dark shadow and silvered moon-glow. The keep sat dark and sullen, pockets of light leaking from shuttered windows. Riv could see Revenants like ants massed in the courtyard before the keep's doors, others climbing upon the walls, but it looked as if the keep was still secure. Immediately below her, Byrne and her small band—twenty or thirty strong—were making their way through darkened streets, skirting around the hill Dun Seren was built upon and then down the slope towards the northern boundary of the fortress. Riv swept ahead, dropping lower, checking for Revenants in Byrne's path.

There were none, all of them seemingly concentrated on the assault of the keep.

Or with Arvid, their leader. In this tunnel Hadran spoke of.

Riv rejoined them at the northern wall, Byrne and her group pausing to unbar a smaller gate, the iron hinges creaking as it swung open. Then they were out on the riverbank amidst a tangle of boathouses and barns, the smell of pitch and pine resin thick in the air. The river was dense with tied rafts of timber: trees felled from Forn Forest and floated here for trade. They rose and fell, *clunking* together in the swell and heave of the river.

Byrne led her crew along the riverbank; she clearly knew the exact location of the tunnel Hadran had spoken of and led them unerringly through the trees and undergrowth. She paused for a moment and then, pushing through a dense thicket of branches, disappeared from view.

Riv saw the other Ben-Elim dip out of the sky and vanish into the treeline. She followed Meical into the shadows.

There was a narrow path that looked like a fox trail, and Riv followed Meical's back through a snare of branch and thicket. The path sloped down towards a wall of reeds, then cut under an overhang of earth where exposed tree roots as thick as Riv's waist curled in and out, looking like dark wyrms burrowing through the earth. To her right, willow branches draped in thick curtains.

Sound changed, echoing, as they entered a tunnel, the darkness slick and dense as oil, a sense of weight around her oppressive and sinister. Riv bumped into Meical's back as he stopped suddenly. The air had changed, though Riv could see no further than her outstretched hand. It was less oppressive and stifling.

A whispered word.

"*Lasair*," and a spark of light, followed by a sharp crackle of flame as a torch ignited. Byrne was holding it high. She touched it to another torch set into a sconce in the wall, light flaring, and Balur lifted it out, touched it to more torches hidden in the wall, took them and handed them out. Meical took one.

Riv blinked and looked around.

They were in a chamber. The floor was raw-carved rock, the walls braced with flagstone, earth oozing between slabs. It was wide enough for all of them, and more besides. The torchlight did not penetrate high enough to reveal the roof.

Byrne turned and looked at them.

"I don't know how Arvid knows of this tunnel, for it is a secret way into Dun Seren. It leads directly up into the keep. Arvid will try to enter the keep, to surprise and slay those within, but thanks to Hadran—" she nodded to Meical and the Ben-Elim—"we are forewarned, and now Kill will prepare a welcome for them. If they reach that far. We are here to make sure that Arvid does not escape." Byrne paused, drew in a deep breath. "Arvid *cannot* escape. She must die in here, tonight. We know what's at stake if she does not." She looked at the warriors gathered about her, including Ethlinn and Balur, a handful of other giants, and Meical and the Ben-Elim. Her gaze hovered on Riv a few moments longer. "We of the Order have sworn our oaths and sealed them in our blood, pledged ourselves to truth and courage. But you who have not said the words, I know that you are the same as us, in your hearts. Warriors, brothers and sisters bound to a cause. Otherwise you would not be here now, standing at our side, risking your lives. This is the sharp edge of who we are. We will stand and fight, together. There is no retreat this time. We win or we die."

Riv felt her blood stir at Byrne's words. She had always thought of the Order of the Bright Star as the White-Wings' rivals, a faction of warriors who were inferior in every way. The truth was something altogether different. Riv had come to respect their martial prowess, but more than that, she respected *them*. She respected their values and their courage. It made her ashamed of her upbringing and her opinion of them, and made her wish that she were one of them. And in Byrne's momentary glance and few words, she suddenly felt that she *was* one of them. Bound by something deeper than Elyon's Lore.

"Truth and Courage," Byrne said, and turned, leading them into the darkness.

"Truth and Courage," Riv whispered, though it must have been loud enough for Meical to hear, because he turned and gave her a quizzical look.

She glared defiantly back at him.

Byrne led them on, a handful of torches leading the way, Meical holding his torch high just in front of Riv. They left the huge chamber and padded into a narrower tunnel, though it was still wide enough for seven or eight abreast, the roof just visible in the flickering torchlight. Water gathered and dripped from rocks above, and huge worms oozed from the damp earth where roots had cracked the stone. The scrape of their footsteps echoed around them. Riv felt frustrated at the back of their group; Balur's bulk all but obscured her view of anything else.

A sound ahead of them. Byrne held up her hand, their short column rippled to a halt.

"What is it?" Riv whispered.

"If you'd keep silent, we'd have more chance of finding out," Meical said. Riv bit back an angry retort and kept quiet, mostly because she knew he was right and wanted to know what was happening up ahead.

Shouts. A scream. The clash of arms.

"Quickly," Byrne called out, and then their party was moving more swiftly through the tunnel, Riv's wings twitching with the urge to fly. The sounds of combat grew louder, a corner turned in the tunnel and they spilt into another chamber, this one far larger than the first. They spread either side of Byrne, staring at the scene before them. Torches flickered on walls, the room filled with swirling shadows, on the ground, in the air, all around her there was constant, chaotic movement.

At its centre was a stone pedestal, before it a long table that had been overturned. It was on fire, flame and black smoke billowing from it in sheets. Chairs were strewn about the table. Riv noticed all this with a fleeting glance, her eyes drawn to the people in the room.

There were Revenants everywhere, surging about the room like a kicked nest of ants, climbing the walls, a great knot of them swarming at the far end of the chamber. It was impossible to tell how many of them there were: a hundred and fifty, two hundred? The smoke and flame made all chaos, and something else was adding to Riv's confusion. The Revenants were fighting other people.

People with wings.

Even as Riv stared, her eyes trying to make sense of what she was seeing, a figure swooped through the air above her, the wind of its wings shifting her warrior braid. A Revenant that had half-climbed the wall, long talons puncturing stone and hard-packed soil, launched itself away from the wall and slammed into the winged creature, the two of them spiralling down and crashing to the ground, an explosion of dust. The two figures rolled, thrashing, the Revenant's distended jaws latching about the other's throat. The winged warrior stabbed at its attacker, a burst of blue fire as its knife pierced flesh, but the Revenant did not let go. The sharp tang of blood as its head wrenched, and the winged warrior was slumping, weapon falling from its grip.

They came to a halt before Riv, the Revenant atop the winged creature. It looked up at Riv, dark blood coating its lips and chin. Its muscles contracted as it bunched, leaping at Riv, and Meical's spear took it through the throat, blue fire crackling. A gurgled hiss and the Revenant was slumping at Riv's feet, its head landing on her boot.

She was hardly aware of any of it, her eyes fixed on the winged creature before her. A woman, tall, lean muscles, a bow fallen from her dead fingers. Riv stared at her wings. Dark feathers. Not a Kadoshim half-breed, as had been her first thought.

Feathers. Her wings are made of feathers.

Meical stared, frowning.

"What is this?" he said.

"She is a Ben-Elim half-breed, like me," Riv whispered.

CHAPTER TWENTY-SIX

DREM

Drem froze for a moment, staring into the chamber. Fire and smoke, blood and death. Momentarily he had been pleased to step out of the relentless claustrophobia of the tunnel, the sense of weight all about him constricting his chest and causing him to walk with one hand almost permanently taking his pulse, but the rolling black clouds of smoke and the snarl of bodies in the chamber made his relief short-lived.

He had been here once before, brought by Byrne. That journey had started from Byrne's chamber high up in the keep. On that visit the oak and stone table had been set before a stone pedestal and upon that had been a thick leather-bound book. A guarded, treasured secret of the Order of the Bright Star, from which a select handful learned the ways of earth magic and became Elementals, able to exert some measure of control over earth, air, fire and water.

The pedestal was enfolded in smoke and flame.

"No," Byrne gasped.

She moved forwards, sword and shield in her fists. Utul, Shar and a dozen others spreading behind her like a trailing cloak. Byrne looked back at Drem.

"Find Arvid," she growled.

Drem was moving, Cullen and Keld beside him.

Byrne and her companions hit the Revenants like a silent wave, an explosion of blue fire as their blades struck. The

Revenants had their backs to them, their attention focused on the figures swooping down from the rooftop. There must have been more of these winged warriors holding the tunnel exit at the far side of the chamber, because Revenants were congested there, a heaving mass trying to break through, some using their talons to scramble up the walls, trying to reach the tunnel that way. Drem saw a dark-winged warrior filling the space, stabbing with a spear, a flare of blue light.

They have rune-marked blades.

What are they? They have feathers, but they are not white, like the Ben-Elim. Are they half-breeds, like Riv? Drem remembered his only visit to this chamber, how he had felt that he was being watched, and how a huge brown feather had floated down out of the darkness.

They are the guardians Byrne spoke of.

Then he was amongst the Revenants, his shield slung across his back, seax and hand-axe in his fists. He chopped and stabbed left and right, ripples of blue fire stuttering around him. For half a dozen heartbeats he and his companions carved a wedge into the Revenants, but then the creatures were turning, realizing they were attacked from behind, throwing themselves at Drem and the others in frenzied fury.

One leaped at Cullen, talons reaching, and Drem chopped one of its hands off at the wrist. The creature howled; Cullen smashed it in the face with his shield, sending it staggering backwards, and Keld stepped in and buried his sword in the thing's belly. They fought together, the three of them, Drem losing track of the chamber around him, Byrne and the others lost from view as he, Keld and Cullen formed a half-circle and step by step cut their way into the Revenant rearguard. Two Revenants forced a gap between Drem and Cullen's shields, broke them apart, another creature clawing at Drem, blood appeared on his thigh below his mail coat. Drem struck at its head; his wrist was caught in a taloned grip, pale face and gaping maw lunging at him.

An arrow crunched into the creature's skull, a blue flash, and dark wings swept over Drem.

I need to find Arvid. No point just fighting blind.

He quickly glanced around. All was smoke and chaos, flame-cast shadows, Revenants all around him, giving no sense of how the fight was going. He searched the room, glimpsed the stone pedestal ahead of him.

"Keld, Cullen," he called as he lurched forwards, cutting into the skull of a Revenant rolling on the ground with one of Byrne's honour guard. Keld and Cullen pushed forwards either side of him, the three of them breaching a way through the havoc. Flames from a burning chair gave a little space— Revenants were avoiding it. Drem leaped over the chair, through the flames, ran on through a black cloud of smoke billowing off the table, and then he was at the pedestal. It was as broad as a tree at the base, with a flat top about as high as his chest. He slipped his axe into a leather loop on his belt and gripped the top, shook his foot at Cullen.

"What?" Cullen said, then stabbed a Revenant.

Keld stepped forwards and cupped his hands for Drem's boot, hoisting him up. He clambered onto the pedestal, stood straight, wobbled a moment, then found his balance.

Directly ahead of him he could see the bulk of Balur and Ethlinn, black figures swarming them, Balur bellowing. Byrne was close to them, a handful of her honour guard about her, another island in a sea of Revenants. To his right Drem caught the flash of Utul's flaming sword, Shar fighting with her back to him. Bodies were piled around them, but there seemed like no end to the creatures. Winged warriors were still swooping in and out of the darkness above, loosing arrows, stabbing with spears. Drem saw a Revenant scale the mound of the dead around Utul and Shar and leap, slamming into a winged warrior, the two of them spinning and crashing to the ground.

There are too many of them.

A Revenant hurled itself up at Drem. Cullen crunched his

shield into it, sending it careening away, rolling, scrambling on the ground. A shouted order from Keld, and Fen and Ralla rushed in from the shadows, tearing at an arm and leg, Keld stepping forwards and chopping into the Revenant's face.

"Whatever you're doing up there, make it quick," Keld called up to Drem. "You're making a target of yourself."

"Stay up there as long as you want," Cullen said, grinning as another figure launched itself at Drem. He swung his sword, chopping through its neck into clavicle bone. The Revenant collapsed in a heap, dragging Cullen's trapped sword with it. Keld stepped over Cullen, covering him with his shield while Cullen tried to wrench his blade free of the dying creature.

"Ignore the idiot who can't even keep hold of his own sword, and *hurry up*," Keld shouted up to Drem.

Drem kept searching, and then he saw her.

"ARVID!" he bellowed at the top of his lungs. He saw Ethlinn's head turn towards him, Utul's as well, and he pointed towards the far end of the chamber, to the right of the exit, where Revenants were crammed tight, all of them fighting to get at whoever was holding the tunnel's entrance.

Arvid was there, a knot of motionless Revenants guarding her. It was their stillness that had drawn Drem's eyes. He saw a winged man swoop down out of the shadows, thrusting a spear close to Arvid. She pointed with her axe and half a dozen of the stationary guard around her burst into motion, scuttling up the wall, stabbing their long talons into the earth of the walls and then launching themselves into the air. Four of them missed the flying warrior, two of them crunched into it, teeth and talons raking. The warrior fell from the air in an explosion of feathers. Drem watched as the man was dragged struggling to Arvid. She reached down and grabbed him by the throat, effortlessly lifting him up in front of her. The man kicked and punched. Arvid opened her mouth unnaturally wide and bit into his face. A high-pitched scream cut through the clamour in the chamber, then the warrior's arms and legs were slumping.

Arvid threw the corpse away.

Drem felt a wave of nausea, and anger.

He jumped from the pedestal, landed unsteadily and broke into a run. He heard the thump of Keld and Cullen's boots behind him, the snarling of Fen and Ralla. A Revenant loomed out of the smoke and he chopped and slashed, axe into the face, seax across the chest. It reeled away and Drem was holding his breath through billowing smoke, bursting out of it to see Arvid and her guards, twenty or thirty Revenants. He kept running, knew there was no time for stopping and thinking now.

Speed and surprise are my best chance. Like a predator's strike. He'd been on enough hunts to know how this worked.

Get in amongst them fast, don't slow to fight. Cut, stab, move until Arvid is in front of me.

From the right he glimpsed Ethlinn ploughing through the chamber, from the left a flare of Utul's flaming sword and Shar fighting silently alongside him. They were all converging on Arvid, but Drem was there first.

Arvid didn't see Drem coming, and in a handful of heart-beats three Revenants were dead or dying, Drem carving through them. Another went down with Drem's axe in its skull, wrenching his arm as the blade stuck. He slashed with his seax as he juddered to a halt, tugging on his axe.

There was sudden pain in his left leg: talons raking him, blood welling. He stabbed down, his seax slicing through flesh, grating on bone. Another leaped upon him, mouth wide, teeth snapping at his throat. He jerked away, rotten breath washing over him; he lashed out with his seax, a crackle of blue flame.

Drem limped forwards, the pain in his leg burning. Cullen and Keld had been brought to a standstill a few paces ahead of him. Revenants were swarming them, a frenzied mass of teeth and talons. Drem felt wounds opening up, links in his mail tear-ing. Beyond them a snatched glimpse of Arvid, her black eyes staring at Drem. She lifted her axe and strode towards him.

More Revenants threw themselves at Drem, Keld and

Cullen. He saw Cullen drop to one knee as one jumped onto his back. A frozen moment as Drem tried to reach them, the Revenant's head coming back, mouth wide, teeth bared. Keld turned, swung his sword, but another Revenant slammed into the huntsman, the two of them crashing to the ground. Fen and Ralla leaped in.

Cullen screamed. The figure on his back was biting the red-haired warrior, jaws clamping between his neck and shoulder. Cullen was wearing mail, but Drem saw the spurt of blood.

A flash of flame and Utul was there, his sword leaving a trail of blue fire, the Revenant falling away from Cullen, dead before it hit the ground.

Revenants hurled themselves at Utul, but Shar stepped into Drem's view, her curved sword making short work of Utul's assailants. Shar stood with her sword raised in stooping falcon, guarding Utul as he dropped to one knee to check on Cullen.

The Revenants parted. Arvid appeared, standing half a head taller than any around her. She met Drem's gaze and he saw recognition flare in her eyes.

"Fritha did not catch you, then," Arvid said, her voice somewhere between a whisper and a hiss, somehow cutting through the din of battle straight into Drem's head.

"No," Drem said, straightforward as always.

"Good, Gulla will be well pleased with me, when he hears of your death at *my* hands."

"Come on and try," Drem grunted. He rolled his hand-axe, shifted his feet.

Arvid's eyes shifted from Drem to Cullen, Utul and Shar, who were only a few paces before her.

Faster than expected, her axe swiped at Shar. There was an explosion of sparks as Shar parried hurriedly and took a step backwards. She ducked another axe blow, stepped in with her own sword slicing at Arvid's belly, the Revenant's mail tearing, but deflecting the blow. Shar stepped away on light feet, but Arvid surged after her, axe sweeping low in one hand, talons clawing with the other. Shar caught the axe, deflecting it with a clang of iron, but Arvid's talons raked across her face, blood spattering, sending Shar spinning with the strength of the blow, falling, Arvid striding after her.

"NO!" Utul yelled, exploding from his crouched position.

He threw himself between Arvid and Shar, who was on her knees, spitting blood.

Utul's blade flashed, an incandescent rain of fire as he struck at Arvid; she stumbled backwards, blocking Utul's attack with her axe. Blue light flared as Utul's blade slashed across her chest, cutting through mail and flesh. Arvid screamed, Revenants around her leaping to her aid.

Utul dropped two Revenants in as many heartbeats, but another raked him with its claws. Utul slashed even as he staggered away, his flaming sword opening its throat. He took a few stumbling steps, trying to right his balance, blood sluicing from the claw marks.

Arvid surged after Utul, axe swinging and crunching into his hip, biting deep, then she ripped it free in a spray of blood and mail. The Revenant's taloned hand grabbed Utul's throat, holding him upright. Utul slashed with his sword, Arvid smashed the weak blow away. The sword clattered to the ground, flames sputtering and going out.

Arvid squeezed. Utul spat in the Revenant's face, even as his eyes bulged, veins purpling. An audible *crack* as his neck snapped.

CHAPTER TWENTY-SEVEN

RIV

Riv was dimly aware of the battle raging in the chamber, of more winged figures swooping down from the shadows, others at the far end, holding an entrance to another tunnel. She was still lost in her thoughts, gazing at the dead half-breed at her feet.

How many of them are there?

A world of questions opened up to her, spiralling like a whirlpool in her mind, but one thought blotted out all else.

I'm not alone.

A sound—looking up, she saw the shape of Revenants speeding towards her, three, four, more of them. Before she had a chance to move, Meical and the Ben-Elim were in front of her, others rising, the air churning as wings beat, spears stabbed.

A ripple of blue flame.

"Come," Meical said, turning and looking down at her.

"*Look!*" she said, pointing at the dead warrior.

"There are questions that need answering," Meical said. "But the only way to those answers is through these Revenants. There is a battle that needs fighting."

She looked down again at the half-breed and it was like a struck spark to Riv.

These mist-walkers killed one of my kind. They need to pay.

Her rune-marked sword hissed into her hand and she took to the air. Revenants were everywhere, swirling around clusters of the Order. Ethlinn and Balur were at the far end of the chamber, Ethlinn striding towards some point in the chamber she seemed desperate to reach, Balur trying to follow her, Revenants clinging to him like rats.

Meical flew into the chamber; Riv took his left side, the surviving eight Ben-Elim spread around them in the shape of a wedge. They swept low, stabbing down at enemies.

Meical led them inexorably forwards, closing in on each beleaguered knot of Order warriors. They set two groups free, were too late for the next, but slew the Revenants that were crouched, feasting on dead warriors' corpses.

Flames and black smoke obscured Riv's vision, but then the cloud rolled on and Riv saw a Revenant, taller and broader than the rest. A woman, an axe in one fist. In her other she was holding a warrior of the Order by the throat, squeezing. Revenants formed a ring around them.

Arvid.

Riv saw a burning sword fall from the warrior's grip.

Utul.

Even as Riv watched, she saw Arvid's grip tighten, Utul's head lurch to one side, flopping at an unnatural angle.

Riv exploded into movement, Meical calling after her.

She sped through the chamber, felt movement above, glanced up to see dark-winged figures flying there, watching her. She was almost upon Arvid, who had thrown Utul's body to the ground. Ethlinn and Balur were closing in, though they were set upon from all sides. Drem was standing over Cullen, slicing and chopping with his seax and hand-axe, Keld's wolven-hounds close by, ripping and biting. Shar appeared from nowhere, face twisted in a wordless scream, sword raised over her head, carving a way through Revenants towards Arvid.

A roar from the tunnel drew Riv's gaze; an explosion of flame boiled into the chamber, Revenants falling back, alight. Then warriors were leaping through the flames into the chamber: Kill, Byrne's captain, and Tain the giant. Close behind them was Queen Nara with a spear in her hand, Madoc her first-sword at her shoulder, others following.

Below her Shar cursed as she tried to break Arvid's guard. This was the first Revenant Riv had seen use a weapon, twice as dangerous now with her strength and speed. Iron clanged and Shar reeled back, tripping over a body, falling, and Arvid was towering over her, axe rising. Riv beat her wings, sword levelled, but knew she was going to be too late. She pulled her arm back to throw her sword, and then a net flew through the air, wrapping around Arvid, lead weights swinging about her limbs and torso.

Arvid bellowed, thrashing in the net, and stumbled backwards, Revenants leaping to her aid, tearing at it. Keld appeared, sword and shield in hand, blood sheeting from a wound on his head, a flap of skin hanging.

Shar climbed to her feet.

Arvid tore an arm free from the net, Revenants were trying to rip the rest from her.

"Kill them," she hissed, talons gesturing at Shar and Keld, Drem just behind them, still protecting Cullen's prone form.

Then Riv was amongst them, wings beating as her feet skidded on stone, sliding, Meical and the other Ben-Elim behind her, stabbing, killing. Riv skewered a Revenant, shifted her weight, her momentum carrying her on, sword ripping free. More Revenants were in front of her, protecting Arvid as she frenziedly tore the last scraps of net from her arms.

Meical took to the air, other Ben-Elim joining him, jabbing down. Dimly Riv knew that Meical was using the right strategy, using his wings as an advantage. But the red haze had filled Riv's mind, and all she wanted to do was be in the thick of it, to stab and slice and kill.

A crash behind her: Ethlinn and Balur reaching the fight, heads and limbs flying. Both giants were bleeding from a multitude of talon and puncture wounds. Byrne was there, too, eyes fixed on Arvid, all of them carving their way through the ring of Revenants that had formed around their dark captain.

A snarling figure lunged at Riv but its head exploded as she hacked downwards, tore her blade free from the mess that collapsed to the ground, leaped over the corpse.

And then Arvid was in front of her.

Riv did not pause.

A beat of her wings powering her forwards, sword stabbing. Arvid swung her axe, deflected Riv's sword, threw the remnants of the net in Riv's face, sidestepped and slashed talons at her as she stumbled, half-blinded by the net.

Riv instinctively dropped to her knees, ripped the net from her face, felt air hiss over her head, rolled on one shoulder, tucking a wing, and then she was back on her feet, turning. The axe was swinging again, this time Riv's legs bunched, propelling her into the air, a beat of her wings and she was jumping above the axe, flying over Arvid, cutting down at her. Arvid hissed, clutching her shoulder at the blue-flamed line that appeared there.

Riv landed, lunged, Arvid's axe swinging around, blocking, stumbling backwards. She snarled and swept forwards, axe and talons a blur. The blade sliced through air a finger's width from Riv's throat, talons raking across Riv's belly, mail links shattering, a burning sensation.

Riv ignored it, found her balance and ducked beneath the backswing of Arvid's axe, darting in close, and then her sword was stabbing into Arvid's belly, angled up, pushing deeper, under the ribs, piercing her heart. Riv ripped her sword free in a burst of blue sparks, Arvid stumbled away. The Revenant dropped her axe, hands grasping at the wound in her belly. She looked at Riv with her black eyes, sighed, toppled to the ground.

A change around her, the sounds of battle fading, and Riv turned.

All about them the surviving Revenants were gasping, limbs flopping as they collapsed to the floor.

Drem looked up and gave her a weary smile. "You took your time, didn't you?"

CHAPTER TWENTY-EIGHT

DREM

Riv gave Drem a fierce grin, her wings and limbs trembling. Then she punched her sword into the air and the survivors in the chamber were cheering, echoing louder and louder. Drem felt a moment of relief and elation, the realization that he'd looked death in the eye and survived, again. That was followed by a wave of exhaustion.

He looked down. Cullen was lying still on the ground.

Drem dropped to one knee, put his hand to Cullen's neck, searching for a pulse. For a long, agonizing moment he couldn't find it, but then, faint but steady, he felt it.

Cullen groaned.

A fist unknotted in Drem's belly.

I would not be losing you, Cullen.

His own wounds were clamouring for attention, the claw marks on his leg the worst, a pain that throbbed with each beat of his heart. He tore a strip from his linen undershirt and quickly bound the wound, then checked himself over, found a few sets of puncture wounds from Revenant teeth on his arms, and blew out a relieved sigh that Arvid was dead.

The bears will be all right, now, he thought.

Close by, Shar dropped to her knees besides Utul's body. She lifted him, cradling his head in her lap, and stroked his face. Tears streaked lines through the grime on her cheeks.

There is no coming back for Utul. Drem felt a deep wave of grief for the warrior. He had not known him long, but he'd liked him, had felt that Utul was a man he could trust. *And now he's gone.* He could not pull his eyes away from Shar, holding Utul on her lap, her tears falling onto him. Their position dragged Drem back over half a year and sixty leagues north into the Desolation, to him kneeling beside his father, holding Olin as he died.

So much death.

Keld limped over to him, one side of his face covered in blood. A flap of skin was hanging from his temple.

"That'll need stitching," Drem said, tearing another strip of linen from his undertunic.

"Aye, soon enough," Keld said. His hounds were with him. Both were matted with blood. Drem saw puncture wounds on Fen's chest.

"Cullen?" Keld asked him.

"Unconscious. Cracked his skull when he fell with a Revenant on his back. But he's breathing."

"I'm not unconscious," Cullen croaked. "Help me up."

The relief in Keld was obvious.

"What did I miss?" Cullen groaned, trying to sit up. "My head hurts. Where's my sword?"

"You dropped it, again," Keld said, kneeling beside them both. "And it's a fine time to be sleeping on the job. The fight's done now, no need to rush."

"Done?" Cullen said. "But I haven't killed Arvid yet."

"Riv beat you to that," Drem said, as he wrapped his strip of linen around Keld's face, holding up the flap of skin.

"Damn it," Cullen muttered. "That's not fair, she's got wings. We had to cut our way through a hundred of these *things*—" he prodded a dead Revenant next to him—"to even get close to Arvid."

"Riv did her fair share of Revenant-fighting," Keld said, "don't be worrying about that."

"Still," Cullen muttered, picking at blood that was scabbing on his head, "I wish I had wings."

Fen licked Cullen's face.

"Ach," Cullen muttered, "your breath smells."

"He's been chewing on Revenants, what do you expect?" Keld ruffled Fen's fur. Ralla pushed in for some attention, too. Drem scratched her neck.

Byrne appeared, looking down on them. She rested a hand on Drem's shoulder. A long look from her as she assessed their wounds, and then she nodded.

"You'll live," she said.

"Aye, though Keld may as well be dead, with his pretty looks all ruined," Cullen said.

Keld cuffed Cullen across the back of his head.

Byrne shook her head and strode away, threading her way to Riv, who was still standing over Arvid's corpse.

Byrne put a hand on Riv's shoulder and smiled at her.

"You saved us tonight," Byrne said. "Saved more than you know. We are in your debt."

Riv shuffled her feet, looked at the ground.

"We fought together," Riv said. "I was just the first to pin Arvid down. I got lucky."

No, you weren't, Drem thought, looking at Utul and Shar. *Luck had nothing to do with it. And Utul and Shar are blade-masters.* He looked at Utul. *Was.*

Meical and the Ben-Elim landed around Riv and Byrne.

"Thank you," Byrne said to them.

"We are allies," Meical said, then paused, looked into Byrne's eyes. "And friends, I hope." He offered his arm.

Byrne looked at him, then down to his arm. A hush fell over the chamber.

"Aye, friends," Byrne said, taking his arm in the warrior grip.

"Good," Meical said. "I hoped to right a wrong I committed against Corban. I feel now that I have."

"You fought with me, bled with me. Risked your life." Byrne shrugged. "That is the most any man or woman can do."

"So, there are no thanks needed between us," Meical said. "But there *are* questions that need answering." He looked up.

Shadowed figures circled near the ceiling.

Byrne gazed up at them and nodded.

"Faelan," she called out.

A winged figure flew into the air from the tunnel that led out of the chamber, slow, powerful beats of his dark wings. Others fell in behind him, swooping down from the shadows, thirty, forty, more of them. The one Byrne had called Faelan circled above them and landed before Byrne. He was shorter than the Ben-Elim, though broader, his hair and eyes dark, where the Ben-Elim were fair. Clothed in mail and a hunter's belt, quiver, knife, axe in loops on the belt, a sword in his fist.

"Who are you?" Meical asked, frowning.

Faelan looked at Meical, dark brows knotting. Slowly he looked away, at Byrne.

"I am no friend to the Ben-Elim, and I do not answer to them," he said. His voice was strange to Drem, deep and halting, as if he didn't use it much.

Abruptly there was a tension in the air, a score of Faelan's kin alighting behind him, all glowering at Meical and the surviving Ben-Elim.

"Peace," Byrne said, holding a hand up and stepping forwards. "You cannot judge all Ben-Elim the same. These are my allies." She looked at Meical. "And my friends."

"They are not *my* friends," Faelan said, looking Meical up and down.

"I am no Ben-Elim," Riv said, stepping forwards. Her wings rippled, dapple grey. "And Meical is my friend."

Faelan looked at Riv, eyes widening as he took in her wings.

"Then things have changed in the world," he said.

"Ha, that is a truth." Meical laughed. "A moon ago I was imprisoned in iron."

Another blink from Faelan as he stared at Meical. "You are...Meical? Who fought Asroth?"

"Aye, I am Meical. And I still fight Asroth. I'd fight along-side you, if you'd allow it."

Faelan stared at Meical, his frown returning.

"This is a conversation for another time," Byrne said. "Faelan, you held these creatures. My thanks. I was worried for you."

"We would never let you down," Faelan said. "We owe a great deal. I have something for you." He sheathed his sword and dropped to one knee before Byrne, hands reaching inside his cloak. He pulled out a leather-bound book and offered it up to Byrne.

"Ha, you are a good friend to have, Faelan," Byrne said. "And never, ever kneel to me," she added, putting a hand under his arm and pulling him to his feet.

Faelan rose, Byrne taking the book from him and embracing him.

"Well, I'm glad that's done," Cullen whispered to Drem and Keld. "Now can we go and find something to drink? I've worked up a thirst."

CHAPTER TWENTY-NINE

JIN

Jin held up her hand, reining in her horse, and her warband rippled to a disciplined halt behind her.

"What's wrong, my Queen?" Gerel said, his eyes darting left and right, scanning the dark trees and shadows of Forn Forest, his hand resting on the clip of his bow-case at his hip.

"Nothing is wrong," Jin breathed, staring at the sight before her.

The road they were upon was edged with Forn's tall trees. To Jin's left, between her and the treeline, a river frothed and foamed, the water cold and clear. Ahead of her the trees thinned, fading into meadows. The road and river ran on, side by side, cutting a wide line through the meadows. They led up to a towering cliff, a wall that filled the horizon and rose high as the sky. The river cut a stark line through it, cascading white-spumed from the great heights down to the meadows, not quite a waterfall.

"The plateau of Arcona," Jin whispered. The road led up to the cliff face, and carried on, weaving its way up the cliff. To the Sea of Grass.

Home.

Moths fluttered in her belly.

All my life I have longed for this moment. To return home. Many a night I would lie awake, thinking of my triumphant return to my people. But never did I imagine it under these circumstances. My father, Uldin, King of the Cheren, slain by my betrothed.

She clenched her teeth, the moths in her belly incinerated in a flush of anger, and she glanced back over her shoulder, staring beyond her warband to the road that faded into the dark of Forn.

Is he riding on this road? Fleeing to his people? Or is he doing as Asroth said, following his half-breed southwards, like a dog in heat?

She felt her fist clench around her bow, knuckles white.

"Onwards," she shouted, spurring her mount on.

Wind tore at Jin's warrior braid. She was a long way up, the treetops of Forn just a smudge far below. Her second horse was tethered behind her. Each of her warriors had a spare horse, allowing them to ride hard and switch mounts to maintain their pace. Less than two ten-nights to reach Arcona from Drassil, and she was proud of that. Now that she was queen, everything was a challenge. Every task asked the same question. Was she good enough? Could she lead her people well and accomplish great things? These were exceptional times, a time for warriors to make their name, to stake a place and live for eternity; or to fail, and die two deaths. The death of flesh, and the death of shame. A sharp, indrawn breath to control the fear that thought stirred in her veins.

Her warband rode behind her, four hundred and seventy-eight warriors spread along a switchback path that was carved into the cliff's face. It allowed three or four to ride abreast, no more. Just room enough for one large wain. There were other roads into Arcona, but not for a hundred leagues north or south. Her hawk banners snapped in the wind; the river tumbled in a roar, deafening.

And then she was at the top, the path spilling out into tall grass, black granite boulders protruding from the earth around the river's lip. An ocean of grass spread before her, undulating and sighing into the horizon, a cold wind rolling off it. She breathed deeply, drawing in the chill air, let it fill her lungs, scouring away the filth of Drassil, of her life as a slave. Exhaled it out in a long, slow breath.

The river cut a dark line through the ocean of green, in the distance flowing from a lake, a dark stain upon the land. In the lake's centre was an island of tree and rock.

The Isle of Kletva.

To the north of Kletva lay Jin's lands and her people, the Cheren. She longed to see them. Jin let her eyes wander south and east, far into the distance. To the lands of the Sirak.

"Soon," she promised to the wind, grass and sky.

Warriors rode out to greet them, a dozen scouts guarding the Cheren's borderlands. They wore no mail and were dressed for speed, deels of blue felt and wool, leather jerkins, strung bows in their fists. Jin's banners told them most of what they needed to know, but they were still alert.

Jin reined in and waited for them, her warband settling behind her. Leather harness creaked, a horse whinnied. She reached inside her deel and took out a long strip of embroidered cloth, a tablet weave of wool in blue, green and grey, a hawk still clearly entwined upon it, all beak and talons and wings. Her father's blood stained the fabric. It was his king's band, all that the Cheren needed to signify his status in their Clan. Jin remembered Gerel untying it from her father's corpse and giving it to her, that night in Forn. Her hands had been slick with Erdene's blood, her grief over her father and elation at having slain their enemy's queen still thick in her veins. When Gerel had given it to her, she had not been able to wear it, the grief of Uldin's death was so heavy upon her. She had not felt that she deserved it. She still didn't. But she knew there was no other choice now.

She offered the king's band to Gerel, who took it, and she held her right arm out.

Gerel nodded, a grunt of approval, and tied the strip of tablet weave around her upper arm, knotted it.

"My Queen," he said. "Our Queen."

The scouts drew near, all of them except two reining in just outside bowshot. The other two rode on, a steady canter until they were a dozen paces from Jin. A click of the tongue from their riders and their mounts stopped.

"I am Tark," one of the scouts said, a man who looked more like leather than flesh. He looked from the hawk banners to Jin, eyes fixing on the king's band upon her arm.

"No," he whispered.

"Take me to the Heartland," Jin said. "Uldin is dead." She paused. "And we are at war."

Jin saw the gers from half a league out: white patches speckling the green, like snowdrops in spring, blanketing the ground.

The Cheren Heartland.

The Cheren Clan was made from a few hundred smaller families, all related, all Cheren, but they lived a nomadic life-style, moving with their herds and the wind, and rarely came together as one. When they did congregate as a Clan, it was usually here. The Cheren Heartland was as close to a fortress or town as the Cheren had, with huge gers built to house thousands. It had stood for as long as Jin could remember. The last time her Clan had gathered here had been a ten-night before she was taken from Arcona by the Ben-Elim. Her Clan had gathered here, summoned by Uldin, where they had prepared to fight the Sirak over the death of her mother. She could remember the cheering for her father, the proud faces of her Clan, their warband sounding like a thunderstorm as they rode south to face the Sirak. But it had gone so terribly wrong. On the day her Clan had met the Sirak on the field, literally as the battle had just begun, the Ben-Elim had arrived, crushing both Cheren and Sirak alike, and taking her and Bleda as wards, a bridle to control the Clans.

And now I am home, a king's band upon my arm.

"It is as your father told us," Gerel said as he cantered beside Jin, "the Clan is gathered, waiting on his word for war."

The Heartland could stand empty for moons at a time, even

years, but now it was full, lines of smoke marking a thousand fire-pits, the sound of life rippling out from the encampment.

That was just as Uldin had planned. His small warband that now rode behind Jin was to lure Erdene out into Forn, while back in Arcona the full strength of the Cheren was gathering here, waiting to strike.

Your plan will bear fruit, Father. The Sirak will be destroyed, our blood-feud settled. I will be Uldin's Fist.

They rode between the first gers, round tents of felt, though these were far larger than usual. Children *whooped* and dogs barked, chasing them. Tark had ridden ahead to announce Jin's arrival, and he appeared before her now, leading a hundred or so riders, an escort to bring Jin before the gathered Clan. He nodded to Jin and fell in at her side.

Eventually the tents gave way to an open space that was heavy with the rich tang of horse dung. Paddocks were everywhere.

Not like the idiots in the west, Jin thought. *We keep our horses close to us, safe, they are the heart of us.*

A gentle hill rose up before Jin, around it a mass of mounted warriors, men, women, more riders than Jin had ever seen in her life. Two thousand, three thousand, she could not tell. Uldin had taught her to count riders by their banners, usually fifty or sixty around a banner. There were too many banners here to count.

Stern faces stared at Jin, hard and weathered by Arcona's constant winds. Jin did not glance left or right, but set her cold-face and rode up the hill to its peak. Fear fluttered in her belly.

What if they will not follow me? Blame me for my father's death?

She swallowed, fear, grief, rage, all mixing within her, coalescing into something new.

Determination.

Jin reined in, her horse turning.

Thousands of men and women stared up at her, the wind a constant moan through the grass. Somewhere above Jin a bird screeched. She looked up, saw the silhouette of a hawk diving from the grey skies, wings closed, talons outstretched as it swooped into the long grass, disappearing from view. Heart-beats passed, and then the hawk rose from the grass, a hare clutched in its talons.

Deep inside Jin she felt a certainty settle upon her.

I am the hawk.

"My Queen," a voice filtered through to her. It was Gerel.

She sat tall in her saddle.

"My father, your King, is slain," she cried out, her voice tugged by the wind. Murmurs rippled through the crowd, though word would have spread from Tark.

"He was slain by the coward Bleda, Prince of the Sirak."

Shouts now, oaths of vengeance called out.

Jin raised her right arm, showing the king's band. She clicked her tongue, touched her knees to her horse and it turned in a tight circle, letting all see.

"I am your queen, now. I slew Erdene, Queen of the Sirak. I drew a knife across her throat and watched the life drain from her eyes, and I will do the same to her heir." She paused, feeling the blood rushing in her veins, pounding. "Bleda is King of the Sirak now. But what is a king if his Clan are all DEAD!"

She screamed the last word.

"DEATH TO THE SIRAK!" she yelled, spittle spray-ing, standing tall in her saddle, letting her cold-face slip. Tears streamed from her eyes, her father's dying face floating in her mind. She was amongst her kin, her Clan, her people, and she was paying them the highest honour, showing the heart of her feelings, her grief and rage in all its rawness.

A moment's silence, only the cold wind soughing through the grass, and then the crowd roared back at her.

"DEATH, DEATH, DEATH!"

Gerel raised his voice beside her, and the warband around her.

"DEATH!"

Jin smiled.

I will take everything from you, Bleda. Your people, your kin, your friends, your lover. And when that is done, I will take your life.

CHAPTER THIRTY

FRITHA

Fritha sat alone in a chamber, staring into the dying embers of a fire. She was in a room above Drassil's Great Hall. Some said it had belonged to Corban, the one they called the Bright Star. Now it was a cold and empty room. The unshuttered window was open, darkness leaking in, just the scrape of wind in branches. Torches flickered on walls, pools of orange light, shadows pressing upon them.

I like this time. The darkness before dawn. It is like the world is taking a breath, still and silent for a moment, before the chaos of day.

She rubbed her eyes, looked at her hands. They were black with the work of the forge, coal and oil and sweat. But Fritha's chest was filled with a sense of joy. She looked at a linen-wrapped bundle at her feet, lifted a wine skin and took a long, sweet draught.

A knock at the door.

She wiped wine from her lips.

"Enter."

The door scraped open, a sudden through-draught causing the torches on the wall to crackle and hiss, sending shadows leaping. Elise slithered in. Behind her came Elise's father, Arn, and behind him, the broad bulk of Morn, her leathery wings folded across her back like a cloak.

Elise and Arn both looked better than when Fritha had seen them last, a ten-night ago, fresh from their journey to Drassil from the Desolation. This was the first time Fritha had seen them alone. Asroth had worked her hard, elated with the success of his new hand, and in truth she had become lost in that work. Now, though, looking at Elise and Arn, she was sorry that she had not seen them sooner.

Elise came to a halt before her. The scales of her lower torso were a pale, milky-white, her tail wrapping into a circle beneath her. Her upper torso was clothed in linen and wool, a belt at her waist with sword and knife. Her fair hair and freckles blended with her skin, almost glowing in the half-dark of flame and shadow. Fangs protruded from her lips, a gleam of saliva. She looked at Fritha with pain in her eyes.

"You left usssss," Elise said, echoing the words she had said to Fritha in the Great Hall.

Fritha stood, the effort making her realize how exhausted she was.

"I am sorry," Fritha said. "I love you, Elise, and I am sorry."

And that was all it took; Fritha saw the pain lift from Elise's face. A hesitant smile twitched her lips.

She is like a puppy, forgiving her master for a beating.

Fritha stepped forwards and stroked Elise's cheek. The smile grew broader.

"I will never leave you again, you are too precious to me," Fritha assured her.

Elise's tail shuddered, a rattle.

Arn came to a halt beside them, his face stern. He was altogether a different case from Elise.

We have spent years together in the wild, protected each other, saved each other's life in battle. But we do not have the bond I have with Elise. Of creator and created, like mother and child.

"You abandoned us. Left us for dead," Arn said.

"I am sorry, Arn." She took a deep breath. "I had to be here, to set Asroth free, or all would have been for nothing. If I had not come, then Gulla alone would have set Asroth free. A representative of humankind had to do it, to be involved, for our future." She blew out a long breath. "I sent Morn to find you."

"You did not *send* me," Morn growled. She was standing a few paces behind Arn, beneath a wall torch. Her arms were folded, her features in shadow. "I am not your slave, to do your bidding."

"No, that is not what I meant," Fritha said hurriedly. "I *asked* you to search for Elise and Arn. I pleaded with you."

"Yes, that is more like the truth of it, and now my father is angry with me," Morn said.

Fritha stroked the white scar on her arm, testament of her blood-oath with Morn. Remembered their words together, two outcasts seeking vengeance, and finding strength in each other.

You are a good ally to have. If you will be true to me, your loyalty not divided.

"It is a sadness that Gulla does not see your qualities," she said. "You are strong, courageous. A skilled and fierce warrior." Though Morn remained silent, Fritha noted the ripple that went through the half-breed's wings, the shift in the set of her shoulders.

You are not used to compliments.

And you like them.

"And to prove my gratitude, and my friendship, I have something for you." She looked to Elise and Arn. "Something for all of you."

Fritha leaned forwards in her chair and pulled loose a cord that bound the linen bundle at her feet, opened it up. She raised a hand-axe, the shaft veined wood, the blade bearded iron. The metal was dark. It did not gleam in the torchlight.

"For you, Arn," she said, offering it to the old warrior.

He stepped forwards hesitantly.

"Is that...?" he trailed off.

"The blade is starstone metal, forged from the same metal that once made the Seven Treasures. It is priceless beyond measure. And deadly." She held it out to Arn. "Take it," she said.

Arn reached out tentatively, his fingers wrapping around the wooden haft.

"The wood is cut from Drassil's great tree."

"I, I do not know what to say," Arn said.

"Say thank you, and that you forgive me," Fritha said.

Arn cut the air with the axe, a soft hiss.

"Thank you. I forgive you. A thousand times, I forgive you." He smiled.

Fritha dipped her head to him, then reached into the bundle again. She lifted up a scabbarded knife, the hilt bound with leather, silver wire threading around it.

"For you," she said to Morn.

The half-breed strode to her, no hesitancy in her step, and took the knife. The blade was long and narrow, black as night. A small cross-guard. Morn held it up, ran her thumb along its edge, watched as a pearl of blood appeared. She looked at Fritha, their eyes locking for long moments.

"Better vengeance than grief," Fritha whispered, repeating the words Morn had said to her. It seemed like a long time ago, back in the starstone mine.

"Better vengeance than grief," Morn echoed, then sheathed the knife. She gave a curt nod of her head, her teeth showing in a smile, and Fritha knew then that Morn's loyalty was hers.

She reached down one last time and lifted a spear. The shaft was long, dark wood, the spear blade crow-black, shaped like a leaf, the belly of it curved, so that it would not snag in meat and bone. A weapon made for killing.

"For you, my Elise," Fritha said, holding the spear out in the palms of both her hands.

Elise looked at it, a gentle hiss escaping her lips, and then she slithered forwards, scales rasping on stone. Elise took the spear, hefted it, testing its weight and balance. Then she was slicing it through the air, reversing her grip from overhand to underhand, switching to double-handed, the air rushing with each stroke.

"It issss beautiful," Elise said.

"Not as beautiful as you, my perfect creation," Fritha said quietly.

Elise smiled at her, fangs bared. Fritha felt a warm glow in her belly.

I have her back. Her and Arn, and now Morn. And Wrath, of course. Her draig was in Drassil's great chamber, curled before the stairwell that led to this room. He had grumbled that he could not fit up the stairs when Fritha had climbed them, but Fritha knew this needed to be a private conversation, and that Wrath's presence at the foot of the stairs would ensure that no one came within earshot.

And my Ferals, though few of them are left. They will breed.

But it is something. A place to start.

"How have you done this?" Arn asked her, still staring at the axe blade, turning it in his hand.

"I am Asroth's queen," she said, then smiled, knowing how fragile that position was. "I have made myself useful to him. Forged his hand and gauntlet, and made him weapons from the starstone. He is well pleased and wished to reward me. He gave me a portion of starstone."

"And you made these for ussss, when you could have made anything for yourself?" Elise said.

"In truth, I am not *that* selfless. I did make myself a little something." Fritha patted a short-sword hanging in a scabbard at her hip, like the swords she was trained with in the White-Wings. "But there was metal to spare." She shrugged. "I could have made myself more, but…you are important to me. I wanted to show you that, with more than words."

She stopped, drew in a deep breath.

"There is something that I would tell you. And something that I would ask."

Fritha looked at them all in turn.

"You must swear to secrecy. If you breathe of this to another soul, it would…endanger me."

Another silence, only the crackle of torches on the wall.

"Tell ussss," Elise said. Arn and Morn nodded.

"Asroth's seed is in my belly. His child grows within me."

Their eyes grew wide, a sharp intake of breath from Morn. Elise's tail rattled.

"I would have you swear to protect my baby. She will be the future of the Banished Lands. But there are factions within Asroth's court that would not be best pleased with this news. Factions that would see my child as a threat. And soon we will march to war; dangerous times lie ahead for us."

"She?" Arn said.

Fritha stroked her belly.

"Yes. She." Even now Fritha could feel the warmth of her child, a presence deep within.

"Will you do it?" Fritha asked, a tremor in her voice.

"Yessss," Elise said.

"Aye." No hesitation from Arn.

Morn looked at Fritha. "I thought there was something different about you," Morn said. "Now I see it. You have hope, again, where you had none. It has made you scared."

"Yes," Fritha admitted. "Will you swear to me?"

"I will," Morn grunted.

Fritha drew her new short-sword, the blade black as night. "Then let us make a new scar, and bind ourselves, one to the other." She drew the blade across her palm, blood welling, and looked at them, feeling her heart pounding in her chest.

Elise, Arn and Morn each put their starstone blades to their hands and drew blood.

CHAPTER THIRTY-ONE

DREM

Drem stood with his friends.

Byrne was before them. She had a large, flint-grey stone in her hands, and she turned and placed it upon a cairn.

They were standing in a field of cairns, a part of Dun Seren that Drem had not seen before, to the north-east of the keep, the river Vold a black smear beyond stone walls. Hundreds of people filled the field around Drem. Thousands. Warriors of the Order and their families, Queen Nara with Elgin, Madoc and her people. Riv, Meical and the handful of the Ben-Elim who had survived the battle were close by, and Drem also saw that Faelan and a few score half-breeds from the caverns beneath Dun Seren were there. They looked uncomfortable in the open space, the sky cloudless and blue above them, a beautiful summer's day.

"Your sacrifice was not in vain, and it will be remembered," Byrne said, her voice loud in the silence. "We will never forget."

The crowd echoed her words, Drem adding his voice to theirs.

"We will never forget."

There were one hundred and twelve new cairns; Drem knew exactly how many, for he had helped raise them, rocks brought up in wains from the river below. It had been a sobering deed, seeing linen-wrapped bodies slowly disappearing as the rocks were piled around them. Most of them were warriors of the Order, those who had fought with rune-marked blades, but some were Ben-Elim, and half-breed Ben-Elim, and some from Nara's warriors.

People from across the Banished Lands, torn to pieces by a horde of blood-mad Revenants. Drem pinched his nose, the strangeness and injustice of it filling him with a deep melancholy.

They stood in silence a long while, Drem lost in his thoughts, the wound in his leg starting to ache and throb. Cullen's hand upon his shoulder brought him back to himself. He saw that only a few were left, the crowds around him melting away, back to the work of repairing and healing.

And preparing.

Half a ten-night had passed since the Battle of Dun Seren, as it was starting to be called, and almost with the rising of the sun that same day Kill had gathered a team and taken them to the forges. The fires had been blazing night and day since then, the sound of hammers a constant ringing as rune-marked blades were forged.

"Come on, lad," Cullen said.

Why does he insist on calling me "lad," when I am older than him?

They walked through the field of cairns together, Drem looking at the inscriptions on stones as they passed them. To his right Drem saw movement, the flicker of wings deep amongst the cairns. He tapped Cullen and pointed.

It was a Ben-Elim, on his knees before a cairn.

Drem and Cullen threaded through the cairns, approaching the Ben-Elim. He was talking, head bowed.

"I am sorry," Drem heard the Ben-Elim say. He must have heard their footsteps, for abruptly he froze, his head snapping round to look at them.

It was Meical, and tears were streaming from his eyes.

He stood quickly, a beat of his wings and he was airborne, rising higher into the blue. In heartbeats he was just a smudge in the sky, blurred by the sun.

Drem shared a look with Cullen. There were two cairns closer together than the others.

"Why would Meical be kneeling before a cairn?" Drem asked. "And whose cairn is it?" He found the stone at the foot of one of the cairns.

"I know," Cullen said.

Drem leaned closer to read the inscription on a flat stone at the foot of the cairn.

"Here lies Corban, the Bright Star, our captain, our friend."

He was silent a moment, feeling the weight of history behind those words.

Our friend.

"He was a hero," Drem said. "We have all heard the tales."

"Aye, he was," Cullen said, unusually solemn.

"But out of all that could have been said about him, the word *friend* is on his cairn. He was a man. Like us."

We are just people, all of us the same. Flawed, fragile, stubborn, angry, happy. And life treats no one differently. We are born, and we live, and then we die. It's what we do while we are here that counts. And if we can be called friend, then we are lucky indeed.

That thought rocked Drem. He shook his head and stared at the cairn. It was the same as all the others, the stones weathered, moss-grown, flowers poking out of gaps. He shifted, looked at the other cairn. It lay across the foot of Corban's cairn, and Drem moved so that he could read its stone.

"Here lies Storm, friend of Corban, protector of her pack. Faithful unto death."

Drem blew out a long breath. "Corban's pet wolven?"

"She was never his pet," Cullen said.

Friend of Corban. Those words echoed in Drem's mind. *Friend.*

So much of what we are and do is shaped by that. Our friendships. Those we love, those we choose to stand beside.

"There's a story that goes with that inscription," Cullen said. "Corban died here, an old man, in his sleep. He was placed within his cairn, his sword upon his chest. Afterwards a feast was held in Corban's memory. Storm, the wolven, did not want to leave the cairn, but Coralen, Corban's wife, coaxed Storm to go with her. Well, later that night, during the feast of remembrance, Storm started to growl. Then she howled and went running off. Coralen and all of the Order went after her, and she led them back to Corban's graveside. Kadoshim were here, attempting to desecrate the cairn, and Corban's body."

Cullen paused, emotion twisting his mouth, putting a tremor in his voice.

Drem sucked a breath in. After the life that Corban had led, standing against the Kadoshim and their evil, that was the most unbearable act. It looked as if Cullen agreed with him, the young warrior's face pale, his mouth a thin line.

"Because of Storm they were interrupted before they could carry out their plan, but they did take Corban's sword."

Drem's fingers brushed the hilt of his own father's sword, hanging back at his hip again.

I am glad to have this, something that was a part of you, my dear father, Drem thought.

"The next morning," Cullen continued, "Coralen dressed for war and rode out of Dun Seren, with Storm at her side. She never came back."

"But Storm did," Drem said, looking at the huge cairn.

"Aye. Ten moons later. She loped into the fortress, the story goes, ignored everyone, and made her way to Corban's cairn. When she got here she lay down at his feet, and refused to leave his side ever again. She lived a while longer, I'm not sure how long, days, a moon? But she never left Corban's side again."

"Faithful unto death," Drem said.

"Aye, just so." Cullen nodded.

The stable yard was busy. Warriors of the Order and a score of giants were repairing splintered doors and frames. Drem saw Keld working on the post-and-rail fence before the bear-paddocks. Fen and Ralla were close by, lying in some shade beneath a hawthorn tree.

The huntsman's face was cut and bruised, stitch lines along the whole of his cheek, temple and across the side of his head where Revenant talons had sliced a huge flap of skin.

"Ach, but you're not getting any prettier," Cullen said as they stopped before Keld.

"Don't think I'll lose any sleep over that," Keld grunted. "Hold this," he said, pointing at a wooden rail.

Drem lifted it, held it in position, bracing it with his knee while Keld nailed it in place. He looked into the paddock, eyes searching.

"He'll be along anytime now," Keld said with a wink.

Just then a huge shape lumbered into view, the white bear appearing from behind a stand of trees. Hammer followed behind him.

After the battle in the caverns beneath the fortress, Drem had hurried back to the enclosure, hoping that the white bear was still alive. Alcyon the giant had been tending them both, cleaning wounds and preparing for stitching. Hammer, although at more risk than the white bear and closer to death, had been easier to stitch, because she was verging on unconscious. But the white bear had taken none too well to Alcyon stabbing him with a sharp needle. It had taken a lot of honey to get the white bear's wounds stitched.

Drem felt a jolt of happiness at the sight of him.

He saved me in the skirmish on the plain, and carried me all the way home.

Heavy footsteps, and Alcyon strode up to them. He had a huge saddle slung across one shoulder and a big bundle of leather tack in one arm, a hemp sack in the other. He looked at Drem and the others.

"Time to see if Hammer is up to a saddle on her back."

Her wounds had been so bad that Drem was amazed that the giant bear was even up and walking.

But I have seen her fight a giant bear and a draig and survive. She is a strong one. But what else should I expect? She was Sig's companion for countless years.

The white bear and Hammer were close now, and Drem climbed the rail that Keld had just nailed, earning him a *tsk* and a dark look from the huntsman.

Cullen followed him over.

"Just testing your work," he said, with a flashed smile at Keld.

Alcyon went the long way around, using the gate.

Drem walked up to the white bear, who stopped and lowered his head, rubbing his muzzle into Drem's chest. It nearly knocked Drem to the ground, but he set his feet and leaned into the bear, scratching one of its ears. His other hand stroked the bear's neck and chest, his huge shoulder, checking that wounds were healing well, flesh knitting, scabs thick and starting to peel away.

"You are a survivor, my friend," he whispered. The bear rumbled quietly in agreement.

Alcyon reached them and put the saddle and tack on the grass, then dropped the hemp sack with a thud.

"What's in there?" Drem asked the giant.

"That's Hammer's coat of mail. If she's going into battle, she'll need to be wearing it." He looked up at the bear looming over him.

"Well, Hammer, how do you feel about having a giant on your back?"

The female bear regarded Alcyon a moment with her small dark eyes, and then she dipped her head and one shoulder. It was the way that the giant bears of Dun Seren gave permission for a rider to climb upon their back.

"*They are not pets, or dumb animals broken to service,*" Keld had told Drem when he'd seen it the first time. "*This is a partnership. A bond of friendship and loyalty between rider and bear. These bears are as intelligent as you or I. They know what they are doing, and choose it willingly.*"

"Ah, well thank you, great bear, you do me much honour," Alcyon said, patting Hammer's shoulder and stooping to lift the saddle. "Some help?" he said to Drem, who grabbed one side of the saddle and grunted with the weight of it. Together they heaved it up onto Hammer's back, let her shake a little so that it shifted into place.

Drem and Alcyon reached for the saddle-girth, but a

rumbling growl stopped them. It wasn't from Hammer, but from the white bear.

"Think you better have a look at this," Cullen said, slapping Drem's back.

Drem turned to see that the white bear had dropped his shoulder and dipped his head, like Hammer had just done to Alcyon. He was looking at Drem with intelligent black eyes.

Drem froze, staring. Then he stepped forwards, around the white bear's lowered shoulder, gripped a handful of fur and leaped up onto the bear's back. He teetered a moment, almost falling, but the white bear stood and rolled its shoulder, shifting Drem onto his back.

Drem sat there, the world looking different from this high vantage point. Men, women and giants were staring at him; Cullen open-mouthed, Keld with a wry smile on his face, Alcyon nodding. Drem felt...overwhelmed. A happiness soared through him, such that he hadn't felt since before the death of his father. He leaned forwards, patting the bear's neck, and whispered in his ear.

"Thank you, my friend," he breathed.

The white bear looked up over his shoulder at Drem and gave a contented rumble.

"Well, I think that bear deserves a name. We can't keep on calling him *white bear*," Cullen said from down below.

"Time for a naming," Alcyon agreed, grinning.

"What's it to be, then?" Cullen said. "Death From Above? Avalanche?"

The white bear rumbled a growl in Cullen's face.

"Terrible Breath?" Cullen said, pinching his nose.

Drem sucked in a deep breath, emotions still flowing through him. He looked at his friends about him, felt such a sense of belonging at this moment—the act of the white bear's friendship sealing something in him. It was an act of loyalty that would never be forgotten.

"Friend," Drem said. "His name is Friend."

CHAPTER THIRTY-TWO

FRITHA

"Help me," Fritha said to Bune, as she struggled with a shirt of mail that was laid out across her bed.

The Kadoshim stepped close and took one side of the shirt. He touched it hesitantly, respectfully.

It was forged from starstone metal.

The links were black, greased for protection, so it looked like liquid oil as Fritha and Bune lifted it, rippling and shimmering in the light. They settled it over Asroth's outstretched arms and around his back. He was on the dais in Drassil's Great Hall, their bed behind him, a hundred Kadoshim surrounding them, Asroth's personal honour guard, all of them hand-picked by Bune. Wrath lay a short distance away, enjoying the warmth of a beam of sunshine that sliced down through a window in the domed wall. Fritha and Bune pulled the mail coat along Asroth's arms, over a shirt of padded linen, across his broad shoulders, and then each of them was stepping behind Asroth. Unlike a normal coat of mail, it was not one enclosed piece that would have been threaded over the head. The Kadoshim had wings that had to be tailored for. Fritha and Bune stepped behind Asroth, buckling straps that pulled the mail tight and snug around the arched mounds of muscle where Asroth's wings met his back.

"There, my beloved," Fritha said with a grunt, as she threaded the last buckle. She stepped back in front of him and watched as he rolled his shoulders and shifted his weight, letting the mail coat settle around him. He swung an arm, punched the air.

"It feels good," he said.

"This will make it feel even better," Fritha said, taking a belt and buckling it tight about his waist. It had a long knife hanging from it, almost as long as Fritha's short-sword. A knife with a black, starstone blade. Fritha pulled some of the mail coat up above the belt, let it hang so that the belt took some of the coat's weight.

Asroth grunted. "That is better on the shoulders."

Fritha lifted a helm of black iron. Asroth dipped his head as she placed it upon him, adjusting the nasal bar, settling the curtain of iron rings over his neck and shoulders. Black cheek-plates hung as protection; they were engraved with silver. She buckled the chinstrap, then stepped back.

"Ah, but you are fine," Fritha breathed as she looked at Asroth. "A god of war."

Asroth smiled at her. "*The* god of war," he corrected.

Fritha dipped her head in agreement.

She had worked to exhaustion and beyond to craft Asroth's war gear, seeking out the finest smiths, metal crafters and leather-workers within their ranks, overseeing everything, and blending all with her blood magic and words of power.

Asroth looked at Fritha and held his hand out. His new hand, wrapped in a black metal gauntlet.

"Give it to me," he said.

Fritha stepped behind Asroth and nodded to Bune. This was definitely too heavy for her to lift alone. Bune stepped forwards and together they lifted a long axe, turned and placed it into Asroth's fist.

His gauntleted hand closed about the shaft. Thick wood, ringed with bands of black iron. Asroth touched the butt to the stone floor, a black iron cap on the haft's end scraping on stone. The axe blade stood at a height with Asroth's head, single-bladed and bearded, a wicked-looking spike on its spine. There were pits in the iron and dark mist curled around the blade. Asroth wrapped his other hand around it and swung it in a hissing circle. A trail of mist marked where it sliced the air. Fritha had the distinct impression that he could have decapitated a giant with that blow.

Asroth inspected the blade, scraped his gauntlet against the spike, tested the balance of the haft, then looked up at Fritha.

"I am ready," he said to her.

"I have something for you, a surprise," Fritha said, barely able to contain her excitement. She opened a hemp sack and reached inside, took out a rolled bundle and held it out.

A whip, the handle made of leather-bound wood. The whip comprised a dozen strips of leather twined with thin black wire. Towards the end of each strip were three hooks, the heaviest ones on the tip. They were made of black metal.

Asroth took the handle, the strips of leather dropping to the stone with a slap and clink of iron.

The whip swung loose in his hand, then he was bringing his arm back, and with a fluid *snap* the whip *cracked*, twelve barbs of iron lashing out at his bed, some snaring in the sheets and straw mattress, others in the wooden frame. A flick of his wrist and the bed seemed to just explode, a cloud of straw and linen and splinters of wood filling the air. Fritha raised a hand over her face.

Asroth stared at the whip.

"I *like* it," he said.

He rolled the whip and hung it on his belt, then spread his wings wide. A few powerful beats and he was rising, turning and hovering.

He is truly formidable. Clothed in starstone metal, wielding star-stone blades. A man to follow, to lead a nation, to conquer a world. And he is father to my child. Tendrils of pride and fear coiled through her.

"This is our time," Asroth said to Fritha and to the

Kadoshim about him, one hundred warriors. "This metal," he said, raising an arm and looking at the sleeve of his mail coat, "it was my prison for over a hundred years. Now it is my weapon and my shield." He nodded an acknowledgement to Fritha. "How long have we fought the Ben-Elim and their tyranny?" he asked the Kadoshim. "Our Long War. More than two thousand years we have struggled against them, and now we will end it. We will end *them*."

CHAPTER THIRTY-THREE

RIV

Riv sat in a high-vaulted chamber, a cup of wine in her hand and a plate of bread, cheese and fruit before her. She was high in a tower, large windows with shutters flung open looking out over the land about Dun Seren. Meical and Hadran were there, Balur One-Eye and Ethlinn sitting opposite. Queen Nara of Ardain was with them, her hair jet black, a wolven-fur about her shoulders. Her battlechief, Elgin, sat beside her, and Madoc her first-sword stood behind her chair. Other chairs were empty.

Riv drummed her fingers on the table.

The creak of a door.

"Welcome," Byrne said as she strode into the chamber. Kill marched one side of her, Tain the crow master at the other, Craf perched on his shoulder. Others followed behind them: Shar, Drem, Keld and Cullen.

And Faelan, the half-breed.

Riv's breath caught in her chest.

She had so many questions.

Byrne sat down, the others settling into seats around her. Faelan's wings rippled, glossy dark-brown feathers, almost black. His eyes glanced over Meical and Hadran, then settled upon her. He looked as if he had questions of his own.

"And welcome to this, our council of war," Byrne said.

Close to a ten-night had passed since the Battle of Dun Seren. That time had not been spent sitting idly. "This meeting is long overdue," Byrne said, "but there has been much to do. The dead deserve our respect." She hung her head a moment, genuine grief twisting her features. She had lost a lot of people, Riv realized.

And she is a leader who actually cares about her warriors. I am so used to the Ben-Elim, to Israfil and then Kol. They saw us as servants, pawns. Byrne is not like that.

"But before we talk of war, and the way forward, there is something that must be resolved. Something that has long been hidden, and is now in the light." She looked at Faelan, who returned her gaze, unblinking.

"This is a moment I have long dreamed of," Faelan said, "but now that it is here, I do not know where to begin."

"Let me help you, then," Byrne said gently. "Faelan has been here more years than I have drawn breath. His mother brought him to these walls in the year 65 of the Age of Lore."

"That means you are at least seventy-three years old," Riv snorted. Faelan did not look that old.

"Aye," Faelan dipped his head. "Remember, the blood of Ben-Elim runs in my veins. I suspect I am not immortal, like my father; I am but a half-breed, blessed or cursed with long life."

"Who is your father?" Riv asked.

"I do not know," Faelan said. "My mother took that secret with her to the grave. Who is your father?"

"Kol," Riv said.

I will keep his dirty secrets no longer.

Byrne frowned at that.

Faelan nodded slowly.

"Why do you live in darkness? A secret hidden in the dark." Riv looked at Byrne, feeling her anger pulse. "You speak of truth and courage here. I do not see much of that at work in this." Her lip curled in a sneer.

She saw people tense, Drem sitting straighter, Cullen scowling at her. She did not care.

"I understand your saying that," Byrne said. "I have long struggled with it. Faelan's secret was handed to me by my predecessor, the day I became high captain of the Order. With it came an oath of secrecy, sworn in blood. Right or wrong, I do not know, but here is the logic of it." She drew a deep breath. "Faelan's mother came to my predecessor, a babe clutched in her arms, barely a moon or two on this earth. She told my predecessor and his captains of the Ben-Elim's ways, their dirty secret. Of what they did to hide that secret."

Hadran shifted in his seat, looked at the floor.

"She told us of the cabin in the woods," Byrne continued. She looked at Riv. "You will know of this place, I presume?"

"Aye. I have seen it," Riv said. "I have seen the cairns."

"I was told that the captains of the Order discussed it; at first they were outraged, and were of a mind to confront the Ben-Elim. Who knows how that would have gone? Faelan's mother pleaded against taking that course, for Faelan's sake. She said the Ben-Elim would not rest until he was dead. You must remember, Israfil was their lord. He would not brook such an affront to Elyon's Lore. To him Faelan would have been an abomination." She looked at Drem. "We nearly went to war with the Ben-Elim over you," she said to him. "Just imagine what would have happened over us sheltering a Ben-Elim half-breed."

"It would have been war," Riv said, remembering Israfil hacking the wings from a Ben-Elim who had committed the crime of kissing a human. "Israfil would not have stopped until Faelan and all who protected him were dead. There is no question about that."

"Yes," Byrne said. "That is what my predecessors believed." She shrugged. "So, the decision was made to acquiesce to Faelan's mother. The Order agreed to give her and her child shelter, to protect them and keep them secret. The tunnels were the obvious place."

"That is no place to live," Riv said.

"I like it," Faelan said. "The tunnels are safe. My people

have been safe there for over seventy years, and we leave at night by secret ways, feel the wind in our wings, patrol the night skies and the darkness. We watch over Dun Seren at night, a small way to repay our debt."

"*Craf's crows watch over Dun Seren,*" Craf squawked.

"Aye, and a grand job you make of it," Faelan said. "But even crows have to sleep."

Craf ruffled his feathers.

"Aye, we sleep safer in Dun Seren knowing that you protect the skies from dusk till dawn," Byrne said.

"Your people?" Meical interjected. "How is it that there are so many of you?"

"I met a woman." Faelan shrugged, a ripple of his wings. "One of the Order's high captains. The chamber we fought the Revenants in—that is where those of the Order go to learn their Elemental ways."

"The captains of the Order have always been party to this secret," Byrne said. "They would meet with Faelan, teach him. His letters and history, martial skills. Orina was in Kill's rank, fifty years ago."

"Ah, but she was beautiful as the moon," Faelan breathed. "We had seven children, and those children met others within the Order." He shrugged. "We have lived a good life, thanks to the Order; thanks to Byrne."

"It is no thanks to me. I have just kept the oath I swore, though I have questioned it every day. I have long felt the weight of it."

"It is no fault of yours," Faelan said. "That blame lies with the Ben-Elim." He glared at Meical, who returned the gaze, sadness in his eyes.

Hadran looked up then. "Do not blame Meical for this. He was imprisoned in a gaol of iron. And in truth, before that came to pass, he was the only Ben-Elim who spoke of you humans as…people, and he was mocked and mistreated for that. We Ben-Elim have been so wrapped up in our war with the

Kadoshim that all else has paled. We saw you as…unimportant." He hung his head. "I am ashamed to say those words out loud. And I am as guilty as any Ben-Elim. I was part of Kol's faction." He shook his head. "I cannot speak for any other Ben-Elim, but for my part, I am sorry, and I will do all in my power to make amends for the past."

Faelan stared at Hadran a long time, his gaze unblinking.

"I will watch you, and see if your words ring true," he said eventually. "Forgive me if I am not disposed to place much faith in the word of a Ben-Elim."

"That is fair enough," Hadran said. "My deeds will attest to the truth of my words."

"Time will be the judge of that," Faelan said.

A silence settled over the room.

"So, we are kin," Riv said to Faelan. "I am not alone in this world."

"Just so," Faelan said, a shy smile twitching his mouth. Riv felt her own smile spread across her face.

"Well, I'm glad that's sorted out," a voice said. Cullen. "Now, can we talk about the business of killing Asroth?"

Balur One-Eye rumbled a laugh.

"Yes," said Byrne. "There is much to discuss." She looked at Meical and Hadran. "You came here for a reason, but Nara and her people arrived before we could speak properly."

"I apologize for the inconvenience," Queen Nara said, though Riv saw a twitch of her lips.

"No inconvenience," Byrne said, "we are glad to have another thousand warriors in our ranks."

"We are glad to be alive," Nara said.

Byrne looked back to Meical and Hadran.

"We came to tell you of Drassil's fall, of Asroth's return."

"You have done that already," Byrne said, "and yet you stay?"

"Aye." Meical dipped his head. "There was a battle to fight, and a friendship to prove."

"Granted," Byrne said. "And yet you are still here."

"We are allies in the war against Asroth. We should talk of the way forward. Together."

"I agree," Byrne said.

"We should share all we know," Ethlinn said. "Our expedition in the north, the news from Drassil. Questions we both have may be answered that way."

"That is wisdom," Byrne agreed. "Meical, Hadran, when you arrived we had not long returned from the north, where we fought with a warband of acolytes and other creatures."

"Ferals and mist-walkers?" Riv said through a mouthful of cheese. "Like the ones we fought here?"

"Aye," Balur grunted.

"Amongst other things," Cullen said.

"Other things?" Riv raised an eyebrow.

"A snake-woman," said Byrne. "A terrible creation, born of the earth power, a corruption of blood and bone."

"And a draig with wings," Keld said.

"Where have these creatures come from?" Meical frowned. "This is not the Banished Lands I remember."

"Fritha." The name was whispered. It took Riv a moment to realize that Drem had uttered the name. He was looking down at the table.

"Fritha has done this," he said, looking up and meeting Meical's dark gaze. "She is called *priestess* by the Kadoshim and their acolytes. It was Fritha who *changed* Gulla, made the Revenants, the Ferals, a draig with wings, all of them."

"She was at Drassil," Riv said, sitting up straighter. "With her draig. They smashed the shield wall like twigs. She freed Asroth with a black sword."

"My father's sword," Drem said. "Forged from starstone metal with the purpose of slaying Asroth."

"Well, that didn't go quite according to plan," Riv remarked. "Did your da think this through?"

"Fritha murdered him and took his sword," Drem said.

"Oh." Riv looked down.

"I will take the sword back from her and fulfil my father's oath," Drem said. His face was flat, emotionless. At this moment he reminded Riv of Bleda and his face of stone.

He thinks he's going to kill Asroth.

It was a ludicrous claim, especially when Drem was sitting in a room with some of the greatest warriors in the Banished Lands. Byrne, Balur One-Eye.

Me.

And yet there was something about the way he said it that gave Riv pause.

"Aye, well, to kill Asroth we've got to find him. And to find him we need to get off our arses and go after him," red-haired Cullen said. "What are we waiting for?"

"*Whisht*, Cullen," Byrne snapped. "Not every problem is solved by charging at it."

Cullen looked as if he disagreed and was about to say so, but Keld shifted beside him and Cullen winced.

Did Keld just stamp on Cullen's foot?

"There is wisdom in Cullen's words," Meical said.

"See?" Cullen muttered.

"Every moment you remain here is another day that Asroth grows stronger, tightens his grip."

"You all saw those Revenants, what they can do. I will not throw my warriors' lives away because we rushed into battle unprepared," Byrne told him. "I aim to put a rune-marked weapon in the fist of every warrior here—man, woman and giant." She paused, drew in a long breath. "But I know time is vital. The longer we wait, the longer Asroth and Gulla have to consolidate their grip on the Banished Lands. The more innocents will die." She looked between Hadran and Meical. "What is your plan? Your purpose for coming here?"

"Asroth is free, his enemies should work together," Riv said. "Otherwise Asroth will pick us all off one by one."

Ethlinn nodded. "There is wisdom in that," she said.

"What allies?" Balur said. "Who is left?"

"Kol still lives," Hadran said. "He leads the survivors of Drassil—Ben-Elim and White-Wings—south, to join with our garrison at Ripa. There are over seven thousand White-Wings spread along the borders of the Land of the Faithful, but most of them are at Ripa or close to it. He asks that you join us there, and that we face Asroth together."

Riv felt a stab of worry thinking about Aphra marching south through Forn.

Byrne steepled her fingers, brows knitting.

"Ripa is a long way," she said.

"Drassil's closer," Cullen said. "Best we go there, kill Asroth, toast our victory."

Byrne and Keld tutted him. Balur chuckled.

"What are your numbers here?" Meical asked.

"Around two thousand warriors of the Order. Less, since the battle."

"Two hundred giants," Ethlinn said. "Some with bears."

"A thousand warriors of Ardain," Nara and Elgin said together.

"That is not enough to take Drassil," Riv said.

"We've fought the Kadoshim long enough to know how to beat them," Cullen said, a curl of his lip.

"There are too many of them," Meical replied, shaking his head.

"There cannot be so many Kadoshim." Byrne frowned. "A hundred years of battle and hunting them has seen their numbers dwindle."

"They have bred an army of half-breeds," Hadran said with a scowl. "Thousands of them."

A widening of Byrne's eyes, then she nodded. "Gulla has planned long and well, it would seem."

"I've seen you train," Riv said, "and had the honour of fighting alongside you. You are a force to be reckoned with, of that there is no question."

Cullen snorted.

"But if you go alone you will be outnumbered and over-whelmed. They have warriors in the air, acolytes, *thousands* of these mist-walkers—"

"Revenants," Drem interrupted.

"What?" Riv said.

"They are called Revenants. I told you, that's what Fritha named them, and she created them, so she should know." He looked agitated.

"Fine. Revenants," Riv continued, scowling at Drem, "and Cheren horse-archers."

"The Cheren are allied to Asroth?" Byrne asked.

"Aye. They made a deal with Gulla, betrayed us. It was the Cheren who used a ruse to open Drassil's gates for Gulla's acolytes."

Byrne drummed her fingers on the table.

"The greatest warriors in the world could not hope to win against these odds," Riv continued. "Even with your magic swords."

Byrne just looked at her.

"We need each other," Meical said. "You need the Ben-Elim to fight in the air, the White-Wings to hold the ground with their wall of shields. The Order of the Bright Star and Ethlinn's giants would be the hammer against their anvil."

"What of the Cheren?" Byrne said. "I have seen their bow and horse work. They are not a force to be taken lightly. We would need to counter them, somehow."

"We have the Sirak," Riv said with a smile.

"The Sirak are allied to you?" Byrne said. "Truly? I doubt they have much love for the Ben-Elim."

"My Bleda has given his word. He is riding to Arcona now, to raise his Clan."

"Your Bleda?" Balur rumbled, raising an eyebrow.

"Yes," Riv said, feeling her face flush with colour. "*My* Bleda." She liked saying it out loud.

Byrne studied Riv, slowly she nodded. "Love is the strongest oath," she said.

"The warriors you have here," Meical asked, "is this your full strength?"

"No," Byrne said. "I summoned many for the campaign into the Desolation, but our holds have been left manned."

"There is a garrison at Balara," Shar spoke for the first time. Her eyes were still red-rimmed and sunken. "Two hundred swords. They would be disappointed to miss a battle with Asroth."

"Balara?" Riv said.

"A giant ruin in the south. It is not far from Ripa," Byrne said.

Meical smiled.

"There are others at Brikan and other places," Kill said. "Perhaps another thousand in all."

"We will need them all," Meical said. "The battle is coming that will decide the fate of the Banished Lands for the next thousand years. Every man, woman and giant who would stand against Asroth and his Kadoshim should be there. It will be our only chance. We must wipe them all from the face of this earth."

"To my mind it is the Revenants that pose the greatest danger," Byrne said. "You saw them at Drassil?" she asked Riv.

"Aye. Impossible to tell their numbers; they moved in the forest and were shrouded in mist, but I saw five hosts converging on Drassil, each similar to the host we have just fought."

"We have burned over four thousand Revenant corpses," Tain the giant said.

Cullen wiggled his fingers, frowning. "Twenty thousand?" he said.

"Aye," Byrne nodded. "Even if every man, woman and giant here went into battle with a rune-marked blade we would be overwhelmed by such numbers."

"And their numbers swell with every victim," Ethlinn said.

"All the more reason to move quickly," Cullen muttered.

"We have to kill their captains," a voice said: Drem. "There were seven of them. Seven people that Gulla drank from that night. Ulf and Arvid are now dead, and their broods with them."

"Do you remember them?" Byrne asked him.

Drem frowned.

"Scar-faced Burg." He put a hand to his throat, fingers brushing a discoloration around his neck. "He tried to hang me; I won't be forgetting his face. Tyna, Ulf's wife. She made good soup. Thel and Ormun, two brothers, they were trappers, like me and Da..." He trailed off a moment, looked out of the window to the north. "The last one I did not know. His head was shaved short, like one of the Kadoshim acolytes. He was tall, slim. A scar over one eye, making it droop, like this." He pulled the skin down over his right eye.

"Well, let's find them and kill them," Balur growled.

"Aye, that's a plan I like," Cullen said, snapping his fingers. "Find the five that still live and kill them. That would just leave us with Kadoshim, half-breeds, fanatical acolytes and the Cheren to fight." He grinned. "Easy."

"I have a better plan," Drem said. All in the room looked at him. "Kill Gulla, and the five will fall and all their Revenants with them."

CHAPTER THIRTY-FOUR

BLEDA

Bleda sat on his horse and stared, the long grass of Arcona sighing in the wind about his horse's legs.

"No," he whispered.

He was staring at a Sirak camp. Flames crackled, gers burned to charred husks, and great clouds of black smoke billowed across the plain. Bodies scattered the ground, arrows and spears protruding from their charred, twisted remains.

We are too late.

A click of his tongue and his horse walked forwards. She was a skewbald mare, her name Dilis, which meant *Faithful* in the old tongue. Ruga, Ellac and Yul spread around him, his warband shifting into motion behind him. They had ridden hard to reach here, over a moon. The hardest part of the journey had been travelling through the snarl of Forn from the cabin to the east road. After that they had moved fast, the road cutting like an arrow from Drassil to the plateau of Arcona.

On the road they had found signs that had troubled Bleda: hoof-prints and dung indicating a large body of riders was ahead of them, the gap widening with every day. Wyrms of worry had been coiling in his belly since then.

Grass turned to ash beneath his horse's hooves, his warband spreading wide, ninety-eight riders, all that was left of his honour guard and the warband his mother had brought to Drassil. Bleda passed a charred corpse clutching a spear in their belly, another face-down with three arrows in the back. More and more. Here and there a horse stood over a corpse, head low. Such was the bond between rider and horse that Sirak mounts would often return to their riders, dead or alive.

A touch of Bleda's ankles and Dilis stopped. He leaned and gripped a spear shaft, tugged it free from another corpse.

"A Cheren spear," Ellac grunted beside him.

"Aye." Bleda sighed. He hefted the spear—the balance was excellent—and slipped it into the leather ring on his saddle.

"Search for any survivors," he said. "Gather the horses and arrows."

Smoke in the distance, faint screams on the wind.

They were three days deeper into Sirak lands, following the trail of destruction the Cheren were leaving. Seven more Sirak camps, hundreds dead. They had a change of mounts, now, though, which made their progress faster, and they were gaining. Bleda also had another twenty riders in his warband, survivors they had found, unconscious, wounded, all somehow overlooked by the Cheren.

They are moving fast, not taking the time to check the dead or even gather up their arrows. We will use them to slay those that made them.

A gentle rise in the land, beyond which the shouts were louder. Bleda signalled, the column of riders behind him spreading wide, like wings. Another signal and a score of riders peeled away from each wing, circling wider.

We should scout our enemy out, learn their numbers, approach cautiously, a voice in his head whispered. But there was a fire in his belly, his heart pounding with the frustration of seeing his people slaughtered.

Fresh cries on the wind, louder.

He slipped his bow from its case, gripped a fistful of arrows and took Dilis to a gallop, leaning low to the arch of her neck.

He glimpsed Yul smile to his right, heard the drum of Ellac and Ruga's horses' hooves close behind.

And then he was cresting the ridge. Black clouds rolled up the slope, engulfing him for a moment. He rode on, blind, burst out into bright sunlight.

Instantly he knew that he was outnumbered. There were Cheren riders everywhere, a flock of warriors swirling through the camp before him in their sky-blue deels, mail and leather, bows in their fists. Impossible to tell accurately how many, but there were more than his hundred and twenty. Gers were on fire, flames reaching for the sky, Sirak warriors on the ground. The old and children as well. Others running for their horses. Bleda saw one leap onto her mount, an arrow taking her in the shoulder, throwing her back to the ground. She scrambled to her knees, but the Cheren rider was rearing over her, hooves crashing down, trampling her.

Another Sirak warrior was running up the incline, straight towards Bleda, three Cheren riders pursuing him. The Sirak stumbled, unsure of who Bleda was as he burst from a cloud of smoke. The riders behind him were galloping, screeching their battle-cries like the hawk that filled their banners. Bleda nocked and loosed, leaning over his mount's neck; the first Cheren rider was punched from his saddle with Bleda's arrow in his eye. The second Cheren fell backwards over his saddle with an arrow in his chest, Bleda slowing to look down at the Sirak warrior stumbling to a halt before him. Yul and Ruga swept past Bleda, their arrows pin-cushioning the last Cheren rider.

"Who are you?" the Sirak warrior breathed.

"I am your kin," Bleda said. Ellac reined in beside Bleda, a small shield strapped to his right forearm, a spear in his left fist.

"Ellac?" the warrior said.

"Aye, it is me, returned to give you a kick up the arse, Oktai. Now turn around, put some sharp iron in your fist and fight for your Clan."

Bleda's warband swept over the rise, bursting out of the smoke, and rode screaming battle-cries into the camp. Bleda grabbed more arrows from his quiver and rode on, Ruga and Yul sweeping wide and circling back to join him.

In a handful of heartbeats all turned to chaos. The slope had given some sense of the conflict, a detached view, but down here amidst the smoke and flame, warriors appeared from nowhere, horses thundering, the whistle of arrows through the air, iron clashing, screaming, smoke choking and stinging eyes, flames swirling. Bleda's horse jumped over a Sirak warrior lying on the ground, trying to hold his intestines in, purple rope glistening between his fingers.

Bleda nocked and loosed, nocked and loosed, one arrow slamming into a Cheren's back, throwing him forwards in his saddle. He took another through the throat as they raised a spear to skewer a Sirak on the ground.

"UP," Bleda yelled at the fallen warrior as he rode past him, swerving amongst a cluster of gers, putting another Cheren down. His blood pounded through his veins: anger, fear, exhilaration combining into a heady joy that swept through him. Finally, to *do*, to *fight*, instead of thinking, chasing, worrying. His body took over, virtually no room for thought as he charged through the Sirak camp. Countless years of training, of allowing muscles to act in pre-programmed patterns. His arrows left a trail of the dead in his wake. Dimly Bleda was aware of Ellac at his left shoulder, a shadow protecting his flank. He was not sure if Ruga and Yul were still with him. A cloud of smoke billowed across him, the sound of hooves and clash of iron loud in his ears. Bleda slipped his bow back into its case and reached over his shoulder, drawing his sword. Then he was through the smoke, a knot of Cheren riders in front of him, eight or nine warriors stabbing and slashing down at a handful of Sirak, all of them on foot, desperately trying to stay alive a few heartbeats longer.

"ERDENE!" Bleda screamed, and spurred Dilis into them. A jarring crash as horseflesh collided, Bleda chopping right, a downwards, diagonal slash that opened the face of a Cheren warrior as he turned at Bleda's scream. Bleda swayed in his saddle, a spear-point stabbing past his eyes, the upswing of his sword striking the spear shaft, Ellac finishing the woman holding it, his own spear punching into her throat. Bleda urged his horse on, constant movement, steel sparks as he parried a clumsy strike at his torso, a counterstrike at his opponent's head, denting his helm, blood sheeting the man's face, blinding him for a moment, Bleda's sword opening his throat.

Then he was through the knot of riders, Ellac following. Bleda pulled on his reins, Dilis turning in a tight circle, just in time to see Yul and Ruga emerge from the smoke and crash into the Cheren. Ruga snarled as she fought, mouth twisted. In four or five breaths she severed a hand at the wrist, cut into a shoulder, links of mail spraying, and slashed a warrior's thigh. Yul, beside her, moved like a warrior from the tales. Bleda could only track the man's blade by the arcs of blood that it left in the air and the warriors slumping or falling in their saddles. A head spun through the air, thumped to the ground and rolled up to the hooves of Bleda's horse.

The Sirak on the ground dragged the last Cheren from her saddle and she disappeared from view. A scream cut short, and then there were no more Cheren breathing.

"Up!" Yul shouted, holding the reins of a Cheren mount and offering them to one of the Sirak on the ground. There were four still standing, all of them grabbing weapons and leaping into Cheren saddles.

"WITH ME!" Bleda cried, and turned his horse, riding on into the camp. Yul, Ruga and the others caught up with him.

Like a wave they swept through the spaces between gers, Cheren falling, confused by this new attack from behind. Bleda's sword was notched and slick with blood when he burst out of the far side of the camp. A score of Cheren riders were ahead of him. Their leader, an older warrior, his warrior braid grey as it curled beneath his helm, sat on his horse a moment, the animal dancing.

He hesitates, unsure what to do.

Ruga put an arrow through the warrior's throat, the man swaying and toppling.

More Sirak emerged from the gers, a line forming either side of Bleda. The remaining Cheren turned away and spurred their mounts into a gallop.

"They can't get away," Ruga snarled.

"They won't," Bleda said.

The two score riders he had sent wide appeared, curling around the camp and riding towards the fleeing Cheren, cutting off their escape route. A flurry of blows, the clash of steel, and then it was over, Bleda's warriors cantering towards him. Many of them were grinning and whooping.

Bleda felt a rush of joy, at being alive, at being victorious. He looked about him, saw men and women from this camp about him, others joining them, as well as more of his own warband appearing. He patted Dilis' neck, the mare sidling on the spot, the thrill of battle coursing through her muscles, too.

Ruga grabbed Bleda's wrist and punched it into the air.

"BLEDA!" she screamed, Ellac and Yul and the others taking up the chant.

"BLEDA!"

Bleda pulled his arm free and rode on a few paces, turned so that all could see him, waited for the chanting to stop.

"This is not the time to celebrate our victory," he cried. "The Cheren are killing our people. We are the only hope of saving them. Search the camp, tend the wounded, put all who can ride and hold a bow in a saddle. Then we ride."

His warriors turned and made their way back into the camp. Old Ellac was sitting on his horse, staring at Bleda. Their eyes met and Ellac smiled at him, dipped his head.

That meant more to Bleda than a thousand voices shouting his name.

CHAPTER THIRTY-FIVE

DREM

Drem stood in the weapons-field of Dun Seren, dawn's light washing over him, high cloud tinged with pink and orange. The air was sharp and crisp, a freshness to the day's start that filled Drem's lungs.

It feels pure.

Others were rowed either side of Drem, ninety or a hundred in total. Many of them were young, no more than sixteen or seventeen summers. Cullen had told Drem that they were warriors from Ardain who had travelled here with Sig over a year ago, hoping to become warriors of the Order. And then there were the half-breeds from the caverns. Faelan stood with around sixty of his kin, an assortment of wing colours. Faelan appeared utterly focused, his back straight.

Byrne stood before him, Kill and Tain either side of her, Craf perched upon Tain's shoulder. And behind them, all of the Order of the Bright Star. Around two thousand warriors, dressed in their war gear, looking at Drem and those around him. He could see Keld and Cullen watching him, both of them solemn-faced. Rab the white crow was sitting on Cullen's forearm, Cullen absently scratching his feathers. Shar was there, her face still marked by her grief. So many others.

Behind Drem he heard the murmuring of a crowd. Many who were not warriors of the Order were gathered; Ethlinn and her giants, a few hundred warriors, Meical and Riv and the Ben-Elim, Queen Nara, Elgin, Madoc and a thousand others.

So many people, all staring at me and a handful of others.

It was making Drem feel uncomfortable. He fought the urge to put his fingers to his neck and take his pulse.

You have fought two battles. Faced a Revenant horde. Stop being an idiot.

Byrne stepped forwards.

"These are exceptional times," she said, "and they call for exceptional measures. Usually, to join the Order of the Bright Star, you would take your warrior trial before us all; sword, shield, spear, net, the running mount. But to do that would be to disrespect you. You have come through the furnace of combat. You have stood with us, shoulder to shoulder, and risked your lives in the defence of this fortress. Not just the rock and stone, but the values this fortress is built upon, that our lives are built upon." She paused, taking a moment to look each one of them in the eye.

"Truth and Courage. Those are the words that define a warrior of this Order. They are more than words; they are a way of life. Would you choose them? You will be swearing to a life of hardship, a life where you put aside your own pleasures and desires, and place yourself in danger's way. Again, and again, and again."

My mother and father stood here once, on this field, and swore this oath.

A moment's silence. Then, as one, Drem and the others responded.

"I will."

Byrne nodded. "Then say these words after me." She sucked in a deep breath.

"Tru—"

The flapping of wings from above and a figure descended from the sky, dapple-grey wings beating, breaking her fall, and Riv alighted before Byrne. Her wings drew in tight, a twitch and ripple as Riv stood there, dust settling around her.

"Will you take me?" she asked Byrne.

Byrne stared at her.

"You would take our oath?"

"I would," Riv said.

"Have you thought this through? You have other allegiances."

"I have a mother, whom I love more than life. But she is a warrior; she knows the life we choose. She would be proud of me."

"And your father?"

"I care not what he thinks. I have thought this through. Being here, standing with you...it is hard for me to put into words. It is like coming home..." She shrugged. "So, I ask you again. Will you take me?"

A small smile touched the edges of Byrne's mouth. "I would be glad to hear you take our oath," she said. "And proud to call you sister."

Riv looked at her, almost as if she was surprised Byrne had said yes.

"My thanks," Riv said.

"Join the line," Byrne told her, and Riv stepped backwards, Drem shuffling to his left to make room for her. He nodded to her as she slipped in beside him, one of her wings squashing against him.

She looks more nervous than when we went into battle.

Riv drew in a long, deep breath, her shoulders rising, held it and then blew it out slowly.

"Repeat these words after me," Byrne called out, her voice ringing in the morning air. "Truth and courage are the banners I live by."

"Truth and courage are the banners I live by," Drem said, slow and clear, his voice mingling with Riv's and a hundred others.

"Love, loyalty and friendship shall be my guiding light."

Drem echoed Byrne's words, the weight of them resonating within him. He could almost hear his da whispering them in his ear, his father's voice, cracked with the years, the voice that had cared for him, taught him, loved him.

"I will be the bright star in the night sky, the candle in the darkness."

Drem spoke on, tears running silently down his cheeks as the ghost of his father said the oath with him.

Oh, Da, I miss you so.

"The defender of the innocent, protector of the weak. I will bring hope to the lost, give my life for the helpless." He swallowed, trying to get rid of the lump in his throat.

"With Truth as my shield," Byrne called out, and Drem echoed her. "And Courage as my sword, I shall stand against the darkness."

I will, Drem thought. *I belong here, with these people, living this life.*

The field seemed to ring with the words, Drem's heart pounding.

"From this day on, until the time of my death."

The words faded, a ringing echo returning from the high northern wall.

Byrne stood before them, a silence settled.

Drem glanced at Riv, saw tears staining her cheek.

Byrne opened her mouth one last time.

"This is my oath," she cried, "sealed with my blood."

"This is my oath," Drem said, and drew his seax, slicing it across his palm, making a fist that dripped red droplets of blood onto the grass.

"Sealed with my blood."

A stillness settled over the field, Drem staring at Byrne and the Order of the Bright Star behind her. He saw Keld and Cullen, though their faces were blurred through his tears.

Then the Order erupted in cheering.

CHAPTER THIRTY-SIX

RIV

A wall of sound hit Riv, the Order's cheering almost deafening her.

Riv blew out a long, shaky breath, her chest rising and falling as if she'd run a dozen leagues.

What have I done? A White-Wing becoming one of the Order of the Bright Star, our greatest rivals. She wanted to laugh, felt the emotion bubbling in her chest. *But it feels so right. My life at Drassil was a lie. All of it a deceit to keep me in my place, and to further the Ben-Elim's cause. But this place is not like that. These people are not like that. They accept me for who I am. So I too can accept what I am. The real me, and a fresh start.*

I feel as if I've been reborn.

She smiled, a grin that made her face ache, at everyone and no one.

"Truth and courage," she whispered.

"Welcome, sister," a voice said beside her. Drem. He was smiling at her, and offering her his arm. His smile changed his face. It was not something she remembered seeing on him, unlike his friend, Cullen, who seemed to smile all the time.

And especially when he's going into battle.

She took Drem's offered arm in the warrior grip.

"Brother," she said, liking the sound and feel of that.

Byrne was the first to reach them, a hand on each of their shoulders, emotion bright in her eyes. She stepped back and straightened, looking at them both. Tain and Kill appeared at Byrne's shoulder, each of them holding something. Tain had a folded grey-green cloak of simply spun wool. Kill held something out in her palm, an iron cloak brooch about the size of Riv's fist. It was fashioned into the shape of a four-pointed star.

"Welcome to the Order of the Bright Star," Byrne said formally, taking the cloak from Tain and throwing it around Riv's shoulders. She then took the brooch from Kill and pinned the cloak in place, adjusting the brooch so that it sat upon the left side of Riv's chest.

"My thanks," Riv said, not knowing what else to say, her emotions too complicated to articulate.

Byrne gave her a formal nod and moved on to Drem. Tain grinned at her.

"Welcome," he said.

"Thank you," Riv murmured, still trying to master the emotions in her veins.

Craf was perched upon Tain's shoulder.

"*More warriors with wings*," the crow muttered. He didn't sound too impressed.

Riv looked up at the bird.

"I am honoured to share the skies with you, Craf," she said.

Craf looked at her with a far too intelligent eye. "*Welcome to the Order*," he squawked down at her.

Byrne leaned close to Drem and said words Riv could not hear, but Drem blinked away a tear and smiled, and then Byrne, Kill and Tain were moving along the line and Cullen was upon them, all laughter and hugs. Keld was just behind him, and more of the Order offering congratulations. Even the white crow, Rab, was there, flapping and squawking excitedly. Shar suddenly appeared before Riv, her eyes still red-veined with his grief.

"Welcome, sister," she said. Riv remembered Shar kneeling in the dirt, Utul's body in her lap.

"You slew my Utul's killer," she said. "I am in your debt."

"No, you're not," Riv said. "No debt. I did what any one of us would have done, given the chance."

"What happens in our heads," Shar said, tapping her temple, "and what we actually do, can be a world apart." She shrugged. "Anyway, I have made you a gift, for avenging Utul." She held a linen-wrapped package out to Riv, tied with leather.

Riv stared at it, hesitated. She was not used to compliments, or gifts.

"Do not offend me by refusing," Shar said. "My heart is wounded enough."

Riv tugged on the leather and opened the bundle.

She gasped.

It was two swords in polished leather scabbards. They were short, like her own White-Wing blades, the hilts leather-wrapped. The cross-guards were gently curved, wings engraved upon them.

"They are rune-marked," Shar said, "by my own hand. They will never fail you; they will stay sharp as any razor, never notch or break."

"I-I don't know what to say," Riv said, not able to tear her eyes away. She reached out and took one in her hand. The scabbard was soft and freshly waxed. With a hiss of steel she drew the first sword, then drew the other one and touched them together, a gentle chink, and held them close to her ears, listening to their sword song.

She smiled and held them before her, rolled them in her wrists. They caught the rising sun, glowed red.

"Beautiful," she whispered. "You honour me, Shar. My thanks. A thousand times, my thanks."

Shar smiled at her. "We shall kill Revenants together," she said. "And avenge Utul again and again, until these Revenants are no more."

"That is a pact I will gladly agree to," Riv said, unable to keep a grin from splitting her face.

She sheathed the swords and Shar helped her strap them to

her weapons-belt. When she was happy that all was right and that no adjustments needed to be made, Shar bade her farewell and left.

Riv stood there, looking about the field. Drem was close by, with Keld and Cullen, others of the Order congratulating the new recruits. Byrne and Kill were talking with Faelan.

A tremor in the ground and Riv turned.

Balur One-Eye was looking down at her, Queen Ethlinn beside him.

"Well, you have come a long way since you failed your warrior trial a year ago," he rumbled.

"Ha," Riv said. A flash of Israfil the Lord Protector, High Captain of the Ben-Elim, as he fought her, goaded her with insults and half-truths, testing her temper and self-control.

That did not end well.

"I have not thought on that for a long while," Riv said. "At the time I thought my world had ended, that my life was over."

"And look at you now," Ethlinn said. She gave Riv a long, appraising look that made Riv feel uncomfortable. "I am glad for you, young one," Ethlinn said. "You blaze bright as the sun. The world is a better place for having you in it."

Riv blinked at that. She could not remember ever having spoken to Ethlinn before, although she had admired her many times in the weapons-field, especially her skill with a spear.

"Well, got nothing to say to my daughter?" Balur grunted.

"Forgive me," Riv said. "I am not often lost for words."

Balur barked a laugh at that.

"I did not know that you had even noticed I was alive, all my years at Drassil," Riv said to Ethlinn. "And, I should also say that I am not used to compliments."

"Ha, Ethlinn notices *everything* and everyone." Balur smiled. "It is her gift. And she is not given to handing out compliments, either."

"A warrior does not just fight," Ethlinn said, a wry smile on her face. "First a warrior must *see*. And I give compliments where I see them due," she added, looking at Balur.

He chuckled at that, too.

He laughs a lot more here, at Dun Seren, than he ever did at Drassil.

"I've watched you, too," Balur said. "You've still got a bit of a temper, though." He ruffled Riv's hair.

"Aye," Riv conceded. "I'm still working on that."

"Self-control is overrated," Balur said with a smile.

"Truth and courage," Ethlinn said, tapping Riv's new cloak brooch. "You could do much worse than live your life by those values."

"That's what I think," Riv said, looking at the cut on her palm, starting to scab, now. "That is my oath. That's what I'll do."

A horn rang out over the field, long and haunting. It fell silent and then sounded again.

All conversation stopped.

"That is it, then," Balur said. "It's time to go."

"What is that horn?" Riv asked.

"The call to war," Ethlinn said.

Riv stood on the wall above Dun Seren's gates, staring at the statue of Corban and Storm. Meical and Hadran were beside her, seven more Ben-Elim close by. They stood in silence, waiting.

The crack of hooves on stone, and the thud and rumble of bears.

Byrne appeared, mounted at the head of a host. She was clothed in mail and leather, sword at her hip, a spear couched in a saddle-cup. Kill rode one side of her, gleaming in mail, Tain striding on the other, a long spear in his fist. Behind them rode the Order of the Bright Star, the sun shimmering on their helms and coats of mail, spear-tips glinting, shields with the bright star painted upon them slung across backs or hanging from saddle straps. Amongst them all, one warrior stood out to Riv: Drem, black-haired and tall in his saddle, his mail glinting, a helm and shield hanging from saddle straps. His new cloak brooch shone bright upon his chest.

He was riding the white bear.

Riv grinned to see it. The warriors of the Order were all around him, Cullen and Keld there, but Drem sat above them. He was a big man, tall and broad, but he still looked small upon the bear's back.

Byrne rode through the courtyard, looking up at the statue of Corban and Storm as she passed them, then looking up at Riv and Meical as she passed through the gates and out into Dun Seren's streets.

A raucous squawking and flapping of wings and Riv saw a cloud of crows burst from the keep's tower, swirling lower and following the battle-host.

"*WAR*," they croaked, as they passed over Riv, "*WAR*," repeating their chant again and again.

In the courtyard the last of the Order passed through the gates, over two thousand warriors, and then Queen Nara rode in, Madoc at her side and Elgin behind, leading her warriors. A grey-cloaked warband a thousand strong, the banner of a snarling wolven rippling above them.

Nara and her warband passed through Dun Seren's gates and finally Ethlinn and her giants appeared, wrapped in mail and leather, the ground trembling with their arrival. Riv guessed at a hundred and fifty bears that came lumbering into the courtyard, perhaps fewer, another hundred or so giants striding amongst them. As they passed through the courtyard Meical nodded down at Balur and Ethlinn, and then his wings were spreading and beating and he was airborne. Riv crouched and jumped, wings powering her up, Hadran and the Ben-Elim around her.

Wind filled her wings and she laughed with the joy of it, Meical glancing at her, a smile cracking even his serious face. They spiralled upwards together, and from behind the keep Riv saw more winged figures appear: Faelan and his kin, flying to join the war-host as it left Dun Seren.

Meical led Riv, Hadran and the Ben-Elim on a wide loop of the warband, swooping back over Byrne as she rode through the outer gates of Dun Seren, out into a rolling meadow. Byrne reached a fork in the road and she turned east, towards the dark of Forn Forest.

At Byrne's council of war they had talked long into the day, debating the best strategy to pursue. A strike on Drassil, Cullen had advocated. Meical had petitioned that Byrne march south-east to Ripa and join forces with Kol and the White-Wings. In the end they had all agreed that they could not waste time at Dun Seren while scouts travelled the land to ascertain where Asroth was. Byrne proposed that they wait at Dun Seren until all who were fit to march to war were equipped with a rune-marked blade. It had taken fifteen nights for that goal to be achieved. In the meantime crows had flown east, sent to scout Drassil and report.

"Asroth and Gulla are our goal," Byrne had said. *"Slay them and this war is over. We will go where they are."*

Meical had not been happy about this decision, but as yet they did not know where Asroth was.

"He may have marched south after Kol and his host," Meical had said. *"That is what I would do. Strike my foe where they are strongest, before they have time to grow stronger."*

"Maybe," Byrne had agreed. *"If that is the case, then we shall march for Ripa. But I will not march blind."* So they had agreed to march eastwards until they received words from Craf's scouts.

Riv hoped that the final decision would be to travel to Ripa, for that was where she had asked Bleda to meet her.

If he is successful in Arcona and gathers his Clan. If he even still lives.

She felt a pang of worry at that, and a stab of anger, already swearing to slaughter any who dared lay a hand on her Bleda.

He still lives, she told herself. *And I will see him again. If we do not fly for Ripa, then I will get word to him, somehow. We shall meet where the Kadoshim are. Wherever we fly, the Kadoshim will be there. That is where the great battle of our time will take place.*

CHAPTER THIRTY-SEVEN

JIN

Wind whipped tears from Jin's eyes as she leaned forwards in her saddle, the feathers of an arrow tickling her cheek as she drew and loosed. Two more arrows followed in quick succession before the first one hit its mark, a Sirak warrior standing open-mouthed before the opening to his ger. She imagined him with Bleda's face. He fell back into the tent, clutching the arrow sprouting from his chest.

She rode on, slowing her mount with her knees, loosing an arrow into the darkness of the tent opening, just in case someone else was about to emerge. A scream followed her as she sped past the ger, telling her she had guessed right. Slowing again, she reached for another handful of arrows, searching for her next target. There was no shortage of them, Sirak all about her stumbling from their tents in the cold half-light of dawn. Men, women, children. She saw two of them fall with her arrows in them. The drum of hooves, Gerel appearing to her right, a blazing torch in his fist. He tossed it onto the roof of a ger; flames leaped skywards as the felt started to crackle and burn. All about, Cheren riders overtook her, forming a line of torches, some thrown, trailing flames through the air. In a dozen heartbeats the camp was on fire, entering its death-throes as her warriors carved their way through another Sirak encampment.

Jin reined in, looking around. This was the seventh Sirak

holding she had struck. She had lost count of those that had died by her own hand, each death a personal message to Bleda.

It is not enough.

She reached for another fistful of arrows.

It was midday before they were done, the sun a furnace in the sky, sweat running from Jin's face. The elation of battle had dimmed, leaving her tired and thirsty. Gerel offered her a water skin and she took it without comment, drinking deeply, and watching as Tark rode towards her. The old scout had a rope tied to his saddle, a score of Sirak bound to it by their wrists, being dragged across the plain. Behind them their camp burned, bodies cooking in the flames.

Tark rode up and reined in, yanked on the rope and warriors stumbled to their knees before Jin.

"Kneel before your Queen," Tark said.

One of the Sirak, a woman with grey in her warrior braid, her body lean and striated with muscle, looked up at Jin and spat at her.

Tark's spear stabbed her in the throat, in and out like a fast punch.

The woman swayed, tried to say something but only blood issued from her mouth. She fell on her face, a twitch of her foot and then she was still.

"Be respectful, or die," Tark said. He looked at Jin. "We have saved some, as you wished," he said.

"So I see," Jin said. "Put them with the others."

Tark slipped from his saddle and took an axe from his weapons-belt. He calmly chopped at the wrists of the dead Sirak, hacking through meat and bone. When he was done, he climbed back into his saddle and led the prisoners away, towards a row of wains that were rolling into view, ten of them, already stuffed full of Sirak prisoners.

At first Jin and her people had glutted themselves on the

slaughter of the Sirak, the fulfilment of a dream long hoped for. Seven camps they had put to steel and flame, a frenzy of killing, their bloodlust an endless wave. But Jin had realized that this would soon come to an end. It was almost too easy. She decided to take some prisoners, just a handful from each camp, so that once all of the Sirak camps had been hunted down and destroyed, they would have something to do during their celebration feast.

I will miss the screams of the Sirak, but no matter how many I hear, they do not take away my pain, or my hatred for Bleda.

I wish he were here, so that he could see the destruction of his people. I will wipe their name from this earth, so that there is no thought or memory left of them.

Her warband were moving out of the Sirak camp now. Close to a thousand riders. An overwhelming number for any of the Sirak camps they had come upon, the largest only numbering a hundred and seventy souls. The rest of her Cheren war-host she had split into bands of two hundred and cast them wide. Like a net they had set upon the Sirak borderlands, a net sixty leagues wide, and together they had swept into the Sirak lands, all travelling inwards, towards the Heartland. The Sirak were like the Cheren, with a nomadic life, extended families living and moving in camps. Setting up for a ten-night or a moon, then moving on. But they had a Heartland, just like the Cheren did. A traditional, holy place where they would gather, for a coronation, or a royal wedding, or a birth.

That is where we shall end this. Where we shall end the Sirak.

Jin sat looking into the fire-pit. A pot hung over it; Tark was stirring porridge. Grey light was seeping into the world, darker shadows shifting into the outlines of men and women, the silhouettes of gers beyond them. They had set up their site in the shadow of another fallen camp, little more now than ashes and blood beneath her hooves. There had been more resistance this time, Jin's slower pace allowing for word to run ahead of her charge towards the Sirak Heartland. They had faced mounted warriors, a pitched battle half a league before the camp, but it had helped the Sirak little. Jin liked to think that it was Cheren skill that had prevailed, but in truth she knew it was their numbers. The Sirak had been a hundred and sixty, against Jin's thousand. It had been over almost before it had started, although she had lost twenty-seven riders.

Jin had sat at this fire-pit last night and drunk with her warriors. She had been too inebriated to make her way to a ger and had fallen asleep beside the fire, listening to them drinking and toasting their victory. Toasting her.

"Great Queen," a voice said, Tark offering her a bowl of porridge.

Great Queen, they are calling me. Because I have led them to the greatest victory the Cheren have ever known. Even if we stopped now, got on our horses and rode away, this moment will live in the Cheren Clan forever. When we swept like wildfire through our enemy's land.

She felt relief, that she had led her Clan to this, that she had not failed.

I think Father would have been proud of me.

That thought caused something to hitch in her chest, and for a moment tears threatened.

No. She took a long, deep breath and pushed that emotion away.

"My thanks," she said, taking the bowl from Tark. It was hot, so she blew on it and stirred it with a wooden spoon.

She noticed Tark staring at her and raised an eyebrow.

"You are not like the Cheren," he said. "Your skin, it is smooth, soft."

Jin scowled. "I am like the Cheren, in here," she said, putting a hand over her heart. "Just because I do not look like a weathered saddlebag, like you."

Tark's lips twitched a smile, his moustache jumping.

Gerel shifted beside her, leaning forwards to ladle a bowl of porridge for himself. He blew on his porridge and spooned up a mouthful, slurping and huffing because it was too hot.

"You should wait for it to cool," Tark said to him.

"I know, but I hate waiting," Gerel said. "And my belly is cold, so the heat is no bad thing."

"Ha, tell that to the skin peeling from your lips," Tark said.

Jin snorted a laugh, the first she could remember in a long time.

"Today is the day, my Queen," Gerel said to her, smiling good-naturedly at Tark's comment.

She looked at him.

"Today we shall take the Sirak's Heartland," he said.

"Yes, we will," Jin said. There was no doubt in her mind about that. There were not enough Sirak left to stop her.

Even knowing this, Jin felt an emptiness. A knowledge deep in her belly that taking the Sirak's Heartland was not enough.

"Something troubles you?" Gerel said to her.

She sighed.

"There is more to be done," she muttered.

"More? What more?" Tark said.

"My father's vengeance," she said quietly. "This is not finished. It never will be; not while Bleda still lives."

Tark shrugged, a pragmatic gesture. "First one sows, then one reaps," he said.

"Aye. One step at a time," Jin said. "I know. But I am like Gerel. I hate waiting. I want Bleda's head on a spike *now*."

"If that were so you would have nothing left in life to look forward to," Tark said. "It will be the greatest revenge, my Queen." He looked at her over his bowl. "And it will happen. You are the Great Queen, she who has raised the Cheren up higher than a thousand generations. We will follow you to the ends of the earth, kill a nation of enemies to bring you joy."

That made Jin's blood quicken. The Cheren were a hard people, weathered by a hard life on the Sea of Grass. To hear them speak of her like this, it was another dream come true.

She smiled, an act of trust, her gift to Tark.

He looked away into the distance and ate some more porridge.

"Here comes Hulan with his riders," he said.

Jin followed his eyes, saw the shimmer of riders on the grassland, a banner in the breeze. Hulan led one of the smaller bands Jin had sent into the Sirak borderlands. If the plan had worked, all ten bands would join her today. And then they would strike the Heartland together.

Jin sat on her horse, looking into the distance. Tark and Gerel were mounted beside her, her warband gathered and waiting. Six more captains had ridden into her camp after Hulan, all with tales of victory and slaughter, but the other three groups had not been seen. No one had arrived since midday, and the sun was now sinking into the horizon.

"We can wait no longer," Tark said quietly, as Jin scanned the grasslands.

Where are they? she thought, looking to the west.

Only the sinking sun and leagues of undulating grassland.

"I know," she said. "We must ride without them." She raised her fist and Tark put a horn to his lips. With a sound like rumbling thunder, the war-host of the Cheren began to move, Jin leading them. She gave one more glance over her shoulder, hoping to see riders with the hawk banner on the horizon, but they did not appear.

Where are they?

CHAPTER THIRTY-EIGHT

BLEDA

Bleda waited in silence. He was mounted, leaning low over Dilis' neck, the felt roof of a ger brushing his head.

How long? Are they coming? Have I made a mistake?

Dilis' ears pricked forwards. He strained a moment, and then he heard it.

The drum of hooves.

"Steady," he whispered, patting her. He lifted his helm from its saddle hook and pulled it over his head, buckled the chinstrap.

The hooves louder, now, and then the first scream, a Cheren war-cry.

Bleda put a horn to his mouth and blew, at the same time touching his feet to his mount, and she burst into motion, exploding out of the ger. Daylight bright around him. Bleda dropped the horn and grabbed his curved bow from its case, a fistful of arrows, and he was nocking and drawing.

A swarm of riders were galloping towards him, blue deels, hawk banners, bows and burning torches in their fists.

He loosed at the wall of riders, a touch of his knees to keep Dilis moving—to stay still with a hundred Cheren war-bows aimed in his general direction meant certain death. A dozen arrows slapped into the space he had just been filling. One slammed into his shoulder, rocking him. He grabbed the arrow shaft, twisted and pulled the arrow out. There was no blood.

The arrowhead had pushed apart two of the iron plates of his lamellar coat, but the leather and wool beneath had snared the point. He threw the arrow away.

All around him Sirak riders burst from more gers, Yul, Ruga, Ellac, scores more, and in seven or eight heartbeats they were galloping towards the Cheren, Bleda leading them, all leaning low over their horses, arrows flying from their bows. Bleda heard a scream behind him, an arrow skimmed past his face, another *tinging* off his helm. He emptied his fist of arrows, saw riders falling in the Cheren line, so close now he could see faces, expressions of surprise and doubt amongst his enemy.

You will see how it feels to have a fair fight; this time you are not falling like hawks upon an unsuspecting mouse.

Bleda and his warriors had caught up with this Cheren warband and circled wide around them during the night, a long, arduous journey, leading their horses at a walk through the darkness. Just before dawn they had found the Sirak camp the Cheren were headed for, and warned them.

Bleda slipped his bow back into its case and reached for his sword. Sirak war-cries echoed and he knew that more of his warband would be riding at the Cheren flanks now, the trap sprung. His blade hissed into his hand and he grinned.

The hunter is now the hunted.

There was a concussion as the two lines collided, horseflesh crashing together, bones jarred, Bleda grunting with the impact as he parried an overhead blow, swept the sword down and away, a backswing counter that he felt meet the resistance of leather and then flesh. He sawed his blade free, heard a scream and then his horse's momentum carried him on, no time to check if his opponent was dead or just injured. He swayed and chopped to the right, too quick for his enemy's parry, his sword glancing off a helm, carrying on to bite between neck and shoulder. His target grunted with the pain, but still lunged at Bleda, sword stabbing at his chest.

A spear took the Cheren in the shoulder, punched through

boiled leather into flesh, Ellac appearing at Bleda's side. He shoved, pushing the Cheren from his mount, the warrior falling with a shriek and disappearing amongst churning hooves.

Bleda rode on, hacking and slicing either side of him. It was a jostling mass. Sweat stung his eyes, battle-cries and screams filled his ears. And then he was bursting into air and space, pushing through the enemy line and pulling on his reins to turn.

He paused. The battle was all but done. There had never been any doubt of the outcome. His own warband had swelled with the Sirak he had saved, over three hundred riders added to his original force. And the warriors of this camp had joined them as well, another hundred and fifty. In total almost six hundred Sirak rode with him now. There were at most only two hundred Cheren riding against them here.

Sirak warriors punched the air in victory, an ululating cry going up amongst them. Bleda felt their joy. It was a terrifying and exhilarating thing, facing another man or woman in battle, knowing that in a short space of time one of you would likely be dead. Just to see that through, to come out the other side of that conflict and realize you were alive, brought with it a rush of elation and relief. And combined to that the Sirak had the exultation of facing an age-old enemy in battle and triumphing.

"Another victory," Ruga said as she cantered up beside him, Yul and Ellac following, others behind them, chiefs of the camps Bleda had saved.

Bleda nodded at her.

"It is good to see the Cheren fall," a warrior in mail said, an older woman, her warrior braid more silver than black. Her name was Saran, chief of this camp. "But it was over too soon."

"There are more Cheren out there for you to kill," Bleda said. "There will be more opportunities to bloody your steel."

"Good," Saran said.

But how many more?

They had questioned a wounded Cheren at the last camp.

At first the woman had refused to speak a word. She was clutching at her belly, trying to stop her intestines from squeezing through, and failing.

Bleda had respected her courage, though that had not stopped him letting Yul introduce her to another level of pain. He had questions that needed answering.

And now he knew what he had suspected.

Jin is behind this.

It is no spring raid, snatching cattle and a few souls. This is a planned, organized attempt to destroy my Clan. We have slain close to six hundred Cheren warriors, now, but I fear it is just the spume of the wave.

How will we beat them? How will I save my people?

He rode slowly amongst the dead, looking down at the Cheren warriors in their sky-blue deels, now blood-soaked from one wound or another. He stopped beside a corpse, a lamellar vest upon this one, over a coat of boiled leather.

A young man, a fine sword lying in the trampled grass beside him, its leather hilt wrapped with silver wire.

Their chief, judging by his war gear.

"Strip them," Bleda said. "Gather their weapons, their armour, and any deel that isn't too damaged."

Sunset drenched the grasslands red, a sea of blood. Bleda had called a halt on their journey south and east. It was clear where Jin was headed, and they weren't going to get there before full dark.

To the Sirak Heartland. It was over half a day's ride before they would reach the floodplain the Heartland was built upon, and there was no point pushing on into darkness, risking their horses. Many of the animals were close to exhaustion. *They are our lifeline. An injured horse will result most likely in a dead warrior.* So, camp was being made beside the banks of a river, though the midsummer sun had dried it up to little more than a stream. Bleda had ordered no fires, just dry biscuit, cured meat and hard blocks of goat's cheese. Ellac had grunted approvingly, which was starting to unsettle Bleda. It was happening too often from the usually silent and stoic warrior. Paddock lines had been set, gers erected, and warriors were beginning to sit and talk, while going through the daily ritual of checking and repairing their kit. Soft kit first, then armour, whether it was boiled leather or mail, and finally weapons, checking for notches and dried spots of blood which would eat away at the steel, then sharpening. It was a continual cycle of stitching, cleaning, fixing, maintaining, all of it essential to the art of staying alive in combat.

Bleda was walking along the riverbank, within the boundaries of the camp. He was aware of Ruga following him, ten or twenty paces behind. He knew as Lord of the Sirak he had to accept this, but Bleda felt suffocated, overwhelmed, and had just needed to walk and think. Since leaving the last camp he had been preoccupied with finding Jin, and her warband. The Cheren prisoner had spoken of the strength of the Cheren, every last man and woman that could sit on a horse and wield a bow.

That is a lot of Cheren to kill. What am I to do?

He felt the weight of his newfound leadership. It was taking some getting used to. Especially as he had felt that he'd failed so disastrously with his first command. His hundred honour guard. He'd led them into a forest full of mist-walkers, and never seen most of them again.

But I still live, though I do not deserve to. I will think, this time. Not charge blindly at my enemy and just expect a victory. Courage is good, but it must be tempered with wisdom and strategy.

And that is what he had been trying to do; to use his wits first, an attempt to win battles with the fewest casualties to his warriors. Like at the last camp, hiding in wait for the Cheren, surprising them, and crushing them with a flanking force. It had worked this time. Only five Sirak slain, a dozen wounded, for two hundred dead Cheren.

But he knew it would not be so easy against Jin and her horde.

The prospect was overwhelming. He was not scared. Well, not scared of dying, anyway. He had come face to face with death the night his mother had died, when he had cut Uldin's throat and then stood open-armed, waiting for the arrows to pierce his body.

No, he was scared of failing. Of letting his people down, of letting Riv down.

He came upon the stump of a willow, lightning-struck and fire-blackened, the dead trunk fallen into the river. He sat, looking into nowhere, just thinking, took a wedge of cheese from a pouch at his belt and carved a slice. A sound filtered through his thoughts, a tapping. He looked up and saw a huge black crow sitting on the blasted tree trunk. It had a snail in its beak and was bashing it against the fallen tree. The snail shell was proving to be remarkably resilient, the crow banging it harder and harder against the tree, its feathers becoming more and more ruffled with the effort.

"Here, have some of this instead," Bleda said, cutting a slice of cheese and throwing it at the crow. The cheese landed close to a taloned foot. The crow stopped its frustrated banging, the snail still in its beak, and eyed the cheese. Its head swivelled, looking at Bleda, then back at the cheese.

It dropped the snail, then took one sidestep closer to the cheese. The black beak stabbed down, skewered the cheese, threw it into the air and swallowed it whole.

Bleda smiled.

"*Thank you,*" the crow muttered, looking at Bleda with a beady eye.

Bleda nearly fell off the tree stump.

He blinked, staring at the crow.

"Pardon?" he said.

"*Thank you,*" the crow croaked. It took a few sidling steps closer to Bleda. "*Nice cheese. Got more?*"

I did not imagine it, Bleda thought. *Or am I losing my mind?* Then he remembered something Riv had told him.

"You are from Dun Seren," Bleda breathed. Riv had told him of a talking crow, a messenger from the Order of the Bright Star, who lived at Dun Seren. It had been bringing word to Israfil. Riv said its name was Flick.

"Are you Flick?"

"*Dun Seren, home, yes,*" the crow squawked. "*Flick, no. Me Durl. Flick dead. Flick brother.*" The crow hung his head.

"Ah, I am sorry to hear that," Bleda said. "It is always hard to lose kin. Here, have some more cheese." He cut a slice and threw it, Durl catching it deftly.

Ruga stepped out of the twilight, frowning at Bleda.

"Who are you talking to?" she asked suspiciously.

Bleda pointed at the crow. Ruga scowled at him.

"Who are you talking to?" she asked again, eyes scanning the riverbank.

"*Talking to Durl,*" the crow said, rocking from one taloned foot to the other.

Ruga stumbled back, reached for her bow.

Durl squawked and flapped his wings.

"No, Ruga," Bleda said. "This is Durl. He is an ally, from Dun Seren."

"A talking crow!" Ruga said.

"*Obviously,*" Durl muttered, eyeing Ruga with disdain and running his beak through a ruffled wing.

"Sit, Ruga," Bleda said. "You're upsetting Durl."

Ruga looked as if she didn't want to get any closer to Durl, but she sat on the stump beside Bleda.

"You are a long way from home, Durl. What are you doing here?" Bleda asked. Ruga was looking at him as if he was insane.

"*Tain give Durl important task,*" the crow cawed, puffing out his chest feathers. "*Looking for someone.*"

"Arcona is a big place," Bleda said. "It can't be an easy task."

"*No, not easy,*" Durl agreed. "*Durl been flying long time. Wings ache.*" He eyed them. "*You help Durl?*"

"If I can, I will," Bleda said. "Who are you looking for?"

"*Durl looking for Raina. Giant. She needs to go home. Back to Dun Seren.*"

"There are no giants in the Sea of Grass," Bleda said.

"There were, though," Ruga said thoughtfully. "There were tales, remember? Of a giant Clan who dwelt near Kletva."

Bleda did remember, but he had never given the tales much credence, thinking them faery stories designed to keep young riders from swimming the lake for the island.

"*Yes, yes, the Kurgan,*" Durl squawked. "*Raina one of Kurgan.*"

"Why don't you look at Kletva, then?" Bleda said, pleased that he might have helped. "It's a lake, north and west of here."

"*Durl already been there,*" the crow said despondently.

"Have some more cheese," Bleda said. It seemed to cheer the crow up.

"*Thank you,*" Durl cawed. He swallowed the cheese, then flapped his wings. "*Durl keep looking. Can't give up, must keep trying,*" he said, jumping and beating his wings, taking to the air. "*If you see Raina, tell her Durl looking for her.*"

"I will," Bleda said.

"A nice crow," Ruga said with a shrug as they watched Durl disappear into the twilight.

"And wise," Bleda said with a frown. "Don't give up, keep trying," he breathed to the night air.

Bleda crawled through the grass on his belly, up to the ridge of an incline. The scraping of grass either side of him, a handful of others joining him: Ellac, Yul, Ruga and Saran. They all stopped at the ridgeline and stared.

Bleda swore softly.

The Heartland was in flames. A Sirak encampment, the closest thing to a town or fortress that the Sirak had. It was not fortified; it had never needed to be, situated at the centre of the Sirak's land, a hundred leagues in all directions of Sirak-controlled plains and Sirak warriors about it. But it was big. A sprawling mass of gers, many of them up to ten times the normal size of a travelling ger, their wooden framework more solid, timbers planted into the ground, felt and animal skins stretched wide and high on the frames.

And it was all burning.

Bleda could see Cheren riders speeding between the gers, hawk banners everywhere, could hear the faint screams on the wind. He tried to count those banners, to try and gauge how many Cheren Jin had mustered, but in the chaos it was too difficult. Even so, it was obvious that there were thousands of his enemy down there.

And we are six hundred and twelve.

Something drew Bleda's eye, a dust trail. He followed it, saw on the plain between him and the Heartland a column of wains that tracked the river Selen, wide and dark that curled across the plain, a long way from its meltwaters in the Kalevala Mountains, far to the north. There were maybe ten or twelve wains, Cheren riders spread around them.

Is that their baggage train? Food? Not likely. The Cheren usually ride light, and they would have been plundering the Sirak camps they have destroyed.

He squinted, straining his eyes to see the wains. They were wide, and had some kind of structure atop each one.

Like ... bars on a cage.

He swore again, and then signalled for the others to follow him back down the incline.

"We cannot beat them," Bleda said. "They are too many." Yul and Saran and many others scowled back at him. These were words that no Sirak ever wanted to hear about the Cheren.

They were sitting in a great circle beyond the ridge Bleda had climbed, letting their horses drink at a stream. Over six hundred Sirak were staring at him.

"We strike hard and fast, and hope that works. If it doesn't, we do not stay and fight. We will run, and live to fight another day. I have not saved you from the Cheren horde only to see you throw your lives away now."

Bleda had his plan firm in his mind, knew there was a chance it would work. But equally, he had seen many a plan fall apart. And he knew his people. They were proud, stubborn, stiff-necked. He knew they would not be inclined to flee from the Cheren, so he had to deal with that possibility here, now.

A ripple of muttered curses confirmed his worries.

"I will not run from the Cheren," Saran said, voices behind her murmuring agreement. "I will not show them my back. I am not weak."

"To die now *is* the weak choice," Bleda said, his Sirak cold-face still and emotionless. "Die now, and the Cheren will dance on our bones and wipe the Sirak name from this earth. Follow me, stay alive, and I vow to you a chance at fulfilling our vengeance."

Ellac quietly grunted his approval. Bleda was glad for the encouragement.

"How can we ever hope to beat them?" another voice called out. "You said it yourself, they are too many. Better to die fighting, in our Heartland, defending our Clan, than to die running. Chased and hunted down like a stray goat."

"Aye," agreed Saran and others.

"There is another choice," Bleda said. "We have friends in the west. Allies. We lead Jin and her horde there. And once we are there, with our allies beside us, we will turn and kill them. Jin, her honour guard, and every single Cheren warrior who follows her."

"Allies? Foreigners! The Ben-Elim are as much our enemy as the Cheren," Saran spat. "What use are they? They would betray us."

"Things have changed in the west," Bleda said. "I thought of them like that, but war with the Kadoshim has altered everything. It has brought out the best, and the worst." Bleda remembered the road in Forn, as he fought alongside his mother against a swarm of Ferals, he remembered how Kol and the Ben-Elim had abandoned him, flown away and left them.

But not everyone abandoned me.

He bowed his head, thoughts of Riv filling his mind, how she had flown out of the darkness at Uldin's camp and saved him from certain death; he saw her fierce smile, could almost taste her breath. How her wings felt as they wrapped around him, soft feathers against his back. His hand strayed to his chest, where beneath his lamellar coat and woollen tunic sat a dapple-grey feather, pressed against his heart. He would go back for Riv, if nothing else.

Where are you? Did you succeed in your task with the Order of the Bright Star? Will they stand with us on the field of battle against Asroth?

Asroth.

There was more to go back for than love, though that alone would have been enough for Bleda. He hated Kol and did not trust him, but he did trust Meical. He had only known the Ben-Elim a short while, but his words at their brief council had filled Bleda with something he hadn't felt for a long time.

Hope.

Meical will keep his word. Will gather all who would stand against Asroth and his Kadoshim. And they are a great evil, even more than Jin and her Cheren scum. Asroth must be beaten, and the Sirak are needed in the west for that to happen.

"We have allies in the west, and they are worthy of our friendship. Some amongst the Ben-Elim. Giants. The Order of the Bright Star."

His warriors looked at each other, a hundred conversations beginning. Even in Arcona the Order of the Bright Star was known, though mostly through tales and fables.

"But our *people* are here. Our *home* is here," Saran said.

"No, my home is here," Bleda said, touching his heart. "And here." He put a hand upon Ellac, and then on Ruga, moved on to touch Yul, and then gestured, taking them all in. "We are kin, Clan; *we* are the Sirak, not this dust we stand upon. Wherever we are, there is our home."

Nods of agreement.

"I am your King, last child of Erdene. You follow me, or you do not." He shrugged. "It is your choice. Either way, I will not change my course."

Without hesitation Yul was beside him.

"You slew Uldin; I will follow you to the ends of this earth." He looked at Saran and her followers. "I am a simple man. I love my kin and my Clan. I give and keep my oath. I can aim an arrow and wield a sword, but I do not know much about strategy. I *do* know that Bleda promises me revenge for Erdene's death." He paused a moment, a tremor in his cheek. "Bleda promises me a chance at defeating the Cheren. He promises me *vengeance*." He shrugged. "That is enough for me."

A silence settled over them.

"Will you follow me?" Bleda asked.

"HAI!" the crowd called out. Saran met Bleda's eye and she gave a curt nod.

"Good," Bleda said. "Now we ride, and show our enemies what it means to fight against the Sirak."

CHAPTER THIRTY-NINE

JIN

Jin reined in and wiped sweat from her face, spat a glob of blood onto the ground. Her jaw ached, blood leaking from her lip where a sword-pommel had been punched into her face. She probed it with her tongue, found a tooth was loose.

I came off better than you, though, she thought, looking down at the woman who had injured her. Her head flopped to one side, half-severed by Gerel. He had seen the blood on Jin's face and gone into a frenzy that had seen him hack the offending warrior from her saddle, and then swept him on into another knot of Sirak warriors. Jin shifted her weight in her saddle and rode after him, her honour guard in a line behind her.

They crashed into the Sirak, a storm of swords and spears, of snarling faces and screams, Jin's sword moving fast in short, economic strikes. She sliced and stabbed, lunged and swayed. The Sirak fought with a wild abandon that only the cornered can do, but her honour guard were too many, too skilled, and in a score of heartbeats all the Sirak before Jin were dead.

She looked at Gerel, saw him sitting on his horse, covered in blood, his face a red mask, his chest heaving. Jin grinned at him.

We are here, at the heart of my Clan's enemy, dealing them their death-blow. Think not of Bleda and the future. Enjoy the now.

"On," she said, urging her horse forwards.

The encampment was burning, smoke and flame destroy-ing a thousand years of culture, her Clan sweeping through it, slaughtering those that had built this place, who lived here, refusing to leave.

I admire that about them. They knew I was coming, saw our host approaching on the plain and knew they were outnumbered. But they chose to stay. They chose to stand.

The battle had roared through this part of the Heartland and moved on, the sound of skirmishes here and there floating through the wide spaces between the great gers, so much bigger than a normal camp. They were built to accommodate the whole of the Sirak, a few thousand people.

By nightfall it will be burned to the ground.

Exhaustion draped over Jin like a shroud, every muscle in her body burning, aching, throbbing. She leaned back in her saddle, the high back supporting her, and for a moment she lacked the strength to lift her sword.

Dead Sirak were all around her.

She had fought her way through the encampment, through the chaos and blood, and somehow now found herself back on the outskirts of the camp, close to where she had originally entered. Half a league behind her the wains full of Sirak prisoners were waiting on the plain. Jin had ordered that they keep their distance until the battle was done. She didn't want to risk them entering the Heartland and catching fire somehow, or being attacked by any survivors. She was looking forward to the entertainment her prisoners would bring.

Tonight, when we celebrate.

Gerel was close by, his battle-frenzy gone. He sat straighter than Jin, though, his eyes everywhere, alert as always. She was becoming used to his constant presence, and reassured by his vigilance and watchfulness. More of her honour guard were around her, seventy or eighty. The others had either become separated from her in the confusion of battle, or they were dead. Tark was there, too, his spear red almost the length of the shaft.

Just beyond Tark survivors were being herded out from the

blackened husk of the encampment, Cheren warriors leading handfuls of bound prisoners out and depositing them on the plain. There were at least a hundred, so far.

I do not like these warriors being grouped together, while my force are still spread through the encampment, rooting out any last resistance.

"Tark," Jin called out. "Take those prisoners out to the wains. Load them up, lock them away. I don't like them just sitting here. There are too many of them." Their numbers had grown again, a hundred and twenty, maybe. "Take as many riders as you need to get it done."

"*Hai*," Tark said, dipping his head to Jin. He rode off, barking at Cheren as he passed them, rounding out forty or fifty riders. They circled the captured Sirak, spent a while checking they were bound securely, and then they were prodding them to their feet with spears and setting off across the plain towards the wains.

"You have done it, my Queen," Gerel said to her.

"What?" she said, still watching Tark escorting the prisoners.

"What no Cheren king or queen has done before. Taken the Sirak Heartland, destroyed their Clan. How many of the Sirak do you think still live?"

"We have maybe three hundred prisoners, now," Jin said.

"Aye, but they won't be breathing for long," Gerel said.

"That is a truth," Jin said.

"Once the prisoners are gone, the Sirak will be no more."

"Apart from Bleda, and however many he has with him."

"Ach." Gerel spat. "There could not have been more than a score that rode away from their raid on our camp," he said.

"It doesn't matter," Jin said. "While Bleda breathes, the Sirak still live. We will stay here a day or two, celebrate our victory." She looked at the prisoners moving across the plain, close to the wains now. They would play a large part in that celebration. Perhaps she would make them fight each other, like Asroth had done to the surviving White-Wings at Drassil. She smiled at the thought of that.

"What is that?" she said, still looking out onto the plain.

"Where?" Gerel asked.

Jin pointed; out beyond the wains, there was movement on the plain. Riders. A hundred, more. Jin's fist tightened around the hilt of her sword.

"They are ours," Gerel said. "The hawk banner flies above them, and I can see blue deels."

"Ah," Jin said, the banner clear to her, now. "It must be Duya or one of the other chiefs, arrived late to the battle."

CHAPTER FORTY

BLEDA

Bleda cantered across the plain. He shifted in his saddle, rolled his shoulders, trying to settle the lamellar vest he had buckled over a blue deel. He'd taken them both from the dead Cheren chief. It wasn't a bad fit, but Bleda had lived and breathed in his own lamellar coat, and this was no comparison. He felt lighter, though, as if he could move as fast as the wind.

I will need to, if this doesn't go to plan.

He was riding across the plain, parallel to the great river Selen. The midsummer sun had made the water low and the riverbanks steep. A hundred and eight warriors rode behind Bleda; that was as many Cheren deels as they could salvage. Ruga and Yul were as close to him as shadows. Ellac was not there, and Bleda felt uncomfortably aware of the old warrior's absence. He had ordered Ellac to stay behind, his stump marking him out and making him a risk. Ellac was the only warrior missing a hand still to be riding in a warband upon the Sea of Grass. The Sirak and Cheren were masters of the bow, and what use was a warrior who could not draw a bow?

A great use, is the answer to that, Bleda thought. Ellac had proved he was no waste filling a saddle. With his one hand he had slain more Cheren than Bleda could count.

And he gives good counsel, when he can be bothered to open his mouth.

But Ellac would have been a danger, now. Because everyone

knew that Ellac was Bleda's companion, which was why Bleda had ordered the old warrior to stay behind. The look on Ellac's face had given Bleda pause, though. It had been as if Bleda had given him the greatest insult. So Ellac had been given a new task.

Only one hundred and eight of us. How many prisoners are in those wains?

Bleda and each warrior with him had a spare mount tied to their saddles. That would not be suspicious to anyone looking at them—the Cheren often rode with spare mounts, and especially so on this campaign, where speed had been their greatest weapon. The only odd thing about the spare mounts was that they were already saddled.

If we need more horses we can take them from the Cheren. I count fifty Cheren guards around the wains, maybe another ten driving them. If we are quick and do this right, we should be away without any trouble.

A movement caught Bleda's eye. Further away, beyond the wains. More riders, approaching from the Heartland.

Hells.

Beyond them Bleda saw flames and smoke curling up from his ancestral home, the Sirak Heartland. There were Cheren warriors at the fringe of the encampment, blue deels marking them.

Bleda felt a sharp rush of shock, a frozen moment where his breath caught in his chest, followed swiftly by anger. The Sirak Heartland, in flames. The urge to kick his horse into a gallop and slaughter the Cheren before him was overwhelming. But that would mean more than his death. It would be the death of his people, of the Sirak. He drew in a shuddering breath and focused on the Cheren around the wains.

Sharp-eyed Ruga had noticed the riders approaching. She pointed.

"How many of them?" Bleda asked her.

"Maybe fifty," she said, after a moment's silence. "They are escorting more Sirak to the wains."

"Ah," Bleda brightened. "More of our kin that we can save, then, and more horses we can take."

"Why not ride on and slay the whole Cheren horde, while we are at it?" Ruga said cheerfully.

"Perhaps we will," Bleda said.

He did not feel so confident, his eyes scanning the plain, running along the river's edge.

Am I mad, leading a hundred warriors towards a warband of my enemy, at least two thousand strong?

Should we have just left, ridden away with the warriors I have saved? Six hundred Sirak is a fearsome warband.

No. These are my people. I owe this to them.

He sucked in a deep breath, his hand dropping to the leather clip on his bow-case. He undid it.

This will be bow work, quick and fast, or we are in trouble.

He looked ahead now, as they drew closer to the wains, Cheren riders looking at him and his warriors. Behind them the wains were becoming clearer; the Sirak prisoners within them were crushed and piled tight, no room to move. The stench of urine and excrement wafted on the air. Bleda felt his anger stir, alongside his fear, his blood pounding in his veins, the imminence of violence sharpening everything. Sight, sound, smell, all seemed brighter, clearer. His fingers twitched for his arrows.

In his peripheral vision he saw Ruga and Yul rest their hands on their bows.

The riders from the Heartland had reached the wains. Cage doors were being opened, Sirak prisoners forced to clamber in, spear-points encouraging them. Bleda saw an older warrior leading the prisoners. He stared towards Bleda.

He said something to a Cheren rider close by, and that warrior started to ride towards Bleda. He raised his hand in a greeting, then dropped it casually to rest upon his bow.

A voice in Bleda's head told him it was time, to hesitate now would mean disaster.

Faster than thought, his bow was in his hand and arrows in

his fist, the first one nocked, drawn, loosed. Two more arrows in rapid succession, the first one punching into the rider approaching him, a spray of blood as he toppled backwards over his saddle. The second arrow took a more distant Cheren in the shoulder, the third arrow piercing his throat as he opened his mouth to scream.

A whispered word and touch of his heels, and his horse leaped forwards, moving from canter to gallop, the horse tied behind following.

Yul, Ruga and the rest of his warband burst into motion, spreading wide, a hail of arrows flying from them a few hoof-beats later. Cheren tumbled from their mounts, twenty, thirty, more, the remaining warriors reaching for their bows. Bleda's warband surged forwards, only the drum of hooves betraying their charge, no battle-cries this time.

We will be as silent as wolves in the night, Bleda had ordered.

Arrows came back at him. He bent low over his saddle, a touch of a knee and Dilis was swerving right, though a little sluggish with the spare mount tied to her saddle. Arrows *zipped* past him. A few screams behind him, the thump of Sirak bodies falling. Bleda saw the old warrior stab a Sirak prisoner with his spear. Other prisoners were turning on their guards, leaping up at them, dragging them from their horses.

Another fistful of arrows, gone in a few heartbeats, and then another fistful. He was almost amongst them now, his warband in a loose line. An arrow slammed into his saddle-arch, a moment later another arrow punching into his left arm, like being hit by a rock. It threw him backwards, almost toppling him from his saddle. He swayed, righted himself, felt his grip going on his bow and managed to slip it back into its case. He looked around wildly, searching for where the arrows had come from.

The old warrior. He was reaching for more arrows.

Ruga saw him, too, screeched with anger that her lord had been wounded, aiming. Loosed two arrows in the time it took Bleda to draw a breath.

The old warrior ducked and yanked on his reins, the first arrow punching into the horse's shoulder; it screamed and reared, the second arrow piercing the warrior's thigh. He fell from his saddle; his horse's hooves crashed to the ground and it bolted, dragging the warrior fifty paces before his leather stirrup snapped.

Blood pulsed from Bleda's bicep. He grabbed the arrow shaft protruding from his flesh, tried to snap it, a jolt of pain and nausea that threatened to empty his stomach and sent dots flashing in front of his eyes. He left it and reached over his back, drawing his sword.

Movement from his left, the thud of hooves as riders appeared from the riverbank. He grinned to see Ellac leading another hundred of their warband. They had made their way down to the river Selen and dismounted, leading their horses by foot along its steep banks. Taking advantage of the low waters, they had crept closer, hidden from view by the steep-sided banks.

Now they were charging into the flank of the wains and remaining Cheren, arrows flying. Bleda saw Ellac reach the wains first, an arrow pinging off his buckler. Ellac put his spear into the belly of a Cheren standing on the wain's driving bench.

Bleda raised his sword, searching for an enemy to slay, and instead saw the last of the Cheren fall from his saddle, his throat opened by Yul's sword. He held back a cry of victory, instead riding to the nearest wain and chopping at the bolts that kept it locked. Sparks flew and the bolts fell, the cage door swinging wide, Sirak within spilling out. He gave the first one the reins of his spare horse. More Sirak riders were there, helping prisoners into saddles.

Ellac was throwing the cage doors wide on another wain, a mad scramble for empty saddles. Saran and other Sirak riders were rounding up empty Cheren horses, others leaping from their saddles to gather up quivers of arrows from the fallen enemy. Bleda saw Ruga take the reins of the old warrior's horse, then ride back to where he lay upon the ground. He moved and Ruga's spear arm rose.

"Hold," Bleda called to her, and Ruga's spear-point hovered.

Bleda cantered over to her, looked down at the old warrior.

He tried to rise, spat a curse at Bleda, but he had an arrow in one leg, his arm was broken from his fall and it looked as if his back had been ripped open from being dragged by his horse, a trail of blood smearing the grass.

Bleda took his spear from its saddle-cup and stabbed down, held it a finger's breadth from the warrior's eye.

"I am Bleda ben Erdene, Lord of the Sirak," he said. "I slew your King. Remember me to your Queen."

"You lie," the old warrior said. "All know that Bleda is the whipped dog of the Ben-Elim. He is in the west with his half-breed whore. He does not have the stones to come here."

Ruga's spear twitched.

"Hold," Bleda snapped.

His wrist flicked, a red line opening along the old warrior's cheek.

"Just so you know that I am no ghost," he said. The old warrior looked away.

"Look at me," Bleda said. "Look at my face. Describe it to your Queen. Tell her that I chose a half-breed Ben-Elim over her. And tell her that I will kill her, soon. Maybe not cut her throat, like I did her father, but she will die by my hand. Erdene will be avenged."

The old warrior stared at him, then, hatred bright in his eyes. "The Great Queen will see you dead," he said.

"Ha." Bleda laughed. "Let her try."

A sound drifted over the plain to him. A high-pitched screeching, followed by a horn blowing from the Heartland. He looked up, saw riders massing at the encampment's rim, two hundred, more joining them; some of them were already breaking into a gallop towards him. At their head was a woman. That was where the screeching was coming from.

"Jin," he breathed.

A cold anger swept him, then, the world shrinking to Jin upon her horse. The woman who had killed his mother. Who had slaughtered his people. His hand reached for his bow. A sharp pain from his shoulder. Ruga touched his wrist.

"This is not the time," she said.

A long, lingering moment, then he took a shuddering breath.

"Tell her," he snarled at the old warrior, and then he was tugging on his reins, his mount turning. Most of the Sirak prisoners were mounted, Saran and Ellac leading them back across the plain, away from the Heartland. Bleda saw three of his kin still on foot. He kicked Dilis into a canter, rode to one of them, his hand out, and pulled them up into the saddle behind him. Ruga reached the other two, gave one the reins to the old warrior's horse and grabbed the other one's outstretched arm, and then they were galloping away from Jin, the wind whipping their warrior braids, horns blowing wildly behind them.

CHAPTER FORTY-ONE

JIN

Jin galloped across the plain, a wild rage flooding her, filling her veins and powering her limbs, a feral, kinetic energy that needed to be released.

Never had she felt such hatred.

She had stared at the riders in their blue deels beneath the Cheren hawk banner as they'd approached her wains, at first pleased that more of her warriors were alive. She had been worried about them, and troubled by their absence.

Her eyes had been drawn to their leader. A dark-haired warrior, sun glinting on a lamellar vest.

And then she had seen the same man draw his bow and start putting arrows into her warriors.

For a dozen heartbeats she had stared open-mouthed, struggling to understand what she was seeing. His riders had moved from a canter to a gallop, spreading behind him, and sent a hail of arrows into her warriors. She'd seen Tark shouting a warning, killing prisoners, then reaching for his bow, putting an arrow into the leader in the lamellar vest.

Somehow, she had been frozen; confused, unbelieving.

"It is the Sirak," Gerel had said, his hand gripping her arm.

"It is *Bleda*," she had whispered back at him. By then other Sirak were surging up the bank from the river. Tark was down, prisoners pouring from her wains, and Bleda was cantering over to Tark.

"It cannot be Bleda." Gerel frowned, straining his eyes.

"It is BLEDA!" Jin screeched.

Her shock was burned away in a flare of hot rage, incinerated by it.

She had screamed for her warriors, Gerel putting a horn to his lips and blowing, summoning the Cheren, wherever they were, even as Jin was kicking her horse into motion and reaching for her bow. In heartbeats she was hurtling across the plain, her body one with her mount's, the two of them moving in unison, muscles and hooves flowing in the perfect rhythm of the gallop.

The Sirak were fleeing, now, the one she thought was Bleda leaving last, pulling another Sirak up behind him onto his mount. She reached for arrows, knowing they were out of bowshot, but nocking and loosing anyway. It fell infuriatingly short of the last riders.

A cloud of dust was swept up by the fleeing Sirak, marking their retreat, four or five hundred riders at least, by the look of it.

There must have been three hundred prisoners, maybe more.

They were riding up a ridge, now, beginning to disappear over it by the time Jin reached the wains. The ground was littered with Cheren dead, ninety, a hundred of her warriors. Jin dragged on her reins, a spray of grass and dry earth, pulling her horse to a trot, stopping where she'd seen Tark fall.

"My Queen," she heard a voice call, saw Tark close by, trying to drag himself upright. He was badly wounded, blood sheeting his leg from an arrow wound, one arm hanging at the wrong angle.

Hooves drummed, Gerel catching up with her, the first of her riders with him, around a hundred and fifty. More were riding from the Heartland, a steady stream, though she could still hear the faint din of battle, swirling on the wind.

"See to him," Jin said, and Gerel slipped from his saddle, kneeling beside Tark. He cut Tark's breeches around the arrow protruding from his thigh, gave Tark a drink from his water skin and then poured the rest over the wound, washing it clean. He touched the arrow, probed the wound. A grunt from Tark.

"Will have to cut it out," Gerel said. He took Tark's arm, a protruding lump on the forearm where the bone had snapped. "Bite on this," Gerel said, slipping his knife's sheath from his belt.

"Wait," Jin said. "The one who spoke to you." She paused, blew out a long, unsteady breath. "Was it him?"

Tark looked up at her, pain, anger, shame mingled in his eyes.

"He called himself Bleda," he said.

Jin sucked in a strangled scream.

"What did he look like? Describe him."

"Young, like you," Tark said. "He was arrogant, though I put an arrow in his arm. Dark. His face was soft, for a Sirak."

"Aye, like mine. Because we have not ridden the Sea of Grass for ten years." She looked at the last riders disappearing over the ridge line. "What did he say to you?"

Tark's eyes flickered away.

"Tell me *everything*. You will heal, ride the grass again. If you wish to ride at my side, you will tell it all to me."

A grunt and nod from Tark. "He said he would kill you, soon. He boasted of cutting Uldin's throat."

A memory of her father, black blood jetting as Bleda's knife sliced through his neck.

"What else?" Jin said, a tremor in her voice. She focused on Tark. "There is something else."

"And that he chose a half-breed whore over you."

The fire in Jin's veins turned to ice.

I will kill him. By Elyon above and Asroth below, I will kill him, if it is the last thing I do.

"Set his arm," she grated at Gerel. There were Cheren riders all around now. Maybe five hundred of her warriors, a trickle as more crossed the plain to join her.

There was a grinding sound as Gerel pulled on Tark's arm. The old warrior hissed, went rigid as Gerel manipulated his broken bone back into place, boot-heels scraping in the grass.

They must have numbered close to two hundred. Then the prisoners, another two to three hundred, though most of them are weak, injured, weaponless.

She made a decision.

"WITH ME!" she cried, standing tall in her saddle, and then she was riding towards the ridge line. The drum of hooves behind her, Gerel calling out, but she ignored him, setting her face to the dust cloud that still hovered in the air.

Cheren riders settled around her, grim-faced men and women. Jin reached for her bow, slipped it from its case, took a handful of arrows from her quiver, holding her reins loose and guiding her horse with her knees and ankles. She was riding up the ridge, now, a steady canter. She was angry, angrier than she had ever felt before, but the wild heat was gone, replaced by an icy rage that she could think through.

I will not rush blindly into some trap. She signalled right and left, a few score riders branching off, sweeping wide. Then she was cresting the ridge, arrow nocked, leaning low over her saddle to give a smaller target. She was expecting the snap and whip of arrows.

Nothing.

The ridge was empty, trails flattened through the grass. Jin rode on a short way, so that she wasn't silhouetted upon the crest of the ridge, and then touched her reins, her mount stopping while she surveyed the land, using the high ground. A series of dried-out stream-beds clustered below her on the plain, separating again to thread their way to the river Selen. Where the streams met there were signs of her enemy, the ground churned by hooves, bloodied clothes and bandages discarded. Jin raised her hand and pointed. A handful of warriors rode down to the streams, searching. At the same time the warriors she had sent wide around the ridge appeared. They had been sent to root out any flanking ambush, or to undertake their own flanking manoeuvre if Jin had ridden into a fight. They signalled that all was clear.

Jin was satisfied no ambush was imminent, and so lifted her gaze further afield. Riders were in the distance, a large mass riding away from her. They were riding hard, stirring up a dust cloud, travelling fast, not caring about hiding their passage or their numbers.

They are fleeing for their lives. Bleda knows he has stuck his head too far into the wolf's mouth; he has seen my strength. Survival is all he has on his mind. He is running scared.

The drum of hooves behind Jin. She twisted in her saddle, but it was only Gerel. Tark was with him, his broken arm in a sling, the arrow that Jin had seen protruding from his thigh was gone, a bandage wrapped around it, blood starting to seep through.

Tark reined in with one hand and a word; his new mount stopped. Bleda and the Sirak had taken his old horse. His eyes scanned the scene, taking in the stream-bed and then the fleeing warband. They were already over a league away.

"Prepare to ride," Jin called out.

"No, my Queen, they are too many," Tark said. "They could be hoping to lure you out, away from the strength of your host."

"No, Bleda is fleeing; he is scared," Jin said.

"Is he?" Tark said. He shrugged. "Either way, you have five hundred riders here. They have more."

"How many?" Jin snapped. Her father had taught her how to count and measure riders on the plain, but usually by noting the banners flying above them. Bleda's warband had no banners.

"Nine hundred, a thousand horses," Tark said. "They may have spare mounts, but I don't think so."

Jin sat there a few moments, not trusting her mouth. Her teeth ground, muscles in her jaw bunching as she thought.

"Let me track them for you; they shall not escape," Tark said.

"You?" Jin said, expelling an angry breath and looking him up and down. His arm in a sling, his leg bound but bleeding.

"You are not fit to ride."

"I am," Tark said. "What is a little pain. My arm and leg are seen to; they will heal. Besides, I could ride with no arms."

This was true, not some idle boast. The Cheren learned to guide their mounts through pressure from their knees and feet, far better than clumsy yanking on reins.

"But you cannot fight," Jin remarked.

"Maybe not." Tark nodded. "But I am the best tracker in Arcona, I have other uses. And I would make up for my failure to kill Bleda. Let me find him for you."

Jin gave Tark a long, measuring look, and then nodded.

Tark snapped an order and a score of scouts set off after Bleda, moving down the ridge and onto the plain at a steady canter.

"They cannot gallop forever," he said to Jin. "And they are unlikely to have spare mounts. We will catch them. Send word back to the Heartland, gather your warband about you. They will wish to see the death of Uldin's killer."

Jin smiled coldly.

CHAPTER FORTY-TWO

FRITHA

Fritha leaned over Wrath's back.

"There they are," she shouted, a flutter of joy in her belly at the sight of Asroth's war-host. It had been over a ten-night since she'd seen it. "Time to land." The wind whipped her words from her mouth even as she spoke them.

Wrath heard her, though, tucking a huge wing and turning in a wide, looping half-circle.

They were flying above the treetops; the sun sinking into the west was turning the canopy of Forn to molten gold. Below Fritha was a line of her warriors riding a narrow road. Arn and her honour guard, her hand-picked warriors, on course to intersect a far wider road that carved through the trees. It ran from Drassil in the north to the Bairg Mountains in the south and was called Lothar's Road, for some reason that Fritha could not remember from her histories.

I was taught those histories at Drassil when I was trained, indoctrinated, as a White-Wing.

Fritha still could not quite believe how much the world had changed in so short a time.

Drassil fallen. The Ben-Elim routed. Asroth free. His child in my belly.

It made her feel dizzier than Wrath's spiralling descent.

Below them was a sight that took Fritha's breath away. A warband, the like of which the world had never seen before.

First were the Kadoshim and their half-breed offspring, close to two thousand winged figures speckling the sky. Below them, upon the road, marched nearly four thousand acolytes. They were starting to move like professional warriors now, rather than the brigands and outlaws that most of them had been. Not that all of them were cut-throats, criminals and murderers. Many of them had been outlawed by the Ben-Elim for petty crimes or had turned to brigandry as a response to the harsh regime of the Ben-Elim. Arn and Elise had been such as these. Others were from a more martial background, like Fritha herself, or Aenor, chief amongst the acolytes. He too had been a White-Wing, disillusioned and outlawed for his own personal reasons.

The warband on the road below Fritha was not in any discernible formation, just a disorganized rabble.

They have been used to skulking in the dark places for the last ten years, in forests and mountains and caves, trying not to be seen. And now they are marching down Lothar's Road for the whole world to see them, although that can hardly be called marching.

The White-Wing warrior within her curled her lip at their haphazard progress.

She swept down through the Kadoshim and their half-breeds, and then lower, Forn's trees rising either side of her. Crows squawked, lurking in the shadows of Forn, some circling the warband.

They know that death and slaughter are coming.

Fritha eyed the crows suspiciously, remembering Flick, the talking crow from Dun Seren.

There could be talking crows amongst them, she thought, *spying on us. But there are so many of them, we could never root out the spy.*

Horn blasts echoed up to her, people pointing up at Wrath.

The acolyte warband filled the road as far as Fritha could see, a slow-moving river of men and women, leather and steel. At their head she saw Asroth. Although he was often in the skies, he also liked to ride at the head of his war-host, sitting upon

the largest horse Fritha had ever seen. A piebald stallion found
in the stables at Drassil, all muscle and mane. Fritha suspected
that he had been used more for ploughing than battle, but he
was broken to ride and responded well to all of the usual commands, and most importantly of all, he could take the weight of
Asroth in all his war gear, which was impressive. Fritha felt her
heart beating faster at the sight of him, clothed in his armour,
shimmering like black oil in the setting sun.

Horns sounded and the warband stuttered to a halt. A hundred wains were pulled to the roadside as men and women began
to unload them and set up camp.

Warriors were cheering and shouting, welcoming Fritha's
return.

Wrath landed, a running crash, his wings beating to break
their fall, Fritha clinging on. People leaped out of their way.

"Still need to work on those landings," she said to the draig
as she unbuckled herself and climbed down from her saddle,
dropping the last few feet to solid earth. She breathed a sigh of
relief. As much as she was becoming used to flying upon Wrath,
and had made her saddle and harness more secure, she still preferred her feet upon solid ground.

"*Sorry*," Wrath growled.

Fritha patted his scaled neck and began undoing the girth
of his saddle, warriors of her honour guard hurrying to help
her. She heard the sound of hooves and the scrape and slither of
scales on the ground and turned to see Elise rippling sinuously
towards her, Arn riding at her side. A hundred of Fritha's honour guard rode behind Arn, heading for a newly erected paddock. Elise smiled to greet Fritha, her fangs bright.

"You have returned to me," Elise said. She had not come on
Fritha's task, unable to match the speed of mounted warriors
that Fritha needed. Elise was shockingly fast, but she lacked the
endurance to move at such speed for days at a time.

"Of course I have," Fritha said.

One of her Ferals loped past Elise to greet Fritha, pushing

its head against her. She staggered with its strength, though she smiled and stroked its muzzle, tugging on a huge protruding canine. Elise slithered up, coils pushing the Feral away. It growled at her, and she hissed back, tail rattling.

"Peace," Fritha said, smiling, "we are all friends here." She stroked Elise's cheek, the snake-woman's scowl melting away.

"Well met, Father," Elise hissed as Arn slipped from his saddle, passing his reins to an acolyte. Arn's hand rested upon the head of his starstone axe, which was hanging on a belt loop at his waist.

"What news?" Elise asked them.

"Asroth will call a meeting, soon. Stay with me and you shall hear it then."

Elise nodded.

"This war-host needs to move faster," Fritha commented.

Arn shrugged. "If Gulla's Revenants hadn't eaten most of the horses at Drassil then this warband would be riding, not walking."

Fritha pulled a face, agreeing. By the time anyone had realized what the Revenants were doing in Drassil's stable-blocks it had been almost too late. Little more than a hundred horses had been saved. Fritha had taken most of those for herself and her warriors, and scouts were riding the rest.

"*Wrath hungry,*" the draig rumbled, talk of eating horses obviously stirring his appetite.

"Go and fly, find yourself something to eat," Fritha said.

"*Have to fly far,*" Wrath moaned. "*Mist-walkers eat everything.*"

"Yes, I know," Fritha said, tight-lipped. "Happy hunting," she said and patted Wrath's muscled neck, then shielded her eyes as he beat his wings, stirring up a cloud of dust, and winged into the sky.

"Come with me," Fritha said to Arn and Elise as she walked away, a score of her honour guard following a few steps behind them.

"Welcome back, my Queen," Asroth said as Fritha approached. He slung a leg over his saddle, slipping to the ground, took two long strides towards Fritha and swept her up into his arms, crushing her to him, kissing her passionately.

"Ah, but this world of flesh is a constant joy to me," he said as they parted. "Two thousand years of living in the Otherworld as a spirit is really very dull."

Fritha laughed, still reeling from his kiss.

"Come, our tent awaits," Asroth said. He gestured to a Kadoshim guard, who raised a horn to his lips and blew, summoning Asroth's captains, then Asroth was striding through the entrance of a huge, hastily erected tent. Torches were already burning, a table being laid out with food and wine. Asroth thumped his long axe down onto the table-top and sat in a chair, draped one leg over the arm and held his cup out, an acolyte appearing at his shoulder to pour. He drained it in one long draught, then held the cup out for another. Bune and a handful of Kadoshim followed behind Asroth, some sitting at the table, others taking up various positions around the tent.

Fritha unstrapped her weapons-belt and laid it over the back of her chair, then sat and sipped from her own cup. Arn stood behind her, Elise slithering into the smoky shadows of the tent.

Aenor strode through the opening, short and squat. He poured his own cup of wine and sat at the table. Asroth held his cup out to him in greeting, drank that down, too.

"Well met, Fritha," Aenor said, a dip of his head to her before he drank. "I am glad to see you returned to us safe."

"So am I," Fritha said. She liked Aenor. They had had their differences over the years, and Aenor could be rude, obstructive, a pain in the arse, but she knew that he was honest, and if he said he was pleased, then he was.

"The warband looks bigger since I left," Fritha said to Aenor.

"Aye, it is, thanks to you," Aenor said.

Since leaving Drassil Fritha had taken to flying ahead of

their warband, Arn and fifty of her honour guard riding on the road beneath her. Together they had visited the towns and villages scattered along the great road, declaring the Ben-Elim routed, and proclaiming the new order of the Kadoshim and humankind, working together in harmony.

A draig with wings had made an impression, though many had run screaming at the first sight of Wrath. Once Fritha had proved he would not eat anyone without her say-so, though, people had seemed to be far more open to listen to her message.

She asked all if they would join her warband. Well, not exactly *asked*. She told them of Asroth and his great army, and made it clear what would happen if they refused. Even this was no guarantee, and sometimes Gulla and his Revenants were needed to show what would happen to those who refused Fritha's generous offer. One night Fritha had flown back to see what exactly Gulla's lesson was. She had heard the screams long before she had seen the village. So, their ranks were swelling.

Every man and woman in the Banished Lands learned weapons-craft from childhood. Spear and axe, mostly, as a sword was a costly weapon, so they were valuable additions to the warband. Once they joined, Aenor would teach them how to fight as a unit, in the shield wall or just as part of a fighting company.

Many had joined, Fritha suspected, because they were in equal measure awed and terrified of Wrath. Over a thousand had swelled the ranks of the acolytes since their journey from Drassil had begun.

"It is you who has to train them, not I," Fritha said to Aenor.

"A task I am happy to do," Aenor said, raising his cup.

While Fritha had been locked away within the forge at Drassil, working her dark magic upon starstone metal, Aenor had been working his own kind of magic upon the acolyte warband. He had been drilling them in the weapons-field every day, from dawn till dusk, and every evening since they had left Drassil, too. Even if they were not a match for the White-Wings' discipline, Fritha was becoming confident that they could form a shield wall and hold their own in a fight. The new recruits were fitting easily into that routine.

Aenor had also plundered the armouries of Drassil, and his warband looked like warriors now, many in shirts of mail, or if not mail then in boiled leather coats and cuirasses and carrying the White-Wings' rectangular shields. The white wings embossed upon shields and armour had been painted black, though. Weapons had also seen a significant upgrade, thanks to Drassil's armouries. Most of the acolytes had fought with spear and axe, but now the bulk of Aenor's host had a short-sword at their hip.

I suppose Aenor chose the right skill to teach first; fighting is more important than marching.

A beating of wings and a dark silhouette filled the tent's entrance, blocking out the last rays of the sun. Gulla entered the tent, his wings closed tight, a travel-stained cloak swirling about him like mist. He dipped his head to Asroth and sat at the table, ignoring Fritha. Black mist curled around him like smoke.

He hates me, after what I said to him in Drassil's Great Hall. I have made an enemy. Though better an enemy of Gulla and a friend of Asroth than the other way around.

"Now that we are all here," Asroth said, "a warm welcome back, my bride. We are overjoyed to see you. Now, report." His smile of a few moments ago was abruptly gone, all earnest focus now. This was something she was becoming used to: Asroth's ability to switch from one mood to another in the beat of a heart.

"Haldis is empty," Fritha said. "It is no risk to us. There were signs that the fortress has been lived in recently, but its inhabitants are gone now."

"What inhabitants? How many? And gone where?" Asroth said.

"Maybe a thousand White-Wings," Fritha said. She had flown to Haldis with a hundred half-breeds in the air around her, Arn leading her honour guard on the ground. They had gone to scout out the fortress, to discover if it was inhabited and a potential threat to their flank.

"There has long been a White-Wing garrison at Haldis," Fritha said. "It has always been around a thousand strong."

"Aye," grunted Aenor. He had served at Haldis, long ago.

The sound of wings beating outside the tent and Morn alighted beyond the entrance. She didn't block out as much light as Gulla as she swept inside, her frame shorter and broader than her father's.

"My King," she said to Asroth, dipping her head.

"Sit," he said, nodding at a chair, and then Morn was sitting at the table, beside Fritha.

"Continue," Asroth said to Fritha.

"We found evidence of a large force heading south. The tracks were old."

"How old?" Asroth asked.

"Hard to tell," Fritha said, looking at Arn.

"Maybe a moon, could be longer," Arn said.

Asroth nodded. "And where are they going, these White-Wings?"

Fritha took a sip of her wine. "They travelled south. We have long thought that our Ben-Elim enemy would have fled south to Ripa, where the White-Wings have their largest fortifications outside of Drassil. It would make sense that these White-Wings were going there, too. Perhaps they heard news of Drassil's fall. Ripa is the obvious place for them to regroup."

Asroth leaned back in his chair, sipping thoughtfully from his cup of wine. He turned his heavy-lidded gaze onto Morn.

"And what news do you bring me, child of the Kadoshim?"

"There is life in Brikan," Morn said, colouring at Asroth's words.

Asroth cocked his head, inviting more.

"There are warriors on the walls, though I did not see many.

I would guess there is a skeleton garrison left at Brikan," Morn said.

"You would guess," Asroth said. "You flew a long way to guess."

Morn's face flushed even redder. She looked at the ground.

"I was ordered not to set foot on the ground," Morn said sullenly.

"By whom?" Asroth said, his voice cold.

"By me," Gulla answered, his voice a rasp. "For her safety."

Asroth stared from Morn to Gulla.

"My eyes are good," Morn said. "I saw much. Warriors of the Order of the Bright Star, curse them." She spat. "I counted fifty, on the walls, the bridge, the courtyard, a patrol along the riverbank."

"The Order of the Bright Star fielded a sizeable warband in the north," Fritha said. "I should know, I fought them."

"And lost to them," Gulla said quietly.

"So, it is likely the numbers at Brikan are low," Fritha continued, ignoring Gulla.

Asroth sighed.

"It would be foolish to march beyond Brikan with our eyes fixed on the south," he said, carefully putting his cup of wine on the table. He sat up straight, slipping his leg off the arm. "That would leave enemies at my back. And I am no fool," he said, his smile and relaxed demeanour vanished. He looked from Fritha to Aenor, to Gulla.

"But, it would be a shame to halt our march south, as well," he said after a moment's silence. "I will send a force west. Strong enough to overcome any resistance." He drank more of his wine.

"Gulla, take as many of your Revenants as you need and ensure that Brikan is filled only with corpses."

"Yes, my King," Gulla said.

"That will be good, it might leave some food in the forest for the rest of us to hunt," Fritha said, sharing a look with Aenor.

Feeding a warband on the march was not easy, especially when there were ten thousand Revenants lurking in the darkness of Forn, eating their way through the forest's population; whatever manner of beast or bird, the Revenants were sucking the animal population of Forn dry.

Better than turning on us, I suppose, Fritha thought. She was acutely aware that Gulla and his Revenants outnumbered the rest of Asroth's warband two to one.

Gulla turned his one eye upon Fritha.

"There is food enough in the forest for all of us," he said in his grating hiss of a voice.

Asroth waved his hand, dismissing the subject as if he found it boring. "Gulla, be quick with this task. I am eager to be out of this forest. Does it go on forever? How much longer until we reach our destination?" He waved his hand again. "Ripa? I am eager to catch Meical, Kol and the rest of the Ben-Elim maggots and make them pay for their crimes."

"At this pace we will not see the Bay of Ripa before Hunter's Moon," Aenor said.

"Three moons." Asroth frowned, then he shrugged.

"If we had horses, my King," Aenor said.

Another sore subject, Fritha thought, but she said nothing, thinking she had goaded Gulla enough.

"It will take as long as it takes," Asroth said. He looked at Gulla. "And Sulak is in the south?"

"Yes, my King," Gulla said. "With our allies."

"Ah, yes." Asroth smiled. "I am looking forward to meeting them."

CHAPTER FORTY-THREE

RIV

Riv dropped through cloud, moisture coating her wings, glistening on her mail, and then she was through it, the land spread like a tapestry below her. Forn Forest lay to the east, an endless ocean of green, while below her lay multi-hued meadows dissected by glistening streams. They wound their way to the river Rhenus, which the warband had recently crossed.

Close to three and a half thousand warriors of the Order of the Bright Star.

At first they had headed east from Dun Seren, taking the road to Drassil, but little more than a ten-night into their journey crows had returned, bringing the news that Drassil was empty, Asroth and his warband marching south.

Riv had wanted to fly to Drassil, to scout it out and see for herself what the Kadoshim had made of her home. But Byrne had forbidden it.

"The skies are dangerous," Byrne had said. *"No longer are they the sole domain of the Ben-Elim. Best to send Craf's crows. I imagine a murder of crows already fills the sky wherever the Kadoshim go."*

Riv knew that Byrne's logic was sound, although she was not so keen on being ordered.

Still, I am a warrior of the Bright Star, now, she thought, one hand brushing the cloak brooch at her shoulder. *I have to take the bad with the good.*

The warband below her was heading south, skirting the edges of Forn Forest, their destination Ripa, far in the south.

Ripa. Where Aphra waits for me.

Riv felt a flush of happiness at the thought of her mother. She had never gone so long without seeing her.

And Kol, my father.

That was not a reunion she was looking forward to.

Though I am looking forward to telling him that I've joined the Order of the Bright Star.

A figure swept into her peripheral vision, dark-winged Faelan. He flew closer to her, nodded a greeting, then pointed at the ground.

"Time for the next shift," he shouted to her.

Byrne had put the warriors with wings into teams, three units to scout the skies immediately about the warband. The crows travelled further afield. The winged warrior units were to rotate in shifts, to prevent exhaustion.

"Battle could fall upon us at any time," Byrne had said. *"We must be ready, and not exhausted from flying every hour of the day."*

Riv had shrugged at that. She loved to fly, but the logic made sense to her.

She raised a hand to Faelan and he grinned at her, then he was turning a wing and veering left, banking to round up the rest of his unit. Riv dipped her head and began a spiralling descent to the ground. Queen Nara was at the head of the warband, her warriors taking the vanguard today. Beyond them small specks dotted the ground, Riv's sharp eyes picking out solitary riders and wolven-hounds loping through meadows and groves, the hunters of Dun Seren scouting the land. Branches shook in the eaves of Forn and she saw Drem upon his white bear. Then she was turning and looping down towards Byrne and Ethlinn, ready to make her report.

Riv dipped a chunk of dark bread into her bowl of pottage stew. She was about to put it into her mouth when she stopped, turning to look at Cullen.

He had his own bowl of stew, and just like Riv he had dipped his bread into it. Now he was sucking on that bread, slurping, pottage dribbling down his chin.

Riv felt her face twist in disgust.

Cullen must have felt her eyes on him, for he looked at her.

"What?" he said.

"You eat like a pig," Riv snarled.

"Aye." Cullen shrugged. "But I kiss like an angel." He gave her his broad smile, stewed barley stuck between his teeth.

Riv stared at him, unblinking.

"That's not funny," she said.

Cullen's eyes dropped, downcast. "Wasn't trying to be *funny*," he muttered.

"Ignore him, he's an idiot," Keld said. The old huntsman was standing with his two wolven-hounds.

"Eat your stew," Cullen said, waving a bowl at Keld.

"When I'm done," Keld said.

Riv looked at Keld, and the two wolven-hounds standing next to him. They were huge, of a height with Keld's chest, and broadly muscled as well, their muzzles shorter than a wolven, jaws broader. Riv remembered seeing them tearing chunks out of Revenants.

"I'm glad they're on our side," she said.

"Ah, these two, they're the best of friends to their pack, the worst of enemies to any that try to harm their pack." He smiled. "They're my babies." Keld grunted as he unbuckled coats of mail from them.

"That's quite the job, each morning and night," Riv said.

"Aye, it is," Keld said. "But it's worth it. Once upon a time I would only pull their ringmail out if we were going into battle, but these days..." He looked up at the trees of Forn looming in the east, a darker wall of shadow as twilight settled about them. "With Revenants and who knows what lurking in the dark places, it's safer this way," he muttered.

"Aye," Drem said as he strode into their small camp. It was one of a hundred fires burning within the picket-line of the

295

warband, spread over half a league of land. Drem had a bag slung across his back stuffed full with his white bear's coat of mail. "Friend has a coat of mail, too. We all saw what the Revenants did to them. Mail is worth its weight in gold; it stopped a Revenant making a meal of me. Alcyon helped me make this. Most of it we patched together from other bears' coats. Bears that fell, that night."

Riv knew exactly what night he was speaking of, could still remember all too vividly the dead bears littering the courtyard, Revenants swarming over them like flies.

Drem dropped the sack of mail onto the ground. "Wish it wasn't so heavy, though," he grunted.

Keld took the bowl Cullen was waving at him, and Drem ladled himself a bowl from the pot hanging over their fire. They both came and sat down.

Riv was not sure why she found herself at their fire each night, when Hadran and Meical were always inviting her to eat with them. She had spent time with Faelan as well; the two of them had so many questions for each other. But when evening and tiredness began to set in, Riv always found herself searching out the company of these three men. Perhaps it was their easy way with each other that she found settling, reminding her of her own kin and friends.

Keld threw a crust of bread to his wolven-hounds. The red-furred one, Ralla, jumped and snapped it out of the air before Fen had opened his jaws.

"Ach, you're getting slow, my lad," Keld said, waving a crust at the slate-grey wolven-hound. The hound padded over to Keld, took the bread and rubbed his head against Keld's shoulder, nearly knocking the huntsman over.

The pad of footsteps, and figures walked into their camp. Byrne, with Meical and Hadran.

"I thought you'd be here," Byrne said with a nod to Riv.

"We've been looking for you," Meical said.

Keld stood and offered them bowls of stew. Byrne took one,

and the ladle, too, filling her own bowl and offering some to Meical and Hadran.

"Meical wishes to leave us," Byrne said. "He thinks word needs to be taken to Ripa; of us. Of Asroth's war-host."

"There is news of that?" Cullen asked.

"Aye. Our crows have returned. Asroth moves down Lothar's Road. He is almost at the southern fringes of Forn."

Riv was silent, she knew what was coming.

"Meical wishes for you to fly with him."

"Riv's one of us, now," Cullen said. "She doesn't need to go flying off half a thousand leagues."

"You're right, Cullen," Byrne said. "You *are* one of us," she said, looking at Riv over the fire. "Meical suggested that you might want to go, as you have kin in Ripa. Rather than discuss this behind your back, I thought it best to find you and ask. If you wished to go, I wanted you to know that there is no problem with that; I would give you leave."

Riv nodded, thinking over Byrne's words.

"Aphra I do long to see," Riv said. "Kol, not at all."

"I can understand that," Byrne said with a grimace.

"I would like you to fly with us," Meical said. "I feel that you have been at the heart of this, since I have been awakened. And—" he smiled—"you could be the representative of this Order. The thought of Kol's face..."

Hadran coughed into his bowl of stew.

Riv grinned at that.

He won't be too happy that I've swapped the white wings for the star.

"It's true, a representative of the Order of the Bright Star in Ripa would be good," Byrne said, a half-smile on her face. "I could not send Faelan. I fear he would kill Kol within half a sentence of their first conversation."

"Not the best way to begin an alliance," Meical observed.

Riv smiled. "I will go," she said, then dipped her head to Byrne. "My thanks."

"You are welcome," Byrne said, a warm smile, rare from her, softening her hardness. "But come back to us."

"Of that there is no doubt," Riv said, already a sadness in her gut at the thought of leaving these people.

"Good," Meical said, "then we will fly with the sun."

"One thing I would ask of you," Byrne said, standing. "Stop at Brikan, our outpost in Forn. There are a hundred and fifty of our Order there. Tell them of what is happening. Have them prepared to leave. Tell them we will be there in a ten-night, at most."

"I will," Meical grunted. He looked to Riv. "We fly at dawn," he said, as he and Hadran followed Byrne out of the firelight.

Riv sat and stared into the flames a while, her thoughts filled with Aphra and Kol, of Jost and Fia and her White-Wing friends. And of Bleda.

Ah, Bleda, where are you? she thought. *Will I find you in Ripa?* That thought sent moths fluttering inside her belly.

"Don't know why Meical thinks he can drag you halfway across the Banished Lands," Cullen muttered as he poured himself another bowlful of stew. "Feels safer with you in the sky above us."

"Faelan and his kin are here," Riv said. "They guard the skies."

"Well, it's not the same," Cullen said. "They're not...you."

Riv looked at Cullen, slightly confused.

"What Cullen is trying to say, lass," Keld said, "is that we shall all miss you."

"Aye, that *is* what I said."

"No, it isn't." Drem pulled a face.

Riv looked at them, realized she had come to care for these three.

"I shall miss you, too," she said.

"Ach, it's all right, lass," Keld said, patting her knee. "We are brothers and sisters in arms, we four." He looked at Drem and Cullen. "I've had something on my mind to say, but have been thinking on it a while. Your departure makes this a good time to speak of it, I suppose."

"What?" Riv and Cullen said together. Drem sat silent, intently focused as always.

"At the Order of the Bright Star we often form a crew," Keld said to Riv. "We recently lost someone, someone dear to us. She was a good lass—"

"Lass!" Drem exclaimed. "She was two hundred and forty years old."

"Aye, well. She was the best of us, brave and fierce, like you, Riv. Maybe not quite so..." he paused, looked like he was trying to think of the right word. "*Spontaneous*," he said.

Drem cracked a smile at that.

"Ha." Riv laughed. "You mean angry."

Keld shrugged. "We've one hot-head already, why not two? What I'm saying, lass, is that you'd be welcome in our crew." He looked at Drem and Cullen. "I haven't asked these lads, yet, but I'm certain of their answer."

Drem and Cullen nodded.

"You'd be welcome," Cullen said.

"Aye," Drem agreed.

Riv looked at all three of them, felt a swell of emotion in her chest, and her eyes blurred with tears. For so long now, she had felt alone. The Ben-Elim had taught her that she was an abomination. Her temper had lost her friends, caused her to fail her warrior trial, and yet these three saw past all of that.

"I would be honoured," she said.

CHAPTER FORTY-FOUR

BLEDA

Bleda reined in his mount, staring at the river that cut across their path. It was wide and slow.

"A big river," Ellac observed.

"Aye," Bleda agreed. He twisted in his saddle and looked back, over the heads of his warband to the dust cloud that hovered in the distance, marking Jin's pursuit behind him.

"They are still following," Ellac said. "And getting closer."

Bleda looked at Ellac.

"I know," he said.

They had ridden south-west for a ten-night, a fast pace, though not as fast as Bleda would have liked. They had around a hundred and eighty spare mounts, and between nine hundred and eighty-three riders that was not particularly helpful. Even less, when a dozen of those spare mounts were carrying provisions and bundles of arrows gathered from the Cheren they had slain. The initial gap that Bleda had opened between him and Jin's following warband had closed steadily over the last seven days.

He frowned, looked back at the river, then rode Dilis on, down a gentle slope and into the water until it lapped at her hocks. It looked as if the waters did not rise any higher. Bleda patted Dilis' neck and she dropped her head to drink from the river.

Ellac joined him, Yul, Ruga and Saran following.

"A ford," Bleda said.

"Aye. A good place to cross," Ellac said, "or—" He paused, looking left and right, following the river as far as he could see, both north and south. He touched his reins, his horse moving left, through the slow-flowing water. He stopped after a hundred paces or so, turned to look back at Bleda.

"What?" Bleda asked. He felt his nerves starting to fray. Constant riding, exhaustion and the weight of responsibility heavy upon his shoulders.

If Jin catches us, we will die. All my people, the last of the Sirak. Because of me. My leadership. My decisions.

"I am thinking, we could ride a league or two in these shallows, until we reach another ford."

"Why? The Cheren would find our trail when we leave the river," Bleda said.

"Yes, they would," Ellac said. "But first they would have to stop here, send riders to the far bank, and ride both north and south until they found our trail again."

That will slow them, help to widen the gap again.

Bleda rolled his left shoulder as he thought on Ellac's suggestion. His arm ached where the old warrior's arrow had pierced him. Yul had pushed the arrowhead through, clean out the other side of Bleda's arm, then snapped the shaft and pulled it free. Bleda had his lamellar coat back on, now, and was thankful for it, though his wound was itching and he could not reach it to scratch it. It was driving him insane.

Yul and Saran both grunted their approval of Ellac's plan.

"That is a good idea," Ruga said.

"Ellac, you are wise beyond your years," Bleda called out.

"Then that would be wise indeed," Ellac said, water splashing as he cantered back to them. "The old wolf is the more cunning," he said as he reached them.

"Cunning is good," Bleda said. "Cunning is what we need

right now." He clicked his horse on, riding along the shallows, his warband moving into the river after him, churning the water brown.

"Ruga, what river was that?"

"The Ider," she said.

"I don't remember these lands," he said, much to his shame.

How can I lead my people when I do not even know the land?

By asking for help. Pride can be a poison.

"You were taken when you were eight," Ruga said, with a shrug. "You have not ridden the Sea of Grass all your life, like most Sirak."

"No," Bleda said.

"But you are Sirak, here," she said, fingers brushing her heart. "And here—" a tap of her temple.

Bleda glanced at her and smiled.

"Thank you," he said.

They were riding at the head of the warband, the Ider River three days and sixty leagues behind them. They were deep in the south of Arcona now, heading for the southern passages, running for Ripa. The grass was not so green, the earth dustier. Groves of trees spotted the distance, mostly twisted, sunblasted husks. He turned in his saddle and looked back. His warband was riding in tight formation at a steady canter, scouts on the flanks and ahead. He looked behind them into the distance and swore under his breath.

Jin was back.

For two days the dust cloud of Jin's warband had disappeared, Ellac's idea at the river slowing his enemy. But now they had caught up again. He turned and looked forwards.

"You know when you stopped me killing that old warrior," Ruga said, "the one that put an arrow in your arm?"

"I know the one."

"Why did you say those things to him, insulting Jin, goading her?"

"Because I needed to make sure she would follow us. If she wasn't sure it was me, she might have sent a warband a few hundred strong after us. And I wanted her and all the Cheren in Arcona to follow me, to give any survivors in the Heartland a chance to escape."

Ruga looked back at the Cheren warband, then forwards.

"Your plan may have worked a little too well."

"Ha, that is the truth of it." Bleda laughed. "I think Jin must be angrier than a hornet-stung bull."

In the distance he saw the shimmer of hills and mountains, marking the southern rim of Arcona. Beyond those mountains were the deserts of Tarbesh. To the east Arcona's plateau was bordered by the southernmost reaches of Forn Forest. That was his goal.

"How well do you know this land, and the route to the Tethys Sea?" Bleda asked her.

"Well enough," Ruga said. "As well as anyone, better than most. My kin travelled often in the south."

"Good," Bleda said. "Out of my captains, who would you say knows these southlands as well as you?"

"Ellac," Ruga said without hesitation. "Out of all, he is the only one I would say knows them better. He was born here."

"Ellac," Bleda said, an idea starting to form in his head.

"I won't do it," Ellac said.

"You will, because I am Lord of the Sirak, and it is my wish," Bleda said. "But even if I were not, you would still do it. Because you know it is our best hope, and because I ask you as my friend, not my subject."

"Ach, don't try your clever words on me," Ellac spat. Bleda saw panic in his eyes. "My place is with you. At your side. That is the oath I swore to your mother."

"You swore to do all in your power to protect me," Bleda said. "That is not staying at my side. Do what I ask, that will be protecting me. It will be the best chance at protecting us all."

A silence between them, Ellac looking from Bleda to the others—Ruga, Yul, Saran. All stared back at him, stony-faced.

"You could go," Ellac said to Yul.

"I could, but I would get the warband as lost as a deaf and blind rabbit." Yul shrugged. "I do not know these lands."

"You, then," Ellac said to Ruga.

"I am asking *you*," Bleda said. "It is the most important task, and I only trust you to do it."

A long, indrawn breath from Ellac, expelled angrily.

"All right," Ellac said. He pointed a finger at Bleda. "But you better live to see me the other side of this."

"I will do my absolute best to honour that," Bleda said.

"And you—" Ellac pointed at Yul—"make sure he keeps his word, and his head."

"If it is within my power, then it is already done," Yul said.

"Good, that is settled," Bleda said. "Now, strip every bush, every tree, I need as many campfires as we can make."

CHAPTER FORTY-FIVE

JIN

Jin raised her hand, a horn blast echoing her command to halt.

It was the dark end of twilight, when shadows had merged and night was settling into full dark. Riding any longer would risk broken legs for mounts.

But Jin's heart begged her to continue.

We are so close. I can almost smell the sweat of Bleda's warband. Their fear.

It had been a hard chase, even with spare mounts they had ridden their horses close to exhaustion. And when they had reached the Ider River and fallen behind by another day, Jin had almost screamed with frustration.

But we are close now. On the morrow we shall catch them and I shall have my vengeance. I think I will nail Bleda to a tree and watch him skinned.

In the distance campfires prickled into existence, like stars in the night sky.

"They are making camp," Tark said beside Jin. "A wise idea."

Gerel gave Tark a dark look. "It is wise when my Queen says it is wise."

Jin smiled.

Gerel would say day was night if that was what I commanded.

"It is wise," Jin said, looking around. Streams ran like veins of black blood in the darkness. "A good place to make camp."

Calls rippled along the wide column of Jin's war-host, horses were led to streams, paddock posts and ropes hammered into the ground.

Jin dismounted and led her mounts to the paddocks, unsaddled them, rubbed them down, checked their hooves, Gerel her constant shadow. When she was done she slung her saddle over her shoulder and found a campfire, sat and leaned against her saddle. Gerel passed her a spit of roasted lamb and onions wrapped within a stone-warmed flatbread. She ate silently, thinking on what the morrow would bring.

"My Queen." A hand shook Jin awake. "They are moving out." It was Tark, his arm splinted and wrapped in a bandage.

Jin sat upright, a sharp pain in her neck where she'd slept awkwardly on her saddle. It was as dark as pitch, embers glowing in the remains of the scraped-out fire-pit. Gerel grunted close by, pushed himself up onto one elbow.

"What do you mean?" Jin said, reaching for her water bottle and standing. She drank, then poured water over her face, blinked.

"See for yourself," Tark said.

They strode through the camp, Jin picking her way through and over sleeping bodies. Tark stopped and pointed.

Jin squinted into the darkness.

A thousand pinpricks of light were moving in the distance. Torches. Moving south, away from her. Jin looked to the east, saw no sign of dawn, no patch of grey on the horizon.

"What are they doing?" Gerel asked, joining them.

"They are risking their horses," Tark said, disgust in his voice.

"A desperate act," Jin said with a sneer. "Bleda thinks I will not follow until dawn, that I will not risk broken legs for my horses on this ground." She looked to the east again. "How long until dawn?" she said.

Tark shrugged. "The night is far from done."

Jin looked at the moving torches, kicked the dusty ground.

"Raise the warband," she said.

Gerel put a horn to his lips.

The ground was rising beneath Jin's feet, a gentle incline. She held a torch in front of her, checking the ground before each step, leading her horse by the reins, another mount tied and following behind.

The glow of Bleda's torches was far in the distance, but still visible. Jin stepped around a cluster of rabbit-holes, came across a guttered campfire, saw another at the edge of her torchlight.

"This is where they made camp," Tark said beside her. He was bending low, studying the ground.

"We need to move faster," Jin said, staring at the faint glow of torches in the distance.

"We should check their camp, this could be a trap, an ambush," Tark said.

Jin had thought of that, but in the end the thought of losing Bleda was so horrific that it made the risk worth it.

I have close to four thousand warriors. Even if this were an ambush, we would crush him.

"I will not lose Bleda," Jin said.

A long moment, Tark frowning, then he dipped his head.

"Onwards, then," he said.

They carried on, following a thousand torches into the night.

CHAPTER FORTY-SIX

BLEDA

Bleda called a halt. Grey light was seeping into the world, an orange glow in the east as the sun clawed its way over the edge of the world.

"Douse your torches," he called out, throat dry. He thrust both of the torches he was carrying into a stream, then walked along the flank of his horse, took the torch strapped to his saddle and plunged that into the water, another hiss and burst of steam. Finally, he strode back to his second mount, Dilis, having a long-earned rest from carrying him, and took the torch fastened to her saddle, too, and doused that one. Behind him a hundred and eighty warriors did the same.

He squatted beside the stream, drank from a cupped hand, then filled his water bottle.

"Drink," he said to his horses, leading them to the stream-bank. "We will not be stopping for a while."

They dipped their heads to the cold water, Bleda standing and looking behind. His warriors were spread along a hillside path that followed the stream bubbling out of these hills. They were tired, dust-covered, but an air of satisfaction rolled off them. Of a ruse gone well.

Yul was sitting on a boulder, running a whetstone along his sword-edge.

"They followed us, then," Ruga said.

"Aye," Bleda said, looking past his small warband and into the distance. "And it looks like all of them."

Behind them, threading between two gentle hills, was Jin's war-host, thousands of lit torches making the air about them glow. They were low in a valley, dawn not touching them, yet.

The most vital part of his plan had been for Jin's warband to cross his campground long before there was a hint of dawn's light. Otherwise they would have seen the tracks of eight hundred horses heading south-west, away from Bleda's force of one hundred and eighty, who Ruga was leading south-east, towards the mountains that bordered the desert lands of Tarbesh.

"They will know, now, though," Ruga said. "Even the Cheren can count."

"Aye," Bleda grunted.

"They could still turn back, once they realize they've been tricked," Ruga said, "or split their force and send half of them back. It will be a long journey, and a big gap, but they still have spare mounts. Ellac doesn't."

"I know. They must continue to follow us. All of them." Bleda strode to his horses and unbuckled a strap, pulling out a rolled package from behind his saddle. He shook it and held it out. A blue deel, blood staining the left arm, and a vest of lamellar armour. He dropped it on the ground beside the stream.

Ruga looked at the clothing, then at Bleda.

"You are relying heavily upon Jin's hatred for you," she said.

"I killed her father. Shamed her with a Ben-Elim half-breed."

Ruga nodded. "I would hate you, too."

"MAKE READY TO RIDE!" Bleda cried out. He took his bow from its saddle case and strung it, checked his sword over his back, made sure it wasn't sticking in its scabbard. Finally, he checked the hidden knife in his lamellar coat, the one he had used to cut Uldin's throat.

His warriors went through similar routines, then they were climbing into saddles, leather and iron creaking and jangling.

Bleda shifted in his saddle, then looked at Ruga.

"It's going to be a long day. Lead us on," he said, and then they were moving out, the drum of hooves filling the air.

CHAPTER FORTY-SEVEN

JIN

Jin reined in her horse and stared down at the ground.

Behind her the war-host was letting their mounts drink from the stream, filling water bottles, chewing on cured meat and hard biscuit.

Jin felt frozen, just staring at the blue deel and lamellar vest on the grass beside the stream.

Tark was already on the ground, looking at tracks. He approached the deel and vest, prodded it with the butt end of his spear shaft.

"That is what he was wearing," Tark said. "When he gave me this." He touched a red scar on his cheek, still raw, not quite healed.

Rage bubbled up inside her, a pressure within her chest. It had been close to boiling over from dawn's first light, when she had seen Bleda's warband on a hillside in the distance. Not the thousand she thought she was following. Not even two hundred. She had been tricked.

Tark squatted and stuck his spear butt into the stream, fished out a sodden torch.

"A good trick," he said.

Jin flashed him a dark look.

"We could go back," Tark said. "They have spare horses here, many hoof-prints were deeper, heavier than others. My guess is the bulk of the warband went south-west from their camp, but it is these who have the spare mounts. That would make sense now. Speed is their only hope of escaping from us."

Jin pulled in a deep breath, trying to dispel the red fog in her head. All she could think about was Bleda, of pushing a sword into his chest, slowly, watching his mouth open to scream, seeing in his eyes the knowledge that Jin had won.

She shook her head, looked behind, then forwards. Gerel sat his horse close by, silent and brooding.

"No, we go forwards," Jin said. "Bleda is here. We find him, kill him, then the Sirak have no lord, they are finished."

"And the other warband, the bulk of their strength?" Tark asked.

"The other warband is heading for the Tethys Pass," Jin said. "Once we have killed Bleda and his two hundred, then we shall travel west. We shall either catch them before the pass and kill them, or follow them into the west and kill them there." She shrugged.

"I like it. Either way, all the Sirak die," Gerel said.

"Yes. But Bleda first," Jin said.

Tark prodded the deel and lamellar vest.

"This could be a ruse, to keep you on this trail, stop you from turning back. Bleda might not even be here."

"It could be a ruse," Jin acknowledged. "But I don't think so. Bleda is too proud. He would not allow someone else to lead this band, so outnumbered and unlikely to survive. He is too noble to allow that. No, Bleda is with them, I am sure of it."

"Well, then," Tark said, swinging up into his saddle with a grimace, his arm not healed yet. "Let's be about catching him."

"Find Bleda, help me catch him, and your place and fame amongst the Cheren will be guaranteed for all generations."

"I will find him for you, my Queen. It is what I do."

Tark slowed in front of Jin.

They had been riding hard for more than half the day, the sun high and hot. Beneath them the ground was changing.

Rolling foothills shifting to steeper inclines, valleys and cliffs, the ground moving from grassland to dusty shingle.

"What is it?" Jin asked as she reined in beside him.

"Something…strange," Tark muttered, swinging from his saddle.

They were in a wide, stony valley, a number of gullies separated by cliffs leading up into the mountains. Tark walked to the end of the valley, stooping before the entrance to each gully. Jin clicked her tongue and her horse trotted after him.

"What is it?" Jin asked again.

Tark looked up at her, shaking his head.

"He is a clever one, this Bleda."

"Tell me," Jin said.

"They have separated. Riders have entered each gully."

Inside, Jin screamed.

"Bleda *must* be heading for the west," Jin said. "Not Tarbesh in the south. If he goes to Tarbesh he would be trapped. From there he would have to sail to the Land of the Faithful. So, which route leads west?"

"It's impossible to say," Tark said. "Unless you know the land. This is the Sirak southlands. I have raided Sirak territory all my life, but never have I been within fifty leagues of these southlands. To answer your question would need local knowledge. Does anyone know these lands?" he asked.

Jin's captains were all standing together. Hulan, Jargal, Vachir, Medek, Essen, all captains who had led smaller warbands in Jin's campaign against the Sirak Heartland. They all shook their heads, said no.

Jin drew in a long breath.

"Then we must split up," Jin said. "How many different routes, Tark?"

"Six," the scout said.

Another indrawn breath, Jin struggling to control her simmering rage.

"Hulan, Jargal, Medek, Essen, Vachir, take five hundred warriors each. The rest with me."

The gully steepened rapidly, the ground littered with shingle and rocks. It was slow going, Jin felt the passage of time like a burning candle in her chest. The wax melting, the light fading. Tark was in front of her, riding a while, then slowing, observing the ground.

He pointed to lichen on a boulder as Jin passed it, a scuff, horsehair stuck to it. A little further up the gully, a pile of horse dung.

It was still warm.

The sun was starting to dip into the horizon, the temperature dropping.

No. If darkness falls we will never find him.

A shout from Tark, other warriors behind Jin calling out.

The silhouette of a horse and rider up ahead, standing beside a boulder. The horse's head was dipped, eating a patch of grass. The rider sat straight-backed, clothed in a leather surcoat and iron helm, apparently uncaring that Jin was riding up the gully towards them, fifteen hundred Cheren at her back.

Before she knew it Jin had her bow in her hands, an arrow nocked and sent speeding through the air. It punched into the rider's shoulder.

The rider swayed, then was still. No cry of pain. They didn't even look Jin's way.

The sound of arrows loosed all around, a dark cloud rising and falling, a ripple of *thunks* as thirty arrows slammed into the rider. They toppled from the saddle, disappearing. The horse shied slightly, then calmed and continued to eat.

Jin kicked her horse into a canter, oblivious of the terrain, and was the first to reach the horse and rider.

Cheren were about her heartbeats later, bows pointing in all directions, waiting for the ambush and arrows that all thought was coming.

The gully levelled off here, a pool of clear water, dark green grass growing about it. More horses and riders were here, scattered about. Some of the horses were drinking from the pool, others cropping at grass, all of their riders strangely straight-backed and wholly uninterested in Jin and her Cheren warriors.

Jin looked at the warrior on the ground, a mass of arrows protruding from him.

Protruding from *it*.

Jin jumped from her horse and kicked the warrior. The leather coat fell away to reveal a branch of wood, the coat stuffed with grass and straw. She stood and stared at it, for a moment her mind struggling to understand what she was seeing.

Then she raised her head to the sky and screamed.

Far in the distance, horns echoed through the mountains.

CHAPTER FORTY-EIGHT

BLEDA

Bleda held his bow ready, an arrow nocked, his right hand holding two more. He glanced at the jagged skyline, the sun sinking into the mountains.

We almost made it. He'd thought the scarecrows on horseback would have saved them, had almost kissed Ruga when she'd come up with the idea. Twenty of their spare horses slapped and sent galloping up each gully, each with a scarecrow of branches and shrubs stuffed into Sirak armour and tied to their backs.

It had hurt him to lose a hundred of their horses, but if that bought them enough time, then it was the difference between life and death. Bleda and his hundred and eighty warriors had set off up the gully that Ruga was certain led to the Tethys Pass. The only problem was that there had been a fall of rocks across the gully, and Bleda and his warband had been forced to dismount and clear a passage through. It had taken too long, and although after that they had moved quickly, given the rocky terrain and steepness of their trail, it was not long before riders from the rear were cantering forwards and warning Bleda that there were sounds of pursuit.

Soon after there had been shouts and the sound of arrows, one of his warriors falling with an arrow through the back of his neck.

Bleda had led his warband on, a burst of reckless speed, hoping to maintain a gap long enough for the sun to set and night to fall. But then they had come across a second rockfall. It was too late. The Cheren were upon them.

And so here he was, sitting in his saddle with a hundred riders lined around him, bows in hand, waiting. He patted his horse's neck, a gelding taken from the Cheren. It whickered at him. Bleda had ridden Dilis through the day and she was salt-stained with sweat, resting with their other spare mounts. Yul was beside him, bow in his fist.

"No foolish bravery," Yul said to him. "I swore an oath to Ellac."

"We have a plan," Bleda said. "I will stick to it."

Yul grunted.

They formed a row across the gully, cliffs and boulders guarding both flanks.

A good, defensible spot, Bleda thought, *if I were a White-Wing. Their wall of shields would work well here, and this ground is not made for horses. We need space, the open plain to wage our war.*

But who knows how many Cheren are riding up this gully after us?

The sound of horses' hooves, a whinny, and figures appeared around the curve of a huge granite boulder. One horse, two, a handful more, spread out across the gully, moving carefully.

Scouts.

Bleda drew his arrow, felt the tension build as his bow bent, feather scratching his cheek, and loosed. His left arm quivered a little; the wound in his bicep had healed, but the muscle inside was still weak. His arrow flew well enough, took the first scout in the chest, punching through leather vest and wool deel, the rider toppling backwards over his high saddle.

All around Bleda bows thrummed and arrows flew, the handful of scouts entering the gully falling in a matter of heart-beats. One put a horn to his lips and blew, the call being taken up behind him, horn blasts echoing up the ravine, deafening.

An arrow hurled the last scout from his saddle.

Will they come slowly, or rush us?

The horns kept ringing, but over them Bleda heard the thunder and crack of hooves.

"READY!" Bleda called out, another arrow nocked, his blood thumping in his veins.

The first riders cleared the boulder, a solid line, warriors riding hard, leaning over their mounts' necks, keeping low to reduce how much of a target they were. More riders behind them.

"LOOSE!" Bleda cried, and his line of warriors released their first arrows, all of them nocking and loosing, nocking and loosing, again and again.

He saw the Cheren doing the same, the sound of arrows whipping through the air like a kicked nest of hornets.

A drawn breath as Bleda reached for a fresh fist of arrows, before his first three had found their marks. He heard screams from the Cheren, saw riders fall. Screams around him, as well, Sirak tumbling, swaying, falling from mounts.

"LOOSE!" Bleda yelled again, his bowstring thrumming as he loosed another three arrows in quick succession. Saw the Cheren were sweeping around the boulder and into the gully like a tidal wave, filling his sight. More Sirak fell about him. An arrow *tinged* off Yul's helm, rocking the warrior in his saddle.

"Now," Yul said beside him.

"RIDE!" Bleda cried, touching his reins, his mount turning, and then he was giving it its head, letting it gallop up the gully, away from the Cheren. All around him Sirak broke into a gallop, Yul close by. He looked over at Bleda and grinned, the first time Bleda could remember such an expression on the warrior's face.

Bleda grinned back.

If we are to die, we will make a song of it.

He looked back, saw at least a score of his warriors littering the ground, wiping the smile from his face.

They followed me, and now they are dead.

They sped around a bend in the gully, out of sight of the

pursuing Cheren, arrows stopping for a moment. Up ahead Bleda saw the second wall of tumbled rocks that had blocked their way. They had tried to clear a path through this rock-fall, too, but it had quickly become apparent that there was no chance of doing it in time.

Ruga had been inconsolable with shame and had tried to throw herself upon her sword.

I have led you to your death, she had said. Bleda had grabbed her wrist and Yul had told her it was more shameful to die before her King, unless it was in defence of Bleda's life.

Bleda saw her now, a face looking out at him from high up in the rocks. There were another eighty Sirak around Ruga, all waiting with bows ready. All knew the rocks had ruined their plan of staying ahead of their pursuers. Now the only option was to turn and fight, to kill all who followed them, or to die. Bleda hoped to lure the Cheren into a charge, to get them to fill the ravine, no slow, stealthy attack from them, just a killing ground full of the Cheren. From the sounds of thunder sweeping up the ravine, this plan had worked well.

Maybe too well. They are too close, number too many.

Battle-cries behind Bleda, the *whip* of arrows as the Cheren surged around the bend in the ravine. A strangled cry close by, a Sirak tumbling to the ground.

Bleda turned in his saddle, leaving his horse to choose her own path, only his knees guiding her, and he looked back, bow drawn, sent an arrow flying at the mass of Cheren behind him. And another. Yul and other Sirak riders did the same, and Bleda heard the *snap* and *twang* of arrows flying from bows behind him, a hiss as arrows flew overhead from Ruga and her eighty.

Cheren fell, scores of them, horses, too, and in heartbeats the ravine was a tangled mass of horses and warriors.

More arrows flew, more death rained upon the Cheren. Bleda drew and loosed.

Cheren began to flow around the snarl of horseflesh and

limbs, arrows flying up the ravine. Yul cried out and swayed in his saddle, an arrow high in his back.

Shouts amongst the Cheren, a hail of arrows flying Bleda's way.

They see me, my lamellar coat.

Arrows spattered around him, Bleda twisting in his saddle, a jerk of his knees sending his horse galloping right, towards the ravine's boulder-strewn edge. Arrows followed him, ricocheting off stone. One thumped into his mount's flank, another its back leg, and the gelding faltered, an arrow flew spinning, deflected by Bleda's lamellar plates. A trio of arrows slammed into his horse's side and neck. It screamed, stumbled and fell, Bleda suddenly airborne, flying weightless through the air, his bow slipping from his grip.

He hit the ground with a crash, breath flying from his lungs, rolled and crunched into a rock, rearing black above him. Spots dotted his vision, a wave of nausea, and then he was scrambling to his knees.

All he could think of was his bow.

His brother's bow.

Where is it? If I am to die, I want it in my hands.

So much of him was caught up in that bow. Life, when it had been happy, as a child in Arcona with his kin. And then, again, when Riv had returned it to him.

Riv.

Her face filled his mind.

His hand moved, desperately searching the ground.

The thunder of hooves. Cheren were pouring up the ravine, only a few hundred paces behind him. His horse was lying on the ground, bloody froth on his lips. He couldn't see his bow.

A scream to his right: Yul, realizing that Bleda was not with them. He was dragging on his reins, turning, galloping back to Bleda, leaning in his saddle.

"No," Bleda said.

A volley of arrows slammed all around Yul, speckling the ground, piercing his horse, the animal's front legs folding, collapsing, and Yul was hurled through the air. He hit the ground, rolled, cried out, the arrow in his back snapping. He came to his feet and stumbled towards Bleda. His bow was gone, his arm was reaching over his shoulder, sword hissing from his scabbard and then he was standing before Bleda, a human shield.

Arrows flew at them, Bleda staring up at Yul. The warrior's blade moved, a blur slicing through the air, and arrows fell about Bleda, chopped in two. One slammed into Yul's thigh, another skimming from his helm. Others punched into the boulder behind Bleda.

Shouts, war-cries, and Bleda looked up the ravine to see Ruga leading a charge from the rocks, scores of warriors behind her. And the Sirak he had been riding with were all turning, riding back towards the flood of Cheren.

"No," Bleda whispered.

It will all be for nothing. They will all die here.

Another volley of arrows at Yul, the warrior's sword moving impossibly fast, only the hiss of air, the crack of wood, broken arrows falling on the ground around Bleda. Yul grunted, staggered back, another arrow punched through mail into his side, high, around his ribs, blood seeping.

"Come, death," Yul snarled at the wall of Cheren warriors.

Bleda threw himself at Yul, crashed into the back of his legs, knocking Yul to the floor. More arrows hammering down around them. Bleda dragged him back, tight to the boulder, a partial overhang giving them slight cover.

Yul struggled, trying to regain his feet.

"LOOK AT ME!" Bleda yelled, grabbing Yul's face.

Yul froze, stared at Bleda.

Bleda pulled an arrow from his quiver. He pressed it into Yul's hand.

"Take this arrow and give it to Riv. Tell her to slay Jin with it. Tell her I love her, that I tried..."

"No," Yul grunted. "I will not abandon you."

"I am your KING," Bleda growled, "and my command is this. Lead my people, help Riv. She is with the Order of the Bright Star in Dun Seren. Help them, too."

Yul stared at him a long moment. His faced twisted, a battle going on within him.

A flight of Cheren arrows peppered the boulder about them, striking sparks.

"No," Yul said. "My Queen died without me by her side, a shame I struggle to bear each day. I will *not* leave you here to die alone." He looked down at himself, his body studded with Cheren arrows. "And besides, I do not think I would get very far. Let us die together, as a Sirak king and his oathsworn man should. Killing our enemies." He gripped his sword.

Bleda looked into Yul's eyes, then nodded.

A grating sound behind them, a hiss, like steam, and the boulder that Bleda and Yul were leaning against moved. Disappearing, as Bleda tumbled backwards onto his back into a cave or tunnel as the wall vanished. A huge face peered down at him, a woman, all slabs and sharp angles.

She looked down at them, scowling.

No, she's not human. She's a giant.

"What in all the hells is going on?" she growled.

CHAPTER FORTY-NINE

DREM

Drem swayed in his saddle, moving with the rhythm of Friend's gait. It was unlike a horse's movement, more a rolling, lumbering, permanent swaying, like being at sea, rather than the precise movement of a horse, and his body used different muscles to keep him sitting in his saddle. After his first day of riding upon the white bear, Drem's legs and lower back had ached more than he could ever remember. The next morning he had hardly been able to move from his cot, his muscles were so stiff and painful. Now, though, after over a moon of travelling, it felt as natural to him as walking. He leaned forwards and patted the bear's thick-muscled neck through a coat of mail, and received a rumble in response.

Drem was riding down a hard-packed forest path, more like a road. To his left the forest was cut back thirty or forty paces, and to his right the river Rhenus flowed, wide and dark. Branches curled over the path, a lattice of canopy above him, though it thinned over the river, allowing beams of sunlight to intrude on this twilight world. Drem marvelled at the forest, the trees so much bigger than anything he had ever seen before. He'd thought the forests of the Desolation were impressive, but this...

"Put your eyes back in your head," Keld said, riding a horse beside him, "they're only trees, and there's a lot more where they came from. It's what they're hiding that we need to be looking for."

"Aye," said Drem, taking his eyes from the canopy above to search the gloom that pressed about them. He saw loping shadows flitting amongst the trees: Fen and Ralla and other wolven-hounds that were part of their scouting party.

"There it is," Keld said, pointing ahead. A bridge appeared, crossing the river into a dark-stoned fortress, walls thick with ivy surrounding a squat keep. "Brikan, garrison of the Order."

They were riding at the head of a score of warriors, all huntsmen and women of the Order, sent ahead by Byrne to lead the garrison of Brikan out of Forn and join the warband in their march southwards, to Ripa.

"*Brikan, Brikan.*" Rab flapped down from above, setting other crows in the trees to squawking.

"We know," Keld said to the crow, "but thank you, anyway."

"*Welcome,*" Rab croaked, as he spiralled above their heads.

Drem saw figures upon the wall. A horn call rang through the forest.

"Shouldn't be here long," Keld called out to all in the scouting party. "Rest your mounts, a bite to eat and drink. Reng, soon as you've done that, round up a crew and scout out a perimeter. Don't want any surprises."

"Aye, chief," Reng said, a slender warrior, lean-muscled. Drem had sparred with Reng many times in Dun Seren and been surprised by his wiry strength. He had expected him to be fast, which he was, but the strength in his lean frame seemed to exceed the man's weight.

They reached the bridge that crossed the river and led directly into the fortress. Hooves clattered on stone, Friend's claws scratching gouges. Warriors of the Order lined the gate-house wall. Keld raised a hand to them, and the gates swung open. Drem rode into a wide courtyard, feeling a hundred pairs of eyes upon him and the white bear. The courtyard was edged with a moss-covered stone wall, a score of buildings around the sides. Stables, forge, grain stores, water barrels, a haybarn. Drem saw a handful of wains fully loaded, auroch harnessed and ready, and a few score horses tethered to rails; they were all saddled and ready to ride. In front of Drem a set of wide steps led up to the keep, a squat building wrapped in vine. Warriors lined the walls, others were in the courtyard and on the keep's steps. Drem counted over a hundred.

A man strode down the steps of the keep, grey hair tied back except for his warrior braid, a beard grey and dark as storm clouds, his eyebrows jutting from his brow. He was dressed for war in a coat of mail, a surcoat of the Order worn over it, black wool with the bright star upon his chest. He was of average height, with a lightness to his step that spoke to Drem of ability and speed, despite his age. Sword, knife and axe all hung from his weapons-belt.

"Well met," he called out to Keld, as the scouting party spilt into Brikan's courtyard, wolven-hounds loping amongst them, all wrapped in coats of mail.

"Well met, Halden," Keld called back to him. He dismounted, a stablehand taking his reins, Fen and Ralla falling in either side of him as he strode to Halden. They took each other's arms in the warrior grip.

"Mind if my crew eat some of your food and drink some of your water?"

"Course not," Halden said, gesturing towards the stables and water barrels. Drem saw that a long table had been laid out, food and drink upon it.

"We've packed all we can carry," Halden said, "might as well try and eat the rest."

Most of Keld's crew dismounted and led their horses towards the stables and water.

"You look ready to ride," Keld said, nodding to the saddled horses and loaded wains.

"Aye," Halden said. "We had visitors, three nights gone. Winged visitors."

"Meical, Riv and the others," Keld said.

"Aye," Halden said. "Strange times we are living in. Meical

free of his skin of metal. A half-breed Ben-Elim flying the skies in broad daylight."

"That's Riv," Drem said. "She swore the oath."

Halden looked up at Drem upon Friend's back.

"I'm glad to see it," he said. "It's about time, been too long in coming. And I'm guessing we can use all the help we can get." He stepped back, staring at the white bear. "And this big lump is a pleasant surprise. I've seen keeps smaller than this bear." His eyes drifted up to Drem. "Big as you are, you're the smallest giant I've ever seen," he said.

"Ha, he's no giant," Keld said. "You're looking at Drem ben Olin. He's Olin and Neve's boy."

"Well, I'll be," Halden said with a grin. "You'd best be getting your arse down here, then, so I can give you a proper welcome."

Drem lifted one leg over Friend's saddle and slid to the ground. It was a long way down, but he had mastered it now. Alcyon had adapted Friend's saddle, added a set of leather hoops to the stirrups, a little like a ladder, but Drem only used them to climb up into the saddle. Getting down was much easier.

As falling is easier than climbing.

Hooves clattered on stone as Reng led a crew of five out of the courtyard, dipping his head to Keld and Halden as he went. A handful of wolven-hounds followed them, loping out of the gate and across the bridge.

Halden stood and looked Drem up and down.

"Well, you're a big one." He slapped Drem's shoulder. "I can see Olin in you, and your mother. They were fine people. Friends."

Drem just nodded. It still felt strange, that so many people at the Order had known his mam and da so well.

Better than me.

Halden looked up at the white bear. "Well, there's a story there, I'm guessing. You're the first man I've ever heard of to ride a giant bear."

"There is a story," Keld said, "a long one. Drem and this bear have saved each other's lives, many times each now, from Kergard in the Desolation to Dun Seren. And likely will again, before this war is done."

"So, it's happening, then," Halden said. Drem thought he saw hints of excitement and apprehension mingled on the man's face, though he could not be sure. He'd never been a very good judge of what a man was thinking by the expressions he pulled. Olin had tried to give him lessons.

"Asroth awakened, the Kadoshim taking Drassil, the Ben-Elim routed. The last battle of the Long War, ending in our times." Halden blew out a long breath, then smiled. "We've waited a long time for this, my friend," he said to Keld.

"Aye. And we'd best be riding soon, if we don't want to miss it," Keld said. "Byrne and the rest are half a day's ride west. Don't want to let them have all the fun."

"As you see, we are all ready. You and your crew refresh yourselves, and we'll be off."

Drem saw that Keld's scouts were already at the table. Wolven-hounds were snarling over a trough of butchered scraps.

The bear swung its head, snuffling, raised his head, sniffed the air and then growled.

Drem was learning to tell the difference between the bear's growls. Some were playful, or mournful, or friendly.

This one was none of those.

Wolven-hounds lifted their heads from their gnawing of bones, looked to the open gateway of the keep and also growled.

A horn blew upon the walls.

"Rider approaching," a voice called.

The thud of hooves beyond Brikan's walls, and Drem looked out through the open gateway, across the bridge and into the forest.

Reng appeared, riding hard, a wolven-hound bounding at his side. There was blood on the hound's muzzle. Blood on Reng.

Behind them a mist boiled from the forest.

CHAPTER FIFTY

BLEDA

Bleda stared at the giant. She was shaven-headed, apart from a ridge of black spiky hair running down the middle of her head.

"Dun Seren," she said, her voice like rusty iron. "You said Dun Seren. You said the *Order of the Bright Star*."

Other figures loomed behind her, more giants, heads shaved, clothed in mail, leather and fur.

"Yes," Bleda said. "I am allied to the Order of the Bright Star."

Screams filtered into the cave he was half in. The pounding of hooves and a Cheren rider appeared, horse rearing, his bow drawn. He hesitated a moment, seeing the cave opening and a giant leaning over Bleda, but only for a heartbeat and then his arrow was leaping from the string of his bow, straight at Bleda's chest.

The giant swung her arm, a huge round shield covering Bleda and Yul. The arrow punched into it, a spray of splinters near Bleda's face as the arrowhead pierced wood. Bleda heard a scream cut short, the splatter of blood and the Cheren warrior crashed to the ground, lifeless eyes staring at him.

The shield withdrew, the giant stared at him again, a spear in her fist dripping blood.

"Help us, please," Bleda said.

"Do giants still stand with the Order?" the giant asked him.

"Aye," Bleda said. "Ethlinn, Balur One-Eye...Alcyon." They were the only giants Bleda knew well enough to recall in an instant.

The giant recoiled, her face twisting in a scowl, Bleda thought she was going to kill him. Instead she stood, said something to the giants behind her in a language he didn't understand. One of them raised a horn to his lips and blew, the sound deep and ominous, echoing through the cave and out into the ravine.

Other Cheren riders rode at them, reining in their mounts, bows nocked and drawn—warriors searching for Bleda and Yul. At the sound of the horn they hesitated.

The giant stepped out in front of them, her shield high, and threw a spear. It pierced a rider, hurled him from his horse, flying through the air to crash into another horse and rider behind him. The giant took a few long strides forwards, startlingly fast, at the same time pulling a one-handed hammer from her belt and hefting it. She smashed it into the chest of the second Cheren rider, the sound of bones shattering and the rider disappeared from her saddle.

"With me," the giantess cried over her shoulder.

"Kill the ones in blue," Bleda shouted to her. "Those in grey are with me."

She nodded.

Other giants issued from the cave, striding over Bleda and Yul and out into the ravine, just as the charging ranks of Cheren and Sirak met with a deafening crash. Along the ravine other granite doors opened, more giants emerging from them. The giants bellowed a war-cry and charged, wielding long-hafted hammers, axes and spears. They slammed into the flank of the Cheren like a wave into kindling. Cheren warriors and their horses fell in an explosion of limbs and blood.

Bleda scrambled to his feet, gave Yul his arm and pulled the warrior up. He was wounded many times, arrows protruding from his leg and torso.

One by one Yul gripped the arrows and snapped them, a grimace of pain. Then he hefted his sword and grinned at Bleda.

"Let's kill some Cheren."

CHAPTER FIFTY-ONE

DREM

"Revenants," Drem breathed.

Keld and Halden ran to the wall, speeding up the stairwell, Drem behind them, others from the courtyard following.

Reng was galloping for the bridge, a black mist rolling along the path behind him, curling from the trees either side, then his horse's hooves were cracking on stone and he was bursting through the open gates of the fortress, his wolven-hound leaping behind him.

"Ware Revenants," Reng cried out.

Feet pounded on steps; warriors manned the wall, Keld's scouts amongst them.

"Halden, best be closing those gates," Keld said grimly.

"CLOSE THE GATES!" Halden bellowed, then looked to Keld. "What are Revenants?"

"Look," Keld said.

The mist boiled along the path, spilling out onto the riverside. More vapour flowed from the wall of trees beyond the river, rolled up to the bridge and stopped, churning sluggishly. Shapes moved within the mist.

"How many ways out of here?" Drem asked.

"That's it," Keld nodded at the bridge.

The flapping of wings—Rab all but fell from the sky above them.

"*Revenants, Revenants,*" the bird was squawking, alighting on the wall before Drem and Keld.

"Will that bird ever tell us anything before we already know it," Keld muttered.

"*Worried,*" Rab croaked.

"Rab, fly to Byrne as fast as your wings will take you, tell her what is happening here."

"*Rab not leave friends,*" Rab protested.

"Go now," Keld said. "If Byrne doesn't learn of this, and soon, then none of us will be leaving here."

Rab hopped from claw to claw.

"*Rab fly, save friends,*" he said, then leaped into the air and flapped over their heads, spiralled once and flew west.

On the riverbank a figure stepped out from the mist.

A man once, now twisted. He was tall, his head shaven, pale as parchment, black veins mapping his skin. He looked up at Drem and the others on the wall, hissed at them, revealing a mouth too full of razored teeth. One eye drooped shut, a scar running through it. His chin was crusted black with blood.

A memory flashed through Drem's mind, of Gulla rising before a bloodstained table, of seven figures stepping forward, raising their chins and baring their throats to the Kadoshim lord.

"That's one of the Seven," Drem said.

"Revenants? The Seven?" Halden said.

"Dark spawn of Gulla and twisted magic," Drem replied.

"Rune-marked spear," Keld cried, turning and looking down into the courtyard. One of his scouts threw a spear up to him.

Keld caught it, in one motion turned, arm whipping back and then forwards, the spear hurtling from his grip. It flew down from the wall, across the water.

The Revenant on the riverbank saw it, watched, then swayed. A spark of blue fire as the spear's edge grazed the creature's ribs, sailed on to disappear in the mist. There was a gurgled scream, a flare of blue light inside the mist.

"Bollocks," Keld muttered. "Do you have a rune-marked blade?"

The figure on the riverbank raised a taloned hand and pointed at the keep.

"Aye," Halden said, patting his scabbarded sword.

"Brothers, sisters, be ready to FIGHT," Keld called out. "All with a rune-marked blade to the wall and gates."

"Only a runed blade will hurt them," Drem said to Halden. "Anyone without such a blade will die a quick death at these creatures' hands."

The Revenant on the bank opened its mouth and screeched. A high-pitched, scratching sound issued from its mouth, like a thousand flies trying to crawl into Drem's brain. He fought the urge to put his hands over his ears.

The mist moved, slid onto the bridge, gaining momentum, flowing across, towards the barred gates.

Keld turned and sprinted down the wall's steps, running for his horse.

Drem drew his sword and thrust it into Halden's hands. "It's runed—give it to someone who needs it." Halden grunted and turned, barking out orders to his warriors as he strode along the wall, heading to the gates. Everywhere was motion: warriors running to the gate, racing to the walls. Drem glimpsed Keld's scouts handing out their weapons—all of Keld's crew had more than one runed blade, whether it be spear, axe or sword.

Drem drew his seax and hand-axe, hefted them, felt the excitement and fear of imminent battle flutter through his veins.

The mist slammed into the gates, burst upwards like a dark wave, wisps curling over the wall. The barred gate shook as bodies slammed into it, hundreds, the sound of wood creaking.

Keld appeared beside him, his bow and quiver of arrows in his fist. Fen and Ralla were with him, snarling, muscles rippling in their coats of mail. Drem looked to the white bear, saw he was standing below in the courtyard, facing the gates, snarling and scratching the ground.

Keld rested his quiver of arrows against the wall and strung his bow. Impacts against the gate echoed through the courtyard, a tremor Drem could feel in his boots and bones. He leaned over the battlement, peering at the bridge and gate.

That gate is not like Dun Seren's. It is not going to hold.

Revenants appeared, swarming out of the mist, climbing the gate and towers in a tangle of snarled limbs, just as they had done at Dun Seren.

"BURN THEM!" Keld cried out as he drew an arrow from his quiver, leaned out over the wall, loosed at the Revenants climbing the gate. A spark of blue fire. Another arrow loosed, then another and another. Bodies fell from the wall, into the river.

Drem bounced on his toes, feeling both frustrated that he couldn't get at the Revenants and a sense of building dread in his gut about the numbers they were facing. There had been no warning of this attack, no time to tell Halden and the warriors of Brikan that fire was the greatest weapon against the Revenants, and no chance to explain the urgency of identifying and killing the Revenants' leader. It was all happening too fast.

The Revenants clambering the wall were close to the top. Some of Keld's scouts were there, stabbing with rune-marked spears, other warriors of Brikan with runed blades or burning torches. Drem saw a constant crackle of blue flame in the swarm at the gate, a Revenant here and there falling away, flames sprouting from face or body, but the throng of creatures swallowed their dead and kept hurling themselves at the gates, others surging upwards in a mass of bodies.

Keld loosed his last arrow, saw a Revenant tumble into the river, disappearing with hardly a splash.

With a growl, he dropped his bow and shrugged his shield onto his arm, drew his sword.

"With me, Drem," he said, and strode along the wall towards the gateway.

Revenants were clawing their way onto the wall, tendrils of

mist curling up around them, grabbing at limbs even as they were stabbed. A warrior of the Order was dragged screaming over the wall. Then another. A Revenant leaped out of the mist, landed on all fours, threw itself into a warrior, the two of them falling into the courtyard.

Drem reached the press, leaned and stabbed a Revenant as it climbed, saw a hundred more beneath it. The mist on the bridge seethed and swarmed with dark figures.

There are too many.

"We must find their captain," Keld grunted, thrusting his sword into the mass of enemies in front of him.

Revenants were clambering over the wall, now too many of them to push back. One threw itself onto a warrior of Brikan. She swung a sword but the creature was too fast, surging inside her guard, jaws wide, teeth searching for flesh. Drem stabbed it in the waist with his seax, a burst of blue flame, saw it spasm and scream, chopped into its skull with his axe, bone and rotten flesh exploding. The Revenant collapsed, the woman pushing it away in revulsion.

A loud crack from the gates, vibrating up through stone. Drem and those around him froze for a moment. Another crack, louder, the iron hinges of the gate squealing.

Then in a burst and screech of iron and splintered wood the gates exploded inwards. Drem and those around him on the wall above the gates were thrown to the ground.

A frozen moment, a cloud of dust filling the courtyard, slowly settling. Drem clambered to his feet, saw Keld rising.

Black mist poured through the shattered gateway, followed by countless Revenants.

"SHIELD WALL!" a voice yelled in the courtyard, Halden, standing with forty or fifty warriors of Brikan. Round shields came together with a crack, sharp steel glinting. The Revenants hit it like a wave, the wall staggered, straining, but it held against the first rush, swords and spears stabbing out, flashes of blue flame and Revenants fell back, screaming.

They have no chance, Drem thought, *the shield wall is too short, its flanks unprotected.* Even as Drem looked he saw Revenants pouring around the shield wall's edges, leaping and tearing at warriors.

There was a deafening roar as Friend waded into the Revenants on the shield wall's right flank. He swiped with his claws, his huge jaws clamping onto bodies and shaking them. Revenants went flying through the air like sticks, bellies opened, torsos and limbs shredded. Drem saw a severed head spinning through the air.

It gave a moment's reprieve; the shield wall took a step forwards, stabbing down at the scattered Revenants. But the tide of creatures through the smashed gates was relentless, the courtyard filling. A new wave threw themselves at Friend, swarming over him.

"No, not again," Drem breathed, and leaped into the courtyard.

He slammed into a knot of Revenants, scattered them, though they were instantly twisting and turning, leaping back to their feet. Drem slashed and stabbed with axe and seax, crackling blue flame as Revenants fell about him. Then Keld was at his side, Fen and Ralla throwing themselves at the creatures, ripping at limbs, Keld working with them, his runed sword stabbing and hacking at any Revenant the wolven-hounds pinned or distracted.

They cut a way through to Friend. The bear was covered with Revenants biting and slashing at him, frenziedly trying to rip through his coat of mail. Friend let out a deafening roar, spittle flying, and he reared onto his back legs, throwing a dozen black figures in all directions, slammed back down to earth, crushing a fallen Revenant; the ground shook. Drem chopped into a skull, stabbed through a back, ripped his blade free, sliced another Revenant across the face. Keld punching Revenants with his shield, stabbing, chopped into one between neck and shoulder, his blade snaring in bone, dragged down, his booted foot on the dying creature's chest, yanking his blade free.

And then the bear was free, a space cleared around them, dead or dying Revenants all about, gurgling, scratching. Fen and Ralla crouched either side of Keld, snarling. Drem strode to Friend, stood with his back to the bear's shoulder, looking into the courtyard.

Halden's shield wall was swamped: dead Revenants piled before it but so many more were climbing over the dead. Drem saw one grab a shield rim and drag the warrior holding it out from the ranks, three Revenants falling upon her, tearing and biting. A warrior stepped into the breach from the second rank with a two-handed spear and pierced a Revenant, blade punching into its chest and bursting out of its back. But the spear was not rune-marked. The Revenant gripped the shaft piercing its chest and dragged itself along the wood towards the warrior, grabbing him by the throat, talons raking flesh to red ribbons.

A scream from above, shadows flitting across the courtyard, and Drem looked up, saw winged figures swooping down. Their wings were black and leathery.

"WARE THE SKIES!" Keld cried as Kadoshim and half-breeds fell upon the courtyard. Drem saw a half-breed woman swoop at the shield wall and stab down with a spear, a dozen more winged warriors following her.

It's her, Gulla's daughter.

The shield wall shattered with her attack, a hole opened that Revenants poured through, the shield wall breaking and splintering.

"TO THE KEEP!" Keld yelled, started to run, stopped and grabbed Drem by the shoulder, half dragging him. Drem turned and ran with him, Fen and Ralla bounding ahead, leaping up the wide steps. "Friend!" Drem bellowed. The bear was swatting at another Revenant, then turned and lumbered with them.

The keep's doors were open. Brikan was built from stone by giants in an age long past. Drem ran through into a deep hall, turned at the entrance. Friend trudged past—there was room enough for him.

Keld stood at the gateway and put a horn to his lips, gave it three short blows, the sound echoing in the hall, ringing out into the courtyard.

"WARRIORS OF THE ORDER!" Keld yelled. "TO ME! The doors," he called to Drem, and the two of them began to heave them closed. Warriors leaped up the stairs, ran into the hall, ten, fifteen. All about the courtyard battle raged. A knot of warriors from the shield wall were fighting their way up the steps, others caught in scattered melees. Horses bucked and screamed as Revenants fell upon them, a stampede as ropes were snapped, some horses galloping for the gateway, trampling Revenants and clattering across the bridge, others falling to the horde, dragged down by a wave of teeth and talons. Their screams filled the courtyard.

Reng burst through the doorway, his wolven-hound still with him, a handful more of Keld's scouts following. They turned and helped Drem and Keld with the doors, some reaching for the wooden bar. Halden was leading a knot of warriors up the steps. Drem ran to join them, chopped his axe into a Revenant's wrist, severing the hand that had just grabbed a warrior's shield. He ducked a swipe of talons from the other hand and stabbed upwards with his seax, punched into the creature's belly, on, upwards and deeper, found its rotted heart, twisted his blade and then pushed it away.

"YOU!" a voice cried. Drem looked into the courtyard to see Gulla's half-breed daughter staring at him. She hurled her spear; Drem stumbled to the side, the spear striking stone and flying through the keep's doors.

She beat her wings, moving towards him.

Drem turned and ran, throwing himself into the hall just behind Halden.

Keld and Reng were closing the doors.

Drem hefted the wooden bar, ready to set it in the doors, another warrior helping him.

Something changed in the courtyard, a stillness settling upon the Revenants, all of them halting whatever they were doing. They all looked up. Survivors of the Order took the opportunity, running to the keep's open doorway, flying through.

Drem saw the Revenants' captain again, standing in the wreckage of the smashed gateway. He was looking up, too.

Drem followed their stare, saw half-breeds descending, maybe fifty of them, alighting in the courtyard amongst the dead, then a score of Kadoshim. They spread through the courtyard, forming a ring. Another figure descended, dark wings wide, beating slowly, dust stirring on the ground. He was a Kadoshim, but different. Taller, limbs stretched, musculature striated. He wore a coat of dark mail, a nimbus shadow about him like a dark halo, and he had only one eye, which glowed red.

"Gulla," Drem whispered, though all in the hall heard him; the silence in the courtyard was absolute.

Gulla looked about him, surveying the dead, saw warriors of the Order scattered everywhere, the courtyard slick with their blood. He smiled, then looked up at the keep, saw Keld, Reng and Drem.

Keld slammed his door shut, Reng a heartbeat behind him.

CHAPTER FIFTY-TWO

BLEDA

Bleda sat on a stone chair too big for him; he felt like a child with his feet dangling. He was exhausted, limbs heavy, his very bones aching, but there was also an energy flowing through him.

I am alive, when I thought I was dead. Should have been dead.

He looked about. They were in a huge cavern, wide bowls burning with blue-tinged fire set around the chamber.

Yul was lying on a table, his mail and deel stripped away, the giant cutting arrows from his body. All around them injured Sirak warriors were being tended. About a hundred of his warriors were still breathing, survivors of the battle in the gully.

"Are you . . . Raina?" he said.

The giant's head snapped up at him and she frowned, brows bunching.

"How do you know that?" she said in her voice of iron.

"A crow from Dun Seren was looking for you. Durl. He hasn't found you yet, then?"

"No," Raina grunted, her frown deepening.

The battle in the gully had been short and fierce. All of his Sirak had ridden at the Cheren, trying to get to Bleda and Yul, but the Cheren numbers had been overwhelming. But then the giants had charged from their hidden tunnels, crashing into the Cheren's flank, axe and hammer and spear smashing the Cheren into pulped, bloody ruin. In less than a hundred heartbeats it had been all but over, close to five hundred Cheren lying on the rocky floor, bleeding into the mountain's bones.

Other giants came and stood around Raina, tall and brooding. All of them had shaved heads, strips of hair down the middle of their heads. Most of them wore leather and mail. One that was standing close to Raina wore a long, short-sleeved coat of lamellar plate, like Bleda's, except that each iron plate was as big as Bleda's fist. He was fair-haired, a twisted scar running through his nose.

He said something to Raina in a language Bleda didn't understand.

"This is Ukran, Lord of the Kurgan," Raina said to Bleda.

"Oh, you are not their lord, then," Bleda said to her. For some reason he'd thought that she was.

"She is not," the giant said haltingly. His voice deeper and rustier even than Raina's.

"The Kurgan are not used to speaking in the Common Tongue," Raina said with a shrug. She dug a knife into Yul's back, coaxing an arrowhead out, soaking up blood with a linen rag. Yul grunted. With a sucking sound the arrow pulled free. Raina set to stitching the wound, a hooked needle on the end of a thread as thick as a bowstring.

"So small it hardly needs stitching," Ukran grated.

Raina ignored him, carried on stitching.

Bleda was proud of Yul: he made not a sound.

When she was done Raina cleaned the wound, packed leaves and honey onto it and then wrapped a linen bandage around Yul's back and chest. She took his arm and helped him sit upright.

That was the third arrow she had cut from Yul's body, the third wound she'd stitched and cleaned.

"I am in your debt," Bleda said to her. "To all of you."

"You are, little man," Ukran agreed. "I was of a mind to kill you all. I don't like strangers." He scowled at Bleda.

"Well, I am doubly thankful that you joined *with* us," Bleda

339

said. "I am Bleda ben Erdene, Lord of the Sirak. Well met, Ukran, Lord of the Kurgan."

The giant just looked at him.

"We are all strangers until we meet," Bleda said with a shrug. He held his arm out, offered the warrior's grip.

Raina's mouth twitched at that.

"Hmm," Ukran rumbled. Then he took Bleda's arm in a huge fist.

"And my thanks, for not killing us," Bleda said.

"You have Raina to thank for that," Ukran said.

"You spoke of Dun Seren and the Order of the Bright Star," Raina said. "Of Ethlinn and Balur and...Alcyon."

"Aye," Bleda said. "You know them?"

A smile ghosted Raina's face.

"Aye," she said. "Alcyon is my husband."

Bleda nearly fell off his huge stone chair. Alcyon was the giant he had known the longest. Bleda had ridden upon Alcyon's bear saddle all the way from Arcona to Drassil, so many years ago. Despite that, he had liked the giant. There had always been a sense of kindness behind his dark, quiet eyes.

"So, what news from the west?" Raina said. "Why is Durl searching for me?"

"The news is war," Bleda said. "The Kadoshim have risen, Drassil is fallen, Asroth awakened. The Ben-Elim are routed."

Raina was silent, her face unreadable. "And what of the Order?" she asked.

Bleda looked at Raina. Was aware that he was giving her much information, while hardly knowing who she was.

But Durl is seeking her, a crow from Dun Seren, so she must be allied to them somehow. Alcyon is her husband. And most importantly of all, she saved my life, and the lives of my warriors. I am in her debt, and the least I can give her is the truth.

Bleda sucked in a deep breath.

"In truth I know little of them. Only that one I love has gone to them, asking for their aid."

"One you love?"

"Aye. Her name is Riv. She is a half-breed Ben-Elim. She has gone to Drassil with Meical and other Ben-Elim—"

"Meical!" Raina interrupted.

"Aye. He was freed along with Asroth. Riv saved him, helped him escape from Drassil." He felt his chest swell with pride at that.

Is she not the fiercest, bravest warrior in all the Banished Lands?

"And what are they asking the Order of the Bright Star to do?" Raina asked. "What is Meical's plan?"

"To meet at Ripa. There is a garrison of White-Wings there, the largest force outside of Drassil. All those who survived Drassil are heading there. I too have promised to raise my people and take them to Ripa."

Raina looked around the chamber.

"One hundred Sirak will not make so much of a difference," she said.

Yul grunted at that. He clearly disagreed.

"There are more of us than this. I led these brave warriors as a diversion, allowing eight hundred of my people to make it to the Tethys Pass."

Raina looked at him a long while, then at Ukran.

"You are an interesting man, Bleda ben Erdene," she said at last.

"Aye," Ukran said. "I think I am glad we saved your life."

Bleda dipped his head to them both.

"So, you are bound for Ripa?" Raina said.

"Aye. Can you help me get there? These mountains are full of a Cheren warband hunting me."

"We will kill them," Ukran said.

"Although I do not doubt your skill, they number three to four thousand riders," Bleda told him.

"Hmm," Ukran rumbled. "Perhaps we shall leave them be, then."

"I will help you get to Ripa," Raina said. "I will do more than that. I will come with you." She looked at Ukran. "I have news that the Order needs to hear, news that Ukran's scouts have discovered. I am hoping that Ukran and his Clan will march with me, that they will join in this war against Asroth."

"We are safe here," Ukran replied with a shrug. "Why march my people to death, when they can stay here and live?"

"Because if Asroth and the Kadoshim win, then death will find you, even here," Bleda assured him. "This is no political war, one king seeking land and titles. This is a war against evil. I have looked into a Kadoshim's eyes and seen it. They would kill us all. Every living, breathing creature that walks the Banished Lands." He raised his hands, palms up. "That is why I fight. To protect those I love from death."

"That is the only reason to fight," Raina said.

Ukran regarded him with dark, brooding eyes.

"What is this news that the Order of the Bright Star needs to hear?" Bleda asked Raina.

I have been truthful with her, told her all I know. Will she do me the same courtesy?

She gave him another long, unreadable look.

"The Shekam giants are riding to war, and Kadoshim fly above their Clan."

CHAPTER FIFTY-THREE

DREM

"Bar the doors," Keld said. Drem and the other warriors were only too happy to oblige. A thick oak bar slammed into place, latched with four thick hooks.

They stepped away from the doorway.

"That Gulla you spoke of, their leader, he's out there?" Halden asked. He was bleeding from claw marks across one cheek.

"Aye," Keld said.

"And his half-breed daughter," Drem said.

"And one of the Seven," Keld added.

Halden snorted and shook his head.

Drem looked into the hall. There were seventy or eighty warriors there, a mixture of Keld's scouts and Halden's warriors of Brikan. All had rune-marked blades; those who didn't were corpses outside, bleeding into the courtyard's stone. Friend loomed behind them, and Fen and Ralla padded in the shadows, four more wolven-hounds snarling at the keep's doorway. The hall was vaulted, shuttered windows along two walls.

"Ways out? Somewhere more defensible?" Keld asked.

"Rooms in the tower," Halden said, a jerk of his head towards a stairwell at the back of the hall. "Or the dungeons below."

Drem already knew that, whatever the decision, he wouldn't be leaving this hall. The keep was built for giants, but Friend would struggle to fit through stairwells and corridors, and

343

would certainly have no room to turn or fight. Drem walked to Friend's side, leaned against the white bear.

"I've led you into another tight spot," Drem said sadly.

Friend rumbled a growl, nudged Drem with his muzzle. Revenant flesh hung between his teeth.

"I'm not of a mind to run," Halden said. "Let's try and kill the bastards here."

Keld nodded, grinned.

Warriors took water skins from their belts, drank deeply, some tending to wounds, ripping and tying makeshift bandages, no time for more. Some sat at benches in the hall, cleaning weapons.

A slow banging on the door, a fist shaking dust from timbers.

"I saw you, son of Olin. Slayer of my son. I know you are in there. My daughter is out here with me. She *dreams* of your death." Gulla's voice seeped through the door like a scratching hiss, squirming into Drem's head, making his ears itch.

Drem looked at Keld.

"I am coming in. You will all soon be dead. Best you say your last words, but know this: your time is over, the Long War is already won, the Banished Lands ours. You are already dead, you just do not know it yet."

"Less talking, more fighting," Halden called back, "and then we'll see who will be doing the dying."

A hissing laugh, then silence.

Warriors looked at one another, hefting weapons.

"Ready," Keld said.

"Kill Gulla's captain and many of the Revenants will fall," Drem said into the silence. "Kill Gulla and *all* the Revenants die."

"He speaks the truth," Keld said. "Kill Gulla." He said it again, louder. "Kill Gulla."

Voices joined him, becoming a chant.

"KILL GULLA, KILL GULLA, KILL GULLA."

A silence settled again, no sound of movement from the other side of the doors.

A sudden bang, a shutter across a window imploding, splinters of wood showered in. A Revenant crashed through into the hall, crunching into the long table, rolling to its feet, snarling, talons slashing. All along the wall Revenants smashed through the shuttered windows, falling and rolling, rising, running.

Battle erupted, warriors of the Order cutting down the incomers with their rune-marked blades, more Revenants pouring through the open windows. Halden threw himself at a Revenant standing upon the long table, chopped into its ankle with his sword, severing its foot. The Revenant swayed and fell, Halden's sword hacking into its neck. Another Revenant leaped upon Halden's back; Reng stabbed it with a spear.

A huge thump against the keep's doorway, an explosion of dust.

Drem stabbed a Revenant through the belly as it leaped upon him, the creature hurtling into Drem, its momentum sending them both tumbling to the ground. Drem kicked and rolled, extricated himself from the dead weight, climbed back to his feet.

Another crash, the doors rattling in their hinges. The bar creaked, fissures opening.

Friend grabbed a Revenant in his jaws, shook his head and body pieces flew in different directions.

Another blow against the door, fracture lines crackling through it, the bar bending, a series of snapping sounds.

Winged shapes swept through the open windows, half-breeds and Kadoshim, flying up into the eaves of the hall, hovering. Spears flung, warriors of the Order falling.

Keld punched a Revenant in the face with his shield boss, sent it staggering, Fen and Ralla leaping forwards, jaws clamping on its arms, dragging it down, Keld stepping forwards, stabbing it in the face, an eruption of blue fire.

A deafening crash, the doors exploded inwards, shards of

splintered timber flying through the air, one impaling a warrior of the Order, hurling her into a wall.

For a frozen moment, all stared at the shattered doorway, a beam of light flooding in, then gone as bodies filled the entrance. Revenants poured into the room, mouths wide, jaws snapping, talons reaching. Kadoshim and half-breeds flew above them.

Death comes for us all, Drem thought. *But we'll take some of you with us.*

He slashed a Revenant across the face, saw it fall in a spray of teeth, a horizontal chop of his axe into another's throat, blue fire sizzling, ripped the blade free as the Revenant collapsed. Pushed back by the press of bodies. Friend roared, lashed out, eviscerating three Revenants with one swipe of his razored paws.

Then Drem saw the Revenant captain. In life he had been an acolyte, hair shaven short. His lower jaw was covered, thick with blood. He exploded into the room, ducked a warrior's sword-swing, ripped the shield from her arm and leaped in close, jaws opening wide, clamping on her throat. They fell to the ground, the Revenant's head shaking, blood spurting. The warrior's feet drummed on the ground.

"KELD!" Drem yelled, pointing at the captain. Keld nodded, the two of them cutting a way forwards, Fen and Ralla following Keld, Friend with Drem.

The churning of air above Drem. He instinctively ducked, a spear stabbing where his face had been. He turned and looked up—Gulla's half-breed daughter was glaring down at him.

"My name is Morn," she snarled. "It is good to know the name of your killer." Her spear stabbed again, Drem twisting, steel scraping on his shoulder, links of his mail coat tearing.

Drem chopped with his axe, splintered the spear shaft. Morn flung it at him and he batted it away. She drew her sword.

Friend roared, swiped at her, Morn's wings beating, moving her, but claws raked a wing, sending her spinning. She screamed as she fell, and more half-breeds swooped from the sky, jabbing spears at Friend. A red gash opened along one cheek, mail tearing on his flank. Drem grabbed the net at his belt, swung it overhead and released, lead weights spreading, wrapping around one half-breed, crushing his wings together and he plummeted from the air, crashed to the stone floor. Friend stamped on him, blood and bone erupting.

There were half-breeds and Kadoshim all around now, the air a turbulence of wings, stabbing at Friend, forcing him back, away from Drem.

More wings behind Drem, an impact in his back, throwing him to the ground. He fell and rolled, looked up into Gulla's face. Gulla had a longsword in his fist and swung at Drem's head. Drem lashed out with his seax, rolled at the same time, a clang of steel and sparks flew. He swayed right, a vertical cut from Gulla's sword missing him by a finger's width. Pushing to his feet, he slashed at Gulla with his seax.

Gulla roared, parried Drem's seax and beat his wings, swept close, a boot kicking Drem in the chest, sending him tumbling. Stamped on Drem's forearm, pinning his axe. Drem stared up at Gulla, saw his sword rise.

A piercing scream, echoing through the room. Something in the air changed, Revenants pausing, looking.

Gulla and Drem looked, too.

Keld was standing before the Revenant captain, his sword in the creature's chest. It was screaming. Blue fire crackled like lightning through its torso, and then Keld was ripping his blade free, the Revenant collapsing at his feet.

All around the room Revenants sighed and dropped to the ground.

"Rald," Gulla snarled, shock and hatred leaking from him.

"WHO'S NEXT?!" Keld bellowed, glaring about the room.

Gulla took a step towards Keld.

Drem slashed desperately at Gulla with his seax, a blue line opening up along his thigh. Gulla screamed and stumbled, his face filled with shock.

"That's three of your Seven dead," Drem grunted as he scrambled to his feet, swept up his axe. "Him, Ulf, Arvid." He leaped after Gulla, another slash of his seax catching the Kadoshim across the forearm, mail links tearing, rage and fear washing the Kadoshim's face.

"Soon it will be *you*. We can hurt you, we can kill you," Drem yelled, brandishing his seax and axe.

Gulla snarled and beat his wings, rocking Drem backwards, and swung his sword. Drem parried with both his weapons, the power in the blow sending him stumbling. A roar shook the room as Friend lumbered between Drem and Gulla, teeth bared. Gulla looked at the white bear, opened his mouth and screamed his rage, wings beating, and he rose into the air, shouting commands to his Kadoshim who swept towards Drem and the bear. Gulla flew towards Keld.

"No," Drem breathed, then screamed Keld's name, the huntsman turning, seeing Gulla flying at him. He grinned, set his feet with shield and sword.

Drem started to run, swerving around Friend and ducking beneath the slice of a Kadoshim sword. Revenants leaped at him.

How are there Revenants still standing? Rald is dead. The hall was thick with dead Revenants, but a few were still standing.

They are Gulla's Revenants.

A roar from the white bear. Drem turned back to see a Kadoshim hovering in the air, stabbing his sword at Friend's eyes. Drem sheathed his seax and swept up a spear, hefted it once, finding its balance, and threw. It flew straight as an arrow, pierced the Kadoshim in the waist, sinking deep, angling up. The Kadoshim shrieked and dropped from the sky like a stone. Friend finished him off as Drem started running again towards Keld.

Gulla was close now, wings beating hard. The huntsman was perfectly still, in a half-crouch, shield and sword ready, eyes fixed on Gulla.

Then something crashed into Keld's back, throwing him forwards, onto his knees, his shield spinning from his grip.

Morn. She stood behind him, a long, black knife in her hand, and stabbed down. The blade punched through Keld's mail, pierced deep into his back.

Keld screamed.

Fen and Ralla leaped at Morn, jaws clamping on her face and arm, the three of them tumbling backwards. Drem saw the black knife in Morn's fist, bloody to the hilt. They disappeared from view. A wolven-hound yelped, whined.

Drem was sprinting now, axe back in his fist. A Revenant in front of him. He shouldered into it, his seax slashing its throat open, ran on as it spun and fell.

Keld was pushing himself upright, sword still in his hand. Blood speckled his lips.

Behind him Drem saw Fen flying through the air, thrown into a wall.

Gulla landed in front of Keld, the huntsman swung his sword. The blow was weak, Gulla sweeping it away, a backswing chopping into Keld's arm, his sword clattering onto stone. Gulla reached down, grabbed a fistful of Keld's mail and heaved him up, into the air, feet dangling.

Drem, almost sobbing, skidded to a halt, hefted his axe and threw it.

Keld's hand was at his belt, trying to find the hilt of his knife.

Gulla's jaws opened unnaturally wide, rows of razored teeth bristling, and bit down onto Keld's throat. Dark blood spurted.

Drem's axe spun through the air, sinking with a wet slap into Gulla's back. He screeched, dropped Keld, tried to reach the axe, couldn't. A beat of his wings and he was rising, twisting into the air, snarling, Keld's blood thick on his chin. Dripping.

Drem was close now, saw Keld on the ground. The huntsman was moving, though weakly, hands clamped around his throat, blood leaking between his fingers. A figure rose behind him: Morn, her face a bloody mask, mail coat rent and tattered. She had a new spear in her fist, eyes fixed on Drem.

Drem ran at her, a cold rage filling him.

Morn hefted the spear, pulled her arm back, aiming at him.

An arrow punched into her, high in the chest, spinning her.

Drem ran on, dimly aware of Kadoshim and half-breeds dropping from the sky, crashing to the ground, arrows sprouting from them, Revenants falling around him, blue flame crackling around arrow wounds.

Drem saw it all in blurred half-images, his eyes fixed on Keld. He dropped onto his knees, skidded to Keld's side, lifted the warrior's head and shoulders, cradling him on his lap.

"Hold on," Drem said.

Keld looked up at him, tried to say something, blood bubbling from his mouth, choking.

Beyond Keld, Morn was on the ground, slowly rising, an arrow protruding from high in her chest, blood running down. At her feet lay a tangle of red fur, the wolven-hound Ralla, lifeless eyes staring.

Morn stood.

Arrows slapped onto stone around her, one punching through her wing.

A Kadoshim fell from the sky, crunched onto stone, an arrow in his throat. Drem looked up, saw a winged figure at a window, Faelan, with a bow in his hand. Other half-breed Ben-Elim were swooping into the room, all loosing arrows while in flight.

A horn blew, high and otherworldly. Morn looked up, more arrows flitting at her, one skimming off her mail-coated arm. She looked at Drem, then up at the half-breed Ben-Elim. Back at Drem.

"ARGH!" she screeched. "Soon," she snarled at Drem, and leaped into the air.

Keld's body started to twitch.

"No," Drem said, part order, part denial.

Keld's eyes fluttered.

A whine, scratching on stone and Drem glanced right, saw Fen stumbling towards them. The wolven-hound was bleeding, swaying. He collapsed at Keld's side, lay his big head on the huntsman, whined.

Keld stared at Drem, an intensity in his eyes.

"Look…after…" Keld breathed, bubbles of blood forming on his lips.

Drem wiped them away.

"Please, Keld, no. Not you. I can't lose you, too," Drem whispered, tears blurring his eyes.

"Look…after Cullen, and my babies," Keld whispered, his breath a rattle. "This'll go…hard on them."

"You'll look after them yourself," Drem said.

Keld's hand fell from his throat, scraped on the ground.

Drem buried his face in Keld's chest and sobbed.

CHAPTER FIFTY-FOUR

JIN

Jin picked her way amongst the dead, crows rising in a squawking, protesting mass from their feast.

The sun was not long risen, tall shadows stretching across the gully. Jin had ridden hard upon realizing she had been tricked yet again. But by the time she and Tark had led her warband out of their own ravine and back to the valley, darkness had settled and the sounds of distant battle had long since fallen silent. She had made the frustratingly difficult decision to make camp for the night and to rise before first light.

By that time Jin's other captains had all returned to the valley, only Medek and his warriors were missing. As the sun had crested the peaks, Jin and Tark had led their reunited warband into the gully Medek had taken.

And now she had found him.

Or at least, she thought it was him. His skull had been caved in, most of his face missing, the rest pulped.

"What happened?" Gerel muttered, shifting another Cheren corpse with his boot.

They had found the battleground quickly enough. The ravine was thick with the dead. Men, women, horses, all lying still and twisted, most with empty, red-staring sockets where their eyes had been, taken by the crows. Tark had set his scouts to searching the area; so far, no survivors had been found.

"There are Sirak here," Cheren said, crouching beside a

dead warrior in a grey deel. She was lying on the ground, legs twisted unnaturally beneath her, two Cheren arrows protruding from her chest.

"Aye, there are," Jin said.

"But not enough," Tark grunted, dropping Medek's bow upon his corpse and moving on, picking his way through the corpse field.

"Find Bleda," Jin said. "Check every body."

"Aye, if he is here, I will find him." Tark nodded, but Jin knew the huntsman did not expect to find Bleda's body. Because she didn't, either.

He is making a fool of me.

Jin sipped from a water bottle in the shade of a boulder, the sun hot in the gully. Gerel stood close by, a dozen of her honour guard about her. Everyone else was working at the task before them.

Bodies were being piled, Cheren and Sirak, weapons and war gear stripped from the dead, anything valuable. There were things here that Jin did not understand.

"Report," she said, as Tark approached her.

"Five hundred Cheren dead. Eighty Sirak."

That staggered Jin for a moment. The dead had been so tangled and intertwined that it had been impossible to tell numbers or Clan.

How has this happened?

"And Bleda? Where is he?"

"Bleda is not amongst the dead," Tark said. There were others with him, a handful of his best scouts, and Jin's captains, Hulan, Jargal, Vachir and Essen, all of them lords of large families within the Cheren.

"Where is he then?" Jin asked, trying to keep her voice even and calm, suppressing the rage that was churning within her, a pressure building in her chest.

"I do not know," Tark said, a frown knitting his brows.

"Perhaps over those rocks." He gestured to a tumble of boulders that blocked the gully. "Though I can see no tracks that way. He would have had to go on foot, no way for horses to get through."

Jin drew in a long breath.

"Tark, what happened here?"

The scout looked at her, confusion, uncertainty in his eyes.

"All right," Jin said. "Tell me what you do know."

"There was clearly a fierce battle fought," he said. "A charge from both sides; you can see where the lines met." He pointed to the gully, to a point where the corpses of warriors and horses had been piled thickest, the stony ground still dark with their blood.

"But battle spread all along this part of the gully. And then, there were more Cheren dead there." He pointed again. "As if they were attacked on the flank."

"An ambush?" Jin said. She shrugged. "Bleda is proving to be cunning."

"Aye, that he is," Tark replied. "And yes, it looks like a flanking attack, but where from? There is no cover to hide such a force." He looked at the cliffs and boulders whose shade they were standing in. "And then there are the wounds. Only on our Cheren."

"Go on," Jin said.

"They are . . . unnatural," Tark said. "There are many Sirak arrows amongst the dead, sword and spear wounds. But there are others as well. Men and women crushed. Dismembered. Wounds too big for Sirak sword or spear."

Jin just looked at Tark. "It *is* strange," she admitted. "How, then, do you explain these things? Who gave these wounds and death blows to my people?"

"I do not know," Tark said.

You are saying that a lot. Too much, for my liking.

"Giants?" Jin said. She had seen old Balur One-Eye training in the weapons-field at Drassil. He could have made wounds like this, with his war-hammer.

"Giants do not live in Arcona," Tark grunted.

"The Night-Walkers," a voice muttered, Vachir, one of Jin's captains.

"What?" Jin said.

Vachir looked away. He was an older warrior, grey streaks in his warrior braid, and wore a fine coat of mail, edged with leather and gold wire.

"Creatures of campfire tales," Tark said, with a frown. "Mountain-dwellers, cave-lurkers that come out in the dead of night and steal our goats and children."

"Monsters," Vachir said.

"Huh." Jin snorted. "I believe in monsters, but only the ones I can see."

"Believe or not," Vachir said, looking at a huge gaping wound in a dead Cheren warrior's chest, "the dead tell no lies."

"And where are the horses? Our horses," Jin said. "Five hundred Cheren rode into this ravine. Their bodies are here, but I only see a hundred or so dead horses. Where are the rest? The way ahead is blocked by rockfall, and we came up the gully this morning. Where are they, Tark?"

He opened his mouth to speak.

"Do not say *I don't know*," Jin snapped. "You swore to me that you would guide me, that you would lead me to Bleda. *That is what I do*, you said to me. So, find him."

Tark looked at her, then looked away.

"Where are my horses, Tark?"

"Lining a monster's belly?" Vachir said, quietly, but loud enough for Jin to hear.

"And where did this monster gut and skin our horses, quarter them, cook them?" Jin snapped.

Vachir shrugged. "You lead us, you tell me," he said, a twist of his lips. He looked at her then. "Or can you not? We have followed you; sixty leagues from the Cheren Heartland, been tricked, lost a warband of our kin." He gestured to the piled dead. Then he hawked and spat.

"You question my leadership, Vachir?" Jin said quietly.

He stared into her eyes, looked about at Cheren warriors, working at stripping the dead, but listening. He stood straighter.

"The leader of the Cheren must be able to do more than slaughter a bound prisoner," he said loudly. "Skilled with bow, blade and wits, that is what the Clan requires in their king, or queen."

A silence settled between them.

"Aye, that is how you slew Erdene, is it not? A sword-thrust from behind, Erdene bound and beaten, on her knees." He sneered. "My youngest bairn could do such a thing. No great honour in that. No great skill."

Others were listening now, Cheren warriors up and down the valley, pausing at their tasks.

"And now you lead us blindly, following this Bleda like an auroch bull with a ring through your nose. Tricked, our kin slaughtered." Vachir looked at the Cheren dead. "Where are your wits? Where is your skill?"

Gerel took a step forwards, hand rising for his sword hilt.

"Hold," Jin said, a gesture at Gerel.

"I will show you my skill," she said quietly, resting a hand on the bow in its case at her hip, "if you wish. If you challenge me."

He stared at her, silence thick and heavy around him.

Then he was reaching for his bow, his other hand grasping a fistful of arrows.

Jin's bow slipped into her hand, her other hovering over her quiver. She waited, aware of the gradient, the wind, the ground about her feet.

Vachir's first arrow was nocked, drawing back to his ear.

Jin moved as he loosed. She grabbed three arrows, dropped to her left, tucked her shoulder and rolled, right hand in her quiver. Vachir's first arrow hissed through the space she had been standing in, came out of the roll as the second arrow crunched into the stony ground a handspan from where she knelt. Her first and second arrows nocked, drawn, loosed in quick succession. She rolled again, Vachir's third arrow skimming her shoulder, mail links tearing.

A yell, a thud.

She came out of her roll with her last arrow aimed.

She didn't need it.

Vachir was on the ground.

She stood and strode up to him, her heart pounding, chest heaving, the thrill of violence and the closeness of death surging through her veins. Gerel was a shadow at her shoulder, Tark and the others following behind.

Vachir had one arrow in his hip and another between shoulder and neck. It had punched deep, through mail, wool and linen into flesh, just below his clavicle. Blood pulsed from both wounds.

"I lead the Cheren," Jin said, standing over Vachir. "I have *earned* that right." She drew her bow, aimed her arrow into Vachir's face, her blood yearning for his death.

He stared back at her, a brave man facing his end with a snarl.

She blew out a long breath, loosened the tension on her bow.

"Your life is mine," she said to Vachir. "Mine to take, mine to give. Death or life, your choice. Will you follow me?"

He looked up at her, mastering his pain, a change in his eyes, the slow realization that he could live, if he wanted to.

"I will follow you," he grunted.

She slipped her arrow back into its quiver and offered him her hand, pulled him upright. He grunted with the effort, but stood beside her.

"You were close," she said, showing him the split links on her mail coat.

"Not close enough," he breathed, then bowed his head to her.

"My Cheren people," Jin called out, turning to look at her warriors. Thousands of faces, shaven-haired, long warrior braids, a hard, strong people. Her people. "I have slain our enemy's queen, led you into the Sirak lands, crushed and burned

357

every hold, turned their Heartland to ashes. All that remains is to destroy their homeless king and his handful of vagabond followers."

She saw pride fill Cheren faces, shoulders straighten and chests puff out.

"I do not know where Bleda has gone," she cried, "but I do know where he is going. To the Tethys Pass and then Ripa, to meet with his puppet-masters and his half-breed whore. That is where I am going to lead you. And if he has reached there first, then we shall follow him, to the ends of the earth if needs be. Until our victory is complete, until he and his followers are dead, and the Sirak name is nothing more than a bloodstain at our feet."

"*HAI!*" cheered the Cheren.

CHAPTER FIFTY-FIVE

DREM

Drem sat in the hall of Brikan, Keld's body in his arms. Time passed, people moving before him, crouching, saying things. Drem thought one of them had been Halden, blood-spattered and angry. He was gone now. All Drem could see was Keld's face, his empty eyes, blood congealing on his lips.

Like my da.

Horns rang in the distance.

Fen lay against Keld's body, blood crusting in his fur. The wolven-hound was whining quietly, a plaintive, melancholy sound. To one side the white bear stood, head bowed as if he were in mourning, too.

A hand on Drem's shoulder, the whisper of wings.

Faelan knelt beside him, looked down at Keld.

"Ah, but this is a *grave* loss," the half-breed said sadly. He rested a hand upon Keld's chest, murmured words. "You should let him go," Faelan said. "He is gone."

"No," Drem said. He did not want to let Keld go. It was strange, he had known the man only a short time, but they had been through so much together. Keld had saved his life, countless times over. Without even knowing it, Keld had become a man that Drem loved. Like a brother. Like a father. Like a friend.

He had had few friends in his life, his da filling that space for so many years, and that had been enough for him. But since the Order had come into his life it had seemed that there was a family about him. It felt strange, and good. And yet they all just kept on dying.

My father. Sig. Stepor. Now Keld.

He felt short of breath, a cold fist around his heart, squeezing.

The flapping of wings, talons scraping on stone and Rab was there.

"*No, no, no,*" the bird squawked. "*Not Keld. Brave Keld, Keld Rab's friend.*" He bobbed his head, hopped about on the stone, then laid his white-feathered head against Keld's hand, ran his beak over it. The crow looked up at Drem, hopped up to him, a flutter of wings and he was on Drem's shoulder.

"*Rab sad, Drem sad,*" the crow croaked in Drem's ear.

"Yes," Drem breathed.

Horn calls again, louder, now, the sound of hooves across Brikan's bridge and into the courtyard. Voices calling out. Someone shouting his name, and Keld's.

Cullen.

Hooves clattering on the keep's steps, louder, echoing as a horse was ridden into the hall.

"Drem," Cullen cried, the young warrior leaping from his saddle, boots slapping on stone, and he was running, falling to the ground beside Drem, throwing himself upon Keld's body.

"No, no, no, no, no," Cullen was murmuring. He rocked on his knees, cupping Keld's cheeks in his palms, and looked up at Drem. Tears streaked his cheeks, snot hung from his nose.

"Who?" Cullen said, face twisting between grief and snarl.

"Gulla, and Morn, his daughter," Drem whispered. "I tried…" He felt a wave of guilt, that he had not saved Keld. The huntsman had saved him so many times, always watching out for him, guarding his back.

"Where are they?" Cullen said, one moment terrifyingly cold, the next weeping, grimacing.

"Gone, back into the forest," Drem said. In truth he did not know. "Kadoshim, half-breeds, Revenants," he murmured.

More people were entering the keep, orders shouted. Drem heard Byrne's voice.

"Thank the Bright Star you live," she said, appearing beside him, crouching and throwing her arms around Drem, hugging him tight. She let him go, looked down at Keld.

"Ach," she said, her lips twisting. She stroked Keld's head, blinked tears from her eyes.

The sound of feet. Drem realized that Cullen was no longer beside him. He turned, saw Cullen leaping into his saddle, drawing his sword.

"Cullen, what are you doing?" Byrne cried.

"Hah," Cullen shouted, urging his horse into motion, dragging on his reins, and the animal was turning, cantering out of the keep, across the courtyard.

"What is that fool doing, now?" Byrne snapped.

"He wants revenge," Drem said. Gently he lifted Keld's head from his lap and laid it on the cold stone, then stood.

"I'll bring him back," he said, climbing into Friend's saddle. The bear lifted his head, rumbled a growl at Drem and then they were moving.

"Faelan, take some of your kin, watch over them," Drem heard Byrne call out behind him. Then he was out in the courtyard, the place full of the dead, warriors beginning to gather them. He glimpsed Queen Nara with her battlechief, the two of them lifting a body together.

Cullen was halfway across the bridge, his horse close to a gallop. Drem leaned over in his saddle and whispered in Friend's ear. The bear increased his speed, heading for the shattered gateway. People leaped out of the way and then they were on the bridge, a few heartbeats later beyond it, trees rising tall, branches closing overhead, twilight settling about Drem like a cloak.

"CULLEN!" Drem yelled, but if he heard, he gave no indication of it. Cullen galloped on, guiding his horse down a hard-packed road that led away from the keep, travelling roughly north-east, by what Drem could make out from the sun and his memory of maps Keld had shown him of Brikan and the surrounding terrain.

Keld.

A knife in his heart, the pain surging all over again.

He glanced behind him. Brikan was fading into a pale light at the end of a rapidly narrowing tunnel.

In front of Drem, Cullen galloped on, bent low over his saddle. But he was riding a horse. Friend was bigger, surprisingly fast when he needed to be. His lurching gait was gaining on Cullen.

The world was degrees of shade now, the odd beam of light where sunlight managed to pierce the canopy. Something flitted across the ground before Drem, the hint of a shadow. Drem glanced up, saw broad, feathered wings, others further away.

Faelan and his kin.

Behind him, faint as morning mist, the sound of hooves.

"CULLEN!" Drem called again.

His horse cannot gallop forever, they must slow soon. Gulla and his Revenants must be long gone by now.

On into the forest they thundered.

Curls of mist crept across the forest path. Drem felt a seed of worry. His hand went to his belt. His scabbard was empty, sword given to Halden. His axe was gone, lodged in Gulla's back, only his seax was in its sheath.

Cullen slowed, then dragged on his reins, his mount skidding to a halt. A moment's pause as he stared into the forest, and then he was spurring his horse off the path, into the trees.

"NO!" Drem yelled, but Cullen was already gone. A whispered word and Friend slowed. They reached the point where Cullen had left the road. Dark mist churned sluggishly on the forest path. A fox's trail ran through thicket and vine. Drem stared into the shadows, thought he saw the hint of movement, heard the drum of hooves. He looked up, saw the silhouette of feathered wings high above.

"Friend?" Drem said, unsure if the bear could move into the forest here, the foliage so dense. Friend lurched forwards, pulverizing a path into the darkness.

Well, that was easier than I thought.

They moved into a twilight world, Friend unexpectedly nimble, threading amongst wide-boled trees, able to find a way through branch and tangled brush, and when he couldn't, he simply smashed through any obstruction in front of him.

Not much good at stealth, though. We won't be sneaking up on Cullen like this.

There was a flicker of movement up ahead, and then Cullen's horse came into view. It was drinking at a stream, Cullen gone from its back. The forest grew thicker here, a snarl of thicket and thorn.

Mist grew denser about them. Now that Friend had stopped moving, Drem noticed a change in the forest.

It was silent. No birdsong or crow-call, just the rustle and scrape of branches high above. A spot in the undergrowth that had been hacked, a ragged trail. Movement between the trees, what looked like the flash of Cullen's red hair. And something else, further ahead. A shape flitting through the forest.

A Revenant?

"On," Drem said, and Friend shifted into motion, smashing a line through the dense overgrowth, straight after Cullen and whatever it was that the warrior was chasing.

They gained, Cullen having to thread his way through the underwood where Friend just walked through it. The thing Cullen was chasing was closer, too. Human in shape, mist curled around it, and it had that stuttered motion that marked it as a Revenant.

But it moved oddly, though.

It was limping.

The forest grew lighter.

Fifty paces between Drem and Cullen now. Ten paces between Cullen and the Revenant. It seemed to be alone, no wall of mist nearby, no other Revenants moving through the forest here.

It is injured, has fallen behind.

It was stumbling through the brushwood, snatching glances back at Cullen, who was shouting and raging, swinging his sword wildly at the undergrowth in front of them, frothing and snarling like a mad man.

Drem was thirty paces away, now, and then Cullen leaped at the Revenant, the two of them falling, crashing into the bushes. Friend ploughed on, lumbered to a halt a dozen steps from where Cullen had disappeared. Drem slid from his saddle, slipping his seax from its scabbard. He hit the ground running, ready to stab the Revenant and drag Cullen free.

But they were gone.

Drem prodded the ground with his seax, could see where it had been flattened. He followed the trail a few paces, and then saw the ground fall away. A steep slope down to a stream forty or fifty paces below, some kind of ravine, a sheer cliff rising on the other side.

The forest was lighter here, daylight filtering in where the canopy thinned over the ravine.

Shouts, screams echoed up to Drem. He leaned, peered down, saw Cullen and the Revenant fighting. Then he was scrambling down the slope, his seax back in its scabbard, clinging to roots and vines as he fell more than climbed down the slope. He tumbled out onto the ravine floor and drew his blade.

The Revenant was dead. More than dead. Cullen was swinging his blade, chopping at the creature as it lay upon the ground, hacking it into something unrecognizable. He was screaming, and crying, his voice hoarse.

Drem sheathed his seax again, and wrapped his arms around Cullen. The warrior resisted for a moment, then dropped his sword and turned into Drem, hugging him back. His body shook with sobs.

"Keld," Cullen said, over and over, as if his name would

bring the huntsman back. Drem felt fresh tears filling his own eyes, an ocean of grief swelling inside him.

He did not know how long they stood there like that, only that eventually Cullen's sobs quieted, and then they were stepping apart.

"I'll kill them all," he said, wiping his nose. "Gulla, Morn, every last Revenant that walks this earth. Pile their skulls at Keld's feet."

"Leave a few for me," Drem said, in his mind Gulla and Morn looming large, and Fritha behind them.

And Asroth, the ultimate creator of all of this grief.

A rumbling growl drifted down to them. Friend was standing at the top of the ravine, peering out through the trees, looking at them.

"Where are we?" Cullen said.

"Somewhere in Forn." Drem shrugged. "I just followed you."

"Forn Forest is a big place. Bigger than a country."

Drem looked around, a fast-flowing stream was close by, bubbling around moss-covered stones, the ground soft and green.

In the shadows of the cliff something dark loomed.

"What's that?" Cullen said, bending quickly to pick up his sword.

Drem stepped closer, hand on the hilt of his seax.

"It's a cabin," he said, approaching it. He stepped lightly across the stream, boots splashing in water, and then he was on the other side, walking up wooden steps onto a cabin porch. The timber creaked, damp and rotten.

Footsteps splashing and Cullen was behind him.

A tree had grown through the floorboards of the timber porch, wood splintered and rotten. Drem could just make out shuttered windows, thick with vine. A door hung half-open, one hinge gone.

Above the door a skull had been nailed to the timber frame. The bone was bleached by weather. It was human in shape, but somehow different, bigger, the planes of cheek and brow sharper, more angular. And to either side of the door were nailed two wings. Dark, leathery, desiccated and crumbling, only the bone and cartilage of wing-arches intact.

Even so, it was clear to Drem what it had been in life.

"A Kadoshim," he breathed.

Drem pushed the door open with one hand, peered inside, waited for his eyes to adjust to the shadows, then stepped into the cabin.

A single room, a table and chair. The air was thick and musty.

Cullen squeezed in behind Drem, his sword pointing into the corners of the room.

On one wall more skulls were nailed, all of them similar to the one outside, a dozen Kadoshim.

"Whoever lived here, I think I like them," Cullen whispered.

In the corner was a bed.

Drem strode over and gazed down at it.

A skeleton lay upon the bed. Clothes hung in tatters on bones, a rusted mail coat. A book and a longsword lay across the skeleton's chest, hands that had clearly once gripped the hilt had fallen away.

"The room's clear," Cullen said. Then the pad of footsteps and Cullen was behind Drem, peering around him.

A gasp.

"It can't be," Cullen said.

Drem's eyes were fixed on the hilt of the sword. A-hand-and-a-half grip, the pommel fashioned into the shape of a howling wolven.

Drem had seen that sword hilt before, on a carved statue that stood in the courtyard of Dun Seren.

"It's Corban's sword," breathed Cullen.

CHAPTER FIFTY-SIX

BLEDA

"Tell me of the Shekam," Bleda said, as he rode beside Raina. They were at the head of a long column of Sirak and giants, threading through a wide, high-ceilinged tunnel. He was on Dilis, had been so relieved when he'd seen the skewbald mare led into the cavernous halls of the Kurgan giants. It was their third day of travelling underground, the dark constantly pressing in upon them, and Bleda longed for daylight and the sight of the sky.

"The Shekam are a giant Clan," Raina said, "like my Clan, the Kurgan, who walk with us."

"But these giants, the Shekam, are allied to Asroth?"

"Aye, it looks that way," Raina said. "They have been seen marching from their secret lands, and Kadoshim fly above them."

"That's not a good sign," Drem said. "I have fought the Kadoshim. They are more than just an enemy. They are a sickness. A plague. How many of these Shekam are there?"

"Two hundred, three hundred, maybe more."

"Ah." Bleda did not think that was too great a number. Of course, giants were formidable warriors; he had just seen what a hundred could do to the Cheren, but he knew the White-Wings at Ripa numbered in their thousands.

"You think that is not so dangerous," Raina said, glancing at him.

Bleda shrugged. "A formidable foe, but their numbers— they're not so great."

"Ah, but they are riding draigs," Raina said.

"Draigs!" Bleda almost spat. He had never seen a draig, had thought them more a campfire tale than real, living creatures. From the stories he had heard told, one of them was supposed to have been a match for a score of warriors.

"Aye, draigs," Raina said.

"Let's hope Ethlinn and her bear-riders are marching for Ripa, then."

Raina said nothing, just held her torch up and stared ahead. Silence settled between them.

"You are Kurgan?" Bleda asked after a while.

Raina looked at him.

"You ask a lot of questions," she said.

Bleda smiled. "It's a long walk in the dark, and I don't like tunnels. Better to talk."

"I am Kurgan," she said.

"And your husband Alcyon, he is Kurgan?"

"Aye."

"Then why is he with Ethlinn, and not here with you?"

Raina blew out a long breath. "That is not a short story," she said.

"I am going to be at your side for a hundred leagues," Bleda answered.

"A fair point. But it is also a tale that I do not like to think on. I will not talk of it," she said.

Bleda nodded.

They walked on in silence awhile. Just the sound of boots and hooves on stone, the drip of water. One hundred of Bleda's Sirak had survived the battle in the ravine, though most of them bore injuries of one sort or another. Yul, despite his wounds, was still sitting straight in his saddle. They had close to five hundred horses with them, taken from the Cheren dead and led into the tunnels.

That will speed our journey to Ripa, if we are reunited with Ellac. I hope he made it to our meeting point, that Jin has not caught up with him somehow.

Bleda heard something, at first thought it was the sound of wind, roaring through the tunnel. It got louder. And then he saw a pinprick of light, beyond Raina's torch.

"We are here," Raina said.

The roaring grew louder, constant and close to deafening. It was a waterfall, cascading over the exit to their tunnel. Fractured sunlight broke through in multi-hued beams.

"Control your horse," Raina shouted to him over her shoulder, Bleda straining to hear her. She doused her torch in the water, and then walked on. The path they were following narrowed to a ledge. Bleda twisted in his saddle and looked back, over the three horses he was leading, and saw Ukran behind him, then Yul and Ruga. He signalled to them, and they moved into single file.

Then Bleda was moving forwards. Raina had disappeared, the path twisting just beyond the tunnel's mouth. Water fell only a handspan from his horse's hooves, the ground slick and slippery. He rode into a dense mist, moisture thick in the air. Bleda rested a hand upon his bow in its case, though he knew that it would be useless—the bowstring would be ruined by this water. He blinked as bright sunshine seared his eyes, and then he was outside, the sky opening up above him. He breathed in happily and rode on a few paces. Raina was ahead, standing on green grass, a wall of trees behind her.

The waterfall crashed into a wide pool that frothed and spumed, a permanent mist of water hanging in the air before the tunnel entrance. Yul, Ruga and Ukran appeared through the mist, blinking as Bleda had done. Riders and giants filed out into the daylight behind them. Bleda looked up, following the waterfall. It fell from a great height, a cliff rising almost to the clouds, it seemed.

"Where are we?" Bleda breathed.

"Arcona is up there," Raina said. "We are now in the Land of the Faithful. Those trees mark the south-eastern fringe of Forn Forest."

Bleda looked around, imagining the maps he had pored over during his lessons in Drassil. He wished he'd paid more attention. Vaguely he could see it in his mind's eye. The plain of Arcona filling the east, Forn Forest its western border. To the south-west lay Ripa, on the coast.

But before Ripa I must find Ellac and my Clan.

"Can you take us to the Tethys Pass from here?" Bleda asked.

Raina pointed to the south, at something that shimmered on the horizon.

"That is the Tethys Sea," she said, "and your kin should be less than half a day from here."

"There it is," Raina said, pointing.

Bleda was sat upon his horse beside Raina, Ukran and Ruga. The rest of Bleda's warriors were stationed deeper in the forest with Yul and over a hundred giants.

They had ridden south from the waterfall, seen the plateau of Arcona sink towards the sea, turning into a white-rocked land of mountains and sheer cliffs.

Raina was pointing at a wide road that led from the forest into those mountains.

"Where is your Clan?" Ukran asked.

Bleda looked at the road, at the forest it emerged from, and the mountains it disappeared into. Beyond the road the land slowly levelled and the sea shimmered, a glistening blue. Bleda could smell salt on the air, and the cry of gulls drifted on a breeze.

"I don't know." He shook his head. "I have never been here before, and Ellac only as a child."

"That would be a hundred years ago, then," Ruga said.

Bleda snorted a laugh.

"Ellac?" Ukran said. "Is he a giant?"

"No," Bleda said. "He is just old. Ruga was making a joke."

"This is not a joking time," Ukran grunted.

That is a truth.

Is Jin out there?

Raina had assured Bleda that it was impossible for Jin to have ridden through the mountains and reached this pass before they had, using the giants' tunnels. Three days it had taken them to reach here, and Raina said above land it was a four-day journey, at least.

But Jin rides fast, and rage and revenge will be a fire in her belly.

"I told Ellac to wait for me at the Tethys Pass," Bleda said.

"For how long?" Ukran asked him.

"One day. Any longer, and the gap he'd opened between him and Jin could have been closed." He scanned the mountains and forest again. There was no sign of Ellac, or of Jin, but either of them could have been hidden in the ravines or shadowed forest.

Hooves drummed and Ruga was riding out from their cover into the stretch of land that separated mountains from forest.

Bleda made to go after her but Yul put a hand upon his reins and held him there, the warrior grimacing as his wounds pulled.

"It is too late," Yul said. "The deed done. Following will not help."

"He is right," Raina said.

Bleda watched as Ruga trotted across the open ground. It was stony, with patches of sun-bleached grass. She reached the road and reined in, looking east and west to the mountains and then the forest. A touch of her reins and her mount turned in a tight circle, showing herself to any eyes that might be watching. Ruga wore a Sirak deel of grey, a coat of mail over it, sleeves ending at the elbow for bow work, splits up each leg for riding.

"It is I, Ruga of the Sirak," Ruga called out. "If you are hiding in the shadows, Jin of the Cheren, come out and fight me. Or are you too much of a coward?"

Bleda heard Yul grunt his respect.

A silence, only crows squawking in the forest.

Ruga turned a circle again.

Where the road met the trees of Forn a rider emerged.

Ruga's hand dropped to her bow in its case.

The rider was a man, dressed in grey and mail. His head was shaved, one long, grey warrior braid coiling around his shoulder. He raised an arm to Ruga, revealing a stump where his fist should be.

Ellac.

Bleda clicked his tongue and spurred his horse on, bursting from the trees. Yul was close behind him, and together they rode across the ground ululating a welcome, Raina and Ukran following them.

Ruga was already with Ellac, but Bleda saw the old warrior staring at him. They met upon the road, Bleda grinning at the old man, gifting him with his open emotions. He did not think he could have hidden them if his life depended upon it.

"Ah, but my old heart soars to see you," Ellac said as Bleda leaned in his mount and gripped the old warrior's arm.

"You made it," Bleda said.

"Of course," Ellac grunted. "That was never in doubt. You, on the other hand." He looked into Bleda's eyes. "I have worried..."

Other riders emerged from the forest where Ellac had appeared, more Sirak, some fanning wide, bows in fists, eyes on the mountains.

"We should move from here, it is too open," Yul said, looking up at the mountain pass.

Ellac looked at the bandaged wounds on Yul.

"You have a tale to tell," he said.

"Aye, and allies to introduce to you," Bleda said, gesturing at Raina and Ukran.

Ellac raised an eyebrow, then dipped his head to the two giants.

"Well met, Ellac of the Sirak," Raina said.

"We should move," Ukran said. He was looking up at the mountains.

Bleda followed his gaze, into the mountains, and then up, to where something was becoming visible in the sky, a few leagues distant.

A cloud of dust.

"Jin," Bleda said. "Best we save the introductions and ride."

CHAPTER FIFTY-SEVEN

DREM

Drem stood by the stream, looking up at warriors climbing down the ravine wall. Ropes had been tied to trees, making the descent easier and safer than his had been. Faelan and a handful of his kin circled in the stark sky. Drem looked over his shoulder, saw Cullen still standing over the bed in the cabin, looking down at the skeleton and sword.

Faelan had taken word to Byrne at Drem's request.

And there she was, Byrne almost at the ravine's floor. Her feet touched onto ground and she strode towards Drem, a handful of her honour guard about her. She glanced down at the corpse of the Revenant as she passed it, then looked up at Drem. Their eyes met, no words. Byrne strode up the creaking steps and into the cabin, eyes flickering to the Kadoshim skull nailed above the doorway.

Drem followed, saw Cullen lean forwards, reaching out. Gently the young warrior extricated the sword from the skeleton and held it up, his eyes bright with emotion. Byrne stopped in front of Cullen.

She just stood and stared.

"By the Otherworld," she breathed.

"It's *his* sword," Cullen murmured, turning the blade in his hand. It was long, a-hand-and-a-half grip, the blade wide at the hilt. Dust had thickened to a kind of congealed skin upon the blade, but Drem had a feeling the blade beneath was sharp and bright. Cullen sliced the air with it, then a roll of his wrist, turning it, holding the hilt out to Byrne.

She took it, her eyes wide, contemplated the blade for long, silent moments. Then she looked down at the skeleton upon the bed.

"It must be Coralen," Byrne said. Drem remembered Cullen telling him of the tale, Coralen riding out of Dun Seren with Storm after Corban's cairn had been defiled. Byrne knelt beside the bed, tentatively put a hand out and lifted long strands in her fingers.

Hair, Drem realized. It was mostly grey, though Drem caught a hint of red.

"Coralen had red hair, flaming like fire, the tales say," Byrne said. She looked up at Cullen. "Like yours."

Cullen smiled then, an awed, joyful expression sweeping his face.

Gently Byrne lifted the book from the skeleton's chest. She held it as if it could crumble in her fingers, blew dust from the leather cover, wiped more away. The leather was cracked and worn, but Drem could see markings upon it. Letters, like the ones he had seen upon his seax, runes. And two symbols; one shaped like a black teardrop, the other the eyes and snarling teeth of a wolven.

Byrne gasped. "This book bears the sigils of Cywen and Coralen."

Cullen leaned over Byrne's shoulder.

"*A chaitheamh amach*," he said clumsily.

"To cast out," Byrne breathed.

Drem checked Friend's wounds. Dawn was brightening the world around him, mist from the river and dew dripped from trees. Drem looked at the vapour curling up from the water and onto the bridge, but this was ordinary mist, not black and seething with taloned monsters.

He was standing in Brikan's courtyard, cleared now of

countless Revenant corpses and the bodies of fallen warriors. Dark stains dotted the flagstoned ground. Everywhere was movement, warriors mounting horses, giants climbing onto bears. Auroch bellowed and stamped their feet, harnessed to wains.

Friend had new wounds, most of them shallow. Only one had needed stitching. Thankfully there had been no bites. Drem was spooning fresh honey onto a gash beneath Friend's eye, the bear's mouth open, huge tongue lolling, trying to reach some of the sweet liquid.

Mostly the wounds were around his muzzle and face, where spears had been jabbed at him. His coat of mail had served him well. Drem had tended to the rent links last night, patching them up, and his own mail coat as well. He'd had a pile of harness to fix and stitch, buckles torn loose, a gash in his coat of mail, more rips in his breeches.

"Here you go," Drem said, dolloping a spoonful of honey onto Friend's tongue. The bear rumbled contentedly.

Horns blew, the warband preparing to move out. Queen Nara had led a force out already, a vanguard moving along the road out of Forn Forest.

Drem sucked in a deep breath and stroked Friend's cheek.

"Something I need to do, first," he muttered, then walked away, across the courtyard. Friend eyed him, then followed.

Drem skirted the keep. He paused at a wain, prised open a barrel and pulled out a butchered leg of lamb, wrapped in linen. He walked on until he was in a walled area behind the keep, strode past an open gateway, the entrance to Brikan's weapons-field, and on, past buildings and then trees, until he saw cairns before him. Lots of cairns.

There was a row of fresh-built ones. Cullen stood before one, head bowed. Rab was perched on his shoulder and Fen the wolven-hound lay close to the stones.

Drem walked up, stood silently at Cullen's side, and looked at Keld's cairn.

He felt the pain again, a fist around his heart as grief bubbled within him.

Cullen knelt and placed a hand upon the cairn.

"I never had the chance to tell you anything," Cullen whispered, voice thick with grief. "But you were my rock, my friend. I loved you like a father, and I miss you more than I can bear. Only the thought of avenging you, and Sig, keeps me moving." He looked up at Drem, tears in his eyes.

Drem looked back through blurred vision, images in his mind of his father in the snow, of Sig strapping herself to a post, of Keld in his arms.

"We will never forget," Drem breathed.

"We will never forget," Cullen echoed. He stood. "Gulla's a dead man walking," he snarled.

"And Morn," Drem breathed, remembering her black knife punching into Keld's back.

Cullen drew his knife from his belt and cut a red line along his forearm, held it out.

Drem, understanding, took his seax and sliced his arm, drawing blood.

"For Keld," Cullen said.

"For Keld," Drem replied, and gripped Cullen's arm, blood mingling and dripping onto the stones of Keld's cairn.

A horn rang through the fortress.

"*Rab peck Gulla's other eye out,*" the crow squawked.

"Good," Cullen said. He looked at Drem. "Let's go find those bastards and kill them," and then he was striding off.

Drem looked down at Fen, the huge wolven-hound lying beside Keld's cairn. Fen still wore his coat of mail, blood crusted in patches. Another cairn lay beside Keld's. Ralla's body was inside it. Wolven-hounds of the Order were honoured and remembered, just like any other warrior who fought for the Bright Star.

"Ah, but you're a faithful lad, and you're grieving, too," Drem said, kneeling beside Fen and placing his hand upon the hound's chest. "Keld has been like your da, your pack leader from when you were a cub." Fen looked at him with one yellow eye, gave out a mournful whine.

"You can't stay here, Fen," Drem said. He looked the wolven-hound in the eye, stroking his furry, scarred cheek. "I don't know if you understand me, but you should know that Keld asked me to look after you. With his last breath he did that, caring about you." He reached inside his cloak and took out the leg of lamb. Friend sniffed behind Drem.

"This isn't for you, Friend," Drem said to the bear, and offered it to Fen. The wolven-hound sniffed the meat, then opened his jaws and took it. Dropped it on the ground and put one of his paws over it.

"I can't look after you here. You have to come with me and Friend, Cullen and Rab. We're going after those that slew our Keld, and we are going to make them pay. It'll be dangerous, might not live through it. But at least we will have tried." He stood. "What do you say? Coming? We are pack, now; you, me, Friend, Cullen and Rab. Riv when she comes back. And we are going to make Gulla and Asroth wish we had never been born."

Fen looked up at him, a rumbled growl deep in his chest. Then he stood, sniffed once at Keld's cairn, whined, picked up the leg of lamb and padded after Drem.

CHAPTER FIFTY-EIGHT

RIV

Riv sat in the dark and chewed on a hard biscuit. She missed Cullen's pottage stew. In truth, she missed more than that. She missed the Order of the Bright Star. She missed her crew: Keld, Drem and Cullen.

She had been honoured and deeply touched when Keld had invited her into their group, and flying away the next morning had been a difficult thing to do. But she knew information had to be exchanged, the lines of communication opened up between the Ben-Elim and the Order of the Bright Star. And she missed her mother, too, was looking forward to seeing her.

Aphra, I hope that you are safe, and that you have made it to Ripa. I have so much to tell you.

A ten-night of hard flying, close to a hundred leagues travelled, and now Ripa was close. Riv looked up, a sky full of stars shimmering above her. The temperature had risen with every day travelled, although summer was waning. They had made camp tonight in a small dell, a few scattered alders around them. Meical had said no fires, as they had seen distant silhouettes in the sky that day. Kadoshim, circling far to the east.

Riv had been tempted to scout closer, but they only numbered eleven, and they were not looking for a fight.

Not yet.

Meical was sitting opposite her, his head bowed in thought.

He's not much of a talker, for someone who has been Lord of the Ben-Elim, she thought.

Hadran and five other Ben-Elim sat with them, in a loose circle in the grass, the other three Ben-Elim on their watch shift. The night was warm, cloudless and bright, so Riv wasn't missing the fire. She was feeling a tremor in her blood, though, but it was nothing to do with the cold. It was the thought of seeing Kol.

My father.

She thought of the last time she had seen him, at their make-shift council of war at the cabin in Forn, and the things that had been said.

"What did Kol mean," Riv asked Meical, "about you being in chains, the last time he saw you?"

Meical looked up, eyes unfocused for a moment.

"I was a prisoner, put in chains and thrown into a cell," Meical said.

Riv scowled. "Who by?"

Meical was quiet, looked at his hands.

"By us," Hadran said with a frown. "By the Ben-Elim."

"I don't understand," Riv said. "I thought you were High Captain of the Ben-Elim. Why would they throw you in gaol?"

"I *was* their high captain," Meical said. "But it was decided by the Ben-Elim Assembly that I had become too close to humankind; to the people of the Banished Lands I had been living amongst. They thought my judgement was clouded by my emotions."

"Your emotions? What do you mean?"

"My friendship with Corban."

A long silence, then a twitch of his lips. "They were right, but I do not regret it. In truth, I thought that my emotions had finally opened my eyes, not clouded them."

"What was wrong with being friends with Corban?"

Meical glanced at Hadran, who sat with his head bowed. The other Ben-Elim were shifting where they sat, wings twitching uncomfortably.

"You could tell her," Meical said to Hadran. "I would not speak ill of you."

Hadran looked up, his dark hair glossy in the starlight. He drew in a deep breath.

"The Ben-Elim decided that Meical had lost sight of our task, and our plan. We had strategies in place that had taken hundreds of years to come to fruition, and Meical was putting those plans at risk. He was no longer prepared to make the... sacrifices, that war sometimes requires." Hadran's voice was stiff, wooden as he spoke.

"I still don't understand," Riv said. "What did you do for the Ben-Elim to imprison you?"

Meical looked at Hadran and the other Ben-Elim. Hadran just nodded.

"I told Corban the truth." Meical shrugged. "That he had been lied to. That he and his kin, his family, were pawns in a great game. That they were a *strategy* in our Long War with the Kadoshim."

Riv shook her head. "Why am I not surprised," she said bitterly. "The more I learn of the Ben-Elim, the more a fool I feel for blindly following them."

Hadran stiffened. He opened his mouth, then stopped, his shoulders slumping.

"I am sorry," he said. "For my part, I regret much that has been done." He looked up at Riv, pain in his eyes.

She looked at him, wondered when exactly this cold, aloof warrior had gone from being her guard to her friend.

She smiled at him. "The past is done. Now, the next day. That is what is important. What truly matters."

Hadran nodded. "Thank you," he whispered.

"Riv is right," Meical said. "The past is done. Over. My only regret is that it took me away from the fight, from Corban and the others."

"You were there at the end, though, at the battle. At the Day of Wrath."

"I was," Meical said. "But only because Corban ventured into the Otherworld and set me free. His friendship taught me much." He looked at Hadran and the other Ben-Elim. "For my part, I forgive the mistakes of the past. As long as lessons have been learned, and the same mistakes are not repeated, over and over."

"What lessons are those?" Riv asked him.

"That what we fight for is love and friendship. Not schemes and strategies, but people. Our kin, our friends. Our loved ones." He sighed. "That is what Corban taught me. The mistake is to forget that."

"That mistake will not be made by me," Hadran said. "Never again."

Meical offered Hadran his arm. There was a moment as Hadran looked into Meical's face, and then he took it in the warrior grip.

"What of Kol, though?" Riv said.

Meical sighed. "I cannot speak for him. But I will not stand by and watch him do wrong. If I can stop that, I will."

"So will I," Riv snarled.

Meical smiled.

"I have no doubt of that, warrior of the Bright Star."

The ground below Riv changed from the undulating green of Sarva's trees to open meadows, a wide river flowing from the forest towards the sea. Ripa appeared, a fortress and town nestled in a bay of glistening blue, the river's estuary curling around the town's western border. A tower of white stone stood like a spike upon a hill, sharp cliffs on its south side dropping down to the bay. It was surrounded by a stout wooden fortress, buildings of wood and thatch spilling in tiers down the hill and rolling up to the bay, where scores of piers and jetties jutted into the sea. Masts were thick on the water, gulls crying above them.

Riv and her companions had been seen, other Ben-Elim spotting them a dozen leagues further inland, scouts guarding the approaches to Ripa.

And that is wise, from what we have seen.

Now an escort of white-winged Ben-Elim were leading them into Ripa, flying lower, swooping over sun-baked meadows that surrounded the fortress. Riv saw a hive of activity on the plains. A tall, long, palisaded wall ringed a half-circle about Ripa, roughly a league out from the fortress. Closer to the fortress there was a well-organized camp: rowed tents, hundreds of them, if not thousands, which was reassuring. Paddocks, fire-pits, cook-houses, grain stores. Riv could make out figures as small as ants sparring, others on marching drill. Her eyes lingered on the paddocks, hoping to see Sirak horses, smaller and hardier than the mounts the White-Wings used, but from this height she could not tell.

Erem, one of the Ben-Elim leading them in, shouted and gestured and they tucked their wings, diving out of the bright blue towards the tower on the hill. Horns were blowing, now, announcing their arrival, figures becoming clearer, warriors pointing up at them.

Riv and the group of Ben-Elim circled the tower and swept in close. At the tower's peak Riv saw huge windows facing north, south, east and west. Erem checked his wings, slowed, and flew through one of those windows, disappearing into the tower.

They followed.

Riv beat her wings, slowing and hovering, then alighted upon a stone floor. The room was the interior of the tower, at its centre a huge table, a map of the Banished Lands carved into its top. Around it were a dozen Ben-Elim, elegant and beautiful, and standing about them were a handful of White-Wings, men and women with short-cropped hair, gleaming mail and polished cuirasses, the white wings of their order emblazoned upon their chests.

Kol stood at the centre of it all, leaning upon the huge table, staring at it. The last time Riv had seen him he had been pale-faced and battered, his mail torn, bandages seeping blood. Now, he was dressed and glowing like a god. His golden hair was tied back, bound in a thick warrior braid, a coat of mail trimmed at neck and sleeves with gold. A sword and knife hung at his belt, both scabbarded in soft leather bound with gold wire. He looked up as Riv flew in, his eyes flickering over her, settling upon Meical and Hadran.

"Well, I was wondering where you were," Kol said. He looked Hadran and the other Ben-Elim up and down. "Fetch them food and drink," he said, waving a hand. "There were more of you when you left."

"We have seen battle," Hadran said. "A Revenant horde."

"Aye. Well, report," Kol said.

Hadran looked at Meical, who gave a slight nod. Kol saw it, his mouth thinning to a tight line.

"The Order of the Bright Star are marching here, willing to unite with our forces," Hadran said. He paused. "The plan is proceeding as Meical proposed."

"It was *my* plan," Kol said defensively.

Hadran gaped at Kol, opened his mouth.

"It does not matter who suggested the plan of uniting here against Asroth," Meical interrupted. "So long as that is what we do. Unite with our allies."

Kol shot Meical a hard look.

"I do not think you should be here. You were removed from your position of authority, deemed unfit and imprisoned. You have no right to be party to our council of war."

Hadran gazed at Kol in shock.

"This is *wrong*," he said. "Meical has fought with us, fought *Asroth*, he has every—"

"Be *silent*, Hadran. You were in the Assembly that voted him removed from power; you were in the Assembly that voted me Lord Protector of the Banished Lands. *My* plan is going well. We have close to six thousand White-Wings here, another thousand marching from Haldis due any day, and a thousand Ben-Elim, those stationed on the southern coasts, or survivors of Drassil. We hardly need the Order of the Bright Star."

"You know that's not true," Meical said calmly. "We all saw Asroth's host at Drassil. And it is stronger now."

"Well, be that as it may," Kol said, "we certainly don't need an outcast Ben-Elim's help." He glared at Meical. "You disregarded the Ben-Elim Lore. Made a mockery of our traditions. Perhaps you *should* go back to a cell."

I've had enough of this.

Riv strode forwards, Ben-Elim around Kol staring at her, standing in her way. She did not change her pace or direction, just walked through them, shoving them out of her way.

"Talking of disobeying the Lore," she said, looking into Kol's eyes fiercely. "Well met, *Father.* Have you missed me?"

A silence settled over the room, all staring at Kol and Riv. Slowly Riv saw understanding dawn in Ben-Elim eyes.

Dumah, a Ben-Elim that Riv remembered from the Assembly, stepped forwards.

"You told us no one knew who her father was. You *swore* it, in front of the Assembly."

"I..." Kol said, eyeing Riv with disgust. "She's lying."

"No, she's not," a voice spoke from the back of the room.

Riv turned, saw her mother, Aphra, standing there. Like Kol, she was gleaming in mail and leather. She looked strong, and back in the best of health. She strode through the room, Ben-Elim and White-Wings parting for her.

"I am Riv's mother, and Kol *is* her father," Aphra said to the room. She looked at Dumah and the other Ben-Elim and drew in a deep breath. "I'm sick of living this lie, it has been a poison in my life. Do to us what you will."

Dumah looked between Kol, Riv and Aphra. Kol was pale, a tremor in his cheek.

Fear, or rage? Riv wondered. *Probably a bit of both.*

For herself, Riv felt no fear. Just a soaring elation, and a swell of love and pride for her mother. She reached out and took Aphra's hand in hers.

Dumah turned to Kol, holding his gaze. Kol tried to return the look, but his eyes faltered and he dropped his head.

"I may be an outcast Ben-Elim," Meical said quietly, "but I say Aphra and Riv are innocent in this. You," he said to Aphra, "were manipulated and seduced by someone you believed to be almost a god." He looked at Kol. "If anyone should answer for this, it is *you*." Murmurs of agreement rippled around the room. "But," Meical continued, "my advice is that any judgement should wait. There is a war out there. Asroth marches here, we have seen his war-host, and there is no room for discord amongst us. Not now. All who are the enemies of Asroth should put aside our differences and *fight*." He snarled the last word, wiped a hand over his face. "Because, let me tell you; divided we will fall."

Dumah, Hadran and the other Ben-Elim all stared at Meical, as did the White-Wing captains.

No, Riv thought, *let Kol be tried and cast out now.* She felt her rage bubbling, the thought of Kol finally receiving some small measure of justice intoxicating to her.

"Meical speaks wisdom," Hadran said. "Asroth is our enemy."

Dumah frowned. "Lies and deceit within our midst, though," he muttered.

"Deal with it after the war, if any of us still live," Meical said. "A Ben-Elim Assembly. I would demand it, anyway. I have my own grievances to air." He held Dumah's gaze.

Riv breathed in, deep and slow. She had come to trust Meical, knew that what he said had logic in it, though every fibre of her being wanted to see Kol humbled and laid low.

"I would be in agreement with that," Dumah said, "if the other captains amongst us agree."

"Most of them are here," Meical said. "What say you?" he asked, looking around the room.

There were nods, mutters of agreement.

"That is settled, then," Dumah said. "An Assembly when Asroth is defeated. Though until then Kol forfeits his title of lord protector. Decisions will be made by the Assembly."

"In consultation with our allies," Meical added.

Dumah looked at him, then nodded.

"Good," Meical said.

"Good," Kol echoed, as if this had been his plan all along.

Riv stared at Kol, stunned by his audacity.

"Well met, *daughter*," he said, the twist of his crooked smile through his scar. "You are a great deal of trouble, you know. And a disobedient soldier. A White-Wing should do as they are ordered."

"I'm not a White-Wing," Riv said, tapping her cloak brooch with a cold smile of her own.

Kol looked at it, frowned.

"What have you done now?"

"Made the right choice," she said. "Truth and Courage."

Kol rolled his eyes. "Dear Elyon above," he said.

Aphra put a hand on Riv's shoulder.

"I have been so worried for you, missed you so much," she said, and smiled at Riv, tears in her eyes.

In front of them all Riv wrapped her arms around Aphra and kissed her cheek.

"I have missed you, too, *Mother*."

CHAPTER FIFTY-NINE

FRITHA

Fritha poured a bucket of hot water over Asroth's back; steam rose from the bath and she passed him a cup of wine.

"Ah, by the Otherworld, but that feels so good." Asroth groaned. "The pleasures of this world of flesh are never-ending." He twisted in the bath to look back at her, water spilling.

She was refilling the bucket from a barrel in the corner of their huge tent and hanging the bucket to warm over a fire-pit.

"Let someone else do that. Join me," Asroth said.

It was not a suggestion.

Fritha unbuckled her weapons-belt, lay it over a chair, then jumped and wriggled out of her coat of mail. Then her boots and breeches came off and finally her tunic. Quickly she lifted a leg over the bathtub rim and gasped as she eased herself into the hot water, sat facing Asroth, steam rising in curls between them.

He took a sip from his cup of wine, a red stain on his lips.

"You are beautiful," Fritha said to him, taking in the sharp lines of his cheeks, the black wells that were his eyes, muscle of shoulders and chest thick and striated.

He just smiled at her.

"You cannot hide it from me," Asroth said casually.

Fritha raised an eyebrow.

He leaned forwards, his hand moving beneath the water. Fingertips brushed her stomach, making her shiver.

"Your belly. My *child*," he said.

They had not spoken of it up until now. Fritha had guessed that Asroth knew, but she did not want to risk being banned from battle, so hadn't mentioned it.

She smiled at Asroth. "I am honoured that your seed grows within me," she said.

"As you should be," he replied, brushing away a strand of silver hair that had fallen across his face. "Your name will live on in history, long after your bones have crumbled to dust."

That was not a particularly warming thought for Fritha. She did not care much for glory, or for what may come to be after she was dead and gone. She wanted things now. Revenge. Success. A child. A family to belong to, to look after.

"A child. My child," Asroth murmured. "It is a strange thought, but not unpleasant. I think I will enjoy being a father."

"You will be a good father," she said.

"Maybe." He sipped more wine. "Can you fight, with our child in your belly?" He sounded genuinely interested.

"Aye," Fritha said. She shrugged. "There will come a time when I can't, but the war should be won by then."

"Good," Asroth grunted. He stretched in the bath, his foot rising beside Fritha's shoulder, black-nailed toes wriggling. "I am eager for battle now," he said, a smile creasing his face. "How long until we reach Ripa?"

They had left the trees of Forn Forest behind them a tennight ago, travelled through the passes of the Bairg Mountains and were now marching across leagues of gently rolling meadows and dells. Their pace had picked up each day, with Aenor finally teaching his acolytes the rudiments of marching.

"A moon and a half, perhaps two moons." Fritha shook her head. "You were in no rush to begin this march, and yet now you wish it were over?"

Asroth looked at Fritha a long while, under heavy-lidded eyes.

"I find your company refreshing," he said. "And I am inclined to tell you a truth. Can I trust you?"

"Of course you can," Fritha said. "I would rather cut my unborn child from my belly than betray you." Though even as she said the words, she knew she did not mean them. Her child was *everything* to her.

"I will hold you to that," Asroth said.

Fritha looked at him. "A truth," she prompted.

"I wanted to leave Drassil much sooner, but I . . . feared."

"Feared what?" she asked with a frown.

"Losing." He looked to the entrance of their tent where a curtain hung, saw the shadow of a Kadoshim guard outside.

"Gulla," he breathed. "He is much changed. More powerful now. And he has the Seven about him, and his host of Revenants. He is my captain, has always been loyal, but since I have returned, there is a change in him. He has tasted his newfound power, and liked it."

Fritha nodded. There was always a knot of worry in her belly about Gulla, and what he was capable of.

"You made him this powerful," Asroth said. "But at Drassil I knew I had the starstone metal, and that the forge was somewhere within the fortress. I needed those weapons." He looked over at the long axe leaning against his coat of mail that was hung on a cross-frame. His battle-helm and whip hung over one arm, his weapons-belt with his black-bladed knife over the other.

"When I awoke, I felt weak. And discovering I was missing a hand did not help that." He lifted his arm out of the water and looked at his new right hand, made a fist. Fritha could see the scar-line and stitch marks a little way above his wrist, and to her eye the flesh of his hand looked slightly paler than the rest of his arm, but to most it would look almost normal.

"I am stronger, now, and the starstone strengthens me more. It was created in a place between this world of flesh and the Otherworld, and took power from both. I can feel its strength when I wear it. I am not so worried about Gulla now."

Fritha stroked the swell of her belly beneath the water.

"I have a truth to share with you, too," she said. "You know that Gulla and his Revenants do not feel pain like us. They can take a wound that would slay or disable any one of us."

"Aye." Asroth nodded.

"In the Desolation, Ulf, one of the Seven, was with me. He was slain with a rune-marked blade." She paused. "I worked such runes into your long axe and knife. And my short-sword."

Asroth stared at her a long while, then chuckled.

"No wonder Gulla fears you," he said.

"Fears me?" Fritha said. "Hates me, more like."

"You need not worry about him, my bride," Asroth said.

"I am worried where he is," Fritha said.

"He has been gone too long," Asroth agreed.

Over a moon ago Gulla had left them, taking Rald, one of his Seven, a Revenant horde and a guard of Kadoshim and half-breeds. Their destination was Brikan, with orders to destroy whatever skeleton guard remained. It should have been a simple task and they should have been back by now. Fritha was most worried because Morn had gone with Gulla.

"And I worry about other things," Fritha said. "Where are Jin and her three thousand Clansmen? We are a moon from Ripa. She should be with us by now."

Asroth waved a hand. "With or without her the Ben-Elim will fall."

Fritha was not so sure.

Drassil was a well-timed ambush. We took them by surprise. Ripa will not be like that. I do not trust Gulla and his Revenants, and without them we have four thousand acolytes, plus the Kadoshim and their half-breeds. I have seen what a White-Wing shield wall is capable of and the Ben-Elim are more than a match for the Kadoshim.

"We have *other* allies, remember," Asroth said, sipping his wine.

"Allies we have never seen or spoken with," Fritha said.

"Gulla has spoken with them, and Sulak is in the sky, watching them," Asroth said. "You worry too much."

And you worry too little. Have these pleasures of the flesh over-whelmed you? We need strategy, not brute force. We must not underestimate the Ben-Elim and their forces.

It was the next morning that Gulla swept into Asroth's tent, Morn a few steps behind him. Kadoshim guards were stationed inside the tent now, Fritha seated at a table with Asroth. Aenor was there, too. Elise was lurking in the shadows. Wrath lay outside the tent's entrance—he was too big to fit through the opening.

"More wine," Asroth said, holding his cup out, an acolyte servant hurrying forwards with a jug to fill it. Wine was offered to Fritha, too, but she held a hand over her cup.

A clear mind, whenever Gulla is around. It seems that Asroth enjoys his wine too much to care.

Gulla was walking with a limp, a bandage around his thigh, and another wrapped around his chest and back, threaded between his wings. His brows were knotted in a glower over his one red eye. Behind him Morn looked worse. Her face was a lattice of red-scabbed wounds, a bandage wrapped high around her chest, a spot of blood on the linen, and one of her wings was frayed and tattered.

"What happened?" Asroth asked, looking Gulla up and down.

"There were more of the Order at Brikan than expected," Gulla said. "And Byrne's vanguard arrived before we had finished them."

"Vanguard?" Asroth said.

"They were half-breed Ben-Elim," Morn said. "Skilled with bow and spear."

Fritha sucked in a breath, felt as if she had just been punched.

Half-breed Ben-Elim, like my daughter.

My daughter, who the Ben-Elim murdered.

Fritha had seen one of these half-breeds in Drassil, at the battle within the Great Hall when Asroth had been freed. A fair-haired warrior with dapple-grey wings. She had dragged Meical to safety. Fritha felt an unnatural hatred for her, that she was alive where her own daughter was dead.

"We slew many of them," Gulla said, "but the battle was hard fought, and we were forced to retreat before more of Byrne's advance arrived."

Asroth's lip curled. He gestured for Gulla to sit and offered him a cup of wine.

"I do not drink that anymore," Gulla said. "I have other tastes."

"Of course," Asroth said. "I keep forgetting. You are wounded," he added. "I did not think you could be wounded now, or that you did not feel the pain from it." He waved his hand.

Gulla reached inside his cloak and drew out a hand-axe. He threw it onto the table with a clatter.

"There is worse news," he said. "The Order of the Bright Star have forged weapons that can hurt us. Slay us. Me, my Revenants."

"Like Ulf in the Desolation," Fritha said. Gulla shot her a glowering look from his red eye.

"Rald is dead," Gulla said, bowing his head. "Thousands of my Revenant horde fallen with one blow."

"That *is* a blow," Fritha murmured. She reached forwards and took the axe, lifted it and turned it. It was well balanced, a single, slightly hooked blade, weighted for throwing. She ran her thumb along its edge, saw pearls of blood bead on her thumb. She smeared the blood over the blade.

"*Nochtann,*" she whispered.

The blade seemed to shimmer a moment, her blood bubbling, and then runes appeared, carved into the iron of the axe-head. Fritha bent closer, studying the runes.

"*Misneach,*" she murmured, looked up at Gulla and the others. "Courage."

Morn made a disgusted sound in her throat.

"Where did you get this?" Fritha asked.

"Morn pulled it from out of my back," Gulla snarled. He rolled his shoulders, grimaced.

"Drem threw it," Morn said, staring straight at Fritha.

"Drem?"

"Aye, the man who slew my brother."

"I know who he is," Fritha said.

The man she had chased from one end of the Desolation to the other. Who she had offered a place at her side.

And he spurned me.

I did kill his father.

"I tried to kill him," Morn said, "came so close."

"It looks as if he came closer to killing you," Asroth said drily, looking at Morn's wounds.

"This was not him," Morn said. "The huntsman's wolven-hounds tried to eat me. I put a knife in one of them. Father tore the huntsman's throat out," she said, with a smile at Fritha.

"He slew Rald," Gulla growled.

"The huntsman who led the escape through the Desolation," Morn said to Fritha.

"Good," Fritha said, remembering him. A man she guessed was high in the Order of the Bright Star.

"The Ben-Elim half-breeds put an arrow in me," Morn continued, touching the bandage across her chest, "that Father cut out." She clicked her neck. "And that white bear did this to my wing." She extended one wing, showing Fritha where claws had raked it.

"The *white* bear?" Fritha asked. She had come across a white bear before, and was not fond of it.

"Yes, the white bear," Morn said. "And I will *kill* it."

A rattle sounded from the shadows of the tent, Elise emerging. "I hate that white bear," she hissed. During the battle in the Desolation the white bear had nearly crushed Elise.

"So does Wrath, don't you, my darling?" Fritha called out.

A deep rumbling growl echoed in from beyond the tent's entrance, the wind of Wrath's breath stirring the curtain.

"You fought that white bear, didn't you?" Fritha called out to her draig.

"*Wrath smaller then. Wrath big now. Wrath eat white bear if see it again.*"

"That's the spirit," Asroth said, laughing. He looked at them all. "So, my grudge with Meical is not the only one that will be settled before the walls of Ripa, then."

"No," Fritha answered, thinking of Drem. "Not if the Order of the Bright Star are marching to Ripa."

"I hope they are," Asroth said. "All our enemies in one place. I am growing tired of this constant marching. Better to fight them all and be done with it."

Although if they unite that would make our enemies stronger. Better to fight them separately, divided and weaker.

"They are marching south," Gulla said. "Whether they are marching to Ripa to unite with our allies, or just pursuing us, I do not know." He lifted his palms. "Either way, we shall face them on the battlefield soon."

"Don't look so worried about that prospect," Asroth said.

"I have just lost thousands of warriors." Gulla tried to keep the anger Fritha could see clear upon his face from spilling out in his voice.

"They were only Revenants, though. Surely you can just make more," Asroth said, waving airily, and smiled. "After all, there are plenty of blood-filled humans between here and Ripa in the south."

Gulla nodded thoughtfully at that. A slow smile crept across his face.

CHAPTER SIXTY

RIV

"Has there been any sign of Bleda?" Riv asked Aphra, who was striding in front of her through the warren of the White-Wings' camp beyond the walls of Ripa.

"No," Aphra said, looking over her shoulder. She saw the look that settled over Riv's face.

"Should be any day now," she added reassuringly.

Riv just grunted, chewing her lip.

She followed Aphra through the camp, the rising sun already hot, casting the world in red and gold. Tents were set in orderly rows, thousands of them. Despite dawn only just breaking, everywhere was motion, the camp waking into life like a living, breathing machine. Fire-pits burned, meat turning on spits, pots boiling, porridge bubbling, people sitting on benches, eating and drinking. In another section White-Wing warriors sparred, drilled the shield wall, voices and the *clack-clack* of practice blades.

"Here we are," Aphra said, as they passed through a long row of tents and stepped into another open space of cook-fires and sparring ground.

Conversation stopped, those sparring stuttering to a halt, as all paused in whatever they were doing to look at Riv.

So many faces.

Familiar faces: Aphra's garrison of White-Wings, the survivors from Drassil. Riv saw Ert, the old sword master, and

Fia scooping water from a barrel with a ladle and washing her baby. Avi, how he had grown, a shock of dark hair on him. Bull-muscled Sorch was there, on his knees with a practice sword in his hand, a young boy attacking him.

Tam.

There was a silence and then a cheer rose up amongst them.

"Why are they cheering me?" Riv said.

"Because none of us would be here if not for you, Riv," Aphra said. "You saved us."

"Meical helped," Riv said, uncomfortable.

"Aye, he did," Aphra said. "But without you, we would have been food for crows that day, and they all know it."

People came forward, slapping Riv on the shoulder, offering their arm in the warrior grip, hugging her, welcoming her back. Aphra ushered her through the crowd, Riv nodding and smiling, and then she was being sat upon a bench and given a pot of porridge and a board of sliced meat, fried onions and bread.

"Riv," a voice called, a figure shoving through the crowd around her.

"Jost!" Riv said, putting her food to one side and standing, embracing her friend. They held each other tight, silent for long moments.

"I've missed you," he said when they parted. "It's been too quiet. No brawling fights, no having to guard your back. I haven't had a black eye in at least three moons."

"I'm sure I can fix that for you," Riv said, and they both grinned.

"Sit, eat with us," Aphra said, and Riv did, Jost hurrying off to fetch a jug of water and a handful of cups. Fia joined them, carrying Avi under one arm.

"Wings," the boy said, pointing at Riv.

"Aye, aren't they fine?" Fia said. "One day you'll have your own wings, just like that." She held her hand out and squeezed Riv's shoulder.

"So, what's the news?" Jost asked, as he sat down beside Riv.

"There was a battle at Dun Seren, a host of Revenants chasing the survivors of Ardain."

"Revenants?" Aphra asked.

"Mist-walkers," Riv said. "They were created by Fritha, High Priestess of the Kadoshim. She changed Gulla using dark magic and Asroth's right hand, made him into something new. The first Revenant."

"Fritha," Aphra said.

"Aye. It was her at Drassil, who rode upon the winged draig."

"I know her," Aphra said, going pale. "Or *of* her. She was a White-Wing. Just... disappeared. I suspected that Kol or one of his inner circle were the reason." She looked at Fia, who nodded.

"Well, she hates us and the Ben-Elim, sure enough," Jost said. "I saw her at Drassil."

"If she was anything to do with Kol, then she has good reason," Riv muttered.

"Careful," Aphra said, looking about. "You are amongst friends now, but Kol is powerful here, and he has many eyes and ears in this camp."

"What happened, in this battle?" Jost asked Riv.

So Riv told them of the battle upon the meadows where Nara and her people were saved, and then of the assault upon Dun Seren, about the effects of being bitten, about the Revenants' towers of bodies and limbs, how flame deterred them, about the Order's rune-marked blades. About the rush for the tunnels beneath the fortress and of Arvid's fall, though she did not say that it was her who had killed Arvid.

And then she told them of Faelan and the half-breed Ben-Elim.

"Elyon above," Aphra breathed. "So many years, so many lives damaged by Kol and his hubris."

"Aye," Riv grunted. "They will be here soon, with the Order of the Bright Star." She looked at Fia and Avi. "Your son will not be as alone as you feared. The Order protected them, kept them secret and safe for over sixty years."

"Sounds as if you like this Order of the Bright Star," Jost said. "I thought they were supposed to be a poor image of us. Weaker, less skilled."

"The truth is something altogether different from that," Riv said. "I like them a great deal. I took their oath. I am one of them." She showed them her cloak brooch, the bright star gleaming, freshly polished.

"But you are a White-Wing," Jost breathed, "one of us."

"No, I failed my warrior trial, remember? I was never deemed good enough by the Ben-Elim. And now, even if I wanted to be a White-Wing, I do not think I would fit so well into a shield wall." She gave her wings a ripple. "That *is* where you White-Wings are more skilled than the Order of the Bright Star, the shield wall," she said.

Jost sat a little straighter at that.

"In all else martial, the Order of the Bright Star excel. But that is not why I took their oath."

"Why *did* you swear their oath?" Aphra asked.

Riv had thought on this long and hard in the days since she had alighted on the weapons-field at Dun Seren.

"Because of what they stand for," Riv said. "Even their battle-cry is Truth and Courage. Truth. Not the lie I have lived at Drassil. That we have all lived. Just speaking to Meical on the journey here has revealed so much more of the Ben-Elim's deception." She shook her head. "And Courage. That is something that we all value and believe in. I am a fighter." She shrugged. "Born and trained to kill. But when I fight with the Order of the Bright Star, I know it is for the right reasons."

She looked up, saw Aphra, Jost, Fia, all staring at her, and others had joined them, were sitting or standing, listening attentively. Ert, Sorch, many others.

"We share the same enemy, the Kadoshim," Riv said, "and they are a great evil that must be fought. But when this war is done, if I am still breathing, I want nothing to do with Kol or his Ben-Elim." She gazed at Aphra, took her hand. "I love you,

you should come with me. All of you." She looked at Jost and the others. "There would be a life for us at Dun Seren, amongst people we can respect. Not pretty, egotistical arselings with wings who use us as pawns."

A silence settled about her, some nodding, some frowning.

Aphra blew out a long breath. "Much to think on." She nodded, squeezing Riv's hand. "But you are right, the Kadoshim are the enemy of all. I will consider what you've said, but one battle at a time, eh?"

Riv nodded.

"I would say this, though," Aphra continued. "The Ben-Elim are no different from you and I. Good, bad and everything in between. Some are honest, honourable, others are...less so."

"Aye. Hadran is all right, and Meical," Riv acknowledged.

"All right?" Jost said. "Meical fought Asroth to a standstill. He's a *legend*."

A small figure pushed through the press around Riv, Tam. He threw himself at Riv and hugged her. The huge figure of Sorch loomed behind him.

"You've come a long way from Drassil, Tam," Riv said. "I saw you in the weapons-court, you're fierce with a blade."

Tam grinned. "Sorch has been teaching me."

"Looks as if he's doing a fine job of it," Riv said, and nodded at Sorch. She'd never liked him much but the Ben-Elim had a way of making friends out of enemies, and her feuds with Sorch seemed so long ago.

I have fought a host of Revenants since then, people who wanted to tear my throat out with their teeth or fingernails. Sorch doesn't seem so bad now.

She stood and looked at him.

"So," she said. "Which am I? Abomination or sword-sister?"

He looked her up and down.

"Sword-sister, I'm thinking," he said with a grin.

Riv offered her arm in the warrior grip, and Sorch took it.

The beating of wings up above and Meical descended from

the sky. He was dressed for war, as always, with the rune-marked sword and spear the Order had fashioned for him in his fist and at his hip.

"A hard-fought journey since I saw you last in Forn," Aphra said to Meical, as she offered him her arm.

"Aye," Meical answered as he took it. "That is the way of the Banished Lands. Your daughter brings you much honour. She slew Arvid, one of Gulla's Seven, and with that blow destroyed the Revenant host."

Murmurs and gasps of appreciation rippled around them.

"Well, you left that bit of information out." Aphra's eyes gleamed with pride as she looked at Riv.

"Forgot," Riv muttered, shuffling her feet. "So," she said, changing the subject. "Tell me, how do you plan to face a horde of blood-hungry Revenants?"

CHAPTER SIXTY-ONE

BLEDA

Bleda sat and chewed on some flatbread and cold lamb. To the south mountains reared, to the north, the trees of Forn Forest. They were camped upon the banks of a river, in a wide valley that cut through those mountains.

Dawn's glow was beginning to seep into the world, pushing the darkness back.

He was up first every morning, liked this time to sit in silence and think on the coming day.

"More?" Ruga asked, using her knife to cut slices of meat. She was his constant shadow.

Bleda shook his head, too full of what the next days might bring.

Ripa. Battle. Riv. Will she be there? Does she even still live?

A tremor in the ground and Raina joined them with a large black pot in her hands. She set it upon the stone next to Ruga's lamb, then saw that the fire-pit had burned out. Reaching down to a pouch at her belt, she pulled out a small jar. A foul smell like curdled cream hit Bleda as Raina wiggled open a wooden stopper. The giant carefully took a pinch of powder from the jar and sprinkled it onto the dead embers in the fire-pit. She stoppered the jar, put it back in her pouch, then took a water skin and washed her hands clean. Finally, she drew a striking iron and kindling stone from her pouch, struck some sparks that went scattering over the embers and powder.

There was a *whoosh* and blue flames burst into life, filling the fire-pit.

Raina gave a contented grunt, stirred her pot with a wooden spoon, then sat beside Bleda.

"What *is* that?" Bleda asked, staring at the blue flames.

"Giant's fire," Raina said with a shrug.

"I've heard of it," Bleda said. "I thought it was like oil."

"No." Raina smiled. "It is this powder. You can add it to anything, oil, water, wood—it will make everything burn, and a little goes a long way."

"I can see that," Bleda said, looking at how the whole fire-pit was crackling with blue flame. Raina stirred her pot again.

"You're an early one." She grunted, rubbing her head, stubble scraping.

"Aye," Bleda said. "Tell me again, where are we?"

"Those mountains are the Agullas." Raina pointed. "And the land we are moving into was once known as the realm of Tenebral. Now it is just one more province in the Land of the Faithful."

"Not for much longer," Bleda said. "Win or lose this war, the world will change. Kol and his Ben-Elim will not rule."

"Will they not?" Raina said, raising an eyebrow. "I can't see the Ben-Elim relinquishing their power so easily."

"They won't have a choice," Bleda said.

Raina shrugged. "I hope you are right."

There was a flapping and cawing above them and a crow spiralled out of the sky.

"*RAINA, RAINA!*" it called, getting closer and bigger, setting dust swirling as it landed in the grass.

"*Durl found Raina*," the crow squawked.

"Durl," Raina said, a smile on her face. "I was wondering when you'd finally find me."

"Well met, Durl," Bleda said to the crow. "I told Raina you were looking for her." He reached for some lamb and tore a shred off, throwing it to the crow, who caught it in his big black beak and swallowed it whole.

"*Tain say hello,*" Durl said, hopping from foot to foot. "*Alcyon say they need you. War. Asroth. BAD MEN!*"

"I am already going to them," Raina said.

Durl cocked his head to one side, regarding Raina with one eye.

"*Truth?*" the bird croaked.

"Aye, truth," Raina said.

"*Alcyon say he miss you.*"

Raina paused, looked away.

"I have missed him, too," she murmured. "You can help us find them," she said, louder. "Bleda here says that the Order of the Bright Star are marching to Ripa, to join with those who stand against Asroth. You could fly there and find out if they are there yet."

"*Durl fly to Balara,*" the crow said. "*Durl's friends at Balara.*"

"That's close enough," Raina said.

"*Durl hungry, thirsty, tired. Rest first. Been looking everywhere for you.*"

"Of course," Raina said. She stirred the pot. "Break your fast with us. Meat or *brot*?"

Durl hopped closer, eyeing the food.

"*Both,*" he squawked.

Raina scooped a spoonful of the porridge-like substance into a bowl.

Bleda tore off more strips of lamb and threw them at the crow's feet. Around them the camp was coming to life, giants and Sirak emerging from tents, setting about the process of breaking camp.

We shall be gone soon. Bleda looked to the east, wondering how far behind them Jin was. She was still following them. Seven days had passed since Bleda had seen the dust cloud of her host at the Tethys Pass, and it had followed them steadily southwards. With the extra horses that Bleda had captured, his warband had moved faster, and he had been stunned that he had not needed to slow down for the giants. They had run at a steady, ground-eating pace. Jin had followed them, but not gained. He judged she was a day and a half behind them.

"How long since you last saw Alcyon?" Bleda said to Raina.

"Thirty years," Raina said.

Bleda blinked. "That is a long time. Why?" he asked.

Raina slowly looked at him.

"I love someone," Bleda said. "I have been parted from her, and it hurts, like a physical pain. I cannot imagine being parted for so long."

Raina blew out a long breath.

"My apologies," Bleda said, "I should not have pried."

"You are honest," Raina said. "There is a sincerity about you that I like. And we are allies, so perhaps a little truth does not hurt."

She gave a sigh. "Many, many years ago, our Clan, the Kurgan, were attacked," she said. "I and my son were taken prisoner, and Alcyon was forced into slavery to a Kadoshim lord. The rest of our Clan were scattered. Years passed." She paused. "And then two good men set us free," Raina continued. "Maquin and Veradis were their names. And as we emerged into the world again the Long War was happening. Coming to its end, we thought, at Drassil."

"The Day of Wrath?" Bleda asked.

"Aye, that is what it came to be called. We fought alongside Ethlinn. She united the giant Clans. Benothi, Kurgan, Jotun, we all fought against the Kadoshim and the Black Sun. And we won. But the war was not over. Kadoshim fled the battleground, hid, and then fought again. Dun Seren was built, the Order of the Bright Star established. But all the while, my heart was drawing me back to Arcona, to search for my people. Alcyon came with me, but eventually he wanted to stop, said that Ethlinn needed us. That the Kadoshim were a danger that we could not turn our backs on. I did not want to go, still believed there was hope of finding our people." She shrugged. "Alcyon left."

"And you stayed, and you found them."

"I did," Raina said. "I asked them to come back with me to Ethlinn, but they would not. They felt safe, in their caves in the dark. They would be staying, still, if not for the Shekam, and for you."

"Me?" Bleda said.

"It was the words you spoke the night we found you. About standing against the Kadoshim. About standing against evil. They struck a chord in Ukran's heart."

She looked at him and spread her hands wide. "And now I am travelling with you and my Clan. Going back to Alcyon, and to war."

The sound of hooves and jangle of harness. Bleda looked up to see Ellac leading Bleda's horse to him, saddled and harnessed.

Time to ride.

"Aye," Bleda said, standing and thinking of Gulla and Jin, and of Riv. He reached for his weapons-belt and buckled it about his waist. "To war."

CHAPTER SIXTY-TWO

JIN

Jin rode along a valley that cut through a range of mountains. They loomed to the north-west and south-east, peaks flecked with snow.

The Agullas, she remembered from her history lessons in Drassil.

It was starting to feel as if she'd been chasing Bleda forever. In reality, it had only been a ten-night since she had picked up his trail at the Tethys Pass. She could see that same trail on the ground now, many hooves. There were other prints, too, of booted feet, unnaturally large.

"Giants." She spat. As soon as Tark had shown the footprints to her at the foot of the Tethys Pass Jin had known. Here were the Night-Walkers Vachir had spoken of.

They may look intimidating, but an arrow through the eye will put one on their back, no different from any other foe.

Up ahead Jin saw some of her scouts. They were stationary, waiting beside a river.

Jin signalled to Gerel and he put a horn to his lips and blew, the call taken up by others along the three-thousand-strong warband.

Slowing to a canter, Jin drew close to Tark and his scouts. Tark nodded to her and slipped from his saddle.

"They camped here," Tark said, gesturing to fire-pits and heating stones, areas of grass that had been flattened.

"How close are we?" she asked, though she already guessed.

Tark walked to a mound of horse dung, bent and broke a piece off, sniffed and chewed on it. Spat it out.

"A day," he said.

Jin controlled the urge to snarl. Once she had reached the Tethys Pass and found Bleda's tracks she had ridden her war-host hard, but when her horses had started to fall, with injuries or exhaustion, she had had to slow the pace.

Jin's captains rode up around her. Vachir nodded respect-fully to her, bandages still bound around his wounds at chest and hip.

"We are far into the Lands of the Faithful now," Tark said to her and her captains. He looked uncomfortable about that.

"These lands don't belong to the Ben-Elim now," Jin said. "The Ben-Elim are routed. Asroth thought they had fled to Ripa, a fortress to the south." She looked up to the sky, check-ing the sun and mountains. "And Bleda rides that way."

She knew a time was coming, approaching fast, where she would have to make a decision. Continue to follow Bleda, or abandon the chase and ride in search of Asroth. That is what she had sworn to do. But Bleda was so close, she could almost taste her vengeance.

But he will reach Ripa before I catch him, and then I will likely be the outnumbered one.

"My Queen," a voice pulled her out of her thoughts. Gerel. He was pointing up.

Jin looked into the sky, putting a hand over her eyes. It was cloudless, an endless blue, the sun hot, despite the fact that it was Hunter's Moon, summer long departed. And in that blue there were black dots. She stared, and the dots grew larger.

Bows were lifted from saddles and strung, hands hovering over quivers.

Ben-Elim or Kadoshim? Jin wondered, her own hand resting on her bow.

The dots were becoming winged silhouettes, twenty or

thirty of them, and one of them was far larger than the others. And this one had a tail.

Fritha and her draig.

"Peace," Jin called out. She looked at Gerel. "But be ready. They may be our allies, but that does not mean I trust them."

She heard gasps and murmurs from amongst her warband as the draig swooped lower, its wings beating up foam and spray from the river. It circled over Jin's head, a wide loop, and swept down to land on the far side of the river. The ground shook as its feet hit the surface, wings still beating, slowing its momentum, but it ran on, into the river, an explosion of water hurled into the air, crashing back down, spray reaching as far as Jin, spattering her face.

The draig stood in the middle of the ford, water up to its bowed belly, Fritha upon its back, wearing a bearskin cloak.

"*Wrath thirsty,*" the draig said, and lowered its head to drink noisily from the river. Fritha leaned forwards and stroked the beast's muscular neck.

That beast's hide is so thick, its scales look like plates of lamellar armour. I wonder, would my arrows even pierce it?

Around Fritha other shapes descended, thick-muscled men and women with wings like leather and spears in their hands. Not Kadoshim, but their half-breed spawn. Jin recognized the one named as Gulla's daughter, Morn.

The draig lurched into motion, eruptions of water with each footfall as it splashed across the river, then stomped up the riverbank. It lumbered onto the meadow, stopping a dozen paces before Jin. Her horse danced on the spot, not liking the sight or smell of this draig before her. She calmed the mare with a soft word and a hand on her neck.

"Well met, sister," Fritha said to Jin, which took her by surprise.

Sister?

Jin looked up at Fritha a long moment.

"Well met," she replied.

"I have been looking for you, hoping to find you soon," Fritha continued. "You are a welcome sight, and needed." She looked from Jin to the war-host gathered at her back. Fritha smiled. "You have kept your oath, I see, and gathered the strength of your Clan."

"Three thousand Cheren riders; finest warriors in all of the Banished Lands," Jin said.

"Hmm." Fritha nodded. "And the Sirak?"

"Most are feeding the crows. I am in pursuit of the last of them." She looked to the south. "Bleda leads them."

"Ah. The one who slew your father."

Jin nodded.

"How far ahead is he?"

"A day or so." Jin shrugged.

"You should break off that chase now, and come with me. Asroth and our war-host are two score leagues west of here. You will not catch Bleda before he reaches land held by the Ben-Elim. Seven thousand White-Wings, over a thousand Ben-Elim in the sky. Even the finest warriors in the Banished Lands will struggle against *those* odds."

"You do not command the Queen of the Cheren," Gerel said.

Fritha looked at Gerel, and so did Wrath. A snort of air exploded from the draig's nostrils, a line of saliva dripping from one long tooth.

"*He looks tasty,*" Wrath rumbled.

"We do not eat our friends," Fritha reminded him. "I was not ordering, merely advising," she said to Gerel. "Your Queen is a strategist and cunning thinker. What is the point of charging into death, when she could wait a little longer, join our host, as she promised, and attack with a warband of fourteen or fifteen thousand at her side? That is just wisdom, is it not?"

Gerel gazed up at Fritha.

"That is for my Queen to decide, not I," Gerel said.

"Loyalty, I like that. You are a good man. And it takes a good leader to inspire that kind of devotion." Fritha looked at Jin.

"What say you? Come west with me, to victory. Or continue south, to an almost certain glorious death. Better vengeance than grief, don't you think?" Fritha's eyes flickered to Morn.

"Better vengeance than grief," Jin said. "I like that."

"So do we." Fritha smiled, another fleeting glance at Morn. Jin saw even a twitch of lips upon her glowering face.

"We will ride with you to Asroth," Jin said.

CHAPTER SIXTY-THREE

DREM

Drem rode through the sentry-line, one of the last to return from a day scouting ahead of Nara's vanguard. Warriors parted for Friend, nodding a greeting up at him as Fen loped at his side and Reng the huntsman trotted beside him. Since Keld had died, Drem had ridden ahead as scout every day. Reng had led, taking over Keld's position amongst the huntsmen of Dun Seren, but had given Drem point on many occasions, having seen first-hand Drem's skills as a woodsman and tracker.

They passed through countless lines of tents, the smell of woodsmoke from a hundred fire-pits drifting on the breeze. Up above, winged figures circled: Faelan and his kin, as well as Craf's crows.

He glanced to his right, saw the spike of a tower beyond their camp. The fortress of Jerolin, its black tower pointing like an accusatory finger at the sky, a glistening lake beyond it, wide as a sea to Drem's eyes. The fortress was empty; word of Asroth's horde had sent all fighting men and women south to Ripa, those left behind running to hide in the wooded hills and forests of this land. It had been the same for over a moon: every hold, village, town and fortress empty. The people of the Banished Lands were afraid. Drem could feel it, a creeping sensation in his gut, a shiver down his spine, as if a spider's legs crawled across his neck.

The end is coming.

He wiped sweat from his eyes.

"It's Hunter's Moon, how can it be so warm?" he muttered to Friend. "Though I don't know why I'm complaining; you're the one covered in fur."

They reached the bear enclosure and Hammer lumbered over to them as they entered, a deep rumbling sound in her chest. She rubbed her head against Friend's neck and he rumbled back, pushing against the huge bear.

"We're pleased to see you, too," Drem said to Hammer, "but let me climb out of my saddle first."

Alcyon laughed, the giant following Hammer. Drem dropped to the ground, stretched his back and patted Fen's neck. The wolven-hound padded off to the shade of a tree, turned a circle and flopped to the ground, mail coat clanking. Drem saw Alcyon looking up at Jerolin's tower.

"You've seen this place before?" Drem said.

"Aye," Alcyon growled. The memory did not seem like a pleasant one. The giant sighed and rubbed a hand over his eyes. "Those Kadoshim have caused a lot of hurt in this world. Too much."

"That will end soon," Drem said, his mind full of Gulla and Fritha and Morn.

"Aye, it will," Alcyon said. "One way or another."

The giant was helping Drem unbuckle and remove Friend's saddle and coat when Cullen ran into the enclosure.

"Byrne wants us," Cullen said. "Riv's back from Ripa."

Byrne was in her tent standing beside a table, pouring mead into a handful of cups. Riv was there, wings furled tight across her back. Meical was there, too, and Kill was at Byrne's shoulder.

Riv looked over at Drem and Cullen as they walked into the tent, gave them a tentative smile that faded.

"What's wrong?" Riv said. Then she looked at Fen, who had followed Drem and now padded into the tent. "Where's Keld?"

Byrne handed Riv a cup of mead. "I haven't had time to tell her," Byrne said to Drem and Cullen.

"Keld…" Cullen began, a tremor in his voice stopping him.

"Keld fell, at Brikan," Drem said, his voice flat, monotone. He felt the grief, though, a nausea deep in his gut and a prickling behind his eyes.

"How?" Riv asked, colour draining from her face.

Drem drew in a deep breath. "Keld led a scouting expedition to Brikan. While we were there, Revenants attacked. Gulla was there. He and his daughter, Morn, slew Keld."

"And I will slay *them*," Cullen snarled.

Rage helps him.

"Keld put a rune-marked sword through the heart of one of Gulla's Seven," Drem carried on. "Thousands of Revenants fell."

Riv shook her head and put a hand to her temple, rubbed it. She drank her cup of mead.

Byrne refilled the cup.

"Keld is a loss we all feel," she said.

"Aye," muttered Kill beside her.

"I—" Riv started, but words would not come. Her face twisted in a snarl. "Asroth, Gulla and all his scum need to die." She took a long, shivering breath, looked at Drem and Cullen. "I am *so* sorry," she said.

"Asroth does need to die," Byrne said.

"The Long War must come to an end," Meical said beside Riv. "And killing Asroth is the start of that, but it will only be over when every last Kadoshim is wiped from existence."

"So, let us be about that end," Byrne said. "What news, Riv?"

"You are ten, maybe twelve nights from Ripa," Riv said slowly. "But Asroth is closer. He has crossed the Agullas far to the east of here, and is marching due south to Ripa. I have not had a close look at his warband, his scouts were thick in the air, but I saw it from a distance. It is…vast. Though much of it was cloaked in mist. The work of Gulla and his Seven, no doubt."

"They are four, now," Cullen said with a fierce snarl.

And soon they will be none.

"How long until Asroth reaches Ripa?" Byrne asked.

Riv looked at Meical and shrugged. "If his host were as

disciplined as White-Wings, they would travel the distance in five days. But he is slower. Nine, maybe ten days. It is hard to tell."

Byrne's mouth formed a tight line. "Can he be delayed? It would be best for us to reach Ripa and fight him together. Divided we are both easier to destroy. And we have rune-marked blades, unlike the warband at Ripa. Until we reach there they are vulnerable to a Revenant attack. It would be overwhelming."

"Aye. Like Drassil," Riv said. "But Kol is in no hurry to join with you."

Byrne raised an eyebrow.

"He has seven thousand White-Wings around him, over a thousand Ben-Elim. He thinks he is invulnerable."

"Idiot," Byrne muttered.

"Fortunately, he is not in total control of the Ben-Elim and White-Wings anymore," Meical said. "Thanks to Riv."

All looked at Riv.

"I named him as my father," Riv said, "in front of his Ben-Elim and White-Wing captains."

"Ah, well, better the truth be brought out into the light," Byrne said. "What happened?"

"Kol will be tried before the Assembly after the battle with Asroth is fought, if anyone lives to try him."

Byrne nodded. "But who commands at Ripa, now?"

"Technically, the Ben-Elim Assembly," Meical said. "But that is too unwieldy. In reality it is spread between a handful of Ben-Elim: Dumah, Hadran, a few others. Kol still holds some power. He has many followers."

"So," Byrne said, "is there any way that Asroth can be slowed?"

"Defences have been laid. Ditches dug, barriers built, but how long will they slow him?" Riv shrugged. "Who knows?"

"We must hurry, then," Byrne said, looking at them all.

"There is something else I wanted to talk to you about," Riv said. "To ask you."

Byrne sat down.

"Sit," she said, "and tell me all about it."

CHAPTER SIXTY-FOUR

FRITHA

Fritha led three White-Wing warriors by a leash, two men and a woman, beaten bloody, staggering, half insensible. They had been caught by Morn and her half-breed kin, scouts spying on Asroth's camp.

They were foolish to think they could come so close. They deserve what is about to happen to them. She walked out beyond the last tents of the camp and into the shade of a copse of alders. Behind her and the captives strode Arn, Elise there, too, slithering across the ground, and a handful of Fritha's honour guard behind them. Fritha put a hand to the small of her back, rubbing knotted muscles. Her swelling belly was affecting all parts of her body. The child within her was growing, and quicker than a human child, she felt. Something in her spirit told her this baby would not be much longer in her womb.

Just wait for the battle to be done, she thought, stroking her belly.

The three captive warriors started to pull on the rope leashes tied around their necks and wrists.

"Can you smell him?" Fritha said to them, as she dragged the warriors on. They were pitifully weak after being put to the question, all three of them missing some body part or other, whether it be fingers, toes or teeth. "Or is it death that you can smell? Either way, I am sorry, but this is a cruel world. At least your deaths will be quick, and they are for a good cause. My Wrath will need his strength over the next few days."

She heard Wrath's rumbling growl, a reverberation in her boots and chest, and saw a hulking shadow move between the trees.

She stopped and let the warriors go. Just dropped the ropes. They tried to bolt backwards but Elise was there, her tail lashing and mouth wide, hissing, Arn and Fritha's warriors pointing sharp steel at them.

The White-Wings turned from Elise, panicked by her proximity, and ran straight into Wrath.

His neck darted out and one was in his jaws, bones crunching, blood spraying. One of the men. The other two warriors ran stumbling in different directions.

Fritha smiled, watching Wrath eat the first warrior, shards of bone spilling from his jaws.

"The other two are going to escape," Arn said.

"No, they won't," Fritha said, gazing lovingly at Wrath. She looked at Arn. "He likes to hunt."

Arn nodded.

"Come," Fritha said, "I am supposed to be in Asroth's tent. He has called another council of war."

An acolyte pulled the tent opening wide for Fritha and she stepped into Asroth's portable throne-room. She strode in and then stopped, staring.

Asroth was sitting in his high-backed wooden chair, Bune standing behind him, other Kadoshim in the shadows that pooled between burning bowls. Another Kadoshim was kneeling before Asroth. With a gesture from him the Kadoshim rose and looked at Fritha.

"Behold, my bride," Asroth said to the Kadoshim.

The Kadoshim eyed her. He had jet black hair where Asroth's was silver, his face pale as a fish's belly, a scar running down his cheek and through his mouth, making one corner curl in a permanent sneer.

"Beautiful," the Kadoshim said, his eyes running over Fritha. They hovered over her belly. Although she was strapping it with linen, it was still showing through her mail shirt. Her cuirass did not fit and needed the buckles adjusting.

"Fritha, this is Sulak," Asroth said.

"Well met," Fritha said, approaching Sulak. She held out her arm for him. "My Lord Asroth has spoken much of your loyalty and fierce bravery."

Sulak regarded her. Slowly he wrapped his long fingers around Fritha's forearm, squeezing her leather vambrace.

"Well met, Fritha, high priestess and bride of the King," he said, his voice quiet, almost gentle. It did not match his dark gaze.

"Come, sit," Asroth said, "eat, and drink wine." He snapped his fingers and acolytes came forwards with jugs and platters.

Fritha sat at Asroth's table. Elise and Arn entered the tent, Arn to stand at Fritha's shoulder. Sulak's eyes followed Elise as she slithered around the tent, coiling and settling in a shadowed corner.

Aenor entered brusquely, sweating. He grunted a greeting and then sat and poured himself a cup of wine, filled his wooden trencher and started eating.

Fritha stared at him.

"Hungry work, catching White-Wings," he mumbled through a mouthful of cheese. It had been Aenor who had captured the White-Wing spies Fritha had just fed to Wrath.

More movement at the tent's entrance and Gulla and Morn swept in, black mist curling around Gulla like a cloak. Fritha noticed that he was still walking with a limp, and that his shoulders were hunched.

His wounds from Drem at Brikan still trouble him.

Fritha felt unduly pleased about that.

Four figures followed Gulla, what was left of his Seven:

Burg, Tyna, Ormun and Thel. The smell of decay entered the tent with them, of things long dead and rotted.

"Sulak," Gulla said with a dip of his head, and he sat at the table, too. Morn slammed down into a chair between Gulla and Fritha.

She does everything angrily.

Another shadow at the tent entrance and Jin stepped into the tent. She wore her blue deel tunic, a coat of riveted mail over it. Weapons bristled on her belt: bow, quiver, two knives. A curved sword jutted over her shoulder. A Cheren warrior followed her, Gerel.

Fritha smiled at them both, pleased to see them. Jin's presence gave her a new confidence. Three thousand warriors that were not Revenants. Experts of warfare on horseback. Now their war-host was beyond formidable.

Jin nodded a greeting and Fritha patted the chair beside her.

"Welcome, my captains," Asroth said. "So, to business. How long until we reach Ripa and I get to put my boot on Meical's skull?"

"Three days' travel," Aenor said. "We will see the fortress of Balara in two days."

"Balara?" Asroth said, raising an eyebrow.

He has been told countless times, Fritha thought, trying not to roll her eyes. *He does not seem concerned with any details of the impending battle.*

"A fortress belonging to the Order of the Bright Star, my King," Aenor said. "It lies upon a hill on the northern fringe of the Sarva Forest, a day's journey from Ripa. We should take it first, don't want enemy at our back when we assault Ripa." Aenor shrugged, slurping on his cup of wine. "We do not expect much resistance there. It most likely has a skeleton garrison, much like Brikan did, in Forn."

"Although that was not as easy to crack as some thought," Asroth said, eyeing Gulla.

Gulla said nothing.

"Aye. It should be scouted out thoroughly," Aenor said.

"So, three days until we reach Ripa," Asroth said. "Most excellent." He grinned.

"What is the plan, my King?" Fritha asked. "The strategy of attack?"

Asroth looked at her over his cup of wine.

"I shall lead the centre, you and Aenor at my side. Jin will watch the left flank, Gulla and his Revenants the right. Morn and Bune will lead the aerial attack. And you with me, of course," Asroth said to Fritha. "Your Wrath will cause quite the impression, I am thinking." He raised his palms. "And then our enemy shall die."

"You will remain on the ground?" Fritha asked him.

"Aye," Asroth said. "To begin with. It will be a battle, no plan lasts past the first hundred heartbeats. We have over-whelming numbers, both on the ground and in the air. Meical's defeat is inevitable."

"The numbers are in our favour," Fritha said cautiously, "but we are not facing a rabble. Seven thousand White-Wings, possibly more. They are skilled at field combat."

"We shall tear them to pieces." Asroth smiled. He looked at Fritha, then pulled a sad face. "Do not look so worried, my bride. Our war-host is vast, unstoppable. But to add to that, Sulak has joined us; my loyal friend. He leads a thousand Kadoshim and their...children. He will join us at Ripa, with his winged forces, and our allies, the Shekam giants. Our enemy will not walk away from this fight."

"The Shekam giants," Fritha repeated, looking at Sulak. "En route from Tarbesh? That is a hard journey. How close are they to Ripa?"

"They are speeding to Ripa as we speak," Sulak said. "Have no doubts, they shall be there when you need them. As will I."

"And what is the planned attack with them?"

Sulak raised an eyebrow. "Have you seen a warband of giants, three hundred strong?"

"Yes," Fritha said, thinking back to Balur One-Eye charging up a hill upon his battle-bear, hundreds of giants and bears behind him. The ground had shaken.

"Well, then you have some idea. But these giants will be riding draigs. Three hundred draigs. There will be no stopping them, no defending against them. Seven thousand White-Wing warriors, ten thousand, the end will be the same. Their corpses trampled into the ground."

Fritha hoped it would be that easy, but life had taught her never to underestimate anyone.

CHAPTER SIXTY-FIVE

DREM

Drem sat, unstoppered his water bottle and took a long, deep drink.

"Thirsty work, riding bears," Alcyon said to him. "And sore on the arse."

Drem nodded. Riding a bear was not the same as sitting in a horse's saddle. The legs were pushed wider, different muscles used to maintain your position, and a bear's movement was different to a horse's. No walk, trot, canter and gallop. It was just shifting from one lumbering speed to the next.

"Here," Alcyon said, passing Drem a wrapped parcel of dried, salted pork.

"My thanks," Drem said, cutting himself a slice, and then passing it on to Riv, who sat the other side of him.

They were camped in the Sarva Forest, beside a black-flowing river, wide and languorous as it approached the sea. Night had fallen. Drem, Riv, Alcyon and Meical were sitting on the riverbank, a dozen warriors of the Bright Star with them. Cullen and the rest were on first watch, silent and still amongst the trees of Sarva. Fen was somewhere out in the forest, too.

Friend was with Hammer beneath high-boughed trees, close to the wains. The white bear was nibbling Hammer's shoulder, and she swiped him with a paw.

"How long?" Drem asked.

"We'll see Balara on the morrow," Meical said. "We've made

good time. Pulled ahead from Byrne and the Order by a day or two." They'd been riding hard for six days. Switching the horses harnessed to the wains every half-day, and the ease of travelling on the wide, hard-packed road, had seen them cover around sixty leagues in six days.

"My thanks," Riv said. "These weapons that we are carrying may well save my mother's life."

"You're welcome," Drem said.

Wings flapped and Rab fluttered down out of the canopy above.

"*Rab's wings tired*," the crow said. Riv cut a slice of pork and threw it to the crow, who stabbed it with his sharp beak, flung it into the air and gulped it down.

"*Thanks*." He burped.

"What news, Rab?" Alcyon asked.

"*Saw Kadoshim in the sky, long way away. Two days from Balara, three from Ripa, maybe.*" The crow ruffled his feathers, a semblance of a shrug.

Meical grimaced. "That is too close. A hard ride to Ripa on the morrow."

"We'll do it," Riv said.

Drem thought Riv was capable of making most things happen by sheer will.

I like her. She sets her mind to a task and does what is necessary to make it happen.

"How does it feel, to be so close to the end?" Alcyon said. He was looking at Meical.

The Ben-Elim shook his head. "I do not know. Is it the end? I hope so, but for it to really be the end, Asroth, Gulla and every single Kadoshim must die." He looked around at them all. "So much has happened, for you the last hundred years full of battle, victory and defeat. But my last memory was fighting Asroth in the hall at Drassil. Corban was there, going sword to sword with Asroth; Storm and Cywen, too." He shook his head. "Part of me feels that I am still in that fight." He blew out a long sigh.

"Asroth and all who follow him must die," he said. "That is all I know. If that were to happen, how would it feel?" He looked into nowhere. "Like standing on the brink of an abyss. This is the last breath before the fall." He shrugged. "Thousands of years this war has been waged, so to think that this battle will settle it...I hope so, and at the same time it is a...daunting thought. I am scared, excited." He looked at them all then: Alcyon, Riv, Drem, the other warriors of the Order.

"Win or lose, I am proud to fight beside you. That is the lesson I have learned, that changed me. Love, loyalty, friendship. You humans have such a great capacity for these qualities. It makes me want to be like that."

"You are," said Riv.

"I made mistakes, in the past."

"Yes, the past," Alcyon rumbled. "This is now. You are here, with us, not in a high tower with Kol and the rest. Aloof. Superior. You are our friend, willing to stand beside us. Willing to die beside us."

Meical nodded. "I am," he said quietly.

Drem slipped through the forest, almost as quiet as Fen, who was shadowing him. It was his watch, and he was looking for Cullen.

A sound in the darkness. A slow, rasping scrape. Drem altered his direction and saw Cullen, sitting with his back against a tree. Moonlight filtered through branches, trees losing their leaves in Hunter's Moon, casting dappled silver and black across him. He was running a whetstone across his sword, head bowed, staring at his blade as if it contained all the answers in the world.

Drem crept up behind him, purposely cracked a twig under his boot.

Cullen jumped and looked, sword out. Half rose from his position. The moonlight showed tears glistening on his cheeks.

"Oh, it's you." Cullen slid back to his sitting position.

"Your watch," Drem said. "It's over."

Cullen nodded, but made no move to leave.

"What's wrong?" Drem asked, reaching out to squeeze Cullen's shoulder and sitting down beside him.

"What isn't wrong?" Cullen mumbled, carried on sharpening his sword.

Fen appeared from the darkness. He sniffed at Drem's face, licked him, then turned and sat, shuffling backwards until his back haunches were pressed against Drem.

"He's telling you he trusts you," Cullen said. "Keld explained what that means. Fen is telling you he trusts you to guard his back." He went back to rasping the whetstone along his blade.

"I trust him, too," Drem said, and scratched Fen's neck, just above the leather collar of the wolven-hound's mail coat.

"We had a chat," Drem said. "Fen's part of our crew."

"Damn right he is," Cullen muttered.

"And Keld asked me to look after him."

"When did Keld ask you that?" Cullen said, a slight break in the rhythm of his whetstone.

"With his last breath," Drem said.

Cullen grunted.

"He asked me to watch over you, too," Drem said. Cullen deserved to know Keld's last words. "He said his death would go hard on you."

A gulp from Cullen, though he did not stop sharpening his sword. "He wasn't wrong."

"We are kin," Drem said. "We look after each other."

"Aye." Cullen sighed.

"That's a rune-marked sword," Drem said. "I doubt it needs sharpening."

"No," Cullen agreed. He stopped his work. "This is a cruel world," he breathed. "Keld. Sig. Before that my mam and da. All of them slain by Kadoshim."

"How old were you, when your parents died?"

"Twelve summers," Cullen said. "Since then, it was always Sig and Keld there, looking out for me."

"Cullen, you are fearless and brave. A mighty warrior."

"Fearless and brave," Cullen said bitterly. "Not inside. Inside, I feel the fear, every day. Of fighting Kadoshim, of dying, of not living up to my heritage, of letting my mam and da down. Of letting Sig and Keld down. I'm scared of *everything*."

"But you laugh in a fight, you are the first to charge. You even like getting hurt."

"Aye, that's right," Cullen said fiercely, "because fear won't rule me, that's why. If I didn't laugh, I'd run away crying. Why do you think I challenge Balur One-Eye on the weapons-field every day? Do you think I want to fight that big oak tree? He beats me every time." He looked at Drem. "Fear will never be my master. But Keld dying—it's too much. I feel...alone." Fresh tears rolled down his cheeks.

Drem nodded. He knew what fear and loneliness felt like. He turned his arm, ran his fingers along the gap in his leather vambrace, felt the ridge of a scar beneath his linen tunic. A reminder of his oath over Keld's cairn.

"You're not alone, brother," he said quietly.

Cullen looked up at him, tears bright in his eyes. He reached out and squeezed Drem's hand.

"I know," Cullen murmured.

Drem saw the top of Balara's tower as he and their small band spilt out of the forest onto the road that curled around the fortress and led towards Ripa. Drem twisted in his saddle and looked to the south. He saw a curving wall of timber surrounding a plain that led towards the coast. On the horizon the sea shimmered a deep, sparkling blue, and when he squinted he could just make out a rise in the land, a white spire upon it.

The tower of Ripa.

Drem looked about, saw Alcyon glowering up at Balara's tower.

"Are you all right?" Drem asked him.

A tear rolled down the giant's cheek.

"Bad memories?" Drem asked.

"Aye. My wife and son were imprisoned here once. By the Kadoshim and their servants, the Vin Thalun."

"Your son. Tain?" Drem asked.

"Aye. Tain, and my wife, Raina."

"I cannot imagine you allowing that to happen," Drem said. "It must have been a bad time."

"Huh." Alcyon grimaced. "It was the worst of times. I was enslaved to a Kadoshim by dark magic. My wife and son were kept here as a surety of my obedience."

"What happened?"

"It is a long story, but the short of it is that Maquin Oath-Keeper rescued them. Brought Raina and Tain to me." He wiped a hand over his eyes.

Rab looked up to the sky and squawked, flapped his wings.

"*Brother coming*," he croaked.

A black dot was swooping over the fortress and down the hill towards them, coming from the east and circling lower.

"*Durl, Durl*," Rab squawked, as the black crow spread his wings, slowing his descent.

"*Rab, Rab*," it answered, alighting upon one of the wains, saw Cullen and hopped onto his shoulder, ruffled his beak through Cullen's red hair.

"Well met, Durl," Cullen greeted the crow.

"*Durl happy Cullen here*," Durl said.

"Why do all of Craf's crows love you so much?" Drem asked.

"Because of my wonderful personality and kind nature," Cullen said.

"Nothing to do with your regular visits to Pella, that lass who works in Crow Tower helping Tain," Alcyon said.

"Nothing at all," replied Cullen.

Durl the crow jumped at Alcyon's voice, then started hopping on Cullen's shoulder, squawking excitedly.

"*Alcyon, Alcyon*," the crow squawked.

"Aye," Alcyon rumbled. "What is it?"

"*Durl found Raina. Tain sent Durl to find her, said Alcyon sad, need Raina. Durl find her. Durl find Raina, Raina, RAINA.*"

Alcyon's face drained of colour.

"Where is she?" he asked.

"*On plain, running to Ripa.*"

"Ripa. Why?"

"*She helping Bleda and the Sirak.*"

"What?" It was not Alcyon who said that, but Riv.

"*Who are you?*" Durl asked Riv.

"I will be the one who plucks all your feathers out if you do not answer me, and quickly," Riv said. "Who is Raina with?"

"It's all right, Durl, this is Riv, and she's one of us," Cullen said.

Durl bobbed his head.

"*Riv rude,*" Durl muttered.

"Be polite," Cullen whispered.

"Please, Durl," Riv said, her feathers twitching.

"*Raina with Bleda and Sirak. They on plain, riding for Ripa.*"

"Durl, I could kiss you," Riv said, winging into the air.

"On the plain," Alcyon repeated.

"*Yes, Raina close, close.*"

Hammer lurched into motion, Alcyon urging her on past Drem and the others towards the plain before Ripa's walls.

"Where are you going?" Cullen shouted after the giant.

"To find my Raina," Alcyon called back joyfully.

"Drem, Cullen, follow us to the plain before Ripa," Riv called to them.

She was already speeding away before Drem or Cullen had a chance to answer her.

CHAPTER SIXTY-SIX

RIV

Riv sped through the air, her wings beating fast, wind ripping tears from her eyes.

Bleda.

Balara shrank behind her and, in a score of heartbeats, she was level with Alcyon and Hammer, the bear heading east, down Balara's hill and onto the rolling meadows that dominated the landscape. Riv left the giant and bear behind, sped over meadows dotted with clustered woodland. To her right the sea and Ripa edged the south, but Riv was looking to the east. She saw a cloud of dust, about a league away, moving south-west, towards Ripa. Her wings beat harder, propelling her faster than she had ever flown before.

The dust cloud grew larger, figures within it taking shape, a lot of horses, maybe a thousand, the riders moving at a fast canter, a column roughly ten horses wide. Giants were amongst them, running.

Closer still and Riv saw banners amongst the riders, a stallion rearing on a field of green. Her heart lurched in her chest.

It is them. That crow was not lying.

And then she saw him.

Bleda.

Riding at the head of the column, straight-backed in his coat of lamellar armour. His face was partly covered but she *knew him*. His shape, the way he carried himself, his effortless ease in the saddle.

A horn call from the column, faces looking upwards, hands pointing. Some reached for bows.

This would not be a good time to die.

Riv slowed a little, spreading her wings and gliding for a few heartbeats, letting them see her wings and see that she was no Kadoshim.

Bleda was looking now, calling out. He shifted on his saddle, climbed to stand upon it, reins in one hand, the other raised to her. He was grinning.

Riv swept down, a curling dive, had a glimpse of faces, mouths opening when she didn't slow, and then she was flying into Bleda, wrapping him in her arms, lifting him from the saddle. She shifted the angle of her wings, beat them hard, rising steeply, and Bleda was hugging her, kissing her face, her lips, and all the while they rose into the sky, Riv returning his kisses with a joyful passion. They hovered in the sky kissing, laughing, crying.

"You missed me, then," Riv said, a grin so wide her jaws were aching.

"Aye, a little," Bleda said. He gifted her his beautiful smile.

"Ah, but it is fine to see you, Bleda ben Erdene," she sighed, laughed again.

"I have missed you like a flower misses the sun," Bleda said.

Riv laughed, the joy in her belly uncontainable.

Slowly they descended, turning gently, her wings beating slowly, until their feet touched the ground.

"You should ask next time you are thinking of taking my King half a league straight up into the sky," Old Ellac said to Riv. "My heart is thumping in my chest."

She grinned at him. "It is good to see you, Ellac, and you, Ruga," she said, seeing Bleda's oathsworn guard. "And you, Yul." She nodded to the warrior, noting the bandage around his thigh, another high about his chest and back. Her eyes took in the Sirak, all warriors in leather or mail, bows and quivers at their hips, heads shaved apart from their long, thick warrior braids. Most of them bore the marks of battle, bandages somewhere on their bodies.

"You have seen a scrap or two, a tale to tell," Riv said to Bleda.

"Aye." He nodded. "Much like you, I am guessing."

"And who is this winged woman?" a giant rumbled. A woman, a huge round shield strapped across her back, head shaved apart from a strip of thick black hair running across the centre.

Like Alcyon shaves his head. Looking around, Riv realized all of the giants wore their hair the same way. There were a lot of them, sweating and travel-stained.

"This is the one I told you of," Bleda said. "My Riv, the one I love."

"I should hope so," the giant rumbled. "I would be disappointed if you greeted every woman you meet in such a way." She looked Riv over, saw her star-shaped cloak brooch. "You are one of the Order of the Bright Star. A half-breed Ben-Elim! *Pfah*, how the world has changed since I walked east." She smiled at Riv. "But for the better, it seems."

"This is Raina," he said, "one of the Kurgan Clan. Ukran there is their lord." Bleda pointed at another giant, wearing a coat of lamellar plate, much like Bleda's, the strip of hair running down the middle of his head golden as wheat. "They saved my life, and many of my Clan. I owe them a blood debt."

"Ha, you'll have your chance to repay that, I'm guessing," Ukran said.

"Aye," Riv said. "Asroth is two days' march from Ripa."

A silence settled then, all eyes sharply on Riv.

"My thanks, Raina, Ukran, for saving Bleda. This world would be an empty place without him." She stroked Bleda's cheek, smiling, unable to stop herself from touching him. She wanted to kiss him again.

A rumbling in the ground, and Riv turned, saw a shape approaching them across the ground, dust rising about it.

Bleda reached for his bow, others too.

"No," Riv said, "it is a friend." She glanced at Raina.

Hammer approached at a lumbering run. A hundred paces away and she began to slow. Alcyon sat there, head shaved, a strip of black hair down the middle, two single-bladed axes crossed upon his back. Twenty paces away and Hammer skidded to a stop, dust and sun-bleached grass erupting. Alcyon leaped from the bear's back, landed in a stumbling run and ran on, straight towards Raina.

He threw himself to the ground at her feet, skidded up to her, wrapping his arms around her hips and burying his face in her stomach.

"My Raina," he was crying, over and over again. "I should never have left you. Forgive me."

Raina put a hand on his head, tears streaming from her own eyes.

"There is nothing to forgive," she said, prising his arms from about her waist. She sank to the ground, pressing her forehead against Alcyon's, and folded her arms around him.

Riv turned away; something about this reunion was so raw and intimate that she felt it was wrong to be watching.

Bleda stroked her face.

A warning cry from Ruga, pointing into the sky, and another winged figure was descending from the sky. It was Meical.

"Well met, Bleda," Meical said as he landed. He looked at the Sirak and Kurgan giants. "You have honoured your word, brought a warband that could turn this battle."

"They are fine warriors, each and every one," Bleda said. "But I have also brought a warband of Cheren on my tail, at least three thousand strong." He looked behind him, to the northeast. "Though I think they've thought better of galloping into Ripa after me."

"Most likely they've joined with Asroth's war-host," Meical said. "You'll see them soon enough."

Riv looked to the north, her eyes picking out black specks in the sky, at the edge of the horizon.

Kadoshim.

"We'd best make for Ripa," she said, turning towards the timber wall that ringed the plain and fortress.

Bleda remounted and offered Riv a horse. It had been a long time since she'd sat in a saddle, but she did not want to leave Bleda's side, so she accepted.

"You do not look so comfortable," Bleda said to her, "as you do in the air."

"It's been a long time," she said with a shrug.

They rode at a slow canter through plains of yellowed grass, the ground stony, clusters of poplar and olive trees. The giants kept pace with long, ground-eating strides. Alcyon chose to run beside Raina, Hammer lumbering along with them. Ripa loomed on the horizon, Ben-Elim circling the skies, and half a league ahead of them Ripa's newest wall loomed. Riv could see White-Wing warriors walking upon it, more clustered around the gates they were approaching. On the plain to the west she saw a band of riders, three wains, and a giant white bear.

"Time for you to meet my new friends," Riv said, and led Bleda and his warband towards them.

CHAPTER SIXTY-SEVEN

BLEDA

Bleda was struggling to take his eyes off Riv. She glowed like the sun to him. He glanced towards the newcomers, then looked again.

That's a very big bear. And it's white.

He stared at the white bear. It was huge, much bigger than Hammer, who was making the ground shake a dozen paces away from him. The white bear was wrapped in a coat of mail, muscles shimmering as it moved. The mail was buckled and harnessed under its torso, much like a horse's saddle-girth, though more complex.

I've often thought our horses should have those. It would slow them, but would protect them, too. And they would adjust to the weight, as I have adjusted to my coat of plate.

What Bleda was most surprised about, though, was that a man, not a giant, was riding upon the bear's back. He was dark-haired and broad, a leanness to his musculature. He wore a coat of riveted mail, sword and axe at his belt, and the biggest knife Bleda had ever seen. A grey cloak draped his shoulders, pinned with a brooch fashioned into the shape of a four-pointed star. A helm and round shield with the same four-pointed star hung from hooks on his saddle.

Like Riv's. The Order of the Bright Star.

A wolven-hound loped at the bear's side; it, too, wore a coat of mail.

Does everything in the north wear mail?

Behind the white bear a red-haired warrior sat on the bench of a wain, driving a brace of horses. Two crows sat on the bench-back, one white and one black. The black one was Durl. Two more wains rumbled along behind them, warriors driving them, others riding around them, about a score of hard-looking men and women in mail, all with the four-pointed star on their shields and pinned across their chests.

"So, this is the master of horse and bow that you won't stop telling us about, then," the red-haired warrior said, grinning broadly, looking from Riv to Bleda.

"That's Cullen, ignore him," said Riv, though she was smiling, too.

"Well met, Bleda of the Sirak," Cullen called out, "and welcome to the we-are-going-to-kill-Asroth clan."

Bleda liked him already.

"The talkative one up on the giant bear is my friend Drem," Cullen continued. "He's pleased to meet you, too."

Bleda looked up at Drem, who nodded down at him.

"I am glad to see you reunited," Drem said. "Riv has spoken much of you."

"Well met, Drem," Bleda said. "And I'm pleased to see you're fighting on our side, and not the enemy's." He looked from Drem to the bear to the wolven-hound.

Drem smiled. "I've had the good fortune of making some excellent friends since I've come out of the north."

"Talking of friends," Meical said, looking up into the sky, "we have visitors."

Ben-Elim were flying in their direction, maybe a score of them, their white wings gleaming in the bright sunshine. Even from this distance Bleda could see they all held spears.

Meical looked at Drem and Cullen. "You should go," he said. "Byrne wants you back, and I gave her my word. Stay and you're likely to get caught up in Ben-Elim politics, and then you'll never make it back to the Sarva before Asroth's vanguard is in sight. You'll be stuck in Ripa."

Drem and Cullen looked from Meical to Riv.

"Meical's right," Riv said. She passed her reins to Bleda and dismounted, striding to the wain and climbing up onto the driver's bench, taking the reins from Cullen.

"My thanks," she said, "you have given my mother and friends a chance at surviving the Revenants. This would not have happened without you."

Cullen shrugged, gripped Riv's arm. "I'll tell Byrne you'll see her soon," he said, then leaped from the wain onto the back of a horse.

"Alcyon?" Drem called out.

"I'll be staying here a while, I'm thinking," he said. "Tell Tain why."

"*Durl tell Tain, that Durl's job*," the black crow squawked, ruffling and puffing his feathers out.

"We will all see you soon," Drem called down from the back of his bear. He looked to Bleda and gave him a nod.

"I'll look for you on the battlefield," Bleda said, dipping his head.

"He's not hard to find," Cullen laughed. "He rides an avalanche."

And then the white bear was turning away and breaking into a run, heading towards a green smudge on the western horizon. The warriors driving the other two wains climbed onto spare mounts, and then Cullen and the other riders were following Drem, having to break into a fast canter to keep pace with the bear.

Riv sat in the wain, watching them go. Two of Bleda's Sirak dismounted and climbed onto the driving benches of the other two wains. Riv flicked her reins and they were moving out. Bleda rode up beside her.

"Interesting friends you have made," he said.

"Aye, that they are. And good in a scrap."

"That's good, because there's a big one coming."

Riv looked at him, another grin as bright as the sun.

"Asroth is coming here, to us?" Bleda said.

"It looks that way," Riv said.

"So this will be our battleground?" Bleda asked, looking about him.

"Between here and Ripa," Riv said. "Probably the other side of that wall." She nodded ahead. "But the ground is much the same."

They were riding across an undulating plain of sun-bleached grass, clusters of trees here and there, to the south-east a ridge of hills leading up to the coast. The tower of Ripa stood upon the westernmost of those hills, a town on the slopes rolling down into a bay. Much of the land between Bleda and Ripa was obscured by the wall they were approaching, but Bleda could see that a huge, sprawling camp lay across the hillside that Ripa's tower stood upon.

They reached the gates in the wall. Bleda held up a fist and his warband came to a disciplined halt.

The gates were barred, White-Wing warriors peering down at them.

"Open the gates," Riv called up to them.

"We need permission," one of the warriors called down, a woman that Bleda did not recognize.

"We are your allies," Riv called up. "Come to fight with you against Asroth."

"I need a Ben-Elim's permission for the gates to open."

Meical spread his wings. "What am I?" he said. "Open the gates."

"I wish I could, but I cannot," the warrior said. "I have had my orders."

"Orders?" Riv echoed. Bleda could see her muscles starting to twitch in her face. He knew what that meant.

The White-Wing looked up, saw Ben-Elim in the sky above.

"We'll wait for them," she said. She looked relieved.

Shadows dappled the ground and Bleda saw the Ben-Elim that had been flying their way were above them now, circling downwards. Fifteen of them.

"Declare yourselves," one of the Ben-Elim called out, alighting in front of Bleda, the others hovering over them or landing on the palisade's walkway. The one in front of Bleda was brown-haired, handsome as all Ben-Elim were, a spear in his fist, and he was frowning, eyes moving from Riv to Bleda.

"Erem, you know full well we are friends and allies," Meical said, stepping out in front of the Ben-Elim.

"We are at war, Meical; I cannot allow just anyone to wander inside our lines. Who are you?" he said, looking at Bleda.

Bleda drew in a deep breath, all of those years at Drassil and the Ben-Elim's airs of entitled superiority flooding back to him. He could feel the tension in those around him, Ruga and Yul closest. He saw Ruga's fingers twitching.

She wants to put an arrow in his eye and I don't blame her.

"I am Bleda ben Erdene, King of the Sirak," he said.

"And what is your purpose here?"

"Enough," Meical said furiously. "You are insulting our allies, Erem. These warriors have travelled far, and through great danger, to join us in the fight against Asroth. What are you doing?"

"Kol's rules are very clear," Erem began.

"Get out of the way and open the gates before I do it myself," Riv snarled.

Shadows on the ground again and more Ben-Elim were in the air, a score or so. They swooped down to the wall and gate, one of them landing on the ground close to Erem. It was Hadran.

"Open the gates," he called up to the White-Wings on the wall.

"Kol's orders—" Erem began again.

"Are now overruled," Hadran said sternly. "These are our allies, and our friends. They will be treated with respect."

There was a creaking of timber and the gates opened.

"My thanks," Riv said to Hadran, and flicked her reins, the wain rolling on.

Bleda clicked his horse forward, a fast walk, and rode in front of Riv, towards Erem. His warband broke into motion behind him. "Kol is not *my* master," he said to Erem as he drew near. "I am here because Asroth is our mutual enemy. Not because the Ben-Elim summoned me, not because I like you, or even respect you."

The Ben-Elim blinked, a curl of his lips as his spear twitched, but a thousand hands dropped to bows in a heartbeat, and Hammer let out a low rumbling growl.

"I wouldn't," Alcyon said, striding past the Ben-Elim.

Erem leaped into the air, his face twitching with anger.

"Kol will hear of this," he called down.

"Good," Riv shouted up to him.

Bleda rode close to the wain.

"I think I hate the Ben-Elim almost as much as the Kadoshim," he said.

"They are not all the same," Riv said. "Meical is one of us. And Hadran."

"That is good." He looked at her. "And I would tolerate all the Ben-Elim in the world to be at your side again."

"That's the correct answer," she said, grinning.

Bleda followed Riv as she drove the wain along a column made by two rows of tents. The sun was sinking, long shadows merging. White-Wing warriors were everywhere, more people than Bleda had ever seen in his life. He was feeling uncomfortable, closed in after riding across the Sea of Grass. Worse, he had left his warband to make camp. It would have been impossible to ride his whole Clan through the camp like this, and Riv had asked him to accompany her, so he'd left Ruga in charge, Hadran escorting Bleda's warband and assisting them in the organization of their camp. Raina, Alcyon and Ukran were setting up their own settlement close to Bleda's warband. Ellac and Yul were the only Sirak accompanying him.

Riv pulled on her reins and turned into an open square roped off into two sections. More White-Wings were here, most of them lined along a trestle table, helping themselves to the evening meal laid out in pots and bowls. All stopped and stared as Riv drove in, the other two wains following her.

"Riv," a voice called out, and Bleda saw Aphra running towards them. She looked older than Bleda remembered, more grey in her short-cropped hair, lines deeper in her face.

The last few moons have taken their toll on all of us.

Riv leaped from the wain and fell into Aphra's arms, the two of them hugging.

"Well met, Bleda," a voice said, Bleda looking to see Jost beside him. He didn't look much changed at all. Tall and slim, a surprising strength in his lean frame.

Bleda slipped from his saddle and gave Jost his arm. Jost slapped it away and wrapped his arms around Bleda, hugging him tight.

"It's good to see you," Jost said. "Lots of White-Wings here, but not many friends."

"It's good to see you, Jost," Bleda said.

"White-Wings, gather round," Aphra called out, and Riv beat her wings and flew up onto the bench of the wain.

"Asroth's war-host is almost here," Riv said, as Aphra's warriors gathered close. Bleda thought there were around two hundred, maybe more.

"On the morrow they will reach Balara. The day after they will be here. You all saw the mist-walkers that attacked Drassil. Revenants, they are called, a dark magic spawned from Gulla and his priestess. These Revenants will be with Asroth. Ten thousand of them, maybe more. Normal weapons do not hurt them. You know these things already, you've *seen them*, know what they can do." She leaned over the wain, undid a knotted rope and swept back the hemp sheet, revealing bundled weapons.

"These weapons are rune-marked blades. They will hurt the Revenants as any normal wound would hurt us. These weapons will kill them, as a normal blade would kill us. There are short-swords, though few of them, for the front row of the shield wall. More spears and long axes for the deeper rows." She looked around at them all. "I wish I could have brought more. But at least if you come up against these Revenants in the coming battle, you will have a fighting chance. And give them a reason to fear you."

Aphra looked into the wain, touched a spear blade.

"We cannot thank you enough for this," Aphra said. "I have been racking my mind trying to think of a way to stand against those things."

"Well, now you have it," Riv said with a grin. "They are a gift from the Order of the Bright Star. Each and every warrior in their warband has a rune-marked blade, close to four thousand warriors, and they are no more than three days away. If we can hold Asroth's horde for one day, they will be here. So, Aphra, distribute them as you see fit. Apart from the arrows. They are for the Sirak."

Bleda grinned.

Ruga held open the tent curtain, Bleda and Riv ducking to enter. Bleda looked around, nodding.

It is not a Sirak ger, but it will do.

The night was growing late, much discussion having taken place at Aphra's camp, and Bleda was abruptly feeling exhausted. Now they were safe, within patrolled pickets and no chance of Jin galloping into his warband, he felt weariness creeping through his limbs. Torches burned in sconces, smoke rising through a hole around the central pole. A bed in one corner, a table and two chairs, jug and cups, a platter of food. Fruits and cold meats, cheese. And a stand for his armour and weapons.

"How did you manage all this?" Bleda said to Ruga.

"I told the Ben-Elim you are a king, so Hadran organized this."

"It will be strange, not sleeping under the stars," Bleda said.

"Aye, warmer, and better for the back and bones," Ruga said.

"For that I am grateful," Ellac added as he entered behind Bleda and Riv. He and Yul were carrying bundled sheaves of arrows under each arm. They put them upon the table.

"Five hundred arrows there," Riv said. "These Revenants, you have all seen them?"

Bleda and the others nodded.

"Fire hurts them, but these—these will kill them." She touched one of the arrow-tips. "Each one has been forged with a rune of power. But there are thousands of the monsters," Riv said. "Kill their captains, and those they have turned fall with them."

"Their captains?" Bleda said.

"Gulla was changed, transformed, into a new creature, by their priestess, Fritha. He chose seven captains, who became the first Revenants, and he sent them out to create a legion of monsters, all blood-hungry. Kill one of the Seven, and those they've turned will fall. I have seen it happen. Kill Gulla, and we believe all will fall."

Bleda grunted, thinking that through. "That could change the whole battle; win it."

"Aye," Riv said.

"How do we find these Seven?"

"There are only four, now," Riv said, a brief smile ghosting her lips.

There is a story there.

"From what we've seen, they are different from the others. More intelligent, they wield weapons and they have guards about them." Riv pulled a face. "It will not be easy. But we have one more day to prepare. There will be a council of war on the morrow, and you will be invited," Riv said. "I will make sure of it."

"And Raina, Alcyon and Ukran?" Bleda asked.

"Yes," Riv said. "All those allied against Asroth must be represented."

"Good," Bleda said. "Then tonight I will have a cup of wine, and not sleep with my weapons-belt making indentations in my flesh."

"As long as it stays close," Ellac said.

"Aye." Bleda nodded.

He poured them all a cup of wine from the jug on the table, then held his own cup out.

"My friends, we have come a long way, through much," he said. "And more danger and death is only a night or two away. But this night, sleep well, and be proud of what you have accomplished."

Nods and murmured approval as they touched cups, and they all drank.

Ellac looked at Bleda and Riv.

"I am for my bed," he said, "better to face death without yawning." He walked to the tent entrance and lifted the curtain, then looked back. "That means all of us," he said, gesturing at Ruga and Yul. They stood slowly and left the tent. Ellac looked at Bleda, and smiled, closing the curtain behind them.

Bleda looked at Riv and she smiled at him over her cup of wine, her eyes shining in the torchlight. A tremor shuddered through her wings.

"Ah, but you look fine to me, Bleda ben Erdene," she said.

A slow, shy smile touched his own lips. He unbuckled his horsehair helm from his belt and set it upon his weapons-stand.

Riv unfastened her cloak brooch and took her cloak from her back, reverently placed the cloak and brooch upon the table. "Help me," she said, turning her back on him.

Bleda stepped close to her and began unbuckling her coat of mail, a set of leather buckles down the middle of her back. She sighed as it came loose, her linen tunic beneath damp with oil and sweat.

"It's been a while since I've stepped out of this," Riv said, laying the mail over the back of a chair.

"Aye," grunted Bleda. Being close to Riv was blurring his concentration, his blood pounding in his head like a drumbeat.

"Here," Riv said, gently turning him, "a favour for a favour," and she unbuckled his lamellar coat. He wriggled and it slipped down from his arms. Riv stepped close. "Battle looms, and none can know the outcome, who will live or die, but I know this. We have now. This moment." She leaned close and brushed her lips against his, her fingers at his deel, unfastening the ties. They would not open, so she gripped the deel and ripped it open, both of them laughing and kissing as the deel fell to the ground. He stepped away, pulled his linen tunic over his head, and something fell to the floor.

Riv laughed, breathless. "How much do you keep secreted away in your clothing?" she said. Then looked at the floor. There were two things. A dapple-grey feather and a dried flower. She looked in his eyes. "One of my feathers, and the flower I gave you, in Forn."

"Aye," Bleda said. He looked away, then raised his gaze to meet her eyes. "You are my heart, my life, Riv. So I have kept them over my heart. The feather is part of you, and the flower…" He smiled at her, shrugged. "I knew then, when you gave it to me."

"Knew what?" Riv whispered.

"That you felt the same as I."

A silent moment, and then they were in each other's arms, kissing, Riv's wings wrapping about them.

CHAPTER SIXTY-EIGHT

FRITHA

Fritha braced herself as Wrath crashed into the gate tower of Balara. There was an explosion of rock and masonry cascading down into the courtyard beyond the wall, a cloud of dust enveloping Fritha.

"*Wrath sorry*," the draig growled, shaking himself.

The rising sun sent Wrath's shadow stretching across an empty courtyard. Fritha peered into Balara and saw a deserted fortress, gates open and streets empty. The sound of hooves behind her as the Cheren approached and Jin cantered through the gate arch, Cheren riders behind her, spreading out, bows bristling.

Jin looked at the rubble in the courtyard, then up at Wrath and Fritha, perched on a half-destroyed section of the wall. She raised an eyebrow.

"He is still working on his landings," Fritha said. She looked around. "I don't think anyone is here."

"I'll find out," Jin said, a touch to her reins and she rode on, along the central street that led to Balara's tower. Fritha watched the Cheren filter into the fortress, three thousand riders. They broke into groups, some dismounting, going through building after building, checking every room, alcove and hidden space. Others stayed mounted, patrolling the streets. Fritha was impressed with their methodical thoroughness.

There were more hoofbeats on the hill beyond the wall and

Arn rode into the courtyard, a hundred of Fritha's hand-picked warriors with him. Elise was there, gleaming in her mail, her scales shining in the sunrise. Ferals loped around her, some sniffing the ground, others looking up at Fritha.

Asroth had given Fritha the honour of leading the attack on Balara. She had chosen Jin and Morn as her captains. Morn had scouted the fortress from high above last night, before the sun had set, and reported that it looked deserted, but that was not to say that there was not some nasty ambush-in-waiting lurking in the shadows.

"Hold this courtyard and the gate," Fritha said to Arn and Elise. "Let the Cheren do the hunting. There are enough of them."

A shadow passed over the courtyard and Morn swept down to her, two score half-breed Kadoshim behind her. Morn alighted on the wall beside Fritha, her kin spreading over the fortress, swooping low.

"It looks empty," Fritha said.

"Aye," Morn grunted. "A pity. I would have liked to kill some more of the Order of the Bright Star."

"Where is your father?" Fritha asked.

"With the war-host, half a day behind us," Morn growled.

"This has been a long time coming, hasn't it?" Fritha said. "And yet, now we are a day away from Ripa and the Ben-Elim, it feels so far away."

"Yes, I am sick of this waiting, eager for the battle to begin."

"Let's get a better look." Fritha leaned over Wrath's neck.

"Take me up, my darling," she whispered.

Wrath shook, snapped his wings out and stepped off the gate tower. They fell towards the courtyard, Arn's eyes flaring wide, but Wrath's wings caught the air and they started to glide, then his wings were beating and they were rising, over the rooftops of the fortress, up, towards the tower, circling around it, spiralling upwards, until they were at the very top of the tower.

"Can you land there, without destroying the tower and killing all the Cheren on the ground?" Fritha asked Wrath.

"*Don't know, Wrath try,*" Wrath growled.

Fritha laughed.

Wrath's wings changed angle and he hovered above the tower, slowly descended, his bowed legs searching for purchase. Tiles cracked, crumbled to powder, and Fritha felt the whole tower strain. And then Wrath was balanced, the tower holding, though stones and timber creaked and groaned. A tile slid and skittered down the roof, fell spinning into air, a long drop and then the tinkle of it splintering on the ground.

Morn circled them, then landed.

"He's learning," Morn said.

"Well done, my darling," Fritha said, patting Wrath's neck. The draig rumbled contentedly.

Fritha looked to the north and saw the mist of Gulla's Revenants, moving slowly across the land like spilt oil. In the sky Kadoshim and their half-breed offspring circled like crows, all moving inexorably south, towards Balara. As Fritha looked she saw some of those specks in the sky were much closer. They were moving fast, with every heartbeat growing closer, larger.

"He is coming," she whispered.

Asroth was easy to spot in the sky, bigger than the others, his black mail and helm seeming to suck all light into it, a dark shadow around him, the very air dimmer.

He saw Fritha upon Balara's tower and angled towards her, hovered over her a moment, his long axe slung across his back, his honour guard of Kadoshim swirling around them, a storm of wings, and then Asroth was alighting beside Fritha and Morn, his wings snapping closed.

"Are they here?" Asroth asked them.

"No, my beloved," Fritha said, "they have fled your coming."

"Ah, that's a great pity," Asroth said, looking genuinely disappointed. "I wanted to whet my axe in battle. It is different from executing prisoners. And this Order of the Bright Star were founded by Corban. Killing them will be the next best thing to killing that maggot."

"You'll get your chance, I'm sure," Fritha said. "But first, you'll have to make do with Ben-Elim and White-Wings."

She looked to the south, Asroth and Morn following her gaze.

To the south a plain of sun-dried grass rolled towards the sea, dotted with low hills and clusters of woodland. A curling timber wall enclosed the plain before Ripa.

Someone's been busy, Fritha thought.

"There it is," she said. "Ripa, and our enemy."

"On the morrow they will all be dead," Asroth growled, his voice cold as a winter's grave.

CHAPTER SIXTY-NINE

RIV

It was not long after dawn, part of the rising sun still merged with the horizon, sending long shadows creeping across the world, but Riv was dressed in her war gear and was standing in Ripa's highest tower room.

She had been summoned to a council of war.

The memory of Bleda was fresh in her mind; she could almost feel his body, still curled against her in sleep, feel his touch on her skin, his lips upon hers. She turned, smiling, to look at him, standing close to her, Ellac, Ruga and Yul with him. Their eyes met, a flicker of a smile from him.

Meical was studying the table in the centre of the room, which had a map of Ripa and the surrounding area laid out upon it. Raina, Alcyon and Ukran were talking about good staging points with Aphra and a score of White-Wing captains, leaders of the regiments that would defend Ripa's walls.

Ben-Elim swept into the room, entering through the huge windows. Twenty, thirty of them. Riv stepped back as Kol entered, his blond hair tied and braided with silver wire, his coat of mail gleaming. He strode to the centre of the room, giving Meical a disdainful look. Other Ben-Elim joined him, Dumah and Hadran amongst them.

"The Kadoshim have taken Balara," Dumah announced. "They are a day from our walls."

A silence as that news settled into everyone.

"Our White-Wings will man the new wall and form three lines on the plain between the wall and Ripa," Kol said. "Three shield walls: a centre and two flanks. Bleda and his Sirak will guard one flank, the giants—"

"Stop," Bleda said.

Kol stuttered to a halt, confusion on his face.

"Kol, you will not command my forces in this battle," Bleda said. He looked at the other Ben-Elim. "I was of the understanding that Kol had been removed from his position of authority until he stands trial before the Assembly."

"You are right," Dumah said, "but Kol has led the defence strategy for seven moons. We—" he gestured to the Ben-Elim around him—"believe it is better for him to lead this campaign. It will be a battle. It cannot be run by a council."

"Let Meical lead, then," Bleda said. "He has actually defeated Asroth before. And I will not fight under Kol's command."

"Meical!" Kol sneered. "Unacceptable." He looked at Dumah. "Let this petty child leave, if that's what he wishes. We don't need him, anyway, our victory is obvious. Asroth leads a rabble. At Drassil we were surprised, but now Asroth has no chance. A collection of acolytes and some half-breed Kadoshim, they are no match for us, or our White-Wing legions."

Dumah looked from Bleda to Kol.

"We *do* need him," Dumah said. "I have seen the reports of Asroth's warband." He looked at Bleda. "Kol is right for this task."

"Then I will leave, and take my warband with me."

"If the little man goes, I will leave with him," Ukran said.

Kol glared at the giant.

Dumah sucked in a long breath, his mouth a tight line. He looked at the Ben-Elim behind him, some shuffling, nodding, rippling of wings.

"Then Kol will step down as commander of this battle."

"I am in agreement for Meical to lead," Hadran said.

"I will not lead," Meical said quietly. "But I will fight Asroth, and let no man, woman or Ben-Elim try to stop me."

Something in Meical's words set Riv's blood thrumming, the first hint of her battle-joy.

"It would not be fitting for you to lead," Dumah said. "If the Assembly agrees, I shall lead. I have been here since the defences began and know the terrain as well as any."

The Ben-Elim nodded and murmured their agreement.

Is this the first time the Ben-Elim's leadership has ever been questioned? And that they have changed their course as the result of a human's objection? The thought that it had come from Bleda made Riv's chest swell.

"Does that settle this?" Dumah asked Bleda. "Are you prepared to accept my leadership?"

Bleda looked at Meical, who dipped his head.

"I am," Bleda said.

"Good. Then let us proceed. We have close to seven and a half thousand White-Wing warriors gathered here. One thousand Sirak riders, and a hundred Kurgan giants. Ripa is not large enough to contain one third of our troops, and what little space there is will be given to the protection of the innocent, the old and young, those who cannot fight."

Are the Ben-Elim finally learning compassion for us mere mortals? Riv wondered.

"So, we will have to meet them on the field. That is, in part, why we have built a wall out on the plain. Asroth approaches from the north—" he pointed to the map on the table—"with a host of Kadoshim, half-breeds, acolytes and these mist-walkers."

"Revenants," Riv said. Dumah looked at her. "They are called Revenants."

Dumah gave a curt nod.

"What are their numbers?" a voice said, quiet, calm. It was Meical.

"Impossible to tell," Kol said, not even looking at Meical.

There was a flapping of wings at the tower window behind Riv and a white crow flew into the chamber, Rab alighting on Riv's shoulder.

"*Well met, friend*," Rab croaked in Riv's ear.

She smiled to see him and scratched his chest.

"*Byrne and Order in Sarva*," Rab muttered.

"We are outnumbered," Dumah continued. "Our scouts have flown as close as possible to Asroth's host, but they have more wings in the air than us, so it is difficult. We have had losses."

"How *many* do we face?" Meical asked again.

"Maybe twenty thousand," Dumah said, "but most of the host move under a cloak of mist, so it is impossible to tell accurately."

"Aye, Gulla and his Revenants," Riv said.

"Yes. They will prove difficult. Kol has told us that we need to take their heads for them to fall."

"And do all you can to avoid their bite. If they put their teeth in you, you will be turned into one of them, within a day. Armour, helms, gloves, greaves. Cover all you can," Riv advised.

Dumah nodded. "That information will be spread."

"Taking their heads is one way to put them down," Riv said. "The best way is to stab them with a rune-marked blade."

Dumah frowned at that.

"The Order of the Bright Star wield them," Riv said.

"But the Order of the Bright Star are not here," Dumah pointed out.

"They were supposed to be," Kol muttered. "I sent for them. But they are late."

"They are one day behind Asroth," Riv said, trying to keep the anger from her voice. "And they have marched from the north, after defeating a host of those Revenants."

"We will have to fight without them," Dumah said.

"Aye," Riv agreed. "If we can hold Asroth for one day, then the Order of the Bright Star will be here." She looked at Kol. "How do *you* propose to fight these Revenants? You have been here for nearly seven moons. You have fought our enemy, know what we face. How have you planned to meet them?"

"Be careful, half-breed," Dumah said. "You are close to being disrespectful. We will meet our enemy with more than just our courage. We have not been idle over the last few moons. A wall has been built around the plain of Ripa. We do not expect it to hold our enemy indefinitely; not when they have aerial troops who can fly over it. But the bulk of their war-host will fight on foot. We hope it will hold back their acolytes, and these Revenants, if the walls are manned thick enough. We have over five hundred scouts and hunters, skilled with the bow. They will be split between the outer wall and Ripa's tower."

You have a thousand Sirak, but they are not best used on a wall. They need space, to ride.

"Aye," Meical said. "It will help, though the Revenants are adept at scaling walls. We saw them climb Dun Seren's walls and breach them in short time. They swarm at points and inter-link, make a tower of limbs."

"That is good to know," Dumah said.

"Pouring fire on them slowed them," Hadran said.

"We have pitch and oil, but the walls are timber, they could catch fire," said Dumah.

"Soak the walls first, it may not stop them catching fire eventually, but it will slow the process," said Meical.

"And a burning wall would hold them," Hadran added.

"For a while, until it burned itself out," Meical said.

"We are not expecting the wall to stop them. More likely it will hold them a while, and maybe allow us to thin their num-bers," Dumah said. "Behind the wall there is a league of land before the camp. We are expecting that to be the primary bat-tleground. In that space two trenches have been dug around Ripa, both filled with stakes and barricades, both flooded with water channelled from the river. They are designed to slow our enemy. In between those barriers are hidden pits, positioned in a way to channel our enemy into choke-points. At each of those points a White-Wing shield wall will be stationed, each one a thousand strong." He looked at the White-Wing captains. "We will have reserves close by. From what we know, these Revenants will not tire, so rotating fresh troops will be vital to holding those points. If a choke-point breaks, all fall back behind the second trench, where we do the same again."

Meical nodded. "This is a good plan, against Asroth's acolytes. I am not so sure those trenches will hold the Revenants, or channel them where you want them to go. And the skies will be dangerous."

"What else can we do?" Dumah asked.

"Kill Gulla, and all his Revenants will die," Riv said. She waved a hand as everyone in the chamber looked at her.

"That is *very* good to know," Dumah said. He looked at the Ben-Elim in the room. "We shall put together a strike force. If Gulla is spotted, we will go for him. But if Gulla does not join the attack, if he remains at the rear?"

"Then we do it the hard way," Riv said. "Kill them one Revenant at a time. They don't like fire. What about the channels you've dug?"

"Those channels are leagues long, and filled with water," Dumah said.

Riv turned and looked out of the window. To the south Ripa was protected by a bay. To the west the river curled out of the Sarva, wide and deep feeding into the bay. It was a natural border to Ripa's town and also a good natural defence. Masts, piers and boathouses lined the riverbank. Riv could see where the two channels began, the first only a few hundred paces behind the new wall. There was about half a league between the first and second channel, both curling in half-circles from the river around the entirety of Ripa, ending at the foot of hills to the east of Ripa. The space between the two channels was a good killing ground, mostly undulating grassland. Riv could see clusters of pits, designed to feed the enemy into three narrow points.

"The flanks are weak," Riv said. "To the west, if Asroth has forces that can cross the river, and east, where the wall ends and the hills begin."

"I will protect the east flank," Bleda said, staring at the land from their vantage point.

Riv looked at him. She had thought that he would prefer the plains to the hills, better ground for horses and manoeuvrability.

"The start of an idea," Bleda said, tapping his head. "I would like to take a ride through those hills, later today."

"I like it when he gets that look," Ruga whispered. "Previously it has ended in Cheren dying."

"And I will watch over your west flank, guard the river," Ukran said.

"Good." Dumah nodded.

"What about the air?" Meical asked. "What are our numbers?"

"Around a thousand Ben-Elim," Dumah answered.

"They outnumber us in the air, as well, then," Meical said. "Have you planned for that?"

"We will stay close to Ripa, and low. There will be archers in the tower, on the walls."

"Lead the Kadoshim and their offspring over my Sirak," Bleda said, "and we shall teach them to fly high."

Riv looked back at the channels dug into the land.

"Raina," she said. "That powder you have, that sets blue flame burning on anything. Does that include water?"

"It does," Raina said, her voice like an iron rasp.

"How much do you have?"

CHAPTER SEVENTY

FRITHA

Fritha padded through the darkness along a stone-flagged street, a skin of wine in one hand. Behind her the sounds of revelry echoed out from Balara's hall and tower. She did not feel like merrymaking.

I will save that for after the battle.

All had their own way of finding their courage before a fight. Fritha wanted quiet but the noise in the hall was filling her head with chaos. She walked along the wide street that led from Balara's tower towards the gates. Behind her she heard the slither and rasp of scales on stone, and then Elise was beside her.

"What issss it?" Elise asked her, "enemy in the treesss? A night attack?"

"No, my love, I just wanted some quiet," Fritha said.

"May I ssstay?" Elise asked.

"Of course," Fritha said, her fingers brushing Elise's hand.

They walked silently through the fortress, passing guards stationed along the way. Iron braziers burned in the courtyard, flames swirling in a breeze. Acolytes sat around the fires, others lining the walls. They moved out of the way as Fritha and Elise scaled the stairs and walked along the wall.

Arn was already upon the wall, staring out towards Ripa. He nodded a greeting and fell in silently behind them. Stone turned to timber beneath their feet as they crossed sections of the wall that had crumbled to ruin and been repaired by men. Fritha eventually found a spot that she deemed right for her mood, dark and silent. It was to the west of the gate tower, overlooking the dense shadows of the Sarva Forest. She sat, dangling her legs over the wall, and took a drink from her wine skin. Arn sat one side of her and Elise coiled the other.

Silence settled about them, only the soughing of wind in trees, the creak and scrape of branches. In the distance, from within the forest, Fritha heard the howl of one of her Ferals, taken up by others.

My babies are hunting in those woods. And guarding us, too. Nothing on the ground could slip past them.

"A long time," Fritha said into the darkness, "since my Anja was murdered by Ben-Elim, and you both found me, somehow brought me back from a darkness worse than death." She looked at them both. "You both saved me."

"We have sssaved each other, countless timessss," Elise hissed, her tongue flickering.

Arn grunted his agreement, his hand on the starstone axe at his belt.

"And everything we have done, strived for, it will be decided on the morrow," Fritha said, taking another sip of wine.

And if we win, what then? A brave new world. One where Asroth rules, with me at his side. She felt a shiver at the thought, pleasure and fear. *Will Asroth keep his word, once we have helped him win? I do not know, and that is why I am gathering my friends. Wrath, Elise, Arn; and Jin will be next. She is no fool. Together we are a force that Asroth cannot discard. Or easily destroy. But these are thoughts for another day. Right now, there is only the morrow.* She felt so many things; excited, melancholic, fearful, angry, all of those emotions swirling through her blood, mixing and blending. She reached out a hand and put it upon Elise's, squeezed it, then reached out to Arn, too, and squeezed his hand.

"Together we shall face all that this world throws at us."

"Aye," Arn said. "Together. We are as close as kin now."

"We are," Fritha agreed.

"We shall avenge my fallen mother, hung from a rope by Ben-Elim for no real crime," Elise hissed. "We shall wipe the Ben-Elim from the face of the earth, and make thisss a better world for those who follow after usss."

"We shall," Fritha said. Her hand went to the swell of her belly. She felt a kick, as if her unborn child agreed with her.

"No flying away if thingsss go bad, thisss time," Elise said.

"No," Fritha said. "This is one battle that there is no running from. Tomorrow we will win or we will die."

CHAPTER SEVENTY-ONE

BLEDA

Bleda sat on a stool as Riv scraped her sharpest knife across his head. Dawn's first rays filtered through cracks in the fabric of their tent curtain, along with sounds of the camp stirring. They had both woken in the dark, lying there, silent, holding each other.

Today is the day. Today we fight. Live or die, this is the day.

Bleda blew out a long breath, felt knots of tension and excitement building in his stomach and chest.

"I know," Riv murmured, as she shaved stubble from the last part of his head, leaving only the long warrior braid.

"All done," she said, wiping her knife clean and sheathing it.

"My thanks." He stood and looked into her eyes.

"Well, it's a special day, you should look your best," Riv said.

"It is," Bleda agreed. "For so long, I have just been living from one day to the next, not knowing if I would see the next dawn. This day, this battle, has always seemed so far away. And now it is here, upon us."

"I feel it, too," Riv said. "Like a song in my blood."

"Aye, that is it." He looked at Riv, so strong and beautiful, her wings magnificent.

"I want to...thank you," Bleda said. "You have given me so much. My heart was buried in a deep, dark place for so many years. You awoke it, the day you gave me my brother's bow. That act of kindness, of friendship, when I felt so alone..." He paused.

Riv smiled and stroked his cheek. "I love you, Bleda ben Erdene," she said, and leaned forwards and kissed him. "I have one more gift for you," she said, and reached into her bundled cloak. She drew out a long knife in a scabbard. "It is rune-marked," she said. "You have runed arrows, but, just in case."

"My thanks," Bleda said. He threaded the scabbard-loops onto his weapons-belt, which was draped over his lamellar coat.

"Come, let's get you dressed," Riv said. She was already in her coat of mail; Bleda had helped her into it earlier. Riv passed him a tunic of wool, which he shrugged over his head, and then his grey deel of felt. A lot of layers beneath his lamellar coat, but the combination of felt and wool would help to snare an arrow if it found a gap in the iron plates of his armour.

A cough beyond the tent's entrance.

"Come," Bleda said.

Ruga entered, carrying two clay bowls. "Porridge and some honey," she said. "It's going to be a long day."

Bleda took his bowl and stirred it, steam rising, blew on a spoonful and ate. Ellac and Yul entered the tent behind Ruga, silent and grim, both in coats of mail, leather vambraces on their forearms, their grey deels clean and bright. Ellac had a sword across his back. Yul had the same, and his bow and quiver at his waist. The rune-marked arrows were easy to pick out, their feathers grey, where the rest were goose-wing white.

Bleda had given out twenty-five runed arrows to twenty hand-picked warriors, including himself. They were the best archers in his warband and Riv had told him of the importance of putting Gulla or his captains down.

Without a word Ruga helped Riv with Bleda's lamellar coat. He stood with his arms out, helping them thread it over him, then cinching it tight at the back and buckling it. He rolled his shoulders, enjoying the welcome weight of it. Riv and Ruga slipped his weapons-belt around his waist, Riv buckling it, his bow-case and quiver comfortable on each hip. Finally, his sword-belt was looped over his shoulder, a leather baldric, and the scabbard settled across his back. It was not his father's sword, which Erdene had given to him. That had been taken from him by Jin and Uldin when he had been taken captive in Forn Forest. But this was a good Sirak sword, taken from a fallen warrior. He reached over his back, gripped the leather-bound hilt, checked that it did not snare in the scabbard. It was perfect.

He and Ruga helped Riv with her weapons-belt. The bow he had made her in its case, a quiver of runed arrows. Two short-swords and a knife.

Riv went through a routine of checking her blades for their draw, adjusting the straps of her quiver, brushing the palm of her hand across the feather-tips.

"I think we are ready," Bleda said. He took a moment, looked at all of them.

"My brave warriors," he said to them. "You have followed me, saved me, proved your courage and heart to me a thousand times." He nodded to himself. "Whatever happens this day, I am proud to know you, and call you friends."

Ellac, Ruga and Yul looked back at him, tears in their eyes.

Bleda drew in a deep breath. "Let's kill our enemies, and live to drink and boast of it together," he said, and all four of them grinned back at him. From Ruga, Ellac and Yul that was the deepest honour they could give.

Ruga swept the curtain open and went out before him, moved to one side, Bleda stepping out into bright morning sunshine.

His warband were arrayed in front of him, a thousand war-riors all mounted, staring silently. Horse breath steamed in clouds on the chill of morning. A horse whinnied, leather har-ness creaked. Bleda strode to his mount, Dilis, one fist on the saddle pommel, and he vaulted onto her back, then looked at his warriors.

"You have followed me this far, fought countless battles beside me. Spilt your blood. And it all comes to this day. Now we have our chance to avenge our kin; now we have the chance to put our enemy in the ground. The Cheren die today."

"*HAI!*" his warband cried, and then they were breaking into motion, Bleda leading them out. Riv's wings snapped open and she leaped into the air, rising above them.

Bleda looked at the battlefield. He was positioned halfway up a low hill on the eastern fringe of the plain, Riv standing beside him. The wall curved before him, circling out and away from the hills he had his back to, a huge semi-circle that took in leagues of open plain before it curled back in towards the coast, ending on the banks of the river that spilt from Sarva's darkness. Bleda could make out Kurgan giants massed along the riverbank.

White-Wing warriors walked the palisade, over a thousand warriors in their polished black cuirasses and mail. Archers were amongst them, and at scores of points Bleda saw the heat-shimmer in the air, marking where great iron pots of pitch were being heated. On the walls about them warriors were tipping barrels of water down the timber palisade and walkways, soaking the wood, preparing it as well as they could for the imminent fire and pitch.

On the plain immediately behind the wall the ground was empty. Two or three hundred or so paces back the first ditch cut a dark line across the plain. It ran parallel with the wall, the water in it glistening, spikes bristling. Makeshift portable bridges were laid across it at the moment. Scores of pits had been dug into the ground on both sides of the ditch, filled with stakes and kindling and pitch, though it was not lit yet. The pits were covered with latticed branches and had loose earth and grass thrown onto them. Each pit had a stone placed upon it, painted with limestone whitewash so that Bleda and all the allies would be able to see them and know where the pits were. They gleamed in the sun, now risen over the hills and cliffs at Bleda's back.

Further back still, behind the pits, were three regiments of White-Wings, each a thousand swords strong. Bleda had never seen a shield wall with such great numbers. Behind them was open plain, then the second ditch, and then behind that ditch were another two regiments of White-Wings, reinforcements or to protect any retreat. Arrayed behind them was the camp, spread across the hill that Ripa's tower stood upon. Bleda could see gulls circling, a glimpse of the sea shimmering behind it all.

"A lot of warriors," Ruga said beside him.

"Aye," Bleda said.

"But not as many as them," Riv said. She was standing beside Bleda.

"No," Bleda said. They were far enough up the hill to have a view over the outer wall. On the plain to the north, still a league or so away, Asroth's war-host approached. It filled the land like a dark stain, creeping towards them. On this eastern fringe, their right flank, banks of black mist rolled over the land, everything within it hidden. The mist was thinner in the centre, though, and Bleda could see warriors with shields marching, the same rectangular shields that the White-Wings used.

The western flank was wreathed in mist.

Where is Jin?

Above the warband Kadoshim and their half-breed offspring flew.

Wings from above and Bleda looked up, saw a score of Ben-Elim dropping towards him. Meical led them.

"Well met," Meical said as he landed, his wings stirring up dust from the ground. Hadran alighted with him, other Ben-Elim hovering in the air above them. "A good day for a fight," he observed, looking up at the sky. It was cloudless, the sun at their backs, a gentle breeze taking the heat out of the sun, but not too much to foul bow work.

"It is," Bleda said.

"The Ben-Elim thank you for standing with us, Bleda ben Erdene," Hadran said.

Bleda nodded. "I am happy to stand alongside you, Hadran, and you, Meical. There are many reasons I am here. The

Kadoshim are an evil that must be purged, there is no running or hiding from them. My greatest enemy stands with them, Jin of the Cheren. But above all, I am here for her." He looked at Riv.

"There is much strength in love," Meical said. "You humans have taught me that."

He held his arm out and Bleda looked at it a moment, and then leaned in his saddle and gripped it.

"Whatever this day may hold for us, it's an honour to fight alongside you," Meical said.

"Aye, and you too," Bleda said. "Ha, you are a legend from our histories. How can we lose?"

"So is he," Meical said with a frown, looking out at Asroth's host. They could not see Asroth, but everyone *felt* his presence. A dark malignance approaching them.

"Even legends can die." Bleda shrugged. "If you put an arrow in their eye."

Behind him he heard Ellac grunt his approval.

"Yes," Meical said, staring at the dark host on the plain. "Riv, it is time," he said. She looked at Meical, then at Bleda.

"Kill your enemies, and live to boast of it with me tonight," she said to him, as her wings snapped out, repeating his words from earlier in the tent. She bent her knees, jumped and beat her wings and then she was airborne, hovering a moment before Bleda, looking into his eyes. He smiled at her, and then she was rising with Meical, Hadran and the other Ben-Elim.

Just live, Bleda thought, watching her shrink into the sky.

CHAPTER SEVENTY-TWO

FRITHA

Fritha rode upon Wrath's back, swaying with his bow-legged gait, her eyes fixed on the wall before them. The sun was rising slowly, hanging low in the sky behind the hills and cliffs of Ripa, making Fritha squint.

They have the advantage of the sun at their backs, Fritha thought, not liking that. Only half a league separated her from her enemy now. Her heart was beating faster, a nervous energy in her limbs building, making her movements twitchy.

"Fritha, something strange is happening to me," Asroth said.

She looked over at him. He was riding upon his huge stallion, clothed in his starstone mail and helm, his long axe slung across his back, his whip and knife at his belt.

He looked like a god come to earth.

Which I suppose he almost is.

"What is it, my beloved?" she said.

"I can feel my blood pumping through my veins, my heart beating faster, and look—" he held his gauntleted hand out and Fritha saw a tremor pass through it.

"Is this *fear?*" he said.

"I think it is," Fritha said. "Fear, excitement, the knowledge that we are about to face our enemy, and either you or they will be food for crows by the end of the day. The prospect of imminent death can focus the mind and make your heart pound."

Asroth nodded. "I was thinking about that," he confessed.

Then he smiled. "This *fear* is delicious. I have never felt anything like it. The possibility of death is...euphoric. Fear will not rule me, though. I will fight, despite my fear." He looked at Fritha, grinning. "No wonder you mortals cling so desperately to your lives, if it is so full of this. It is intoxicating."

Asroth looked down at one of his acolyte honour guards, riding a few paces behind.

"Summon my captains," he said.

The warrior put a horn to his lips and blew two short blasts.

In moments Gulla and Morn were sweeping from the sky, Bune and a dozen other Kadoshim as well. Aenor cantered up from further down the line, and a few moments later Jin was riding across the warband, her oathsworn man at her shoulder, as always.

"It is upon us," Asroth said. "The last battle of our Long War. Can you taste it?" He grinned at them all, heads nodding back at him. Fritha *could* taste it, everything heightened at this moment.

"We all know what to do. To kill our enemies, we must get past that wall," Asroth said, abruptly focused. "Gulla, send the two of your Seven and take their flanks. Aenor, now is your time. You have served me faithfully and so the honour of striking first at the Ben-Elim is yours. Take the wall." He looked at Jin. "You, my violent friend, will wait until there is a hole in that wall. It won't take long. Once it's there, and we've cleared it, you will lead us."

"Aye," Jin said, nodding.

"That is a nice sword," Fritha said, looking at the weapon that jutted across Jin's shoulder, its leather-bound hilt threaded with silver wire.

"It is Bleda's," Jin said. "I am going to give it back to him. In his skull."

Fritha smiled. She liked this woman more and more.

Asroth looked up at the sky, saw Ben-Elim circling beyond the wall, but they were no great host.

"Where are they?" he murmured quietly.

Fritha watched Asroth, sensing a change in him.

He is more focused and assertive than I have seen him. There is a sharpness to him that I have not seen on this whole long journey. It gave her a rush of confidence that she had not been feeling.

"This is close enough," Asroth said, and horns blared, the war-host stuttering to a halt. Wrath growled, saliva dripping from his teeth. Fritha could sense it in him, too, a tremor in his skin, scales rippling. He wanted to tear and rend and feast. They were only a few thousand paces from the wall now. Silence settled over the plain like a shroud, thick and heavy.

"Gulla, Aenor, start the assault," Asroth commanded.

Behind them the sound of drums began, a steady, pulsing beat. Aenor marched past them, leading his warband of acolytes, thousands of them in wide columns. They passed around either side of Asroth and Fritha's honour guards. Elise's tail lashed and Ferals snarled, pawing the ground. Aenor looked up at Fritha as he passed her, their eyes meeting. She dipped her head to him, respect both for coming so far and for what he was about to do. Then he was past her, the bulk of his warband following, over three thousand warriors committed to the assault. Long ladders cut from Sarva's trees were gripped amongst them.

"Kill them," Fritha whispered.

Left and right, on the edge of Fritha's vision, she saw banks of black mist swirl forwards, moving across the plain towards the eastern and western flanks of the wall.

CHAPTER SEVENTY-THREE

RIV

Riv glided close to the ground with Meical, Hadran and a score of Ben-Elim. They were flying low, behind the wall, Hadran calling out encouragement to the warriors around them. Pockets of Ben-Elim were stationed about the battlefield, strike forces tasked with the support of the wall, having the speed to reach beleaguered points quickly. They were also hunting parties for Gulla or his captains, if they were seen. The bulk of the Ben-Elim were being held in reserve, though, waiting. They would try to counter the Kadoshim aerial attack, when it came.

"One thing I need to do," Riv called to Meical. She saw Aphra on the western fringe of the wall, working hard with her White-Wings at dousing the timber palisade and walkway with water. Riv sped towards them, with a flurry of beating wings alighted beside Aphra.

Her mother emptied a barrel of water and wiped sweat from her brow.

"Stay safe," Aphra said.

Riv smiled and reached out a hand to stroke Aphra's face. "It's a battle, Mam," she said.

Aphra smiled, too, and pulled Riv into a tight embrace.

In the distance, drums began to beat.

"Here they come," Jost said, close by.

"I'll see you after," Riv growled, and leaped into the air, speeding along behind the wall to join Meical and the others.

She reached them and together they rose over the central section of the wall.

The plain north of Ripa spread before them, Asroth's war-host filling it. Banners rippled in the breeze, black wings upon a white field.

Three fronts were advancing across the ground. In the centre a block of acolytes were moving forwards, thousands of them, though Riv could still see deep columns of warriors held behind in reserve. The line of warriors advancing was roughly a hundred fighters wide, twenty or thirty deep. Rectangular shields were raised, though they were not in tight order. They looked like White-Wing shields, but with black wings, not white. Riv spied ladders in the deeper ranks. A volley of arrows flickered out from archers upon the wall as the acolytes came within range. Most thudded into shields, a few screams drifting on the wind.

Riv's eyes were drawn to the two flanks. Two banks of mist were surging forwards, roiling like wind-whipped storm clouds, already sweeping past the acolytes. The sound of drums rolled across the plain, like thunder rumbling within the storm. Faster and faster the banks of mist swept forwards, an unstoppable river tumbling down a hill. Wisps of vapour curled and frayed at its edges as Revenants charged the wall's western and eastern tips.

The charge to the west hit first. An explosion of black mist sprayed upwards, like a great wave crashing into a cliff, spume hurled high. Revenants appeared, a tangle of limbs and torsos as they merged together, massing into their tower of bodies that climbed frighteningly fast up the timber wall.

White-Wings on the wall above the Revenants were shouting. Cauldrons of boiling pitch were hurled over the wall.

Revenants screamed, audible even from Riv's distance, bodies tumbling from their living tower, catching fire, limbs flailing.

To the east another crash as the second bank of mist crunched into the wall. Riv's head snapped that way. The wall shook, a tremor running through it, but it held.

A roar of voices as the acolytes in the centre closed ranks, shields coming together with a crack. Their pace doubled. Arrows rained down upon them now, rattling upon shields, more screams as they found flesh. Another dozen heartbeats and the acolytes were running, shields still tight, a few cracks here and there. Lines of warriors appeared with ladders, sprinting for the wall, others holding shields above them. Some dropped as archers targeted them, but many more sped on. The first ladders reached the wall, spiked legs set into the ground, the tops slamming onto wood. Riv's hand reached for her bow, but she stopped herself, knowing all her arrows were rune-marked.

Save them for Revenants.

Screams rang out from the west.

Half a dozen Revenant towers were surging up the wall, boiling pitch being hurled upon them. Flames were bursting into life from Revenant flesh, towers collapsing, but other Revenants were reaching the top of the wall, taloned hands gripping timber, heaving themselves over onto the walkway.

Aphra is stationed down there.

"My mother," Riv yelled, pointing to the west. Without waiting for a response she was tucking her wings and stooping into an angled dive. Wind ripped at her, snatching tears from her eyes as she hurtled down. Everything grew larger, quickly. Riv unclipped her bow, pulling it from its case and snatching a fistful of arrows. One, two, three arrows nocked and loosed in quick succession as Riv aimed at the top of the Revenant towers climbing the wall, not wanting to shoot into the combat. Her aim was not that good, not when she was moving so fast her vision was blurred.

She did see the crackle of blue flame, though, evidence that her arrows had hit their mark. Revenants tumbled through the air, crashed to the ground. More blue fire drew her eye, a series of bursts on the walkway.

Aphra and her warband.

She shifted her wings, changed her angle and slipped her bow back into its case. Then she drew her swords.

More ripples of blue flame on a section of the wall, White-Wings fighting desperately. Riv crashed into a knot of Revenants, her swords swinging and slashing. Blue fire crackled and Revenants fell away screaming. Riv's feet hit the timber walkway and she chopped at a Revenant climbing over the wall, fingers spraying as it fell backwards. A stab into another's mouth as it leaped over the wall. A tide of creatures swarmed the walls, so many, moving so fast. Riv saw one grab a White-Wing and hurl the warrior over the wall. Riv ducked talons, punched her sword into a belly, ripped it free in a burst of blue flame, a beat of her wings as more claws slashed and grabbed at her, lifting her up. She swung her swords, severing grasping hands, swiped at a head, her blade biting into a skull, wrenching it free, the Revenant dropping like a stone.

Another figure leaped at her but was skewered by a spear as Meical swept down behind her. Hadran and the other Ben-Elim followed, raking the Revenants on the walkway, clearing a space in heartbeats. White-Wing warriors cheered to see them.

More Revenants came over the wall, an endless tide.

"SHIELD WALL!" a White-Wing yelled, Riv recognizing her mother's voice from a thousand battlefield drills. Aphra was twenty paces ahead of Riv, a dozen warriors were lifting shields with her. Aphra was trying to protect a team working the pitch and cauldrons. Shields thudded tight, a small wall formed across the walkway, and rune-marked blades stabbed out, swords, spears, long axes chopping, Revenants falling before them. Riv beat her wings, passing over her mother, landed beside the four or five White-Wings gathered around a huge iron fire-pit with crackling flames. Cauldrons were upon chains attached to wooden beams and posts that could be swung from the fire to the wall, where a lever upended them. But the incomers were climbing too fast, too high. The cauldron swung towards the wall as a snarl of Revenants appeared, surging over and dropping to the walkway. Riv leaped upon them, stabbing and slashing, but one slipped past her, a slash of its talons opened the throat of the White-Wing swinging the cauldron upon its timber frame, and then the Revenant hurled itself into the beam that suspended the cauldron. There was a creak of timber, the beam snapped and then the cauldron fell. A huge crack as it hit the walkway, a shower of boiling pitch exploding, the stench of sizzling flesh, White-Wings and Revenants screaming. The cauldron rolled, hot pitch spreading across the floor, engulfing a Revenant's feet. It howled, fell into the black-bubbling liquid, hands submerged where the flames ignited, hungrily burning up the creature's arms. Then the timber of the walkway and wall was smoking, more flames sparking.

The wall burst into flame.

CHAPTER SEVENTY-FOUR

BLEDA

Bleda saw the flames ignite on the western wall, snatching into the sky like grasping fingers. Black smoke billowed. Worry coiled and slithered in his belly. He'd seen Riv diving down to join the battle, saw Meical and the other Ben-Elim follow, but now Riv had been swallowed in the chaos, too far away for Bleda to make out individuals on the wall, even from his vantage point on the hillside.

She is fierce, resourceful, he told himself, and tore his eyes away, looking back to the section of wall before him.

Bleda felt revulsion as he watched the Revenants swarm the wall, first in their tens, then scores and now hundreds of them gaining the walkway. He had fought them in Forn Forest. Well, fought one of them, seen it rip the throat out of Tuld, his oathsworn man. He knew how strong and unnaturally fast they were, and how hard they were to kill.

White-Wings on this eastern tip of the wall were fighting hard, hacking with swords, sending heads spinning, smashing Revenants back over the wall as they appeared. It was a losing battle, the wall was starting to break down into knots of combat as the enemy just kept on coming.

"DISMOUNT!" Bleda cried out, swinging his leg over his saddle and dropping to the ground. As he strode forwards he drew his bow from its case, took a rolled, waxed bowstring from a pouch at his belt and strung the bow.

Scores of burning braziers stood in a row before his war-band, barrels full of arrows sat close to each one. Each arrow-head had a strip of linen soaked in pitch tied about it. Bleda and his Sirak had been tasked with keeping the walkway clear, but he was loath to start using the fire arrows so soon, especially after he had just seen the western wall burst into flame.

"RUNED ARROWS!" he called out, taking one grey-fletched arrow from his quiver. His twenty chosen archers did the same, Ruga and Yul either side joining him. "AIM AND LOOSE!" he called out. He drew and loosed, saw his arrow fly through the air and punch into the temple of a Revenant claw-ing at a White-Wing's belly. Bleda saw a spark of blue fire in the creature's head as it was hurled from its feet, fell toppling back over the wall.

All along the wall twenty Revenants fell, a ripple of blue sparks. But still the wall was filling with them, White-Wings falling, throats ripped out by talons and fangs. Some of the Revenants were breaking away, forging their way towards the wall's centre. One rolled off the walkway and fell to the ground, climbed to its feet and began running towards Bleda.

There is no choice, Bleda realized. *Five hundred runed arrows will be gone in a hundred heartbeats, and it will not stem the tide. And we need those arrows for Gulla and his captains. We must risk the fire arrows or the wall will be lost.*

"FIRE ARROWS!" Bleda cried, taking a pitch-soaked arrow from the barrel and dipping it into the burning brazier. A *whoosh* as it ignited and Bleda held it up for his warriors to see.

This time a thousand Sirak drew their bows, each with a flame-wrapped arrowhead. As one they loosed, a swarm of flames arcing through the air, slamming down into Revenants upon the wall. A dozen arrows pierced the Revenant running at Bleda; it was thrown backwards, rolling to a halt. It started to rise but flames crackled, engulfing it, and it collapsed. Screams from the walkway, the hiss of flame in flesh, clothes igniting as Revenants fell.

"AGAIN!" Bleda cried, and another thousand arrows were in the air, and then another volley, and then another. Revenants fell spinning, pin-cushioned with arrows, became living torches, an inferno raging across the walkway. White-Wings used their shields to hammer the invaders back over the wall, or hurl them down to the ground.

And then, like a held breath, the wall was clear of Revenants.

White-Wing warriors raised their weapons and cheered.

Bleda felt a moment of elation, believed that these creatures were stoppable.

Hands appeared at the wall, a fresh tide of Revenants dragging themselves up and onto the walkway.

And Bleda saw patches of timber blackening and glowing. Flames crackled into life.

CHAPTER SEVENTY-FIVE

FRITHA

Fritha stared at the wall. All along it, battle raged. The White-Wings on the eastern flank had looked close to being overwhelmed, Gulla's Revenants swarming up the wall like an unstoppable wave, cauldrons of pitch slowing but not stopping them. Then a storm of arrows had held that tide and reduced them to living torches. But Gulla's horde was relentless and now sections of the wall were starting to burn, flames licking at the sky. In the centre Aenor and his acolytes had gained the wall, though many had fallen. As Fritha watched, ladders were pushed from the wall-top and sent crashing to the ground, crushing a score of warriors. On the western flank the Revenants' black mist was merging with clouds of smoke as a section of the wall burned. Around it Fritha glimpsed white-feathered wings and saw the odd crackle of blue flame. It brought back terrible memories of when she had seen weapons of the Order of the Bright Star slay Ulf's Revenants. It had been during the battle in the Desolation, and she had seen that same blue flame.

Are the Order of the Bright Star there?

But their scouts had seen the Order's warband moving into Sarva Forest only a day ago, so they could not have reached Ripa before Asroth's host. It was impossible, even with a night march. Fritha scanned the rest of the wall, could see no evidence of those weapons elsewhere.

There are too few of them. It is only there, on the western tip. Perhaps it is the garrison from Balara, fled here instead of joining with Byrne.

Screams from the centre drew Fritha's eyes, another ladder pushed away from the wall, swaying for a moment and then toppling to the ground.

"Aenor needs support," Fritha said. "Surely the time is here for Morn."

"No," Asroth said. "It is too soon. Wait until the walls are harder pressed, all of their troops engaged."

There was a certainty in Asroth's voice that reassured Fritha. For some time she had been concerned about his strategic skill, or more importantly his lack of it. But she had seen a change in him yesterday, during their council of war at Balara. Scouts had returned, reporting on the movement of Byrne's warband, stating that they had just entered the western fringes of the Sarva Forest. Gulla had asked whether they should wait for the Order of the Bright Star to join Ripa's warband, rather than risk having an enemy at their back.

"*No,*" Asroth had said. "*Divided, they will fall. We strike Ripa on the morrow, hard. The Ben-Elim will fall. And then we will turn and face Corban's offspring.*"

Fritha had agreed. Gulla had been a fool to suggest waiting. The only danger was that Byrne's warband would appear before Ripa was taken. But that was beyond unlikely. The last report soon after dawn that morning was that Byrne was a day's march away. So, if Ripa fell today, all would be well.

If.

"Now," Asroth said, beside Fritha, drawing her from her thoughts.

Bune put a horn to his mouth and blew a long, ululating note.

Behind her Fritha heard the beating of many wings. Morn flying over them, leading all of her half-breed kin. Eight hundred warriors. And every single one of them carried one of Aenor's acolytes. They flew low to the ground, approaching the wall like a swarm of hornets, the sound of their wings drowning the din of battle.

Warriors on the wall saw them, horns sounded. Arrows

flickered out from the wall, faint screams, a handful of half-breeds plummeting to the ground. Ben-Elim appeared in the sky, small clusters of them, scattered in the air along the length of the wall, all of them speeding towards the centre, where Morn and her warriors were aimed.

But they were too late.

Morn and her kin were close to the wall now, and they began to rise. Fritha could see acolytes in their grip drawing weapons, warriors with long axes, swords, spears. None of them carried shields. This was a force intent on slaughter and ruin. They had accepted their own deaths were likely. Morn was the first to crest the wall, dropping the acolyte in her arms onto the walkway. Within heartbeats Morn's kin were swooping and releasing the acolytes in their arms. A hundred, two hundred, three hundred warriors dropped onto the wall in less time than it took Fritha to unstopper her water skin and take a long sip.

Still more acolytes were dropping from half-breed arms as the first of the Ben-Elim reached them, a score or so, carving into the flank of half-breeds as they turned in the sky, their orders to return to Asroth's host on the plain. Winged shapes fell, twisting, wings broken or lifeless. More Ben-Elim arrived as the last of Morn's kin released their human cargoes.

Fritha drummed her fingers on her sword hilt. She was restless, filled with energy.

I need to fight.

"They are holding longer than I thought," Asroth growled. All along the wall battle raged, sections beginning to burn, the fire spreading, clouds of smoke billowing, and in the sky above the wall Ben-Elim fought half-breed Kadoshim.

"If we wait long enough the wall will burn to the ground. There, and there, first," Fritha said, pointing to the western and eastern tips of the long wall.

"Too long," Asroth said, looking at the sun. To Fritha's surprise it was high in the sky, midday already upon them. Asroth looked at Fritha. "It is time," he said.

Those words set Fritha's blood thrumming through her veins.

She buckled herself in, checked the bindings. Then she took a helm from a saddle loop, a simple iron cap with cheek-plates and a curtain of riveted mail hanging from the back to protect her neck. She buckled the leather strap under her chin. Then she checked her weapons, longsword and short, hanging at her hips, a spear couched and strapped in a saddle-cup, a round shield with black wings painted upon it strapped to her saddle harness.

Asroth leaned over and placed a hand on her cuirass, low, over her belly. "Keep to the plan, no undue risks," he said, "I would see my child when this is done."

Fritha smiled at him, felt a flush spread through her chest and into her neck.

"Go, then, priestess and bride, earn your fame in the histories of this world," Asroth said to her.

Fritha leaned forward in her saddle and patted Wrath's neck.

"It is time, my love," she whispered. "You know what to do."

"*Destroy, kill, eat?*" Wrath growled.

"Exactly," Fritha said.

Wrath broke into lumbering motion, his wings spreading wide, and then he leaped into the sky, wings beating. She looked back, saw Arn urge his horse into a canter as he followed her, her honour guard, over a hundred strong, riding at his back. Elise was powering across the ground, coils undulating, her shield and spear raised. Ferals loped on their flanks. Fritha smiled, seeing them following her into battle. Then she set her face to the south, to the wall that was looming ever closer. Arrows flickered up at her, one hissing past her head. Another passed through Wrath's left wing, the draig lurching for a moment, then steady again. And then Wrath was diving, aiming straight at the wall, a section to the left of the central gates. More arrows came at them. Wrath's wings pulled in tight, their speed increasing, and Fritha leaned low over his neck, her gloved hands holding on tight to the leather harness. She felt a moment of absolute terror as the wall seemed to hurtle towards them, a fractured image of faces staring, mouths opening to yell, some leaping, realizing what was about to happen.

Wrath hit the wall, a lurching impact, a moment of resistance, Fritha thrown forwards in her saddle, leather harness about her straining, and then the wall exploded like kindling, timber thick in the air, warriors hurled up, high into the sky. A moment of weightlessness, then another impact, Fritha rocked and shaken, Wrath crashing to the ground, his legs buckling, claws gouging the earth, sending up an explosion of grass and earth. The draig fell, a half-roll, wings beating frantically to right himself, skidding to a halt.

Timber and bodies fell about them, thudding to the ground, a cloud of dust enveloping them.

Fritha lay with her arms wrapped around Wrath's neck, for long moments unsure if she were dead or alive, if she was unhurt or if she'd broken every bone in her body.

Wrath lurched to his feet and shook himself, splintered timber and earth flying off. Then his neck darted out and he snatched up a White-Wing warrior in his jaws, bit down hard, a scream cut short as Fritha heard bone shatter and crunch. The draig shook his head, blood spurting, the White-Wing hanging limp.

The dust settled and Fritha pulled her spear from its strap. White-Wing warriors were all about her—reinforcements for the wall, she guessed—others running down from wooden stairwells. Aenor's acolytes were up on the walkway to either side of her. One stairwell was almost taken by them. Behind her she heard the thunder of hooves, Arn and her honour guard pouring through the huge hole Wrath had smashed. Elise appeared at Fritha's side, warriors freezing for a moment at the sight of her.

Fritha looked at an open plain, a scattering of White-Wing warriors before her, grassland behind them, studded with more organized blocks of White-Wings, and behind them, a hill and the tower of Ripa.

Wrath dropped what was left of the White-Wing in a heap at his feet, opened his jaws wide and roared.

CHAPTER SEVENTY-SIX

RIV

Riv was thrown from her feet, a huge concussion rippling through the wall, timber frames and wall bracers screeching in protest. She fell over the walkway's edge, White-Wings and Revenants tumbling about her, the ground rushing up towards her. A frantic beating of her wings and she checked her fall, stabilized and then climbed into the air, hovering for a moment, trying to understand what had just happened.

Smoke and flames billowed, clouding her vision. A deafening sound rang out, a roaring that filled the air, making Riv's ears ring. She climbed higher, escaping the smoke, and then froze.

Part of the wall around the central gate was just...gone, smashed into a thousand pieces. And standing on the ground immediately before the hole in the wall was a winged draig, a woman upon its back. Riv had seen them before, in the Great Hall of Drassil, charging and smashing Aphra's shield wall apart.

Fritha.

As Riv watched, enemies poured through the breach, riders in mail, and Ferals and something else. At first Riv thought it was a giant snake, like the white wyrms that she had heard Cullen tell of, because its thick, sinuous body was pale as curdled milk. But this snake had a woman's torso and head, wore a coat of mail and gripped a shield and spear.

Riv shivered, a moment of intense revulsion.

In the air above them Ben-Elim and Kadoshim half-breeds swirled and fought and died.

Time to retreat.

That had been the plan, Dumah had been adamant. The wall closest to Riv seethed with combat, the Revenants were being kept at bay by Aphra and the White-Wings with runed blades.

And this wall will not hold much longer.

Timbers were blackening, the wall creaking, swaying.

"RETREAT!" Riv bellowed, saw White-Wings look her way. Her mother lifted a blade in acknowledgement, barked an order and her small shield wall took a step forwards, stabbing and hacking down Revenants in their way as they cut a path to the closest stairwell.

Meical and Hadran appeared out of the smoke, other White-Wings about them, twelve or fifteen left of their original score.

"The wall is breached," Riv said, pointing with one of her short-swords. "And Asroth has not come yet. Why?"

"I don't know," Meical said, scanning the plain. "Perhaps he uses his *allies* as fodder." He shrugged. "He will come." He looked at the wall, Revenants still scaling it, then he looked to Hadran. "We must help with the retreat."

"Aye," Hadran said, a shift of his wings and he was leading the surviving Ben-Elim back at the wall, spears stabbing at Revenants blocking the path to stairwells. Riv saw her mother with a knot of warriors. They were carving a way to a stairwell, almost there, but Revenants were thick upon the wall before them.

Riv beat her wings and flew at them, crashing into the creatures like a boulder, scattering them, her twin swords slashing and stabbing. Blue flame crackled like a ring around her as she sliced throats, opened bellies, stabbed and hacked and thrust. And then she was standing on the walkway, her chest heaving, her mother before her.

"MOVE!" Riv shouted, jumping into the air. Aphra led her band of warriors down the stairs at a run. Riv glimpsed Jost and old Ert amongst them. Revenants were swarming on the walkway, running after them. Riv landed and stood at the top of the stairwell, blocking their way.

The black figures threw themselves at her. She severed a taloned hand as it grasped at her, stabbed a Revenant through the chest, felt her sword grate on bone, kicked the collapsing body back, snaring and tripping creatures behind it. Sliced a throat, stabbed into a face, an overhead swing that cracked a skull, ripples of blue fire everywhere, but where one Revenant fell, two more replaced it. Riv leaped into the air, evading grasping talons and snapping teeth. Feet thudded on timber and then Aphra was on the ground. She ran on fifty paces, then paused, yelling for more of her warband to join her. Sixty or so warriors were gathered around her, others flocking to her, yet more shouting from other stairwells as they hurtled down from the walkway.

Revenants were surging over the wall now, an unstoppable tide. Meical, Hadran and the Ben-Elim were hovering, stabbing with rune-marked spears, choking the stairs with the dead, buying White-Wings a few heartbeats to break away. Revenants started leaping from the walkway, forgetting about the stairwells. They crashed to the ground, fell in heaps, but then rose in their jerking, stuttered movement.

"RUN!" Riv yelled, as she swooped over Aphra and saw her mother retreat towards the outer ditch, leading a mass of White-Wings with her.

Riv swept higher. On the eastern fringe she saw the wall in flames, sections starting to crumble, caving in, explosions of flame and ash. She looked for Bleda, saw that he had led his Sirak higher into the hills, though they were still loosing volleys of flaming arrows at the Revenants. Battle raged at the centre, where the draig had broken through the wall, most of the White-Wings there unable to extricate themselves from the acolytes and riders who had swept through to confront them.

Riv saw the draig lumbering forwards, jaws lunging, long-taloned claws slashing, Fritha upon its back, stabbing with her spear. Riv paused in the air, her blood surging with the urge to go and put her sword in Fritha's belly. Screams from below drew her attention and she saw Revenants starting to catch up with White-Wings, leaping and crashing into their backs.

Aphra?

Riv searched below, saw one Revenant speeding, closing ground on a White-Wing, but then in a burst of grass and earth it was gone, falling into one of the many pits. Others were falling, White-Wings using the whitewashed rocks to guide their way, swerving amongst the traps. Riv flew over one of the triggered pits, saw a Revenant within it pierced upon spikes. It was writhing, squirming, slowly disentangling itself.

Are those pits deep enough to hold them?

She looked to the south, to the block of a thousand White-Wings standing in loose formation before the second ditch.

Come on.

Behind them she saw smoke billowing and the flare of ignited torches. Then, as one, five hundred Ben-Elim took to the sky, their white-feathered wings blindingly bright in the midday sun, all of them with a burning torch in each hand.

They rose over the White-Wing formation, sweeping forwards. Riv flew higher and they passed beneath her, throwing their burning torches into pits that had been triggered, flames igniting, the Revenants trapped within screaming. All across the plain flames burst into life like stars breaking into light at nightfall.

Riv searched for her mam, saw her reach one of the makeshift bridges laid across the first ditch of water. Aphra stopped, turned, urging her warriors to cross. Riv sped towards her, landed beside her, a shared look between them as White-Wings pounded across the bridge.

The world was different down here, a chaos of sounds and smells. The last of the White-Wings crossed the bridge, Aphra following. Riv saw a Revenant come stumbling intact through the maze of pits, swerving and leaping, then it was running towards her, arms reaching, mouth gaping.

Riv stood, waited. The Revenant was thirty paces away, twenty, ten. It leaped.

Riv's knees bent and her wings snapped out, launching herself into the air. The Revenant hurtled through the space beneath her. Riv twisted in the air to see Aphra and a dozen White-Wings gripping the timber planks of the bridge, heaving and throwing them into the ditch. The Revenant fell, the ditch too wide, and it screamed as it was impaled upon a long spike of timber. It thrashed, limbs flailing, teeth gnashing, but could not free itself. All along the ditch Riv saw White-Wings doing the same thing with the bridges, then turning and running again.

More Revenants were navigating the burning pits, running at the ditch, launching themselves into the air. It was too wide for them to clear it, all of them splashing into the deep water, submerged, many pierced by spikes. But some avoided the spears and clawed their way at the far bank, scrambling up onto the plain, breaking into a run again.

That ditch will not stop the horde, but it is slowing them.

Elsewhere on the field the pits and ditch were having a greater effect upon the acolytes. Riv saw Aphra and the retreating White-Wings reach the ranks of the shield walls before the second ditch, three wide regiments, each a thousand swords strong. Riv saw giants close to them, Alcyon upon Hammer's back.

Riv turned in the air and looked at the battle on the field, wondering who to kill next.

CHAPTER SEVENTY-SEVEN

FRITHA

Fritha stabbed down at a White-Wing, her spear slapped aside by a shield, the warrior slashing at Wrath's side. A line of blood welled, but the cut was not deep; Wrath's scales and skin were thick and hard. Then the warrior was collapsing, Elise's spear punching through the back of his neck and bursting out of his throat. She whipped the blade free, tendrils of black smoke curling around the spearhead.

Fritha gave Elise a quick nod of thanks, pulled on Wrath's reins, trying to slow his frenzied onslaught. The draig stamped on a White-Wing running past them, pinned the screaming warrior down. Wrath's jaws clamped around her head and she stopped screaming.

"Stay here!" Fritha shouted. "Eat."

Wrath rumbled his thanks up at her, then set about tearing the warrior beneath his claw to pieces.

Fritha took the opportunity to look around.

Smoke billowed, obscuring much. Fritha glimpsed White-Wings retreating from the wall, Revenants and acolytes in pursuit. Directly ahead of Fritha the ground was unbroken by these fire-pits, a seemingly unhindered path towards Ripa. In the distance she could see a long wall of shields, waiting.

A screech, a hissing through the air and a Kadoshim half-breed crashed to the ground, wings tattered and limp. A wound gaped in its belly. Fritha looked up, saw hundreds of Ben-Elim

486

filling the sky, the last of Morn's half-breeds speeding away, back to Asroth's lines on the northern plain. As she watched, the Ben-Elim wheeled in the sky, reforming, most of them flying back towards Ripa.

More shrieks and Fritha saw acolytes in front of her disappearing, sprays of water erupting, other warriors falling on spikes.

We need to pull back. Getting sucked into a mindless charge into that shield wall is not the best idea.

"Pull everyone back," Fritha called out to one of her guards. Her own troops had stayed close to her, Arn and her honour guard all mounted, curled around her flanks. Even her Ferals had remained near, though they were savaging any White-Wing who came within reach.

Her guard put a horn to his lips, blowing out two notes, one short, one long, then repeating it. Acolytes ahead of Fritha slowed, stopped, began to filter back to her through the maze of fire-pits.

The Revenants did not.

On both the eastern and western flanks they poured over the wall and through the fire-pits, though on the eastern flank their numbers were being thinned by a constant hail of fire arrows.

"What are we doing?" Arn called up to her. "They are fleeing."

"No, they are retreating," Fritha said, her gaze flickering across the plain. "This is planned. And that is what we shall do. We shall keep to the plan." She remembered Asroth's words to her, his hand upon her belly. "Breach the wall and clear it. Hold it for the next move, that was our task." She twisted in her saddle, looked back over her shoulder, through the wall, saw a line of horses, hawk banners rippling above them.

The sound of wings and Morn was in the sky above her, hovering. She had a cut across her forehead, blood sheeting one side of her face, but she was grinning.

"Well met, sword-sister," Fritha said to her. "You can tell Jin the way is clear for her."

CHAPTER SEVENTY-EIGHT

JIN

Jin sat in her saddle, waiting.

She had felt a fierce exultation watching Fritha upon the draig's back, the two of them hurtling out of the sky like a hammer and smashing the wall before her to kindling. Even Tark had grunted his satisfaction. Then Fritha's warriors had passed through the breach, followed by a lot of screaming. To either flank Revenants were still swarming the walls, a never-ending stream of bodies climbing and disappearing. She glanced to her right, saw Asroth sitting upon his horse, wings furled tight to his back. Kadoshim were all about him, on the ground, some circling lazily in the air, and behind them a large number of acolytes. Around a thousand warriors, kept in reserve. A bank of mist churned sluggishly beyond Asroth, showing that not all of Gulla's captains had been committed to the attack on the wall.

A winged figure flew out from behind the wall and sped towards her. Morn. She descended, alighting in front of Jin.

"Fritha has cleared the way," Morn said. "Our enemy have retreated. They have dug pits, but they are all on fire, so you can see them." Morn looked back at the wall. "There is a central pathway wide as a field that cuts through the pits, a shield wall of White-Wings at the end of it."

"Room to manoeuvre?" Jin asked.

"Aye, there is," Morn said, "it is maybe two hundred men wide, but it is clear they are guiding us that way. And there is a water-filled ditch cutting across the plain before the White-Wings."

"How wide?" Fritha asked.

Morn scratched her arm-pit. "Maybe three men, lying head to toe."

Jin nodded. "We can jump that," she said, "but we will need room to move between the ditch and the shield wall."

"There is much room," Morn said. "More than from here to the wall."

Good, Jin thought. *That will be enough.* She dipped her head to Morn. "My thanks," she said.

Jin took her helm from a saddle hook and slipped it over her head, buckled the strap under her chin, looked at Gerel.

"Begin," she said.

Gerel blew out a long horn call, Jin flicking her reins and touching her heels to her mount's ribs. She moved forwards at a fast walk, three thousand Cheren following behind her. The wall grew closer, the crackle of flame louder. A cloud of smoke billowed out of the hole in the wall, Jin sucking in a deep breath and riding into it. She came out the other side of the cloud, inside the wall, now, and saw Fritha upon her draig, standing to the right of Jin. Pits of fire burned across a wide plain, only a central channel directly in front of Jin clear of flame. A dark line shimmered, marking the water-filled ditch. A fair distance beyond the ditch Jin could see a long row of rectangular shields, white wings emblazoned upon them.

They want us to approach down this line, think their wall of shields is strong enough to resist whatever comes at them. I shall teach them to regret such arrogance.

She looked elsewhere, searching for a sign of Bleda, but could only see smoke and flame.

He is here somewhere, and I shall find him, but first I will show these White-Wings what it is like to stand before the Cheren.

She clicked her tongue, shifted her feet, her horse moving from a walk to a slow canter. Jin dipped her head at Fritha as she passed her.

She rode on, focused now on the path before her. Jin called out to Gerel, more horn blasts, and a line of riders formed up either side of Jin, sixty wide, a ripple as lines formed behind her, the warband slipping into a huge column. Their passing rumbled like constant, distant thunder.

The ditch was closer now, Jin saw spikes with bodies impaled upon them. Another touch of her ankles and flick of her reins and her horse was leaping into a gallop. She bent low over the arch of her horse's neck, felt the wind snaring her warrior braid, her heart pounding in her head. The ditch rushed towards her, forty paces away, and Jin tapped her heels into her mount's flanks, urging him on, then she was rising in her saddle, taking her weight from her horse's back, and they were flying, weightless, leaping across the ditch, a flash at the edge of her vision of Gerel and Tark and so many others doing the same, for a long, timeless moment all of them sailing through the air. And then with a thud and drum of hooves she was landing on the other side, turf spraying, and she was galloping on.

A wide stretch of plain opened up between Jin and the White-Wings, the warriors closer with every heartbeat. A horn blast and the White-Wings stepped together, moving from loose order to tight, another signal and their shields were coming up, interlocking with a crack. A hundred warriors wide, ten rows deep, it was the largest shield wall Jin had ever seen.

Over ten years I have waited for this moment, planned it in my mind. How I will show the Ben-Elim and their White-Wings that a wall of shields is no match for the Cheren.

Her mouth twisted, part snarl, part smile, and she reached for her bow, drew it from its case, then her other hand was grasping a fistful of arrows. She knew her warriors were all doing the same.

A hundred and fifty paces at full gallop, she wrapped her reins around her pommel, guiding her mount with her knees, passed her arrows to her bow fist and nocked the first arrow, drew it and loosed, the next two arrows flying before the first one hit. She heard bowstrings *thrum* left and right of her, a hail of iron hurtling through the air. The rattle of stones on wood as arrows slammed into shields, screams as the missiles found gaps in the wall, a head too high, an exposed ankle.

One hundred paces away from the wall, a new handful of arrows, nock, draw, loose, nock, draw, loose, the arrows punching deeper now that she was closer. More screams as arrowheads pierced wood and bit into the arms holding the shields. A ripple as warriors fell, others stepping forward to fill the gaps.

Fifty paces, another trio of arrows loosed, their impacts rocking warriors not fully braced. One of Jin's arrows took a warrior in the cheek as he risked a glance over his shield rim.

Idiot.

He dropped, dead before he hit the ground.

Almost on top of the shield wall now and Jin touched her reins, a pull to the left, pressure from her knees and ankles, and her mount slowed, turned, thirty riders doing the same, the other thirty from Jin's front row peeling right, all of them galloping along the length of the shield wall, loosing arrows at almost point-blank range, White-Wings hurled back into the warriors behind them. At the same time the row of riders behind Jin began loosing at the shield wall.

Jin reached the end of the shield wall and steered her mount left again, dropped to a canter and rode back along the flank of her galloping column, riding three hundred paces back down the channel before touching her mount and riding back into the centre, reforming a line again with Gerel and Tark meeting her, all of her sixty riders slipping back into a disciplined row, moving forwards at a slow canter, horses blowing and sweating. Jin saw the last few rows of her column galloping at the shield wall, peeling left and right, others cantering back down the line, reforming into rows behind her. The shield wall appeared before her, their shields studded with arrows, some cracked and splintered, dead White-Wings heaped on the ground, and then she was urging her horse into a fresh gallop, reaching for more arrows, bending low in the saddle.

CHAPTER SEVENTY-NINE

BLEDA

Bleda stared at the Cheren as they galloped across the plain, hurtling at the White-Wing shield wall positioned at the field's centre. He felt his jaw clenching, muscles bunching as he watched the Cheren loose a storm of arrows at the shield wall at full gallop, the front row peeling left and right in perfect timing, galloping along the front of the shield wall, loosing more arrows as the row behind charged, then peeled away, a perfect manoeuvre repeated in constant cycle, giving the shield wall no respite, no time to clear their dead. He heard warriors scream, saw them fall. He felt a grudging respect for the Cheren, to see them galloping into battle, their courage as they charged the shield wall, the beautiful lines of their columns, their skill.

He hated them.

Jin is down there, leading them.

But there was no way to get at her.

He had repositioned his force higher on the hills, taken the barrels of fire arrows with him. His endless hail of missiles had thinned the Revenants flooding the wall, and after that flying draig had smashed a hole in the wall's centre, he had helped to hold the Revenants back as the White-Wings had retreated.

But his position meant that there was now a river of Revenants between him and the Cheren.

Strangely, even though he and his Sirak had slain far more Revenants than all of the White-Wings on this eastern edge of the battle, the Revenants were completely ignoring him and his warriors, were still charging in a frenzied mass at the White-Wing shield wall on the plain behind the first ditch.

He lifted his last fire arrow, nocked it, drew and loosed. The arrow flew through the air, trailing fire and smoke, hundreds of other arrows arcing and dropping through the air, punching into Revenants as they swarmed across the fire-dotted plain.

The creature Bleda had aimed at stumbled, the arrow catching it in the shoulder, spinning it. For a long moment it teetered on the edge of a fire-pit, arms flailing, then it fell backwards into the flames.

A knot of Revenants were moving across the plain, threading in between the burning pits of fire. They were moving differently from the others. A solid mass of them, slower, but with more purpose. As Bleda watched, they stopped, one of them at the centre looking up at the hill from where the flaming arrows had been coming. Straight at Bleda. It was a woman, long hair lank and stuck to her skull. She pointed at Bleda, opened her mouth and issued a ululating cry, that felt like insects crawling inside Bleda's skull, behind his eyes.

Revenants stopped in their steady stream towards the White-Wings, looked up the hill, began to run at Bleda.

"One of Gulla's captains," Bleda hissed, fingering the twenty-four grey-tipped arrows he had.

He turned, ran to his horse and leaped into his saddle.

"Ellac, you're in charge here. Rune archers, with me," he called, and then he was spurring his horse into motion, breaking into a canter. Ruga, Yul and a score of riders following him.

They charged at the Revenants.

Creatures were running towards them, converging on Bleda, but he ignored them, eyes fixed on the woman who had pointed at him. She was still there, standing between two pits of fire, staring at him.

Bleda felt for his bow, his other fist reaching for arrows, a glance to make sure they were grey-fletched.

Smoke billowed in front of him, hiding the Revenant captain.

Another Revenant appeared at the edge of his vision, leaping at him, arms outstretched. Two arrows punched into it, a spurt of blue flame as it was hurled to the ground. Ruga and Yul.

"Cover me," Bleda cried, his thighs and knees tensing, putting pressure on his horse, and he was swerving between pits of fire, turf spraying, smoke rolling over them. Heat flared from one pit as his horse's hooves skidded and they swerved too close to the flames, the stench of singed hair, then they were balanced again. Revenants leaped at him, then fell away with flashes and spurts of blue flame, his companions' arrows keeping him safe.

And then he saw her again, moving now in her swift, jerking fashion, away from him, through the maze of pits. More Revenants were swarming towards him, hundreds of them. Bleda loosed an arrow, then another, took a long breath, then let the third fly.

The first arrow slammed into the Revenant captain's side, staggering her, a ripple of blue flame shimmering up her ribs. The second sliced into the back of her leg and she stumbled, dropping to one knee, more blue flame. She looked back at him with a snarl on her face.

Revenants leaped at him, ten, twelve, more. Too many for his guards to cull.

His third arrow punched into the Revenant captain's eye. Blue flame pulsed, spiralling out from her eye socket, juddering through her whole body. She collapsed on the ground, legs jerking, arms twitching, then she was still.

The Revenants jumping at him fell like rocks, thumped still and lifeless to the ground.

Bleda reined in his mount, Yul and Ruga catching up with him, his other warriors with them.

All around them Revenants gave a collective sigh and dropped, collapsing to the ground. Hundreds of them, thousands. A still silence hung in the air, and then cheers rang out from the shield wall.

Bleda twisted in his saddle, looked up at his warband on the hill, saw Ellac punching the air with his spear. Bleda grinned. A flick of his reins and his horse walked on, over to the Revenant captain. He dismounted and knelt by her corpse, pulled his three runed arrows free. They came out with a sucking, tearing sound. He wiped them clean and slipped them back into his quiver.

One of his palms was flat on the turf, bracing him as he crouched beside the Revenant's corpse. He felt a tremor in the ground, heard screams filtering across the field. A few strides and he was back in the saddle, looking to the west.

Where the Cheren were still charging the centre's shield wall in a perfect loop.

There was no longer a river of Revenants blocking his way.

He gave Yul and Ruga a cold smile, leaned in his saddle and spoke quickly to them.

CHAPTER EIGHTY

JIN

Jin was galloping at the shield wall, arrows flying from her bow, slamming into linden and flesh. She saw a White-Wing collapse, the warrior behind too slow to fill the gap, a dozen arrows flitting into the hole. Screams, more White-Wings dropping, the gap widening.

They are close to breaking.

Jin glimpsed split shields, other White-Wing warriors exhausted, trying to rotate back in the wall, but her Cheren spied every movement, every chink, filling any weakness with arrows. And there was nothing the White-Wings could do to stop them—the Cheren horse were always out of reach.

Jin was enjoying herself.

Her war-host had made over a dozen passes and put about thirty thousand arrows into the shield wall. She had glimpsed shadows flitting across the ground as Ben-Elim gathered in the sky above her, and Jin was waiting for their inevitable diving attack. But that was what Jin wanted. Her Cheren would move their bows from the shield wall and aim them at the sky.

Jin realized something had changed on this flank: there was an absence of sound. She glanced around, saw that the entire eastern section of the plain was still. There were no Revenants moving in their constant, animated thirst for blood.

What has happened? Have they retreated?

The hiss of an arrow and the Cheren rider in front of Jin

swayed in his saddle, toppled slowly to the side, a white-fletched arrow protruding from his neck. His foot caught in a stirrup and he was dragged along the ground.

The *thrum* of bowstrings and instinctively Jin ducked. More Cheren riders fell in front of her, four or five, screams and thuds behind her.

She looked to the east, the direction the arrows were coming from, and frowned.

Horses were standing in a line, maybe a score of them, and upon their backs were...Revenants. And they were loosing arrows at her Cheren riders. A bank of smoke swept across them, Jin squinting to see. The Revenant riders appeared again, trotting out of the smoke, sending more arrows flying. Jin swayed in her saddle, an arrow hissing past her.

The Revenant riders broke into a canter, and then a gallop, charging at Jin and her war-host. Another volley of arrows from them, the rumble of their hooves in gallop, more Cheren hurled from saddles.

"WARE!" Gerel was crying, Jin raising her bow, grasping for arrows, nocking and drawing. She put her first arrow into the chest of a Revenant, her second and third into its face. Three more arrows punched into it in quick succession, Gerel unloading his bow into the creature. It rocked back in the saddle, swayed and fell to the side, crunched to the ground.

And Jin's heart froze in her chest, ice suddenly in her veins.

There was another rider sitting in the saddle behind the Revenant, who wore a deel of grey beneath a lamellar coat, horsehair flying from an iron-spiked helm.

Bleda.

He was galloping towards her, bow in his fist, loosing arrows at her Cheren riders. The sheer bold audacity of it sent a pulse of rage through her, even as she threw herself forwards, barely avoiding two arrows in the chest.

A handful of arrows flitted from Jin's warriors, more Revenants pierced and falling to the ground, revealing Sirak warriors in the saddle. They were close, now, thirty or forty paces away. Cheren warriors gathered about Jin, seeing this new threat, and launched volleys of missiles at the charging line. Bleda was already turning in a tight half-circle and riding away, cantering between the pits of fire, his warriors following him, back into the flames and dark vapours.

Without thinking, Jin was guiding her mount off the wide channel and into the maze of fire-pits. Gerel saw her and followed, his horn at his lips, blowing blast after blast, and then her Cheren were following her, three thousand warriors riding into a fire- and smoke-filled wasteland.

Jin glimpsed Sirak riders ahead of her, clicked her mount into a trot. No reckless gallop through this maze of fire, another trap of Bleda's, no doubt. Dimly, she was aware of horns blowing, to the north. Fritha's voice, high and shrill, calling Jin's name. She knew this was breaking away from the plan, that she had not yet accomplished her task of cracking the White-Wings' shield wall, but she did not care. The horn calls changed and a glimpse to the north showed ranks of acolytes massing around Fritha. They began to move forwards, down the wide channel towards the shield wall.

I will return. Once Bleda is dead, his corpse hanging from a spike, I will lead my Cheren back and finish what I've started. But Bleda is right there...

Another glimpse of horses ahead of her, three or four hundred paces, grey deels. She loosed a trio of arrows, heard screams, both human and horse. Picked up her pace, moving into a fast canter, becoming accustomed to finding the winding path between the pits of fire.

Corpses littered the ground, emaciated, their clothing in tatters, and Jin realized she was riding amongst a field of Revenants.

This is where he took the Revenant corpses from. He killed their captain.

Fritha had told Jin how the Revenants could be slain, and what had happened when their captain had fallen in the Desolation.

Smoke cleared and Jin saw Bleda and his riders breaking into a gallop. They were free of the pits and riding up a hill.

Jin bared her teeth in a snarl, resisted the urge to gallop after them, she was almost through the field of fire. And then the ground cleared before her, no more pits, no more fire, her view unhindered.

Bleda had crested the rise of a hill and had stopped, was looking down at her.

Ice slithered through her veins, a hatred of this man before her that chilled her blood. Her hand twitched but she knew he was out of bow shot. Jin reined in a moment, allowing her warriors to gather behind her as they emerged from the smoke.

A score of Sirak surrounded Bleda, Jin recognizing Ruga, one of Bleda's oathsworn, and also Yul, who had been Erdene's first-sword.

You didn't save her, and you won't save Bleda.

Bleda saw her. He lowered his bow and slowly drew one finger across his throat.

The ice in Jin's veins erupted into a white-hot fire.

"BLEDA!" Jin screamed.

Then she flicked her reins and touched her heels to her mount, felt the animal's muscles bunch and she was leaping forward, breaking straight into a gallop.

Bleda looked at her a moment longer, and then he was turning and riding down the far side of the hill, disappearing.

CHAPTER EIGHTY-ONE

FRITHA

Fritha ground her teeth, watching as Jin led her warband away from the White-Wing shield wall.

She will answer to Asroth for that.

She scanned the battlefield, knew that Jin had come close to breaking the shield wall.

I shall finish the shield wall in Jin's place and I will take her glory, and Asroth's praise.

Wrath led the way, Elise and Arn either side of her, Aenor and his acolytes massed behind her, maybe fifteen hundred to two thousand who had survived the assault upon the wall.

We must strike now, before the shield wall has a chance to recover and reorganize.

Wrath was lurching forwards, head low, moving side to side, tongue flickering. The ditch was close now, maybe fifty paces ahead. Spikes and corpses were becoming visible.

That will not keep us out.

Fritha looked to the east, flame and smoke shielding much from view, but she could see Jin and the first of her riders galloping hard up a gentle hill beyond the field of flame. Other than the Cheren on the hill, the whole eastern quarter of the battlefield looked strangely still. Fritha had seen the Revenants fall, knew instantly that their captain must have been slain. The shield wall they'd been tearing to pieces was still standing there, looking like a half-mauled animal, stunned and in shock. The skies were clear, which bothered Fritha. She knew Asroth was waiting for the Ben-Elim to commit to the fight, and she had thought that moment had arrived when the Ben-Elim swept forwards with their torches. But they had flown back, behind the shield wall, and now the skies were mostly clear of white-feathered wings, maybe a few score of them circling beyond the shield wall.

To the west Fritha saw more wings, but they were low, swooping at the Revenants that were attacking the western shield wall. The White-Wings looked swamped, close to break-ing. Fritha glimpsed grey-feathered wings and blonde hair diving low over the Revenants, recognized the half-breed Ben-Elim that she had seen in Drassil.

You chose the wrong side.

The ditch loomed, waters swirling with blood, the stench of death in the air, voided bowels. Flies buzzed on corpses. Wrath spread his wings, broke into a run and leaped into the air, wings beating, and he glided over the ditch, landed with a crunch on the far side. Fritha let him walk on a few paces, then told him to stop.

"*Not smash enemy?*" the draig asked, confused.

"Soon," Fritha said. "We should wait for our friends."

A splashing behind her as Arn rode into the ditch, water coming up to his horse's chest. Elise slithered into the water, swam sinuously across, both of them navigating the obstacles and climbing up the bank. Then they were either side of Fritha, more of Fritha's honour guard negotiating the water, Aenor leading his acolytes into it, wading through the filth. It was not long before a thousand swords were massed about and behind Fritha, all dripping, more wading through water and climbing up the ditch's bank.

The shield wall was still and silent before her, maybe five or six hundred paces away. Behind it was more open ground, even-tually rising into a hill, a vast camp spread upon it. And beyond that, the town and tower of Ripa, framed by the sinking sun.

Fritha leaned in her saddle towards Aenor.

"Form a wedge behind me," she said. "You know the shield wall as well as any. I'll punch the hole, you widen it."

"Aye," Aenor said, hefting his shield. Blood crusted his mail, a flap of skin was hanging from his chin, but he looked animated. This was a moment they had all waited for, to take on the fabled White-Wing shield wall.

"We'll teach those arrogant bastards a lesson," he said, giving Fritha a grim smile.

She nodded, then looked to Arn.

"Hold back, don't follow me into this, horses won't help where I'm going. Harry the flanks as the wall splits."

He dipped his head in acknowledgement.

Then Fritha was sitting tall in her saddle, hefting her spear, eyes fixed on the wall of shields.

"Smash them," she said to Wrath.

The draig let out a bellowing roar, and then he was lumbering forwards, a shuffling, broken-gaited run. Behind her the acolytes broke into a jog. Within the shield wall, orders were shouted, shields tightening up.

It won't help them. Nothing can, now.

Closer now, fifty paces away, forty, the ground flashing by in a blur. Spears flew at her, cast from far back in the wall. Some hit, striking Wrath's neck and shoulder, but were shaken loose as he continued to charge, blood flowing over his scaly skin. He roared again, his wings giving a sharp beat, a final burst of speed, and then he was smashing into the shield wall. A concussive *whoomph*, Fritha rocked in her saddle, and warriors were flying through the air, voices screaming, trampled, bones shattered like kindling.

Wrath ploughed on, his momentum carrying him deeper into the shield wall. He lashed out with jaws and talons. Fritha righted herself, gripped her spear and stabbed, took a White-Wing in the neck, dragged her spear free, stabbed again, into the opening of a helm. Shields and swords were coming back at them, now, stabbing. Wrath bellowed, jaws crunching on a shield and the arm that held it, ripping it from its socket.

Fritha glanced, saw Elise beside her, round shield in one hand, her black-bladed spear in the other.

Shields started pushing in, Fritha jabbing left and right, adrenalin coursing through her, fuelling her limbs. Elise was hissing and snarling, her black spear carving ruin. A roar from behind: Aenor and his acolytes. White-Wings fell, the acolytes cutting into their ranks, widening the existing gap like water freezing to ice within a cracked stone, prising it open from within, and then the shield wall began to break. Like a dying animal taking a last, deep breath, there was a moment's pause, and then the shield wall shattered, fracturing into a hundred smaller parts. Horns blew, a frantic sound from deeper back in the shield wall. White-Wings were disengaging and retreating where they could, though many were falling to Aenor's acolytes and Arn's mounted warriors.

We cannot let them regroup.

More horn blasts and the tramp of feet, Fritha looking to the east. She saw the shield wall that had been fighting Revenants marching towards her. It was six or seven hundred strong, shields locked and tight. Ahead of her the shield wall was retreating and regrouping, maybe two or three hundred swords left.

Wrath could smash it again, but our flank is threatened. This could become far too even a fight in a very short space of time. She twisted in her saddle, looking back to the hole in the wall. *We need reinforcements.*

Asroth, I need you.

But nothing was there, the hole in the wall an empty place, no sign of movement.

Her troops were massed about her, milling, waiting for her leadership.

A long look at the two shield walls before her.

We should retreat, pull them after us, or send word for reinforcements.

There was a burst of light, like a soundless explosion, and then a wall of blue flame was leaping up, higher than two men, spreading across the field of battle in a wide, looping curve.

Giant's fire, like in the hidden forge in Drassil's great tree.

"No," she said, even as the wall of flame ignited the ditch in front of her, cutting across the channel she was about to use to retreat, flames crackling on, rippling around the whole battle-field, the entire ditch a barrier of blue flame, heat haze rolling from it in waves.

Realization dawned upon her.

The ditch was not to keep us out. It was to keep us in. We are trapped.

CHAPTER EIGHTY-TWO

JIN

Jin galloped down a steep slope. Gerel and Tark were either side of her, her war-host surging down the hill like an avalanche. In front of her she glimpsed Sirak riders disappearing behind the swell of another hill.

"CAUTION!" Tark yelled, as he galloped alongside her.

Jin's heart was pounding, her blood boiling, the sight of Bleda and his reminder of how he had slain her father incensing her. But Tark's words filtered through her rage.

Tark is right, Bleda has tricked me before.

She slowed, her warriors doing the same about her, shifting from a gallop to a steady canter.

Tark dipped his head to her, and then rode ahead with his men to the hillside where the Sirak had disappeared. Tark reined in and waited for Jin as his scouts fanned out around him, moving on, disappearing from sight.

"He is planning something, this Bleda," Tark said. "I do not like the look of this." He pointed: two hills rose either side of a valley, curling and disappearing behind a stony slope. Jin looked up at the sky, saw the sun starting to dip towards the west.

"He is a cunning one, this Bleda," Tark said, "and we must be cunning, to catch him."

"What do you suggest?" Jin asked him.

"Let my scouts go first. Then choose a captain to lead a

vanguard. And more scouts up on those slopes. Then we move forwards. No blind charge."

Jin nodded, though her blood surged with the need for speed, the sense that Bleda was slipping further away with every wasted breath.

"Do it," she said. "Quickly," she added.

In less time than it took Jin to change her bowstring and drink from her water skin, Tark had sent fifty riders up onto each slope, and Jargal, one of her captains, was riding into the valley, a thousand warriors at his back.

"Now we proceed," Tark said.

The valley began as wide and grassy underfoot, but soon became stonier, with a steady, gentle incline. Other vales branched off, but Tark and Jargal led them on. Slopes began to rear around them, the route becoming narrower. Jin lost sight of the scouts on the slopes above her.

Hooves crunched on stone and Tark rode back to Jin.

"I don't like this," he said.

A sound on the wind. A scream?

"Where are your scouts?" Jin asked him.

Tark's eyes flitted over the slopes.

A sound above them, movement behind a huge boulder. Jin's bow was in her fist, pointing. But it wasn't something behind the boulder that she'd seen moving.

It was the boulder.

It lurched into movement, began a slow roll down the slope, quickly gathering momentum. All along the slope other boulders began to move, tumbling down towards Jin and her warband.

CHAPTER EIGHTY-THREE

BLEDA

"PUSH!" Bleda grunted, his shoulder to a huge boulder. All along the ridge other Sirak were doing the same, boulders careening down the slope.

It had taken Bleda half a day of scouting the hills yesterday to find this spot, another half a day to manoeuvre the boulders into the right positions, teams of horses harnessed up to move them. Alcyon, Raina and the Kurgan giants helped.

At that point he hadn't even known how he was going to get Jin to follow him. He only knew that he had to try. All the time, sweat and toil could have been for nothing.

But as Bleda stood and watched the boulders hurtling down the slope towards the Cheren warband, all that labour and pain were very definitely worth it.

Shouts and screams were ringing out from the valley floor, Jin and her warriors bursting into motion, horses turning, jostling to move back down the valley. Some did, but there were close to three thousand horse down there, and the valley had become too narrow for them to all turn and gallop to safety.

Bleda's boulder slammed into the Cheren, the bone-crunching sound of impact, the rock rolling on, leaving a crushed mass of blood and bone in its wake. The other boulders hit the valley floor, pulverizing all in their way.

Bleda reached for his bow, grabbed arrows, close to a thousand Sirak warriors around him doing the same. They sent a volley up, arcing down into the valley, another volley, and then another. The *patter-slap* of arrows striking leather and flesh, like hail on shutters, more screams ringing out. Then the Cheren were retreating, horns blowing, a frantic gallop back along the valley floor. Bleda watched them go.

The sound of hooves on gravel and Bleda looked up, saw Ruga leading her warriors along the crest of the slope. A hundred Sirak riders. They were at the head of a long train of riderless horses. Maybe fifty of them.

"A gift from the Cheren," Ruga said. "Their scouts were not expecting their ambush to be ambushed."

Bleda smiled at her.

"And they have given us a gift," Ruga said, pointing to bundles of quivers tied to the first few horses, all full of arrows.

Even Yul smiled at that.

Bleda strode to his horse and climbed into the saddle, looked back towards the west and the battlefield. Between the curve of hills he glimpsed the flicker of blue flame.

"We'd best be getting back," he said.

CHAPTER EIGHTY-FOUR

DREM

Horns rang out, echoing along the forest road. Drem looked over his shoulder, saw the warband rippling to a halt. He ground his teeth, turned to look ahead. The road continued into shadow, bordered on their left by a wall of trees, branches arching overhead. To Drem's right a wide, sluggish river flowed, winding its way to the Bay of Ripa. Patches of sky were visible, angled beams of sunlight from the sinking sun sparkling on the river and sending shadows stretching along the road.

"Why are we stopping?" Drem called to Cullen, the sense of dread in his belly flaring.

We are too late, the battle is under way. How can we stop now?

Cullen shrugged, his own desperation for speed etched on his face.

"Horses to the river," a voice cried out. Elgin, Nara's battlechief, was leading the vanguard of Ardain's warriors to the river's edge. Warriors dismounted, knelt to refill water bottles, horses' heads dipping to drink.

From further down the line Rab fluttered above the warband, squawking Drem's name.

"*Byrne wants you,*" Rab croaked at Drem and Cullen. Drem touched his reins, Friend turning and lumbering back down the forest road, Cullen riding in the emptiness of his wake. Warriors hurried out of their way.

Byrne was standing amongst the first line of trees, a handful of figures around her—Ethlinn and Balur, Tain with Craf upon his shoulder, Queen Nara and Kill. Byrne was holding the book she had found upon Coralen's skeleton in the cabin.

"Drem," Byrne said as he joined them. "Riv is close to you and Cullen. Did she speak to you of the fall of Drassil? Specifically, of her rescue of Meical?"

"She spoke of the priestess Fritha and the winged draig," Drem said.

"Aye," Cullen nodded.

"And Meical, when she lifted him into the sky?"

"*Did she speak of starstone metal that had encased him and Asroth?*" Craf squawked impatiently. "*Craf saw it when Cywen made it, like black oil, all over them.*"

"Be polite," Tain whispered, stroking Craf's neck.

"No, Riv never spoke of it," Cullen said, shaking his head.

Drem frowned, searching his memories. "She said the skin of starstone metal exploded, the blast of it throwing all in the chamber to the ground."

"But what happened to the metal?" Queen Nara asked.

Drem and Cullen shrugged.

"Riv did not say," Cullen said. "In truth, I think she was more focused on escape."

"A fair point," Balur said.

"Why?" Drem asked.

Byrne looked at the book in her hands. "There may be an answer to our war with the Kadoshim, but we need starstone metal. A lot of it."

"Perhaps it is still in Drassil," Balur rumbled. "If it was shattered and blown in all directions by the explosion. Like stone smashed by a war-hammer."

"Would Asroth just leave it there?" Ethlinn mused.

"Impossible to know." Byrne grimaced. With a snap she closed the book. "Well, if no other answer comes to light, then we must return to Drassil, when we can, and search for the starstone metal. But not today." She smiled grimly at them. "Today we ride to battle and blood." She looked at the warband spread along the forest road, many remounting now, water bottles filled, the thirst of their mounts slaked.

"A black-bladed knife," Drem whispered.

"*What? Speak up*," Craf squawked.

"I saw a black-bladed knife, at Brikan," Drem said. "It cut through Keld's coat of mail as if it was nothing."

"A new starstone weapon?" Ethlinn growled.

"Who wielded it?" Byrne said.

"Gulla's half-breed daughter," Drem said.

Byrne nodded slowly. "We must consider the possibility of new starstone weapons, then, and if Asroth allows warriors such as that to wield one, then there must be more."

"It will make him stronger," Ethlinn said.

"Aye," Byrne said, looking at the ground. She shrugged and looked at them all. "But forewarned is forearmed, and this was never going to be an easy fight. We must fight it one step at a time, first we must get to Ripa, and I fear we will not reach its walls before the sun sets, but we must try."

Grunts of agreement. They had abandoned their baggage train two days ago, packing provisions for a few days and riding hard for Ripa, making the most of every moment of daylight, and walking further during the night, but they were still not close enough.

Drem climbed back onto Friend's back.

We must try, he thought. *Riv is there, fighting for her life.*

CHAPTER EIGHTY-FIVE

FRITHA

Fritha looked at Aenor, the two of them realizing how this was going to go. The shield wall in front of them had reformed, maybe three or four hundred strong. The shield wall from the east was marching towards them, at least six hundred strong. Together they were roughly equal to Aenor's acolytes, and they were White-Wings. They were better trained. She had Elise, Arn and his riders, and she was upon Wrath, who could do a lot of damage, but he was not invincible.

Something on the battlefield changed, a prickling on Fritha's neck drawing her eyes to the west, where Revenants were swarming a beleaguered shield wall.

Except that the Revenants were collapsing.

A silence, like an indrawn breath, followed by a long sigh. A winged figure rose up from the ground, dapple-grey wings, two short-swords raised.

"The half-breed," Fritha whispered.

The half-breed Ben-Elim let out a victory cry, echoed by the White-Wings below her.

She's slain another of Gulla's captains.

And as Fritha stared, horns blared and voices cried out. The shield wall beneath the half-breed reformed and was beginning to march, straight towards Fritha; maybe four or five hundred shields, a handful of Ben-Elim circling above them. And behind them all was another ditch and two more legions of White-Wings, both at full strength.

We are going to die. It dawned on Fritha in a moment, like a candle being snuffed out.

Where is Asroth and his Kadoshim? Where is Jin and her Cheren? Where is Morn and the half-breeds, or Gulla and his Revenants? There are still thousands of them left, but none of them are here.

She looked down at Aenor, at Arn and Elise, and she stroked Wrath's bloodied neck.

A glorious death, then, and take as many of them as I can with me.

"Let's do this," she said, her companions hearing her. They all hefted their weapons, shifted their feet. Prepared themselves for one last charge.

And then she saw the White-Wings in front of her staring beyond her, eyes wide, mouths gaping.

Fritha turned in her saddle, looked at the blue flame barring her way.

The earth around the ditch was moving, crumbling away, as if something were burrowing beneath it, sucking it down. The blue flames rippled, flickered, thinned. Fritha heard a voice.

"Crochnaíonn an talamh an lasair, buail mo shliocht. Lasair, bogha do do rí..."

"Earth, smother the flame, bear my passage. Flame, bow to your king," she whispered, the hairs on the back of her neck standing on end.

The earth began to seethe and bubble.

"CROHNAÍONN AN TALAMH AN LASAIR, BUAIL MO SHLIOCHT. LASAIR, BOGHA DO DO RI," the voice bellowed, and earth exploded upwards in a great gout, spraying over the blue flames, raining back down into the ditch, and with a hissing crackle the flames went out. A ridge of earth rose up from within the ditch, wide enough for a score of men abreast to cross.

Asroth rode across the hard-packed earth, blue flame still

crackling either side of him. Warriors marched behind him in ordered rows. Behind them Fritha glimpsed a wall of dark mist concealing Gulla and his Revenants. And above them all flew the Kadoshim and their offspring. Fritha saw Morn amongst them, a spear in her fist.

And then Asroth was beside Fritha. He looked at her, smiled, for Fritha the world fading for a moment. Asroth dismounted, marching forwards to stand between Fritha and the White-Wing shield wall.

Asroth stared at them, his coat of mail and dark helm glistening and shimmering like oil. Then he shrugged his long axe from his back and gripped it in both hands, swirled it around his head in a looping circle, leaving a trail of black smoke in the air.

"Who is first to die?" Asroth said.

CHAPTER EIGHTY-SIX

RIV

Riv froze in the air, hovering, speechless.

"Asroth," Meical breathed.

It felt as if the whole world had stopped. Was holding its breath.

For a moment Riv felt…scared. A wyrm uncoiling in her belly, fear slithering through her.

He looks…unstoppable. No Ben-Elim, no warrior, not even Balur One-Eye, carried the same aura of malice and menace.

"Who is first to die?" she heard Asroth call out, his long axe circling his head.

The shield wall in front of Asroth did not move, though to their credit they did not turn and run, either. And then Asroth was striding forwards. He loomed over the first row of the shield wall, Riv seeing shields tighten up, warriors bracing themselves, setting feet and leaning shoulders into their shields.

Asroth swung his axe, a cracking, splintering sound as the blade hacked into shields, an explosion of timber and blood, screams, and three or four warriors fell, shields and flesh sheared by the axe. A warrior at the edge of the axe's reach stumbled forwards, her shield snagged. Asroth's second swing chopped into her at the waist, a wet, sickening crunch and she was hurled to the ground, her body almost severed in two. Asroth put one boot on her corpse and wrenched the axe blade free.

The shield wall moved, warriors stepping forwards to fill

the gap left by the dead, countless years of drill making the act subconscious.

"ADVANCE!"

Riv felt a flush of pride and respect for whoever called that.

The shield wall took a step forwards, towards Asroth, and another. He stood a moment, as if surprised, then swung his axe again, more screams, shields and warriors shattered and broken, a spray of blood, but the shield wall did not falter. They stepped forwards again, closing on Asroth, and spears stabbed out, grating on his mail.

Asroth roared, a rage-filled sound, his right leg going back as he swung his axe again, more White-Wings hurled from their feet, blood spraying.

Horns blew from Ripa's tower. She looked up to see Ben-Elim leap into the sky, hundreds of them, white feathers glowing red in the sinking sun. They swept down the hill, towards the plain and Asroth.

A cry rang out from the Kadoshim and half-breeds behind Asroth, wings beating as they rose higher in the air, powering towards the Ben-Elim.

There was another roar, louder and deeper than Asroth's, filling the whole field, and Fritha's draig lurched forwards, lumbering into a run. It smashed into the wall beside Asroth, hurling a dozen White-Wings through the air, trampling a dozen more.

The acolytes behind Fritha yelled and broke into a jog, shields up, charging at the White-Wings.

Riv shook herself, a spell had been lifted, as if she'd been mesmerized by Asroth's appearance.

Now she just wanted to kill him.

She looked a Meical and Hadran.

"Let's end this," Meical said, and the three of them shared a grim smile.

Without another word, their wings spread wide and they flew towards the battle.

The acolytes hit the White-Wings, a concussive crash echoing, warriors thrown to the ground, most of the White-Wing shield wall holding. The din of battle rang over the field again.

In the air the Ben-Elim and Kadoshim met above the warriors on the ground, an aeons-old rage palpable as they clashed, the battle breaking down into a myriad of individual conflicts as Ben-Elim, Kadoshim and half-breeds swirled around one another, spears and swords stabbing, feathers and wings slashed, blood pouring from the sky like rain.

Kadoshim and half-breeds saw Riv, Meical and Hadran, a dozen, maybe more, and they hurled themselves at them. Riv snarled, a fierce joy sweeping her.

She tucked her wings, a burst of speed, and spun between two Kadoshim, swords slashing. The clang of steel on one side, a spray of sparks. On the other side her sword bit through mail and flesh, mail links shattered and blood flowing. The wounded Kadoshim screeched, lurched in the air and then gave out a gurgling scream as Meical's sword chopped into its neck.

The world condensed to a swirl of noise and fractured images as Riv snarled and raged and killed.

She heard a voice calling out, filtering through the red haze that filled Riv's mind.

"ASROTH!" Meical yelled. Asroth paused in his death-dealing and looked up. Silver hair spilt over his shoulders. He smiled and raised his axe at Meical, an invitation.

Meical closed his wings and dived.

"No," Riv whispered. *We have to attack Asroth together.*

A pulse of her wings and she was flying after Meical, but then a weight slammed into her side, a leather-winged half-breed crashing into her, the two of them spinning through the air, locked. The half-breed had a spear in one fist, a knife in the other, and Riv felt white-hot pain lance along her thigh. She could not bring her swords to bear, snared in a spinning dive, not knowing which way was up or down. A glimpse of a snarling face, black-stubbled hair, and Riv punched her sword hilt into that face, again and again. The half-breed fell away; Riv stretched her wings and pulled out of the dive, hovering in the air.

She saw the half-breed dropping, then its leathery wings snapped out and it was rising, turning to look at Riv. A woman, her nose and lips pulped and bleeding from Riv's sword hilt.

She still gripped her spear and knife.

A long, black-bladed knife.

Drem had told her of a half-breed with a black-bladed knife.

"Morn," Riv said. "You slew Keld."

The half-breed smiled, blood on her teeth.

"Aye, and now I'll do the same to you."

"Come and try," Riv said, curling her lips, holding her short-swords wide.

CHAPTER EIGHTY-SEVEN

FRITHA

A voice rang out somewhere above her.

"ASROTH," and Fritha looked up, many upon the ground pausing, doing the same.

It was Meical, hovering in the sky, brandishing a longsword.

Asroth lifted his axe, an acceptance of Meical's challenge, and then the Ben-Elim was tucking his wings and diving. Close in the sky Fritha glimpsed Morn, locked in a spinning embrace with the Ben-Elim half-breed.

Meical descended from above like a well-cast spear, his sword pointing straight at Asroth's heart.

The long axe swung, a huge loop, at the last moment Meical shifting the angle of his approach, sweeping up, the axe skimming his belly. Meical's sword slashed down, clanged on Asroth's helm, staggering him, and then Meical was sweeping up into the air.

Asroth bellowed at him, his wings snapping out, beating, and he was rising into the air after Meical, dust swirling in a whirlwind upon the ground. Meical turned and flew at him again.

Asroth gripped his axe two-handed, like a staff, blocked an overhand swing from Meical, steel sparking, turning as Meical swirled around him, blows struck faster than Fritha could see, always answered with the clang of steel, a stuttered staccato of blows that lasted a dozen heartbeats, ending with a crunch and

Meical spinning away, dropping from the sky, crashing to the ground before Fritha. He rose unsteadily, blood sheeting from his head.

Asroth descended slowly, landed before Meical, a grin upon his face.

"You've had more than two thousand years to prepare for this," Asroth said. "I thought you'd be better."

Meical shook himself, a ripple through his wings.

"*Cré a bheith ina bholg, coinnigh mo namhaid*," Meical shouted, and ran at Asroth, sword held high, two-handed.

The ground beneath Asroth's feet shifted, seemed to melt, and Asroth lurched, sinking into the earth. He swayed, straining to heave a leg free, but the ground had become a sinking bog, sucking at Asroth's legs.

"*Lig saor mé*," Asroth snarled, and the ground solidified, seemed to spit him out.

Meical slashed down as Asroth stumbled and raised his axe, steel grating as their weapons caught in a bind. Meical broke away, a flurry of blows at Asroth, head, thigh, shoulder, ribs, all blocked, Asroth standing there like a rock before a storm, Meical swirling, moving faster than Fritha's eyes could follow.

Meical stepped back, breathing hard.

Asroth put his gauntleted hand to his cheek, wiped away a thin line of blood. Gripped his axe again.

Meical stepped in fast, a straight lunge at Asroth's chest, dipping under Asroth's block, sweeping back up and in, stabbing high. Asroth stepped away, Meical's blade touching him, sparks on mail. A twist of Asroth's arms and his axe shaft had locked Meical's blade.

Asroth kicked Meical in the groin, dropping the Ben-Elim.

A beating of wings and more Ben-Elim were swooping down, a score at least. Kadoshim were close behind them, Bune leading Asroth's honour guard, who had been fighting in a loose circle above Asroth.

Fritha recognized some of these Ben-Elim. Dumah was there,

whom she had served under for a time. He flew at Asroth, Ben-Elim either side of him, the three of them breaking through Bune's guards. Spears stabbed out at Asroth. He stepped back, away from Meical, who was still on his hands and knees, retching onto the grass.

Asroth set his feet and swung his long axe, an explosion of splinters as he sheared through the Ben-Elim's spear shafts, a backswing and the wicked spike on the reverse of the axe crunched into a Ben-Elim's skull, the warrior dropping like a stone, crashing to the ground. Asroth tugged the blade free, bits of bone and brain in the air, slammed the butt into the second Ben-Elim's belly, doubling him over, Asroth's knee crunching into his face, sending him flying, slamming onto the ground.

Dumah swept past Asroth, turned, dropping his shattered spear shaft, reaching for his sword hilt, and Asroth's axe sliced into his neck, a spurt of arterial blood and his corpse collapsed to the ground.

A swarm of Ben-Elim were swooping around Asroth now, Kadoshim interweaving amongst them, trying to hold them back.

Fritha urged Wrath towards Asroth, swiping a path through White-Wings in her way.

Meical was back on his feet, his sword in his hand. He charged at Asroth, but Bune slammed into him, knocking him back to the ground. Meical rose, sword swinging in an arc around his head, chopping at Bune's neck, parried, Bune stumbling away, then coming back at Meical. A furious exchange, steel clanging, grating, Meical eventually stepping out of range. Bune followed, relentless, sword swinging in a horizontal blow with enough force to take Meical's head.

Meical dropped to one knee, sword stabbing straight out and punching into Bune's belly. It tore through mail, then leather and flesh. Bune's sword dropped to the ground and he fell to his knees, staring at Meical. Then toppled backwards.

Asroth was backing towards Fritha, half a dozen Ben-Elim

setting upon him in a frenzied attack. His long axe kept them all back. Fritha saw another Ben-Elim land to his right, beyond Asroth's vision, spear poised, waiting for an opening to stab in.

Fritha felt her heart freeze in her chest.

It was Kol. The father of her child, Anja.

She had loved him once, with a passion that burned as bright as the sun. She hated him now, with a passion just as fervent. He had ordered the murder of her baby.

"KOL!" she screamed, the White-Wing hearing, turning.

"Wrath, crush him," Fritha snarled, and the draig leaped forwards, head swaying, sending any White-Wings in their way hurtling through the air. Kol saw them charge, turned, wings opening to leap into the sky, but the air was thick above him with fighting Ben-Elim and Kadoshim. He dived to the right, just as Wrath's head lunged out, jaws wide. The draig's teeth snapped on air, claws raking the ground, turf spraying as he skidded to a halt, Fritha dragging on her reins, Wrath turning.

Kol was on the ground, rolling. He grabbed a White-Wing shield as Wrath swiped at him with a taloned claw. The shield exploded in a spray of splinters, Kol flying through the air, over the heads of fighting warriors, crashing to the ground thirty or forty paces away, disappearing amongst the turmoil.

Fritha searched for him, screamed.

CHAPTER EIGHTY-EIGHT

RIV

Riv twisted in the air, Morn's spear jabbing at her, fast as a snake. She curled around the spear as it stabbed past her, one short-sword hacking down at the spear shaft, splintering it, the head falling away, her other sword stabbing at Morn's belly.

The Kadoshim half-breed swayed, too slow, Riv's sword slicing into her hip, shattering mail and grating on bone.

Morn screamed, hacking at Riv with her black knife. She felt the blade score a red line across the side of her neck, then slammed her head forwards, headbutting the half-breed across the bridge of her nose. A burst of blood and cartilage and Morn's eyes rolled back into her head. She began to fall, fingers limp around the black knife.

Riv's hand snatched out and grabbed the knife, watched Morn fall, crashing into a knot of combat below.

Hadran was spinning through the air, two Kadoshim pursuing him. She flew at them, crunched into one's side, slashed wings with her short-sword, stabbed Morn's knife into the Kadoshim's chest. The weapon pierced mail like a hot knife through butter. Riv twisted the blade, pulled it free and the Kadoshim was falling. Hadran had dispatched the other Kadoshim.

"Meical," Hadran said, and they looked down at the battle-field below them.

Asroth was standing amongst a swarm of violence. Dead

Ben-Elim and White-Wings ringed him like storm-wreckage left by the tide.

Meical was the only Ben-Elim trading blows with Asroth.

Hadran's wings folded and he dropped into a dive, Riv following him. They smashed through the combat. Somehow Asroth glimpsed them coming. He stepped away from Meical and swung his axe at Hadran. The Ben-Elim swerved, the axe slicing through his wing as he hit out with his spear, punching into Asroth's bicep, but the black mail held, the spearhead glancing away, and Hadran crashed into a knot of acolytes and White-Wings.

Riv was right behind Hadran, hidden from Asroth's view, and she flew straight at him. He saw her, then pulled his axe back, the spike swinging at her, but she twisted her wings and flew under it, skimming the ground, and lashed out with her short-sword, felt it bite through wool and flesh.

Asroth bellowed in pain.

Riv's momentum swept her on and she ploughed into the acolytes where Hadran had crashed. She swung and stabbed with sword and knife, righted herself. Grabbing Hadran's arm, she dragged him upright. They turned and ran at Asroth.

Meical was there before them, leaping in, striking down in a powerful two-handed blow, right to left, Asroth's long axe parrying, knocking Meical's sword wide, Meical twisting, a burst of speed that avoided the counter-swing from the butt-spike of Asroth's axe. He swung his sword at Asroth's waist, slashing into mail, black smoke bursting from the starstone coat. Asroth grunted, twisted on his feet, axe swinging in a circle, its blade slashing through part of Meical's wing. Meical stumbled, dropped to one knee, one wing hanging limp, Asroth followed him, a booted foot crunching into Meical's chest, hurling him twenty or thirty paces through the air, crashing to the ground.

"*Cré, coinnigh mo namhaid,*" Asroth growled as he strode after Meical, and the ground around Meical began to bubble and seethe. Roots burst from the earth, wrapping around

Meical's wrists and ankles. Meical struggled and heaved, veins bulging purple, but he could not break free.

"*Fréamhacha agus sosanna*," Meical gasped, and the roots began to wither, some snapping.

"*Greim a choinneáil air, fréamhacha an domhain*," Asroth commanded as he approached Meical, his long axe rising. More roots burst from the ground, snaring Meical. "You are no match for me, with blade or with the earth power." He smiled, looming over Meical.

Riv slammed into Asroth's back, her sword cutting into the small of his back with all of her strength. Impossibly, his mail held, the sword turned away, only scraping across it. Asroth twisted, snarling, his elbow crunching into Riv's nose, even as she lashed out with the black knife. It stabbed into Asroth's arm, piercing the black mail easily, on into the meat of his bicep. He cried out, dropped his axe, swung his arm, throwing Riv off, his gauntleted fist crunching into her head and she spun through the air, hit the ground, slammed into Meical.

Black stars speckled Riv's vision. She shook her head, pushed herself to her knees.

"Help, me," Meical grunted beside her, straining against his bonds. Riv still had sword and knife in her fists. She slashed with the knife at the roots about one of Meical's ankles and they fell away.

A battle-cry behind them: Hadran was thrusting his spear at Asroth's chest, a blow that should have torn through the coat of mail and stabbed deep. But the spear just...exploded in a shower of splintered wood. Hadran gazed down at the shattered shaft, confusion on his face.

Asroth laughed and backhanded Hadran with an iron-gauntleted fist, lifting him from the ground, sending him spinning through the air to land a dozen paces before Riv and Meical.

Hadran climbed to his feet, blood dripping from his mouth, and stood guard before Meical and Riv, drawing his sword from his scabbard.

Riv slashed at the roots binding Meical's other ankle.

"You can't save him from me," Asroth said. He drew a short-sword from his hip with a grimace of pain, blood dripping from his arm where Riv had stabbed him. With his other hand he unclipped a whip from his belt. Riv saw the gleam of iron shards and black wire in the leather. Asroth looked up at Hadran and smiled.

Riv cut Meical's last bonds. Meical lurched to one knee, grasping for his sword.

Asroth threw his arm out and flicked his wrist, the crack of leather and iron as the fronds of the whip hissed out.

Hadran screamed, iron hooks biting into him, wrapping around his arms and torso, his neck and face. Tentacles of black mist swirled around him. He slashed his sword at the leather strips, but they did not break, only pulled tighter.

Asroth heaved on the whip, Hadran fell, screaming, dragged until he lay at the Lord of the Kadoshim's feet, lacerated and bleeding into the ground.

Riv started to run.

Asroth stabbed down with his short-sword and there was a gurgled cry as Hadran spasmed. A tremor through his wings, then he was still.

Riv screamed, behind her Meical was yelling.

Behind the demon king a bank of black mist poured through the gap between the blue flames. A figure emerged from it, one red eye glowing.

Gulla.

He alighted behind Asroth, stabbing his spear at a cluster of White-Wings locked in combat with shaven-haired acolytes.

A horn rang out from behind Riv and Meical, a voice shouting.

"RETREAT!" it cried, the horn blasts taken up, blaring across the battlefield. All around Meical and Riv, White-Wings were turning and running, filling the space between them and Asroth. Above them Ben-Elim tried to disengage from their battle with the Kadoshim.

Riv looked for Asroth, glimpsed him through the crowd. She took a step towards him.

A fist grabbed her arm, part turning her. Meical.

"Stay and die, or fly and live," he said to her, an echo of the words she had said to him, so long ago, it seemed, on the day she had saved his life in Drassil.

Riv snarled, her face twitching, tears blurring her eyes.

"Hadran," she said.

A twist of Meical's lips. "Only alive can we avenge him." He looked beyond Riv, at the black mist spreading. "We can't win this battle, not with a fresh wave of those Revenants. Not here, not right now."

Riv let out a strangled growl, then grabbed his arm, part dragged him through the air, over the ranks of acolytes and White-Wings. Below her she saw Raina preparing to light the second ditch.

CHAPTER EIGHTY-NINE

BLEDA

The world opened up before Bleda, a cold wind blowing off the bay, stirring his warrior braid. It felt good on his skin, which was damp with sweat. To his left was a clifftop and the sea glistening far below. Straight ahead he saw Ripa's white tower, and down to his right the camp of their war-host spread across a hillslope and vale, and beyond that, the plain of the battlefield.

Far out on the plain the wall was a burning, smouldering wreck. Within its boundaries the field was studded with fire, clouds of smoke billowing across it. He saw the outer ditch had been lit with Raina's giant's fire, a blue line curving around the battleground. Either side of the blue-flamed ditch black mist swirled, crossing into the southern part of the field through a small gap.

Bleda's lip curled. *More Revenants.*

Even as Bleda was staring, trying to make sense of the battleground, he saw the second ditch spark into blue flame. It began around the centre, flowing rapidly in both directions, in heartbeats dissecting the battlefield again, curling as far as the river to the west and the hills to the east.

The sign to retreat. We've been pushed back, then. Gulla needs to die. It would make this battle winnable.

Gulls screeched and Bleda looked to the south, out to sea. Black specks on the horizon, swirling in a slow-moving circle.

They could not be birds, they were too big. He strained his

eyes, peering hard, saw the faintest silhouette, and felt a sliver of ice run down his spine.

"Ruga, what do you see?" he asked, knowing her eyes were as keen as a hawk's.

"Kadoshim and ships," she eventually said.

They curled around the headland, into the bay, moving steadily towards Ripa.

"I don't like the look of that," Ellac muttered behind him.

Bleda touched his reins and his horse turned away, breaking into a canter.

Hooves drummed as Bleda rode through the empty camp, the plain below him. He could see the survivors of the battle now. Ben-Elim in the air, above the giant's fire, two blocks of White-Wings, the reserves that had been held back, each over a thousand strong. Between those blocks milled more White-Wings, maybe a thousand. Bleda searched for Riv, but couldn't see her, a seed of worry in his belly.

"Get their attention," Bleda said to Ruga. She put a horn to her lips, others behind her doing the same, and then horn blasts were ringing out. Bleda saw figures turning, looking up at him on the hillside, and then he saw what he was searching for: grey-dappled wings rising into the air, flying towards him.

Riv gave him a relieved smile as she drew close. She was covered in blood, sweat-stained, a gaunt, haunted look in her eyes.

"There are Kadoshim flying above the bay," he called up to her, "and ships fast approaching Ripa."

Riv's wings beat and she rose higher in the sky, straight up, hovering. After long moments she dropped back down to him.

"Help me spread the word," she said, "and meet me at the quayside."

She turned, speeding back towards the war-host at the foot of the hill.

Moving into a fast canter, Bleda led his warband on.

"Kadoshim and ships in the bay," he shouted, his Sirak

taking up the cry. Bleda turned west, riding along the rear line of the war-host. Word spread quickly, and Bleda saw Riv descending to the front lines before the fired ditch. Behind him he heard the tramp of many feet, looked back to see one of the White-Wing reserve regiments marching after him, towards Ripa's port. Others were moving his way, too, giants, and many of the White-Wings. They were battered and bloody, survivors from the wall and battlefield, he guessed.

He entered Ripa through a wide street, buildings of timber and thatch rising about him. The calls of gulls grew louder, the smell of salt and fish oil thick in the air, and then he was cantering onto stone, the port and harbour of Ripa spread around the curl of the bay. Wooden piers jutted out into the sea, all manner of ships bobbing on the swell, anchored or roped to piers.

Bleda reined in, his warband spreading behind him in disciplined rows.

The Kadoshim were clear in the sky now, flying low over a fleet of red-sailed ships. They were huge vessels, low in the water, moving sluggishly. As Bleda watched, sails were furled and oars appeared, banks of fifty a side. They dipped into the water, the ships moving faster.

The sound of wings and two shapes were dropping out of the sky, alighting beside him. Riv and Meical. He was cut and bloody, pale-faced, a bandage wrapped around the arch of one of his wings.

Marching feet behind them and the White-Wing regiment moved into the harbour, spreading wide along the dockside. They were around a thousand strong: a hundred shields wide, ten rows deep.

The ground shook, Alcyon upon his bear, a coat of mail rippling across its muscles. Raina, Ukran and the Kurgan giants came with them, a hundred warriors in mail, leather and fur. A few hundred White-Wings marched with them, led by Aphra.

"Why is the whole war-host not coming?" Bleda asked. "I don't like the look of those ships."

"Asroth can breach the giant's flame somehow. Some kind of Elemental magic," Riv said. "Someone has to try and hold him."

"So we are likely to be attacked from two fronts?" Bleda said.

Riv nodded grimly.

A fluttering in the sky and a white bird flew down towards them, the crow, Rab. He alighted on Riv's shoulder.

"*Looks bad,*" the crow squawked. "*Follow Rab, leave now. Rab take you to Byrne and friends.*"

Bleda looked to the west, the river and giant's fire a barrier, beyond it a plain and then the trees of Sarva.

"We can't just leave everyone," Riv said to Rab.

The sound of many wings above and Ben-Elim were flying over the port, some sweeping down. Kol and a dozen others alighted on the ground before Bleda, Riv and Meical. Kol's face was a mask of cuts and blood, splinters of wood embedded in his cheek and forehead. A bruise was spreading across one eye and cheek, and he held his left arm close to his side, as if to protect his ribs.

Bleda withheld a smile.

"Our White-Wings will meet them, whoever they are," Kol said. "Bleda, try to contain them, stop them from flanking the shield wall. Thin their numbers."

"You don't command here," Bleda said, even though the strategy was sound. It was exactly what he intended to do, anyway.

"I do for now," Kol said. "Dumah is dead, Hadran is dead, every high-ranking Ben-Elim fallen or unaccounted for."

Bleda blinked at that.

"Hadran?" He looked at Riv, knew they had been close. She said nothing, but her cheek twitched.

The ships were closer, now, movement on the decks discernible. A banner was unfurled, above the high prow of the first ship. It was a red, long-taloned claw upon a black field.

"A bear's claw?" Kol said, frowning.

"No," Raina said, approaching them. "A draig's claw. They are the Shekam, and they ride upon draigs."

Kol looked up at her, his face draining of what little colour it had left.

"*Rab told you things bad,*" the white crow squawked.

CHAPTER NINETY

RIV

Riv felt those words hit her like a fist in the belly. Raina had warned them that the Shekam were marching to war. But Ben-Elim scouts had flown out to watch all the approaches to Ripa from the east, and there had been no reports of them. No one had thought to watch the sea.

How do you get a draig on a ship?

Raina stepped forwards with Ukran and a dozen giants. They were carrying three chests between them.

"Guard us from above," she said to Kol.

The ships were close now, oars powering them towards the many piers and quays that jutted out from the harbour-side.

Raina and the other giants strode down a wooden pier, put the chests down and unbolted them, started taking out long chains and cook-pots.

Raina was pouring something into her pot; Ukran and the other Kurgan were all doing the same. Riv saw sparks and blue flame ignite. Then Raina was gripping chains in her fist, swirling the pot around her head in wide, looping circles. Once, twice, three times around her head, and then she released it, the pot arcing high into the sky, trailing blue flame. It began its descent, crashed onto the deck of the closest ship, just below the mast. An explosion of blue flame, flaring bright, catching on the wooden deck immediately, running up the mast like a hungry beast, the furled sail igniting with a crackle. Other pots were flying through the air, three more smashing into the same ship, others flung higher, further. Some splashed into the sea, a ripple of blue fire on the waves, but others landed onto other ships, blue flame spreading in heartbeats.

Shrieks in the sky and Kadoshim were sweeping down, a hundred, two hundred, more, straight at Raina and her kin on the pier.

Riv heard Bleda curse and then his horse was leaping forwards, his bow rising, Sirak behind him following in a thunder of hooves.

Riv jumped into the air, wings beating, shouted at Kol to help. Meical's wings beat but he rose into the air with difficulty.

Riv drew her short-sword and black knife, and flew at the Kadoshim.

There were flames in the bay, the ship closest to Raina a maelstrom of blue flame, black smoke billowing into the sky. Timber was cracking, breaking, water flooding into the hull, and Riv heard a terrible roaring, screaming as the ship began to sink.

More pots of flame flew through the air. They crashed onto ships, flames exploding.

Kadoshim swept around the fire and smoke, forcing Raina and the Kurgan to turn and run back along the pier, one pausing to hurl one last fire-pot. Many ships were burning. Spears were flung by the Kadoshim, a giant on the pier crying out, toppling to her knees. Riv saw Raina slip her huge shield from her back and run back for the fallen giant. Ukran and others were faltering under the attack of the Kadoshim, gripping weapons in their fists—axes and war-hammers.

Riv slammed into the first Kadoshim. It never saw her coming, so intent was it upon Raina and the giants. They rolled in the sky, Riv's sword sheared through its wing-arch, knife jabbing into its throat, and it was plummeting through the air, sinking into the sea with hardly a splash. Riv flew on, amongst the Kadoshim, now, slashing and stabbing, arcs of blood, bodies falling, but there were too many.

Screams from below, giants.

Riv glimpsed white-feathered wings, saw that Kol and the Ben-Elim with him had entered the battle.

There is much I'd say about Kol, but my father is no coward.

Time passed in fragmented moments, punctuated with blood and screams. Riv felt impacts, some blunt, some lines of white-hot fire, saw a burst of her dapple-grey feathers floating through the air, but she fought on. It was who she was, what she did. She was rolling in the air, locked in a grip with a half-breed Kadoshim, the thick muscles of its arm binding her sword arm. She saw its other arm reach for a knife at its belt. Then it was choking, gurgling, dark blood vomiting from its mouth, an arrowhead bursting through its throat.

Its grip went slack and the half-breed began its slow, spiralling tumble to the sea.

Riv looked down, saw Bleda upon the pier, Sirak all around him, scattered along the quayside, their arrows reaping Kadoshim from the skies. Raina and her giants were back on solid ground, running back to Aphra's shield wall.

Bleda was waving for her, signalling for her to fly clear.

She did, or she tried to, but Kadoshim were swooping for her. Arrows hissed through the air, more Kadoshim dropping around her and then Riv was clear of them and flying over stone again, circling above Aphra and Raina.

Bleda came cantering back, Ruga and a hundred Sirak with him.

"My thanks, little man," Ukran said.

"Ha, we have taught them to fly higher," Bleda said.

Riv looked and saw that the skies were clear, the Kadoshim retreating higher into the blue.

Ships were burning, flames and smoke sweeping across the bay, but more vessels appeared, rowing through the chaos, navigating the sinking hulls. One of the burning ships was still moving through the water; it crashed into a jetty, wood splintering. Blue flames jumped from the ship to the jetty, found some wood and crackled into furious life.

Oars banked and a ship's hull grated on wood, others crunching into the quayside. Riv had not realized how huge the ships were. They towered over the piers and harbour.

Ropes with iron hooks were cast from the deck, sinking into the timber of quays and jetties, wrapping around pillars and buildings on the dockside.

There was a moment of silence, ships creaking on the rise and swell of the sea.

A shouted command from the shield wall, bodies shuffling tighter together. A thousand shields came up and pulled tight with a crack, like a thunderclap.

Muted voices from within a ship grating against the dockside. The sound of great bolts being drawn, a creaking sound, a thud, and then an enormous panel in the ship's prow dropped down, crashed onto the harbour-side, leaving a hole in the hull of the ship, like a gaping mouth.

A shadow loomed within that hole, and then a draig was bursting out of the ship and lumbering down the gangplank, a male giant upon its back. The draig thundered onto the dockside, long, razored talons scraping on stone, short legs bowed, its body wide, heavily muscled and low to the ground. The giant upon its back barked an order, pulled on reins and the draig stopped. Its head swayed from side to side, scaly skin a greenish brown, tail lashing. Huge, curved teeth protruded from a long, flat muzzle.

Hammer growled, a deep-chested rumble.

Upon its back the giant sat and regarded them. He wore a spiked helm of iron, cheek-guards, a curtain of riveted mail hung from the back. Most of his face was in shadow, but Riv saw a long, drooping moustache tied with leather. He wore a vest of scaled plate, like Bleda's, but the iron plates bigger and thicker, and his body was wrapped in billowing linen. Tattoos of vine and thorn coiled up one arm, and part-way down the other. He carried a long spear, the spear blade longer and wider than a sword, curved and single-bladed, like the blades the Sirak wore strapped across their backs.

The draig opened its jaws and roared, spittle spraying, the sound filling the harbour, drowning out all else for a moment.

"*Bás dár NAIMHDE!*" the giant cried out, bellowing the last word.

The draig charged.

Horns blew from within the ship and more lumbering shapes appeared, surging down the gangplank. All along the dockside more doors crashed open, an explosion of dust, draigs roaring, lurching out of the ships' bellies.

The first draig hit the White-Wing shield wall. A concussive, bone-crunching impact, rippling through the wall, bodies hurled into the air, crashing to the ground. The draig ploughed deep into the wall's lines, six, eight rows in, not quite breaking through. White-Wings pressed around it, pushing close, stabbing with short-swords. Riv saw a hundred red lines open up across the draig. It roared, lashing out with head, claws, tail, more White-Wings falling. The giant upon its back swung his huge spear, carving through wood into mail and flesh. A head sailed through the air.

More draigs hit the shield wall, twenty, thirty, forty of the beasts, still more disgorging from the ships moored along the docks, and Riv saw more ships behind them, rowing into the harbour.

The shield wall disintegrated, a thousand warriors cast into havoc and ruin in a score of heartbeats. The White-Wings fought back, tried to regroup, pressing around draigs, stabbing with their short-swords. One draig reared and crashed to the ground, White-Wings swamping it, stabbing at the animal's softer belly and the giant. But there were too many draigs. They were crushing, tearing, eviscerating all in their path.

Blue flame was spreading across the dockside, the wind

helping it jump from the burning jetty to grain stores and ship-houses.

Bleda and a dozen Sirak drew their bows, loosed. Riv saw arrows skitter off the draigs' thick, scally hides, and from the giants' iron-plated armour. One giant fell, an arrow in his eye.

Kadoshim came swooping from the sky, screaming and hissing their hate.

The din of battle drifted to them from the north. Shouting, screams, the clash of arms.

"Asroth has broken through the second ditch," Meical said.

Riv felt any hope left within her drain away. She gripped her weapons anyway and spread her wings, bent her knees.

Rab squawked, flapped in front of her.

"*Riv warrior of Bright Star*," the bird croaked. "*Can't stay. Stay means die. Fly with Rab, save your friends, save yourself.*"

Meical touched Riv's shoulder.

"The crow's right. This battle is lost," he said.

Riv looked at Meical, then to Bleda and Aphra, even Raina was looking at her, waiting on her word. She saw Alcyon, and the giant nodded at her.

"We will run and live, fight another day," Riv said. "If we can."

CHAPTER NINETY-ONE

BLEDA

Bleda touched his heels to his horse, barking out orders. His Sirak broke and spread around Aphra's White-Wings as they jogged away from the harbour. Raina and Alcyon were leading the way, out of the town, towards the west. Riv leaped into the air, wings taking her away. Meical tried to do the same, but he swayed in the air, his injured wing failing him.

"Here, brother," Bleda called to him, riding close, offering Meical his arm. Meical took it and swung up behind Bleda.

"My thanks," Meical said, and they rode on.

Shrieks from above and Bleda twisted in his saddle, looked back over his shoulder and saw Kadoshim and half-breeds sweeping down after them, calling down to Shekam giants, pointing at Bleda and his companions.

"WARE THE SKIES!" Bleda called, as he reached for arrows, nocked and loosed, guiding his horse on with his knees. The hiss of arrows as other Sirak saw the Kadoshim and loosed at them. A ripple of screams in the air as a hail of Sirak iron slammed into flesh, Kadoshim falling, spinning from the sky. Another burst of arrows raked the Kadoshim and the survivors broke off their pursuit and wheeled away, searching for easier prey.

Bleda rode on, a slow canter as he curved around Aphra's White-Wings. She was blowing on a horn, trying to gather more White-Wings to her as they fled. Bleda saw the horn calls working, scattered White-Wings in the harbour running in their direction. They left the harbour behind, the ground shifting from stone to hard-packed earth, the street wide, buildings of wood and thatch rearing about them.

Sounds of battle swirled around them, from the harbour, from the north, where Asroth must have forded the giant's flame. Between buildings Bleda snatched glimpses of warriors. Some were fighting acolytes, others fleeing. Further off he glimpsed banks of black mist spreading into the town.

Buildings thinned and then disappeared around them and they moved into open grassland. Aphra had swelled the White-Wings to hundreds, warriors filling the road and spilling down its embankments. Bleda led his Sirak wider, riding across trampled grass. To their left the river flowed, lined with boats and jetties and a jumble of buildings, smoke-houses, grain yards, boathouses. A few hundred paces ahead the road was blocked by a wide trench of roaring blue flame, the western tip of the second battlefield ditch.

"The boats," Riv yelled, circling back to them, and Aphra veered off the road, ran for the riverbank. Bleda searched for a way through the fire for his horses, but could not see one.

They reached the riverbank, dozens of boats of various sizes moored to wooden jetties. Aphra barked orders and formed a protective shield wall with a few score warriors, then started ordering the other White-Wings onto the boats, pushing them off, oars dipping into the water. Bleda helped Meical off his horse, Meical staggered and Aphra ran to steady him, helped him onto a boat.

Riv hovered over Bleda.

"Can your horses swim?" she called down.

Bleda grimaced. They could, but arrows, bows, strings, so much would be ruined or useless if they drove their horses into the river.

"Fly on, I'll find a way," he called up to her, "I'll catch up with you in the forest."

"I'm not leaving without you," Riv said.

A small fleet of boats was in the river now, packed with hundreds of White-Wings rowing upstream, towards the trees and darkness of Sarva. More were still leaping into boats.

Raina took her hammer from her belt and marched to a boathouse, slammed her hammer into one of the hinges of a huge door. She shouted something over her shoulder and Alcyon rode Hammer to the other door and began chopping at its hinges with his axes.

What are they doing?

Bleda turned and looked back at Ripa. More White-Wings were running towards them, trying to escape the blue flame that was spreading through the town, belching black smoke. He glimpsed figures between the smoke and flame: giants on draigs, White-Wings, pockets of shield walls. Kadoshim and Ben-Elim fought in the skies, a constant whirlwind of combat, though Bleda saw some Ben-Elim breaking away and flying their way. Others had already passed overhead, in the direction of the forest.

Further north the roar of battle was echoing, and there were more Ben-Elim and Kadoshim in the sky. Black mist was rolling across the ground, seeping into the town of Ripa, and moving their way, towards the river.

The hinges Raina was hammering at came free with a squeal of iron and the door crashed to the ground. Alcyon's door followed a few moments later.

"Help us," Raina said, Ukran and a handful of giants rushing to her and Alcyon's aid. Together they lifted the doors and carried them over to the blue flame that crackled and roared in the ditch, hurled one of the gates down. It snuffed the flame beneath it, forming a makeshift bridge. Alcyon and his helpers threw their door down on top of the first one, thickening and strengthening the bridge.

Ukran yelled at his giant kin, urging them across the bridge.

"Get your Sirak across, quickly," Raina said. "I don't know how long it will hold."

Bleda barked an order, Sirak starting to canter across the bridge.

A roaring and figures burst from the town. White-Wings, hundreds of them, engaged in a running battle with acolytes. Some were moving in good order, a disciplined retreat, others were running in full rout. There were wounded amongst them, stumbling, falling. The acolytes behind were slaughtering the fallen.

We must leave now. Become embroiled in this and there will be no escape. We will be overrun.

Aphra and the White-Wing warriors about her were yelling at their comrades, urging them on. Some of her warriors broke away from the shield wall around the boathouse, moving towards those fleeing the town. Aphra yelled orders, started marching back to help her people.

In the air black figures appeared, rising from the northeast, swirling across the town after the fleeing White-Wings. Kadoshim. A larger figure flew at their head, leathery wings, a long whip trailing from one hand.

Bleda felt fear trickle through his veins. He knew who this was, even before Riv screamed his name.

"ASROTH COMES!" Riv yelled above him.

CHAPTER NINETY-TWO

RIV

Riv stared at Asroth and the host of Kadoshim behind him, looked down at Aphra as she led a score or so of White-Wings to the aid of her warriors. Aphra had reached them, was leading an attack on acolytes, trying to forge a gap, buying time for her comrades to escape. With mounting horror Riv saw Asroth angle his descent towards the snarl of White-Wings and acolytes.

She sheathed her sword and slipped the black knife into her belt, unclipped her bow-case and grabbed a fistful of arrows, at the same time as her wings were beating, propelling her back towards Aphra, Asroth and the Kadoshim. Feathers brushed her cheek as she drew and loosed, her first arrow arcing towards Asroth, flying high, over his shoulder, punching into a Kadoshim behind him. Her second arrow was wide, another Kadoshim shrieked. Her third arrow she thought was aimed straight at Asroth's chest, but his wings folded as he launched into a dive and the arrow hissed past him.

More arrows in her hand as she dipped into her own dive, loosing as she flew. One of her arrows hit Asroth in the shoulder, but it *pinged* off his mail shirt. Riv shouted a curse.

And then Asroth was crashing into White-Wings, scattering them, hurling many to the ground. He alighted amidst them, his black wings beating a storm that battered more to the ground, his whip snapping out, tearing flesh from bones.

A figure rose amidst the fallen White-Wings, a lone warrior holding a battered shield and a short-sword. Riv knew instantly that it was Aphra. Fear swept her and she beat her wings harder, slipping her bow back into its case.

Asroth's whip cracked, iron claws biting into Aphra's shield, Asroth dragging her towards him. Riv saw Aphra release her shield, run in behind it, using the momentum of Asroth's tug. It took the Lord of the Kadoshim by surprise, and before he could do anything Aphra was within his guard, ducking under his short-sword and stabbing her own blade up, into his belly.

It was a perfect blow, struck with Aphra balanced, her weight and strength behind it, a manoeuvre that Aphra would have practised ten thousand times in the weapons-field.

The sword shattered, hurled Aphra onto her back.

Asroth's whip cracked again, this time no shield to protect Aphra. Claws of sharp black iron bit into her, slicing through mail and leather, hooking into her flesh.

Riv heard her scream, echoed it with her own.

"MAM!"

Riv was close now, a hundred paces, her wings tucked, wind ripping at her hair.

Asroth dragged Aphra towards him, more screams, a thick trail of blood smeared across the ground as Aphra was dragged to his feet, and he sliced down with his short-sword.

Riv slammed into Asroth, hurling him away, sending him crashing to the ground. She spread her wings, checked her flight, swept back to where her mam lay upon the ground. Whip-cords were still wrapped around her, strips of flesh hanging, white bone glistening through the blood. Riv swiped at her eyes, blurred with tears, tried to loosen the cords, but Aphra cried out, a weak, broken sound.

"I'm sorry, Mam," Riv said through her tears, tried to lift her in her arms, but Aphra cried out again. Riv knelt on the ground, cradled her mother's head. "I've got to get you out of here," she said.

Aphra stared up at her, eyes full of pain. A long, rattling sigh fading to nothing.

Riv looked up at the sky and howled.

A sound behind her, a mocking laugh.

Riv turned, saw Asroth standing over her.

"I want my whip back," he said.

The red haze boiled inside Riv's head, all else gone from her mind except for a raw, uncontrollable rage. She snarled, tears blurring her eyes, and hurled herself at the demon king.

CHAPTER NINETY-THREE

BLEDA

Bleda rode after Riv. He'd heard her scream, seen her dive into the fray, but he lost sight of her as a handful of acolytes threw themselves at him, grabbing at Dilis' bridle, trying to rip him from her back. He put an arrow into one at almost point-blank range, hurling the man to the ground. The other acolytes fell in a heartbeat or two, more arrows thumping into them, and then Ruga and Yul were riding alongside him.

"Where is she?" Bleda called to them, standing in his saddle as he searched for Riv. All was battle and blood, White-Wings and acolytes fighting, Kadoshim sweeping and screeching, stabbing. The ground trembled as draigs lumbered from the town.

Then he saw her.

A space had cleared thirty or forty paces to his right, White-Wings dead or battered to the ground. Asroth stood there, his dark wings furled behind him, stumbling as Riv slammed into him.

They twisted and turned for a few moments, Riv seemingly trying to gouge Asroth's eyes out with her thumbs.

"Clear my way," he called to Ruga and Yul, then spurred his mount on. In front of him acolyte warriors spun away, pierced with Ruga or Yul's arrows. They shot a path in front of him, filled with the dead, and then Asroth and Riv were clear before him. His heart lurched into his chest. Riv was hanging limp in Asroth's grip, he had one hand clasped around her throat, a black gauntleted fist pulled back for a blow that would surely crush her skull.

The space between them disappeared as Dilis galloped towards Asroth. At the last moment Bleda pulled on his reins, leaning back in the saddle, a lifetime of learned commands passing through the touch of his knees and feet. Turf sprayed as Dilis skidded out of her gallop, then reared up, hooves lashing out, crunching into Asroth, hurling him through the air. Riv fell from his grip.

Dilis' hooves slammed to the ground and Bleda was leaning low, one hand on the saddle pommel, the other grabbing Riv's arm and hauling her up from the ground, laying her limp form across the saddle in front of him. He spurred Dilis on again, a tight turn and he was speeding back the way he had come, Ruga and Yul skewering any who came close to him. Then the three of them were galloping away, towards the makeshift bridge across the blue fire.

Ukran, Alcyon and Raina were there, guarding the bridge, allowing more White-Wings to cross. They called out to Bleda, urging him on. In a dozen heartbeats Bleda was clattering across the bridge and then he was riding hard along the road, Raina and Ukran running alongside him, Alcyon upon Hammer's back. His Sirak formed around him and they swept along the road and plain, the sinking sun sending their shadows stretching long behind them. In a hundred heartbeats they were disappearing into the gloom of Sarva's trees.

CHAPTER NINETY-FOUR

JIN

Jin crested the brow of a hill.

The battlefield before her was a place of ruin. Some of the pits of fire still burned, most were empty of flame, just black, gaping holes now. Two lines of blue fire curled across the field, and much of Ripa was burning, blue flame creeping up the hill towards the tower.

Most of the field was habited by the dead and those that had come to feast on them. Crows squawked and argued.

Closer to Ripa it looked as if battle still raged, shapes in the sky swirling in combat. Screams drifted on the wind.

"The battle is won, then," Gerel said, beside Jin.

She nodded, the action sending shafts of pain through her skull and nausea flaring in her gut. She leaned in her saddle and vomited on the ground.

Reaching for her water skin, she swilled her mouth out, spat it out, and drank. Then put a hand to her head and adjusted her bandage. It was stiff with dried blood.

Gerel had found her, unconscious beneath her horse. It had taken ten warriors to lift the dead animal enough to pull her out. Her leg still throbbed, but it was not broken.

Damn Bleda to a thousand deaths.

A thousand fewer warriors were riding back with her than had entered those hills. She felt a flush of shame, chased swiftly by rage.

Never again will I chase after Bleda. He longs for my death as much as I long for his. If he still lives, I will let him come to me.

If he still lives.

She looked back to the battlefield and kicked her mount on, trotting down the slope.

Tark and a dozen scouts slipped into the lead. Crows leaped into the sky as they passed, squawking their protests at being disturbed from their feast.

Tark led them to the earthwork bridge across the burning ditch, and in silence they passed across it. The other side was thick with the dead, the stench of blood and excrement crawling into Jin's nose and throat. She rode on, to the next ditch, another earthwork bridge, and she crossed that, too.

Fritha was sitting upon her draig, both of them slumped with exhaustion, both thick with blood. Morn the half-breed sat with her back against one of Wrath's legs. Elise the snake-woman was coiled, leaning over Morn, wrapping a bandage around the half-breed's head.

Fritha looked up as Jin crossed through the flame. She smiled.

"Good," Fritha said. "I feared you might be dead."

"Not yet," Jin said, grimacing. "Where is everybody?"

"Pillaging the town, hunting for survivors," Fritha said. "Gulla is leading his Revenants in a hunt for their supper, no doubt; what is left of them." She frowned at Jin. "You should not have ridden off. I thought you Cheren were masters of your emotions."

Jin opened her mouth to say something, an angry, bitter defence of her actions, but then she thought better of it.

The truth is clear to all. Best to admit to it, deal with it.

"Bleda, he brings out the worst of me," Jin said. She shrugged. "He led me a merry chase through the hills and then dropped a rock on me. It's the last time I make that mistake."

Jin felt a tremor in the ground and looked up to see Kadoshim winging through the sky. Draigs walked below them, huge creatures of slabbed muscle ridden by giants. Asroth strode at their head, acolytes behind him.

As Asroth drew near her, Jin saw he was limping, one leg of his breeches blood-soaked, and his right arm was wrapped in a bloodstained bandage. His long axe was slung across his back, his whip and short-sword in his fists.

"Ah, my fierce hawk has returned to me," Asroth said to Jin. "A little late," he said, a coldness filling his voice.

"I am sorry, my Lord," she said. "I erred. The next battle will be different."

Asroth approached her, reached out and cupped her chin in his palm, looking into her eyes. He held her gaze a long while, then nodded.

"Plans go astray once the blood is being spilt," he said. "But this battle is won, Ripa fallen and our enemies crushed at our feet."

"Not all of them," Fritha said.

"Enough for one day," Asroth said. "Too many even for the crows." He turned and gestured to one of the giants upon a draig. A huge man, tattooed, a wicked-looking long spear in his fists.

"Meet my ally, Rok of the Shekam," he said.

The Kadoshim Sulak descended from the sky, alighting beside Asroth.

"I told you we would be here," Rok said to Fritha, giving her a mocking half-bow.

"I'm glad you were," Fritha replied, dipping her head to the giant.

The giant looked down at her. He unbuckled his helm and lifted it off, revealing a shaven head, tattoos of thorn and vine swirling upon it.

"Well met," he grunted.

His draig snorted.

"*Pretty draig*," Wrath rumbled, snapped his wings out wide.

"Stop showing off," Fritha said to him.

The Shekam draig looked at Wrath, curled a lip and growled at him.

"*I like her*," Wrath rumbled.

"Ha, he has earned that," Asroth said. "We all have. Faced our fear and won, slain our enemies. But even so, the plan has not gone exactly as I'd hoped." He looked up at the tower on the hill. Blue flame wreathed it, and most of the hill about it, smoke belching into the purpling sky as the sun dipped into the west. "I wanted to feast in Ripa's tower."

"It's back to Balara for us," Fritha said.

"Aye," Asroth agreed. "To some wine, a celebration, and then we sharpen our weapons for the Order of the Bright Star."

CHAPTER NINETY-FIVE

DREM

Drem sat in a glade in the moonlight. He glanced up, looking at the moon, saw it was close to midnight.

A rasp as Drem drew his seax, stroked the steel with gentle fingertips. Then he loosened the leather ties of a vambrace and slipped it off his forearm, exposing grimy, sweat-soaked skin. He drew his seax across it and watched blood run down his arm, across his palm, dripping from fingertips to the grass.

"Now we wait," he said to Fen. The wolven-hound was curled at his side, back to a boulder. Its coat of mail shimmered in the half-light.

Time passed, Drem murmuring to Fen, absently tugging on one of the wolven's ears.

Abruptly Fen shifted, climbed to his feet, ears pricked forwards. He growled, almost inaudibly, more of a vibration deep within the wolven-hound's broad chest.

Drem's hand moved to his neck and silently started counting the beats of his pulse.

A sound in the forest, deep within the darkness. The rustle of foliage, the snap of a twig.

Drem slipped his vambrace back on and stood, tightened the leather cords with his teeth, then slipped his hand-axe from its belt hoop. He set his feet, seax and hand-axe ready, eyes flitting across the glade.

Sounds from all around now, moving closer. Padded foot-falls, the whispered crackle of forest litter, bodies pushing through foliage.

Then a growl from something that prowled on the edge of darkness.

A silence, a held breath.

Figures burst from the forest, part man, part beast, creatures of tooth and claw, hunched and muscled, limbs elongated, patched with fur and bare skin.

Ferals.

Ten, twelve, more leaping from the darkness, a whole pack of the creatures.

Fen jumped, colliding with one of the Ferals in mid-air, a bone-crunching collision, a deep-throated snarling, snapping.

A hissing sound filled the glade, arrows raining down from above, punching into Ferals. Faelan and others of his kin swooped down from boughs, bows *thrumming*. Some of the Ferals dropped instantly, pierced many times. Some evaded the iron-tipped death, launched themselves at Drem.

Another explosion from the trees, this one as big as a boulder, a wall of white fur and a gaping maw, and Friend flew into the creatures hurling themselves at Drem. The bear's jaws clamped on one, a paw swiping another, shredding ribs and an arm, the other collided with Friend's chest and was sent hurtling through the air, crashing into a tree.

One evaded the white bear and came straight at Drem. He ducked and spun on one heel, slashed with his seax as the Feral flew past him. It turned, came at him again, ploughing into him. They fell together, rolling in the grass, a tangle of limbs. Drem tried to strike at the creature, found one of his blades was trapped in the Feral's flesh, the other weapon gone from his grip.

The Feral's jaws were close to Drem's face, snapping, teeth clicking, a finger's breadth from his ear.

Another snarling sound, and then jaws were clamping around the Feral's neck and shoulder, the sound of flesh tearing, blood spurting in Drem's face. The Feral howled and whined in pain as Fen tore chunks of flesh. Its claws raked on riveted mail and Fen did not let go, continued to shake the Feral like a rat. Then Friend was there, a paw crashing onto the Feral's back, pinning it.

An arrow punched into the Feral's head.

Drem looked up from the ground, chest heaving as he gasped for breath, saw Faelan hovering over him.

"Trust me, you said," Drem breathed.

Faelan alighted beside him, offered him his arm.

"You're alive." Faelan shrugged.

"How many?" Drem asked as he climbed to his feet. His body ached like he'd been hit with a tree.

"Twenty-six of them," Faelan said. His kin were circling the glade, loosing arrows into any Feral that still moved. "Is that all of them?"

"I don't know," Drem said. "But we can do no more." He patted Fen's neck, the wolven-hound pressing close to him. "My thanks, Fen," he said, then turned to the white bear.

"You're not supposed to be here," he said, the bear dipping his head and rubbing his muzzle against Drem's chest.

Cullen rode into the glade, moonlight casting him in silver and shadow.

"What are you doing here?" Drem asked. "Is the whole war-band coming this way? And you shouldn't be riding in the dark."

"If he's allowed to disobey orders," Cullen said, pointing at the white bear, "then so am I."

Drem shook his head.

The trap had been his idea. Craf's crows had spied the Ferals in the forest, better scouts and guardians for Asroth's warband than any warrior. It would have been impossible to slip past them unobserved. So Drem had come up with this plan. He'd insisted on standing alone, because the Ferals would have smelled the white bear, or hidden warriors upon the ground, and been put off their attack. Only Faelan and his kin had a chance of going undetected.

"Have I missed all the fun?" Cullen asked.

"Aye," Drem said, rolling his shoulder, which throbbed as if it had been dislocated.

"I'll be your guide back to camp, then," Cullen said. "Shouldn't take us long. Friend's made a road as wide as a barn."

Drem's eyes snapped open.

He was lying on the forest floor beside a tree, head on his kit-bag, his cloak pulled tight around him. Cullen was snoring close by. Or it might have been Fen.

Booted feet were in line with Drem's eyes and he pushed himself upright, the weight of his mail coat feeling heavier than normal. Exhaustion was becoming a well-known companion. Byrne was approaching him, threading through sleeping warriors. Beyond her he heard the constant murmur of the river they were following through the forest. Drem sat up, rubbed his eyes, looked up through the trees. It was full dark, long before dawn. He hadn't been asleep long.

Byrne reached him and crouched down.

"You did well," she said, her voice hushed.

Drem grunted.

"Cullen," Byrne said.

The warrior continued to snore.

Drem poked him with his boot.

"What?" Cullen muttered, opening his eyes and, seeing Byrne, sat up.

"Good morning, Aunt," he said.

"It's a long way from morning." Drem sighed.

"Aye, it is," Byrne said. "But when morning comes it will bring battle with it. We are close to the forest's border, and Ripa. Less than half a day's march."

Drem nodded.

"I wanted to see you both, before it begins," she said. Shrugged. "You are my kin."

Drem looked at her, a strong woman, muscles honed, a

sharp intelligence and wisdom in her eyes. She always appeared so strong. Led with strength, but with a streak of kindness also.

"I'm proud to call you my kin," Drem said, speaking his thoughts, as he often did.

Byrne smiled. "And here it was me coming to tell you both that same thing." She looked away, her eyes shining. "Whatever happens on the morrow, know this. I love you both. This war feels as if it has been my whole life, and sometimes it can become hard to remember why I am fighting it. There has been so much death and tragedy." She blew out a long breath, rubbed her eyes. "When it comes down to it, though, when I strip all the politics and strategies away, it is quite simple: I am fighting this war for you. For my kin, the people I love." She smiled at them. "You are worth fighting for." She reached out and squeezed Drem's wrist.

"I'll fight for you until my last breath," Cullen breathed. "Follow you into the Otherworld, if I have to."

Byrne stood, looking down at them. "I know you would." She turned away, paused. "Oh," she said. "Here's something for you, Cullen." She held out something long, wrapped in wool.

Cullen stood up and took it, unwrapped it. Gasped.

"But..."

Cullen held up a sword, drew it slowly from its worn leather scabbard. It was Corban's sword. Sounds came from Cullen's throat, but no words, his eyes bright with tears. The sword glinted in the moonlight.

"But..." he said again.

"It's mine to give," Byrne said, "and I know, here, that it is you who should wield it." She touched a hand to her heart. Then smiled. "Just don't lose it."

Cullen grinned. "That I won't," he said, "not while there's life in my bones."

"Sleep while you can," Byrne said, turning away.

A flapping of wings and loud squawking, they all heard it together, and a white bird came flying above the river.

"*RIPA IS FALLEN*," Rab squawked.

CHAPTER NINETY-SIX

RIV

Riv swayed on her feet and Drem reached out an arm and steadied her, then pulled her into an embrace. She just stood there, her arms trembling, a sea of emotion churning within her.

Drem stepped back, held her at arm's length, looking into Riv's eyes.

"What has happened?" he asked.

Riv just stared at Drem. She did not want to say it, did not want to think it. Her face was throbbing, the taste of blood in her mouth, and she couldn't breathe through her nose. Asroth had broken it. All she remembered was Asroth's gauntleted fist filling her vision, and then nothing, until she'd regained consciousness upon Bleda's horse. For a moment she did not know where she was, could not remember what had happened. And then memory had swept in like a huge wave, destroying everything in its path.

Bleda was standing behind Riv, holding his horse by the reins. He hovered close, worry in his eyes.

"Aphra, Riv's mother, fell in battle," Bleda said. "At Asroth's hand."

Those words seemed to open a floodgate inside her and Riv swayed, almost dropped to her knees, but Drem and Bleda grasped her, held her up. Riv shook her head, fresh tears flowing from her eyes. She felt…everything. A pounding in her head, as if it was about to explode, pain in her chest as if her heart were being squeezed, waves of nausea in her belly. There was a bottomless grief deep inside her, blended with a flickering, white-hot rage, all of it twisting and turning within her veins, spiralling, sweeping her along in a dizzying torrent of misery and fury.

"There is no greater wound, no greater pain," Drem breathed, his face full of care and worry.

"Aye," Bleda whispered behind her, his hand still under one of her arms.

Some distant part of her knew that Drem and Bleda had lost kin in this war, a memory of Bleda's grief as Riv had carried him away from the scene of his mother's death, but all was overwhelmed by the fresh rawness of her own pain.

"Come," Drem said, "let's find some quiet, a place for you to sit, some food and drink."

Riv just looked at him numbly, but when he took her hand she followed.

All around her the Order of the Bright Star's camp was in motion. Torches lit, warriors rushing to help the survivors of Ripa, horses stamping, giants, bears, wolven-hounds, an endless tide of living things. Fia and Ert were standing on the riverbank, shoulders slumped with exhaustion, both of them helping White-Wing warriors climb out of their boats and scramble up the bank. Riv saw fractured moments; Raina reunited with her son, Tain, tears streaming down the crow master's face, Craf flapping his wings and squawking. Someone handing a bowl of porridge to Jost, who took it and just cupped it. Ruga checking the hooves of her horse. Kill unwrapping the bandage about Meical's wing and inspecting the wound. Kol arriving, battered and bloody, a few score Ben-Elim with him. He just sat on the riverbank and looked into his hands.

"Welcome home, child," Byrne said in Riv's ear, her arm around Riv's shoulder. "Go, eat something. Rest. I'll find you soon."

Riv sipped a spoonful of Cullen's stew, holding onto it with both hands. She was trying to stop her hands from shaking. She was not sure if she was starvingly hungry or on the verge of vomiting. Both. Something warm in her belly seemed to help.

Cullen spooned out more bowls from his pot. A lot of people had followed Riv to Cullen's pot. Bleda, Ellac, Ruga and Yul, Ukran, Jost, Ert, Fia and Sorch. All of them were sitting, eating and drinking, all of them lost in their exhaustion and thoughts.

Footsteps and Ethlinn appeared out of the gloom, Balur One-Eye at her shoulder. She looked around the campfire, saw Riv and came to put a hand on Riv's shoulder, squeezed it, then strode to Ukran and crouched beside him.

"Welcome, Ukran of the Kurgan," Ethlinn said. Balur stood over them. "You have travelled far to join us. We are grateful, and I am happy to see more giant kin in this world."

"I haven't come to bend my knee to you, if that's what you're thinking," Ukran said gruffly.

Ethlinn shrugged. "There are more important things than the bending of knees," she said, though Riv was not so sure that Balur agreed, by the way he was glowering at Ukran. "The end of the Long War. The Battle of the Banished Lands is upon us."

Ukran looked at Ethlinn a long while. "It is a battle that cannot be avoided," he said. "I fight now, or when the Kadoshim are knocking on my door in Arcona." He grimaced. "Better to fight now."

"Aye, that is wisdom," Ethlinn said.

"It was the little man's idea. I just followed him here." Ukran pointed at Bleda, who lifted his bowl in a greeting to Ethlinn.

Ethlinn smiled. "Just followed." She laughed. "Over a hundred leagues. You have made your choice, Ukran of the Kurgan, and it is a brave one."

"Sit, eat with us," Cullen said, trying to find bowls big enough for Ethlinn and Balur. He'd already given his other pot to Ukran.

"I think we will," Ethlinn said.

Cullen filled her a bowl and gave it to her, though it looked tiny in her hands.

"Just give me the pot," Balur rumbled. He sat down next to Ukran.

More figures stepped out of the trees. Byrne, with Kill and Queen Nara at her shoulder, and Meical. Byrne looked at Riv and the other survivors of Ripa.

"Meical has told me of the battle," Byrne said. "Of Asroth and his black mail. Of his starstone weapons. He also told me that he saw Asroth bleed today. A knife put through his arm by Riv."

All faces turned to stare at Riv. She had not even told Bleda of her fight with Asroth, her heart so raw and wounded from the loss of Aphra. She was experiencing moments where nothing seemed to matter anymore, but they were swiftly followed by bursts of hot rage, images of vengeance all-consuming.

"Asroth wore a coat of black mail," Riv said, her voice sounding strange in her own ears, flat, emotionless. "I think it is made from the same substance as the knife. I saw Hadran's spear explode when he stabbed Asroth. A blow that would have skewered a wild boar. My mother's sword shattered when she stabbed his coat of mail." Riv paused, felt a tremor in her voice. Breathed deep, then drew the black knife from her belt. "This is the blade I stabbed him with. It pierced his mail. I think this is a starstone blade," she said. "I took it from Gulla's daughter, Morn."

"You slew her?" Drem and Cullen asked together.

"No. She fell. Might have died in the fall, but I cannot be sure." Drem and Cullen shared a look.

Byrne took the blade, studied it, turning it in her hands.

"It is starstone metal," she breathed.

"The point is, Asroth can bleed," Cullen said.

"Aye," Balur rumbled, "and what bleeds can die."

"Yes," Bleda murmured.

"That is good, but there is much more to this," Byrne said, looking up at all of them, a new fire in her eyes. "We *need* this starstone metal. Asroth appears to be wearing or wielding it—a coat of mail, a helm, a gauntlet, black axe, sword and whip. But if this weapon is out there, then perhaps he has gifted starstone weapons to more of his captains. We need it all."

"What for?" Cullen asked.

"To change our world, end the war, forever, not just for a generation. So, on the morrow, if any of you come against an enemy wielding or wearing this starstone metal, take it from them. At all costs."

Nods and grunts amongst them all.

"You have fought hard, fought for Ripa and the Ben-Elim, given your all, and lost much," Byrne said, her eyes resting upon Riv. "But I would ask you to fight once more. One more day, to change our world. To avenge our fallen. Can you do that?"

Riv held Byrne's gaze and gave one sharp, curt nod. *Avenge our fallen. Yes.*

"Good," Byrne said, and gave the black knife back to Riv. "Riv, Ukran, Bleda, I would talk with you, before we move out."

Riv nodded and climbed to her feet.

Kill stepped forwards, until now a silent shadow at Byrne's shoulder.

"Who commands the White-Wing survivors?" Kill asked.

Aphra's name formed on Riv's lips, a fresh twist of pain in her belly. The other White-Wings were looking at one another—Jost, Ert, Fia and Sorch.

"Ert is the best of us," Fia said, Jost and Sorch nodding.

"I am an old man, had some luck on the battlefield, that's all," Ert said.

"Luck!" Jost snorted a laugh. "I stood next to you, and I'm glad I did. What I saw today wasn't luck."

Kill looked him up and down. "I have heard the White-Wings are not bad at the shield wall." The twitch of a smile at her lips.

Ert smiled back. "I have heard that said," he answered.

"We will need the shield wall on the morrow, and you would be welcome in our ranks. I have been thinking during the long journey here, how best to face these Revenants."

"With our runed blades in their hearts," Cullen snapped.

"Aye, but if my thinking is right we will still be heavily out-numbered. They are like a flood."

"They are," Ert agreed.

"Well, I have had an idea, and have been drilling my shield wall in it, but I would be glad if the White-Wings would join us and tell me what you think of it?"

"I am intrigued," Ert said.

"Good," Kill said.

Byrne smiled grimly. "Come, join us, Ert, and together maybe we can work out how to defeat our enemies and take Asroth's head."

"Best thing I've heard all day," Cullen whispered.

Riv stood with her back to a tree, looking at Byrne, who was sitting upon her mare, before the massed warband. Giants, Ben-Elim, the Sirak, White-Wings, Queen Nara and the warriors of Ardain. And the Order of the Bright Star. Talking crows, bears, wolven-hounds.

So many of us, all with one thing in common. An enemy that would take everything from us. All that we love. She glanced at Bleda, who was close by, surrounded by his Sirak warriors.

Pale moonlight gleamed on the water, reflecting into the forest.

"The day is finally here," Byrne said. "The Battle of the Banished Lands upon us. Some here have waited two thousand years for it, some a few score. For me, it feels as if I have been waiting all of my life." She looked at the faces staring back at her. "Our enemy are out there, and they would take everything from us. Take this land, take our homes, our families, our loved ones. Our lives. Make no mistake, Asroth wants it all."

A silence settled over them.

"I say no. Not this day, not *ever.*"

Byrne looked up, along the ranks facing her. "Take your weapons and face your fear. There is only one hope today. And that hope is you." She pointed at a warrior standing before her. "And you." She pointed at another. "And you." She gestured at them all. "We are all the Banished Lands has left, we are this world's last hope. Today there will be a reckoning. Today will be a time of vengeance." She nodded, looked along the rowed ranks, muscles in her face twitching. "Today will be a time of COURAGE!"

Riv felt her blood stir, her weariness washed away.

"Take your Courage, and let's go fight the devil with it," Byrne said.

"COURAGE!" the warband roared back.

CHAPTER NINETY-SEVEN

FRITHA

Fritha woke suddenly.

Something is wrong. She was sitting in a high-backed chair in Balara's feast-hall, a grey light starting to seep in through the doorway and shuttered windows. Asroth was in a chair beside her, one leg slung over the chair's arm, his chest rising and falling in sleep. All around the hall Kadoshim and their half-breed children slept. It had been a night of great celebration, but Fritha had eaten little and drunk less. She felt surprisingly flat, a dark melancholy settling over her. They had won a great victory. A lifetime of hoping and planning, of blood and toil and labour, always working towards one end.

Victory over the Ben-Elim.

And here it was, virtually complete. The Ben-Elim were certainly broken and scattered. Fritha did not know how many had survived yesterday's battle, but it could not be more than a few hundred. White feathers had littered the field.

She looked at Asroth, asleep in his chair.

He was magnificent yesterday. A god of war. He slew and slew and slew. And he saved me when I needed him. When the giant's flame had cut me off and left me to face three thousand White-Wings, he crossed the flame, saved me.

But even that was troubling Fritha.

I never knew he had such power, that he was an Elemental. He commanded the ground to change for him, and it did. Yet there has been no hint or display of that power, until yesterday.

Why didn't he tell me?

I do not trust him.

She shook her head.

Stop being so maudlin.

She stood and padded quietly from the chamber, knew that sleep was beyond her.

Guards stood at the hall's doors, acolytes and Kadoshim. They dipped their heads as she walked past them. A slither and hiss of scales on stone and Elise emerged from the shadows, joined her.

"Can't sleep," Fritha explained.

"I sssleep little, now," Elise said.

Fritha nodded. She looked north, saw a thick bank of black mist filling the street that led into the northern quarter of the fortress.

That is where Gulla sleeps, surrounded by his Revenants. His two remaining captains were supposed to be stationed north and west of Balara, guarding their flanks. They were in the shadows of the forest, most likely stripping Sarva of its blood-filled inhabitants.

Fritha turned south, not wanting to enter Gulla's territory. Elise followed her and they passed along a wide street, its buildings filled with warriors, Aenor's acolytes. The Cheren and Shekam were camped out on the plain, preferring to be close to their horses and draigs.

They reached the gates, barred and guarded, a brazier burning. Fritha and Elise climbed a stairwell and stood on the battlements. A cold breeze stirred Fritha's pale hair, felt good on her skin. The sun was rising, just a thin line of gold on the horizon. To the south Ripa still burned, a blue glow.

Fritha frowned, shook her head.

"What'sss wrong?" Elise asked her.

"I don't know," Fritha said. "It's like something is...missing." Then she knew. "My Ferals." Always she could feel her creations, a distant whisper, a caress in her blood. "They are gone."

Fritha looked to the forest, a dark, impenetrable sea, swaying, stirring in the wind. Gulla's Revenants were supposed to be filling the forest's borders, guarding their flank, but Fritha did not trust them, or Gulla, so she had sent her Ferals deeper into the forest, placing them as scouts against any sneaky tricks Byrne might be thinking of.

But she knew, beyond all doubt, that her Ferals were gone.

Have Gulla's Revenants eaten them?

She felt a stab of fury at that thought.

Then movement caught her eye, on the plain, between Balara and Ripa.

At the same time, a sound grew within the forest, maybe half a league south and west. Branches scraping, shaking, and a shrieking, rising in volume.

"Sound the call to arms," Fritha said.

CHAPTER NINETY-EIGHT

DREM

"There," Drem said.

Dawn was a hint in the air, the solid mass of night breaking down into degrees of shadow. Drem was peering around a wide tree trunk, Faelan and Ethlinn behind him.

He was looking at a dell amongst the trees, a dip in the land before the hill that rose to the fortress of Balara. As Drem stared he saw a denser shadow within the dell, tendrils of mist curling sluggishly from it.

Ethlinn and Faelan looked where he was pointing. Faelan grunted his agreement.

"I can't see them," Ethlinn said.

"They are there," Faelan said.

"Good. Let's do this, then," Ethlinn said. She turned and strode away, Drem following, Faelan taking to the air. Four hundred paces deeper into the forest Drem saw Friend waiting for him, amongst what looked like a wall of giant bears, all of them harnessed and buckled into coats of mail. The Order's huntsmen were scattered amongst them, Drem spotting Reng. Wolven-hounds padded in the shadows.

Ethlinn climbed into her saddle upon a huge brown bear. Alcyon was there, sitting upon Hammer, other giants on foot spread amongst them, including Balur One-Eye and Tain. A murder of crows squawked in the branches above him.

"Revenants are there," Ethlinn said. She lifted a long spear from a saddle-cup. "Remember, only use your runed blades. We need to put these creatures down."

Balur One-Eye reached over his back and drew Sig's long-sword. He gripped it two-handed, sliced the air with it.

Drem remembered that blade, remembered Sig wielding it. Abruptly, he found his chest filling with emotion, found it hard to breathe.

"Today you will be avenged, Sig," Balur rumbled, putting the blade to his lips.

"Yes," Drem murmured.

A bear growled; Drem realized it was Hammer.

"Let's be to it, then," Balur said, looking up at Ethlinn.

Drem climbed into his saddle, settled himself, then drew his father's sword. It still didn't feel a natural part of him, but seax and axe were not right for this, he needed a weapon with a longer reach from Friend's saddle.

He looked around him, saw Fen in his coat of mail.

"You be careful," Drem told him.

Ethlinn rode forwards. A hundred giant bears, another hundred or so giants on foot; a hundred and fifty warriors of the Order, all hunters, accompanied by their wolven-hounds, followed. Drem spotted movement in the air above them, saw Faelan and other wings.

Drem rode with Reng, who led the hunters wide, moving on the left flank of the bears. Balur and the giants on foot filtered to the right flank, Ethlinn's line of bear-riders filling the centre.

They moved through the forest, dawn's grey light all around them now. Birds squawked in trees, startled by their passing. The ground trembled.

This is not a stealth attack. Those Revenants must know we are here.

Trees thinned around them and Drem saw the dell up ahead, the Revenants' mist clear now.

"*Cumhacht an aeir, scrios an dorchadas seo ón talamh,*" Ethlinn called out, as she rode through the forest, lifting her arms.

"*Cumhacht an aeir, scrios an dorchadas seo ón talamh.*" Other giants added their voices to hers, a deep-booming chant like a war-song as they rumbled closer to the dell.

Drem heard sounds issuing from the mist, saw it start to seethe and bubble, shapes moving.

"*Cumhacht an aeir, scrios an dorchadas seo ón talamh,*" Ethlinn and her giants continued to chant, and Drem felt a wind pick up from behind him, swirling through the trees and rushing past him, growing in power and velocity. Drem saw the moment it collided with the mist, a swelling in the air as the mist resisted, making his ears pop, then the mist was tearing and shredding, evaporating, revealing a horde of Revenants within, pale-faced, long-taloned, mouths gaping and razored teeth champing. They were running towards Ethlinn and the line of bears.

I hate Revenants.

Ethlinn levelled her spear and her bear broke into a loping charge.

Bears and Revenants crashed together in a bone-splintering impact, Revenants hurled into the air, trampled, skewered and sliced by rune-marked weapons. It seemed to Drem that a wall of blue fire erupted as the first ranks of the Revenants were decimated.

The bears ploughed on, Revenants screaming their death-rage.

Reng led Drem and the hunters in a looping circle through the trees, cutting back in ahead of Ethlinn's host as they began to slow, the sheer press of Revenants bogging them down. Drem gripped his sword, saw wolven-hounds loping around him, low to the ground as if they were stalking an elk, breaking into a run. Drem shouted a word to Friend and the bear increased his speed, breaking away from Reng and the other hunters, and then he was crashing into the flank of the Revenants, Friend trampling, crushing, rending with his jaws. Drem saw Revenants fall away, chests caved in, half of their face torn away, only for them to jerk back to their feet and throw themselves at Friend. Drem swung his sword, blue flame crackling, and then

Reng and his riders were charging into the flank, spears and swords stabbing, and this time Revenants were falling and not getting back up.

Shadows flitted overhead, arrows hissing down into the press of Revenants between Drem and Ethlinn's bear-riders, more bursts and sparks of blue flame, and far away Drem heard the battle roar of Balur One-Eye and heard the impact as his giants ploughed into the Revenants' right flank.

Drem slashed and hacked to either side of him, cutting the creatures off Friend. To his side he glimpsed Reng stabbing a spear into a Revenant that was rolling with Fen on the ground, all along the line hunters working with their wolven-hounds.

They had slain hundreds in the first few heartbeats of their attack, but Drem saw more, maybe thousands.

A Revenant leaped at Friend, its claws raking across the bear's coat of mail, somehow finding a purchase and scrambling up towards Drem. He stabbed his sword down, into the Revenant's mouth, but before his blade touched the Revenant it was abruptly still, staring into the distance. Then it sighed, slumped and slithered down Friend's side, collapsing into a boneless heap on the floor.

All around Drem the Revenants fell, the echo of battle fading.

Drem looked around, searching for who had slain the Revenants' captain. Then a victory cry drifted down from above, Faelan swooping low. He was brandishing his bow, whooping. Drem cheered, along with three hundred others.

"A great victory," Ethlinn called up to the half-breed Ben-Elim.

"Aye," Balur agreed, striding amongst the Revenant dead. "Now let's get on and find Byrne. Don't want to be late for the battle of the century." He patted his sword and rested it over one shoulder.

Silently they moved on, the trees thinning around them, in the distance Balara's hill becoming visible, and the plain beyond it.

CHAPTER NINETY-NINE

FRITHA

Fritha climbed onto Wrath's back and buckled her helmet strap under her chin.

"Where have you been?" Fritha asked the draig.

"*Humping,*" Wrath growled. "*Shekam draig pretty.*"

"Well, as long as you've got some strength left for today," Fritha said.

"*Wrath STRONG!*" the draig roared, lashing his tail.

The clatter of hooves and Arn was riding into the court-yard, leading Fritha's honour guard. Seventy warriors had survived yesterday's battle. Elise slithered beside them, looking glorious in her mail and helm, a round shield on one arm, her black-bladed spear in her fist. The courtyard was heaving with acolytes as Aenor shouted them into rowed order.

Aenor looked up at Fritha, scabbed cuts across his face, a bandage around his ankle visible beneath his greaves. He hefted his shield, slung it across his back.

"Think I'll be off," he grunted at her.

"Kill your enemies, and stay alive," Fritha said to him. "You fought White-Wings yesterday. The Order of the Bright Star will be easy in comparison. They don't know how to form a shield wall."

He gave her a smile.

"I'll see you after," he said, and led over a thousand acolytes out of the courtyard and down the hill.

Asroth stalked into view, his long axe slung over his back. Kadoshim thick as a cloak trailed behind him. Sulak was there.

Asroth was limping, a fresh bandage bound around his lower leg where the half-breed Ben-Elim had cut him, and he was rolling and flexing his arm where she had stabbed him with Morn's starstone knife.

Asroth climbed into the saddle of his huge stallion, an acolyte standing at its head, holding the bridle. Asroth took the reins, then looked at Fritha.

"Being flesh is not all wonderful," he said, flexing his bicep where he had been stabbed. "I am not so keen on this pain."

Fritha had tended his wounds last night. Cleaned them, packed them with healing herbs, said a word of power over them to speed the healing and then bandaged them with fresh linen.

"Can you wield your axe?" she asked him.

"Aye," Asroth rumbled. "Though it hurts."

"Pain is a badge, an emblem and reminder of what we go through," Fritha said. "Nothing easy is worth having."

"Human wisdom," Asroth muttered.

"The pain will pass," Fritha said. "This victory will last forever."

"Ha, now that is more to my liking." Asroth smiled. He looked out through the gates of Balara, his expression changing, draining of all warmth and becoming something cold. A dark malice pulsed from him. He lifted his helm from its saddle hook and lowered it onto his head, shook the mail curtain into place across his neck, then buckled the chinstrap. "Let's go and take that victory."

Asroth rode out through the gates onto the hill, Fritha behind him. A hundred Kadoshim leaped into the sky and flew lazy circles above them, and five hundred acolytes followed them. They marched through the gates, Asroth riding down the curving road that led to the plain. He reined in about a third of the way down the hill.

"A good spot to see what is happening," Asroth said to

Fritha. The Kadoshim dropped to the ground, setting a guard around them. "We'll attack where we're needed."

The ground spread before Fritha like a map. The blue-flicker of Ripa's burning tower glinted in the distance, but Fritha's eyes were drawn much closer, to the plain before Balara's hill. To the west was the Sarva Forest. Fritha looked at it suspiciously. Her Ferals and one of Gulla's captains were supposed to be lurking in those dark shadows, guardians against any flanking attacks. But Fritha had felt the disappearance of her Ferals and heard strange sounds from the forest, and seen the trees shaking. They were silent now.

She had told Asroth, but he hadn't seemed particularly concerned.

On the plain a war-host was crawling across the ground. They were moving slowly, a block of foot-soldiers leading at their centre, somewhere between one and two thousand strong. Fritha could see White-Wings with rectangular shields at the centre, other warriors carrying round shields with the four-pointed star painted upon them. Horses rode on their flanks and spread behind them.

Aenor had reached the foot of the hill. His warband marched forwards. Fritha felt a vibration in the ground, shivering up through Wrath, and then from the east the Shekam appeared. Rok led them upon his huge draig, over two hundred draigs scuttling across the ground, taking up a position on Aenor's right flank, between his force and the forest. The drumming of hooves and Jin was leading her Cheren riders onto the field, moving into position on Aenor's left flank.

Aenor marched on, the Shekam and Cheren keeping pace with him, all of them inching closer to the Order of the Bright Star. Faint horn blasts echoed up the hill and Aenor's warriors came to a halt, the Shekam and Cheren settling either side of them, like arched wings.

Horns sounded from the Order of the Bright Star as well, and their forces came rippling to a stop.

A stillness lay over the plain. The hissing of the wind, horses whinnying, harnesses creaking. Fritha could feel Wrath's deep breaths, his ribs expanding and deflating, and beneath all of it she felt the beating of her heart. A wild elation coursed through her.

"GULLA!" Asroth cried, his voice echoing across the hill and plain.

Another long, protracted silence, Fritha twisting to look back at the fortress. Black vapour curled up over the walls, a sound rising, like the rushing of the wind, and then the mist was bursting through the open gates like vomit, the fortress disgorging its inhabitants in a dark, talon-filled mass. Fritha had a glimpse of Gulla, wreathed in mist, flying above his creatures as they spilt down the hill, an endless torrent curling to the left and right around Asroth, Fritha and their warriors and reforming lower down the slope, like a river swirling around a boulder. Gulla and his last captain, thousands of Revenants under their control. They swept on, passing across an open space between the Shekam and the acolytes, and then coalesced into a solid block across the front of Asroth's war-host.

They did not pause there, but just carried on towards the Order of the Bright Star.

RIV

Riv stood next to the shield wall on the plain and watched the black wave of Revenants hurtling towards them. Kill stood close to her, the agreed commander of the shield wall foot-troops, with Ert and the White-Wing survivors gathered in the front ranks and heart of the formation.

Further back Riv saw Fritha and her draig upon a hill, a figure upon a horse that could only be Asroth. She felt the heat of grief and rage swell within her.

Asroth, you will die this day, she swore. With an act of will stopped herself from soaring into the air and flying at him. *Keep to the plan. Byrne is right, we can win, we can slay Asroth, but only if we all work together.* She sucked in a long, unsteady breath, held it a few moments before breathing out, trying to take the edge from her rage.

Byrne rode up along one flank of the warband, over a thousand survivors from Ripa at its core, another five hundred warriors of the Order upon each wing, all on foot.

Byrne rode out beyond Kill and Riv, a glance at them, then she was facing the wall of black mist as it came speeding towards them. About a score of warriors followed her.

Byrne lifted her hands into the air.

"*Cumhacht an aeir, scrios an dorchadas seo ón talamh,*" Byrne cried out. "*Cumhacht an aeir, scrios an dorchadas seo ón talamh,*" she repeated, and then Kill and the others were crying out the same words.

"*Cumhacht an aeir, scrios an dorchadas seo ón talamh.*"

A wind rose up, sweeping across the plain, tugging at warrior braids and tunics. It swirled around Byrne and her group of riders, and then burst away from Byrne, almost a physical thing, like a horse kept too long in a stable. The wind swept towards the bank of mist and tore into it, shredding it into tendrils and wisps in a dozen heartbeats, exposing the Revenant horde within. They were charging towards them, a mass of sharp teeth and talons. A Kadoshim flew above them.

"Always better to see who you have to kill," Byrne said as she looked back to Riv, Ert and Kill.

The Revenants were less than a thousand paces away, covering the ground at a terrifying speed.

Byrne drew a knife from her belt and pulled it across her palm.

"*LASAIR!*" she cried out, sprinkling blood onto the ground in front of her. Flames crackled into life. The riders about Byrne did the same, a line of fire leaping up. A flick of her reins and Byrne began to canter along the front of the shield wall, continuing to scatter her blood over the ground, repeating her command of "*LASAIR!*" More fire bloomed. Her riders broke into two groups, half riding with Byrne, the other half heading in the other direction, creating a wall of flame before the shield wall.

"WARRIORS!" Kill cried out, stepping back into the first line.

Riv leaped into the air, beat her wings and rose higher, above the flames. Hovered. The Revenant horde came hurtling on, uncaring of the flames.

"SHIELD WALL!" Kill yelled, echoed by Ert, and rows of shields, both rectangular and round, came up and slammed together, a crack of thunder.

The first Revenants hit the wall of flame, burst through

it shrieking, engulfed. They stumbled forwards, collapsed to the ground, but the screams and death did not deter the horde behind them. Hundreds, thousands crashed through the wall of fire, so many that the flames began to thin. Revenants pounded over the dead, began to avoid the stuttering flames, came on charging at the shield wall.

"WEAPONS!" Ert bellowed, and Riv heard the hiss of blades leaving scabbards, like the wind through grass.

The flames were all but trampled out of existence, suffocated by the weight of bodies crashing through them.

"WARRIORS!" Kill cried out. "SHIELDBURG!"

The warriors in the front row of the shield wall dropped to their knees, warriors on the flanks doing the same, shields still interlocked, but resting upon the ground, now. The second row, still standing, lifted their shields to lock above the first rows. From the third-row back shields came up to sit horizontally over their heads, like a roof. They formed an impenetrable fortress, sealed on all sides, with small gaps between the shields left for stabbing their rune-marked blades through.

The Revenants hit them, an unstoppable wave, a bone-jarring collision. The shield wall buckled, but held. The first ranks of the attackers were hurled onwards, skidding across the roof of shields, scrambling, tearing at the wood and iron, trying to find purchase.

The only gaps had blades slipped through them. Sharp steel stabbed upwards and outwards, and suddenly Revenants were screeching and hissing, blue flame crackling as they were stabbed, injured and slain.

Riv took her bow from her case and reached for a fistful of grey-feathered arrows, began to nock, draw and loose. It was perfect, like having rats in a barrel, the Revenants a swarming, seething, increasingly frenzied mass. Blue sparks of flame burst with every arrow she loosed.

There were so many of them, though. Many were held in the press against the front row of the shieldburg, but their numbers were so great that Revenants began to seep around the flanks of the shieldburg, surrounding it. Shield rims were grabbed, torn at, warriors dragged out of formation and torn apart.

Horns blared behind Riv and the riders on each flank of the shield wall moved forwards. Queen Nara led the left flank, five hundred warriors of Ardain, her battlechief Elgin leading the right flank with another five hundred warriors. All of them were armed with runed weapons, spears in their fists.

They broke from a trot into a canter, riding in at an angle on the Revenants' flanks.

FRITHA

Fritha watched the battle unfold with a growing seed of dread in her belly. The wall of flames she had expected, but she had never seen this shield wall manoeuvre performed and it had worked annoyingly well, holding the Revenants in place with what looked like very few casualties. And now mounted warriors were moving on the flanks of the besieged White-Wings, breaking into a canter and charging at the Revenants. Even from her high vantage point Fritha could see the crackle of blue flame as the riders hit the Revenants, could hear the hissing screams. Fritha huffed her annoyance. Revenants were falling in huge numbers, piling around the tight-packed shields.

Does every warrior down there carry a rune-marked blade?

Asroth made a growling sound in the back of his throat.

"Send them all in," he said to the acolyte beside him. "There will be no waiting. Send them all in."

The acolyte lifted a horn to her lips and blew.

On the plain the Cheren and Shekam began to move, Jin and Rok leading their Clans. The solid block of acolytes in the centre lurched into motion, and behind Fritha she heard the beating of over a thousand pairs of wings.

Asroth looked at Fritha.

"Fly with me, my bride," he said. "No more waiting, no more strategy," he snarled, clenching his fist. "We will crush our enemy, drive them before us, grind their blood and bones into the ground. Right now."

RIV

Riv had almost emptied her quiver of runed arrows, only four or five left. She paused, wanting to hold onto those, in case she saw a Revenant captain, or Gulla himself. The riders of Ardain had held the Revenants back from spilling around the shieldburg's flanks and the creatures were turning upon Nara and Elgin's units now, leaping and tearing at horses, dragging riders from their saddles. But blue flame continued to spark, and Revenants continued to die. The numbers were rapidly becoming more even.

Riv gave a fierce smile. For once a plan was working well. And then she heard the horns. She looked up, saw Fritha upon her draig and Asroth beside her. Warriors and Kadoshim were arrayed about them, around five hundred acolytes on foot, Kadoshim in the air.

The Cheren, who had been deployed upon the plain directly ahead of Riv, moved forwards. Two thousand horse, at least, heading for Elgin's riders. And on the far flank the Shekam lurched into motion on their draigs, lumbering towards Nara's warriors.

More movement drew her eye, up on the hill, behind Asroth and Fritha.

Winged warriors rose into the air from within Balara's walls, Kadoshim and their half-breed offspring. The sky was thick with them, more than a thousand, far more than there were Ben-Elim left in a condition able to fly. They swept over Balara's walls and sped down the hill, low to the ground, over the battlefield.

JIN

Jin lifted her bow from her case, reaching for arrows.

Her head hurt, a throbbing pain with each pulse of her heart, waves of nausea rippling through her belly. Her leg ached, too, had been so stiff and swollen when she awoke before dawn that for a moment she had thought she would not be able to walk. She did not care. Nothing except death would stop her fighting. Yesterday's defeat in the hills had rocked and enraged her. Today she would kill her enemies and prove to her warband that she deserved the king's band.

Gerel and Tark were either side of her, her captains and warriors spreading behind her like the wings of the hawk that snapped on their banners.

The enemy were close, five or six hundred paces away. She saw a banner of a black snarling wolf upon a grey field.

Jin nocked her first arrow, saw a grey-bearded warrior, straight-backed, a fine coat of mail and a sword in his fist.

He is leading them.

A word to her mount and she moved into a fast canter. Two hundred paces away. Close enough to loose, if her target was leather and flesh, but not if she wanted her arrows to pierce mail.

Some amongst her enemy were looking now, had seen this new threat. The old grey-beard was shouting orders, a horn blowing, warriors peeling away, lining up to face the Cheren charge, thirty, forty, fifty warriors, a hundred, more joining them. They spurred their horses on, spears levelling. The grey-beard led them.

Jin grinned. A foe with courage. She liked that.

She bent low over her saddle, drew and loosed, once, twice, three times, saw her first arrow land, the old man sway in his saddle, the second and third arrows punching into his chest. His spear dropped from his hand and he toppled over the back of his saddle.

A storm of arrows flew from behind Jin, slamming into the riders charging at them, the Cheren *yipping* and shouting as they charged.

BLEDA

Bleda felt the tremor in the ground as the Shekam's draigs powered across the plain towards Queen Nara and her warriors. He looked at his warband behind him, saw Yul and Ruga, Ellac, Saran, Oktai, so many more who had followed him. He felt proud of what they had accomplished. He knew the Cheren were on the field, had seen them on the opposite flank before the Revenants had flooded the field between them. But he also knew that they no longer numbered the four or five thousand warriors who had originally given chase to him, right back at the Sirak Heartland.

He was itching to kill more of them, memories of the Cheren's betrayal that day on Forn's eastern road flooding his mind.

The Cheren will have to wait for later. First we must protect our friends, and stay alive.

"Their armour is thick," he cried out, "and the draig's skin is like mail. You must be close for our arrows to pierce them. But they are slow, where we are fast, and our arrows are accurate. Aim for their eyes."

A flick of his reins. "Carry me once more, my faithful friend," Bleda whispered, patting Dilis' neck. She whinnied at him and broke into a canter. He reached for his bow, then for a fistful of arrows. The Sirak cantered behind him, spreading wide like wings, their hooves a rumbling thunder, heading at an angle to hit the Shekam before they could plough into Nara's warband. That would mean destruction for his allies.

Movement in the sky drew Bleda's eye and he saw a cloud of Kadoshim and their half-breed offspring winging across the battlefield, moving fast and low. Hundreds of them, more, over a thousand. He saw them pass over the acolyte foot-soldiers on the plain, who were marching forwards in loose order. The Kadoshim split apart, breaking into two groups, veering left and right of the shieldburg and Revenants, swooping low to stab and slash at Ardain's riders.

Bleda raised a hand, pointed at the Kadoshim flying over Queen Nara's warriors and changed his course. He rode towards them, sweeping in close to Nara, saw her stabbing a Revenant with her spear, Kadoshim above her hovering, jabbing, looping and slashing with swords and spears. Queen Nara's riders were screaming and falling.

Bleda raised his bow and loosed, saw his arrow slam into a Kadoshim's side, punching through mail and leather into flesh. It fell screeching from the sky. Behind him his Sirak followed him in a looping curve towards Nara's warband, sending volley after volley into the sky. Kadoshim and half-breeds were falling, crashing to the ground, studded with arrows.

Many of the Kadoshim saw their kin falling about them and wheeled higher, screeching, moving out of range, giving Queen Nara and her warriors a reprieve. She saw Bleda and dipped her head in thanks. He pointed to the Shekam, who were thundering across the plain towards them. Nara's eyes widened as she stared at the giants and draigs, a ripple of fear, then she was shouting orders, a horn blowing, and her riders were peeling away from the Revenants, forming a loose line a few columns deep and riding at the Shekam. Bleda respected that.

Bleda was ahead of them, riding hard. He swerved away then veered back in, his warband following him like a flock of birds wheeling in the sky. He charged at the Shekam, was close enough to see scales on the draigs' flat muzzles, tattoos of thorn and vine curling up arms and disappearing beneath leather and fish-scale armour.

Fifty paces, forty, twenty, the world a thundering storm around him, the very earth seemed to be shaking.

He leaned low in his saddle and chose a giant, a woman, one of their long-bladed spears in her hands. She saw him, her draig shifting to meet him. He nocked and loosed, nocked and loosed, saw his first arrow skitter off the giant's lamellar coat, the second pierce her thigh, the third punch through her plate coat into her shoulder. Then her spear was swinging at him and he was throwing himself to the side, gripping the saddle pommel with one hand, guiding Dilis wide. The spear hissed through the air above him and he thundered past the giant, dragging himself upright, snatching at arrows and putting all three into the next draig as he sped past it.

Behind him he heard a crunching impact and the screaming of horses. He saw his Sirak were amongst the Shekam, swerving between draigs, arrows hissing through the air like hornets. Giants were falling, draigs screaming, some stumbling and collapsing, their hides pin-cushioned, some with arrows buried deep in their eye-sockets, but Sirak were falling, too, draigs lashing out with claws, lacerating flesh, huge jaws snapping, tearing at horses, snatching riders from their saddles. Bleda snarled and urged his horse back into the blood and death.

FRITHA

Wrath flew over the plain, Fritha watching the battle unfold. Asroth flew beside her, a hundred Kadoshim surrounding them. On the ground below, Arn led Fritha's honour guard down the hill, Elise slithering along beside them. Only the five hundred acolytes remained on the hill, Asroth's honour guard. He had ordered them to hold their position.

Fritha and Asroth passed over Aenor's acolytes, over a thousand warriors marching in loose order.

The shieldburg was still holding, a tide of Revenants swarming over it like ants. On the flanks a swirling battle raged between Jin's Cheren, who were slaughtering mounted warriors, and the Shekam upon their draigs carving into the riders who had attacked the Revenants' flank. She glimpsed other riders, like the Cheren, loosing arrows at draigs, so they had to be the Sirak.

That must be Bleda the Cunning, she thought, remembering how one of Jin's captains had spoken of Bleda during the feast last night.

And above all of this the Kadoshim and their offspring swirled above the battle, swooping and stabbing. Beyond the shieldburg there was a large block of riders, as yet not committed to the battle. They were moving, now, splitting into two groups. That concerned Fritha, as Asroth had thrown all of their host into this battle, with only the acolytes on the hill in reserve, and they were too far away to achieve anything. There was no time to worry, though, the battle was rushing towards them.

"Me first," Asroth said, as he twisted through the air, speeding towards the shieldburg.

The din of battle eddied up to Fritha on a wind from the south, but over it all she heard Asroth's voice, deep and sonorous.

"*Talamh, croith, ceangail mo namhaid,*" he cried, descending towards the battlefield.

The shieldburg still stood, shields battered and torn, but solid, and dead Revenants ringed it like sand piled by the sea.

Asroth alighted on the ground, strode on a few steps, his wings folding behind him.

"*Talamh, croith, ceangail mo namhaid,*" he cried out again, raising his palms.

The ground between Asroth and the shieldburg rippled, as if a huge serpent were passing beneath it. There was a tremor in the shields, gaps opening as warriors stumbled and swayed. Asroth's hundred Kadoshim landed behind him, curled around him, swords and spears raised.

"*TALAMH, CROITH, CEANGAIL MO NAMHAID!*" Asroth bellowed, at the same time shrugging his long axe from his back.

The ground shuddered, soil exploding beneath the shieldburg. Warriors were thrown in all directions, fell stumbling into the open. Asroth strode forwards, his axe swinging in a great looping arc, and shields were splintered, bodies broken.

Part of the shieldburg collapsed, a large area of the ground before Asroth shifting like quicksand, warriors sinking into it, trying to pull free, Asroth's axe chopping into them, cutting them down like wheat at harvest. Asroth pushed into the shieldburg, the rippling shifting away from him, ground solidifying beneath his feet as he trod upon it.

Orders were bellowed as White-Wings tried to reform into better shape, others running at him, weapons raised. Kadoshim swept in, guarding Asroth's flanks, stabbing and cutting, warriors falling, some defending against the Kadoshim, fighting back as Asroth carved ever deeper, like a wedge hammered into the crack of a stone.

And then Fritha was muttering to Wrath, the draig's wings shifting, tilting, banking to the left, hurtling straight towards the eastern flank of the shieldburg, where warriors with round shields were reorganizing into a shield wall.

"Smash them," Fritha said to Wrath.

DREM

Drem's hand moved absently to the pulse at his throat.

He had never seen such a scene before. The battles in the Desolation and at Dun Seren were as nothing compared to this. To the north there was a mass of acolyte warriors marching at speed towards the battle. In front of him giants upon draigs were thundering across the plain, Drem glimpsing Bleda's Sirak and warriors of Ardain flitting amongst them, behind them a shield wall made of White-Wings and warriors of the Order. In the skies Kadoshim and their offspring flew, swooping and shrieking. The noise was deafening—shouting, screaming, roaring, the clash of steel—all of it blending into a colossal, vocal pandemonium. He resisted the urge to put his hands over his ears.

Beyond the draigs and riders something was happening to the shield wall. It was rippling and swaying, warriors falling. A figure in dark mail and black wings was wielding a long axe in great, looping circles.

"Asroth," Ethlinn growled.

He was taller than all those around him. White-Wings ran at him and were hacked down with his axe. He seemed unstoppable.

And then Drem saw something in the sky, low, hurtling towards the shield wall.

A draig with wings. And Fritha was upon its back.

She killed my da. And she killed Sig.

The anxiety in his veins shifted, something both hot and cold running through them. His fingers twitched for his seax.

The draig smashed into the shield wall, a concussive explosion.

"Ach, we're late," Balur One-Eye spat. "Best be getting in there before it's all over. Asroth needs putting down, and his pet draig."

"Yes," Drem growled, a hot anger melting his fear.

"We will have to carve a way to him through the Shekam and their draigs," Ethlinn said.

"Aye," Ukran grinned, as if he were looking forward to it. He hefted a double-bladed battle-axe.

Drem had thought the Shekam and their draigs would be unstoppable; he remembered full well his encounter with one draig in the Bonefells. Even Hammer, a giant bear, had been hard-pressed. But Bleda had spoken to them all during the night, assured them they could be beaten, with the right tactics: his Sirak archers and a flanking attack from Ethlinn and her bear-riders. The draigs outnumbered them, but the bears were all wearing coats of mail, which helped to balance the odds. Drem had believed Bleda and trusted his plan. Now, though, seeing the draigs and giants . . .

Bleda and his Sirak are slowing them, so perhaps he was right. But he is alone, outnumbered, he needs us, now.

"This is as far as you go," Tain said to Craf, who was perched upon his shoulder. Other crows flew in a slow spiral high above the crow and crow master.

"*Craf brave, Craf fight,*" the crow squawked.

"I know you're brave," Tain said gently, "but we need your eyes and your wits more than your beak and talons. Here," Tain said, offering his wrist to Craf. The crow jumped onto it and Tain lifted his arm up into the boughs of a tree that loomed over them.

"*Craf watch, think, help,*" the crow said, and then hopped onto a branch. "*Tain be careful, or Craf be sad.*"

Raina shrugged her round shield from her shoulder and took her single-handed hammer from her belt. Rolled her wrist. All along the line warriors checked weapons, adjusted grips. Drem pulled on the buckle of his iron helm, making sure it was tight. He took his round shield from its saddle hook and checked the grip, then tugged his boiled leather gloves on and drew his sword.

"On me," Ethlinn said, and without another word she was riding out from the trees onto the plain, her long spear in her fist. Balur strode at her side.

Drem looked down at Reng, who led the Order's huntsmen.

"I'll swing wide and hit those big bastards from the other flank," Reng said. "You're welcome to join us, but probably best if your white-furred friend charges with the other bears."

"Aye." Drem nodded.

Reng gave him a grim smile. "I'll meet you in the middle," he said, and then he was riding off, the Order's hunters following him, a pack of wolven-hounds wrapped in mail loping across the plain.

Drem saw the Shekam crashing into the bulk of Queen Nara's warriors, heard the screams of horses.

"We've come a long way from the snow and ice of the Bonefells," Drem said, leaning forwards and patting Friend's neck. He blew out a long breath and then Friend was lumbering out from the trees, Fen loping at their side, the three of them quickly catching up with Ethlinn and her giants. Friend made for Hammer and pushed in between her and another bear. Her head swung towards Friend and she rumbled a greeting. Alcyon looked over at Drem and gave him a nod.

"This is it, lad," Alcyon said. "All the grief they've given us and this world. Time to give them some back."

"Yes, it is," Drem said, his eyes searching for Fritha upon her draig.

And then Ethlinn was charging, all of them following.

Drem shifted in his saddle, felt his blood pounding like a

drum in his head, had a flash of his father's face, blood on his lips, heard his father's voice in his head.

Sometimes the only answer is blood and steel.

The gap between bears and draigs closed. Sirak warriors were swerving and wheeling around the Shekam like a swarm of angry bees, Shekam giants roaring and swinging their huge, long-bladed spears. Drem saw a Sirak decapitated, a horse's side opened up from shoulder to flank, another horse hurled from its feet by a draig's lashing tail. But giants and draigs were falling, too, studded with a multitude of arrows. Some of the Shekam were looking their way now, roaring out warnings to their kin, draigs turning. It was too late, Ethlinn's line of bears was an unstoppable avalanche of meat and bone, leather and steel. Balur bellowed a battle-cry, Sig's sword raised high, two-handed over his head.

Sirak riders were bolting away.

Then the bears crashed into the Shekam.

Friend ploughed into the side of a draig, the giant upon its back thrown from his saddle and disappearing in the crush. The impact threw Drem forwards in his saddle. The draig was shoved a score of paces by Friend, claws scrabbling in the dirt for purchase, and then it was coming back at them. Friend lashed out with his claws, opened red lines down the draig's shoulder and neck. The creature roared, head whipping around, jaws biting into Friend's shoulder and chest. The mail protected Friend from the worst of it, but the draig's canines tore through iron links, sinking into the flesh beneath.

Friend's paw slapped the draig's head, raking a bloody trail down the beast's muzzle. Drem leaned and chopped with his father's sword, saw another deep gash open in the draig's shoulder. The animal released its grip on Friend and stumbled away.

The draig's rider appeared, limping, dragging himself back into the saddle. He drew a curved, thick-bladed tulwar that was strapped to the draig's harness.

"On," Drem urged Friend. Blood pulsed from the puncture wounds in Friend's torn mail.

The giant and draig rushed at them, the draig's jaws wide, the giant raising his sword.

They came together in a crash of muscle, fur and scales, teeth clashing as draig and bear tore at each other. The giant swung his curved sword at Drem, who deflected it on his shield, the blow shivering through his arm. Drem steered the blow wide and lunged with his sword. It stabbed into the giant's belly, scraped along mail plates, slipped between two and sliced through leather. The giant yelled as he swung his sword again, Drem throwing himself backwards as the sword hissed past his face.

Drem and the giant were both shaken in their saddles as bear and draig slammed against each other, biting and tearing.

There was a flash of iron and grey fur and Fen was leaping onto the back of the draig and hurling himself at the giant. Jaws clamped on the giant's shoulder and neck, a savage shake of Fen's head and the giant was screaming, blood erupting. Drem stabbed his sword into the giant's throat and he was toppling from his saddle, Fen falling with him, still snarling and tearing.

Friend's muzzle and fur were soaked red, claw marks raking the bear's neck, but the draig was in worse condition. The two beasts were close in size, but Friend's coat of mail had turned the balance and the draig staggered back, a tremor in its legs, its head and neck lacerated. Friend must have bitten deep, because a gout of arterial blood spurted from the draig. It swayed, then its legs gave out and it crashed to the ground, tail lashing.

Drem cuffed sweat from his eyes, his left arm throbbing from the giant's sword-blows upon his shield. Amidst the ever-moving chaos and madness he glimpsed Balur One-Eye, covered in blood, swinging Sig's longsword around his head, chopping into a draig's neck, half-severing it. Ethlinn was upon her bear, swirling her spear two-handed, a clatter of wood and steel as she duelled with a Shekam giant upon a draig. Sirak riders were swerving and loosing arrows. Raina was battered to her knees, holding her shield up as a giant chopped at her, Alcyon bellowing and hacking with his twin axes, trying to reach her. Reng's charge of horse crashed into the Shekam's flank, sixty wolven-hounds running before them, leaping up at draigs and giants in a snarling, snapping wave. Close by, Tain was trading blows with a Shekam giant, Tain stumbling backwards. A squawking, deafening noise above—Drem glanced up to see a murder of huge black crows spinning downwards, swirling about the giant attacking Tain, pecking, raking him with their talons. The giant bellowed, rivulets of blood running down his face. He slashed with his long spear, birds squawking, an explosion of black feathers, a handful of crows falling dead, others continuing their barrage upon him.

He saw Queen Nara, yelling, wielding her sword, rallying her battered warriors. A Shekam giant rode at her, swung his spear, Nara swaying, parrying, but the spear's angle changed, the blade skimming over her sword, chopping into Nara's neck. There was a fountain of blood as she toppled from her saddle. Beside her Madoc, Nara's first-sword, screamed, his horse pressed tight in a melee. In one fluid movement he lifted his feet from his stirrups and stood upon his saddle, dropped his shield and drew a knife from his belt, then leaped at the giant who had slain Nara. He crashed into the Shekam, sword and knife swinging and stabbing, the giant crying out. They tumbled to the ground together.

Drem hefted his shield, gritted his teeth and looked for a way through to Fritha and her draig. He couldn't see her through the tumult of battle, his vision filled with giants and draigs.

I'll have to carve a way to her, he thought, and looked about for someone else to kill. Friend charged at another draig.

RIV

Riv hovered over the shieldburg, watching warriors hurled through the air by the winged draig. She looked at Byrne, who sat upon a horse with a thousand warriors of the Bright Star mounted behind her.

"Now." Byrne nodded, raised her fist. A horn blew.

Ben-Elim lifted into the air, wings beating, a few hundred of them rising from behind Byrne's riders.

Riv's wings beat, taking her higher.

"Riv," a voice called up to her. Meical, sitting upon a white stallion beside Byrne, one of his wing-arches tightly bandaged. Cullen was upon a horse next to him, the young warrior looking as if he was going to explode with frustration.

"Wait for us. We kill Asroth together," Meical said to her.

She looked at him but said nothing, just drew her short-sword and black dagger, a trail of smoke curling around its blade. She flew higher, joining the flight of Ben-Elim, and saw Kol, still bandaged, his face a lattice of scabbed cuts. He held a spear in his fist, a score of his loyal supporters about him. All Riv could think about was her mother, and her killer, Asroth, down in the shield wall with a winged draig beside him. Behind her she heard horns blowing, Byrne's riders moving.

The shield wall was splintering. Asroth was carving a wedge deep into it, his Kadoshim protecting his flanks. Orders and horns were ringing out, the front rows that had already been split apart were trying to form new, smaller shield walls.

They need to do it quickly, Riv thought, seeing a wall of acolytes moving rapidly across the field towards them.

The din of battle rolled across the field in waves. Bears and draigs were fighting in a frenzied maul, Sirak riders swirling through the combat like mist. Riv's eyes searched for Bleda, but there was no chance of recognizing him, the fight too fluid and fast. There was no telling who was winning.

And then she had no more time to think, the Kadoshim suddenly thick in the air about her. She swayed out of the way of a spear-thrust, the blade stabbing past her face; she beat her wings to sweep inside its range, and pushed both of her blades into the Kadoshim's body. It plummeted to the ground. Riv flew on, weaving amongst the Kadoshim and their offspring. A half-breed slammed into her, the two of them locked, spinning, the half-breed headbutting Riv in the face. She heard her nose crunch, breaking for the second time in two days, tasted blood in her throat, shook her head and headbutted the half-breed back. They separated, a clash of steel as Riv parried a sword-blow, slashed with her knife, leaving a red line along the half-breed's forearm.

Then an arrow sprouted from the half-breed's throat, a rush of blood and he gurgled, dropped from the sky. As Riv looked around, a dozen more Kadoshim fell from the sky, all skewered with arrows.

Faelan swooped in, an arrow nocked, his kin swirling in the sky behind him, fifty of them circling the Kadoshim and loosing their arrows.

"Well met, sister," Faelan said to Riv. She grinned at him and nodded her thanks. Faelan flew on, leading his kin around the edges of the conflict, picking off Kadoshim and half-breeds. The aerial combat was fragmenting now, spreading wide over the field as Ben-Elim and Kadoshim whirled and dived and looped around each other.

Riv used this brief reprieve to look at the battlefield. Jin and her Cheren had decimated the warriors of Ardain on this flank and she was now leading her Clan in sweeping attacks on the shield wall.

Asroth had carved deep into the shield wall's centre, killing all that appeared before him with his fell axe, Kadoshim guarding his flanks as knots of White-Wings and warriors of the Order hurled themselves at the Kadoshim's king.

They need to retreat and regroup, attack him properly.

On the plain a host of Revenants stood, still and silent as death. Many of them had fallen, but there were still so many remaining. Too many. A shiver passed through them and, as one, they surged forwards, rushing into the gap Asroth had forged and hurling themselves at White-Wings and warriors of the Order. Riv thought she saw Kill and Ert with a score of warriors about them, shouting, pulling more to them. They held against the Revenants, were slowly retreating.

Further along Fritha sat upon her draig, amidst a pile of the dead, warriors trampled, crushed, torn to pieces. The shield wall here was utterly destroyed, a few hundred pulled back into a new wall. All about the field White-Wings and warriors of the Order were reforming into smaller walls, a hundred warriors here, forty or fifty there.

A wide line of acolytes marched at these smaller defences, their lines tightening.

The drum of hooves, and Byrne, sword drawn, led five hundred riders galloping around the back of the splintered shieldburg.

"TRUTH AND COURAGE!" Byrne and her warband yelled, the war-cry rippling over the battlefield.

"TRUTH AND COURAGE!" rang out from the western flank of the field, where Cullen was leading the rest of Byrne's mounted warriors.

Riv was about to drop into a dive and try to help Kill and Ert when her eye was drawn to two figures on the plain.

The acolytes had parted for them, swept around them. One Kadoshim, one Revenant. They were standing side by side.

Is that...?

Riv sheathed her sword and threaded the black knife into her belt, then reached for her bow.

Gulla...

JIN

Jin reined in, Gerel beside her, a permanent presence. The enemy she had been sent to attack were all dead, hundreds of riders strewn across the ground. She had set her warband to picking the shield wall apart, but now that had ruptured into smaller parts and had been enveloped by the acolyte shield wall. Jin was looking for a new foe, peering to the west, searching for Bleda. Rok with his Shekam upon draigs seemed to be causing havoc, and the Sirak were there.

That is where I need to be.

"TRUTH AND COURAGE!"

Jin looked to the south, saw a mass of riders galloping straight at her warriors.

The Order of the Bright Star.

"Gerel, form up on me," Jin said.

Gerel put his horn to his lips and blew, Cheren riders peeling away and joining Jin. Her horse leaped into a gallop and Jin leaned forwards, her bowstring thrumming at the riders galloping towards her, a swarm of arrows flying from the bows of her warriors straight at the Order of the Bright Star. Jin saw a warrior at their head, red hair streaming from a helm. He seemed to be their leader.

She aimed at him, loosed.

His shield came up, covering his body, warriors behind him doing the same, the hail-hammer of arrows punching into wood.

A few riders screamed, swayed in their saddles, fell, but not nearly enough, and not their red-haired leader. And then it was too late for another volley as the two warbands came crashing together, horseflesh colliding, weaving in amongst each other. Jin slashed at the red-haired warrior, but he turned her blade, struck with his own sword. She swayed, the sword raking her side, and then their momentum carried them apart. The Order's warriors used their shields well, slashed and hacked with their swords and spears, and Jin heard Cheren warriors crying out, falling. Jin swung her sword, a shield coming up to block her blade, a sword stabbing at her. In a few moments she knew her Cheren were outmatched in this close sword-work. A touch of her heels and her mount was dancing away, taking her out of range. A collision of horses and a grunt behind her, Gerel trading blows with a warrior, the two of them looking well-matched.

Gerel swayed in his saddle, a sword-tip hissing past him, and he lunged forwards, stabbed into his opponent's throat.

All around her Jin saw Cheren falling.

"We need to get out of here, find some space for bow work," she called to Gerel.

A shrieking from above and Jin looked up to see Kadoshim and half-breeds swooping down on the new riders, spears and swords stabbing. Warriors of the Bright Star fell.

"Now," Jin said, and she was riding through the throng, the Order's warriors distracted, defending against the foe from above. Gerel followed, blowing his horn, and her warriors began to disengage, riding out from the throng into open ground.

When they were clear Jin looked back, saw the warriors of the Bright Star focused entirely on the Kadoshim who were swooping down at them. Many in the Order were swirling lead-weighted nets over their heads, hurling them into the sky, the nets wrapping around Kadoshim, the weights pulling tight around wings. Kadoshim fell from the sky.

Over a thousand of her warriors were around Jin now, others still trying to disentangle themselves from the melee.

Jin sheathed her sword.

"It is time," Jin said, looking across the open plain to the Sirak on the western flank. "Time for our vengeance. The Sirak are there, and there are no more tricks that will save them. DEATH TO OUR ENEMIES!" she cried, took her bow from its case and began to ride out across the open plain, away from the Order's riders.

Battle raged on her left. She saw Fritha upon her draig, smashing into a shield wall, her snake-woman and her honour guard about her. Then Jin was past them, riding on, Asroth standing tall like an island in the centre of the field, laughing as he killed with his black axe. Revenants and Kadoshim all around him were battling with more of the fragmented shield walls. Everywhere she looked she saw Asroth's warriors prevailing, the enemy hard-pressed, failing.

Ahead and to her right Jin saw two figures standing amongst the dead. Gulla and his last Revenant captain. They were both staring at the Revenants swarming all over shield walls, looks of earnest concentration on their faces.

Are they guiding their Revenants?

The hiss of an arrow from above. It punched into Gulla's foot, a spurt of blue flame. Another arrow close behind, this one piercing the Revenant captain, into the meat between neck and shoulder, angled inwards. A crackle of blue flame and the Revenant dropped to one knee, hands wrapped around the arrow shaft. It was screaming, a hissing shriek.

Another arrow slammed into the ground, and then one more was crunching into the Revenant's skull, blue flame, and the captain dropped like a stone, dead before it hit the ground.

All across the field to Jin's left Revenants collapsed, hundreds of them. A cry rang out from the beleaguered shield walls.

Gulla looked at his dead captain, then up at the sky. An arrow hissed out of the blue, slammed into his shoulder. He shrieked. Spread his wings, took to the sky, speeding across the plain, back towards Balara.

Coward, Jin sneered.

She looked up to the sky, searching for Gulla's assailant.

And then she saw her.

Riv, hovering in the sky, wings beating slowly, a bow in her fist.

The half-breed bitch. No wonder it took her five arrows to kill one Revenant.

Without even thinking, Jin had a fistful of arrows and was launching them all skywards. She smiled when her first arrow punched into Riv's thigh. The second one skittered off her mail, Riv's wings beating, turning, and the third one slammed into the half-breed's back. Jin heard the scream and saw Riv faltering in the sky a moment, then she began to fall, a lurching, stuttered spiral that sent her crashing into the battle on Jin's left.

Jin smiled.

The half-breed whore is down. Just the betrayer to go now. Bleda, I am coming for you.

BLEDA

Bleda swerved around a draig and loosed an arrow into the giant's face, was already past them before the giant began to topple. He twisted in his saddle and loosed two more arrows into the draig, heard it roar, its tail lashing. Then he was reaching for more arrows, ducking as a Shekam giant swung its long spear at him, air hissing past Bleda's throat, and he was riding away.

He broke into open ground, reined in, trying to make sense of what was happening. The field was pandemonium, the battle with the Shekam spreading wide, up to the first trees of the forest. Ruga was close by, loosing a trio of arrows into a draig, planting one of her shafts into its eye. The beast stumbled on a few paces and then collapsed.

Ruga saw him and cantered towards him. She was bloodied, a gash across her cheek and a bloodstain on her breeches, but she was smiling.

"We are *winning*," she said. "These giants might be strong, but they are too slow."

Bleda smiled back at her.

An arrow punched into Ruga's throat, the iron head bursting out of her flesh, a spurt of blood. She dropped her bow, hands coming up to her neck, and opened her mouth, tried to speak. Blood bubbled out of her mouth.

Another arrow slammed into her side and she fell from her saddle.

Bleda yelled, shock and horror washing through him. Beyond her Bleda saw riders in blue deels galloping towards him, bows levelled. Jin was leading them. He jerked in his saddle as arrows flew past him. Grabbing his own arrows, he urged Dilis into movement and she leaped away.

"SIRAK, TO ME!" Bleda cried out. Yul put a horn to his lips and blew. Ellac and a score of Sirak rallied to him. Bleda pointed to the Cheren and broke into a gallop. He heard Sirak ululations behind him, the drum of hooves.

Ruga's face hovered in his mind. His friend. She had been smiling. Blood in her mouth.

Bleda felt his rage boiling and he snarled, then breathed deep, trying to control his anger, finding the calm. Anger made your muscles tremble and jitter, and that was no good for a steady aim.

Another arrow hissed by. He guided his horse as his mother and brother had taught him, remembered what they had said about the duel of arrows, where two riders charged one another with bows in their fists. Swerve left and right, no pattern that your enemy can read, smooth movement, stay low in your saddle, almost hugging your horse's neck, give your enemy the smallest target.

He nocked, drew and loosed, nocked, drew and loosed, saw Jin sway in her saddle, his arrows piercing a rider behind her, who toppled over the back of his saddle. Behind Bleda the *thrum* of bowstrings as Sirak arrows were loosed. Cheren fell. More arrows coming back at them, Bleda swerving, leaning left and right, loosing more arrows. The pounding of hooves behind him was louder, more Sirak joining his charge. He heard a scream close behind him. One more volley of arrows leaping from his bow and then he was amongst the Cheren, Jin hurtling past him, close enough to touch, her lips pulled back in a rictus snarl. Bleda reached over his shoulder and drew his sword, slashed left and right, felt his blade bite, blood arcing through the air, and then he was through the Cheren warband, galloping out onto the open plain, sheathing his sword and dragging on his reins, turning, reaching for more arrows.

Hundreds of Sirak were emerging from the Cheren warband, Yul first, Ellac close behind. His spear was bloodied to the shaft, the round shield strapped to his arm bristling with arrows.

He charged a Cheren warband without a bow. Bleda felt a swell of pride and love for the old warrior, followed by worry.

Together they turned and faced the Cheren, who were trying to turn for a second pass. They had ridden into the swirl of combat, though—many of them getting caught up in the conflict. Bleda saw Raina hammer a Cheren rider across the chest, hurling him from his saddle. Others were set upon by Sirak warriors still caught up within the Shekam chaos.

Bleda glimpsed Jin ducking a sword-swing from a Sirak warrior, saw another Cheren chop into the Sirak's neck with a sword.

Gerel. Jin's oathsworn man.

Some of the Cheren broke free of the melee and began to ride back at Bleda. He spurred his horse on, nocked and loosed, heard a Cheren scream. Yul, Ellac and the other Sirak behind him broke into a gallop.

The two warbands charged at each other, wind whipping the horsehair plume on Bleda's helmet behind him. A hail of arrows came whistling from the Cheren, one *pinging* off his helm, rocking him in his saddle. He had the chance to loose two more arrows and then he was amongst them, drawing his sword, striking left and right as they galloped past one another. And then he was bursting past them, a snatched glance showing Yul and Ellac appearing. His horse's momentum carried him on, back into the seething mass of draigs and bears. He spied the blue of a Cheren deel, veered that way, swung his sword, a scream, blood spraying, and he was riding at another Cheren, this one seeing him, reaching for their own sword. Bleda's mount came up on the left side, his sword slashing down, parried. Bleda swayed away, the tip of his opponent's blade scraping sparks on the iron plates of his lamellar coat.

They circled one another, horses colliding, jostling, swords a blur, fighting their way across the battleground, in amongst the first trees of the forest.

JIN

Jin ducked, moved, a sword slicing through air where her throat had just been. She slipped her bow back into its case and drew her sword, met her opponent with a flurry of blows. Their swords met, held in a bind, and Jin was looking into her enemy's eyes. He was an old warrior, deep lines in his weathered face. He stared back at her.

"The Fool Queen," he grunted.

A spear-point burst through his throat, was ripped back out, a gush of blood, and he fell from his saddle, Tark appearing behind him.

She dipped her head in thanks, looked around.

It was mayhem: giants, bears, draigs, her Cheren embroiled in a sweeping melee with Sirak, who appeared to be everywhere. And the Order's warriors were there, too, with their swords and shields. Ben-Elim and Kadoshim swirled over their heads, feathers and blood falling from the sky.

Then she glimpsed him.

Bleda, fighting beneath the forest's boughs against one of her Cheren. More of her Clan were riding at him, and Sirak were gathering about Bleda.

The Fool Queen, is that what the Sirak call me? Bleda did make a fool of me, consorting with that half-breed behind my back while betrothed to me.

But I will be the fool that kills Bleda the Cunning.

She pointed with her sword and kicked her horse into movement, Tark and Gerel following her, a handful of others. They rode through the melee, a hurricane of noise surrounding them, swerving around draigs and bears. Jin avoided any combat, her eyes fixed on Bleda. He was flitting between trees, locked in battle with the same Cheren warrior, others fighting around him. A Shekam giant crashed his draig through the trees, Kurgan giants on foot about him.

And then she was breaking out into open space and spurring her horse on. She slipped her sword into the scabbard across her back and pulled her bow from its case, reached for arrows. Nocked.

Bleda slipped behind a tree, part of his horse visible. Jin cursed, rode on, swerving right, saw him again, his sword clashing with his Cheren opponent. She drew and loosed, her arrow leaping from the string, heading straight for Bleda's throat. His opponent's horse crashed into his, and Jin's arrow slammed into the Cheren's neck, slicing through a curtain of mail. The rider cried out, arched his back and toppled from his saddle.

Bleda looked straight at her.

She loosed again, riding directly at him, but he backed his horse up, disappearing behind the tree, her arrow flickering into the forest. She swerved, trying to keep him in sight, and he reappeared the other side of the wide trunk, his sword sheathed, bow in his fist. She threw herself to the side and an arrow hissed past her, iron-tip scraping the cheek-plate of her helm, at the same time as she loosed another arrow. It slammed quivering into the trunk of the tree, a handspan from Bleda's head. Then she was upon him, too close to reach for her sword. She lashed out with her bow, hit him in the face, saw blood spurt as she rode past him, dragging on her reins, turning.

Something slammed into her back, high, just below her left shoulder, felt like a punch. Then the pain came, pulsing out. She twisted, saw one of Bleda's arrows protruding from her. Bleda was riding around her, reaching for more arrows. She ducked, loosed at him, saw her arrow punch into his arm, below the sleeve of his mail coat. He cried out, dropped his bow and ripped the arrow from his forearm, then reached over his back for his sword and spurred his mount at her. She loosed again, a spike of pain in her back, her arrow flying at Bleda's chest.

He chopped it from the air with his sword.

Jin snarled, frustration and respect mixed, then reached for her own sword, rode at him.

Their weapons clashed in a flurry, a spray of sparks, their horses swirling around each other, neighing, trying to bite one another, rearing, hooves lashing out, the two of them moving deeper into the forest.

Jin swayed and ducked, struck and parried, the world around her shrinking down to Bleda, to his eyes, his posture, the ripples of movement that helped her read his attacks. Pain pulsed from the arrow wound in her back, but she ignored it, her hate driving her, filling her with new strength. Dimly she was aware that they had entered a glade, a draig lying dead in its centre, a long spear buried in the beast's chest.

Hooves thudded, steel clashed, letting Jin know other Sirak and Cheren were in the glade about her. She glimpsed Gerel and Tark in her peripheral vision, both of them fighting furiously against Sirak warriors.

Bleda swung at her, a scything blow. She parried, though late, a flash of pain in her wrist, her sword smashed off-line. Bleda backswung and she had no time to bring her sword back into play. She threw herself forwards, inside his strike, and punched him in the face. Blood spurted from his lip and she grabbed at him with her free arm, Bleda trying to pull away, to give himself room to swing his sword. But Jin clung to him, hit him in the head with the pommel of her sword, a clang of iron from his helm. Bleda moved in his saddle, Jin's weight pushing into him, and he began to topple, reached out and grabbed her as he fell from his horse, dragging her with him.

They crashed to the ground, pain erupting in Jin's shoulder

as Bleda's arrow snapped with the impact. She rolled away, sword gripped tight in her fist, felt bile rise in her throat, shook her head to clear the black dots that blurred her vision. Then she was climbing to her feet, saw Bleda on one knee.

Warriors were fighting around her. She saw Gerel was still mounted and was fighting Yul, their swords a blur. Tark was trading spear-blows with Old Ellac.

A crashing and splintering of branches above her and two figures plummeted to the ground, a Kadoshim and Ben-Elim, locked in combat, rolling on the forest litter.

Then she was on her feet, striding at Bleda.

He stood to meet her, raised his blade and parried her overhead blow, slipped to the side, sending her blade wide, putting her off-balance, and he was cutting at her waist. She twisted on her heel, her blade smashing his away, and elbowed him in the face, stepped in as he stumbled. His blade came back up, parried her chop at his head, sliced down, striking her coat of mail, a trail of sparks from her chest to belly, mail links shattering. She stepped away, sword levelled at him.

"No more running," she said to him. Bleda was still, his blade held high, two-handed. "Today you die."

Bleda just watched her, focused on her. She saw recognition dawn in his eyes.

"That's my sword," he said.

"Yes, and I'm going to kill you with it," Jin said.

Two horses rode between them, Gerel and Yul. They were hacking and slicing at one another, blades so fast Jin could only see the after-image of their movement. Blood spurted in the air, raining on Jin's face, and Gerel reeled back in his saddle, blood jetting from his throat. He gurgled and toppled from his saddle.

Jin just stared, struggling to believe what she had just seen. Gerel. He had been with her since her father's first visit to Drassil. Loyal, brave, skilled, a constant reassuring presence.

And Yul had just killed him.

Jin leaped forwards and hacked at Yul in front of her,

chopped deep into his thigh, blood welling. He cried out, kicked his horse on. Bleda was in front of her again.

Their blades clashed, a rush of blows. Jin pressed hard, her attack relentless. Her cold-face was gone, no mask of her feelings. Hate blazed in her eyes, giving her an edge that Bleda could not match. She pushed him back across the glade, past Ellac and Tark, still mounted. Bleda tripped over a branch, stumbled backwards, fell, Jin rushing at him, sword raised.

Yul appeared on his horse, crashing into Jin, sending her flying through the air. She slammed to the ground, rolled, Yul riding after her.

Jin climbed to her feet, saw Yul bearing down upon her and raised her sword. Beyond Yul she heard a cry and glimpsed Ellac toppling from his horse, a spray of blood. Tark twisted in his saddle, saw Jin and Yul. He drew his arm back, hefted his spear.

"NO!" Jin heard Bleda cry.

Tark's spear flew through the air and slammed into Yul's back, shattering mail, slicing through leather. Yul cried out, fell forwards in his saddle with the blow, straightened and reached over his back, pulled the spear free.

Jin stepped forwards and stabbed her sword up, into Yul's belly. He stiffened, gasped, his sword dropping from his fingers. Jin twisted her blade, ripped it free, blood pouring, Yul fell from his saddle onto the ground before her.

A scream: Bleda, he was running at her, sword raised.

Jin set her feet, mouth a hard line.

Bleda struck at her, a flurry that drove her back, his blade a blur, a combination of blows, one merging into the next, Jin parrying, retreating across the glade, no time to counter-strike. He lunged in, stabbing at her belly, and she pivoted, steering Bleda's blade wide, kicked out at his knee, and he dropped to the ground. Jin struck his sword hard, sending it spinning out of his grip, sliced at his throat, but he rolled away, her blade scoring a line across his chest. She followed, felt victory's breath on her neck, so close, her sword slashing. Bleda kicked at her legs, swept her off her feet. She fell with a crunch, a sharp pain, ignored it, rising to one knee, her sword swinging at Bleda as he rolled beneath her blade, his hand grasping at the sleeve of his lamellar coat, then lashing out. Too late she saw the glint of steel, a knife slashing close.

She felt an impact, a few heartbeats before she realized something was wrong. The taste of blood. Tried to take a deep breath, choking as liquid filled her lungs.

A frozen moment as she stared at Bleda. Her sword arm was drooping, the blade suddenly too heavy for her, and she fell back, sitting on the ground.

Fight him, kill him, she told herself. *You are better than him, you have won.* She tried to tell him how much she hated him, choked on more blood, her hands rising to her neck, felt the open wound, slick and slippery.

Bleda stared at her, a bloody knife in his fist. She stared back at him, hating him, hating herself as she realized what was happening.

He had beaten her.

"For my mother," Bleda said, and stabbed his blade up through the bottom of her jaw, thrusting it until the crossguard slammed into flesh.

BLEDA

Bleda tore his knife from Jin's dying body, saw her slump to the ground. He stumbled to his feet, chest heaving, staring at Jin's lifeless face.

I've done it, avenged my mother. It didn't feel real. A vision of Jin stabbing down into his mother's neck. He yelled at her body, a wordless, grief-filled roar.

The sound of combat pulled him back.

He saw Ellac and Tark wrestling on the ground, rolling. Tark had a knife, was trying to stab Ellac, but the old warrior had the huntsman's knife arm in a lock, and with his other arm was punching Tark in the head with the buckler strapped to his arm. The iron boss cracked into Tark's temple and the warrior went slack. Ellac rained blows upon him, again and again, Bleda hearing the sound of bone cracking as Tark's skull caved in.

"Ellac," Bleda called out, and the old warrior looked up, stopped pounding the dead man, raised a hand.

Bleda turned and ran to Yul.

He was lying on the forest floor, blood seeping into the ground. Bleda dropped to his knees beside the warrior, stroked his head, tears in his eyes.

Yul's eyes flickered open. He was waxy-pale, blood on his lips. His fingers twitched and Bleda gripped his hand.

"Mightiest of the Sirak," Bleda said to him. He called over his shoulder, "Ellac, find a healer!"

"I saw you," Yul breathed, a half-smile touching his lips. "My King." A long, sighing breath, and then his eyes closed and his head slumped.

Bleda dropped his head, silent tears running down his cheeks.

The sound of fighting and he turned, saw a Kadoshim and Ben-Elim rolling together, punching, biting at one another. They came to a halt, the Kadoshim on top, pinning the Ben-Elim's arms, reaching for a knife at his belt.

Bleda ran at them.

The knife raised high, was stabbing down.

Bleda chopped into the neck of the Kadoshim, half-severing its head. It fell to the side, blood spurting, a tremor through its wings, and then it was still.

Bleda looked down at the Ben-Elim on the ground.

It was Kol.

Bleda stood there, looking down at Kol. His sword hovered. He hated this man. The killer of his brother and sister. A tremor ran through his blade, the desire to drive it down into Kol overwhelming.

The rustle of footsteps, Old Ellac was walking towards him. He did not say anything, just looked at Bleda.

Bleda looked back at Kol, the Ben-Elim staring up at him with his half-sneer.

With a shuddering breath Bleda lowered his sword.

"I'll let the Ben-Elim Assembly deal with you," he said, and turned away, strode to Ellac, wrapped his arms around the old warrior and hugged him. Ellac hugged Bleda back, shaking with emotion.

A wet cough behind Bleda and Yul moved.

"Ellac, go and find a healer," Bleda exclaimed as he rushed to Yul, saw blood on the warrior's lips, but his chest was moving, his eyes open, fixed on Bleda. He dropped to his knees and gripped Yul's hand.

"Hold on, my friend."

Ellac nodded and hurried limping to his horse. He picked

up his spear on the way, then climbed into his saddle and rode out of the glade.

Behind Bleda, Kol found his spear and levered himself upright with it.

"There is no Assembly left," Kol said. "All of them are dead."

"You'll stand a trial," Bleda said over his shoulder. "Of that I am certain."

Kol curled a lip at him. "If I do, I'll be found innocent."

"No, you won't," Bleda said. He coughed, blood in his mouth, spat it out. "You are a liar and a murderer. I have seen the glade of cairns where slaughtered babies have been hidden to sate your hubris and lust. I will testify that to any who will listen."

The rustle of wings and Bleda half-turned, saw Kol flying towards him. He started to move, then Kol's spear punched into his throat. He tried to raise his sword, but it was too heavy. He dropped it, lifted his arms, tried to grab Kol, but the Ben-Elim ripped the spear free and stepped back.

"Will your kind never learn their place?" Kol said, shaking his head.

Bleda fell to his knees, swayed, toppled onto his back. Kol reached down, plucked an arrow from Bleda's quiver and stabbed it into Bleda's thigh.

Bleda hardly felt it.

Yul grunted, moved.

Kol stood over them both, gripped his spear two-handed and stabbed it down into Yul's chest. A tremor passed through the warrior, a sigh.

Bleda's hand twitched for his sword, but his body would not obey. He saw Kol become a silhouette that spiralled upwards, the sky a bright, white light behind him. Darkness blurred the edges of his vision, crept slowly inwards.

His last thought was of Riv.

RIV

Riv opened her eyes. She could see booted feet, could hear the grunt and yell of combat. Everything was pain. She moved, her wings twitching.

"Careful," a voice said to her. She turned her head, looked up to see Jost looming over her.

"What happened?" Riv said.

"You fell out of the sky, with two arrows in you. Lucky for you that you landed on a pile of dead Revenants."

"Don't feel lucky." Riv grunted, trying to climb to one knee. Nausea swept through her, making her eyes water. Bile rose in her throat.

"Well, you're lucky to be feeling anything at all," Jost said, heaving her up.

Riv saw a bandage around her thigh, put some weight on it. There was a tremor, but it held.

"Had to cut the arrows out of you. The one in your leg was deeper than the one in your back. A coat of mail helps."

She spread her wings, gave them a beat. The muscle of her right wing-arch ached, but she thought her wings would take her weight.

"Here," Jost said, holding out Riv's short-sword and her black knife.

Riv was standing in the centre of a shield square, two rows deep, facing in four directions, maybe eighty or ninety warriors, a mixture of White-Wings and warriors of the Order. Riv glimpsed Kill standing in the front, shoulder pressed into her shield and stabbing her short-sword through the gap. Ert was beside her. They were surrounded by acolytes, grunting and pushing back with their own shields and short-swords. But this wall was made up of White-Wings and warriors of the Order of the Bright Star.

Acolytes were dying.

A half-dozen warriors were standing or sitting in the space within the shield square. Sorch was there, tall and broad. He nodded a greeting to Riv.

Dimly she heard a booming laugh, recognized it from the battle on Ripa's plain.

"Asroth," she whispered.

"Aye. He's chopping his way through shield walls," Jost said, with a shudder. "Fortunately, he's over there, somewhere." He nodded west.

"WARE THE DRAIG!" a voice yelled, from the eastern side of the shield square.

An ear-splitting roar rang out, a tremor in the ground, and then warriors were flying through the air, screaming. A draig's head and shoulders appeared, head lashing, jaws snapping, sweeping up a White-Wing and crunching down. Fritha sat upon its back. She stabbed down at a warrior of the Order with her spear.

The draig lumbered forwards, scattering the wall, warriors thrown, scrambling away. Acolytes started to push into the gap the draig had made.

Riv snarled, flexed her wings and leaped into the air, a wave of pain in her leg, but her wings worked and she flew towards Fritha, building speed.

Something crashed into Riv and she was hurled through the air, crunched back to the ground. She rolled, a shape moving after her, sinuous and reptilian.

Fritha's snake-woman.

She loomed over Riv, rising high on her coils, a fair-haired woman, her arms and torso covered in a coat of mail, a round shield on one arm, a black-bladed spear in her fist.

Black-bladed. Byrne wants that spear.

"*Frithaaaa wants you,*" the snake-woman hissed, and she surged forwards. Riv stabbed with her short-sword, but the snake-woman's shield batted it away, then coils were wrapping around Riv, crushing her legs together, pinning her arms tight.

Sorch and Jost appeared, a dozen warriors behind them. They charged the snake-woman, shields up. Jost's sword rang on her shield boss, Sorch chopped at the white-scaled body of the woman, cutting a shallow gash through thick scales. A pale, milk-like substance oozed from the wound and the creature let out a hissing scream. She slammed her shield into Jost, hurling him away, her strength prodigious. Sorch stabbed at her, his blade sinking deeper, and she shrieked again, turned on him and stabbed her spear. He raised his shield, but the black-bladed spear punched through the layers of linen and linden wood as if they were a cobweb. Sorch grunted, sank to his knees, his shield falling away, a red hole in his chest. He looked at Riv and then fell flat on his face.

Riv yelled, writhed and strained in the snake-woman's coils, but she could not break free.

The snake-woman whirled her spear above her head, a looping slice at the remaining warriors. Her spear cut through the shields like wheat, carving across three warriors, all of them falling back with red wounds gaping. She surged forwards, leaving trails of blood and black smoke in the air, and warriors fell dead or wounded about her. Then she was dragging Riv across the field towards Fritha and her draig, who were only twenty or thirty paces away, destroying White-Wings and warriors of the Order with a savage glee.

Another roaring, from the east, the ground trembling, and Riv saw White-Wings parting, leaping out of the way. A huge white-furred bear lumbered into view, a battered and torn coat of mail upon it, the white fur of its muzzle stained pink with blood. Drem was sitting upon its back, a shield upon one arm, white star upon a black field, a sword in his fist.

The bear paused a moment. Drem looked around, saw Fritha upon her draig, and then the snake-woman slithering towards Fritha.

"ELISE," Drem bellowed at the snake-woman, "LET HER GO!"

DREM

Drem snapped a word to Friend and the white bear burst into a shambling run after Elise, who was slithering away, coils undulating, speeding her across the battleground to Fritha. But Friend was faster. The bear slammed into the serpent-woman, a clawed paw raking her tail, his chest crunching into her torso. Elise screamed, as she was thrown through the air, her coils loosening around Riv, who beat her wings and wriggled free, stabbing deep with her black knife. Riv raised her arm for another blow, but there was a rushing of air and Morn was sweeping down from above. Riv screamed a challenge and leaped into the air, the two of them stabbing and slashing at each other, swirling up and away.

Friend's jaws clamped around Elise's torso, tearing through mail into flesh, blood spurting, and he shook her. Elise screamed, her snake-body shaking like a whip.

Wrath looked up, started to lumber towards them.

Elise lashed out with her tail, Drem blocking it with his shield. The blow cracked timber, numbed his arm. She swung her spear, raked a line along Friend's shoulder, slicing through mail and into flesh.

Friend roared.

Drem leaned in his saddle and chopped down at her, his sword biting into Elise's neck.

Her spear fell from her grip and Friend spat her twitching

body on the ground, then stamped on her head. A hissed cry cut short. A tremor quivering through Elise's tail and then it flopped still.

There was a scream from Fritha, high-pitched, grief and rage mingled, and the draig was charging at Friend, roaring, the ground shaking.

Drem looked at them, a moment of fear, then he thought of his da, hefted his shield and gripped his sword, shouted a word to Friend.

The white bear charged.

Draig and bear crashed together, an impact that rattled Drem to his bones.

Teeth cracked as the draig's and bear's jaws lunged at each other, trying to find purchase in head or neck. The draig's talons raked Friend's chest, the mail coat tearing but taking the brunt of the blow. Friend's paw slapped the draig's head, claws tearing red strips from its muzzle. Fritha stabbed with her spear, the blade turned by Friend's mail. Drem leaned and chopped with his sword, opened a red wound on the draig's thick neck. It roared, backed away, bunched its legs and hurled itself at them again, jaws clamping around Friend's chest and shoulder, biting down.

Mail tore, blood spurted.

Friend roared, pain-filled.

Drem hacked desperately at the draig's head, slicing red strips, but the thick skull turned his blade. Fritha stabbed at him with her spear, Drem swiping the blade wide with his shield, chopped at the shaft, Fritha whipping it back.

A blur of grey fur and iron mail leaped at the draig's head, Fen snapping and snarling, claws scrabbling for purchase, the wolven-hound's jaws biting down into the draig's cheek and eye.

The draig stumbled back, gave a savage shake of his head and Fen flew through the air, disappeared into the crowded battleground. The draig growled, a taloned claw coming up to paw at his eye. It was a lacerated, pulped mess.

Acolytes formed up on either side of Fritha and the draig and marched forwards.

"SHIELD WALL!" Drem heard a voice cry out behind him, thought it was Kill's, then White-Wings were charging in a disciplined line at the acolytes, shields crashing together. Riders poured around the edges of the acolyte shield wall, Drem glimpsing a dark-haired warrior with a black axe chopping down at White-Wings. His axe sheared through shields, iron helms, and left a trail of smoke in the air.

Starstone metal, we need that axe.

The draig hurled itself at Friend again, jaws snapping for purchase. Fritha's spear stabbed at Drem, and he shifted in the saddle, the spear blade skimming past his waist. He clamped down with his shield arm, trapped the spear, swung with his sword. Fritha released the weapon and threw herself backwards, Drem's blade-tip raking the mail over her chest, shattering links.

Fritha smiled at him.

"You've learned a few tricks with your Bright Star friends," she said, reaching for her sword hilt.

The Starstone Sword. My father's sword.

Drem pulled his feet up, stood on his saddle, legs bunching, and leaped at her. Her eyes flared in shock, and then he was crashing into her, tearing her from her saddle, the two of them tumbling to the ground.

They rolled, separated, both coming to their feet, Fritha drawing the Starstone Sword. She swung at Drem, a high blow, and he met it with his shield. The sword sheared through wood, cut from shield rim to boss. Fritha ripped her blade free, trying to slice into Drem's forearm, but he twisted and dropped the shield, hefted his sword, pulled his hand-axe from his belt, set his feet.

Fritha came at him again, another overhead blow. Instinctively he met it with his sword, for a heartbeat wondered if the starstone blade would just carve through his own sword and cut into his skull.

A harsh clang, a ripple of blue flame where the two blades met, and Drem's runed sword held.

A moment's shock between them both, then Drem was pushing Fritha's blade high, shoving her back. She stumbled and he stepped in, chopping with his hand-axe. It crunched into mail, the rings holding, but Drem heard the crack of bone, ribs fracturing. Fritha grimaced, staggered back again.

Drem followed, stabbed with his sword, it was swept wide by the black blade. He chopped again with his axe, Fritha swinging a wild parry, but the blade caught Drem's axe shaft and cut it in two, the axe-head spinning away.

The drum of hooves and Drem instinctively ducked and moved, heard air hiss over his head, the bulk of a horse stamping past him. He stood, stabbed at the warrior who had tried to take his head, saw it was the dark-haired man with the black axe. Drem struck up with his sword, felt the blade pierce mail and flesh. The warrior screamed, arched his back and fell away as the horse walked on.

"No," Fritha snarled, pain in her eyes. "You are killing all I love."

"As you have done to me," Drem snarled back at her.

Fritha pressed in, a flurry of blows, Drem parrying. The black sword sliced through his mail, links shattering, cut a red line along his forearm, a fist to his nose as Fritha stepped in.

A wild, pain-filled roaring filled Drem's ears. He glanced and saw Friend crash to the ground, the draig's jaws clamped around one of the bear's forelegs. Blood was spraying as Friend rolled onto his side, the draig seeing Friend's exposed belly, covered only by a latticework of leather buckles.

"NO!" Drem screamed, made to run to the bear, but Fritha hacked at him. He stumbled backwards, fell over the coils of Elise's corpse, lost the grip on his sword.

Fritha stood over him, the screams of Friend ringing out in the background, and raised her sword.

"This could have been so different," Fritha said. "You were a fool not to join me."

"Go to hell," Drem snarled at her. Glimpsed a black-bladed spear.

Fritha's sword sliced down.

Drem rolled, grabbed the spear and swung wildly at Fritha, black sword and black spear blade colliding. A concussive explosion, hurling Fritha away, sending Drem skidding and scrabbling across the ground. He stabbed the spear into earth and came to a halt, levered himself upright and saw the draig standing upon Friend, pinning the bear with his bulk. The draig's jaws were slick with blood, Friend bellowing with pain. As Drem watched, the draig reared up, jaws opening wide, rushing down to fasten upon the exposed flesh of Friend's belly.

Drem found his balance, drew his arm back and hurled the starstone spear.

It flew straight as a loosed arrow, trailing black smoke through the air and punched into the draig's chest. Deep it sank, halfway up the shaft, dark blood pulsing from the wound.

The draig roared, an ear-splitting sound, a shiver rippling through its body, and it crashed to the ground, rolled onto its side, wings and tail thrashing, jaws snapping, frothing blood. A juddering tremor ran through it and then its head slumped, its powerful neck flopping. A groaning rattle issued from its throat, and it was still.

"WRATH!" Fritha screamed, staggering to her feet, her black sword still in her fist.

FRITHA

Fritha could not see for her tears. She swiped at them, staring at Wrath. Her beautiful, powerful, destructive creation. His flesh was torn, bleeding from a hundred wounds. And he was so very still. She wiped her eyes, drew in a deep, shuddering breath.

Drem has done this.

He is worse than the Ben-Elim, killing my babies.

She looked at Drem. "I'm going to kill you, now."

He swept up his sword and drew his seax, rolled it in his fist.

"Sometimes the only answer is blood and steel," he breathed, and launched himself at her.

The movement was so swift and unexpected that Fritha struggled to get her guard up, blue flame crackling as her black sword clanged against Drem's rune-marked blades. He stabbed with his seax, Fritha shuffling her feet, sidestepping, at the same time throwing his sword wide.

She stepped away as Drem came at her, parrying his attacks, waiting for an opening. He followed with small steps, maintaining his balance, short bursts of blows, always a combination with sword and seax. Fritha felt a white-hot line across her forearm, another across her thigh, mail links on her coat shatter as his seax slashed her belly, all the while her ribs sending pain screeching up her side.

This is not supposed to be happening. He is not this good. She felt her frustration growing, her grief for Wrath and Elise a red rage, but it was tinged with something else, now.

Fear.

She darted away and lifted her black sword, gripped the sharp blade with her fist, squeezed it until she felt her palm slick with blood. Then she smeared her lips with the blood, cupped her fist as more blood pooled.

She saw realization dawn in Drem's eyes.

"*Fuil, sruthán mo namhaid,*" Fritha breathed, her blood spraying, and she flung her blood at Drem. It hissed as it flew through the air, spattered Drem's face and neck, sizzling. She smelled burning flesh.

Drem fell away, screaming, and Fritha followed. He dropped to the ground, rolling, and she stabbed down at him, missed, skewered turf. She raised her sword again.

She heard a snarling, saw movement from the corner of her eye, and then something crashed into her, sent her flying through the air. She landed with a jolt, rolled, stopped. Climbed to her feet.

A slate-grey wolven-hound stood before her. It turned away, loped back to Drem, who was on one knee, patches of his face blistering and smoking. The wolven-hound nuzzled Drem, licked his face, and then turned to face Fritha.

She walked towards it, sword-tip rising.

The wolven-hound growled at her, lips pulled back in a snarl, its hackles rising.

Fritha started to whisper under her breath.

"No," Drem said, rising.

"You need to *stay down*," Fritha snarled, still walking towards him.

"No," Drem repeated, swaying as he stood. "You can burn me, cut me, blind me, I will never stop coming at you. Only death will stop me." His face twisted in pain. "I loved you, and you killed my da."

"I could have killed you, too," Fritha said. "I stood over you, could have killed you so easily."

"You should have," Drem said.

Then Fritha saw he had a new weapon in his hand, not his seax. A black-bladed axe. He drew his arm back and threw it.

Fritha saw the axe coming at her, shifted her weight, raised her sword, trying to both leap out of its way and cut it from the air.

Neither worked, the axe skimming past her sword and punching into her shoulder. Its blade cut through mail links and chopped deep into muscle, spinning her round. She stumbled away, her arm numb, hanging limp, and tried to turn, raising her sword.

Drem was right before her, a handspan between them.

"For my father, and for Sig," he whispered, and stabbed his seax into her. It punched into her mail, piercing and splitting through it, on through leather and linen and into flesh. A terrible pain in her stomach, Drem wrapping one arm around her back, like a lover, and pulled her tighter onto his seax, pushing it deeper, until it was buried to the hilt in her.

Fritha stared into his eyes. They were so close, lips almost touching.

She sucked in a deep breath and screamed.

"ASROTH!"

Then she fell.

RIV

Riv twisted away from Morn, pain shooting up her back, Morn's spear blade sliced across her cheek. She beat her wings and swept away, her body a competing map of pain.

Ignore it. Pain is better than death.

She rolled in the air, spun back towards Morn, slashing with her short-sword, chopping another chunk off the splintered end of the spear shaft. Morn threw it away and drew a knife from her belt, flew at Riv.

They slammed together, Riv feeling the knife blade scraping across her helm, seeking a path inside. They struggled, wrestling, punching, butting heads, snarling and spitting at each other, not knowing which way was up. A glimpse of the ground, rushing towards them, a bone-jarring collision and they hit the floor.

"ASROTH!" a voice screamed, ringing out across the field as they climbed to their feet, stumbling away from each other.

Riv saw Drem and Fritha, in what looked like a close embrace.

Fritha dropped to her knees, toppled to the ground.

Morn cried out, an inarticulate, feral sound.

Riv heard a growling snarl and saw a wolven-hound running towards them. Fen, his mail coat a shimmer, surging across the ground, and then he was leaping, crashing into Morn. They fell, tumbling, Fen's jaws clamping around Morn's face. Riv saw Morn's knife move and Riv beat her wings, speeding to the wolven-hound and half-breed. She landed and stamped her foot upon Morn's wrist, the knife-blade a handspan from Fen's belly.

A frozen moment, Fen pinning Morn, jaws wrapped around her face. Morn looked up at Riv.

"You slew Keld," Riv said. "Fen has something to say about that."

Fen shook his neck, and blood sprayed. Morn screamed; another savage wrench of Fen's neck and the scream faded to a gurgle. Her feet drummed and then she was still.

Hooves on the turf, Cullen riding up. He saw Fen tearing at Morn's corpse.

"Ach, she was mine to kill," Cullen said.

Fen looked up at Cullen, his muzzle soaked red, and growled at the red-haired warrior.

"You had a claim, too, I suppose," Cullen said. He pointed a finger at Fen. "But Gulla is mine."

"I put an arrow in Gulla," Riv said breathlessly, wiping blood from her face. "Saw him flee to Balara."

Cullen looked at the fortress on the hill.

Something around them changed, like a silence amidst the storm. Riv looked around, saw a black shape in the air, winging towards them with slow, powerful beats of his wings.

"Asroth is coming," she said.

Kadoshim followed him, and Revenants upon the ground.

"Good," Cullen snarled.

"ASROTH COMES!" Riv yelled the warning. She leaped into the sky. The whole battleground had disintegrated into a large-scale melee, a hundred different hard-fought battles raging across the field. Close by she saw Kill and Ert with two or three score White-Wings and warriors of the Order rallied around them, holding against twice that number of acolytes. As Riv watched, riders of the Order appeared, Byrne at their head, Meical riding close to her. They charged the flank of the acolytes attacking Kill and Ert, chopping down with swords, and in a few heartbeats the acolytes were collapsing.

Above her Ben-Elim fought in the sky. Riv glimpsed Faelan swirling amongst them, his quiver empty now. He fought with sword and long knife. He and his kin seemed to have done a good job of balancing the numbers.

To the west Riv saw Ethlinn's giants fighting the Shekam draig-riders; Sirak and warriors of the Order were riding amongst them. It looked as if the draig-riders were slowly being overwhelmed. She glimpsed Balur One-Eye trading blows with a huge giant upon a draig's back.

Where is Bleda? Riv thought, searching the swirling combat, but she was too far away and the Sirak riders were a blur as they weaved amongst the draigs.

She saw Asroth again, closer now, bearing down upon her and her friends. Kadoshim flew around him, and the last of the Revenants swarmed upon the ground, following him. In his wake Asroth left a trail of the dead.

A sound filtered through to Riv and she turned, glancing north, towards Balara.

A winged figure was flying towards the battlefield, low to the ground, wings beating slowly.

Gulla.

He flew above hundreds of acolytes; they were marching hard.

Riv looked down, searching for Byrne. Old Ert was trading blows with a broad, squat acolyte, chopping at each other's shields, stabbing over the rims. It was clear he knew his sword-craft. Riv drew her wings in and flew down, intent on putting her sword through the acolyte's heart.

He was on the ground before Riv landed, blood leaking from a sword-thrust beneath his ribs. Ert was leaning on one knee, breathing hard, speaking to the fallen acolyte.

"You betrayed us, Aenor, and chose the wrong side; and now you're dying for them."

"I'd rather die a free man than the Ben-Elim's puppet," Aenor gasped, blood on his lips, then the light in his eyes faded.

Byrne cantered up to them, Meical beside her. She was bloodstained, a long cut on her calf dripping blood, but there was a fire in her eyes. Her riders gathered behind her, the rest either dead or scattered around the field.

"Asroth is coming," Riv said, "a hundred Kadoshim with him, four, five hundred Revenants following him on the ground. And Gulla returns from Balara, leading fresh acolytes."

Byrne looked at Ert. "Can you keep the Revenants and acolytes off us?"

A curt nod. "Or die in the trying. SHIELD WALL!" Ert bellowed, hefting his battered shield and runed short-sword. Warriors on foot ran to him.

Cullen cantered over, Drem following on foot, Fen and Friend limping along either side of him.

"This is the time of reckoning," Byrne said to them all. "Asroth comes, with his Kadoshim." She looked at them.

"Truth and Courage."

"TRUTH AND COURAGE!" they cried back at her, Riv whispering those words.

And then the beating of wings grew louder, Asroth's shadow loomed over them.

"WITH ME!" Ert cried, leading the warriors he had gathered towards the onrushing Revenants.

Byrne walked her horse forwards, the warriors of the Order spreading in a line either side of her. Cullen lingered, looked down at Riv and Drem.

"We are all here, then," Cullen said.

"Aye," Drem said. "I'm glad we're together, now. For the end."

"For *his* end," Cullen snarled, looking at Asroth as he grew larger in the sky. He looked at Drem's fists. "What's that you've got there?"

Drem lifted up his hands. In one he had a sword, in the other, a single-bladed axe. They were both forged of black steel, and tendrils of dark smoke curled around them.

"This is the Starstone Sword my da forged," Drem said. "I swore I'd take it back from Fritha, and kill Asroth with it. This," he said, looking at the axe, "I'm thinking it's a starstone axe."

"Well, now," Cullen said, whistling. He looked at Riv, who had her black knife in her hand. He frowned. "This isn't fair."

"You have a fine sword," Riv pointed out, and Cullen grinned, holding up his ancestor's sword. The hilt was a hand and a half, the blade longer and broader than Cullen was used to.

"Aye, it is a fine sword, and I'm honoured to wield it, but it's not going to be cutting through a coat of starstone mail like those two, is it."

"I'd let you have this sword, but I swore an oath on it," Drem said. "You can have the axe, though, if you like." He held it out to Cullen. "Or there's a black-bladed spear in that draig over there, if you can pull it out. It looks deep, to me."

Cullen looked from the axe to the dead draig.

"Byrne said she wants every starstone weapon we can lay our hands on, and I'm not much for axe work," he said. "Think I might just have a look at that spear." He dipped his head to Drem and Riv and trotted his horse towards the draig.

And then, with a rushing of wings, Asroth was upon them.

He spiralled down from the sky and landed beside Fritha, who lay upon the ground, staring up at Asroth. He bent, and Riv saw his lips move, though she could not hear what he said. Then he stood tall and looked around.

His Kadoshim guards swirled above him, some landing, spreading protectively around him.

Byrne reined in her horse a hundred paces before Asroth. Meical and her warriors lined up either side of her. Beyond them Riv heard Ert shouting orders, shields cracking together, and the hissing roar of the Revenants as they threw themselves at the shield wall.

"Meical," Asroth said, as if speaking to an old friend. "Back for another beating?"

Meical said nothing, just stared at Asroth. He held a shield and sword.

Asroth's face twitched. "Two thousand years you have been plotting my demise, and now you have nothing to say?"

"This is the day you die," Meical said.

"Ha," Asroth laughed. He looked genuinely amused. "Not by your hand." His gaze shifted to Byrne.

"So, you are the leader of this rabble?" Asroth said to her. He took a few strides towards her, shrugged his long axe from his back. Swirled it around his head, like an athlete preparing for a training bout. Black smoke curled around him.

"I am Byrne ap Baradir, High Captain of the Order of the Bright Star, descended from the line of Cywen ap Thannon, sister to Corban, the Bright Star," Byrne said.

"Corban! That pathetic worm," Asroth spat. His hand brushed a white scar that ran along his forehead. "I never had the chance to grind Corban's skull to dust. I shall make up for that with you."

Byrne flicked her reins and her horse walked forwards. She reached inside her cloak and pulled out a vial.

"*Talamh, coinnigh an t-aingeal dorcha*," she said, clicking her horse to a canter. Meical and the line of riders broke into movement.

"Best be joining in," Riv said to Drem.

"Aye," he said. He began to walk towards Asroth, black sword and black axe in his fists.

Asroth frowned at Byrne, looked around him, as if he sensed something. The ground shifted beneath his feet, thick ropes of vine bursting from the ground, wrapping around his ankles. He pulled on one leg, but the vines held it tight.

Byrne's horse came faster, the warriors behind her charging.

The Kadoshim on the ground leaped into the air, the ones circling above swooping down, a winged charge at the riders.

"Let her through," Asroth yelled to his Kadoshim, and they

parted for Byrne, regrouping after she'd passed through their ranks, and they hurled themselves at Byrne's followers. Asroth smiled at Byrne as she bore down upon him, her curved sword levelled at his heart.

"*Scaip*," he said, waving a hand at the vines around his ankles. With a hiss and slither they seemed to just dissolve, evaporating into thin air.

Byrne gripped her sword blade with her free hand, made a fist, crushing the vial and cutting her palm, the contents of the vial mixing with her blood.

"*Cóta ceangailteach*," she shouted, and threw blood and liquid at Asroth. Riv saw it shimmering in the air, changing, growing, the droplets merging, expanding, swirling into a cloak of red sinew, fibrous and slick with blood. It hit Asroth with a wet slap and wrapped around him, like a living skin, pulling tight, snaring his arms.

Asroth writhed, trying to pull free.

"*Lig saor mé*," Asroth grunted, and the net of blood and sinew collapsed around him, dropping to the ground. He raised his axe, Byrne's sword clanging against it as she thundered past him, pulling on her reins to turn.

The line of Kadoshim and riders met, flesh and bone colliding, screams, the ring of steel, horses neighing.

Riv gritted her teeth and flew at Asroth.

Kadoshim swirled around Asroth and Byrne like a shield, fighting with an unbridled ferocity to protect their king, keeping all from him. Riv heard Byrne shouting words of power, glimpsed fragmented images, the ground bucking around Asroth, throwing him to his knees, Byrne flinging more droplets of blood at him, hissing into flame, Asroth screaming as the sizzling blood seared him, but he cried out his own words, a pulse of air battering Byrne's horse away, the animal neighing, rearing, hooves lashing at Asroth, Byrne slashing with her sword, Asroth's axe swirling, chopping into the legs of Byrne's horse, the animal screaming, collapsing.

A Kadoshim flew at Riv and she swerved, swept his spear wide as he stabbed at her and then she was inside the spear's range, was stabbing her black knife into the Kadoshim's belly, ripping it up, the Kadoshim screaming, dying, falling from the sky.

Riv flew on, veering around another Kadoshim, a slash of her knife through its leathery wing and muscled arch and it was plummeting to the ground. Another Kadoshim came at her, and died, and then she was through the Kadoshim's barrier and flying at Asroth.

Byrne was on the ground, rolling as Asroth swung his axe at her. It carved into the ground where she'd been, Asroth ripping it free, an explosion of turf, Byrne back on her feet, darting in, slashing twice at his belly, sparks on mail, then she stabbed at his leg, opened a red line across his thigh, just below the rim of his mail coat. Asroth bellowed, lashed at her with his gauntleted fist, caught Byrne on the side of the head, sending her spinning through the air, slamming to the ground, rolling to crunch against her dead horse.

He strode after her, raising his axe.

Riv crashed into his back, an arm wrapping around his neck, stabbing at him with her black knife. He dropped his axe, grabbed her wrist, twisted and threw her over his shoulder, flying through the air into Byrne, who was clambering back to her feet. They fell in a tangle of limbs and wings.

Asroth picked up his axe.

Riders broke through the Kadoshim around them, three, four warriors of the Order, Meical with them, all of them riding at Asroth, weapons raised high.

Asroth snarled, ran at them, wings beating, axe spinning. He took the first rider in the chest, chopping her almost in two, hurling her from her saddle, then he was spinning, a rider galloping past him, sword hissing through air and the spike of Asroth's axe punched into the back of the rider's head.

"Come, child," Byrne said, helping Riv to her feet.

Byrne rolled her curved sword in her wrist and ran at Asroth. Riv stood, shaking her head, and then followed.

Meical was exchanging blows with Asroth, upon his horse, slashing at Asroth's head and neck.

Asroth just walked through the blows, letting them bounce off his helm and mail.

"*Páirt agus coinnigh mo namhaid, cré agus cloch,*" Asroth yelled, the ground shifting beneath Meical's horse, turning to bog, hooves sinking, and Asroth smashed the butt end of his axe into Meical's chest, hurling the Ben-Elim from his saddle.

Byrne was running now; she leaped at Asroth, holding her sword two-handed, stabbing it at his back, a concussion and explosion of steel splinters as Asroth's coat of mail shattered Byrne's blade.

Byrne fell to the ground and Asroth turned, lifted his knee and cracked it into Byrne's face, throwing her through the air. He swung his axe at another rider, slicing through a shield and severing an arm at the elbow. Then he was twisting, a further backswing as Byrne was rising, the spike of his axe stabbing into Byrne's back.

She cried out as she was thrown back to the ground, where she rolled and lay still.

Riv screamed, threw herself at Asroth.

More figures came bursting through the Kadoshim perimeter: acolytes, in their scores.

Gulla must be here.

DREM

Drem saw Byrne fall and yelled her name. He broke into a run, Friend and Fen beside him.

Revenants were breaking past Ert's shield wall and hurling themselves at riders of the Order, dragging them from their saddles. Acolytes came pouring into the battleground, hundreds of them. Some were forming a shield wall, but most were charging in an undisciplined mass, howling battle-cries. Riders of the Order tried to turn and meet them. Almost directly in front of him Drem saw Gulla swoop from the sky and crash into a rider, ripping her from her saddle, the two of them slamming to the ground. Gulla's jaws opened wide, distending, and he bit down upon the warrior's throat, ripping and lacerating.

Keld, Drem thought.

Revenants flocked to Gulla, forming a ring around him.

"GULLA!" a voice cried out: Shar, charging at the Kadoshim, her sword held high.

She wants her vengeance for Utul's death at Dun Seren.

Gulla looked up, his chin slick with blood.

Drem ran at Gulla, Revenants swarming towards him. He hefted his sword and axe.

Friend reached them first, limping, blood leaking from her wounds, but still prodigiously strong. She smashed into them, sending Revenants hurtling through the air. Drem, moments behind the white bear, hacked and chopped with the Starstone Sword and the black-bladed axe. Blue fire crackled.

These blades are rune-marked, too. The dark blades carved the Revenants to pieces. He ran on.

Shar screamed, slashing and stabbing to either side as Revenants slammed into her horse, ripping at the animal with long talons.

Gulla strode through his Revenants, drawing a longsword from his hip. A Revenant leaped up onto the saddle behind Shar and dragged her crashing to the ground.

"Hold her," Gulla snarled, and stood over Shar.

The Kadoshim raised his sword high, Shar struggling on the ground, a Revenant pinning her.

A thundering of hooves.

"GULLA!" a voice yelled, and Gulla paused, looking round to see a warrior riding at him.

A red-haired warrior with a black-bladed spear.

Fear flashed in Gulla's red eye and his wings beat, lifting him into the air.

Cullen drew his arm back and hurled the spear into the air. It flew, slicing into Gulla's belly, bursting out of the Kadoshim's back. He fell, screeching and flailing. Cullen leaped from his mount's back, hitting the ground, rising, drawing his sword and running towards Gulla. Revenants ran at him and Cullen slashed, blue flame crackling, limbs and heads flying through the air.

Drem reached Shar, stabbed down into the Revenant holding her. Shar grabbed her sword and climbed to her feet. She ran, Drem following.

Revenants were encircling Gulla, who was writhing on the ground, screeching and hissing, holding onto the spear shaft in his belly.

Drem, Shar and Cullen carved into the Revenants. Cullen reached Gulla first, screaming Keld's name as he swung his sword.

A burst of blue flame and Gulla's head rolled away from his body.

A pause, the Revenants switching from their too-fast, stuttered movement to absolute stillness. Then, as one, the Revenants dropped.

All around the battlefield warriors paused, looking at the creatures dropping around them. Cheering rang out across the field. Drem saw Ert turn, shouting orders to the remnants of his shield wall, saw them turn, a tide-line of Revenant dead piled beyond them. A crack as warriors' shields came together, and then they were marching towards Asroth, cutting down acolytes, pushing through the swirl of horses and Kadoshim.

Asroth was surrounded by battle, riders, Kadoshim, Ben-Elim sweeping down from above, warriors of the Order on foot, acolytes in their scores. Drem saw Byrne's body, lying where she had fallen, small and still amidst the swirl of violence. Without thought, he was weaving through the arena of battle, until he burst out into the open space that ringed Asroth. Riders were circling the Lord of the Kadoshim. Meical was there, Riv as well, striking at him, seeking an opening. Kadoshim wheeled amongst them, and at the centre of it all, Asroth laughed his deep, baleful laugh, wielding his black axe and revelling in the bloodshed and death.

A voice in Drem's head whispered of his oath, the black sword in his hand twitching, but he ran to Byrne instead, dropped to his knees beside her. She was lying upon her back, staring at the sky. Blood pooled beneath her, soaking into the trampled turf.

Her head moved as he fell beside her, gripped her hand and kissed it.

"It's going to be all right," he said, though ice coiled in his chest, snatching his breath away. Tears blurred his vision. This was the woman who had taken him in, fought for him, protected him, taught him, made him feel part of a family again.

"My sword," Byrne said, and Drem saw it lying in the grass. He reached out, put the hilt in her fist.

"I keep trying to get up, have to fight him," Byrne breathed, "but I can't feel my legs."

He looked down, saw Byrne's legs were unmoving, one at an unnatural angle.

Screams drew Drem's eyes.

Asroth had disappeared amidst the crush of bodies around him. Horses were neighing, rearing, warriors stabbing and slashing.

"*Cré, caith mo namhaid don ghaoth,*" a voice bellowed. There was a ripple in the earth beneath Asroth, like a restless giant turning in their sleep, and an explosion of blood, horses staggering and falling away, warriors hurled from Asroth in all directions.

Asroth stood there, blood-soaked, his black axe dripping gore, looking at the warriors cast down around him, and he smiled.

"Does he still live?" Byrne asked Drem.

Drem nodded, rose slowly.

"Not for long," he replied.

RIV

The Kadoshim was trying to throttle her, an arm wrapped around Riv's neck. She was struggling, swinging her elbow, kicking, but he held on tight. Riv bit down on the Kadoshim's arm, felt blood spurt between her teeth.

He screamed, his grip loosening, and she was twisting away, slashing with her short-sword across his throat. He fell away, choking on his own blood.

Riv stood there, chest heaving. She saw Meical trying to climb to his feet, using the saddle and harness upon his dead horse to pull himself upright. She stumbled to him, felt the weakness in her leg from the arrow wound, pain pulsing up her back, gave him her arm and helped him stand. They both stood there, battered, bleeding.

A tremor in the ground and Riv looked to the west. A giant brown bear was lumbering across the battleground, Ethlinn upon its back, a handful of giants running alongside her. All in her path were being crushed, hurled through the air. Behind Ethlinn other giants were following, some mounted upon bears, others running on foot. Balur One-Eye was amongst them.

Asroth saw Ethlinn, turned to face her. Kadoshim swooped down at Ethlinn, one of the giants running alongside her crashing to the ground with a spear deep in its chest, the others slowing, forced to fight off the aerial attack. More Kadoshim came, launching themselves at Ethlinn.

"*Bogann an ghaoth iad ó mo chosán,*" Ethlinn cried out, waving a hand. The Kadoshim attacking her were swept away by a tempestuous wind, hurled crashing into each other. Riv heard bones shattering. They fell to the ground, Ethlinn's bear trampling over them.

Asroth bellowed a challenge.

"*Fréamhacha an turais domhain aici, coinníonn sí í,*" he cried, and the ground shifted before Ethlinn's bear, roots bursting from the earth and wrapping around the bear's legs.

"*Faigheann fréamhacha bás,*" Ethlinn shouted contemptuously, and the roots withered and crumbled, the bear stumbling, righting itself and ploughing on. It roared at Asroth, spittle spraying, waves of sound buffeting them. The bear's jaws opened wide, Asroth standing before it, still as stone. He held his axe wide, one-handed, set his feet, raised the axe high. Then he was moving, stepping to the right, turning on his heel, spinning around, and swinging the black axe with all his might. The bear's momentum carried it wide of Asroth, jaws snapping out at him, even as his axe blade crunched into the bear's chest. It cut through the bear's coat of mail, a shower of iron links, carved deep into the bear's flesh, blood erupting, the bear bellowing, its momentum carrying it on, ripping the axe from Asroth's hands and throwing him to the ground.

The bear lumbered on ten or twenty paces, then its forelegs folded and it was crashing to the ground, skidding, turf spraying. Ethlinn was hurled from her saddle, thrown through the air.

Asroth climbed to his feet, strode after the fallen bear, put his feet on its chest and wrenched his axe free. He walked towards Ethlinn, who was rising unsteadily to her feet.

"ASROTH!" a voice bellowed, Balur One-Eye, Sig's huge sword in his fist.

Kadoshim fell from the sky, swirling around Balur, stabbing at him. He ducked, swung his sword, shearing through wings, but more Kadoshim flew at him and his companions.

Asroth turned back to Ethlinn.

Riv leaped into the air, Meical limping after her on the ground.

Ethlinn stood, her spear in her fists.

"This world is not for you," she said as he approached her.

"I like it here." Asroth grinned.

Ethlinn stepped forwards to meet him, swirled her spear over her head, ending with the spear pointing at Asroth's heart.

He stepped in, swinging his axe.

Ethlinn sidestepped, stabbed at Asroth as his swing carried him, her blade scraping across his mail, glancing up, scratching his cheek.

"Your coat of mail cannot save you," Ethlinn said.

"*Tine í a ithe*," Asroth shouted, a hint of panic in his voice, wiping blood from his face and holding it on his gauntleted hand. The crackle of flame and fire grew upon his palm, expanding, and Asroth hurled it like a ball at Ethlinn.

"*Múchfaidh an ghaoth na lasracha seo*," Ethlinn called out, and a swirling wind rose up around her, swept forwards and tore the flames to stuttering ribbons.

"And neither can your words of power," Ethlinn said. "In every way you are outmatched. You have not the skill to best me, only your mail is keeping you alive a few moments longer."

Asroth snarled and rushed in, wings beating, gripping his axe two-handed. Ethlinn stepped in to meet him, holding her spear in the same way, and their weapons met, a series of cracks and clashes. Ethlinn was taller than Asroth, but shockingly fast for her size. There was a flurry of blows, Ethlinn's spear striking Asroth four times, three of them sparking on his black mail, the fourth slicing a red line down one forearm. He staggered away, off-balance, stood and looked at the blood on his arm. He looked at Ethlinn, then up at the sky above her.

"TO ME!" Asroth bellowed, and a swarm of Kadoshim disengaged from combat and swept towards him. Ethlinn disappeared within a storm of wings. Riv heard her shouting words of power, saw Kadoshim swept and hurled by strong winds, but there were so many.

Riv flew towards them, Meical breaking into a limping run, others trying to get to Ethlinn through the swirling Kadoshim. Meical cried out. Riv saw him on the ground, a Kadoshim standing over him. Without thought she threw her black knife, the blade punching into the Kadoshim's back, high, between its wings. It shrieked, stumbled forwards, Meical rolling to one knee, standing, slashed with his sword across the Kadoshim's belly. Mail links torn, a line of blood. The Kadoshim stumbled back.

Riv flew down, wanting her knife back.

"This is why you will lose, Meical," the Kadoshim snarled. "Because you do not see these things for the vermin they are." He sneered at Riv.

"You are the vermin, Sulak," Meical said, "and Riv is my friend." He stepped forwards, a straight stab into the Kadoshim's throat. Sulak fell away, gurgling. Riv kicked him over and pulled her knife from his back.

A cry behind them, both turning to see Kadoshim stabbing down at Ethlinn, and she stumbled, her spear dropping from her hands. Asroth stepped in, Ethlinn's mouth moving as she spoke words of power, but Asroth grabbed her wrist, heaved her towards him and slammed his helmeted head into her face. Ethlinn's legs buckled and she dropped to her knees.

A roar from Balur, Riv glancing to see him running, cutting a Kadoshim from the sky without breaking stride.

Asroth stepped back and swung his axe, a sickening crunch as the blade chopped through mail and carved deep into Ethlinn's back. She collapsed to the ground, her legs twitching, then still. Asroth put his boot on her back and wrenched the axe free.

Riv and Meical hurled themselves at Asroth. He swung the butt end of his axe, smashing into Riv's side, sending her crashing into Meical. They tumbled away, Asroth striding after them, axe rising.

The ground trembled and a white bear shambled to stand over Riv and Meical, Drem upon its back. The bear lashed with a huge paw, caught Asroth halfway through his axe-swing and hurled him through the air.

Drem looked down at Meical and Riv.

"Best be getting back on your feet, we'll need to do this together."

DREM

Drem slipped down from Friend's back.

"You stay out of this," Drem said to the bear. "Kill Kadoshim or acolytes, but leave Asroth to us." He offered his hand to Riv, helping her stand.

"Take this," he said to Meical, offering the black axe.

Meical looked at it, saw black smoke coil, gave a cold smile. He sheathed his sword and took the axe.

Drem turned and faced Asroth.

Asroth beat his wings, righting himself, strode back towards them, his axe rising again.

"You should have seen: I know how to deal with bears," Asroth growled.

"You'll kill no more of my friends today," Drem said, walking towards Asroth. Riv limped on his left side, Meical on the right.

Asroth laughed. "I'll kill *all* of your friends today, and you as well." He shook his head. "Humans, thinking you can actually make a choice about how this will end."

"We'll end *you*, you pale-faced bastard," Cullen called out, running to join them. A Kadoshim swept out of the sky, stabbing, but Cullen sidestepped and sliced with a black-bladed spear, the Kadoshim crying out, his intestines spilling to the ground.

Drem nodded at Cullen as he came to stand beside them.

Asroth looked at them, at the starstone weapons in their hands. Sword, axe, knife and spear. Something rippled across his face.

"Nothing worthwhile is easy," Asroth said grimly, and started walking towards them.

A whistling sound, something huge hurtling through the air between Drem and Riv. Sig's sword, spinning end-over-end. It slammed into Asroth's chest, point first, would have skewered a draig, but his coat of mail somehow held. The sword exploded into a thousand shards but the impact hurled Asroth from his feet, flying through the air, losing his grip on his axe.

Drem turned to see Balur One-Eye running towards them. He slowed at Ethlinn's body, staring down at her, then looked at Asroth. His face was twitching and shuddering, grief a raw wound in his eyes. Slowly Drem saw it shift to rage. A cold, burning rage. Balur stalked towards them. He shrugged his war-hammer from his back, long-shafted, iron banded, a solid lump of pitted iron at its head. He rolled his shoulders, clicked his neck.

Asroth rose slowly, looked at Balur and the others. Looked to the sky.

"TO ME!" Asroth bellowed at his Kadoshim, as he took his whip from his belt, let the iron-bound cords drop to the ground, slid a short-sword from its scabbard.

Kadoshim tried to disengage from their battles, some flying to Asroth, gathering behind him, hovering. Fifteen, twenty of them.

Balur started to run at Asroth, Drem a heartbeat behind. Riv lifted into the air, Cullen and Meical following Drem and Balur.

Asroth's whip cracked, straight at Balur, but somehow Balur swayed and swerved, the cords hissing through the air, past his face, and Balur was leaping.

Asroth stabbed out with his short-sword.

Balur parried the blow with his hammer-haft, iron bands

screaming, a flare of sparks. He swung the hammer into Asroth's head, a grating crunch, sending Asroth stumbling, reeling, his black helm spinning through the air, the leather buckle snapping. Asroth's wings beat, steadying him, and he turned snarling at Balur, silver hair flowing down his back.

Balur strode at him, a Kadoshim diving, stabbing, Balur hammering it into the ground.

"*Talamh a shealbhú mo namhaid*," Asroth yelled, and the ground around Balur's feet shifted into a sucking bog, Balur sinking into it.

Drem was close, ducked a Kadoshim, slashed with his sword, a clang as his blade was parried. Cullen stabbed the Kadoshim with his spear, a shriek. Drem continued moving forwards, closer to Asroth, swept a Kadoshim's spear away, slashed across the demon's throat.

Asroth stepped towards Balur, his sword rising, the giant held firm in the ground. Asroth smiled.

"*Scaoileadh talún mo chara*," a voice cried out, and Drem twisted to see Byrne heaving herself across the ground towards them, her legs dragging limp behind her. "*Scaoileadh talún mo chara*," Byrne shouted again, and the ground around Balur's feet solidified, spitting him out. The giant stumbled, fell to the ground, rolled as Asroth's sword hissed through air.

Asroth bellowed his frustration.

Meical reached Asroth, ducked his sword-swing and chopped the black axe Drem had given him into Asroth's thigh.

A bellowing scream, Asroth lashing a backswing at Meical, Meical ducking, too slow, the sword blade slicing through his wing, sending him staggering a few paces. Asroth's whip cracked again, wrapping around Meical, screams as black iron bit, and Asroth dragged Meical through the air, hurling him away, flesh tearing.

Riv swept down through a storm of Kadoshim, swerved around Asroth and his sword and slashed with her black knife, tearing a long rent in the black mail across Asroth's ribs. Blood

welled. Then she was sweeping up, out of range, Kadoshim falling upon her.

Asroth paused, looked at the blood, snarled, drew his arm
back, cracked the whip at Riv.

"*Scuabann an ghaoth é*," Byrne cried, and a funnel of wind
rose around Asroth, rocking him, sending the strike of his whip
wide.

A wordless scream from Asroth, rage and fury. He muttered
words, eyes fixed on Byrne. Flames crackled to life along the
wound on his arm, tongues of fire materializing; Asroth gathered them in his fist, pulled his arm back to hurl them at Byrne.
Drem slammed into Asroth, staggering him, the tongues of
fire flung to the ground, an explosion of flames and sparks; heat
swept Drem, scorching hair, Drem leaping away.

Asroth roared.

Balur came at him, war-hammer swinging. Asroth's legs
bunched and he launched into the air, wings snapping wide
and beating, the hammer hissing below his feet. He swung his
sword at Balur, who raised his hammer, the sword chopping into
the haft. A crack and the shaft was splintered. Balur dropped
the two halves. Asroth kicked him in the face, Balur falling
backwards, crashing to the ground, and Asroth's whip cracked,
wrapping around Balur's arm, iron hooks biting deep.

Balur bellowed his pain.

Asroth tensed, pulling on the whip, flesh flaying along Balur's arm.

Drem stepped in and swung his black sword, severing the
whip's cords. A crack like thunder, black smoke exploding where
sword and whip met. Asroth tumbled away, the resistance suddenly gone.

Balur climbed to one knee.

"Think I'll see how this suits me," he growled. He lifted
Asroth's long axe from the ground, climbed to his feet.

Asroth stared, wings beating, rose hovering into the air.

Drem saw it in Asroth's eyes.

Fear. He's going to fly away.

Asroth's wings beat, lifting him higher.

Cullen's spear slammed into Asroth's side, punching through the mail, into his ribs.

Asroth screamed, ripped the spear from his body, another lurching beat of his wings taking him higher, blood cascading from the spear-wound.

Riv crashed into him, the two of them spinning together. Drem saw Riv's knife rising and falling, stabbing into Asroth's back, slicing one of his wings to tattered ribbons. Riv was screaming her mother's name, again and again. Asroth bellowed his pain, punched his sword hilt into Riv's head, Riv falling away, limbs suddenly boneless. She crashed to the ground in a heap, Asroth lurching down behind her, his tattered wing failing him. He stumbled to the ground and Cullen leaped at him, slashing with Corban's sword. The blade crunched into Asroth's shoulder, mail turning the blade, but Drem heard the sound of bone breaking. Asroth grunted, slashed his short-sword across Cullen's shoulder, slicing through mail and deep into muscle, blood spurting.

Cullen cried out. Asroth punched him with his gauntleted fist. Cullen's nose broke, blood pouring. He fell flat on his back, Asroth standing over him, short-sword rising.

Drem stepped in, held his sword as his da had taught him, high in a two-handed grip.

Stooping falcon.

He slashed at Asroth, right to left, shattered black mail, a red gash from shoulder to ribs. Asroth cried out, falling away.

Kadoshim swooped at Drem. There was a hiss of air and body parts were raining down upon him—Balur swinging the black-bladed long axe.

Drem and Balur walked after Asroth, stepped left and right.

"TO ME!" Asroth cried, backing away, short-sword flitting from Drem to Balur. But no one answered his call, his Kadoshim dead or entangled in battle. Asroth beat his wings, rose lurching into the air.

"*Fréamhacha an aeir, greim air,*" Byrne yelled, and roots burst from the ground, leaping into the air like striking snakes, wrapping around Asroth's ankles, snaring him, dragging him crashing back to earth.

Drem stepped in, sword in guard across his body.

Iron gate, his father's voice whispered.

Asroth staggered, slashed at the roots, saw Drem and lunged at him, a clang as Drem swept the sword wide, then stepped in quickly, stabbing from low to high, two-handed.

Boar's tusk, his father breathed in Drem's mind.

Drem yelled as his black sword punched into Asroth's belly, pierced mail, deeper, through linen, wool and into flesh. Asroth stared at him, surprise, shock, disbelief crawling across his face.

Drem stepped into the blow, forcing his blade deeper, Asroth grunting, gasping. Black blood pulsed around the wound.

"That is my oath fulfilled, Father," Drem whispered. Then he ripped the sword free, blood flowing. Asroth stumbled back a pace.

Then Balur's black axe crunched into Asroth's neck, a downwards stroke, shearing through mail, collarbone, deep into Asroth's chest.

Asroth opened his mouth to say something, but only blood bubbled on his lips.

He fell backwards, crashed to the ground, and lay still.

RIV

Riv groaned, opened her eyes.

Am I dead?

The pain pulsing through her, from so many places, all clamouring for her attention, told her she was definitely alive.

"Here," a voice said, Meical, standing over her. His arm, shoulder and part of his face were sliced to ribbons, flesh lacerated, blood flowing, but he had a smile on his face.

Riv took his arm and climbed to her feet.

"Asroth?" she said.

"Dead," Meical nodded.

It was quiet.

There was no more combat in the air above, or on the field around them. Riv saw half-breed Kadoshim on their knees, arms in the air in surrender, acolytes dropping their weapons.

Riv and Meical walked slowly, the ground littered with the dead. Cullen was climbing to his feet, his nose twisted, clearly broken, his lower face slick with blood. Together the three of them joined Drem and Balur, staring down at Asroth.

He looked smaller, in death. His skin translucent-pale, silver hair splayed around his head. He was covered in wounds, their collective effort.

You are avenged, Mam.

"Got to admit, he was hard to kill." Cullen was breathing hard. "Good fight, though."

Drem shook his head wearily.

Balur spat on Asroth's corpse and walked away. An arm wrapped around Riv's shoulder and she looked to see Jost. Tall, skinny, impossible-to-kill Jost, his shield arm was hanging limp.

"Should have known you'd be one of the God-Killers," he said, grinned at her.

She hugged him, so much emotion sweeping through her.

The tremor of giant feet and Balur returned. He was holding a figure cradled in his arms.

Byrne.

Drem saw her and stepped aside for Balur. Byrne was pale, pain pinching her features, but her eyes were aware. She looked at Drem and he reached out and squeezed her hand.

"We did it," he whispered, "with your help."

A tear dropped from Byrne's eye.

"Look, Byrne," Balur grated, his voice full of grief. "Look at the accomplishment of your life's work." Gently he stroked hair from Byrne's face and angled her so that she could see Asroth.

"It's over," Balur rumbled.

Those words sank into Riv, slowly, like raindrops into wool.

"It's over," she breathed. Somehow saying the words out loud made it feel real. Her legs felt weak and she held onto Jost, who grinned at her.

"It's over," she said again. Felt a rush of relief flood through her, a flicker of joy. And then all she could think of was one thing. One person.

Bleda.

Because when you love someone, you have to share your joy with them.

She looked around at the gathering crowd, hundreds strong, now, but couldn't see him, or any of the Sirak. She spread her wings, people shuffling away behind her, giving her space.

"Have you seen Bleda?" she asked Jost. He shook his head. Faelan was close by and heard her.

"I saw the Sirak near the forest," he said.

Riv beat her wings and took to the sky, spiralling up.

Most of the field was still now, crows circling. The living were mostly moving to look at Asroth, though others were walking amongst the fallen, searching for survivors, tending to the injured. She saw Kill organizing the guarding of prisoners. Riv flew west, across the field, dead draigs strewn beneath her, and far in the distance one running, its lurching, shambling gait taking it towards Ripa. There was movement within the eaves of the forest. She saw Sirak upon horses, and giants. Her wings beat, taking her further, and she angled downwards, skimmed the treetops, saw more Sirak and giants passing through the forest. And then she was flying over a glade, saw bodies strewn upon the ground, Sirak lined around the glade's edge, in a deep circle.

Worry uncoiled in her belly like a wyrm, slithering, stealing her joy away in a heartbeat.

She circled lower, level with the trees now, then lower.

The Sirak were there, hundreds of them ringing the glade, and she saw Old Ellac, sitting on the grass and staring, at a body.

And then she saw him.

"No," she breathed, felt her stomach lurch, dived the last distance, landing, her wounded leg almost giving way, and she was dropping to the ground, throwing herself upon Bleda's body, holding him, pulling him into her arms, sobbing, kissing his face. His cold, cold face.

"No, Bleda," she said, "it's over, you have to wake up, it's over, we've done it. We can go home now." She shook him, willing him to take a breath, for her to see his eyes focus on her. His beautiful, beautiful eyes, that always seemed to look into her, and *know* her. She stroked his cheek, her tears falling onto him, her body shaking with sobs. She hugged him tight, rocking back and forth.

She didn't know how long she had been there, but dimly she became aware of other people around her. Faelan, looking down at her with sad eyes. His kin were about him; others were in the trees. Drem and Cullen rode into the glade, Drem upon Friend, the bear limping, his fur bloodied and torn. Meical rode with them, fresh bandages wound about his face and shoulder. They were looking at Riv with such concern in their eyes that her grief surfaced again, a fresh wave. She drew in a shuddering breath, then looked up at Ellac.

He had been sitting there, the whole time, just staring at Bleda. He looked so old now. An old man, withered and frail, some kind of spark gone from him.

Bleda was his spark. His reason for living.

"What happened?" she asked him, her voice halting.

"I...don't know," Ellac said. "We fought, here, with Jin and her kin. Bleda slew Jin. Yul was wounded and Bleda sent me to find a healer." He gestured at Yul's corpse, lying close to Bleda. "When I came back, he was..." Ellac swallowed, and tears rolled down his cheeks. They were not the first, judging by the lines on his face through the blood and grime.

"There was no one else here?" Riv asked him.

Ellac looked to the far side of the glade, Riv following his eyes, to where a Kadoshim's corpse lay, its head half-severed.

"Kol was here," Ellac said. "Bleda saved him from that Kadoshim."

"Kol," Riv said.

"Aye, but he was gone when I returned," Ellac said.

Riv looked up at Faelan.

"Find him, bring him here," she said.

Faelan nodded and took to the sky, some of his kin following him.

Drem and Cullen came and sat down beside her, said no words. Fen the wolven-hound loped into the glade, up to Drem, licked his face and then curled down around him.

Riv sat there with them, waiting. More tears came, her grief an ocean inside her.

The sound of wings and Faelan was spiralling down into the glade, his kin with him. Kol flew amongst them, a score of

Ben-Elim about him. He alighted before Riv, looking down at her and Bleda. He was covered in cuts and bruises, his face still raw from the injuries he'd sustained at Ripa.

He bent over Riv, peering at Bleda.

"Ah, that is a shame," he said. He looked at Riv, shook his head. "War is a terrible thing."

"Ellac says you were here with Bleda, alone," Riv said. She lay Bleda's head gently on the ground and stood, Cullen and Drem helping her. Ellac rose, too, with the help of his spear.

"Aye, that is true," Kol said. "I fought a Kadoshim." He gestured to the creature's corpse. "Bleda helped me. He ordered Ellac to fetch a healer for his oathman. I stayed, thanked him for his assistance with the Kadoshim—"

"Assistance!" Ellac muttered. "You'd be a dead man if Bleda hadn't stepped in."

"Aye, maybe." Kol shrugged. "I thanked him, and then left, rejoined the battle."

"How did he die?" Riv asked him.

"I don't know," Kol said, his face flat. He looked at Bleda's corpse. At the wound in his throat, and the arrow in his thigh. He pointed at the arrow. "The Cheren, I'm guessing," he said. "The battle was spread all through the eaves of the forest and the Cheren were everywhere."

Riv looked at Bleda's wounds. She had not been able to bring herself to do so, until now. But something was whispering to her.

Ellac frowned.

"That is a Sirak arrow," he said, crouching to look at it, using his spear for balance.

Kol shrugged again. "I don't know what happened, but that's my educated guess. I'm going to go now. My body hurts, and there is much to do. I have a kingdom to rebuild."

"*Kol does know what happened,*" a voice squawked.

Riv looked around the glade, searching for the owner of the voice.

A branch swayed above them, leaves rustling, shifting to

reveal an old crow, pink skin visible where his feathers had fallen out.

"Craf," Alcyon said.

Kol spread his wings.

"Wait," Riv said to him.

"You don't tell *me* what to do," Kol said.

"Craf, what did you say about Kol?" Meical asked the crow.

Craf hopped from one leg to the next, looking at Kol with dark, intelligent eyes.

"*Kol BAD MAN!*" Craf squawked. "*Kol stab Bleda.*"

Riv blinked, a roaring in her ears. She stared at Craf, then looked at Kol.

"Don't be absurd," Kol said. "Of course I didn't. We are on the same side, for goodness' sake. Why would I do that?"

"*Cairn of murdered babies,*" Craf squawked, "*that's what Bleda said. Then Kol stab Bleda with spear.*"

Kol took a few quick steps towards Craf, his fingers twitching to his sword.

Cullen moved in front of Kol, his sword in his fist, his face dark. "I'd not do that, if you want to keep your head," Cullen growled. Ben-Elim moved, hands on weapons.

Meical stepped between them, holding a hand up.

"Kol is to stand before the Assembly for other accusations," Meical said. "This can be dealt with there."

"Yes, if you like," Kol said, a sneer on his face. "But I hardly think the Ben-Elim will credit the testimony of a crow. Let alone one that is bald and senile."

"*Rude,*" Craf muttered. "*Kol murderer.*"

"Shut up!" Kol snapped.

"You killed Bleda," Riv said, staring at Kol.

"Pfah," Kol spat. "I'm not staying here to listen to this gibberish. Make your claim at the Assembly, and see how that fares for you."

Riv's hand dropped to the pommel of her short-sword. The ocean of grief in her belly had changed, quick as thought. It was rage now, a storm inside her. A red mist filled her vision, her head, a tingling in her veins. Muscles twitched in her jaw.

"Don't," Kol said.

"You killed Bleda," Riv repeated. She lunged forwards, reaching for her short-sword.

Shouts, people grabbing at her, hands and arms snatching at her. But she was too quick. Kol hadn't even had time to react before her sword was out and resting against his throat.

A heavy, breath-held silence.

"You should put that away," Kol said, staring into Riv's eyes. "Don't be an idiot. Do you want to start another war?"

She stared back at him, and he saw the hatred in her eyes. Saw that she didn't care.

"I am your father, you cannot kill me," he hissed.

Riv heard murmurs amongst the Ben-Elim behind Kol, but she didn't take her eyes from his.

He killed Bleda. My Bleda. After we had come through so much, for it to end like this. The red wave inside her turned into a black one, rising high as a wall, a dark sorrow overwhelming her. In one moment life had drained of all meaning, of all colour.

And you took it from me.

Her body tensed for the killing thrust.

An arm wrapped around her waist and dragged her back. She turned her dark glare upon him, saw that it was Ellac.

"You don't want his death on your soul," Ellac said, looking deep into her eyes. "It would change you, leave a stain on your heart. He is your father, your kin."

Riv's lips twisted, tears of anger and grief mingled.

"My thanks," Kol said to Ellac.

Ellac took his eyes from Riv's and looked at Kol. Then he stabbed his spear forwards, adder-fast, the blade piercing Kol's throat. Whipped it back out, blood jetting.

A stunned moment, everyone staring.

"Bleda was as a son to me," Ellac snarled, his voice breaking, tears rolling down his cheeks. "I would slay you a thousand times and risk a thousand wars for him."

Kol staggered back, hands reaching to his throat, blood pulsing over them. He swayed, dropped to his knees.

Ben-Elim shouted, drew their swords.

Three hundred Sirak bows were bent.

"Loose," Ellac said.

As one, the Sirak released their bowstrings, their arrows hammering into Kol, hurling him to the ground. His blood soaked into the forest floor.

FRITHA

Fritha stared at the sky. It was empty of wings now, of Kadoshim and Ben-Elim, though crows were starting to replace them.

They will come for me soon, Fritha thought. *I hope I am dead when they do. I have seen what they eat first. Eyes, and lips. The softest parts.*

"*Fola, croí, a bheith mall, beo, beagán níos faide,*" she whispered, the same words she had been breathing since Drem had ripped his seax from her and she had collapsed to the ground. She knew the words of power she was uttering would not save her, would only keep her alive a little longer.

In truth, she was not sure why she was clinging on to life so desperately.

For my baby. Because she knew, when she died, so would the child growing inside her. But it was inevitable—there was no coming back from Drem's blow.

The blood pulsing from the wound in her belly was leaking sluggishly. She felt her heartbeat beginning to fade, becoming weaker, the gaps between each beat longer, the same with her breaths. Her baby kicked within her, an act of panic. That upset her. She did not want her child to feel fear.

She turned her head, saw the place where Asroth had fallen. She'd watched his fall, was still surprised by it, by Drem and the rest. Asroth's body was gone now, carried away by Balur and his giants. The battleground was empty, still and silent, apart from the squawking of crows, the wet slap of beaks tearing flesh. Nearby she heard the snort of a horse, heard it chewing at a clump of untrampled grass.

A memory of Asroth flashed through her mind, in Drassil's Great Hall, of her dressing him in his war gear. He had seemed invincible, like a god to her.

I thought you would have saved me. Saved your unborn child.

She had said that to him, when he had landed beside her. He had bent down to her, and she had asked him to save her, and her baby.

He had shrugged. *"There are more bellies in this world that I can plant my seed in,"* he had said, then stood and strode away.

She had wept then, knowing that her baby would die.

A sound, a scratching on the ground. She tried to move, but she had no strength, her limbs numb, her body an immovable weight. She twisted her head, saw something crawling towards her.

Arn. Blood pulsed from the stump of his wrist. He was dragging himself through the dirt with his remaining hand, looking at her.

She smiled at him.

He reached her, lay his head upon her.

"Forgive me," he said to her.

"For what? You gave all. Everything," she breathed.

"I swore to protect your child."

A silence, thoughts taking too long to wind their way through the fog growing in Fritha's mind.

"You still can," she said.

"How?" Arn asked. He pushed himself upright, looked at her. She could see some of his strength returning.

"Take my sword, cut my baby free and save her. Take her somewhere far away and raise her."

Arn pulled away.

"I cannot do that," he said.

"You *swore*," she said, a flash of fierce passion in her voice. "I am done, my body broken, my life-blood soaking the earth. But she still lives within me. I can feel her." She looked into Arn's eyes, saw his tears, felt tears of her own.

"Please," she whispered.

He stared at her, emotions rippling across his face. Then he stroked her forehead, kissed her cheek and wrapped his hand around the hilt of the short-sword at her belt, its blade black as night.

CHAPTER ONE HUNDRED AND TWENTY-ONE

RIV

The Year 1 of the Age of Courage, Eagle's Moon

Riv swooped down into a bank of cloud, all becoming white mist for a dozen heartbeats, and then she was bursting through it, moisture coating her like a cobweb. Dun Seren spread below her, glowing in the morning sun.

Faintly, she could hear a bell ringing.

She shifted a wing and began the long spiralling descent.

Dun Seren grew larger, other winged figures flying over the fortress, all of them descending, like Riv, towards the weapons-field.

It felt good to be back, like coming home, and the knowledge that her friends were down there made her heart smile a little. But there was still something, a cloud within her, that kept her distant. She had spent so long with grief wrapped around her heart that sometimes she thought it had seeped into her bones, into her soul.

Oh, Bleda, Mam, how I miss you both.

She sucked in a deep breath and tried to focus on what was about to happen.

People were gathered upon the weapons-field, as small as ants from Riv's great height, others walking through wide streets, making their way to the same place. A section towards the rear of the field, where a new building was under way. A stone dais stood upon a flagstoned floor, wider than Dun Seren's keep. It had been built by Balur and many giants. On the field around it pegs and markers were hammered into earth, trenches being dug, the foundations for a new building. Balur was there, Ukran, Alcyon and Raina, a hundred other giants, all masters of stone-work. Scattered around the new foundations were a handful of old oaks, their trunks wide, the bark thick and knotted. Crows sat upon the branches, watching. Riv spied Rab amongst them.

People were upon the dais; Riv was low enough now to rec-ognize faces. Byrne was there, sitting in her chair, which had poles slipped through iron brackets so that it could be carried about. Furs were draped across her lap. Craf was perched on the chair's back, Tain and Kill either side. Meical was standing with them, his white wings gleaming in the spring's sunlight. He was leaning down and talking to Byrne. Or to Craf.

Probably both.

To one side of the dais Riv saw a mass of white-feathered wings. Ben-Elim, standing silently, looking up at the newly risen sun.

The sound of wings and a voice called to Riv: Faelan, sweep-ing through the air towards her. She raised a hand in greeting and together they spiralled down to the dais, alighting on the grass before it, landing beside her friends.

Drem and Cullen were there, both in wool tunics, grey cloaks wrapped around their shoulders. Riv was not used to seeing them out of a coat of mail, though they still wore their weapons-belts. She *was* wearing her coat of mail, rolled her shoulders to shift the weight.

Cullen grinned to see her, Drem smiling, too, and she strode over to them, pulling her wings tight.

"Glad you could join us." Cullen winked at her.

"This is not something I'd miss," Riv said. "Even if Byrne hadn't ordered me to be here."

An arm wrapped around her shoulder and she turned to see Jost smiling at her.

"Welcome back," he said to her. "How are you?"

Riv had flown to Arcona, to meet with Ellac and the rem-nants of the Sirak. A great cairn had been raised over Bleda's body when they had returned to their homeland, and Riv found herself visiting there often, just to stand before Bleda's cairn and talk to him. Life was calmer in the Banished Lands since the Day of Courage, but grief still darkened Riv's mind. She knew Bleda was gone, and nothing could bring him back, but standing close to his burial mound, knowing there was something of him within, somehow seemed to ease her pain.

"Fine," she said with a shrug.

Jost looked at her as if he didn't believe her.

He wore the grey cloak of the Order, bore the four-pointed star upon his shoulder. There were no White-Wings anymore. The world had changed so much, the White-Wings disbanded. Ert, Jost and the surviving White-Wings had joined the Order the day after the battle on Balara's fields.

A horn blew, Tain on the dais.

"It is time," he called out, when the ringing faded.

Cullen looked at Drem and Riv, and together they stepped forwards; others were stepping out of the crowd, climbing up onto the dais. A mixture of warriors of the Order, Faelan amongst them. Riv stood beside Byrne. She looked up at Riv and smiled at her.

Giants appeared, Balur, Alcyon, Raina and Ukran, carrying a chest threaded with poles between them. They approached the dais, climbed broad steps and walked to its centre, then stopped.

Balur and the others saw Riv and she dipped her head to them.

Raina opened the chest and the four giants tipped out its contents.

A long black-bladed axe, a helm, a coat of mail, a gauntlet, a spear, a sword, a second, smaller axe and a knife. The remnants of a whip, and a short-sword.

Balur and the others took the chest away.

Then Byrne took a knife from her belt and opened a red line across her palm.

"*Cumhacht i mo chuid fola, oscail doras,*" she said, and let it drip into a pewter cup. She passed the cup to Riv, who cut her hand and held her fist over it.

"*Cumhacht i mo chuid fola, oscail doras,*" Riv breathed, as her blood dripped into the cup, focusing hard on the words. Early on the journey back to Dun Seren from Ripa, Byrne had called a number of warriors to her tent: Riv, Cullen, Drem, Faelan, a few others.

"*So many of our number have fallen,*" Byrne said, "*the secrets of the Order could have been wiped out forever. That cannot happen, so I will teach a new generation the earth power. It is a great responsibility, so guard it with your lives, and use it wisely.*" And as simply as that, Byrne had begun to teach them the power of the earth. The journey back to Dun Seren had taken five moons, so a lot had been learned. Having to focus on something so intensely had probably saved Riv's life. Up until that point she had been falling deeper and deeper into a black abyss of grief.

Riv passed the cup on to Drem.

All on the dais performed the same act, and when they were done Balur One-Eye came and collected the cup. He took it to the pile of black metal in the middle of the dais and poured the blood over the weapons.

"*Iarann dubh, réalta cloiche, a bheith nua,*" Byrne recited, and together they echoed her. The black metal on the dais began to shimmer, a heat haze rippling off it, and then, before their eyes, it began to melt, rippling and pooling.

"*Bíodh doras agat, idir fuil agus cnámh agus biotáille,*" Byrne said.

"*Bíodh doras agat, idir fuil agus cnámh agus biotáille,*" they echoed, all of them repeating the words, again and again. Riv felt the tingle in her blood, had learned to recognize that as a sign that the world was changing, reacting to her.

The black iron melted into a dark pool on the stone dais, and then it began to move, to shift and change its shape, rising into the air, slowly becoming something new.

"*Bíodh doras agat, idir fuil agus cnámh agus biotáille,*" they continued to chant, until the black substance stopped moving, seemed to cool with a hiss, steam rising from it, as if suddenly doused with water.

Their voices faded, a silence settling upon them all, spreading across the weapons-field.

Before them upon the dais stood a black-arched doorway, as tall and wide as two giants. On the far side of the dais the weapons-field rolled up to a stone wall, but Riv looked through the doorway and saw something...else. At first it looked like mist swirling sluggishly, a veil, but there were glimpses of what lay beyond. Of purple skies and white-tipped mountains.

Meical stepped onto the dais, walked until he stood before the doorway. The Ben-Elim that were gathered to the side of the dais followed him. Three hundred and twelve of them. Most of the Ben-Elim who had survived the Battle of the Banished Lands, though not all.

Meical turned and looked at Byrne.

"It is time for us to leave the Banished Lands," he said. "We have caused enough harm."

"You will always be a friend of the Order of the Bright Star," Byrne said to him.

Meical smiled, the scars on his face crinkling. "I thank you for that. I was a friend to Corban, in the end, so it means much to me, to be a friend to this Order. It is his legacy, and he would have been proud to know you, proud of your courage."

Byrne dipped her head to him.

Meical looked at them all, eyes coming to rest on Riv.

"It has been my deepest honour to know you," he said, "and to call you friend." He bowed to Riv, and she smiled at him, suddenly realized that she was going to miss him.

Meical beat his wings, rose into the air, then turned and flew through the mist-shrouded door. There was a turbulence of wings as the other Ben-Elim left the ground. They spiralled up, then went through the door in a storm of wings.

Tendrils of mist curled from the doorway.

They all stood there for long moments, staring at the fading shapes. Then Byrne reached beneath a fur upon her lap and drew out a book. There were two sigils upon it, a black tear and the eyes and fangs of a wolven. Byrne's finger traced the sigils, and then she opened the book, looking upon a page of writing in a thin, spidery hand.

"*Cabhraíonn cumhacht na cruinne liom. Gaoth, tine, uisce agus talamh,*" Byrne read from the book, her voice loud, echoing across the field.

Earth power, help me. Wind, fire, water and earth, Riv translated in her mind, even as her voice and of all who stood those alongside her called out the same words of power.

"*Faigh na cinn scoite, créatúir an bhiotáille. Aingil bhán, aingil dorcha, aingeal dílis agus tite,*" Byrne continued.

Find the winged ones, the creatures of spirit. White wing, dark wing, faithful and fallen angels. Riv and the others echoed Byrne's words.

"*Faigh iad agus ceangail iad, agus tabhair chugam iad,*" Byrne finished.

"Find them and bind them, and bring them to me," Riv breathed aloud, then repeated the words in the old tongue. "*Faigh iad agus ceangail iad, agus tabhair chugam iad.*"

The last words echoed, slowly faded, a silence settling. A tingling in Riv's blood as a gentle breeze caressed her face, grew quickly stronger, tugging at her braids. Between Byrne and the black portal the air shifted, shimmered. Air swirled, growing faster, wilder, became a wild spinning force, flecked with flame and water. It roared, spiralling into a tight whirlwind, and then exploded outwards, breaking into myriad strands, hurtling out over Riv's head in all directions, like a thousand ropes of air and flame cast into the sky.

Riv looked at Byrne, but she was sitting with her head bowed, staring at the book. Turning, Riv looked into the sky, saw the tendrils of air had fractured in all directions, streaming through the sky, further and faster than Riv could see.

It seemed that only moments had passed when Riv saw the first speck in the sky. A black dot, growing swiftly larger. A trail of air and flame was returning, a Kadoshim bound within it.

The Kadoshim was dragged kicking and screaming through the sky, faster than Riv could fly, over the walls and fields of Dun Seren, the rope of air and flame contracting, hauling the Kadoshim towards them, closer, closer, until the Kadoshim was held bound before them, wings and arms snared tight to its body. It looked at Byrne, hissed and screeched at her as it writhed and bucked, but it could not break its ethereal bonds.

Byrne just stared coldly at it.

More dots in the sky, a dozen, then a score, soon over a hundred. This time Ben-Elim were amongst them, shouting their outrage, their white wings bound, all of them dragged struggling, shrieking, screaming to hover upon the dais before Byrne and the others. Hundreds of them bound, bunched and jostling together.

Riv searched the sky, saw that all of the tendrils had returned.

"You do not belong here," Byrne said.

"What *outrage* is this?" a Ben-Elim screeched at Byrne. "How dare you bind *us*? We are the Ben-Elim, the firstborn of Elyon."

"You are not welcome here," Byrne continued, ignoring the Ben-Elim.

Yells and cries of shock and indignation, threats and insults spat at Byrne.

"*Caith amach iad, isteach sa neamhní,*" Byrne cried out.

"Cast them out, into the void," Riv breathed, and then raised her voice with the others.

"*Caith amach iad, isteach sa neamhní,*" they called out, like a thunderclap.

Ben-Elim and Kadoshim were dragged into the portal, hurled through it, hundreds of voices wailing, deafening at first, but fading as they passed through, disappearing.

Silence settled.

Cullen looked at Riv.

"Well, that was thirsty work. Don't know about you, but I could do with a drink," he whispered.

She looked at him.

"A drink with friends sounds good," Riv said.

DREM

Drem walked along with Cullen, Riv and Jost. Rab flapped above them.

"Well, that was something," Cullen said.

"Aye, and good riddance to them," Riv muttered.

They left the weapons-field and turned right, passing along a wide street, children playing, dogs running and yapping. The children fell silent as they passed them, whispering and pointing at Riv, Drem and Cullen. Riv noticed, frowned.

"You're famous," Cullen said, nudging Riv with his elbow.

"They're pointing at you, too," Riv said, "and Drem. Why?"

"You three have a reputation here," Jost said. "The God-Killers, they call you. And Balur and Meical. It's not fair, really," he continued. "While the rest of us were getting trampled by draigs and bitten by slavering Revenants, you lot managed to sneak off and steal all the glory." He jumped out of Riv's range, laughing, before she could say anything, or punch him.

Riv scowled at Jost instead.

"Nothing wrong in that," Cullen said. "We *are* the God-Killers. Well, I did most of the hard work, but you two helped, in the end."

Drem shook his head, smiling.

He was reminded, every day, how good it was to be amongst friends.

A trio of wains rumbled past them, loaded with slabs of

stone for the new building. A team of workers followed the wains, amongst them a handful of men and women, squat and broad, thick-muscled, with wings of leathery skin. Half-breed Kadoshim. Drem saw Riv watching them as they walked by. He was still getting used to seeing them in ordinary, daily life.

After the battle a few score of the Kadoshim's half-breed offspring had surrendered. The surviving Ben-Elim had been about to execute them all, but Meical had stepped in. Said that they were as much the victims of the Kadoshim as anyone else. Bred and raised, brainwashed, for a single purpose. The survivors of the battle had met and discussed what to do, eventually offering amnesty to the half-breeds. They were to swear oaths of loyalty to the Order, or they would remain in captivity until the door to the Otherworld was opened, and then they would be exiled there.

All had sworn oaths to Byrne.

Since then they had been kept under a watchful eye, but now, six moons after the battle, Byrne was allowing them to rejoin the world.

A risk, knowing their bloodlines, but they are people, too, and have their own choices to make. Riv is not like her father, so there is hope for these half-breeds, too.

They reached the gateway to the bears' paddock and turned into it, passed through the flagstoned courtyard. Drem saw darker patches on the stone, a reminder of the blood spilt by bears when the Revenants attacked.

Blood always leaves a stain.

The paddock gate creaked as Drem opened it. Riv beat her wings and had already flown over the fence. Cullen climbed over it, at the spot that Keld had been repairing, the day Friend had let Drem upon his back. Cullen always climbed the fence at that same spot, now. Maybe he thought of Keld every time he did it. Of the huntsman's half-smile, his mouth full of nails.

Cullen reached into his cloak and pulled out a leather water bottle and a pouch that he emptied on the ground, a pile of small leather cups falling on the grass.

"Always be prepared," he said, handing out the cups to them all. Then he unstoppered the bottle and poured for them all.

Drem sniffed it. It wasn't water. A sweet, oaky aroma, potent, making his eyes water.

"Careful," Cullen said, "don't sniff too hard, it might singe the hairs from your nostrils."

"Usque," Jost said. "And it's not even high-sun. This day is getting better all the time."

Cullen just smiled and took a sip from his cup.

They all sat in a circle, talking, listening, laughing. Rab flapped down amongst them, shuffling close to Cullen. Drem took a sip from his cup and coughed. Cullen and Jost laughed the hardest. Only Riv was silent. Drem regarded her over his cup. He was worried about her, knew that her grief was a constant shadow on her heart. The loss of her mother and then Bleda, so close together. It would never go, he knew that, memories of his da circling his head, and Sig and Keld. Their ghosts were always with him, brought back when he least expected them, by a smell, or a turn of phrase, a sound. He didn't want them to go—the grief was a sign of his love and respect for them. But he knew it was a sharp knife-edge. There had been a point when his grief could have led him down a different path, suffocated him. It was his oath that had seen him through those darkest times, the feeling that he must keep his promise to his da. And then, after that, it was friendship and love that had seen him through.

Riv has that about her. I hope that it will be enough for her, as it was for me.

A tremor in the ground and Friend and Hammer joined them, as Drem had known they would.

Friend nudged Drem, sniffing him, and Drem scratched the bear's muzzle, felt the ridges and troughs of scar tissue. Drem had a hemp bag slung over his shoulder. He opened it and pulled out a big clay jar, stolen from the hospice, and two bowls, unstoppered the jar and poured honey into both bowls.

Friend and Hammer lapped the honey noisily.

A whisper of movement and Fen loped towards them, across the courtyard, leaping the paddock fence and joining them. The wolven-hound padded around them all, then turned in a circle at Drem's feet and curled down beside him.

Fen was always absent for part of each morning when they were at Dun Seren. He stayed at Drem's side most of each day, walked Drem to his chamber and slept at the foot of Drem's bed. But each morning he was gone. The first time, Drem had been worried and searched for the wolven-hound. He'd found him in the field of cairns, lying beside Keld's cairn.

Drem reached out and scratched the wolven-hound's neck.

He looked around at them all, and sighed, a soft warmth spreading through him.

We have come through so much. Seen so much death and tragedy. He closed his eyes, picturing his father, hearing his voice, felt that acute sense of loss. Then opened his eyes, seeing his friends gathered close. People he had stood beside, who had shed their blood for him, made that choice to live or die together. To stand or fall together. His brothers and sisters in arms. He smiled, loving them.

"So, what are we going to do with ourselves, now those shifty, troublemaking Ben-Elim and Kadoshim have been thrown out of the Banished Lands?" Cullen said.

"We will guard the gate," Jost said.

"Aye," Drem agreed. "Balur and his kin will build their new keep around the gate, and together we will all guard it."

Cullen nodded thoughtfully, sipping from his cup. "I'm worried," he said. "I fear I'm in danger of becoming bored."

"Kadoshim are not the only darkness in this world," Drem said. "Keld told me that, and he's not wrong. There is a darkness in the hearts of men, the potential within us all. Fritha proved that. And there are her creations to hunt. They are spreading through the Desolation, breeding. We shall fight the darkness." He looked at them. "What else can we do?"

They all nodded, sobered by that thought.

"Might give me something to do." Cullen smiled.

"Love, loyalty and friendship shall be my guiding light," Drem breathed, words from the oath they had all sworn. *You are my friends, the people I love.* His eyes came to rest upon Riv. "What do you think?" he said to her.

"About what?" Riv said.

"The way forward?" Drem elaborated.

Riv regarded him, her eyes dark and deep. A silence stretched, Drem thinking she would not answer. Then she drew in a long, ragged breath.

"A wise woman said this to me once," she said. "There is much in life that is beyond our control, events that sweep us up and along, actions that wrap us tight in their consequences." She paused, a faraway look in her eyes. "Stop raging about the things you cannot change. Just be true to yourself and do what you can do. Love those worth loving, and to the Otherworld with the rest of it. That is all any of us can do." Her voice cracked with those last words. A deep breath. "I confess, I can struggle with that. I want to right all the wrongs. And it is hard to let go of... the past. I don't *want* to let go. But I *do* want to protect the victory we have won. To make their sacrifice worthwhile." She looked at them all, mouth hovering between snarl and smile. "To me, that is a task worth doing," then she shrugged, and Drem felt a glimmer of hope for her.

"A toast," Cullen said, filling their cups and holding his high. He looked at Riv. "To Aphra and Bleda." Then he looked to Drem. "To Olin. To Sig, and Keld. To love and friendship, and bonds that cannot be broken. To you all, the greatest of friends." He looked around at them all. "To truth and courage."

"*Friends. Truth and courage,*" Rab squawked.

"To truth and courage," Drem said, the others echoing Cullen, and then they drank.

ACKNOWLEDGEMENTS

So, finally we come to the end of this series, and with it, the end of the Banished Land's tales. Although Of Blood and Bone is a trilogy that can be read as a standalone series, it is also the final chapter of a longer history that involves the four books from The Faithful and the Fallen series. When read together they form around a one-hundred-and-fifty-year history of the Banished Lands, and a sizeable chunk of my life. Roughly seventeen years have flown by, I think, since lifting my pen and writing down my first ideas. I hope that you've enjoyed your time spent here, and that this book feels like a fitting and satisfying conclusion to all that has gone before.

As with any book, it has not been written alone, and there is a whole warband of people to thank.

My daughter, Harriett, was seriously unwell during the time I was supposed to have written this book. Thank God she is well now, but to say it was a dark, difficult time does not really come close. For a long time I did zero writing, and then, when Harriett was home and on the recovery trail, I started going back to the Banished Lands. With a lot of help from my family, and kindness and understanding from my publisher—I'm thinking of you, Bella Pagan—I managed to write this last instalment in something of a marathon sitting. Deadlines were adjusted and I cancelled a lot of what I would call "general life stuff" to get this book finished.

Whilst I was writing, I was reminded of the things that are most important; family, friends, love and kindness. I hope that you find a glimmer of these things in this book—as well as a lot of battle and bloodshed, of course.

So, on with my thanks.

My wife, Caroline, the engine room of our family, a woman I love and respect beyond my meagre powers of description.

My children, Harriett, James, Ed and Will. I love you all dearly, and thank you for being the wonderful, quirky, adorable human beings that you are.

Julie "Bloodthirsty" Crisp, my extraordinary agent and editor. If this book makes you weep at any point, I'm going to point the finger at her...

Bella Pagan, head of Tor UK and an all-round fabulous person to work with, as well as, of course, all the team at Tor UK and Pan Macmillan for their behind-the-scenes work.

The always excellent Priyanka Krishnan, my editor at Orbit U.S., as well as the whole team at Orbit. Your efforts to get the Banished Lands out there are deeply appreciated.

Jessica Cuthbert-Smith, my copy-editor, who never fails to amaze me with the level of depth and detail that she throws herself into all things Banished Lands.

A huge thank you to my small warband of beta-readers. I will never stop being grateful to you for giving up your time to delve into my world, and your thoughts and comments are always gratefully received.

Ed and Will, who I suspect know the Banished Lands better than I do. Our Banished Lands chats (and battle reconstructions) have made for some wonderful memories.

My dear friend, Sadak. Who would have thought our "Tolkien Club" at school (where we were the only members) would have brought us here! Thank you for taking the time to read and chat over this book. I'm still recovering from how organized you were this time round.

Kareem Mahfouz, a force of nature. Your excitement and passion for the Banished Lands and our gang of heroes has been a constant encouragement and source of joy. Chats on the phone with you have become a tradition that I look forward to after every book.

Mike Evans. One of the first friends I made when I embarked on this publishing rollercoaster, always kind and ready to give of your time and thoughts. And your contributions are invaluable,

Acknowledgements

especially on the military details—although I never want to know how you have come by such specific knowledge.

And Mark Roberson, who has been reading drafts of my books as long as I've been writing them. Our Banished Land's chats over a breakfast are becoming a solid tradition.

And, of course, an enormous thank-you is aimed at you, the reader. Without you there would be no Banished Lands. No Corban and Storm, no Drem, Riv or Bleda. Thank you for following me on this adventure. I hope that you've enjoyed reading it as much as I've enjoyed writing it, and that you find this last chapter something to shout a battle-cry about.

And, while I'm saying that this is the final episode in the story of the Banished Lands, while it is most definitely an end, and my next project is taking me to an altogether different world, I would never say never...

Truth and Courage,
John

677

extras

orbit

meet the author

JOHN GWYNNE is the author of The Faithful and the Fallen quartet and the Of Blood and Bone trilogy. He studied and lectured at Brighton University. He's been in a rock 'n' roll band, playing the double bass, traveled the United States of America, and lived in Canada for a time. He's married with four children and lives in Eastbourne, England, running a small family business rejuvenating vintage furniture.

Find out more about John Gwynne and other Orbit authors by registering for the free monthly newsletter at www.orbitbooks.net.

if you enjoyed
A TIME OF COURAGE

look out for

COLD IRON
Masters & Mages: Book One

by

Miles Cameron

A young mage-in-training takes up the sword and is unwittingly pulled into a violent political upheaval in the first book of this epic fantasy trilogy by Miles Cameron, author of **The Red Knight.**

Aranthur is a promising young mage. But the world is not safe, and after a confrontation leaves him no choice but to display his skill with a blade, Aranthur is instructed to train under a renowned Master of Swords.

During his intensive training, he begins to question the bloody life he's chosen. And while studying under the Master, he finds himself thrown into the middle of a political revolt that will impact everyone he's come to know.

To protect his friends, Aranthur will be forced to decide if he can truly follow the Master of Swords into a life of violence and cold-hearted commitment to the blade.

Prologue

It was late in the day when Syr Xenias di Brusias was ready to leave Volta. Almost everything that could go wrong had done so, and he was rushed and was prone, even after the life he'd led, to forget things, so he made himself stand by his fine riding horse in his two-stall city stable and review everything.

He still had not decided what to do by the time he mounted. He set himself in motion, mostly to avoid thinking too much.

His mare was delighted to be ridden; she'd been cooped up for as long as he had himself, and as soon as she was out in the street behind his house she was ready to trot, or more.

He kept her gait down because it was very important that he not be stopped. He was a little overdressed for a common wayfarer, in tall black boots all the way to his thighs and a black half-cloak and matching black hat full of black plumes, but he liked fine things and he lacked the time to change.

He was riding out of a maelstrom, and he needed to stay on the leading edge.

He could hear screams from the north, where the Ducal Palace was. He patted the sword at his hip with his bridle hand then he turned his horse at the first cross street—away from the palace of towering brick on the hillside, and down towards the river, the bridges, and the street of steelworkers where he had a commission to collect.

It struck him that if he collected the commission then he had made his choice; he would never be able to come back to Volta.

It also struck him that a violent political revolution could cover a great many dark deeds. There were already looters on the streets; two men passed him carrying a coffer, and neither looked up or caught his eye. The sound of breaking glass was almost as prevalent as the sound of screaming from the north.

He heard *gonnes* firing, and the snap of crossbows, and a sulphur reek floated past him and made his mare shy. There was the acrid reek of magik, too.

He let the mare trot, and her hooves struck sparks from the paving stones. Volta was one of the richest cities in the west, and it had fully paved streets and running water from the two great aqueducts, which was still nothing compared to the wonders of his home. The City.

Megara. Which he was about to help destroy.

Or not. He still couldn't decide.

The mare stopped abruptly. There was a corpse in the street, and the sound of steel crossing steel. He tugged at her reins, turned along an alley that ran across the back of the shops and emerged on the next broad, empty street, with tall houses tiled in red rising high enough to block the sun.

He looked right and left, but the street was empty. From long practice, his eyes rose, looking at rooflines and balconies above him, but nothing moved, and he gave the horse her head. They flew along the street, past the corner of violence, and down to the riverside, where he reined in and turned the mare into Steel Street, where the armourers were. He knew the shop well; Arnson and Egg, the two families on the gold-lettered sign, had made fine *gonnes* since the principle had first been developed far to the east.

He had a moment of doubt; the street seemed deserted.

But he saw a light burning, and smoke from the chimney, so he dismounted, tethered his horse to a hitching post and moved his dagger back along his belt from habit. Then he pounded at the door despite the darkening eve and the sounds of violence in the high town.

He heard footsteps.

"You came!" said young Arnson.

He pushed in beside the young man.

"I came for my *fusil*."

The lad smiled. "It is done." He pointed at a leather case on the front bar. "Pater is gone; he says it will be bad here. I'm to keep the doors locked and only eat food in the house."

"Very wise." The man paused to admire the case; the fine steel buckles made by hand and blued, and expert leather-work.

Then he took out the weapon.

"You made this?" he asked.

The young man grinned. "I did, too. Pater helped with the lock; I'm not that dab with springs, yet. And I hired the leather-work."

The boy was so pleased with himself that the man almost laughed. He permitted himself a smile instead. "And the compartment?"

"Just as you asked," the young man said. "Not in the weapon, neither." He showed his visitor the cunning compartment built for keeping a secret.

"Superb," the man in the black cloak said, and slammed his dagger into the young man's temple, killing him instantly. The blade emerged from the other temple with admirable precision, and the man in the black cloak supported the corpse all the way to the floor, stepping away from the flow of blood. Then he filled the secret compartment with his deadly secret, wearing gloves; one tiny jewel skittered away across the table and he tracked it down, picked it up with coal tongs from the fireplace, and put it in his belt-purse. Then he threw his gloves—fine, black gloves—in the fire, where they sparkled as if impregnated with gunpowder. He left, satisfied, leaving the shop door wide open to the looters already moving along the street like roaches.

But then he paused. The decision was made; there was no point in being sloppy or sentimental now. He took the tiny jewel from his purse using his handkerchief, covered his horse's head with his cloak, and tossed it back through the open door. It was so tiny he didn't even hear it hit the floor.

He led his horse away. Only after he counted one hundred paces did he trigger the jewel's *power*.

The house behind him seemed to swell for a moment. Then fire, white fire, blew from every window, the glass and horn panes exploding outwards, the shutters immolating, the door blowing off their hinges. It sounded like a crack of thunder, followed by a rushing of wind, and then the fire began to catch the other old houses in the row, even as the first house collapsed inwards in a roar of sparks and a burst of thick black smoke.

He mounted his mare, who didn't like the smell of blood on him or the sound or smell of smoke, and he used some of his *power* to cast an *occulta*. It didn't make him invisible; it merely compelled most people to look elsewhere.

He drew a second pair of gloves from his belt and tried not to acknowledge that he'd always intended this.

The killing.

The secret.

The compartment.

The fire.

The massacre to come.

He had a little difficulty at the bridge; angry, unpaid mercenaries were holding the near end, and they wanted money and no amount of magikal *compulsion* was going to fool them. So he paid, handing over one hundred gold sequins—almost five years' wages for a prosperous craftsman—as if it was his entire purse. They wanted to open his case, the case with the secret and the little *fusil*, and he prepared to fight them, but they lost interest.

There were more unpaid sell-swords in the streets of the lower town, and they were killing. He had to wonder if the duke was dead; and if he was, if the plan was still valid.

He considered changing sides.

Again.

To his enormous relief, there was no one on the Lonika Gate. He rode through unchallenged, and he was tempted to let the mare gallop; he needed to put time and distance between himself and

Volta. The weight of his secret was tremendous; he flinched from it, trying to occupy his mind so that he would not think too carefully of what he was doing or what it would mean. He knew this would end his relationship with his wife.

Myra, his mistress, wouldn't care. She might prefer him alone. She wouldn't even understand.

But he understood all too well what it would mean.

All too well.

People were fleeing the violence; he passed a long line of carts in the winter fields. He rode aside at a barn, dismounted, and took off all his jewellery and his dagger belt, and put it all in his leather case. Sell-swords might search the case, but at least his rings wouldn't give him away. He put his beautiful black doublet in the case as well and pulled on a smock. It was not as cold here as it would be in the mountains, towards the barbaric Arnaut lands, but it was cold enough, and refugees trudged past him carrying beds and bedding, blankets and furniture.

Lonika was five days away; Megara three or four more days beyond. But he had a fast horse, and the money to buy remounts at Fosse and Lonika; as soon as he was free of all the violence, he'd eat up the ground. Nine days travel for a man on foot would be perhaps three for him. He could arrive exactly on schedule, if he was fast. Dark Night. The night the ignorant feared. The perfect night, or so the Servant said. That was not his problem. Delivering was his problem.

He had to make the Inn of Fosse in two days; he'd managed as much on other occasions.

There were soldiers ahead, stripping a wagonload of a poor merchant family as a mother cowered with her children and a man held his split scalp together. Five men in rusting armour threw the family's worldly goods into the mud, rooting for coins. Ten years of falling grain prices and increasingly violent weather had already stripped the countryside of coin and brought out the violence in people.

This was going to be worse.

He rode down a farm lane and well around the soldiers, and emerged on the turnpike into near darkness.

It was a major risk to travel in the dark. But he could see a farmhouse on fire off to the west, and it seemed to him that the whole world had come apart, which gave him comfort for what he was choosing to do. The world might end, but it would be far away and he'd be very well paid. Rich, even. And he'd have Myra. And other entertainments.

He left Volta on fire behind him and rode through the night.

By morning he was just twenty leagues from the Inn of Fosse. He knew the road and the hills, and he was wary, because the Arnauts, although they hadn't made trouble in a generation, were a race of degenerate cattle thieves and sell-swords.

He climbed into the snow-clad hills, his horse tired and hungry, and he was watching the trees either side of the road. But when the road curved sharply into an ancient gully, he had no sight line, and the unpaid mercenaries had chosen their spot perfectly. They had a tree across the road, and he had no warning to turn aside or prepare a *working*, and he had to halt.

He loosened his sword in the scabbard and reached to unbuckle his *fusil*.

He never saw the crossbow bolt that hit him in the chest. It took him ugly hours to die.

1

Aranthur blew on his fingers and cleaned his quill on a scrap of linen. He was too tired to do his best work, and he took a deep breath while he looked through the small glass-paned window in his gable. The glass window was the single greatest attraction in the long room that he shared with three other young men. They each had a gable with horn panes, seven storeys above the cobbled street, which allowed only a fraction of the winter sun to enter. Only the desk window had glass where a student could see to work.

His eye was caught by the sparkle of his talisman, a *kuria* crystal. He waved a hand over it, thinking he'd left it engaged when he was studying for his examination, cursing the waste and then regretting his curses, but the brilliance was only the natural sun tangled in the stone and not an emanation of *power.*

The room was bitterly cold. He glanced at his brazier and his bag of charcoal, counting his coins in his head. He'd bought some things for his mother: elegant ironwork, better than he could afford; fine paper for his sister, leather gloves for his father that he had made himself from expensive ibix leather. He didn't have the money to waste on charcoal.

It was also the last day of classes, and most shops would be closed and most of his tutors had already left.

He looked down at the lines he'd transcribed.

In the beginning there was darkness, and a void, and yet there was the mind of Sophia. And She said the word, and the word was Light, and light filled the whole of the heavens, and there was yet no earth, no water, no fire, no air. All was light.

He looked at the letters he had just formed. *Të gjitha është dritë* in the tongue of home. School—the Academy—so far had been little more than a pile of languages and a lot of writing. A little practical philosophy, and a very, very little magik. And even that little was more theory than practice.

He brushed back his unbound hair and tried not to curse; transcribing sacred words was not supposed to be accompanied by inattention and blasphemy. But it was a pleasure to write in his own tongue and not one of the dry, dead tongues that the Academy seemed to prefer, like Ellene, which drove him mad. He'd almost failed Ellene.

He'd almost failed everything. He hadn't, but it had been close.

690

He sighed and dipped his pen. He could see from the last fifteen characters and the dots over the vowels that his quill was beginning to fray and needed cutting, but he was in a hurry.

And She spoke into the void and there was light, but to the light She sang, and then there were the elements, air, and water, and fire and earth. And the word was song, and the song was the Song, and even as the elements distilled from the light, She desired other voices in Her song, and they joined Her. And there was polyphony, and harmony, and unity. And earth and fire made Earth, and air and water made the Sea; fire and air made the Stars, and earth and water the other planets, and each was a unity, and each was a living form amidst the Infinite; and the Void was not in opposition, but was filled, so that where there had been nothing, there was Everything.

He wrote, and breathed on his hands, dipped his quill, and wrote again. But when his next vowel had an unacceptably sloppy dot, he sat back, managed not to swear, and rummaged for his friend Kati's penknife. She was a student from Safi, a far-off land of burning deserts, and she had already left for home, sixteen days by ship and camel. Her parents were rich, and very demanding, but he envied her. She was going *home*.

She'd left him her penknife, a precious thing, sharp as a razor, just two inches of superb steel. He sat back and took a fresh quill from a tube of them, and cut it: a cut at the reverse angle to help with shape; a squeeze of the fingers to break the quill and form a slit, and then another deft slice to shape the nib. He rolled the quill in his fingers, liked the result, and used the knife to trim the feather to fit his hand, murmuring an invocation to the dead bird for the use of her quill and another to harden the tip. He dipped and tried it on a scrap of laid paper; the line was fine and steady. He went back to his work on vellum, copying out the opening chapter of *The Book of Wisdoms*.

He looked out of the window again and wondered if he was prevaricating. He had an eight-day journey home, and it was warm enough in the City. Arnaud, his Westerner mate, a Frankese from the other end of the world, claimed it was warmer outside than it was in the room. But the City was warm and comfortable in many ways, and the trip home was no little thing; he'd have to work as a deckhand to take a ship, and then he'd have to walk across half of Soulis, his home province, to reach his parents. He felt the temptation to stay—to write them a letter and then go to bed for a few days. He could get some scribal jobs and do more leather-work and use the money to eat his fill.

He could take some extra fencing lessons. He was in love with his sword, purchased in a used clothing market on a whim. With his rent money, because he was a fool. He smiled at the memory without regret, and eyed the blade where it hung on a peg meant for a book sack, by the human skull Daud had bought.

Why did I buy that sword?

It had been a foolish, impulsive purchase—a winter's savings gone in a few beats of his heart, as if he'd been laid under a *compulsion*. It wasn't even the kind of sword he thought he favoured...

He took the freshly cut pen back to his high desk by the cold window and settled himself. He had about a hundred and sixty more lines to copy, and then he could give his sister something truly beautiful for the Day after Darknight. First Sun. A holiday in almost every religion in the City and at home.

He wrote, and wrote. He paused a few times, ate a handful of nuts, breathed on his hands, and, with a wry look, threw some charcoal on the brazier. But he was no longer giving any thought to staying, and he began to write faster, his letters as precise as they would have been on an Academy project. He'd survived his first year at the Academy. He'd learned a few things.

And now he was going home.

if you enjoyed
A TIME OF COURAGE
look out for

THE OBSIDIAN TOWER
Rooks and Ruin: Book 1

by

Melissa Caruso

The Obsidian Tower *begins a bold new epic fantasy trilogy in which the broken magic of one woman will either save an entire continent—or completely destroy it.*

As the granddaughter of a Witch Lord of Vaskandar, Ryx was destined for power and prestige. But a childhood illness left her with broken magic that drains the life from everything she touches, and Vaskandar has no place for a mage with unusable powers. So Ryx has resigned herself to an isolated life as the warden of Gloamingard, her grandmother's castle.

At Gloamingard's heart lies a black tower. Sealed by magic, it guards a dangerous secret that has been contained for thousands of years. Until one impetuous decision Ryx makes leaves her with blood on her hands—and unleashes a threat that could doom everything she loves to fall to darkness.

CHAPTER ONE

There are two kinds of magic.

There is the kind that lifts you up and fills you with wonder, saving you when all is lost or opening doors to new worlds of possibility. And there is the kind that wrecks you, that shatters you, bitter in your mouth and jagged in your hand, breaking everything you touch.

Mine was the second kind.

My father's magic could revive blighted fields, turning them lush and green again, and coax apples from barren boughs in the dead of winter. Grass withered beneath my footsteps. My cousins kept the flocks in their villages healthy and strong, and turned the wolves away to hunt elsewhere; I couldn't enter the stables of my own castle without bringing mortal danger to the horses.

I should have been like the others. Ours was a line of royal vivomancers; life magic flowed in our veins, ancient as the rain that washed down from the hills and nurtured the green valleys of Morgrain. My grandmother was the immortal Witch Lord of Morgrain, the Lady of Owls herself, whose magic coursed so deep through her domain that she could feel the step of every rabbit and the fall of every leaf. And I was Exalted Ryxander, a royal atheling, inheritor of an echo of my grandmother's profound connection to the land and her magical power. Except that I was also Ryx, the family embarrassment, with magic so twisted it was unusably dangerous.

The rest of my family had their place in the cycle, weavers of a great pattern. I'd been born to snarl things up—or more like it, to break the loom and set the tapestry on fire, given my luck.

So I'd made my own place.

At the moment, that place was on the castle roof. One gloved hand clamped onto the delicate bone-carved railing of a nearby balcony for balance, to keep my boots from skidding on the sharply angled shale; the other held the wind-whipped tendrils of dark hair that had escaped my braid back from my face.

"This is a disaster," I muttered.

"I don't see any reason it needs to be, Exalted Warden." Odan, the castle steward—a compact and muscular old man with an extravagant mustache—stood with unruffled dignity on the balcony beside me. I'd clambered over its railing to make room for him, since I couldn't safely share a space that small. "We still have time to prepare guest quarters and make room in the stables."

"That's not the problem. No so-called diplomat arrives a full day early without warning unless they're up to trouble." I glared down at the puffs of dust rising from the northern trade road. Distance obscured the details, but I made out at least thirty riders accompanying the Alevaran envoy's carriage. "And that's too large an escort. They said they were bringing a dozen."

Odan's bristly gray brows descended the broad dome of his forehead. "It's true that I wouldn't expect an ambassador to take so much trouble to be rude."

"They wouldn't. Not if they were planning to negotiate in good faith." And that was what made this a far more serious issue than the mere inconvenience of an early guest. "The Shrike Lord of Alevar is playing games."

Odan blew a breath through his mustache. "Reckless of him, given the fleet of imperial warships sitting off his coast."

"Rather." I hunkered down close to the slate to get under the chill edge that had come into the wind in the past few days, heralding the end of summer. "I worked hard to set up these talks between Alevar and the Serene Empire. What in the Nine Hells is he trying to accomplish?"

The line of riders drew closer along the gray strip of road that wound between bright green farms and swaths of dark forest, approaching the grassy sun-mottled hill that lifted Gloamingard Castle toward a banner-blue sky. The sun winked off the silver-tipped antlers of six proud stags drawing the carriage, a clear announcement that the coach's occupant could bend wildlife to their will—displaying magic in the same way a dignitary of the Serene Empire of Raverra to the south might display wealth, as a sign of status and power.

Another gleam caught my eye, however: the metallic flash of sabers and muskets.

"Pox," I swore. "Those are all soldiers."

Odan scowled down at them. "I'm no diplomat like you, Warden, but it does seem odd to bring an armed platoon to sign a peace treaty."

I almost retorted that I wasn't a diplomat, either. But it was as good a word as any for the role I'd carved out for myself.

Diplomacy wasn't part of a Warden's job. Wardens were mages; it was their duty to use their magic to nurture and sustain life in the area they protected. But my broken magic couldn't nurture. It only destroyed. When my grandmother followed family tradition and named me the Warden of Gloamingard Castle—her own seat of power—on my sixteenth birthday, it had seemed like a cruel joke.

I'd found other ways. If I couldn't increase the bounty of the crops or the health of the flocks with life magic, I could use my Raverran mother's connections to the Serene Empire to enrich our domain with favorable trade agreements. If I couldn't protect Morgrain by rousing the land against bandits or invaders, I could cultivate good relations with Raverra, securing my domain a powerful ally. I'd spent the past five years building that relationship, despite muttering from traditionalists in the family about being too friendly with a nation we'd warred with countless times in centuries past.

I'd done such a good job, in fact, that the Serene Empire had agreed to accept our mediation of an incident with Alevar that threatened to escalate into war.

"I can't let them sabotage these negotiations before they've even started." It wasn't simply a matter of pride; Morgrain lay directly between Alevar and the Serene Empire. If the Shrike Lord wanted to attack the Empire, he'd have to go through us.

The disapproving gaze Odan dropped downhill at the Alevarans could have frozen a lake. "How should we greet them, Warden?"

My gloved fingers dug against the unyielding slate beneath me. "Form an honor guard from some of our nastiest-looking battle chimeras to greet them. If they're going to make a show of force, we have to answer it." That was Vaskandran politics, all display and spectacle—a stark contrast to the subtle, hidden machinations of Raverrans.

Odan nodded. "Very good, Warden. Anything else?"

The Raverran envoy would arrive tomorrow with a double hand-ful of clerks and advisers, prepared to sit down at a table and speak in a genteel fashion about peace, to find my castle already over-run with a bristling military presence of Alevaran soldiers. That would create a terrible first impression—especially since Alevar and Morgrain were both domains of the great nation of Vaskandar, the Empire's historical enemy. I bit my lip a moment, thinking.

"Quarter no more than a dozen of their escort in the castle," I said at last. "Put the rest in outbuildings or in the town. If the envoy raises a fuss, tell them it's because they arrived so early and increased their party size without warning."

A smile twitched the corners of Odan's mustache. "I like it. And what will you do, Exalted Warden?"

I rose, dusting roof grit from my fine embroidered vestcoat, and tugged my thin leather gloves into place. "I'll prepare to meet this envoy. I want to see if they're deliberately making trouble, or if they're just bad at their job."

Gloamingard was really several castles caught in the act of devour-ing each other. *Build the castle high and strong*, the Gloaming Lore said, and each successive ruler had taken that as license to impose their own architectural fancies upon the place. The Black Tower reared up stark and ominous at the center, more ancient than the country of Vaskandar itself; an old stone keep surrounded it, bur-ied in fantastical additions woven of living trees and vines. The stark curving ribs of the Bone Palace clawed at the sky on one side, and the perpetual scent of woodsmoke bathed the sharp-peaked roofs of the Great Lodge on the other; my grandmother's predecessor had attempted to build a comfortable wood-paneled manor house smack in the front and center. Each new Witch Lord had run roughshod over the building plans of those who came before them, and the whole place was a glorious mess of hidden doors and dead-end staircases and windows opening onto blank walls.

This made the castle a confusing maze for visitors, but for me, it was perfect. I could navigate through the odd, leftover spaces and closed-off areas, keeping away from the main halls with their deadly risk of bumping into a sprinting page or distracted servant. I haunted my own castle like a ghost.

As I headed toward the Birch Gate to meet the Alevaran envoy, I opened a door in the back of a storage cabinet beneath a little-used stairway, hurried through a dim and dusty space between walls, and came out in a forgotten gallery under a latticework of artistically woven tree roots and stained glass.

At the far end, a string of grinning animal faces adorned an arch of twisted wood; an unrolling scroll carved beneath them warned me to *Give No Cunning Voices Heed*. It was a bit of the Gloaming Lore, the old family wisdom passed down through the centuries; generations of mages had scribed pieces of it into every odd corner of Gloamingard.

I climbed through a window into the dusty old stone keep, which was half fallen to ruin. My grandmother had sealed the main door with thick thorny vines when she became the Witch Lord a hundred and forty years ago; sunbeams fell through holes in the roof onto damp, mossy walls. It still made for a good alternate route across the castle. I hurried down a dim, dust-choked hallway, taking advantage of the lack of people to move a little faster than I normally dared.

Yet I couldn't help slowing almost to a stop when I came to the Door.

It loomed all the way to the ceiling of its deep-set alcove, a flat shining rectangle of polished obsidian. Carved deep into its surface in smooth, precise lines was a circular seal, complex with runes and geometric patterns.

The air around it hung thick with power. The pressure of it made my pulse sound in my ears, a surging dull roar. A thrill of dread trickled down my spine, never mind that I'd passed it countless times.

It was the monster of my childhood stories, the haunt of my nightmares, the ominous crux of all the Gloaming Lore. Carved through the castle again and again, above windows and under crests, set into floors and wound about pillars, the same words appeared over and over. It was the chorus of the rhyme we learned in the cradle, recited at our adulthood ceremonies, and whispered on our deathbeds: *Nothing must unseal the Door.*

No one knew what lay in the Black Tower, but this was its sole entrance. And every time I walked past it, despite the unsettling aura of power that hung about it like a long bass note too low to hear, despite the warnings drilled into me since birth and scribed all over Gloamingard, curiosity prickled awake in my mind.

I wanted to open it—anyone would. But I wasn't stupid. I kept going, a shiver skimming across my shoulders.

I climbed through another window and came out in the Hall of Chimes, a long corridor hung with swaying strands of white-bleached bones that clattered hollowly in a breeze channeled through cleverly placed windows. The Mantis Lord—my grandmother's grandmother's grandfather—had built the Bone Palace, and he'd apparently had rather morbid taste.

This wasn't some forgotten space entombed by newer construction; I might encounter other people here. I slowed down and kept to the right. On the opposite side of the hall, a slim tendril of leafy vine ran along the floor, dotted irregularly with tiny pale purple flowers. It was a reminder to everyone besides me who lived or worked in the castle to stay to that side, the safe side—life to life. I strained my atheling's sense to its limit, aware of every spider nestled in a dusty corner, ready to slow down the second I detected anyone approaching. Bones clacked overhead as I strode through the hall; I wanted to get to the Birch Gate in time to make certain everything was in place to both welcome and warn the envoy.

I rounded a corner too fast and found myself staring into a pair of widening brown eyes. A dark-haired young woman hurried toward me with a tray of meat buns, nearly in arm's reach, on the wrong side of the corridor.

My side. Death's side.

Too close to stop before I ran into her.

CHAPTER TWO

I desperately flung myself away from the woman, obscenities spilling from my mouth in pure terror. Every piece of me was a deadly weapon I had to redirect: knees and feet and the arms that instinctively windmilled for balance. *No, too near her face, NO—*

My outflung hand hit her earthenware tray, knocking it from her grasp; it was the final push I needed to throw myself aside to the hard floor. The woman yelped, pottery crashed, and meat pies rained down all around me.

I hadn't touched her. She was alive.

Except that I couldn't sense her. I should have felt her heartbeat. This close, her life should have been a warm light in my mind. There was nothing.

"Oh! I'm so sorry! Let me help you—" She reached toward me, brows furrowing in concern.

I scrambled away on the floor, crabwise, my heart still thundering in my chest. "Don't!" I cried. "Stay back!"

She stood, hand still half-extended, meat pies scattered amid shards of pottery at her feet. "Are you all right?"

I lurched upright, stepping away to open more distance between us. A stray chunk of earthenware crunched under my heel. All I could think of was how close I'd come to killing her.

"Didn't anyone warn you? Why were you on the wrong side?"

Her brow creased; I wasn't making any sense, every nerve still jangling. The fear that should have harrowed her face was missing. How could she not know about me?

Unless... "You're not from Morgrain."

That was why I hadn't sensed her before I saw her. My inherited link to the land let me feel the presence of Morgrain-born lives close by, but I had no magical connection to outsiders. And while she looked Vaskandran, the wide bands of colorfully embroidered trim on her crimson vestcoat, along with her golden-brown skin and thick black hair, suggested the lowland domains rather than the gray, pale hill folk of Morgrain.

I'd relied too much on my magical perceptions, allowed myself to get distracted and lazy, and almost killed someone. Again.

My legs trembled beneath me, threatening to dump me on the floor.

The woman smoothed the confusion from her face and dipped a quick bow. "Yes. I'm Kessa, with the troupe of traveling players who arrived this morning. The Foxglove Theater Company; finest in Vaskandar, if I do say so myself. I was trying to bring these from the kitchens for the other players"—she made a grand, tragic gesture toward the fallen meat pies—"and, well, it's easy to get lost in this place."

"I'm so sorry I almost ran into you," I said, which seemed like an appalling understatement given what had nearly happened. "You should stick close to the vines with the purple flowers when you're walking around Gloamingard."

"Yes, someone mentioned that. They were terribly dramatic about it, in fact, but I thought—" Her bright brown eyes came into sharper focus on mine then, and she broke off. I knew what she was seeing: lightning-blue rings around my pupils. Realization broke over her face like a cold wave. Who knew what rumors she'd heard—and if she miraculously hadn't heard any, the staff would have been eager to warn her the moment she crossed the threshold.

Whatever you do, don't go near the Warden. If you touch her, you'll die.

She killed a man when she was four years old. They say she's cursed.

Just last summer a stable boy bumped into her, and his heart stopped for half a minute. He didn't wake up for days, and he may never be the same.

"Oh!" Kessa's eyes widened. I braced myself for the inevitable flick of fingers out from her chest in the warding sign.

But it didn't come. Instead, she dropped to her knees in one fluid movement, head bowed. "Forgive me, Exalted Atheling. I didn't notice your mage mark."

My fingertips flew up self-consciously toward my eyes. "You don't need to kneel. We don't do that here."

Kessa rose, dusting her skirts off, and flashed me a smile. "Better safe than sorry, Exalted. We travel all over Vaskandar, and every domain is different. We just came from Alevar, and if I didn't kneel to a marked mage there, they might have decorated a tree with my head."

"This isn't Alevar." Now that I knew she was safe, I was eager for her to get out of my path so I could head to the Birch Gate. "Please be careful. I don't know what you've heard, but my magic is flawed. If I touch you, you'll die."

Her eyebrows flew up. "I heard that, but I thought they were exaggerating," she admitted. "That's got to be awkward. And the gloves don't help?" She nodded toward my hands.

Sympathetic curiosity wasn't the response I was used to. The only other people outside my family who'd reacted to my power without fear or aversion were a Raverran boy I knew and Rillim, the girl I'd once had mad dreams of courting. A flush crept up my cheeks, and I found myself inexplicably staring at the way dark strands of Kessa's hair lay against her neck as she tilted her head, waiting.

I couldn't get distracted; I had too much to do.

"Through the gloves, a quick touch might not kill you outright," I said. "Skin to skin, it's instant. Now, if you'll excuse me... Wait a minute." A few things fitted belatedly together in my mind, and I frowned. "We're not anywhere near the kitchens *or* the Old Great Hall where the players are rehearsing. You're more than a little lost."

She let out a rich, warm laugh, but something flickered in her eyes. "More lost than I thought, apparently, *and* I ruined the meat pies. My friends will never let me hear the end of it."

"There's nothing in this part of Gloamingard but the old stone keep." And the Door, with all its compelling mystery and power. "You said you came from Alevar. Did you have any dealings with the Shrike Lord, perchance?"

"No, Exalted." She gave a convincing little shudder. "I've heard he doesn't have much of a sense of humor—a rather grave character failing, and one often coupled with a lack of appreciation for theater."

I couldn't help the smile that tugged at my mouth. I wanted to like her—she had lovely sparkling eyes to match her wit, and an easy smile that welcomed me in on the joke. But she'd been too quick with her explanation for being here, as if she'd prepared it in advance. Not to mention that much as I appreciated her relaxed and friendly manner, it didn't fit for a commoner used to domains where you had to kneel to avoid a mage's ire.

If she'd been poking around near the Black Tower, it didn't matter whether I liked her. The Gloaming Lore was quite clear on our duty: *Guard the tower, ward the stone.* The magical protections on the Door were powerful, but that only made tampering with it all the more dangerous.

"Did you see anything interesting, while you were wandering lost?" I asked, deliberately casual.

Kessa hesitated only a fraction of a second. "With respect, Exalted, every inch of this place ranges from interesting to outright bizarre."

A new voice spoke, low and rough as the rumble of an approaching avalanche:

"She's asking because she thinks you're a spy."

My grandmother rounded the corner, her power gathered palpably around her like a cloak of thunder.

orbit

Follow us:

[f] **/orbitbooksUS**

[𝕏] **/orbitbooks**

[▶] **/orbitbooks**

Join our mailing list
to receive alerts on our
latest releases and deals.

orbitbooks.net

Enter our monthly
giveaway for the chance
to win some epic prizes.

orbitloot.com